Elizabeth Elgin is  e *Sweet Promises*. She se Second World War and r marine depot ship. A ke ers and five grandsons ar ge near York.

I am grateful to

Joan Broadbelt
Mary Burton
Ann Osmond
Adeline Polese
Giovanni (John) Polese
Valerie Pratt
and the late Andrew (Dodge) Bailes

who gave generously of their time, knowledge and memories when this book was being written.

By the same author

Whistle in the Dark
The House in Abercomby Square
The Manchester Affair
Shadow of Dark Water
Mistress of Luke's Folly
The Rose Hedge
All the Sweet Promises

Writing as Kate Kirby

Footsteps of a Stuart
Echo of a Stuart
Scapegoat for a Stuart

ELIZABETH ELGIN

Whisper on the Wind

Grafton

An Imprint of HarperCollins*Publishers*

Grafton
An Imprint of HarperCollins*Publishers*
77–85 Fulham Palace Road,
Hammersmith, London W6 8JB

A Grafton Original 1992

Copyright © Elizabeth Elgin 1992

The Author asserts the moral right to
be identified as the author of this work

A catalogue record for this book
is available from The British Library

ISBN 0 586 21198 5

Set in Times

Printed in Great Britain by
HarperCollinsManufacturing Glasgow

1

'Don't agree with them trousers. You're a married woman, and married women shouldn't wear trousers.'

'*Breeches*, Aunt Min, and there *is* a war on.'

Slowly, ponderously, Kathleen Allen gazed around the room as if looking at it for the very last time; a room she would rather not remember, truth known. An over-furnished, over-decorated, overcrowded little room.

Her eyes trailed the back of the sofa to the piano top and the photographs of her husband's parents and Barney – Barnaby, her husband as a little boy, scowling into the camera. Barney with his bronze medal for ice-skating and Barney in khaki, grown fatter now, his toothbrush moustache tilting rakishly with the crooked, Clark Gable smile.

He wouldn't smile when he got her letter, she frowned, wondering why she should feel so guilty about what she had done. But it wasn't so much what she had done, she supposed, but the way in which she had done it. Sneakily, really, it had had to be, because her husband condemned out of hand any woman who joined the armed forces. He always had.

But surely Barney couldn't object to the Land Army? *Army*. In that word the trouble lay. The Land Volunteers or the Farming Corps would have pacified him, but to call it the Land Army at once suggested a group of liberated women in breeches and bright green pullovers, swinging along in ranks of four, pitchforks at the ready.

'And you're still set on going, girl?'

'Doesn't seem I've left myself a lot of choice. I did volunteer.'

5

'Yes, you did. And Barnaby won't be pleased, but you know that, don't you? I suppose you've told him?'

'He knows.' Well, he would when he got her letter, she amended silently. The trouble would start when she received his reply. Because trouble it would contain.

It was unfair, really, that her husband should object to her doing her bit for the war effort, but Barney could, and what was more, he would. He would object loud and long in every letter he wrote, not caring at all that the Censor would read every word.

She had written to her husband immediately the OHMS letter came; the letter that told her she had passed her medical examination and been accepted into the Women's Land Army for the duration of hostilities. That official letter had also told her to report for service on Thursday 18 December, using the enclosed railway travel warrant, and that her uniform, which had already been posted to her in two parcels, would arrive within the course of the next few days. And that had been that. There could be no going back.

The day she had written to Barney was one she would always remember, for it was not only the day on which her calling-up papers came, nor the day on which she summoned up the courage to confess, on a sixpenny airmail letter-card, what she had done, but the day, too, on which her country declared war on the Japanese nation. The day on which, she accepted sadly, the entire world had finally been drawn into war.

But Aunt Min was right. Barney would not be pleased that his wife had joined the Land Army. Hadn't he always made his feelings about women in uniform quite clear? Common, the lot of them and nothing more nor less than comforts for officers. Groundsheets. Why else would women doll themselves up in uniform? Plain as the nose on your face, wasn't it?

No doubting it, Barney would not approve, but on the

credit side, Barney wasn't here to prevent it and for better or for worse she was in the Land Army for the duration; having a baby seemed just about the only thing that would free her from it. And getting pregnant when your husband was in the Army in Egypt was hardly likely to happen.

'Where was it you said you was going?' Minnie Jepson asked yet again. 'In the wilds, I suppose it is?'

'Somewhere in Yorkshire. Alderby St Mary. It's in the North Riding, I think.'

Aunt Min stiffened. Back of beyond, that's what. It wouldn't have surprised her to learn it was cannibal country. To a Londoner, anything north of the river Trent was cannibal country.

'You'll have to watch your step, my girl. Funny lot, up there. And they talk funny, too. Whereabouts in Alderby St Mary will it be?'

'I'm going to a house called Peacock Hey. It's a hostel, really, and I'll be living with other women so you needn't worry, Aunt Min. I'll be fine. There'll be a Forewoman and a Warden to keep an eye on us all.'

'Hmm. And how long will it take you to get there?'

'I don't know, for sure. It'll depend on the train and if we get a good run through.' And if they weren't shunted into a siding to await the passing of something more important; a train carrying vital war supplies or a troop train, maybe. 'I change at Crewe for York, then get a bus to Alderby.'

'Then let's hope you'll be all right, girl,' Minnie Jepson muttered. 'Let's hope they put you off at the right stop.' After all, it would be dark tonight by tea-time. Black as pitch it would be, owls hooting and things creeping in hedgerows. 'Can't say I envy you with all them moors . . .'

'Aunt Min, I'm not going to Wuthering Heights. Alderby isn't in hilly country. It's in the Vale of York. I've looked it up. It's good farming country, not all windswept trees and sheep.'

She sounded far braver than she felt, for her husband's aunt was right. To a city dweller like herself who'd never been anywhere nor seen anything, the countryside was a place of mystery and she, too, hoped she would get off the bus at the right place because in the blackout one bus stop was much the same as any other.

She shivered apprehensively. Suppose she *did* get off at the wrong stop? Suppose she found herself in the middle of nowhere with never a light to guide her and owls hooting like Aunt Min said and eyes watching her and –

'I'll be all right,' she insisted. 'And I'll have to go soon. Why don't I put the kettle on? Goodness only knows when I'll get another cup of tea.'

Had she been stupid, she thought as she filled the kettle. Wouldn't it have been better to have stayed here in Birmingham, where all the factories were on war work and crying out for men and women and good money there for the earning?

No, it *wouldn't*. Last-minute nerves, that's all this was. She'd felt exactly the same before her wedding. Nerves, and doubts. And hadn't she always wanted to live in the country? Hadn't she longed as a child in that green-painted dormitory, to sleep in a room of her own with windows wide open to the silent fields and trees? Even when she had grown up and married Barney, that little aching dream had still been with her. Suddenly she had needed to get away from Birmingham's streets, the sirens and bombs, away from this house, too – Barney's mother's house – and all it reminded her of.

'Looks as if you're going for the duration,' Minnie Jepson mourned, pushing past the suitcase that almost blocked the passageway. 'What ever've you got in there, then?'

'Oh, uniform, mostly.' Kath smiled. 'Dungarees and wellingtons and boots. My own underwear, of course. And shirts and socks, and a working jacket . . .'

'Hmm. Don't know why them blokes at the War Agriculture place didn't think to give you some sort of training. Well, what if they tell you to milk some cows, eh? What'll you do then?'

'Don't really know.' Trust Aunt Min to put her finger right on it. 'I suppose I'll just have to learn, won't I?'

'Bein' on a farm isn't all collectin' eggs and having a romp in the hay.' She took a spoonful of tea from the caddy then shook it level before sliding it into the pot. 'Evacuees from next door to me came home. Couldn't stand it. Wet and smelly they said it was. Couldn't wait to get back to London – bombs or no bombs.'

'I'll manage.' Kath wrapped the knitted holder around the handle of the kettle, pouring carefully. 'I hope you'll be all right, Aunt Min. When I decided to join up I didn't know you'd be coming to live here, though I'm glad you did.'

Very glad. With Aunt Min left in charge, there would be no bombed-out families taking possession of the little house in her absence, she thought gratefully. Aunt Min would keep it clean and warm, though where the old lady would go when the war was over was a problem to be shelved until the war *was* over. 'I'll try to send you something every week to help with the coal and electricity, and I've left my address on the mantelpiece so you'll know where I am. If there's a phone in the hostel I'll let you have the number, though I don't suppose you'll need to ring me.'

'Don't suppose I shall.' Minnie Jepson was used to managing alone. A childless widow from the last war, she had quickly learned to make ends meet and live from day to day on her pension. 'And don't give this house another thought once you've left it. I'll soon have it to my liking, never you fear, girl.'

Housework was Minnie Jepson's religion. Her London

9

home had been her total joy until a direct hit from a German bomb had forced her to seek shelter with her sister in Birmingham. Indeed, it was as if Fate had intervened on her behalf, for her sister had died peacefully in her sleep not six weeks after, her nephew Barnaby Allen had been despatched to fight the war in North Africa and now young Kath was taking herself off to darkest Yorkshire. It could not have suited her better.

'I'll send you a letter every week, Kath, to let you know I've got the money all right. And I'll see your bed is kept aired, just in case they let you home for a holiday, though I don't suppose they will.'

She gazed unblinking at her nephew's wife. A good-looking girl, without a doubt. Small wonder Barnaby had courted her with such ferocity and married her with such determination. Dark, almost black hair, yet eyes of blue; so blazingly blue that you couldn't help noticing them. Thick, dark eyelashes and a nice smile. Irish, those looks were; even her name was Irish. Yet there'd been no one of her own at that hasty little wedding. Only the girl who'd stood bridesmaid for her and even she wasn't family. Some girl, hadn't it been, who'd worked as a parlourmaid in the house next door?

'You can pop a saccharin in my tea,' she murmured. 'And give me the second cup. Can't abide it weak.'

'Yes, Aunt Min.' Can't you wait until I'm out of the house before you take it over? It *is* Barney's after all and I *am* his wife and if anything happened to Barney it would be *my* house. 'Are you going to be able to manage on just one ration book when I'm gone?'

'I'll be all right. Managed before I was bombed out, didn't I?' Of course she would manage. With Kath out of the way and the cleaning and polishing done, there'd be plenty of time to stand in the food queues. It wasn't a bad way of passing a couple of hours – even in winter. 'I suppose you'll be living off the fat of the land? Them

10

farmers'll have plenty of milk and eggs. Don't tell me they don't keep a bit back for themselves.'

'I really don't know. But wouldn't you keep some for yourself now and again? Wouldn't you treat yourself to a nice fresh egg for your breakfast?'

Fresh eggs. They were a thing of the past to ordinary people. Minnie Jepson reckoned that the weekly egg on her ration book was at least a fortnight old when she got it; stood to reason, didn't it, the way they smelled when you cracked one? Only fit for putting in a cake – if you had the butter and sugar to spare.

'What's a fresh egg?' she demanded, truculently. 'And hadn't you better be thinking about getting yourself off? You can't rely on a bus being there when you want one; not with a war on, you can't. That case is going to take a bit of carrying, an' all. Best be on your way, girl. Take it slowly.'

'Yes. No use hanging around, I suppose.' She wished Aunt Min wasn't so anxious to be rid of her. 'I'll just slip across the yard to the lavvy and then I'll be going.'

She wished the churning inside her would stop. She was always like this when something untoward happened. Like the morning she married Barney. She'd wanted to run away. If she hadn't been so desperate to leave the house she'd worked in for the past six years, she would have. A skivvy, that's all she had been. She had exchanged the drabness of the children's home for the drabness of domestic service and only marriage to Barney had freed her from it. Or so she had thought until he'd taken her to the little house he had promised her. Trouble was, he hadn't ever mentioned they'd be sharing it with his mother.

She had felt the same churning that day she walked through the doors of the Labour Exchange and told them she wanted to be a landgirl, surprised that she hadn't needed her husband's permission. The knowledge had made her feel slightly giddy, because for once she was doing something entirely because she wanted to. She was making only the second important decision in the whole of her twenty-three-and-a-bit years and she had been shaking with the enormity of it when she left the counter; when the clerk had already made an appointment for her medical and there was almost no going back.

'Ain't you taking Barney's picture with you, then?' Aunt Min took the Clark Gable photograph from the piano top and dusted it absently with her pinafore.

'I've packed one already. I'll leave that one for you.' Kath smiled, wishing her heart hadn't joined the turmoil inside her with loud, insistent thuds. But this was her first real adventure and being in the Land Army was the only taste of freedom she would ever have.

Oh, she was grateful to Barney. He'd given her respectability, a name. She was Kathleen *Allen*. She knew *exactly* who she was and that no one could push her around any more – unless she chose to let them. Now she was the same as anyone else. She had the same identity card, the same ration book and from today she would wear the same uniform and get the same pay as all the other landgirls in a hostel called Peacock Hey. For a woman who had never quite known who she was, that was something of an achievement. When the war was over and Barney came home, she would settle down, be a good wife and have his children. *When* the war was over. In two years, three years, maybe even longer now that Japan had come into it; now that it wasn't just Hitler they had to see to but all those Japs as well. Funny little slant-eyed men who people said fought and fought and never gave in. How long would it take to beat *them*, she wondered, even with the Americans on our side.

'Well then,' she said, wondering why her voice sounded so whispery and strange. 'I'll just put on my hat and coat.'

A short, well-cut top coat; a round, leather-tied hat, though just how she was expected to wear it she didn't know. She placed it comfortably on the back of her head, picked up her gas mask and said again, 'Well then.'

Minnie Jepson walked down the passage, opened the front door then stood, arms folded, waiting.

Kath picked up her case, manoeuvring it with her knee to the doorstep. Then she put it down with a thump, placed her hands on the elder woman's shoulders and kissed her cheek.

'So-long, Aunt Min. Take care of yourself. I'll write, like I promised.'

'Ta-ra, girl. God bless.'

Kath picked up her case. She didn't turn round – you didn't ever look back in wartime – and she wasn't surprised to hear the door slammed shut behind her. Even before she reached the gate.

Slowly she walked to the top of the street. The churning and thumping were even worse now and she felt strange in her uniform, especially in the breeches and knee-length socks.

'Alderby St Mary,' she whispered. Somewhere in the North Riding of Yorkshire and a million miles away, thank God.

The letter addressed to Rosalind Fairchild came by the second delivery on the 18th of December. It bore the words On His Majesty's Service and she had expected it daily for the past two weeks. Sucking in her breath she opened the envelope with a swift, decisive tear, quickly scanned the single sheet of paper, then looked up, her face a blank.

'It's all right, Gran. They're letting me stay at Ridings. I don't have to be called up.'

Hester Fairchild let go her indrawn breath. She had been worried; useless to deny it. Government departments usually did the exact opposite to what was expected or hoped of them, but for once it seemed they had got it right. She was more relieved than her face showed, for war was hateful to her. War – the last one – had taken her husband and she had no wish for this one to snatch away her granddaughter.

'I suppose it's official, now – puts you in a reserved occupation?'

'Seems it does. I'm exempt from call-up, it says here, but I can't change my job without first asking them.' She shrugged. 'I suppose I'd better let Mat Ramsden know. At least I'm one of his problems solved.'

So now it was official. She had a reserved occupation; work considered so important that she was exempted from call-up. And farming *was* important. Now into the third year of the war, food was becoming alarmingly short. Already it was strictly rationed, with rumours of cuts after Christmas and farmers were left in no doubt that they must grow as much food as they could, and then some, with every acre of land used to capacity. Farms and farm-workers became important almost overnight and vital to the war effort, Mr Churchill said. Britain's run-down farms were suddenly in the front line. For the first time since the last war ended, farmers were needed.

'Read it.' Roz handed over the letter.

She was glad it was all settled, that she could stay in Alderby St Mary, though not so very long ago a small, secret part of her had longed to join the armed forces. She had wanted to wear a uniform, to be *seen* to be doing her bit for the war, but that was before Paul; before she had gone to a dance at the aerodrome and met the tall, flaxen-haired navigator. Once she would have scoffed at the idea of love at first sight. That kind of feeling couldn't be love, she'd have said. Instant attraction, perhaps; something sexual. But something strange had taken hold of her that night; some feeling she had not known to exist had set every small pulse in her body beating exquisitely and her mouth had gone dry as he crossed the floor towards her. He hadn't even asked her if she wanted to dance. He'd held out his hand and smiled as if their meeting was meant to be. They had danced the floor twice round before he said, 'Paul. Hullo.' And she had whispered, 'Rosalind. Roz. Hullo, yourself.'

At least she thought that was what she said, but her heart was thudding in her ears and she'd only been sure of his nearness and the absolute rightness of their being together.

Paul Rennie. Crew member of the Lancaster bomber K-King, based at the hastily constructed aerodrome not two miles away. Paul, who had flown his eighth bombing raid the night before and who would soon be on his thirteenth. Operational flight number thirteen; the dicey one, after which it would all be easy until the thirtieth, which would mark the end of the tour.

His first 'op' had been a swine, he'd said. He couldn't remember a lot about that first raid over Germany save that it had been on Bremen and that the sickness in the pit of his stomach had been nothing at all to do with turbulence. But Paul was like that. He didn't think that flying was a piece of cake; bloody stupid of him, really, ever to have volunteered for aircrew. But he was smiling as he said it and his eyes had been laughing, too. Flying Officer Paul Rennie, who lived near Bath and had a twin sister called Pippa who was a Waaf, somewhere in Lincolnshire.

She would see Paul again tomorrow at the Friday-night dance – if he wasn't flying, that was. If this viciously cold weather continued all week; if a wind from the south didn't banish the frost overnight.

'Won't be long, Gran.' She shrugged into her coat. 'Just going over to the farm.'

Mat would be glad they were letting her stay, just as Gran was. Even if she had never met Paul, it made sense that she should remain in Alderby, because Gran needed her and now Ridings needed her too; a need which had first arisen the day the representative from the War Agricultural Executive Committee – the man from the War Ag. they called him – had come to Ridings. That day, he had gravely and silently paced the boundaries of the parkland surrounding the house, the game-cover and all the grazing Gran rented to Mat for his beef cattle. He had made notes and calculations then said he hoped Mrs Fairchild appreciated that all these idle acres must come under the plough?

'Technically, you see, parkland is grassland and grassland is an extravagance. It just doesn't produce enough food to the acre. It's wasteful, and –' He shrugged away the remainder of the sentence. He had no need to explain or to ask. It was simply a case of going politely through the preamble. The Government needed more wheat and barley, potatoes and sugarbeet and farmers must grow them. A landowner with two hundred-odd acres of parkland doing nothing must contribute too. Or lose her land.

'We'll confirm it officially, Mrs Fairchild. And I think it might be reasonable to expect it to be ploughed –' he waved an all embracing arm, 'by the first of March, next?'

Hester Fairchild nodded apprehensively. 'The beeches?' she asked him, gazing stunned down the majestic tree-lined drive. 'And the oaks? I don't have to – surely you aren't asking me to –' Her lips refused to form the words *have them cut down*. There were more than a hundred, and to fell such magnificent trees was unthinkable.

The man from the War Ag. pursed his lips. 'I think we can leave the trees – plough round them.' He had acquired over two hundred acres for cultivation with less trouble than he'd expected; he was willing to leave the woman her trees. 'I'm afraid, though, that the spinney . . .' He condemned the game-cover with a nod. 'The rough woodland must go. You'll appreciate that?'

'Yes. Of course.' The mistress of Ridings agreed at once; there were no trees of importance there.

So the man from the War Ag. had thanked her, shaken her hand and wished her good-day, well satisfied. She watched him drive off in his official car wondering how she was going to be able to plough up all those acres, tear out game-cover, and cultivate and harvest crops for the war effort.

But at least it would be a means to an end, Roz considered, reluctant to leave the warmth of the kitchen. Ridings was almost a farm now, and she was a farm-worker in a reserved occupation and for that she must be grateful. She could see the war out at home, which was more than most eighteen-year-olds could even begin to hope for.

'Oops! Sorry, Polly,' she gasped, almost colliding with the slight, grey-haired woman who stood in the doorway. 'Didn't see you! Gran will tell you the news.'

'And what in the name of goodness was all that about?' Polly Appleby put down the brown paper carrier-bag which held polishing cloths, pinafore and slippers. 'Rush, rush, rush, that one. Never a minute to spare. Where's she off to now?'

'The letter came.'

'Oh, aye? It's all right, then?'

'It's all right. They're not going to call her up.'

'Never thought they would.' Polly filled the kettle and set it on the stove top. 'Stands to reason, don't it? I suppose she's away to tell Jonty Ramsden?'

'To tell Mat, actually. It's good of Mat to help out with the ploughing and such-like. He hasn't got the time, really, and he certainly doesn't have the men. He's got his own farm to run and there's only Jonty to help him.'

'There's Grace. Works like a man, Grace Ramsden

does. And Mat Ramsden'll do all right out of your park-land – or so talk has it.' She held her hands to the fire. 'But you'll not be interested in village talk.'

Only Polly spoke to Hester Fairchild as an equal. Polly had always been there; had been a housemaid at Ridings when Hester Fairchild came there as a bride, all those years ago.

She stooped to throw a log on the fire, sending white ash falling into the hearth, and red sparks darting up the chimney.

'My, but that's a frosty fire, ma'am. Be a cold 'un tonight.'

'The village?' Hester took cups and saucers from the dresser. 'What are they saying now?'

'Well, talk has it that Mat Ramsden has asked the War Ag. for a landgirl. All Alderby knows. If he's to go into partnership with you, they reckon he's going to need all the help he can get.'

'Alderby seems well informed, as usual,' Hester observed. 'And it won't be a partnership, exactly. But I'm told I must plough up my parkland and grow food on it, and since my acres are next to his, it seems sensible to work them between us as best we can.

'That's why Roz applied for exemption. She might as well work on her own land as join the Land Army and work on someone else's. I was beginning to think they wouldn't allow it. It seemed such a straightforward solution that I was certain they'd tell her she had to join up, or go into munitions, or something.'

'Hmm.' Polly laid traycloth and cups on the silver-handled tray for, war or no war, even a cup of tea was taken in a civilized manner at Ridings. 'And there's talk that the War Ag. is paying farmers well for putting grazing land under the plough. Two pounds an acre subsidy, I heard tell they'd get. That'll be more than four hundred pounds, won't it?'

'Four hundred and eighty.' The information was tersely given. 'There are two hundred and forty acres, to be exact.' Drat the village for its nosiness and drat it again for being right for once. 'And one landgirl won't be enough, Mat told me. He'll need Roz, too, and a good ploughman. Oh, there'll be enough for the girls to do; just for them to take over the milk-round will be a load off Grace Ramsden's mind.

'But my land must be ploughed up, and soon. Those acres have been down to grass since ever I can remember and the sooner they're opened up to the weather the better.'

'I'll grant you that, but a good ploughman is as rare as hen's teeth these days,' Polly brooded. Stood to reason, didn't it? There'd been little money in farming between the wars and small use growing crops that nobody wanted to buy. Ploughs had lain rusting these last twenty years; ploughmen had abandoned their skills and gone to the towns.

'I know that, Polly, but we'll manage between us. We'll have to. If that parkland isn't under cultivation by March, the War Ag. will take it over for the duration. It's as simple as that.'

'But they can't do that, ma'am. Isn't theirs to take!'

'They can, and they will. The War Ag. can take my land just as any government department can take anything it wants. They'd fling the Defence of the Realm Act at me and if I protested I'd be unpatriotic.'

'And lose your land, whether or no.'

'Exactly. So let's hope Mat gets his ploughman and his landgirl.'

'Aye.' Polly settled herself in the fireside rocker, stirring her tea, gazing into the hearth. Just the one fire burning here, now, yet when she'd been a young under-housemaid here, she could have counted five fires at least burning from morning till night, and fires in the bedrooms, too.

19

But coal was a pound a ton then, and logs for the taking from the estate. And the Master had been alive and Miss Roz's mother a slip of a girl.

Ridings had been the place to work at the turn of the century, Polly considered. Far better than being in service at Peddlesbury, ugly old Victorian pile that it had been. Built on wool and inherited coal money and them as lived there then not real gentry, like the Fairchilds. Now Peddlesbury was an aerodrome and Ridings not the house it used to be.

But things had been different before the Master was killed. And before that fire. Twenty-four bedrooms there'd once been and three housemaids and a cook and scullery-maid and a footman. Aye, and a parlourmaid and a housekeeper as well as the outside staff.

But that was another life it seemed, and now she, Polly, lived in one of the gate lodges and came each day to 'do'. She had been a part of a life that was long gone and because she still remembered the Master and Miss Janet, she was as much a part of Ridings as the woman who owned it and the granddaughter who would one day inherit it, and the worry of it.

'You're quiet all of a sudden. Penny for them?'

'Oh, they'm worth more than a penny,' Polly returned gravely. 'Oh my word, yes. A lot more than that.'

'Then I'd best not ask. But sometimes, Polly, I wonder. Have I been wise, urging this exemption on Rosalind? Often, I think she spends too much time with me. Might it not have been better if I hadn't tried so hard to keep her here – if she'd been left free to join the forces, seen a bit of life outside Alderby St Mary?'

'It might have been, but like you said, she just might have opted to join the Land Army and been sent to work on some other farm.'

'I know. But what do you mean, some other farm? I don't have a farm, Poll Appleby.'

20

'You don't? Then what would you call all those acres you've got to cultivate? Seems to me that whether you like it or not you're up to the neck in farming for the duration, and so is Miss Roz. And she's as well staying at home and looking after her inheritance as she is joining the Air Force or the Army.'

'Inheritance? A few hundred acres of parkland and all that remains of a house? And the parkland will go back to grass when the war is over and be left idle again. Some inheritance! And it's all I have to leave her. That, and her name,' she whispered bitterly.

'Now don't get yourself upset, ma'am. I know it's the time of year, but soon it'll be Christmas and afore you know it there'll be a new year to look forward to.'

The time of year. December, when everything awful happened, Hester brooded. They'd taken Martin from her in December and it had been December when Ridings caught fire, the lanes so blocked with snow that the horses pulling the fire engine made heavy going and arrived almost too late.

And did it have to be December when Janet and Toby drove up to Scotland, leaving a two-year-old child behind them at Ridings and never coming back for her?

'Yes, Polly, it'll soon be over. And take no notice of me. I'm just a silly old woman.'

'Old? You? Nay, I'll not have that.'

The Mistress was sixty-four, Polly knew that as fact. She looked nowhere near her age, with those great brown eyes and hardly a line on the whole of her face. A beautiful woman, holding back time; still waiting for her man to come home, and find her unchanged. To Polly, she was still the laughing young girl who came to Ridings all those years ago on Martin Fairchild's arm. And she would always be a fitting mistress for Ridings, no matter how life had treated her.

Thank God for the man from the War Ag. because now

Ridings would be earning its keep again – the Mistress would have a pound or two in her pocket and not have to worry about keeping body and soul together, counting every penny and every lump of coal she put on the fire. Hester Fairchild had kept her pride and reared Miss Janet's little lass to be a credit to the place. High time she had a bit of luck. Heaven only knew she deserved some.

Sniffing, Polly placed her cup on the draining board. 'Ah, well. Best be making a start. What'll it be today, then? Bedrooms or bathroom and stairs?'

The sky was ice-blue, the earth hard underfoot, the grass white and crisp with hoar frost. There was no sun, but the sky shone with a strange, metallic brightness and Roz knew that tonight it would be bitterly cold again. Tonight, the bombers at Peddlesbury would remain grounded.

'I'm back!' she called, slamming shut the door, hurrying to the fire. 'My, but it's cold. No sign of a let-up. It'll freeze hard again tonight, just see if it doesn't. I don't suppose there's a cup of tea in the pot?'

There was. Almost always. Tea was rationed, so the pot was kept warm and used until the leaves inside it would take no more diluting.

'What did Mat say?' Hester poured boiling water into the pot. 'Was he pleased?'

'Mat wasn't there. He's gone to the Labour Exchange again to nag them some more about a farm man, and Jonty's gone to York for spares for the tractor. Grace said he wants to make a start on our ploughing as soon as the frost lets up a bit. It's going to be one heck of a job, you know.

'And good news – they're getting a landgirl very soon. She might even be there tomorrow. Grace said that since I know everybody in the village, it might be a good idea for me and the new girl to take over the milk-round.

'So don't worry too much, Gran love. We'll have Ridings

22

parkland earning its keep before so very much longer. Think I'd better pop upstairs and tell Polly about the letter . . .'

'Polly knows, so don't keep her talking!' Hester called to the retreating back. Then her lips formed an indulgent smile, because it seemed that her granddaughter was right. Between them they would make those long-idle acres grow food and earn money. Roz didn't have to go away and December would soon be over. There'd be another year to look forward to; another spring.

'Thank you, Janet,' she whispered, eyes closed, 'for giving me this lovely child . . .'

Roz walked around the bed Polly was making and picked up a corner of the sheet. 'You know about the letter, Poll?'

'Aye. Charity begins at home.'

'Hmm. Jonty's making a start on Gran's ploughing very soon and Mat's been allocated a landgirl at last, so it's all going to work out, isn't it? We'll make it by March, if the frost breaks soon. Bet it's terrible on the Russian front. They say it's the coldest December for nearly twenty years.' She abandoned the bed-making to wander over to the dressing-table mirror. 'It's *freeeeezing* outside. Just look at my nose. Red as my hair, isn't it?' Frowning, she turned away. 'I'm not a bit like Gran, am I, Poll? Come to think of it, I'm not really like anybody. Where do you suppose my colouring came from?'

'Colouring? With hair like yours, you're complaining?'

'No. Just curious. Gran is dark and so was Grandpa. And my parents were dark-haired and dark-eyed, so who sneaked in my carrot top?'

'*Auburn*.' Carrot top, indeed!

'Auburn, then. But where did it come from?' Not from anyone in any of the portraits, that was certain. All the way up the stairs and on the landing and in the downstairs rooms, not one of the Fairchilds hanging there had red hair. 'Where, will you tell me?'

'Gracious, child, how should I know? From your father's side, perhaps, or maybe you'm a bit of a throwback? Yes, come to think of it, there was one with red hair, I seem to remember. Her portrait got burned, though, in the fire.'

'Yes, of course.' Roz didn't remember, but best not talk about the fire, especially in December, that bleakest of months. 'I suppose it makes a change – my being green-eyed, I mean, and red-haired.'

'Suppose it does. Wouldn't do if we all looked alike, would it? Now are you going to give me a hand with this bed, or are you going to stand there staring into that mirror till it's done?'

'It isn't going to be a barrel of laughs, Poll, my being in a reserved occupation.' Roz straightened the fat, pink eiderdown. 'People look at you when you're young and not in uniform, you know. Jonty's had all sorts slung at him.'

'Then I'm sure I don't know why.' Polly sniffed. 'Jonty is doing a good job for the war effort and so will you be. Growing food is important, or why did they make you reserved?'

'Yes, but when you're as young as Jonty and me, people just expect you to be in uniform. He's taken quite a bit of stick about it. "Get some in!" someone yelled after him. "Why aren't you in khaki, mate? A bloody conchie, are you?", though I know he'd rather have been a pilot, or a Commando.'

'They'd never take Jonty Ramsden for a pilot nor a Commando,' Polly retorted, matter-of-factly. 'When did you ever see a pilot or a Commando wearing spectacles? Jonty will survive such talk and so will you, though it's sad people should say things like that.'

If Martin Fairchild had been in a reserved occupation in the last war, he'd have been alive today, the older woman brooded. Uniforms were all very well, were fine and smart and patriotic, but they got you killed. The Mistress wouldn't have minded the taunts. And now it was happening again. The war to end all wars, they said that one had been, yet only twenty years on . . .

Sad for the young ones, really. This war was none of their making, yet it was young shoulders the burden had fallen on, Polly sighed silently, and so many of them would never see the end of it. The Master hadn't, nor her own young man. But that war was history, now. Their war had been glorified slaughter and because of that she was glad Miss Roz was staying at home with her gran; glad she would never join the armed forces, nor wear a uniform. And if thinking that was unpatriotic, then she didn't give a damn, Polly thought, defiantly. Roz was all the Mistress had left. It was as simple as that.

Now the daft young thing was nattering on about her hair again, and that they could do without. Mind, it came up from time to time and was dealt with by her grandmother. But Roz ought to be told, Polly scowled, picking up dustpan and brush. She'd said as much, not all that long ago.

'Don't you think Miss Roz is old enough to know about –' she'd said.

'About *what*?' the Mistress had interrupted, off-hand. 'That she's a Fairchild? But she knows that, Polly. She's always known it. What more is there to tell?'

What more indeed? The Mistress had probably been right. And even if she wasn't, she had her reasons for acting as she did.

'She'll hear nothing from me.'

'Of course she won't, Poll Appleby. There's nothing to tell,' Hester Fairchild replied briskly. Then her face had taken on that long-ago look. 'Polly, if suddenly I weren't here –'

'Oh, aye? And where, suddenly, are you going, then?'

'You know what I mean! I'm talking about the war;

about nobody being certain of anything any more, and you know it. If suddenly I weren't here, Poll, then it would be up to you. Because you're the only one who knows, apart from me; the only one I'd trust to tell her. But only if she really needed to know, you understand?'

'Aye, ma'am. Only if,' she'd said, and the matter had been dropped for all time. Or so they had thought.

Oh, drat that lass and the colour of her hair! Why did she have to go on about it? Why on earth couldn't she leave well alone?

'*Marvellous!*' Kathleen Allen heaved her suitcase from the bus stop opposite, glad to reach the shelter of the railway station again. 'Flipping rotten marvellous!'

To think she might now be sitting beside the fire at home, her feet snug in Aunt Min's hand-knitted slippers, a cup of tea at her side. But she stood instead in a blacked-out, unknown city and the next bus to Alderby St Mary not due for two more hours.

But it was her own fault. She should have heeded her husband's warning and found war work in a factory or office; anywhere but in the Land Army. Dejectedly she sat down on her suitcase. The journey to York had been a nightmare. She had missed her connection at Crewe, though she strongly suspected there had been no connection to miss, then, after giving right of way to a goods train, a troop train and a train carrying ammunition, they at last pulled out of the station almost two hours late.

You were right, Barney. I should have listened to you. And do you know something else? I'm so cold and hungry that I'd sell my soul for a cup of tea!

She wasn't crying, she really wasn't. It was just that it was so cold and draughty sitting here in a gloomy, grimy station that her eyes were watering, and –

'Hi, mate! Anything the matter?' A Waaf corporal in trousers and battle-dress top stood there, smiling. 'Would

26

one of these help?' She reached into her pocket for cigarettes. 'Go on, it's all right.'

'No! I shouldn't.' Cigarettes were hard to come by. It wasn't fair to take other people's, be what they called an OP smoker. 'I'm all right, thanks. Just a smut in my eye . . .'

'I know the feeling well, but it passes, it really does.' The girl in airforce blue took two cigarettes from the packet, then struck a match. 'You wouldn't be looking for a lift?'

'A lift? Oh, aren't I just.' Kath inhaled blissfully. 'But I don't suppose you're going my way. Not to Alderby St Mary?'

'I can do better than that.' The corporal laughed. 'I go right past Peacock Hey, and I'll bet a week's pay that's where you're going.'

'But I am! I *am*!'

'Then just wait till that lot have unloaded their kit.' She jerked her head in the direction of the airmen who jumped down from the back of the truck. 'They're going on leave, the lucky dogs. Home for Christmas. Makes you sick, don't it?'

'Sick. Yes.' Kath drew deeply on her cigarette, then held the lighted end in the cup of her hand, just as she had seen Barney do; just as the corporal did now. Come to think of it, it was the way cigarettes were always held after dark, for didn't they say that even the minutest glow could be seen from an enemy plane, though she very much doubted it. The real reason for cupping a cigarette, she supposed, was to hide it, for smoking outdoors in uniform was forbidden. Wasn't it wonderful that she, Kath Allen, was in uniform now and being called mate by an Air Force driver? *Mate*. It sent a great glow of belonging washing over her and Barney's expected disapproval was suddenly forgotten. She was a landgirl, wasn't she? Still cold and hungry of course, but she was going to live in the country and work

27

on a farm. Before long she would be at Peacock Hey and with luck there'd be a sandwich and a cup of tea there, maybe even hot water for a bath.

'Thanks.' She smiled at the Waaf corporal. 'Thanks a lot – mate.'

They drove carefully. The streets of York hadn't been laid down with RAF trucks in mind, the corporal said, and there were blacked-out traffic lights which could hardly be seen.

'Isn't it amazing,' Kath murmured when the city was behind them, 'you knowing about Peacock Hey, I mean.'

'Not really. The girls there go to the Friday-night dances at our place and sometimes, if I'm on late duty like now, I take the truck and collect them.'

'Your place?'

'RAF Peddlesbury. There's a big old house on the very edge of the runway called Peddlesbury Manor; it's the Ops Centre and the Mess, now, and some of the unmarried officers sleep there, too. I believe Peacock Hey was once owned by the manor; I think the bailiff lived there. The Peacock girls are a decent crowd. It's your first billet, isn't it?'

'Yes, and I'm looking forward to it. I've never lived in the country, you see – come from Birmingham . . .'

'Well, one thing's certain. It's a whole lot quieter round these parts than Birmingham – or London, where I come from. Not a lot of bombing here, but we get quite a few nuisance raids. On the whole, though, you can expect to get a good night's sleep. Has anyone told you where you'll be working?'

'Haven't a clue. Hope it isn't a dairy farm. Couldn't milk a cow to save my life.'

'You'll learn, mate.' The girl at the wheel grinned. 'When I joined this mob I'd never been in charge of anything more lethal than a push-bike and look at me now, driving this truck.'

Kath sat contented in the darkness of the cab, peering into the rolling blackness as if she were riding shotgun. She wished she didn't feel so smug, so defiant almost, because at this moment she didn't care what Barney's next letter might bring. For just once she was doing what she wanted to do and it was heady stuff. When the war was over and Barney came home, she would be a devoted wife, keep his home clean and always have his meals ready on time. But for now, for the duration, she would enjoy every minute of being a landgirl and living in the country. If the corporal could learn to drive a truck, then Kathleen Allen could learn to milk a cow and maybe even drive a tractor. She let go a sigh of pure bliss.

'Tired?'

'No. Just glad I'm almost there.' Kath smiled.

'Not *almost*. This is it.' Gently they came to a stop. 'Careful how you get down.'

'This is the hostel?'

'Across the road, beside that clump of trees. Mind how you go. See you around.' The engine started with a roar.

'See you. And thanks a lot, mate!'

The front gate of Peacock Hey had been painted white and the stones, too, that lined the path to the front door. Kath walked carefully, feeling for the doorstep with the toe of her shoe. She couldn't find a bellpush, so knocked loudly instead, waiting apprehensively.

From inside came the swish of a curtain being pulled, then the door opened wide.

'Where on earth have you been, girl? We expected you before supper. It's Kathleen Allen, isn't it?'

'That's me. Sorry I'm late. The –'

'Oh, away with your bother.' The tall, slender woman drew the blackout curtain over the door again then switched on the light. 'Trains bad, I suppose?'

'Awful. I got a lift, though, from York.' She looked around at the linoleum-covered floor and stairs, at the

29

row of coat pegs and the letterboard beside the telephone. It reminded her of the orphanage, yet her welcome here had been warm, and there was a vase of yellow and bronze chrysanthemums in the stair alcove. The flowers comforted her, assured her it would be all right. She had a theory about houses – they liked you or they didn't. Either way it showed, and Peacock Hey liked her.

'I don't suppose there'd be a cup of tea?' she asked, nervously.

'There would, lassie, but let's get your case upstairs, then you can come down to the kitchen and have a bite. Cook lives locally and she's away home, but she left you something and I've been keeping it hot in the bottom of the oven.

'Afraid you're in the attic – oh, I'm Flora Lyle by the way. I'm your Forewoman.' She held out her hand and her grip was warm and firm. 'I hope you don't mind being shoved up here? It's cold in winter and hot in summer, but it'll only be until someone leaves and there's bedspace for you in one of the rooms. We shouldn't really use the attics – fire-bomb risk, you know, but I don't suppose there'll be any, and there's sand and water up there, just in case. And you *will* have a room to yourself,' she added, as if by way of compensation. 'It's just that we're so crowded . . .'

'It looks just fine to me.' Kath set down her case and gazed around the small, low-ceilinged room, saw a black-painted iron bed, mattress rolled, blankets folded, a window hung with blackout curtains in the gable-end wall. Stark, it was, like the orphanage; bare like her room had been in service.

'Your cupboard is outside on the landing, I'm afraid.'

'It doesn't matter. It really doesn't.' A chest of drawers stood beneath the sloping ceiling, a chair beside the bed. 'It's fine, truly.'

Kath didn't mind being in the attic. She had slept in an attic the whole of her years in domestic service and shared it, what was more, with a maid who snored. A room to herself was an unknown luxury, far removed from the long, green dormitory she once slept in with nineteen others. Even married to Barney she had shared, not only with him which was to be expected, but with his mother next door, for she'd been sure the old lady lay awake nights, ears strained for every whisper and every creak of their marital bedsprings. Yes, an attic – a *room* to herself would be bliss and she wouldn't care if they left her there until it was all over, and Barney came home.

Barney? Oh, lordy! If only he could see her now.

'I don't suppose you know where I'll be going to work?' Kath hung her coat and gas mask on the door peg.

'I do. You're going to Ramsden's farm, at the far end of Alderby village. You're urgently needed, it seems. They want you there in the morning. Now, lassie, do you want to unpack first, or would you rather eat?'

'Eat – *please*!' Kath followed her amiable Forewoman to the warmth of the kitchen, sighing as the plate was set before her.

She would remember this day for ever, she really would. Thursday, 18th December 1941; the day on which her new life began. It had taken a long, long time, but now she was here in the country and it was near-unbelievable and undeniably wonderful.

'Thanks,' she whispered huskily. 'Thanks a lot . . .'

2

There was no denying that bicycles figured importantly in Kathleen Allen's life. They always had, as far back as she could remember, starting with the orphanage and the little tricycles that were the only memory worth keeping from those days of grudging charity. The bright red three-wheeler with the noisy bell was her favourite and she had pedalled around and around the asphalted yard on this gaudy friend who shared her secret dreams; dreams in which she was not an orphan but a real little girl whose mother dressed her in a buttercup-sprigged cotton dress with knickers to match and whose father gave her rides on the crossbar of his bicycle and boasted, 'Our Kathleen's doing well at school.' *Our*. That lovely, belonging little word.

When her in-service days began, there had been her first proud possession, something entirely her own, paid for at three shillings and sixpence a month, for a whole year. A second-hand bicycle, black-painted, with a bag on the back and a basket at the front.

'Lizzie,' she whispered, remembering. 'Old Tin Lizzie.'

She had ridden Tin Lizzie on her afternoons off and on summer evenings when she finished work. She was cycling in the country the day she and Barney met. Had it not been for a flat tyre, the lorry driver would never have jumped from his cab and offered his help.

'Oh dear, chucks. Know how to mend it?'

She shook her head, knowing only that the cost of repair would take a large bite from the one pound ten shillings she received on the last day of each month.

So the driver put the bicycle on the back of his lorry and

drove to the Birmingham town house in which she worked, offering to remove the wheel and repair the puncture in his own backyard. To her shame she had refused, for where was the guarantee she would ever see her wheel again?

But she saw Barnaby Allen again that very next evening when he knocked loudly on the front door – the *front* door, mind you – saying he was the bicycle repair man. The parlourmaid pointed in the direction of the area steps, reminding him tartly that the kitchen door was the one upon which to knock when doing business with a housemaid.

Barney. His cheekiness had made her laugh and the dedication with which he courted her had been quite bewildering. And now, at six o'clock in the morning she was cycling into her new, exciting life, wishing she knew where Alderby St Mary was, let alone Matthew Ramsden's farm.

She stopped, listening, eyes peering into a darkness that came back at her in dense, rolling waves. 'Alderby's about a mile down the lane,' Flora had told her at the hostel. 'Keep straight on and you can't miss it. Watch out for the Air Force boys, though. Drive those trucks like fiends some of them do . . .'

She set off again cautiously; you had to take care in the blackout. Swollen noses, bruises and shattered spec[s] had become a joke, almost. 'Jumped out and hit you, d[id] it?' Unexpected obstacles had a lot to answer for, especially lamp-posts.

Ahead, the first pale streaks of daybreak coloured the sky, tipping the clouds with yellow, all at once giving shape to houses and trees and the tower of a church. This must be the place, sitting at the end of the longest, darkest, slowest mile she had ever pedalled. Surely she would find someone soon, who could tell her where to find Matthew Ramsden's farm.

She stood still again and listened, breath indrawn. That

was something else about the blackout. You couldn't see, so you listened. Surprising how another sense took over. Someone *was* there and not too far away, either. She pulled in her breath once more, heard the slow, rhythmic grating of cartwheels and the clop of hooves somewhere to her right. 'Hullo?' she called eagerly. 'Hullo, there!'

'Over here! Watch out for the horse-trough!' A pinpoint of light made circles in the darkness and she walked carefully in the direction of the voice. A pony and trap came into focus; milk bottles clinked.

'Hullo?' she said again.

'Here I am.' A woman's voice. 'Looking for someone?'

'Goodness! Am I glad to meet you.' Kath's laugh was high with relief. 'I'm looking for Ridings Home Farm. Is this Alderby St Mary?'

'It is. Just hang on till I check that I haven't missed anybody.' A spot of torchlight shone on the pages of a book, lighting a young face and a fall of auburn hair. 'That's it, then. Just the school milk to drop off, and Polly's, then I'm finished. I'm Roz Fairchild, by the way. I work at Ridings.' A hand reached out.

'Kathleen Allen. Kath.' She grasped the hand firmly. 'I'm pleased to meet you.' She really was.

'Not as glad as Mat Ramsden's going to be to meet *you*. He's desperate for help. Hope you're his new landgirl?'

'That's me, though I've only just joined. It'll be my first farm and I'm a bit nervous.'

'Then don't be, because I'm new to it, too. This is my first day – my first *official* day. We'll muddle through between us.'

'I can't milk, Roz.' Worrying about those cows again, dammit.

'Neither can I, but it's machine milking at Mat's so it won't be too bad. Jonty will show us how. Let's be making tracks, eh? I'm just about frozen.' The weather wasn't letting up, thank heaven. There'd be no ploughing

34

but there wouldn't be any flying, either. Paul would make it to the dance tonight. 'Grace is sure to have the kettle on. C'mon, Daisy. Hup, girl.'

The little pony set off with a toss of its head that set the harness jingling.

Daisy, Kath smiled; Roz and Daisy. Two friends, and she was on her way to hot tea and a welcome.

Happiness flushed her cheeks. She wouldn't spoil one minute of this day by worrying about what Barney's letter would bring. There was a war on and a woman whose husband was away at war must learn to think for herself, make decisions she would once never dreamed of making. No, Kath decided, suddenly headily defiant, she wouldn't worry – well, not until Barney came home.

She smiled with pure pleasure and fell in behind the milk-float that would lead her to the farm. New friends and tea. What more could a girl – a *landgirl* – want on this most special morning?

They came upon Ridings unexpectedly, rounding the broad sweep of lane to see it there ahead of them. It was one of the nice things about the old house, Roz always thought. Now, the fast-lightening sky silhouetted it sharply, sending a glow like candlelight through the empty stone windows, gentling the jagged, broken shell.

'What's that old ruin? An abbey?' Kath gasped.

'That's Ridings,' Roz laughed, 'or what's left of it. I live there.' She always enjoyed telling people she lived in a ruin.

'Oh, goodness, I'm sorry. I didn't mean . . .' Her embarrassment was short-lived, for Roz was smiling. 'I mean – it's an unusual name, isn't it?'

'Ridings? I suppose it is. It's because half of it is in the North Riding and half of it's in the West Riding. The boundary line runs right through the estate. And it isn't all a ruin. There's a bit more to it than that. It was built in the shape of a T, you see, and the top of the T was completely destroyed, but the stem, the bit at the back, survived. That's the part we live in.'

She called the pony to a halt. She loved this aspect of the old house; always from this spot she sent up a thank you that it hadn't been entirely gutted that December day, twenty-four years ago.

'It must have been one heck of a place,' Kath breathed. 'And just look at those gates . . .'

The entrance to Ridings had been built with pride. Sweeping stone gateposts were topped by finely chiselled greyhounds and on either side of them the gate lodges stood splendidly ornate. Kath gazed at the intricately patterned gates and the garish morning light that filtered through the delicate ironwork.

'The height of three men and as old as the house itself.' Roz smiled, though the name of the craftsman who created them had never been known. 'I'm glad you like them. Mind, we live in fear that someone's going to take them away before very much longer.'

She hoped the gates would escape the scrap metal hunters; men who came with the blessing of the Government and removed gates and railings without so much as a by-your-leave, carting them off to be melted down for the war effort. Only field gates were safe, and unpatriotic though it was to harbour such thoughts, Roz was glad that so far Ridings' gates had not been found.

'Who did it?' Kath demanded. 'Cromwell?'

'No. This one we can't blame on him, though the Fairchilds were Royalists, I believe. It was a fire; a wiring fault. Funny, really, that it survived for nearly four hundred years with candles and oil lamps and then my grandfather decided that electricity would be safer.'

'How big was it?' Much bigger, surely, than the orphanage.

'Quite a size – over twenty bedrooms, but I never saw it the way it was. There are pictures, though, and photographs, and I sometimes think the fire was meant to be because Gran and me couldn't have kept it going; not a place that size.'

'It's yours? You own it?'

'It's Gran's. Before my father died – he was an architect – he had the ruins tidied up, sort of. The fire destroyed the roof so everything had to be pulled down for safety, except the outer walls. Then Gran had creepers and climbing roses planted against them and in summer it looks really beautiful. It's mellowed, I suppose.'

'And was much left, at the back?'

'Too much, I'm afraid. It's murder keeping it warm in winter. The part that survived was once the kitchen block and servants' quarters and my father drew up the plans when Gran had it done over. You'll see it, when you meet her.

'But let's get Daisy watered and fed, then we can thaw ourselves out at Grace's fire, and cadge a cup of tea.'

Roz looked at the young woman beside her, seeing her clearly for the first time, amazed by her beauty. There was no mistaking it, even in a face pinched with cold and tied round with a head-scarf. Deep, blue-grey eyes, thick-lashed, and a full, sensuous mouth.

'Is your boyfriend in the forces, Kathleen?'

'My husband is. Barney.' Her lips moved into a brief smile. 'He's in North Africa – a driver in the Service Corps. And call me Kath, will you? I'm used to Kath. What about you?' Too young to be married. Seventeen, perhaps?

'Not married, but I've got a boyfriend. I'm seeing him tonight. There's a – *Damn*!' She reached for a bottle of milk. 'I forgot Polly at the lodge! Won't be a minute. Just follow Daisy, will you? She knows her way home. I'll catch you up.'

Kath turned to watch the girl who ran swiftly back to the gates. A little older than seventeen, she conceded, but in love for the first time if shining eyes were anything to go by. Amazing how important people were in wartime; how easily you got to know them. Before the war you didn't ask such personal questions; you kept yourself to yourself and respected the other person's right to privacy. Yet now it was necessary to make friends quickly, because one thing no one had a lot of was time. For some, there wasn't even a tomorrow. Young as she was, Roz could already have learned that, poor kid.

But tomorrow was a long way off when today had only just begun. Lovely, lovely today. Her first day in the country where she had always longed to be.

'Sorry, Barney,' she whispered, 'but you owe me this one.'

Smiling, she set off after the little pony.

'There now, that'll be Roz. I thought she'd forgotten us.' Polly Appleby glanced up from the porridge pan at the clink of the milk bottle on the back-door step. 'Bring it in, Arnie, there's a good lad.'

She watched the boy dart away. He would expect the top of the milk on his porridge and she would give it to him; after all a growing lad needed a good breakfast inside him. Arnie ate every last scrap of food she set before him with silent dedication and no I-don't-like-this and I-don't-like-thats. His appreciation of food made cooking a joy, even with rationing the way it was. He'd been like that right from the start, come to think of it; a small, hungry seven-year-old, scrawny and unwashed, the last of the bunch.

They had started, that day the evacuees arrived in Alderby, at the far end of the village and house by house the pretty little girls and the clean, tidy boys had been picked out and taken in. Since she was the last call on the list, Polly accepted, it stood to reason she had been given what was left; an evacuee called Arnold Bagley whose clothes didn't fit and who'd scowled at her something alarming.

'I'm afraid,' said the WVS lady who accompanied the billeting officer, 'that he's all we have to offer, but there *is* an allowance of five shillings a week . . .'

Polly had squirmed inside at the injustice of it and her heart warmed to the unwanted boy who stood on her doorstep, his possessions in a carrier-bag, a label pinned to his jacket.

'Just what I wanted,' she said briskly. 'Come you in, lad, and let's get you sorted out.'

She'd have wanted him with or without the five shillings. Arnold Bagley was a challenge, a child to be cleaned and fed and put snugly to sleep in the little back bedroom. And cleaning and feeding he received, for there had been scarcely a pick of flesh on the young bones.

She recalled that first meal. Rabbit pie and rice pudding for afters. He'd eaten it as if it were the first food he'd seen all week, then looked with longing at the pudding dish and asked to be allowed to scrape it clean.

'There was another lady with Roz, Aunty Poll. I saw her.' Arnie took his place at the table again, sitting with spoon erect, waiting. 'She was pushing a bike and she had trousers on.'

'There now, that'll be the landgirl. Mat Ramsden'll be relieved she's come, even though the lass won't know a cow from a bull. Come on, then. Get on with that porridge whilst I make your toast.'

She smiled fondly. The lad was a credit to her, everybody said so. He'd filled out and was three inches taller than when she got him and his two top teeth had grown in straight as a die.

She'd had her anxious moments, though, clothing that ever-growing, ever-hungry frame, but with the help of jumble sales and hand-me-downs she had managed. Arnie was the centre of her lonely life and just let his feckless mother try to take him back to Hull. Just let her try!

She turned the bread on the fork and held it to the fire.

There'd be something fresh to talk about this morning when she went up to the house. Pity the frost hadn't broken in the night. The Mistress was letting that ploughing business get out of all proportion and no use telling her it would get done in the Lord's good time, though it always had and it always would be. They'd manage, somehow.

'Jam on it, or marmalade?' she said to Arnie.

'It looks,' Grace Ramsden pulled aside the kitchen blackout, 'as if our landgirl has arrived.' She nodded in the direction of the dairy where Roz and a strange young woman unloaded the milk-float. 'And making herself useful already. The post has come, by the way. On the table.' She pulled out the fire-damper and set the kettle to boil. Roz had managed the milk-round all right, it seemed. But then, the lass knew the village, didn't she; lived in it since she was a bairn of two, bless her. 'Ready for a bit of breakfast, then?'

She broke eggs into a pan, a contented woman, a rare woman, even, who recognized happiness the moment it came upon her, not like some who saw it only when it was past, and lost. These moments were happy ones, to be lived and remembered. Just this morning when she shook Jonty awake, she had felt such a blaze of happiness to see him there that she had thanked God yet again for letting her keep her son, then sent up another prayer for all the sons who had gone to war and the mothers who had waved them bravely on their way.

Jonty had been their only child, she frowned, basting egg-yolks with spitting bacon fat. She and Mat had never been blessed with a daughter, but now she was to have girls around the place at last; two young lasses to help on the farm and be in and out of her kitchen all day, she shouldn't wonder. Just to think of it gave her pleasure.

'Fried bread?' she demanded of her husband who didn't look up from the letter he was reading.

Fried bread for Jonty, too, when he'd seen to the cows, and the lasses would soon be in for tea and toast, huffing and puffing with cold and warming their hands at her fire.

Daylight had been late coming this morning. Farming was hard enough in winter without the blackout making it worse, Grace considered, but soon the shortest day would be past them. Winter would be half-way gone and the days would begin to lengthen; there'd be the first snowdrop beneath the holly hedge where they always found it and spring just around the corner.

She gave an involuntary shudder. Something, no mistaking it, had just walked over her grave. Or maybe it was only her silly self being so contented with her own little world that Someone up there was sending down a warning.

Grace Ramsden lifted her eyes, offering a silent apology, assuring Him she really did count her blessings and would count them harder, if need be.

'Fried bread, I asked you,' she murmured, 'and you take not a bit of notice. What's so interesting in that letter, then?'

'It's the farm man. They've got us one. He can plough, too, it seems.'

'There you are, then! Problem solved, so why the long face, you daft old brush?'

'Why?' Mat handed over the envelope. 'Read this. Go on – read it.'

'Oh, my word.' Grace frowned when she had read the letter, then read it again. 'This is going to put the cat among the pigeons, all right. Mrs Fairchild isn't going to like this at all. And who's to be the one to break it to her, will you tell me?'

'Mrs Fairchild's land has got to be ploughed and worked for the duration, lass, so she don't have much of a choice,' Mat retorted, tight-lipped. 'Nor do we, come to that. Complain and all they'll do is tell us there's a war on.'

41

'Then if you want my opinion,' Grace laid the letter on the table, 'that lot at the War Ag. are dafter than I thought.'

Trouble, that letter was going to bring; nothing but trouble and heartache.

Polly saw the black and white bird as it slipped sleekly into the holly bush, and crossed her fingers.

'Drat you, bird,' she hissed.

She didn't like magpies; to see one so early in the day and flying away from a frosty sun, she liked still less. Devil's bird; bringer of ill luck. One for sorrow . . .

Taking a deep breath she hurried past the bush. Nor did she uncross her fingers until she opened the back door at Ridings.

'Well now, you'll have heard about the landgirl?' She hung up her coat, hoping the Mistress had not, wanting to be first with the news.

'I've heard.' Hester Fairchild set the teapot to warm. 'It's the other business I find so hard to accept.' Her face was pale, her mouth tight-set. 'How could they, Polly? How *dare* they?'

'Dare they what?' Polly was mystified. She had hoped to have a chat about the landgirl this morning; discover her name and age and if she looked like shaping-up to farm work. 'What's happening, then, that I don't know about?'

'I told Mat; told him to ring the War Ag. at once. But no, they said, there hadn't been a mistake and he'd be arriving on the first of January. Mat says we've little choice in the matter. If we refuse to take him, Ridings will go to the bottom of the list and the man *can* use a horse-plough, they said.'

'So where's the bother? Seems Mat's got what he wanted and he'll be able to make a start on those acres of yours. I'd have thought that things were bucking up a bit and you could've looked forward to the new year with a bit of hope; aye, and money to come once that grassland of yours has been seen to,' Polly reasoned, ever practical.

'Seen to by an *Italian*, because that's what we've been offered.' Her voice shook with anger. 'That's what my husband gave his life for, Polly; to have his land worked by a man who fought with the Germans.'

'Nay, surely not . . .'

'A Fascist, I tell you! We're so short of manpower that we're having to make prisoners of war work. But I don't want one here. Didn't Italy declare war on us after Dunkirk; stab us in the back? He'll be every bit as bad as a German!'

Why must they do this to her, to a woman who had hated all things German with a bitter intensity since the December day the telegram came. From that day on she had never trusted them and she had been right, because now they were at war with us again. And Italy fighting with them.

But thank God that no one at Ridings need speak to the man when he came, for there must be no fraternization, the War Ag. had told Mat. The man would be brought to the farm each morning from the camp at Helpsley and taken back there by a prison guard. He'd be trusted not to try to escape and anyway, who could hope to escape from an island?

Don't worry, they had said on the phone. One or two farmers had already taken Italian prisoners and it was working out all right. Worry? It would be worry enough just to have the man on her land; on Martin's land.

Yet did she have a choice when the first of March would be on her before she'd hardly had time to think? All the lonely years she had struggled to keep Ridings land intact, yet now it would be given to others to farm if she refused the help of a prisoner of war. But to have such a one

43

walking Martin's acres was too much. The world had gone completely mad.

'Tea,' said Polly briefly, setting down the tray with agitated hands. She knew the Mistress almost as well as she knew herself; knew the pent-up emotions that had found no relief with the passing of time, that writhed and festered inside her, still. Pity the poor woman couldn't have given way to her feelings as she, Polly, had done. The day they told her about Tom's death she had walked and walked, hugging herself tightly, weeping until there were no more tears inside her. In Flanders, her young man had been killed, the spring after the Master was taken.

But Mrs Fairchild's sort didn't weep and rage at life. The gentry hid their feelings because that was what they'd been brought up to do. Pity she'd had to stifle all that grief and bitterness, because hating got you nowhere. Thank the Lord that what happened that December day hadn't affected young Roz, she thought gratefully, for the lass was as happy as the day was long. Which was just as well, all things considered, for it would be her and not the Mistress who'd have to work with the prisoner.

'Wonder what Roz is up to on her first day as a farm-worker?' she offered cautiously, but her effort was wasted, for she got no reply. Not that she'd expected one, but it had been worth a try.

If only, she sighed inside her, Mrs Fairchild didn't take on so about Ridings. If only she would accept that none of this was any of her doing, that there was no price to be paid for what happened all those years ago. But she blamed herself and always would, the proud, foolish woman.

'Damn that magpie,' she muttered. 'Damn the evil creature!'

Washing milk bottles and placing them in the sterilizer required little in the way of concentration and allowed for chatter. It must also, Kath decided, be the warmest job on the farm this bleak, winter morning.

'There now.' Roz smiled. 'Just the milk churns to scald and the floor to mop . . .'

'You know so much about it,' Kath sighed, 'and I don't know anything at all. I'm a dead loss.'

'You'll soon learn – get used to the routine and the seasons. It's the seasons that govern farming. I don't really know a lot; it's just that I seem to have been in and out of Home Farm since ever I can remember. It grows on you, I suppose. It was only yesterday they told me officially that I could stay on and work here. I'd half expected to be called up, you know. What's it like, Kath, leaving home and living in a hostel?'

'It's going to be great. The Forewoman is fine and the Warden, too. They were really concerned because there was nowhere for me to sleep but the attic. And I didn't mind at all. I hope they leave me there. It's the first time I've ever had a room to myself – can't get over the novelty . . .'

'You're from a big family, I suppose,' Roz demanded, enviously.

'Yes, you might say that.' Her laugh was genuine. 'As a matter of fact I was brought up in an orphanage.'

Best get it over with; let everyone know, right from the start. You knew where you stood, then, with people.

'Oh, Kath, I'm sorry – well, sorry if it was awful, I mean. I didn't mean to pry.'

'It's all right.' She laughed again at the sight of the bright red face. 'And I don't really know if it was awful – I've never known anything else, you see. I was left outside a police station when I was two weeks old. That much I do know because there was a piece of paper pinned to my blanket with Kathleen written on it and my date of birth. They gave me that paper and the blanket when I left the orphanage and they'd already

45

given me the surname Sykes after the policeman who found me, but I'm Kathleen Allen, now. That name is *really* mine.'

'Then that makes two of us,' Roz hastened, eager to make amends, 'because I'm an orphan, too. My parents were killed in a car crash in Scotland, though what possessed them to leave me with Gran and go careering off just days before Christmas, I'll never know.

'It's just about now that it happened. Gran hates this month. All the awful things have happened in December. And I'm sorry if I seemed rude, but I didn't know –'

'Of course you didn't and I don't mind about it any more. Can't change things, can you, though sometimes I wish I knew who I really am and if my name is O'Malley or Rafferty or Finnegan.'

'Why Irish names?'

'Because that's what I think I am. Kathleen – it's an Irish name, isn't it? And Barney's aunt says my colouring is Irish.'

'Then I wish I had it,' Roz sighed. 'This red hair is no end of a nuisance. Poll Appleby says I'm a throwback.' She laughed out loud. 'Quite an act we're going to be – an orphan and a throwback, wouldn't you say?'

Kath laughed with her. In spite of her accent, Roz seemed not to mind about the orphanage and her not being wanted, because not being wanted was the worst part of the whole thing. She could still weep, if she let herself, for that two-week-old baby; still felt grateful to Barney for giving her an identity. 'That's the floor finished,' she said. 'Now what?'

'Well, the leftover milk is put in the churns for the milk-lorry to collect. Jonty usually does that, but I suppose we'll be doing it now. I'll ask him.'

'I like your boyfriend,' Kath confided. 'Lovely and tall, isn't he? Doesn't look like a farmer, though. More the studious type, but I suppose that's because of his glasses.

46

D'you know, when he took them off he looked really handsome.'

'*Jonty?* You're talking about Jonty?' Roz squeaked. 'He isn't my boyfriend! Whatever gave you that idea?'

'Sorry! Must have got it wrong. I thought, you see, that –' That when a man looked at a girl the way he looked at Roz, his eyes gentle and loving, following every move she made, his face lighting up the minute he walked into the room and saw her there . . . 'that – well, I got it wrong, I suppose.'

'You certainly did! My boyfriend is called Paul. He's aircrew, over at Peddlesbury. I'm seeing him tonight. You'll be coming, won't you, to the dance? But Jonty – well, he – he's *Jonty*. He's been there as long as I can remember. More like a brother, really, and you don't fall in love with your brother, now do you?'

You don't, Kath agreed silently; of course you don't. But he isn't your brother, Roz, and he *is* in love with you; deeply in love, and you don't know it, she wanted to cry. Instead she said, 'Don't think I'll be coming to the dance. Most of the girls at the hostel are going, but I want to get properly settled in, and wash my hair tonight. I'll be there next time, though.'

It was strange that a married woman could go to dances now without her husband – provided she went with a crowd and came home with a crowd. 'What do we do now?' she asked.

'Don't really know. This is my first day here, too, but we'll be all right once Mat decides what to do with us. Think we'd better pop over and ask. Leave your gum-boots at the door, by the way. Grace doesn't allow them in the kitchen. And Kath – I'm glad you're here.'

'Me, too.'

She was. And happy to be living in the country, even though it was winter and unbearably cold. There was such a feeling of rightness about being here, of belonging, that

47

she felt sure she had been born of country stock. She saw nothing of the drabness of dead, cold earth nor of winter-bare trees, only the beauty of skeletal oaks and beeches, stark against a grey velvet sky. This morning, the early light had gilded everything it touched so that all around her had looked like a picture in a shop window.

She wasn't just happy and glad and sure, now, that she had been right to become a landgirl – there was something else, too; something she couldn't define or even begin to understand. Yet it was there, churning inside her like the day she had volunteered, and yesterday, when the front door banged behind her and she had known there was no going back. Now it was there again, only stronger than ever before; a feeling of joy waiting to explode; a certainty that one day, just around a corner, something wonderful awaited her. It made her feel glad and afraid and happy and guilty.

She swallowed hard and kicked off her gum-boots. Guilty? Whatever could there be to feel guilty about?

'Wait!' she called urgently. 'Wait for me, Roz!'

Huddled into her coat, Roz waited at the door of the gymnasium in which the dances were held. Already the music had started, but she always slipped away as the local girls and the landgirls from Peacock Hey climbed down from the RAF truck and filed through the heavily-curtained doors. No use their meeting inside when the need to hold each other and kiss away the time between was so urgent. Always, the first to arrive would wait in the darkness and tonight it was she, Roz, who stood unmoving, ears straining against the music for a whispered, 'Roz? You there, darling?'

She dug her hands deeper into the pockets of her coat, calling back the night of their meeting, marvelling at the intensity of their love. She had never thought it could be

48

like this; never imagined that loving this deeply could have so changed her life.

When she was very small and her prayers had been said, she would whisper, 'And please let me marry a prince, God, so Granny and me can live at Ridings for ever.' And later, when she understood how large bills could be and how very little money they had she would yearn, *Wouldn't it be lovely to fall in love with someone rich; someone who would care for Ridings as we do . . .*

But all that changed the night she and Paul met. Even the old house and the need to hold on to it would come a poor second, had she been asked to choose between it and Paul.

Now she was in love; deeply and for ever in love as Gran had been and most times her happiness was shining and golden. There were the bad bits, she admitted, when the squadron took to the air over Peddlesbury and she was sick with anxiety until they were back and the phone rang and a voice whispered, 'Hi! I love you.' She never minded so brief a message; not when it really meant he was safely home, and that soon they would meet.

But what would happen now with the morning milk-round to be done and she no longer able to wait beside the phone to snatch it up immediately it began to ring, Roz worried. She couldn't ask Gran to take a message because Gran didn't know about Paul, and to wait for a call at the phone box in the village during the milk-round wouldn't work, even with Kath to help, because she never knew when he would be back. She determined to talk to Paul about it. There had to be some other way he could let her know he was all right.

She heard his footfall on the gravel – that was something else about being in love, knowing the way your man walked, even in the blackout. She coughed and he called, 'Roz? Sweetheart?' All at once everything was all right again and they were touching and kissing and oh, dear, sweet Heaven, how she loved him.

'I missed you,' she whispered.

'Two days?' His laugh was indulgent.

'Two *hours*,' she murmured, 'is too long. They're getting worse, Paul, the bits between.'

Practically all she did between their meetings was fervently wish away the hours and days until they were together again.

'Why can't we be married, Paul?'

'Because I'm flying and you aren't twenty-one.'

'That's no excuse, and you know it. And it isn't what I meant. You know what I'm trying to say.'

'Ssssh.' He tilted her chin, searching with his mouth for hers, but she jerked her head aside.

'No, darling! I won't be shushed! It's getting unbearable, the way I want you!'

'And you think I don't want you? Haven't you thought it might be every bit as bad for me? When I'm flying I'm thinking, "Christ, I was mad to get into this mob. Suppose we don't make it back? Suppose I never see her again . . ."'

'Then *why*, darling, when we love each other so much?'

'Because it wouldn't be fair to you. What kind of a mess would you be in if something went wrong, then I didn't get back?'

'*If* you didn't come back, don't you think it's all the more reason for us to have loved – *really* loved?'

'Roz, sweetheart. You might get pregnant and I might be killed.'

'*Don't!*' She stiffened in his arms, sudden fear taking her. 'Don't ever say that word again – not ever! I love you, Paul Rennie. I want to be with you always. Fifty years from now, I want to be with you!'

'I'm sorry.' His voice was low with regret.

'And I'm sorry, too, so let's not talk about it any more

– well, not tonight.' She pressed close again, touching his chin, his cheek, the tip of his nose with little teasing kisses. 'Only I do love you so. And I want you. Nothing will change that.'

'And I love you. I've always loved you. And I want you, too.'

He unbuttoned his greatcoat then wrapped her into it, pulling her even closer. Their lips met and both knew the need to belong and both silently accepted its inevitability.

Roz stood contented against him. She didn't speak. She didn't have to. They would be lovers. The time would come and they would each recognize the moment. If she got pregnant and if she were left alone, then she would manage somehow. Women usually did. Only never to have belonged, even briefly, would be unbearable.

Presently she stirred in his arms. 'Let's go into the dance,' she whispered.

3

1942

A crescent moon lay pale in the sky; the early morning air was sharp. Another year, a new, exciting beginning. Kath pedalled briskly, more sure of the road now, thinking back to the happiest Christmas she had ever known.

It had started with the same too-early call, for even on Christmas Day farm animals must be fed and watered, the cows milked, and she had done the morning round with Roz, touched to find greetings cards and small gifts left beside empty bottles.

When they had finished the dairy work and put out dishes of milk for the seven farm cats, they gathered in Grace's kitchen to drink a toast to victory in carefully-hoarded dandelion wine and wished each other a happy Christmas.

'No more work today,' Mat had smiled, over his glass. 'Off home, the pair of you.'

It was sad, Kath thought, that Barney's letter should be there when she got back to Peacock Hey a little before noon, and even though she had been expecting it for days, she wished it could have waited until tomorrow or have arrived a day earlier, for nothing at all should be allowed to spoil the joy of this special Christmas. This day above all others she wanted to think kindly of her husband, not shrink from his disapproval; wanted to laugh a lot and eat Christmas dinner with the landgirls who were drifting back to the hostel in ones and twos, the remainder of the day their own. Carefully she slit open the envelope, steeling herself against her husband's anger.

The letter from North Africa confirmed her worst fears.

Barney's reply was crisp with dissent, accusing her of deceit when she must have known all along that no married woman could be made to do war work away from her home. It was open condemnation; it hurt her deeply.

Selfish, that's what you are, Kath. The minute I'm gone you're parading around in uniform making an exhibition of yourself and against my wishes, too . . .

She swallowed hard, anger rising briefly inside her. She was not parading anywhere and if getting up at half-past five to deliver milk on a pitch-black winter morning was making an exhibition of herself then yes, she supposed she was.

Well, Kath, you've made your bed so you'll have to lie on it. It's too late now for regrets. You're stuck with it for the duration, so don't come crying to me, Barney warned, *when you realize you'd best have stayed at home*.

She took a deep, calming breath then pushed the letter into the pocket of her jacket, acknowledging that perhaps Barney could be right, that maybe she had been just a little deceitful. When dinner was over, she would sit down at once and tell him how sorry she was; not sorry for joining, she could never be that, but for not asking him first. Then she would tell him about Alderby and Roz and little Daisy; about Mat and Grace and the tractor she was learning to drive. He'd be pleased to hear about the Post Office bank account she had opened and into which every penny of her Army allowance was being paid.

She would not, she determined, tell him about Jonty yet awhile, for young men who did not answer their country's call made Barnaby Allen's hackles rise. Nor would she tell him, ever, about the prisoner of war soon to arrive at Home Farm. Barney held all things Teutonic in contempt and it would do nothing for his peace of mind to learn that his wife might soon be working alongside the Germans' closest ally.

Lastly, she would tell him that she loved him and missed

53

him and thought about him a lot, for no matter what a letter contained or what it omitted to mention, the loving and the missing was an essential part of every letter to every serviceman overseas.

Now that letter was on its way and the new year nearly six hours old. Surely Barney would come to understand that this was the first real freedom she had ever known – might ever know – and that she must be allowed to make the most of every single day. Soon, her loving letters would reassure him, let him know how deeply she cared.

'A happy new year, Barney,' she whispered. 'Take care.'

'Happy new year!' Roz was loading milk-crates on to the trap when Kath arrived at Home Farm. 'Up early, aren't you? Don't tell me you haven't been to bed.'

'No such luck. No parties for me last night; Paul was flying. Make you sick, wouldn't it, flying ops on New Year's Eve and not one of them back yet. Lord knows where they've been all this time. Even if it was Berlin, they should have been back before now.'

'They will be,' Kath consoled. 'It's early, yet.' And dark, and almost two hours still to go before the blackout could be lifted. 'He'll be all right, I know it. You'll see him tonight.'

'Yes I will. I *know* I will. Look, Kath – can I ask you something a bit personal?'

'Try me.'

'Well, were you a – a virgin when you married Barney?' The words came in a tumble of embarrassment. 'What I'm trying to say is –'

'Was I a virgin when we married or had we been lovers?' Kath looked at the downcast eyes, the pink spots on the young girl's cheeks. How naïve she was, how painfully unworldly. 'Well, since you ask, no, we didn't make love. Mind, we got into a few heavy clinches from time to time, but one of us managed to count up to ten in time.' One of

54

us. Always me. 'But it was very different, you see, when we were courting.' They could talk about tomorrow because then there had been a tomorrow; lovers weren't snatched apart and homes broken up, children left fatherless. Once, there had been all the time in the world. 'But what brought all this on?'

'Oh, I don't know. There isn't an awful lot going for it these days, is there – being a virgin, I mean. I wish I weren't. Does that make me sound like a tart, Kath?'

'No. In fact I think it must be awful for you, loving Paul so much. Why is it,' she demanded, 'that we're old enough to go to war but not old enough to get married till we're twenty-one? Crazy, isn't it? You're worrying about Paul, aren't you?'

'Yes. I always do. I'd have thought they'd have started getting back long before this.'

'They're a bit late, that's all – a headwind, maybe. Well, they can't all be –' She stopped, biting back the word *missing*. 'What I'm trying to say is –'

'Ssssh. Quiet!' Ears straining, Roz gazed into a sky still inky dark. 'There's one of them now, I'm sure it is!'

It was several seconds before Kath could hear the faint tired drone of aircraft engines but then, she considered, she wasn't waiting for the man she loved to come back from a raid over Germany; wouldn't keep tally as each one thrashed overhead and circled the aerodrome, asking for permission to land, waiting for the runway lights to be turned on.

'How many went? Did you count them?'

'Yes.' Roz always counted. 'Eleven last night.'

'Fine. Then we'll count them in, shall we?' Kath opened the delivery book. 'Any cancellations?'

'None. Ivy Cottage would like an extra pint, if we've got one to spare, that's all.' She glanced up again, relief in her voice. 'It's them, all right, and that's the first. I wonder where they've been till now?'

'He'll tell you tonight.' Kath smiled. 'By the way, I don't suppose you'd remembered that it's today the Italian is coming?'

'Could I forget? Gran's still going on about it.'

'I wonder what he'll be like.'

'Oh, short, fat and greasy, according to Gran, and every bit as bad as a German.' Roz shrugged, only half listening.

'I always thought Italians were tall, dark and romantic.'

'I couldn't care less what he's like. All I want is for him to keep out of Gran's way and help out with the ploughing. Oh, come on. Let's make a start.'

She glanced up sharply as the first of the homecoming Lancasters roared in low over Alderby. She didn't speak, but already the words 'Ten to go', had formed in her mind and 'Please God, ten more. *Please*.'

Kath was leading Daisy into her loose box when the truck stopped at the farm gate. Arms folded, she stood to watch.

The man who jumped out at a sharp command from the guard was tall and young and fairer than she would have thought.

'Come on, you! Chop chop, there! We haven't got all day!'

The guard was the smaller of the two and a great deal older but he carried a rifle on his shoulder, so size and age didn't count for a lot, Kath reasoned. Perhaps his animosity sprang from a still-remembered Dunkirk or a bomb-shattered home. You couldn't blame him, she supposed, for throwing his weight about a bit.

'The prisoner's here.' She closed the dairy door against the cold. 'A guard has just taken him inside.'

'Damn!' Roz set down a crate of bottles with a rattle. 'I was hoping he wouldn't arrive. Gran swears she'll have rid of him just as soon as Mat can find someone else and she will, nothing's more certain, once the ploughing is done.'

'Is it possible to hate someone so much?'

'Gran can.' Roz ran to the door, wrenching it open, her eyes sliding left and right. 'Listen! There it is. That's eleven back! Now what do you suppose kept them?'

'Does it matter?' Kath flinched as the massive black shape thundered low over the farm. 'They're all home.'

'Yes,' Roz sighed, eyes closed. 'Don't *ever* fall for aircrew.'

'I won't be falling for anyone. I'm married – remember?'

'You know what I mean. Look, I'll scald the churns this morning; you feed the cats, will you?'

Suddenly it was a wonderful day. All at once, at the count of eleven, the cold grey morning was bright with magic. Paul had completed his thirteenth op; the dicey one was behind him. Now surely it would be all right until the last one; until the thirtieth. And tonight they would meet. Perhaps they would dance, perhaps they would walk in the darkness, hands clasped, thighs touching, just glad to be together. Tonight, they might even be lovers.

She closed her eyes, sending silent thanks to the god who had brought eleven crews safely back, knowing that tomorrow or the next day she would once more be counting the bombers out and willing them home again; living through a fresh anguish.

But tonight she and Paul would be together. Tonight was as sure as anything could be in this mad, uncertain world, and tomorrow, and all the uncertain tomorrows, were a million years away.

At eleven o'clock, when they began to wonder if tea-break had been forgotten, Grace called them in to the warmth of the kitchen.

'Sorry it's late. I've been over to Ridings with drinkings for the men and I stayed to watch. Jonty's made a start with the tractor and Mat and the prisoner are trying out Duke, and the hand-plough. It's good to see Duke working. I'm glad we didn't get rid of him.' She smiled.

Few farmers had kept their horses once tractors came within their means, but Mat Ramsden loved horses and the great grey Shire was a joy to him.

'Tractors don't need feeding and mucking-out,' some had scoffed.

'Aye, I'll grant you that, but my Shire runs on hay which isn't rationed like tractor fuel is and it don't have to be brought here, neither, in a convoy. And what's more,' he'd grinned, 'you don't get manure from tractors!'

Duke weighed a ton, almost, and his hooves were the size of a dinner plate. Such creatures were living miracles, Mat declared; tractors were cold, smelly contraptions and bother or not, the Shire horse had stayed.

'I'm glad they've made a start.' Roz watched the saccharin tablet rise fizzing to the top of her cup. 'That ploughing business was really getting Gran down. Will it be finished on time, Grace?'

'It will.' The reply was quietly confident. 'My, but it was grand to see that land getting turned over, coming to life after all those years.'

She had stood there, jug in hand, watching the plough bite deep into the sward; watched it rise green then fall dark and soft as a wave falls on the shore. She had smiled to see the seagulls wheeling overhead then settling in the wake of the plough, grabbing hungrily for grubs. Yes indeed, those long-idle acres were stirring themselves at last.

'Is the prisoner going to be any help?' Roz ventured.

'That he is. He's framing-up nicely. Him and Duke were turning over some good straight furrows.'

'How far must a man walk,' Kath asked, 'just to plough a single acre? And how does he get such straight furrows?'

'He walks miles and miles, that's a fact,' Grace acknowledged, 'and he keeps straight by fixing his eyes on something ahead and not losing his concentration.

'By the way, Roz, Jonty said I was to wish you a happy new year. Said he's hardly set eyes on you since Christmas morning. He wanted to know what you were doing and I said you'd made a start cleaning the eggs.'

'And I suppose he said you were to remind me to be careful?'

Eggshells were fragile, to be cleaned with care when the packers who called to collect them were entitled to deduct a penny for every mark on every egg.

'Well, he did wonder how many you'd broken.' Grace laughed. 'Said he supposed it would be scrambled eggs for breakfast tomorrow. Only teasing, mind. You know Jonty . . .'

She knew him, Roz frowned, or thought she had until Kath had assumed he was her boyfriend. Surely Jonty wasn't in love with her. He mustn't be.

'Teasing? We haven't had a single accident, have we, Kath?'

'Not yet.' Just what was Roz thinking about, Kath brooded, gazing at the suddenly-red cheeks. Jonty *was* in love with her. Why hadn't she seen it when it was obvious to everyone else? And did Jonty know about Paul: was he content to wait for the madness to burn itself out – for madness it surely was – and be there when she needed a shoulder to cry on? 'Come on,' she said more sharply than she had intended. 'Let's get back to those eggs, Roz. There *is* a war on, you know.'

Kath sat beside the kitchen fire, toasting her stockinged toes, eating the sandwiches the hostel cook had packed for her. She was always hungry these days; food had never tasted so good nor sleep come so easily.

'Soup, Kath?' Grace Ramsden stirred the iron pan that hung above the coals.

'Can you spare it?' Food was rationed and she should have refused. 'Just a drop, maybe.'

'Of course I can spare it.' Grace took a pint mug from the mantel-shelf. 'Only vegetables and lentils and barley in it – bits of this and bits of that. Drink it up, lass, and welcome. Whilst you're waiting for it to cool, can you take some outside?'

'To the prisoner, Grace?' Mat's head jerked up from his plate. 'He's brought his rations with him, the guard said, and there's to be no –'

'I mind what the guard said. No fraternization. And how are we all to work with a man and not speak to him, will you tell me? This is *my* kitchen, Mat Ramsden. That lad sitting out there has done a fair morning's work on our land and Kath is going to take him a mug of soup!' She stopped, breathless and red-cheeked, ladle brandished, glaring at each in turn. 'Have I made myself clear?'

'You have, Grace love. You have,' Mat said quietly, though the laughter in his eyes belied the gravity in his voice. 'We'll not tell the guard.'

'Good!' Grace filled the mug to the brim. 'Glad we've got that little matter settled!'

He loves her, Kath marvelled. He teases her, indulges her and his eyes follow her just as Jonty's eyes follow Roz. After all the years, they're still in love, she thought as she carried the steaming mug across the yard. Carefully she skirted a patch of ice, wondering if she and Barney would be as much in love after their silver wedding, confident that they would.

The prisoner sat on an upturned box, his back against the straw stack. He looked up at her approach, then laid aside the bread he was eating and rose to his feet.

Kath stood awkwardly, taking in the height of him, the smile he tried to suppress.

'Hullo. Mrs Ramsden sends soup,' she said slowly, offering the mug. 'For you.'

'The *signora* is kind. I thank her. It smell good.'

'You speak English?' Kath laughed her relief.

'*Si*. I learn it in school for five years. I speak it a lot, since I am prisoner.'

'That's good.' She looked into the young, frost-pinched face. He was tall and painfully thin, his eyes large and brown. 'I'm Kathleen Allen.' She wondered if she should offer her hand, and decided against it.

'Kathleen. Katarina.' He repeated her name slowly. 'And I am Marco Roselli. If it is allowed, you will please to call me Marco?'

'Marco. Yes. Well then, I'll let you get on with it,' Kath hesitated, stepping backward, 'whilst it's hot . . .'

'*Si*, Katarina. And thank you.'

'He's –' no, not nice. We were at war with Italy, so he couldn't be nice. But he was ordinary, she supposed; like Jonty, really. And not stupid, either, as newspaper cartoons showed Italians to be. 'He's little different from us. He said thank you, that the soup smelled good,' Kath supplied, sitting down again, picking up her own mug. 'He seems all right.'

'He is,' Jonty said firmly. 'We had quite a talk this morning. His people are farmers in the Italian Tyrol – there might be a bit of Austrian in him. He'd hoped to go to university, but the war stopped it. There's nothing much wrong with him – and he can handle a horse.'

'Aye. He can't help being in the war any more than you can help not being in it, son,' Grace said softly. 'It's the way things are and he'll be treated decently till he gives us cause not to. What's his name?'

'Marco,' Jonty supplied.

'That's all right, then. Well, we can't keep calling him *the prisoner*, or *the Italian*, can we?' Grace looked appealingly at her husband. Their own son was safe at home; the young man outside had a mother, too.

'Just as you say, love.' Mat nodded. 'And Jonty's right; he knows about horses.' A man who knew about horses would be fairly treated at Home Farm. 'We'd best get back to it whilst the daylight lasts. You ready, son?'

'I hope,' Grace remarked when she and Kath were alone, 'that Mrs Fairchild comes to accept Marco. You'd have thought she'd have been there to see the first few furrows turned over, but not her; not if she has to take help from the other side. It's sad, her being so bitter, but then, she's had more than her fair share of trouble.'

'Trouble? In what way?'

'Losing her man in the last war was the start of it, then having the fire so soon after. And her daughter and son-in-law getting killed in a car accident.'

'Her son-in-law?' Kath frowned. 'Then why is Roz called Fairchild?'

'It's a long story. There was only one child, you see – Janet, Roz's mother. There should have been a son to carry on the name but Mrs Fairchild lost him; a stillbirth, six months on, when Miss Janet was about three. Took it badly, poor soul. And after that, there were no more children. A lot of us wondered why there hadn't been another, but Poll Appleby squashed the gossip once and for all. There was a woman in the village who happened to say that it was certain Mrs Fairchild would soon conceive again like often happened after a miscarriage, and Poll told her off good and proper; told her to watch her tongue and never, ever, say anything like that again, and especially in front of the Mistress, not if she knew what was good for her.

'Then the war came – the first one – and the Master was taken,' Grace brooded. 'They said it was a sniper's bullet, same as took Poll's man. Not long after came the fire, and

62

her under-insured, then Miss Janet and her husband were killed, and there was a young bairn to be brought up.

'But proud, that woman is. Living from hand to mouth sometimes, yet always fretting about that dratted house as if all her trouble had been of her own making.'

Grace poured a kettle of water into the sink, tutting indignantly, shaking her head.

'I'll dry the dishes for you. Might as well, whilst I'm waiting for Roz to get back. But why,' Kath persisted, 'is she called Fairchild? Did her gran change it back, or something?'

'Not exactly. Roz's mother – Janet Fairchild as was – married a Londoner called Toby Jarvis, and he agreed to keep the name. Fairchild-Jarvis, Roz is really called, though Roz will always be a Fairchild while her gran lives and breathes, her being the last of the line, so to speak.

'Still, there's one blessing to come out of this war. At least that old ruin will be giving something back now. All those good acres barren for so long. But Mat and Jonty – aye, and Marco, too, will have them down to potatoes and sugarbeet afore very much longer, and wheat and barley the year after, and – careful, here's Roz, now. Do you think the two of you could take the fodder to the cattle in the far field – hay, and chopped swedes? Take the small tractor, if you'd like.'

The tractor. Kath's eyes gleamed. Her driving was getting better every day. She'd soon be good enough, Jonty said, to drive it on the road. Now that would be something to tell Barney!

Oh, why was life so good? How dare she be so contented, so happy, almost, when men were at war? What would her husband say if he could read her thoughts? Then her chin lifted defiantly.

Sorry, Barney, but there's a war on here, too. We're getting bombed and we're cold and short of coal and next month the sugar ration is going to be cut. So I'm doing my

63

bit the best way I know how and you'll have to accept it.
Sorry, my dear . . .

Hester Fairchild switched off the kitchen light before opening the back door. 'Jonty! Come in. Roz won't be long.' She pulled over the blackout curtain, switching on the light again. 'She's upstairs, getting ready.'

'Mother said you might be able to use a little extra.' He placed a bottle of milk on the table. 'We're a few pints in hand, whilst the school's on holiday.'

Hester was grateful, and said so. Even in the country the milk shortage was beginning to be felt and most agreed that the sooner it was placed on official ration, the better.

'I haven't come for Roz.' Jonty glanced down disparagingly at his working clothes. 'I think she must be going dancing tonight.' With someone else. She usually was, and he couldn't blame her. Most girls would rather be seen out with men in uniform. Tonight, probably, Roz would be meeting one of the Peddlesbury airmen. Most of the village girls dated airmen now. 'Why I really came was to tell you we've started the ploughing, though likely you'll know.'

'Yes, and I'm relieved it's under way. Will it be finished in time?'

'I think so, but the War Ag. isn't going to quibble over a few days. Why don't you come over tomorrow and take a look at it?'

Sooner or later she must come face to face with Marco Roselli; best she got it over with.

'And watch *him*, Jonty, strutting over Martin's land?'

'He doesn't strut, Mrs Fairchild.' The reply was firm, yet without offence. 'He's called Marco and he's my age – a good man with a horse-plough, too.'

'He was fighting for them; *with* them.'

She fixed him with a stare, leaving him in no doubt that further conversation about the prisoner was at an end.

'I'm sorry you feel as you do, Mrs Fairchild.' His voice held a hint of the fatigue he felt. 'Think I'd best be off. One of the heifers was a bit restless when I looked in on her; she's due to drop her calf any time.' A first-calving it would be, that could be tricky. Best he shouldn't be too long away.

'Goodnight then, Jonty. I hope you won't be up all night. Thank you for coming, and for the milk.' Her voice was more gentle, apologetic almost.

''Night. Tell Roz to have a good time.'

A good time! Hands in pockets he kicked out at the tussocky grass of the orchard. Roz had no time for civilians, now. No one had. Even in York, where a different assistant had served him when he called for the tractor spares, he'd come up against the antagonism. Foolishly he'd remarked on it to the middle-aged woman who stood behind the counter.

'What do you mean, where is she?' The reply was acid-sharp. 'She's gone to join the Air Force, that's what. They're calling-up women, now – or hadn't you noticed, young man?'

Yes, he damn-well *had* noticed! He noticed it all the time and if he'd had any choice at all in the matter, he'd have joined the Air Force, too.

He hoped Roz didn't get too deeply involved. Rumour had it that Peddlesbury had lost three bombers in as many weeks. Roz never did things by half. When she fell in love it would be deeply and completely and her grief would be terrible – if she'd fallen for one of the aircrew – if one night he didn't come back.

There had been a lessening of Luftwaffe raids over England, he brooded, yet Bomber Command had doubled its raids over Germany. Stood to reason there'd be heavy losses.

Take care, Roz – don't get hurt, love.

* * *

Roz swept into Ridings kitchen like a small whirlwind, scooped up her coat then placed a kiss on her grandmother's cheek. ''Bye. Got to rush. Don't wait up for me,' and was gone before Hester could even begin to warn her not to be too late back.

She made for the gap in the hedge, walking carefully through the orchard to the small, straight lane that led to the Black Horse inn at the top end of Alderby village. She and Paul often met at the back of the pub, though never inside it; she had no wish for her grandmother to learn about him by way of village gossip. Truth known, she admitted reluctantly, she wanted to keep their affair a secret for as long as she could, knowing as she did that this was not the time to take Paul home or even admit she was 'going out with aircrew' as Alderby gossip succinctly put it.

It was best, she was sure, that for just a little while longer their love should remain their own, if only to save herself from Gran's gentle reminders of her lack of years and the folly of loving too deeply in time of war.

He was waiting beside the back entrance. She was able to pick him out in the faint glow from a starry sky and loving him as she did, the tallness of him, the slimness of his build, his very outline was as familiar to her as her own right hand.

'Paul!' She went straight to his arms, closing her eyes, lifting her face to his. 'I've missed you.' She always said that, but she did miss him. An hour apart was a day, and a day without him dragged into an agonized eternity. 'Kiss me,' she demanded.

His mouth came down hard on her own and the fierceness of it startled her.

'Darling, what is it?'

'Nothing. Everything.' His voice was rough. 'God, I love you. You know that, don't you, Roz?'

'I know,' she whispered, her lips on his. 'I know, Paul.

But something *is* wrong. What happened last night? Let's walk, shall we?' She linked her arm in his, guiding him toward the lane. 'Tell me.'

'Sorry, darling. It's – it's Jock.'

Jock Ferguson, air-gunner. The tail-end Charlie who flew with Paul.

'Where did you go last night?'

'Stuttgart. It should have been a milk run, a piece of cake, but they were waiting for us: fighters, flack, the lot. We went in with the first wave and that's why we got away with it, but the second wave really copped it.'

'And Jock?' Her mouth was dry. Paul's tension was hers now.

'A searchlight picked us up and Jock yelled over the intercom that there was a fighter on to us. Then he said something like, "*Christ! It's jammed. The bloody thing's jammed!*" Then nothing.'

'Yes?' She squeezed his hand tightly.

'Skip told me to go to the tail and find out what was up – see if I could sort it.'

'Jock was hurt?' She pulled him to her, holding him tightly, feeling the jerking of his shoulders and the bitter dragging out of each word.

'The turret was smashed – a great, gaping hole and Jock – hell, Roz, his face was – he was – Jock's dead.'

'Ssssh.' She covered his mouth with her own, stilling his anger and grief. 'I love you. I love you, Paul.' It was all she could think of to say.

'His gun must've jammed. He certainly didn't fire it. He wasn't eighteen, Roz. Not till next week. We were planning a booze-up for him. A kid, that's all he was. A kid on his thirteenth op. It makes you want to jack it all in. He hadn't lived, poor sod.'

'I'm sorry, darling. I'm sorry.' Not yet eighteen. Younger, even, than herself. 'His mother?' It was important to think of her, too.

'She's a widow, I believe, but they'll give her a pension, I shouldn't wonder. And they'll have sent her a telegram by now then follow it up with the usual letter – full of platitudes it'll be, and bloody cant. They've already packed his kit and stripped his bed. In a couple of days' time there'll be someone else in it and hoo-bloody-ray for Jock Ferguson.'

'Was there a lot of damage?'

'The rear turret's gone for a burton; they'll have to fit a new one, that's for sure. Don't know what other damage there was. We were last crew home and how Skip managed to get the thing down I'll never know. We were all frozen. The heating was shot-up and the wind was coming in through – through where Jock was. We just climbed out and walked away from it when we realized we'd made it and left them to get Jock out. The CO was there, but he never said a word; had the sense to keep his mouth shut, thank God. They put rum in our tea, at debriefing – a lot of it, but it did nothing for me. Couldn't sleep afterwards. Just kept seeing that turret. I'm a coward, Roz. I threw up, when we got out.'

'No, Paul! You're *not* a coward! Night after night over Germany; of course you threw up. What do they think you're all made of – *stone*?'

'That's it. Stone. That's what they'd like.'

'Well, you're not. You're all of you flesh and blood. You should go to sick bay tonight and ask for something to help you sleep –'

'Sick bay? Oh, no. One word, just one whimper, and that'll be it. Rennie's cracking up. Rennie's got a yellow streak. LMF, that's what *his* trouble is . . .'

'Stop it! I won't listen! You're *not* a coward and you're *not* lacking moral fibre!'

'You try telling that to those bastards. You try telling them that for every steel-nerved hero in Bomber Command, there are ordinary blokes like me and Jock;

blokes who are afraid sometimes, and afraid to admit they're afraid.

'Try telling the big brass that, Roz. They'd strip us of our rank. We'd be erks again. They'd send us some place where we couldn't contaminate decent airmen and they'd stamp LMF on our papers. In bloody red ink!'

'You're shaking, Paul. You're cold.'

She wanted to hold him, comfort him; tell him to give it time. She needed him to know that she loved him no less for admitting fear; needed him to realize that she understood the terror of take-off, of sitting dry-mouthed till that overloaded, overfuelled Lancaster was safely airborne.

She remembered that eleventh aircraft. It had been Paul's, though she hadn't known it, hadn't realized they'd been fighting for height and praying the undercarriage hydraulics were all right, knowing that below them, down there in the smug safeness of the control tower, they'd already ordered out the crash crew, the fire engine and the ambulances.

'Come with me, Paul?' She saw the haystack ahead. Not that it looked like a stack – just a darker mass, the size of a small cottage. But only this morning she and Kath had cut hay from it to carry out to the far field and she had been happy and relieved because all the Peddlesbury bombers were back. Why hadn't she felt Paul's fear? Why hadn't she been with that eleventh bomber every second of the time it took to land? Why hadn't she known he'd been in need of her love? 'We can shelter behind the stack – it'll be warmer, out of the wind . . .'

She was coaxing him, speaking to him softly as she would speak to a child awakened from a nightmare. But a child could weep away its fears in its mother's arms; a man could not. Paul could not, dare not weep. Paul could only live each day as it came, and count each one a bonus. For him and for all those like him, tomorrow was a brash, brave word, never to be spoken.

'This way, Paul. Can you see all right?' This way, my darling. Let me share the fear. Let me hold you and love you. Don't shut me out.

Kath wrapped her pyjamas around the hot-water bottle then slipped it into her bed, wondering where the next one would come from should this one spring a leak. What would happen, she frowned, if the Japanese armies overran the latex-producing countries in the Far East as easily as they had taken Hong Kong? They wouldn't, of course, but suppose they did? There'd be no more hot-water bottles nor tyres for lorries. And what about teats for babies' bottles? But best she shouldn't think about it – well, not too much. Leave tomorrow to take care of itself. She wondered if Barney had got her letter yet, and if it had made him happier about her being a landgirl. She hoped so. She didn't want to cause him a single moment of worry when she was so happy. Because she *was* happy. To be happy in time of war was wrong, but there it was. Just to be here, in this attic, in this bedroom all her own was bliss enough. Already she had put her mark on it. A jar filled with holly stood on the window ledge, her picture of Barney stood atop the chest of drawers, her dressing gown hung on the door peg and her slippers – slippers Aunt Min had knitted from scraps of wool – stood beneath the chair at her bedside.

And at Home Farm things couldn't have gone better, she sighed. She could almost drive the small tractor and could harness Daisy into the shafts of the milk-float. She could even muck-out the cow shed now without wrinkling her nose.

She wondered about threshing day. Mat had ordered the team, Grace said only this morning, and it would be arriving at Home Farm any day now. Threshing days, Grace told her, were very important, with everyone turning-to and giving a hand, and extra workers to be fed. Wheat, barley and oats were desperately needed; every bushel they had would be sold.

She switched off the light then opened the blackout curtains, gazing out into a sky bright with stars. Tonight had been quiet. No bombers had taken off from Peddlesbury. Somewhere out there in the darkness, Roz and Paul would be together.

Dear, sweet Roz. They had known each other little more than two weeks, yet she understood her so well, Kath sighed, opening the window, breathing in air so cold that it snapped at her nostrils and made her cough. But soon the days would begin to draw out, nights become less cold. Soon it would be spring and there would be daffodils and lilacs, the first rosebud, and –

The cry was sudden, fearsome and high-pitched. It cleared her mind of all thoughts save that somewhere, not very far off, an animal screamed into the night; a wild shrieking, blood-curdling in its intensity. Was some creature trapped and if it was, how was she to find it? Not a rabbit in a snare; something so small and weak couldn't give out so terrible a cry. But what, and where?

Hurriedly she closed the window and with feet that scarcely touched the stairs, ran down to the kitchen.

'Flora! Did you hear it? An animal in pain; such screaming! Come to the door. Listen!'

'Pain?' Flora Lyle laid down her pen and pushed back her chair.

'Oh, *yes*. Quite near, it seems. Maybe it's been caught in a trap. We've got to find it.'

'And then what could we do?'

'We'd let it go. It was *awful*. Listen. Please listen?'

She flung open the door and stood, ears straining, and it came again, that frenzied cry.

'There, now! You heard it, too?'

'Aye. I heard it.' The Forewoman took Kath's arm, pushing her back, closing the door. 'I heard it fine. And yon creature's no' in pain, lassie; no' in pain at all. It's a vixen.'

'A *what*?'

'A she-fox; a female in season. She wants to mate, Kath. She's no' in any trap. Leave her be. There'll be every dog-fox within miles have heard her. January's the month for – well, for foxes and vixens.'

'You're sure?' Kath's cheeks flamed red. 'But it was such a *terrible* sound.'

'I'm sure. Vixens take their pleasures *terrible* serious, you see.'

'Oh, my goodness! Don't tell the other girls?' Kath gasped. 'They'd laugh their heads off, wouldn't they?'

'I'll no' tell,' the Forewoman said solemnly, though her eyes shone with mischief and she struggled against laughter. 'The countryside's a peculiar place, Kath.'

Just a vixen, she thought as she climbed the narrow stairs to her attic. Who ever would have thought it? A vixen, wanting a mate. And such a noise, too. Then her face broke into one of her rare, wide smiles.

'Oh, but you've got a lot to learn, Kath Allen,' she whispered; 'an awful lot.'

But it was as Aunt Min had said. The countryside wasn't all romps in the hay and collecting eggs.

She laughed out loud. 'Oh, get yourself undressed and into bed, you silly woman!' In pain, indeed!

Jonty opened the cow-shed door and called softly to the heifer in the stall nearby.

'Cush, pet. Cush, lass . . .'

Gently he stroked her flank and she turned her head, regarding him with wide, bewildered eyes.

'All right, girl. All right . . .'

She was coming along fine, he nodded. She'd have her calf with ease, though the unaccustomed pain was making her restless.

'Cush, cush,' he soothed.

Oh, yes. She would drop her calf instinctively and with more dignity than ever the human animal could muster. Her pain, though, her *real* pain, would start tomorrow when they took her first-born calf away from her.

'Sorry,' he murmured. 'Sorry, lass . . .'

They sank into the hay on the sheltered side of the stack, pressing deep into it, shoulders touching, hands clasped.

For a long time they were content to be so, taking in the calm after a storm of fear and outrage.

'I love you, Paul Rennie.' Roz lifted his hand, touching the palm with her lips. 'Where ever you are, whatever you are doing; never forget it, not even for a minute.'

'I'm sorry, my darling.' His voice was still rough with emotion and remembered terror. 'I shouldn't have told you. It was wrong of me.'

'It *wasn't*, and you should have. From now on, you must always tell me.'

'So where's your shining-bright hero, now?' The despair in his voice thrust into her like a knife.

'You were never my shining-bright hero, Paul; just the man I loved – *love* – will always love. And I wish you could be an erk again. I wish they'd take you off flying and send you to some place where they'd never even seen a bomber.

'I wouldn't care. Not if I didn't see you again till it was all over, I wouldn't. It's *you* I want, not some cracked-up hero. I want you with me always. And they could stamp LMF right in the middle of your forehead if I thought there could be a future for us together.'

She reached up and pulled his head to her own, closing her eyes, parting her lips for his kiss. As he kissed her, she lifted the hand she had touched with her lips and placed it beneath her blouse to rest on her warm, wanting breast.

'Love me?' she murmured, drawing him closer. 'Please

love me?' Her body strained nearer and she felt the first stirrings of his need, heard the sharp indrawing of his breath. 'Remember this morning, Paul? Remember Jock, who'd never lived? I haven't lived either, and I want you . . .'

He said no, that they shouldn't. They'd be sorry, he said, after. But his protests held no substance against the force of her need and she kissed away the last of his doubts.

'I'll never be sorry.' She slipped open the buttons of her blouse, closing her eyes as his lips touched the hollow at her throat then slid, searching, to her breasts. 'Never in a million years . . .'

Their first loving was a sweet, surprised discovering, a setting free, a soaring delight. It was tender and caring; a coupling without pain or passion. They lay side by side afterwards, breathing unevenly, glad of the darkness.

'There are a lot of stars up there.' She was the first to speak. 'And a moon.'

'It's a new one; a wishing moon.'

Presently she said, 'Was it the first time, Paul?'

'Yes.'

'For me, too. I love you.'

Her love would keep him safe. Now it would always be a part of him. It would wrap him round and keep him from harm, where ever he was, however far.

'Roz – I shouldn't have said what I did. Everybody's afraid, some time or other. It was Jock, you see . . .'

'I know, my love. Nothing will hurt you again.'

'God, but I love you so.' He gathered her to him, his cheek on her hair. 'I'll always love you.'

The hay smelled sweet of a summer past and a summer yet to come.

She had given him back the courage he had feared lost, and he was a man again.

And he was hers, now, for all time.

4

It was not until the last of the milk had been delivered, the last empty bottle collected, that Roz said:

'He's flying again.' The words came reluctantly, angrily. 'After what happened two nights ago, Paul was on ops again last night.'

'But I thought – didn't you say their plane was a write-off? And surely they can't fly without a gunner?'

'They didn't need to. Jock's replacement arrived yesterday morning. As soon as Paul told me, I got a nasty feeling inside.' And cold, frightening fingers tracing the length of her backbone. 'Oh, K-King isn't airworthy; they've already removed the engines and wings to make it easier to move. Then they'll put the whole lot on a transporter and send it back to the factory that made it. It'll be like a new plane when they've finished with it and nobody will ever know that Jock –'

'Hush, now.' Kath pulled on the reins, calling the pony to a stop. 'You mustn't get upset again. You said yourself that Paul is over his thirteenth op; the unlucky one's behind him. He'll be back, all right. Bet everything's gone just fine. It's nearly light; we'll be hearing them soon.'

'No. They didn't leave till midnight. It'll be an hour yet, at least. Unless it's been France or the Low Countries, which I doubt.' She shivered then dug her hands into her pockets, hunching into the upturned collar of her coat, holding herself tight against her anger. 'I thought he'd be all right; when they came back all shot-up I thought at least they'd be given some kind of a break from flying. But no. A crew goes on leave so Paul's lot take over their plane. Hell, but I'd like a few of those desk-wallahs to have a go. Just one sticky op so they'd know what it's like. It was inhuman, sending them out again so soon after what happened.'

'Steady on, Roz. Maybe they had a reason. You know what they say about falling off a horse – that you should get straight back up again? Perhaps that's why they did it – so they won't lose their nerve.'

'Ha!' Roz clicked her tongue and the pony walked on. 'And as if that isn't bad enough, he's going on leave as soon as they've been to debriefing and I won't see him before he goes, though he's promised to ring me. Every night, he said, if he can manage to get through.'

'Then what are you worrying about? Everything's going to be fine. I heard them go last night, but I didn't count. How many went?'

'Nine. I stood at the window. It was a good sky; quite a bit of cloud-cover for them. Oh, Kath. I get sick, just to think about him . . .'

'I know, love. I know. Do you want to take Polly's milk, or shall I?' *Change the subject. Talk about anything but flying.* 'And tell me – why doesn't the other gate lodge get milk from us? Come to think of it, I don't think I've ever seen them.'

'You wouldn't. She keeps herself to herself. Doesn't drink cow's milk – she has her own goat. Bombed out in that first big raid on Manchester, I believe. She's an artist – does illustrations for advertising, or something. Gran was glad to let her have the lodge. It had been empty for ages.'

'She's alone?'

'Yes, but that isn't unusual these days.'

'Suppose not.' *Keep at it. Just don't let her talk about Paul.* 'What's she called?'

'Don't know, but Arnie calls her the Manchester lady.'

'Arnie.' Kath smiled. 'He's a great kid.'

'Hmm.'

'Polly's going to miss him when the war's over.'

'Yes.'

'He's been –' Kath stopped. She was getting nowhere. 'Listen, Roz. Paul *will* be all right and you can't go on like this, every time he's flying. Worrying isn't going to help him – unless there's something else?'

'What do you mean?' Roz jerked out of her apathy. 'Paul's flying. Two nights ago they lost their gunner, then crash landed – isn't that enough? And isn't the prospect of not seeing him for ten days more than enough?' she demanded.

So something else *was* bothering her. She'd been sure of it. All day yesterday Roz had hardly said a word and there had been a tenseness about her, a strangeness.

'Roz. Are you and –' None of her business, but somebody had to talk to her about it. 'Are you and Paul lovers?' There. She'd said it. She turned her head away, not wanting to see the truth of it in the young girl's face; turned away from the anger she knew was to come.

'What the hell has it got to do with you, Kath Allen? Mind your own business – right?'

'Right!'

They walked in silence along Ridings drive, between the rows of shiny-black, dripping trees. They had almost reached Home Farm when Roz said:

'I'm sorry. I shouldn't have spoken to you like that. I know you were only trying to help. Kath – you can't get pregnant, can you; not the first time?'

'They say not, but I wouldn't bank on it.' Oh, the silly young thing; so innocent it just wasn't true. She took a deep breath, trying hard to keep her voice even. 'But best you don't take chances, Roz, next time. Maybe when Paul comes back off leave you should have a talk with him about it? They tell men about things like that, I believe, in the Forces. He'll see that nothing happens.'

'Yes, I will. I must. Only at the time it seemed so – so right.'

'I know. And nobody's blaming you. It had to happen, I suppose, sooner or later. But be careful, Roz.'

Kath sent a jet of water bouncing over the cow-shed floor. 'Cheer up, Roz. They're all nine safely back. Aren't you relieved that Paul has really broken his jinx, now?'

'Of course I am. I was thinking that he'll probably be on his way to the station by now. Wish I could have seen him, just for a second; even a wave as they drove past. I'd have settled for that. Wish he'd asked me to go home with him, though. I want so much to meet his family. Paul said his sister was trying to get some leave to be with him. They haven't seen each other for a year. It must be hard for them, being apart. She and Paul are twins – did I tell you?'

'You didn't, but at least for the next ten days you can stop counting bombers; that should make a change.'

'Yes, but it's going to be a very long ten days, though heaven knows they deserve a break. And he'll phone, if he can get through.'

'Then you'll just have to learn to live from phone-call to phone-call, won't you?' Kath rolled up the hosepipe and hung it on the wall. 'But it wouldn't be you, would it, without something to worry about?'

'Sorry.' Roz smiled briefly. 'I do go on and on about me and Paul, don't I? I'm selfish. I should spare a thought for you. Poor Kath. You don't know when you'll see Barney again; all you've got to look forward to is letters.'

Look forward? My, but that was a laugh, when recently she had come to almost dread the arrival of Barney's next letter. But soon he would receive the one she wrote to him on Christmas Day; a letter full of love and reassurance. She had hoped he would come to realize that many a soldier serving overseas had left behind a wife in the armed forces, and was proud of her, too. She wished that Barney could come to be proud of a wife who was doing everything she could for the war effort; everything she could to help bring him safely home. And she wished with all her heart he would begin to understand, and to trust her.

'Letters? Can't say I'm looking forward, exactly, to the next one. Barney's still mad at me for joining up. And he makes me feel guilty about what I've done because I know I shouldn't be so happy. Wars aren't meant to be happy, are they?'

'I suppose not. And I don't know why I'm going on about Paul asking me home with him. Can you imagine what Gran would say if I told her I was going off with a man she's never even heard of – even if Mat would give me the time off. Why is my life in such a mess?'

'Come on.' Kath grinned. 'You wouldn't change one bit of it, and you know it. And if we don't get this mucking-out finished we'll miss drinkings. Y'know, I'm looking forward to the threshing on Monday, aren't you?'

'Not really.' Roz frowned. 'It's a back-breaking, dirty job; I've had some. I helped out last time. Everybody turns-to; every farm hereabouts who can spare a man sends him along.

'Grace has the time of her life, though she won't admit it. How she'll provide food for everyone who comes I don't know, with rationing the way it is. But she will. She always does. Look, that's Grace at the kitchen window, holding up a mug. Come on – looks as if we're going to be lucky!'

Happy? Kath thought, washing her hands at the stand-pipe, drying them ponderously. Yes, she *was* happy. Indeed, she had never thought such happiness possible and it seemed wrong that Barney could not, would not, understand her need for this one, wonderful experience; wouldn't give her his blessing and be proud of her. But he never would. She was certain of it, now.

'Hang on, Roz! Wait for me!'

* * *

'It isn't fair, Aunt Poll, me having to go back to school the very day the threshing machine's coming to the farm. I'll miss it all, and I wanted to help.'

'Well, you can't. School's more important than threshing day and anyway, you're too young to help. The law says you've got to be fourteen.'

'But I'm big enough.' Arnie's bottom lip trembled.

'Aye, I'll grant you that.' A fine, strong lad he'd grown into. 'But not *old* enough, so you'd best eat up your toast and be off with you. You've got to learn all you can if you're to get that scholarship.'

A place at the grammar school; Polly wanted it for him more than she cared to admit. Arnie was a bright boy, his teacher said. Given to carelessness sometimes, though that was understandable in the young, and too eager to be out of the schoolroom and away into the fields. But bright, for all that. If he'd only take more pride in his handwriting and not cover his page with ink blots and smudges, then yes, he stood a very good chance of winning a scholarship.

He'd look grand in that uniform with the striped tie and the green cap, Polly thought proudly, though where she'd find the clothing coupons and money for such finery she wished someone would tell her. But she would manage. She always had.

'Eat your toast, lad,' she murmured, 'and don't be so free with that jam. That pot has to last us all month, remember.'

'Yes, Aunt Poll.' He eyed a strawberry sitting temptingly near the top of the jar and decided to leave it there for tomorrow. 'I bet you'll be helping with the threshing. I bet you'll be able to get a good look at that engine.' Nobody told grown-ups what to do. He couldn't wait to be a grown-up.

'No, I won't. Doubt if I'll see it at all, noisy, dirty old thing. I'll be helping Mrs Ramsden feed all those

80

people, though how she'll find rations enough for seven extra is a mystery to me.' Grace Ramsden was proud of Home Farm's reputation as a good eating place, in spite of food rationing. Like as not there'd be rabbit pie and rice pudding; good farmhouse standbys. Rumours had been flying, since the Japanese came into the war. No more rice, people said, and if their armies got as far as India, no more tea. Now the rice, Polly considered, folk could do without if they had to, but tea was altogether another thing. 'And anyway, who's to say for sure that the team'll be coming today? Mat will have to wait his turn. There's a war on, lad, don't forget.'

'I know, Aunt Poll.' People said there's a war on all the time these days, as if a war was something terrible. Wars weren't all that bad, Arnie considered. They'd be a whole lot of fun if it wasn't for people getting killed. It would be awful when it was all over and he had to go home. He liked being with Aunt Poll, having regular meals and regular bath-nights, and living in the country was a whole lot better than living in Hull.

He liked Aunt Poll a lot; she was better, he had to admit, than his mother. Not that he was being unkind to his real mother; it was just that he had to try very hard, these days, to remember what she looked like.

'Do you think,' he frowned, taking his balaclava from the fire guard where it had been set to warm, 'that Mam's forgotten where I am?'

'Now you know she hasn't. Didn't she send you a card at Christmas with a ten-shilling note inside it? Of course she hasn't forgotten you.'

No indeed, though she wished she had, Polly mourned silently. What was more, an action like that gave rise to suspicion, especially when such generosity had previously been noticeable by its absence.

But at least Mrs Bagley's visits had ceased after that first year, for now she was on war work; on nights, mostly, though night-work could cover many occupations, Polly brooded, especially when a woman bleached her hair with peroxide and plucked her eyebrows, somehow managing to get bright red nail varnish and lipstick when most other women hadn't seen such things in the shops for months. My word, yes. There was night-work and night-work.

Arnie pulled on his knitted helmet and its matching gloves. He'd been delighted to open the soft, well-wrapped parcel on Christmas morning. He wouldn't mind betting that when he got to school this morning, he'd be the only boy with a khaki balaclava and gloves; *khaki*, like the soldiers wore.

He called 'So-long, Aunt Poll,' then ran out quickly before she could attempt to kiss him; kissing was for girls. Whistling joyfully he squinted up at the Lancaster bomber that flew in low to land at RAF Peddlesbury.

Smashing, those Lancasters were. Great, frightening things, with four roaring engines and two guns and bombdoors that opened at the press of a button. He wouldn't mind flying a Lancaster. Pity he was only nine and a bit, though with luck the war would last long enough for him to be seventeen-and-a-half. He crossed his fingers, frowning. Grown-ups got all the fun.

Climbing the garden fence he made for the long, straight drive and the beeches and oaks that stood either side of it like unmoving, unspeaking sentries. This morning he was taking the 'field' way to school, cutting behind Ridings and the pasture at the back of Home Farm, to pick up the lane that led to the pub and the school nearby. This morning's journey was longer and wetter underfoot and usually taken in spring and summer only, but Arnie felt cheated to be missing the dirt and din of a threshing day and was determined at least to see the monstrous, huffing, puffing engine; to close his eyes with delight as it clattered and clanked past him, making the most wonderful, hideous noises.

Instead, he saw Hester Fairchild. She was standing very still, gazing at the ploughed earth around her and she looked up, startled, as he approached.

'Arnie! Hullo! Taking the long way to school this morning?'

He gave her a beam of delight. He liked Mrs Fairchild; not because Aunt Poll liked her but because Mrs Fairchild liked small boys. She was always pleased, *really* pleased, to see him. And she didn't look at him as if he were a nuisance nor speak to him in the silly voice grown-ups used when they spoke to children.

'I've come this way to see if the threshing team has got here. Are you going to see it, too?'

'No, Arnie. I came to look at the ploughing – to see how they're getting on.' She had come, truth known, because she knew the ploughs would be idle today; because Mat and Jonty and the Italian would be busy all day in the stackyard and she wouldn't have to acknowledge a man she would rather were anywhere than on her land. 'Shall we walk together as far as the house?'

'All right.' Arnie liked Ridings, too; liked it because it was big and full of echoes and hollow noises. He liked the big, painted pictures on the walls; pictures of people with serious faces, dressed in old-fashioned clothes and whose eyes followed him as he walked past them.

He dug his hands into his trouser pockets and matched his step to that of his grown-up friend.

'Did you know,' he confided, 'there's a boy in the village whose dad is abroad in the Army and yesterday the postman brought him a big box of oranges, all the way from Cairo. *Twenty-four*, there were. Can you imagine having twenty-four oranges, all at once?'

'I can't, Arnie. I really can't.' Not for a long time had anyone been able to buy oranges – except perhaps one at a

83

time and after queueing for it at the village shop. Nor could children like Arnie remember the joy of peeling a banana, for that particular fruit had disappeared completely at the very beginning of the war. 'Twenty-four oranges, the lucky boy! Never mind, Arnie. Perhaps someone will send you oranges from abroad one day.'

'Nah. Not me. Haven't got a dad, see? Well, I have, but not an *official* one. Stands to reason, dunnit, when I'm called Bagley and Mam says me dad's called Kelly-godrottim. Glad I haven't got a name like that. Think how they'd laugh at school if I was called Arnold William Kellygodrottim.' He'd do without the oranges, thanks all the same.

'Just think!' Hester's voice trembled on the edge of laughter. What a joy of a child this was. Small wonder Polly adored him. 'But I'm afraid you won't see the threshing team. The driver won't set out with such a big machine until it's properly light. It'll be another half hour before it gets here.'

She reached the orchard gate then turned to watch him walk away, raising her hand to match his wave, thinking how cruel life could be when an unwanted, carelessly-conceived love child like Arnie could grow up so straight and strong and delightful.

And I couldn't give you a boy, Martin; couldn't give a living son to Ridings. Nor, when our babe died, could I try again.

I'm sorry, my love. Forgive me. I didn't know. Believe me, I didn't know . . .

The threshing team clanked into the yard on great, grinding, cast-iron wheels, spewing out coal-smoke, throwing mud in all directions.

'*Good grief*,' Kath gasped.

'First time you've seen one?' Jonty smiled.

It was. She stood still and wide-eyed, thinking so strange

a contraption could only have come from an age that had known Stephenson's Rocket. It was almost a steam-roller, yet with the look of an ancient steam train about it and it pulled a brightly painted contrivance behind it.

'That's the thresher,' Jonty supplied, following her gaze. 'They'll back it up to the stack and the sheaves will be thrown down into it, into the drum.'

'Y-yes.' Kath frowned. 'Does it work on electricity?'

'Nothing quite so convenient.' Jonty shrugged. 'Look – see that big wheel on the engine beside the driver's seat? It's that wheel that connects by a belt to the thresher; and, roughly, is what drives it. And without blinding you with science,' he laughed, 'the straw comes out at one end, the wheat at the other and the chaff – the wheat husks, that is – drop down below it.' He smiled again and his eyes, thick-lashed and blue, crinkled mischievously. 'Got that?'

'Yes. Well, I *think* so.' My, but he was handsome. 'You'll let me down lightly, Jonty?'

'I will. If you aren't afraid of heights you can go on top of the stack with Marco. He'll be feeding the sheaves down into the drum; you can keep them coming to him – okay?'

It wasn't. All at once she was apprehensive, but she said she'd do her best – and thought how foolish she had been to worry about milking a cow, when, had she known about traction engines and threshing machines that day she volunteered for the Land Army, she'd have taken to her heels and run a mile!

'We'll be making a start soon, Kath. They've only to fix the belt, and then we'll be away.'

'What will Roz be doing?'

'She'll be seeing to the filling, most likely. There's hooks at the back end of the thresher, for holding the wheat-sacks. Roz will watch them and tie them when they're full; there'll be a couple of big strong lads to hump them away.

'Last time we threshed, Roz was on the chaff.' Jonty grinned. 'It's a dirty job. The poor love was black all over by the end of the day. She didn't speak to me for ages after.'

Kath laughed with him, biting back the words she longed to say; that if he truly cared for Roz, if he acknowledged what his eyes showed so plainly, then he would wait a while; be there if one day she should need him and the comfort of his safe, broad shoulders. She didn't say them, though, because there was really no need, and anyway, it was no business of hers. But oh, if a man smiled at me the way Jonty smiled at Roz; if his eyes loved me the way his eyes loved her, Kath yearned, I'd be putty in his hands. If, she thought, dismissing such stupid thoughts, she were heart-whole and fancy-free. And not married to Barney, of course.

The thresher was belted-up to the traction engine, the drum rotated noisily. Beside it in the stackyard stood two carts; one for straw, the other to carry away the fat, full sacks of wheat. Roz stood to the rear, a pile of hessian sacks at her side and she waved to Kath who looked giddily down from the top of the stack.

'Be careful,' Marco warned. 'Straw can be slippy. Be careful how you step.'

'I will.' Of course she would. 'Tell me again? I just throw the wheat sheaves over to you and –'

'That is so. And I shall cut the binding-twine, then throw them down, like so.' Gravely, he mimed the operation. 'It is nothing for worry. I show you how.'

The air was frosty and filled with scents of coal-smoke and dusty straw. Kath smiled at Flora Lyle who had come to help, and taken up her position beside Roz.

'All right?' Flora mouthed, and Kath lifted her hand in a reassuring wave.

'Right!' the engineer called. 'Here she goes!'

Marco spat on his hands, rubbed them together, then lifted the first sheaf. Kath took a deep breath. This was better than working in a factory or on munitions. This was where she had always wanted to be; what she had always wanted to do.

She spat on her hands as Marco had done. This was it, then!

She was glad when eleven o'clock came for her arms ached and her mouth was dry with dust; already she had stripped off her pullover and unfastened the top button of her shirt. For the last thirty minutes she had been unable to think of anything but a glass of cool, clear water and the sight of Grace and Polly carrying jugs and a tray of mugs was more than welcome.

'Slack off!' came the cry. 'Drinking time!'

'Come.' Marco held the ladder steady, indicating to Kath to climb down first.

'Water, anybody?' Grace called and Kath answered with a grateful '*Please*,' closing her eyes, drinking deeply.

'All right?' Roz walked over, followed by Flora who carried mugs of tea.

'Just about.' Kath laughed.

'You'll be stiff in the morning,' Flora warned. 'A good hot bath is what we'll all need tonight.'

'Mmm.' Kath nodded to Marco who stood a little apart, unsure amongst strangers. 'Those sheaves get heavy, after a time. Marco works like a machine. It was hard going, keeping up with him.'

Not that she was complaining; far from it. She was part of a team; she was with friends. She belonged here. It felt right, and she never wanted to leave.

They settled into an easy rhythm again. Marco worked steadily, pausing only to mop his forehead or to glance briefly in Kath's direction and smile encouragement. The height of the stack had already fallen by two feet and in time, by mid-afternoon perhaps, when the stack was lower still, the grain elevator would be pushed alongside and the sheaves fed on to it and carried up to the drum, just as people were carried up a moving staircase.

But that would not be yet, Kath knew, already hoping it would not be too long before they stopped to eat and could troop, aching and hungry, into Grace's kitchen.

She looked briefly down. To her left, Roz and Flora tended the corn sacks and to her right, straw was being forked into a cart. She smiled across at Marco and in that instant she felt and saw a fat, black rat, its body soft against her ankle.

'Aaaagh! *No!*' She jumped back, startled, kicking out wildly at the straw beneath her feet. Then she let go a cry harsh with terror for the sheaves were shifting beneath her. She was falling!

She opened her mouth to cry out, but no sound came. She grabbed blindly at the straw, grasping it tightly, halting her fall only a little. The mass beneath her was still moving; she was rigid with panic and fear.

'*Kat!*' A hand caught her wrist with a grip of steel and the sliding and slipping stopped. 'Your hand! Give to me your other hand!'

She lifted her arm slowly, felt his fingers grasp hers. The beater drum flailed and crashed below her, the belt slapped and snaked on and if she fell on it – oh, God! Why didn't they stop the thing?

'Hang on to her.' It was Jonty's voice, above her. 'I've got you, Marco. Don't let her go!'

'Is all right, Kat.' Marco's voice was gentle and calm. 'Be still. Not to struggle.'

Her body had turned to stone; her mouth was dry with terror. Hands tugged at her shirt. They were pulling her back.

'Relax, Kath,' Jonty called softly. 'We've got you. Try not to struggle.'

The straw scratched her face and arms as inch by inch they dragged her back to them. The scream of the belt changed to a soft hum, then stopped; the drum juddered to a halt. Hands grasped the seat of her dungarees. With one grunting, groaning heave she was up and over, landing on top of the stack in a sprawl of arms and legs. For what seemed forever she lay there, shoulders heaving, trying to stop the jerking of her limbs.

'Is all right, Katarina.' Marco gathered her to him, holding her tightly, stroking her hair. 'Is all over now.'

She clung to him and the sobs came; great, tearing sobs of relief. 'Marco, oh, Marco . . .'

'Here now, stop that noise! Come on, lassie; blow your nose!' Flora was there, holding out a handkerchief. 'What was it? What made you fall?'

'A rat. There, at my feet!'

'A rat, Katarina? A little frightened rat?' Marco chided.

'I thought it would crawl up my leg.'

'Help her down,' Jonty said gently. 'I'll take over up here with Marco.'

'No! She stays.' Flora's voice was sharp. 'If she doesn't, she'll never go on a stack again. Snap out of it, Kath! On your feet!'

'I *can't*. The rats. I'm sorry, but –'

'We fix it, yes?' Marco took two pieces of the discarded twine. 'We fix those rats good. Stand up, Kat.'

Unsteadily she got to her feet, watching bewildered as Marco tied round the bottoms of her dungaree legs. 'Is okay, now. No rats in trousers.'

He was smiling. Everybody was smiling. Kath sniffed loudly and pulled the back of her hand across her eyes.

'I'm all right, now,' she whispered. 'I'll stay.'

Grace Ramsden's midday kitchen was warm and steamy, rich with the scents of cooking; a place of safeness and normality after the terror of the stackyard.

'Feeling better now, lass?' Grace asked as Kath hung her jacket on the door peg.

'Fine, thanks. My word,' she smiled shakily, 'but I caused a bit of an upset, didn't I? Marco caught me, you know; just grabbed my wrist. And Jonty was on top of that stack in a flash; held on to Marco's belt with one hand and hung on to the roof beam with the other. Between them – oh, let's just say I was lucky. I still don't like to think what might have happened.'

'Might have, but didn't,' Grace retorted, 'so sit yourself down and let's hear no more about it.'

'But it was so stupid,' Kath persisted. 'And all because of a rat.'

'I'm scared stiff of earwigs,' Grace confided. 'So away with your bother and find yourself somewhere to sit.'

Farms were not duty-bound to feed their workers on threshing days, but Home Farm had a reputation for good food, generously served, and even though now she was reduced to providing less than she would have liked, Grace Ramsden still saw to it that no one went without in her kitchen.

The stackyard workers arranged themselves around the table on chairs and benches, all of them hungry and glad of the break.

'Sorry, Grace, but I don't much feel like food.' The familiar churning was inside Kath still, and if anyone else said one more word about it, even in fun, she would break down and weep again, she really would.

'Then how about taking Marco his dinner? I'll give him yours as well, shall I?'

'You could do worse.' Kath shrugged. 'He did the work of two men this morning.' Apart from saving her life, and holding her comfortably afterwards, not telling her, either, that she was a silly woman who had no place on a farm if she went berserk at the sight of a rat. 'Is this it?' She picked up the tin tray.

'Aye. Hurry along before it gets cold, there's a good lass.'

Marco was sitting where he always sat and she settled the tray on his knees.

'Here you are. It's rabbit pie.' She sat down beside him, chin on hands. 'I want to thank you for saving my life, because you did, you know. I could have fallen into that machine and –' She stopped, remembering the flailing, crashing thresher.

'No. I would not have let you. You are not to think about it.'

'But I must. I can't forget what you did.'

'Jonty was there. He help, also.'

'Yes, and I shall thank him, too.' She made a small, appealing gesture with her hands. 'What can I say?'

'Say you are no longer afraid of rats.' He smiled.

'Oh, no, I couldn't. They'll always frighten me, I think. But at least I know now how to stop them running up my trouser legs.' She smiled, and the smile came more easily. 'Well, I'd best be going, I suppose.' She rose to her feet, then bending quickly, taking his face in her hands, she gently kissed his cheek. 'Thanks, Marco . . .'

She turned then, and ran; back to Grace's kitchen and the men and women who sat at her table. Pulling out the empty chair beside Roz she said, 'All of a sudden I'm hungry. I don't suppose there's any of that pie left?'

Roz kicked off her wellingtons, called 'Sorry I'm late!' then kissed her grandmother's cheek.

'It's almost dark. Did you manage to finish?'

'We did. All over and done with till next year. God! I'm filthy! There wouldn't be any hot water to spare, Gran? My hair's thick with dust and I've got chaff down my shirt and it's itching like mad. I need a bath.'

'I thought you might; towels are on the fireguard. I held back supper till you came in. How did it go, darling?'

'Fine. Well – up to a point, that is. Kath took a tumble

over the side of the stack. She's okay, but still a bit shaken. Marco grabbed her, just in time.'

'The Italian?'

'Yes, Gran. *Marco*. If it hadn't been for him, there could've been a nasty accident.'

'When am I going to meet your friend?' The conversation took an abrupt about-turn. Not that she was not relieved, Hester acknowledged silently, that something awful hadn't happened to the poor young woman, but it could not be discussed at Ridings if the credit must go to an Italian. 'She seems nice. Ask her to tea sometime, and show her the house. You said she was interested to see it.'

'Okay. Sunday's her day off, same as mine. Maybe she'd like that.'

'All settled, then. Perhaps Grace could spare me a couple of eggs for sandwiches,' Hester murmured, 'and there's a little of the Christmas cake left.' An almost fatless, almost fruitless, almost sugarless Christmas cake, she sighed, remembering the take-six-eggs-and-one-pound-of-butter recipe of pre-war days. 'I'll look forward to meeting her. Now upstairs with you. Supper's at six sharp, so don't lie there wallowing.'

'All right now, Kath?' asked Flora as they pedalled back to Peacock Hey. 'Sorry I had to be a bit sharp this morning.'

'I'm fine – you were right to make me stay up there. And one thing I've learned – not to go threshing again without tying my trouser bottoms. Did I make an awful fool of myself?' she asked, frowning.

'No more than I'd have made if it had happened to me. But farms are notorious places for accidents, Kath, so try to forget it. And we'd better get a move on, or there'll be no hot water left.'

A letter was waiting at the hostel; Kath had sensed there would be one. It bore the Censor's stamp and the hand-writing on the envelope was Barney's. She could have done without a letter from North Africa, she thought petulantly. Today of all days she needed Barney's disapproval like she needed a rat up her trouser leg!

Lips set tightly, she returned it to the letter-rack. Right now she needed a hot bath more than anything else in the world. The letter must wait until after supper.

'Ready for your supper?' Grace asked of her son who sat in the fireside rocker.

The departure of the threshing team had not signalled the end of Jonty's day; there had still been cows to feed and milk. Now he was so weary that if the house took a direct hit, he doubted he could get out of the chair.

'Can you keep it warm till I've had a bath?'

'I can. Kath offered to stay on and help with the milking, mind, but your dad sent her back with the Forewoman. She was badly shaken this morning, though she tried not to make a fuss. I like that girl, but just when I think I've got the measure of her and start treating her like I treat young Roz, then a barrier comes down, if you see what I mean?'

'Sorry, Mum, no. Kath seems ordinary and normal to me, and for a towny she's fitted in fine. What do you mean – a barrier?'

'I don't know; not exactly. But I'm right, I'm sure I am. Woman's instinct, you could call it.' Of course Jonty hadn't sensed it; what man would? 'And get yourself off your behind, lad. You'll feel all the better when you've washed that muck off you.' Oh, yes. It took a woman to know a woman. 'And don't forget to rinse out the bath when you've finished!' she called as he slowly climbed the stairs.

There *was* something, Grace insisted, but she couldn't pry – even in wartime, when people had grown kinder and closer, she couldn't. Poor lass. Even in that hostel amongst all those girls, she'd still be alone, she wouldn't mind betting; still holding back that last little bit of herself that no one would be allowed to see, or know.

'Take care, Kath,' she whispered, wondering how she was feeling and what she was doing. 'Take care, lass.'

Kathleen Allen sat beside the common-room fire, a notepad on her knee. Only when she had bathed and eaten her supper had she returned to the letter-rack to pick out the blue air-mail envelope. And she had guessed right; Barney was still angry with her, though when he wrote he had not received the Christmas Day letter she hoped would make things right between them. Things would be better, when he did. When he read of her love; when he realized how she missed him and worried for his safety then perhaps he'd be the Barney she had cared for, and married. It stood to reason, she supposed, that a man should feel resentment when he was parted from all he cared for most.

She looked down at the pad.

Dearest Barney,

Tonight, when I got back to the hostel, your letter was waiting for me. It is very cold here, the skies are grey and darkness comes early. I tried to imagine you sitting there writing to me, with the sun beating down and you trying to keep cool.

She had not mentioned his annoyance in her letter, nor apologized again. By now, surely, he must be prepared to forgive and forget?

Today at Home Farm we all worked very hard, threshing the last of the wheat. Everyone who could be spared came along to lend a hand and we finished just a little before dusk.

She would not tell him about the rat, nor about what happened to her. It might only cause him to worry – or prompt him to say he'd told her so. To tell him was impossible, anyway, because he still didn't know about Jonty who should have been in the Army, and she could never tell him about Marco.

Tomorrow things will be less hectic and Roz and I will be back to normal again. Roz isn't very happy, at the moment. Her boyfriend has gone home on leave and she misses him, as I miss you, Barney.

Yes, she *did* miss him, but not with the tearing ache with which Roz missed Paul. Her eyes misted over. Roz and Paul had no secrets yet she, Kath, must measure every word she wrote to her husband and it was wrong, for he was all she had in the world. He had married her knowing what she was, and given her his name. And having that name, one which was *really* hers, was more important to her than ever she would admit.

Yet how could she tell him? How would he react if ever he was to discover that an Italian – a man who was his enemy – had today almost certainly saved her life? And how could she argue that it had been Marco who was there when she needed help; when she needed comfort?

'Marco is *your* enemy, too,' whispered her conscience. 'His country is at war with your country.'

'Think,' demanded the voice of her reason, 'that if Barney and Marco had faced each other in North Africa and each had carried a gun . . .'

She shivered with distaste. It was all so wrong. Wars were wrong. If women governed the world there'd be an end to war. Women would say, 'No more sons; we will conceive no more children if every score of years you send them to war!'

She clucked angrily. She was being stupid, her with her grand thoughts. Women would never be anything but women. It was the way it was; the way it always would be unless – or until – women stood together and demanded to be as good as men. They'd done it before, hadn't they; had chained themselves to railings and gone to prison, died even. And because of that, a woman could vote and need never tell her husband how she voted. Now women were at war, really at war. They wore the uniforms her husband detested and tried not to be afraid. They *weren't* comforts for officers!

Barney was wrong. He had no right to such opinions and she could not go through life being grateful to him for making her his wife; for marrying a woman who'd been reared in an orphanage and knew neither who she was nor what she was.

She was Kath. She was like Grace and Roz and Flora. She could no more help being abandoned than Marco could help being born Italian. Heavens above, Roz hadn't so much as raised an eyebrow when she'd found the courage to tell her. Roz hadn't cared, so why was *she* so prickly about it? She could no more help being unwanted than Jonty could help being in a reserved occupation, or Paul being an airman. Barney had no right to be so angry when all she was doing was trying to help win the war.

All? But hadn't this war given her the opportunity to do what she most wanted? Couldn't she have helped win the war in a factory, in a shop, or by becoming a nurse? All right. So she'd *wanted* to be a landgirl and live in the country. Was it so wrong? Was every landgirl in Peacock Hey as racked with guilt as she was?

Defiance blazed briefly through her and she looked at the unfinished letter on her knee. Supposing she were to have a brainstorm? Just supposing she were to go completely mad and write, 'Today, at threshing, I could have been killed. I slipped and fell and an Italian caught me and held me, and a young man who isn't in the Army helped him save my life. And afterwards, Barney, I thanked that Italian, and I kissed him.'

Shame flushed her cheeks. Shaking her head as if to remove all such thoughts from it she wrote, *I miss you, Barney. I want this war to be over so we can be together again. Take care of yourself, and come home safely.*

Come home to me quickly, Barney, before I take leave of my senses.

5

'You can say what you like, it's getting a lot lighter now, in the mornings,' Kath remarked, her eyes fixed on the bird that hovered over the churchyard. 'Is that a kestrel?'

'It is. Out hunting for breakfast; mice or voles, a rat, if it's lucky.'

They ate rats? 'Y'know, I think I like kestrels.'

'Thought you might.' Roz paused, then said hesitantly, 'Kath – remember the other day we were talking about – well –'

'About being careful? Not getting pregnant?'

'Yes. And I'm not.' Her cheeks flushed crimson. 'Pregnant, I mean. Thought you'd be glad to know.'

'I'm glad if you are,' Kath said softly.

'What do *you* think?' There was relief in her voice. 'Just think, Kath, in less than three days Paul will be back. I'm an idiot, aren't I, wishing my life away? I miss him, though.' They were walking past the little church, eyes still on the bird of prey. 'My parents are there, in the churchyard.'

'And your grandfather – the one who died in the last war – is he there, too?'

'No. He never came home. He's with all the other soldiers who died there, but Gran has never been to France to see his grave as some wives have. She had a stone put up here for him. I suppose she likes to think he's here in Alderby with all the other Fairchilds.'

'That's sad.' Kath frowned. 'I think I'd want to go, if I could, to see where he is. It might have comforted her, if she had.'

'She doesn't want to be comforted. That's why she still hates Germans. She finds more comfort doing that.'

They left the little graveyard behind them, with its moss-covered headstones, its yew trees and the railed-off corner where all the Fairchilds lay. Roz did not agree with those railings; even as a small child she had demanded to know why it should be so.

'Because they're Fairchilds.'

'Poor things. Aren't they lonely, cut off from the others?'

'I don't think so.' And Gran had said she would understand when she was older, but she hadn't. She still didn't.

'I'm sorry for your gran.' Kath sighed. 'It's a long time ago now. Wouldn't you think she'd have got over it a little?'

'You would, but she hasn't. I told her about what Marco did, but she just cut the conversation dead; refused to listen. I suppose we should hate Marco, too, come to think of it.'

'We should, but I can't; not now. He didn't have to put himself at risk for me, but he did. He didn't hate me, did he?'

'Nope. It's a funny old world. By the way, Gran says I'm to ask you to Sunday tea – if you can call egg sandwiches tea, that is. She'd like to meet you and I can show you paintings and photographs of Ridings as it used to be, if you're interested.'

'Interested? I'd *love* to come.' Kath blushed with pleasure. 'I'll have to wear my uniform, though. I haven't any civvy clothes with me. Will she mind?'

'Of course she won't. Apart from hating Germans – and Italians now, of course – and fussing over Ridings as if it's something special, Gran's quite normal and rather a love, most of the time. I'll tell her you'll come. Will half-past two suit you, then we can have a walk around the ruins while it's still light.'

'Any time at all.' Kath beamed, picking up a milk-crate. Afternoon tea at the big house. Now fancy that.

'I'm getting sick of waiting for it to be summer.' Arnie Bagley scraped his porridge bowl thoroughly and noisily. 'When is it going to be sunny again?'

'Soon, lad. Soon.' Polly longed for warmer days, too. 'Winter's more than half over. Afore very much longer we'll be able to have Sunday tea in the daylight, then we'll know for sure that spring isn't far away.'

Sunday tea in Yorkshire was always taken at five o'clock, just as Sunday dinner was taken at one. They were habits a body didn't break, Polly considered – well, not around these parts – and it was generally accepted that on the second Sunday in February the days would have drawn out sufficiently to enable tea to be eaten in 'the light'. High tea, that was. A knife and fork tea, though heaven only knew how a body was to manage with the weekly sugar ration cut to half a pound. And in February, the Government was to cut fats by an ounce – lard, margarine and butter, too, which would put paid to saving up a little for a cake. No more home-made cakes now, and shop cakes so hard to come by that you could queue for half an hour and still not get one.

'Toast?' she demanded, forking a slice of bread, holding it to the coals.

And as if that were not enough, what about those Japs invading Burma? So what about the tea ration now? Not that she was at all sure that Burma had tea plantations, but those Japanese soldiers had taken a step nearer to India – which *did*.

But before very long there would be American soldiers in Britain which would be a help, she acknowledged, us having been on our own since Dunkirk. It had made a difference in the last war, though they hadn't got themselves over in time to save Mr Fairchild, nor Tom.

'Spring starts on the twentieth of March, doesn't it, Aunt Poll?'

'Spring starts when it thinks it will; when there's no more flowers on that winter jasmine,' she said, nodding to the window and the creeper, bright with yellow flowers, that grew around it. 'You can't say winter's really gone till the last of those little flowers have fallen, so think on. *That's* the day spring starts. Nature don't have a calendar. And there's Kath at the door with the milk. Fetch it in, lad, afore those pesky little blue tits start pecking at the top.'

'It was Roz left it, not Kath.'

'And how do you know that, then?'

''Cos she was whistling. Kath doesn't whistle. Suppose Roz is happy because her boyfriend –' He stopped, not at all sure he'd meant to say so much.

'Because her *what*? Roz hasn't got a boyfriend – well, maybe Jonty, perhaps.'

'Jonty? Nah. Roz's boyfriend is an airman,' Arnie supplied scornfully, throwing caution through the window. 'Her young man's a navigator. And I saw him in the back of the RAF truck that takes the airmen to York when they go on leave. Roz'll be whistling 'cos he'll be coming back, soon.'

'Away with your romancing, Arnie Bagley. Roz hasn't got a young man.' Except Jonty, maybe, and she didn't seem as sweet on him as he was on her, come to think of it. 'And you're not to go saying things like that. Mrs Fairchild wouldn't be pleased if she heard you.'

'But it's true!' He coloured hotly. He *wasn't* telling lies. 'I saw them. *Kissing*. I've seen them ever so many times – well, twice. But they were kissing each other, both times.'

'Now see here, young man; even if you did see Roz and some airman, you're to keep quiet about it or you'll land the lass in trouble with her gran. Roz isn't old enough to have boyfriends – not yet.'

'But she's ever so old, Aunt Poll.'

'You let Mrs Fairchild be the judge of that. You mind your own business and get on with your breakfast.'

Arnie bit savagely into his toast. He'd have thought Aunt Poll would've been interested to know about Roz and the navigator from the aerodrome. He wished now he hadn't told her.

Polly pursed her lips, wondering how much truth there was in Arnie's revelations and how much was the product of his over-active imagination. My word, but Roz had kept the young man dark – if young man there was. Talk went around the village pretty sharpish; surely, if there'd been gossip she'd have heard it, sooner or later. All there was to do in Alderby, most times, was gossip. But there was no smoke without fire. Kissing, were they?

'Beats me how you get to know so much, lad,' she muttered. 'Seeing's one thing; blabbing it all over the village is another.'

'I haven't blabbed! You're the only one I've told!'

'Then let's see to it that it stays that way, shall we?'

Until she'd had time to think about it, that was. Until she'd got to the bottom of it and got the facts right. Only then could she warn the Mistress. Warn Mrs Fairchild? But maybe that wouldn't be a good idea at all. Maybe it would do a lot more good if she were to have a quiet word with young Roz?

Oh, drat Arnie and that inquisitive little nose of his! Drat the lad, though of course he just might be right. After all, Roz *was* nineteen, or would be, come April. Happen who the lass kissed was nobody's business but her own.

'And will you go and bring that milk in,' she said testily. 'Like I told you!'

Kath leaned her bicycle against the kitchen wall and pulled the bell-handle on Ridings' back door. She had thought,

101

for one mad moment to walk boldly up the front door steps and lift the heavy iron knocker, but she remembered her days as a housemaid, and her courage left her.

'Come in.' Roz smiled, taking in the bright green pullover, the collar and tie, the shiny black shoes. 'You do look smart.'

'I was thinking much the same about you.' She had been quick to notice the pleated grey skirt, the pale green blouse. 'It's the first time I've seen you in real clothes.'

'We're in the little sitting-room, this afternoon. Gran said it could do with an airing, but it's really in your honour.' Roz nodded vaguely down the passageway. 'I've been chopping logs for the fire all morning.'

Little remained of the original house, yet the surviving rooms and passages retained the spaciousness of a larger, grander place which the stone-flagged floors and uneven walls did nothing to dispel.

'This house must have been really something,' she murmured, the servant in her taking in the brass door-handles, the hard-to-clean leaded window panes, bellied with age.

'I suppose it was, but what's left suits us all right.' Roz opened a white-painted door. 'Gran, here's Kathleen Allen.'

'My dear, how kind of you to come.' Hester Fairchild's pleasure was genuine, her handshake firm. 'You look chilled. Come to the fire, and warm yourself. You can look at our old ruin later.'

She stooped to place a log on the fire then sank back cosily into the well-cushioned chair. 'Such a luxury these days, Mrs Allen – fires, I mean. And will you allow an old lady to call you Kathleen?'

'Oh please, I'd like that. And you're not old. I got quite a surprise, in fact. I'd expected – well, a *grandmother*, you see.' Her cheeks flushed crimson. 'Sorry. I – I meant –'

'Don't be sorry. Don't spoil it. I'm not too old to enjoy

a compliment. But tell me about yourself. I'm quite a busybody, given the chance.'

'There isn't a lot to tell.' Kath looked around the small, snug room. Every piece of furniture was oddly matched, yet so right. A pair of brocade-seated chairs – Sheraton, were they, like those in the Birmingham town house? – a sofa with a faded, delphinium-patterned cover, china bowls of dried lavender flowers, a hand-embroidered footstool. Things passed down; old things, loved things, safe things. 'I like being a landgirl. It's the first big thing that's happened to me – apart from Barney, that is.'

'Your husband? Roz tells me he's abroad in the Army. You'll miss him.'

'Yes, I do.'

The log began to crackle and flame, shining the brass fender, splashing the walls with fireglow. There were generations of Fairchilds in this room; Roz was lucky, knowing so precisely who she was.

'Have you heard from him lately?'

'Last Monday. Sometimes I don't get a letter for weeks then six arrive, all at once. It's like Christmas, then.' *Was* like Christmas.

'Christmas.' Hester nodded, her eyes suddenly sad.

'Why don't we go out?' Roz had recognized that faraway look. 'Think we might have our walk while it's still light – or take a look at the house if you'd like, and meet the rest of the Fairchilds. They're a rum lot! Would you mind, Gran, if we did?'

'Not a bit. Off you go. I shall sit here by the fire and listen to the wireless.'

'Now don't forget – you must be careful not to mention the prisoner,' Roz whispered when they had closed the door behind them. 'Nor Paul.'

'I'll remember.'

'Right! I shall now bore you silly with the Fairchilds.' With a flourish of her arm Roz indicated the stairs. 'This is really the second-best staircase, by the way. The posh one was destroyed in the fire. And these lot,' she nodded to the chain-hung portraits, 'are all they managed to salvage of my forebears. Meet the folks!'

'This is all so lovely,' Kath said softly. 'Far nicer than I'd have thought. I can understand your Gran wanting to hang on to it; and to think I called it an old ruin. But you love it, too, don't you?'

'Yes, of course, but I wouldn't go on about it like Gran does. I like the outside best – the old walls and the empty windows; so stark, somehow, yet so beautiful in summer.' When the climbing roses were flowering, the honeysuckle and the clematis. 'And if you could just see it, Kath, when the moon is full and it shines through those great, empty windows – now that really *is* something. That's when I love it most, I think – when it's all sad, sort of, as if it's remembering. But let's have a quick look around here, then we'll go out and I'll show you what I mean.'

'So what do you think?' Roz demanded, as Kath saw for herself the strange beauty of a once-great house.

'It's amazing,' she whispered, asking herself how the sight of rose-brick walls and stone-mullioned windows could be so disturbing, so poignant.

'All this lot should have been demolished, really, after the fire but Gran wouldn't hear of it. So my father left just the walls – an outline, I suppose, of what it had once been.'

'I'm glad he did.' Kath gazed fascinated at the forlorn beauty, wondering at its melancholy, and the waste. 'Those windows are like empty eyes, but I don't know if they're looking forward or looking back.'

It was then, exactly, that it happened; when Roz, looking up, saw the predator like a great black bird, low in the sky.

'Kath! Look! God, it's one of theirs!'

Hands clasped they ran, crouching, for the shelter of the walls, heard the scream of the diving bomber and the terrible roar of exploding bombs.

'It's Peddlesbury,' Roz gasped. 'A hit-and-run!' No time for a warning; no time for the wailing, undulating air-raid siren. A lone bomber had slipped in, unseen and unmarked. 'Run, Kath. *Run!*'

Hester was standing in the kitchen yard, her face pale and anxious.

'You're all right! What was it?'

'A sneak raid on Peddlesbury,' Roz choked, breathless from running. 'Another one. Come inside, Gran.'

'Oughtn't we to go down to the cellars?'

'No. Think it's all over now. Short and sharp. Hope it isn't like last time.' Last time there had been many killed and injured. 'Are you all right, Kath?'

'I think so, thanks.' Just that it had brought back the air-raids on Birmingham she had thought forgotten; reminded her of wailing sirens and fearful, waiting silences; of listening, breath indrawn, for the menacing drone of aircraft engines and the sick-making, tearing sound of exploding bombs. And afterwards, leaving the shelter to breathe in the stench of destruction; a mixing of dust, fire and water-doused timbers. Sometimes, too, the stench of death. 'I'm fine. I don't suppose it'll come back – will it?'

'Shouldn't think so. That sort just come in low under radar cover, then get out as fast as they can. That one'll be over the North Sea by now.'

'Yes. Of course.' Kath was thinking about Peacock Hey and how very close it stood to the aerodrome. Most of the girls would be there; today was their day off, too. She was glad that she was here, at Ridings, and felt guilty because she was glad.

'I think,' said Hester Fairchild firmly, 'that after that we could all do with a cup of tea.'

Jonty came, smiling apologetically, as they were finishing tea.

'Thought I'd better come over – just to make sure you're all right,' he said, his eyes concerned.

'Jonathan, how kind. Have you time for a cup of tea?' Hester smiled. 'And we're fine. Have you heard anything about it?'

'Not a lot.' He declined the tea. 'Dad heard in the village that two of the bombs hit Peddlesbury and the other fell in a field.'

'So they're all right at Peacock Hey?'

'I'm almost sure so. One bomb fell near Nab Wood, well away from the hostel and the two that hit Peddlesbury got the runway. By the way, Kath, I'll ride back with you if you let me know what time you'll be leaving.'

'I'll be all right. It's good of you, Jonty, and thoughtful, but I've been in a few air-raids, remember? I'll manage, thanks.'

'He's such a nice young man,' Hester remarked when Jonty had left. 'So kind; so hard-working.'

'Yes, he is, Mrs Fairchild. I owe him my life; him and –' She stopped, remembering Roz's warning. 'I – I think he's handsome, too,' she said, wildly. 'I – I mean –'

'I know exactly what you mean.' Hester smiled obliquely at her granddaughter. 'Though Roz doesn't think so, do you, darling? Roz, I'm afraid, just pooh-poohs me when I tell her I think he's very fond of her.'

'Gran, for goodness' sake!' Roz pouted. 'I like Jonty; I like him a lot, but I refuse to fall in love with him just because you like him and think he'd be good for Ridings.' She rose from the table, pushing back the chair noisily. 'Excuse me, please. Must fill up the teapot.'

'Jonathan,' Kath said hurriedly, wanting to atone for being the unwitting cause of Hester's hurt glances and the flush in Roz's cheeks. 'I didn't realize that was his real name.'

'His Sunday name.' Hester smiled, serene again. 'And forgive Roz her quick temper; we blame it on that red hair . . .'

In the kitchen, Roz already regretted her outburst. She'd almost said that she was in love with someone else, though she'd bitten on her tongue in time. She must learn to be more careful.

Darling Paul, I miss you so, need you so, though she had to be glad he wasn't at the aerodrome when the bombs fell. And she hoped with all her heart that the bombs really had fallen on the runway, like Jonty said; hoped they'd fallen slap bang in the middle of it and made two great craters that would take days and days to repair. She longed for him to phone her. Perhaps tonight he would get through.

The call for which Roz had so desperately prayed came as Kath was preparing to leave; just as she shrugged into her jacket and put on her hat Roz ran to answer its ring, pointedly closing the door behind her.

'I've enjoyed this afternoon such a lot, Mrs Fairchild – bombs and all.' Kath smiled. 'Thank you for letting me see your home. It's – it's just *lovely*.'

'You must come again – often. Don't wait to be asked, Kathleen. I like having young people about the place. Come for Roz's birthday and stay the night, if the Warden will let you. She'd like that, I know.'

'Your gran has asked me to stay the night for your birthday – in April, isn't it?' Kath said to Roz who had offered to walk as far as the gate lodges with her, and to call in on Polly to make sure she was all right. 'I didn't know what to say because you'll probably be out somewhere with Paul. That was him on the phone, wasn't it?'

'Yes. He won't be ringing again; I'm seeing him on Tuesday night, fingers crossed.'

'Look, Roz, I know it's none of my business, but I think you should tell your gran about him. How you get away with it beats me. How do you manage to meet him so often without her knowing?'

'I tell a lot of lies, I'm afraid. I have to, Kath. I know what she'd say, you see. She'd stop me seeing him.'

'Are you sure?'

'I'm sure. I know her better than you do. When you bring up someone else's child, you're just that bit extra careful. Gran's always been like that, where I'm concerned. She's been mother and father and guardian angel to me. She won't ever change.'

'Try her?' Kath urged. 'Just try her?'

'I'll think about it.'

'Promise?'

'I said I would, Kath. Were you very frightened when the bombs dropped?'

'Scared witless, for a couple of minutes.' Okay, Roz. Change the subject, if that's the way you want it. But it isn't going to go away. 'It's times like that I wish I'd been born a man.'

'Why, for heaven's sake? Men can be afraid, too; they just can't show it, that's all,' Roz countered hotly.

'I know, love; I know.' My, but she'd been jumpy today. Missing Paul, of course. 'Don't get me wrong. I know men get afraid. I shouldn't have said what I did.'

'And I shouldn't have been so snappy, but it's awful, sometimes. Gran, I mean. She really would like me to marry someone who'd be good for Ridings and right now Jonty fits the bill, poor love. I wish she wouldn't go on about it.'

'She's only thinking about you, Roz. She's brought you up and you can't blame her for wanting to see you happily married. I wish I'd had someone like her, when I was growing up.

'And that's something else, you know. Does your grandmother know about me – really know, I mean? Does she know I was an unwanted child; that I grew up on charity, in an orphanage? Would I have been so welcome, if she'd known?'

108

'What do you mean, *if* she'd known? She does know. I told her ages ago. I know she can be a bit funny sometimes, but your being brought up in an orphanage wouldn't worry her at all. She'd say it wasn't how you started out, but what you'd made of yourself that mattered.

'But you've got a real chip on your shoulder about that place, haven't you, Kath? You'd think orphanages were dens of iniquity, or something. What you're really so miffed about is your mother having left you. That's really your *bête noire*, isn't it?'

'My *what*?'

'Your black beast, pet hate – your bugbear; just like Gran and her Germans.'

'I suppose it is. And it wasn't all that bad at the orphanage. It was just that I didn't really belong to anybody.'

'Well, you do now. You belong to Barney and to everyone at Home Farm and to me and Gran – right?'

'Right.' Kath smiled. 'Sorry if I got a bit hot round the collar. I meant well and I'm still not going to take back one word about your telling your Gran. Just think about it, will you? She's a lovely person; she might understand more than you think.'

'I know. You could be right.' Roz pushed open the gates then placed a kiss on Kath's cheek. 'It's good to have someone to talk to and I'll think about what you've said. Goodnight, Kath. Go carefully.'

Roz wouldn't think about it, Kath brooded as she rode along Peddlesbury Lane. She'd go on meeting Paul and telling lies about it, nothing would change; except if anything were to happen, that was. And if it did, *when* it did, how was she to tell her grandmother, then?

'Oh, you silly, muddle-headed girl, why do I worry so about you?' she demanded of the darkness around her. 'Just why, will you tell me?'

*　　*　　*

109

Alderby St Mary buzzed with bomb-talk. It ranged from the total destruction of RAF Peddlesbury, to 'a lot of fuss about nothing; only one Jerry plane and all three bombs missed!'

Polly Appleby alone was in possession of the facts for she had got them from Home Farm's landgirl when she left the milk. Peddlesbury *had* been hit; two bombs on the runway but, apart from a lot of broken window panes, no one hurt. And Kath should know, since Peacock Hey was nearer to the aerodrome than Alderby.

Polly said as much to Hester Fairchild. 'Could have been a whole lot worse,' she said, fastening her pinafore. 'Kath knows all about bombing, poor lass; thought she'd be safe in the country, I shouldn't wonder. But it only goes to show that nobody's safe these days from them dratted bombers.'

'It was only a hit-and-run,' Hester observed mildly, 'and this time no one was hurt. We should be thankful for small mercies. Did you know that Kathleen came to tea yesterday? A nice girl. She'll be good for Roz. Roz needs more young company than she's getting.'

'Oh, I don't know.' Polly frowned, filling the kettle, setting it to boil. Roz was getting more company than her grandmother supposed. Polly had thought a lot about what Arnie told her, first deciding that it was nothing at all to do with anyone, then wavering, because Roz had been gently reared and happen it would do no harm if someone were to have a word with the lass. Just a gentle reminder about – *things*.

At that point she had shut out such thoughts at once. Even though it was a known fact that blood ran hotter in times of war, it wasn't for Polly Appleby to sit in judgement on anybody's morals. And who was to say that young Roz's morals were in need of judging? She was surprised, therefore, to hear herself say, 'The lass

110

doesn't do so badly for young company.' She bit hard on her tongue. 'Well, she goes to the dances with the rest of the village and –'

Her cheeks were burning, she knew it. Mrs Fairchild was looking at her in *that* way, and if she wasn't careful the cat would be out of the bag.

'And, Poll?'

'And *nowt*, ma'am,' came the too-sharp, too-ready reply.

'What do you know that I don't – that you *think* I don't know?'

Polly turned, arms folded defensively across her middle. She had said too much.

'Gossip,' she said truculently. 'Nowt but gossip, ma'am.'

'About whom?'

'I don't like, ma'am. You know me. I don't tittle-tattle about what's none of my business.'

'Poll, something's troubling you and I know it's nothing to do with Arnie.'

'No. Not Arnie.' Drat the woman and her probing.

'Then let's sit down and drink our tea and have a talk about it.'

'There's nowt worth the telling.'

'Oh, but there is! You and I have known each other a long time and you only call me *ma'am* when you're cross or worried. Will you pour, Poll?'

Sighing deeply, Polly did as she was asked. There was no escaping it now. Mrs Fairchild was a deep one and she'd not rest till she knew every last word of it.

'It was nowt nor summat, really, and to tell the truth it wasn't village talk, though if Arnie knows about it happen the village knows about it, an' all. And I suppose it's best coming from me; best you don't hear it second-hand.

'It's Roz, you see. Arnie said he'd seen her with an airman from Peddlesbury. Twice. And that's all I know, 'cept that Arnie said the airman had gone on leave.'

'Then Arnie might well be right,' Hester said softly, 'because for the past week Roz hasn't been out at all, nights. It fits, I'm afraid. It all adds up. I've thought for quite some time that she's been meeting someone, and now I know.'

'Not for sure, you don't. Not for sure, ma'am, save that Roz might've met the same young man twice and perhaps danced with him a time or two. But you knew about the dances.'

'Of course I knew. All Alderby goes to the Friday dances. It's the other nights we're talking about, Poll.'

'Then you'd best tackle her about it.'

'How, will you tell me? Do I blunder in like an idiot, demand to know who she's been with and what she's doing?'

'You could, though I doubt it'd get you very far. Stubborn, that one can be and we both know it. But how you're going to do it without causing an upset, I don't know. You're the one who's good at things like that; you'll have to find a way. The lass needs to be told. She's got to know about such things, how easy they can happen and where they can lead. She's your lass, and it's up to you to tell her about – well, *things*.'

'But she's a country-bred girl, Poll. She knows about *things*.'

'She knows about animals and wild creatures; happen it's high time she knew it's much the same for folk.'

'Tch!' Hester clucked. 'I wish we'd never brought the subject up.'

'Oh, aye? Wish we'd stuck our heads in the sand and hoped it would go away, then?'

'No. You're right,' Hester whispered, fidgeting with the chain at her neck. 'It won't go away. Roz is meeting someone and I know she doesn't tell me the truth about where she is. That's the worrying part of it; the untruths. I've asked where she's going and when she'll be in but she never gives a straight answer. I know my own granddaughter and when she's lying to me. For all that, though, I can't risk asking her outright – and being told more lies for my pains. That, I just couldn't take.

'So I shall leave it for the time being and hope she'll tell me. And maybe it isn't all that serious. Maybe she'll have a lot of boyfriends before she meets the right one. Perhaps then she'll tell me about him, and bring him home to meet me.'

'You're taking it very calmly I must say.' Polly sniffed.

'What other way is there? Now tell me, what did young Arnie make of the bombing, yesterday?'

Arnie? They were talking about Arnie, now? The matter of Roz was closed.

'Arnie? Oh, the young monkey enjoyed it. 'Twas all I could do to stop him racing off to see if he could find any pieces of shrapnel. You know what lads are like.' She rose stiffly to her feet. 'Ah, well. Think I'll get the boiler going for the washing, then I'll give the little sitting-room a bit of a going-over.'

She said it sadly, because things were out in the open, now. The problem was far from being solved, but at least it had been given an airing. It was a question of wait and see, and all because of the Mistress and her stiff-necked pride.

But waiting would do no good at all, because Roz was heading for trouble and heartache; Polly knew it, and she didn't like it. Not one little bit!

6

The Peddlesbury raid was over and forgotten and a five-minute wonder, folk said, though they'd been shocked at the suddenness of it, with no time for the alert to be sounded. Nasty, how that Heinkel had managed to sneak in, but count your blessings, they said; no one hurt, this time. And the damage to the runway could easily be repaired, though not too quickly, Kath hoped, since Roz had said it was more the pity that all three bombs hadn't dropped there, and made a proper job of it.

Today Roz was happy. Tomorrow Paul would return from leave and her world would be perfect – until the runway was seen to, that was, and the Lancasters able to take off again.

She must, Kath decided, include Paul in her Sunday prayers. Kath prayed often – a habit, really. Prayers all the time at the orphanage and obligatory church attendance during her in-service years – and in her own time, too. But her prayers held substance now, because she had someone of her own to spend them on: Barney and Roz and everyone at Home Farm. And Paul, too.

Funny how almost everyone went to church these days. It had taken a war to fill the churches, for now almost everyone had someone to commend to divine keeping; everyone had urgent need to beg the Almighty to choose between them and us, and let our side win.

She still regretted not being married in church. To Kath, a church wedding was more permanent somehow, but their small wedding-party would have seemed out of place in such a great loftiness. Only she and Barney there had been, and Barney's reluctant mother and Sylvia who worked at the house next door, and Barney's witness. The Registrar too, of course. Short and businesslike, their joining; a lonely wedding, really. Lonely, but legal.

But this was not a day to think too much on what might have been; this was a rare day that hinted of spring to come. This day was warm from the touch of a wind from the south and a sky so blue it could have been stolen from April. A weather-breeder Mat said it was, and not to be trusted.

Kath held her face to the sun, walking carefully with the near-full jug held between gloved hands.

'Pop over with Marco's drinkings, there's a good lass,' Grace had asked. 'What with Jonty away to the farrier's and Mat wasting his time at the War Ag. and Roz seeing to the calves –' Best keep Roz and Marco apart as much as possible, Grace had long ago decided; best not upset the Mistress more than need be. 'He's working at the game-cover; take along a mug for yourself and have five minutes in the sun. Lord knows, it'll likely be snowing tomorrow.'

The prisoner was working alone, cutting down the smaller, spindly trees in the little wood, dragging them clear with the tractor, stacking them against the time they could be chopped into logs and laid to dry for next winter's burning.

'Marco! How's it coming along?'

'I think we finish, on time. This scrub makes trouble, but we manage okay.'

'Jonty said you'd drag the tree roots out with the tractor.'

'*Si*. We fix a chain.' Smiling, he took the mug she had filled for him. 'You stay, Kat?'

'For five minutes.' She settled herself beside him. 'Jonty's taken Duke to the smithy to be shod. I asked him if he'd bring back one of the old shoes for me – for a souvenir, and for luck. In this country a horseshoe brings luck, you see.'

115

'In my country, also. But this morning you smile, Kat. You have had a letter?'

'No. Not for a week. I think I'm smiling because it's such a lovely day.'

'And tomorrow, maybe, a letter come and you smile some more.'

'Well – at the moment I'm afraid I'm not looking forward to letters. I'm afraid that I – well, I deceived my husband, and –'

'Deceive him? You have a lover?'

'No! Nothing like that!' Why had she started this conversation?

'You tell him lies, then?'

'Not even lies. I'm just not, I suppose, telling him the truth.'

'There is a difference?'

'There's a difference, Marco.' She had said too much; talked about things that should be private between man and wife, talked about them what was more to one who was an enemy. 'Five minutes, Grace said. I'd better go. Bring the jug back later, will you?'

'No, Kat. Wait!' He took her hand and she didn't know whether to snatch it away, or leave it. 'You must tell me why you do not speak the whole truth. If you have sadness it is best you talk about it.'

'All right, then.' She took a deep, defiant breath. 'When I write to my husband it isn't what I write but what I *don't* write. I don't tell him things because he'd be annoyed with me. I haven't told him about you, yet. I can't, because he doesn't like –'

She pulled in her breath sharply, wincing at her stupidity, closing her eyes tightly as if to block out the words.

'He does not like Italians and I am Italian, and working here?'

'Something like that.'

'And?' he prompted softly, his eyes on hers.

116

'And I can't tell him that Jonty isn't in the forces; that a man so young is still a civilian. He thinks all young men should be called up.'

'Your husband is a strange man, Kat.'

'No! That isn't true. It's just that he feels strongly about things. And I've upset him, too, because I joined the Land Army without asking him. He doesn't like to see women in uniform. Well, you wouldn't like it either, would you?'

'If I had a wife and she went to work in the fields for her country, I would be proud of her. Your man spends much time being angry. It is not good.'

'No,' she whispered, eyes downcast.

'It is not good that he makes you sad; not good he does not trust you, though that is to be understood. He is jealous, you see, because his wife is beautiful and he fears other men will admire her.'

'I'm *not* beautiful! I'm – oh, we shouldn't be talking like this!'

'No, we should not. This morning, you see, I have a letter from home. My mother is much sad. She writes that my cousin Toni is missing. Toni is a soldier, fighting in the desert. My aunt fears he is dead.'

'Marco, I'm so sorry. Wars are wrong, and cruel!' And that was a strange thing to come out with, wasn't it, to one who was her sworn enemy. But what else was there to say – that they should have stayed out of the war, not thrown in their lot with the Germans nor invaded Abyssinia, either. But young men like Toni and Barney and Paul and Marco didn't start the wars – only fought them. 'I'm truly sorry,' she whispered, 'and especially for your aunt. My worries are nothing compared to hers.'

'*Si.* Is called making a big hill from a little hill, yes?'

'A mountain out of a molehill,' she said, smiling gently. 'And you *will* forget what I told you? It'll work out. I know it will.'

He watched her walk away; watched her until she was out of sight.

'If you were my wife, Katarina,' he said softly, 'I would treat you good. If you belonged to me –'

He shrugged and refilled his mug. She did not belong to him; she never would. She was a married English woman and he was Italian. They were enemies. It was as simple as that.

Roz whistled loudly and cheerfully.

'Grace says you've had your tea, Kath, so can you give me a hand in the milking parlour? I've fed the calves and filled the trough in the foldyard. There's only the mucking-out to do, then Mat might let us give the men a hand this afternoon. It's such a lovely day to be outdoors.'

'Marco could do with some help. He's there alone. Will Jonty be long away?'

'No. The smithy's only half a mile the other side of the village. He'll be back by dinnertime. Oh, Kath, this day is dragging so.'

'When are you meeting Paul?'

'Tomorrow night. God! I've missed him. I'm grateful he's been away from flying, but it hurts like hell when he isn't near me. Why isn't it nineteen forty-four?'

'Is that when the war's going to end?'

'Wish I knew. It's Leap Year I'm talking about. That's when I'll propose to Paul, and he won't be able to refuse me.'

'Idiot! In nineteen forty-four you'll be twenty-one, and no one can stop you marrying him. Which date in April is it?'

'The twenty-fourth. St Mark's Eve – or so Polly says.'

'And does that make it special?'

'Not really. It's just that on St Mark's Eve – oh, it's a long story! I'll tell you some other time. Let's get the

118

milking parlour brushed out and then we'll have done a fair morning's work for King and Country. Let's work like mad, Kath, then tomorrow will come sooner. And just think – they're saying it'll be a week at least before they can use the runway again.'

'Wonder why they've never thought to take off over the grass,' Kath reasoned, ever practical. 'If they really had to, that is.'

'Couldn't be done, especially now with the ground so soft and wet. Those Lancasters weigh a lot. Bombed-up and with a full fuel load on they'd get bogged down if they tried it. Oh no, Kath. Paul's off flying for another week, thank heaven, and if I'm being unpatriotic, then hard luck!'

Whistling, she picked up brush and shovel and Kath watched her go, eyes sad.

She's so happy. Don't let her get hurt. Please, God, look after Paul and Barney. And all husbands and sweethearts and sons.

Poor God. His ears must be ringing with prayers.

'Roz. I think I've just done something stupid. It – it's about Marco.'

'Oh, yes. And what has Signor So-So been up to, then?'

'That wasn't kind, Roz, and he hasn't done anything. It was me; something I said that I shouldn't have.'

'Like Italians go home?'

'All right – if you don't want to listen –'

'I do. Tell me.'

'Well – it was just that we got to talking about letters – and by the way, he's had bad news from home about his cousin. Anyway, I mentioned that Barney got upset about women in uniform and young men who didn't join up . . .'

'Like Jonty?'

'Yes. I haven't told Barney about Jonty, you see, and if

I told him about Marco, Lord knows what would happen. And as for telling him about what happened on threshing day – well –'

'You're afraid of him, aren't you; you're scared to tell him in case he gets upset, and nothing must upset Barney, must it? Queen Victoria's been gone a long time, y'know. You should stand up to him.'

'Roz, no! You've got it all wrong. Barney is good and kind – it's just that he has strong views about certain things.' She laid aside her brush and took a cigarette packet from the pocket of her dungarees. 'Oh, let's have a smoke! Go on, I can spare it. The WVS ladies came to the hostel last night and they let me have ten. No, it's just that I want him to be proud of me for joining up, that's all. I wanted to be a landgirl so much.' Sighing, she struck a match.

'And so he should be proud of you. But your trouble, Kath Allen, is that you think you owe Barney something for marrying you – but you don't need me to tell you that, do you? And d'you know what I think you should do? I think you should take a long, smug look in a mirror, then tell that Barney of yours to grow up.'

'Roz!' Oh my goodness, hadn't Marco said much the same thing?

'I mean it, Kath. You could have married any man you wanted but you settled for someone like Barney. When are you going to accept that what happened when you were a baby wasn't any of your fault? And that's something else. You said you'd go to the Friday-night dances at Peddlesbury, and you haven't been. Wouldn't Barney like that, either?'

'I honestly don't know. Maybe it's me. Maybe I feel it isn't right for a married woman to go to dances without her husband; not right for me, that is. Yet there are married girls at the hostel who go and nobody bothers about it.'

'So why don't you come on Friday and meet Paul? You'd

enjoy yourself, and a good night out with the girls might stop you feeling so guilty about nothing, or maybe,' she grinned, 'with a bit of luck it just might give you something to feel guilty *about*.'

'You're wicked, Roz Fairchild, and I'll go to that dance, just to show you!'

'Great. You'll have a smashing time. The band's really good and there's loads of partners.'

'You've persuaded me. I do like dancing and I miss not going. And as long as I'm wearing my wedding ring, I suppose it'll –'

'Oh, wear the thing through your nose if it'll make you feel any happier, but *come*! Promise you will?'

'Promise.'

'And you don't have to tell Barney, you know.'

'The way he's acting now,' Kath tilted her chin defiantly, 'I don't think I will.'

'Great! A bit of sense at last! But let's get on with it. Leaning on shovels isn't going to get this war won.'

Kath did not reply. She was thinking about the dance, wishing she'd thought to bring just one nice dress with her, and her dancing shoes. She could, of course, send stamps to Aunt Min and ask her to post them, but Aunt Min might want to know why she needed her gold slippers, and that would never do.

'I think,' she murmured, 'that when I'm due for some time off, I'll look out a few civvy clothes to bring back with me.'

Sneakily, of course. So Aunt Min wouldn't know.

They were walking through the orchard when Kath saw the little white flower. It stood small and frail beneath the holly hedge.

'Roz! A snowdrop. Isn't it beautiful?'

'It is, and a sure sign that winter's on the way out. Think I'll take it in for Gran – cheer her up.' She bent to pick it

121

carefully. 'She's been a bit quiet these last few days. I'll put it in an egg cup in the kitchen window. Come in and say hullo. She'd like that.'

'It was good of Mr Ramsden to let us help the men this afternoon, wasn't it?' Kath kicked off her boots at Ridings' back door.

'It was. He's a lovely man.'

'An older edition of Jonty, I suppose. They say,' Kath murmured obliquely, 'that when a man chooses a wife he should take a long, hard look at her mother, because that's how his bride might look in about twenty-five years.'

'Ah, but I don't intend marrying Jonty, so it doesn't apply, does it?' Roz filled a blue and white egg cup with water. 'And where is everybody? We could make off with the sugar ration and they'd be none the wiser. Still, can't wait.' She placed the little flower on the window sill. 'Polly'll think the little people have left it.'

Polly Appleby thought no such thing. They were only half way across Ridings' cobbled yard when a cry of rage made them turn to see a blue and white egg cup being deposited on the doorstep.

'Who was it, then?' Polly pointed to the flower. 'Who brought that thing into the house?'

'But, Poll, it's only a little snowdrop.' Roz laughed.

'Aye. *One* snowdrop. I thought you'd have had more sense, Roz Fairchild. Asking for trouble, that's what. And the times I've told you!'

'It was a surprise,' Kath insisted, wondering at Polly's dismay. 'To cheer up Mrs Fairchild.'

'Cheer her up? She can do with cheering up when you invite death into the house!'

'Oh Lord, I'd forgotten,' Roz whispered. 'I really had, Poll. I'm sorry, I truly am.'

'And so you ought to be.'

'I'll go and find another. Two would make it all right, wouldn't it?'

'Find as many as you will. The damage is done now, you foolish girl. Oh, be off with you. I'll get rid of it. And next time just think on, will you? Your gran has enough to worry over without you adding to it.'

Indignantly Polly slammed the door; white-faced, Roz whispered, 'How could I have been so stupid?'

'But what did we do?' Kath demanded. 'A little flower; a pretty little flower and Polly gets herself all het up.'

'A snowdrop – one snowdrop on its own – is bad luck brought into the house. Poll even goes so far as to say it's a death sign, but she's so superstitious you wouldn't believe it.'

'Well, *I* don't believe it,' Kath countered hotly. 'I never heard of such a thing. One tiny flower, that's all it was.'

'I know. *One*. You can bring in two snowdrops, you can bring in a bunch, but one – *never*. I should have remembered.'

'I'm surprised at you, I really am,' Kath chided. 'Of course a flower can't bring death. I don't believe it.'

'Nor should I, but Gran does. The last time it happened my parents were killed before the year was out.'

'And your grandfather?'

'I don't know about then. I only know I should have thought. But Polly believes what she calls the signs. Like the St Mark's Eve thing. She swears that's true, as well.'

'St Mark's Eve? You were going to tell me, weren't you?' Kath reminded.

'Oh, forget it,' Roz snapped. 'It's nonsense. Superstition, that's all. For heaven's sake, let's get down to the men before the sun goes in. Let's breathe in some clean, no-nonsense fresh air.'

'But you've got me curious. I want to know.'

'*Later*, I said,' Roz ground. 'We've had enough superstition for one day. Just leave it, okay? Lord, how I want Paul.'

How she wanted him, needed him. Needed his arms

around her and his lips against her cheek telling her it was all right, that one small flower could harm no one.

'Paul!' she gasped, horrified. 'It could be Paul!'

'It could *not* be Paul; it *will* not be Paul. I helped you pick it, Roz, and I helped you put it in water and I'm not one bit afraid. Be reasonable, girl. Say the Lord's prayer, or something. Say something holy and that'll be the end of it. Go on. Do as I say, and it'll be all right.'

'You're sure?'

'I'm absolutely sure. Nothing's stronger than *Our Father . . .*'

Closing her eyes, Roz did as she was told. Of course Kath was right and Polly was a silly, superstitious woman. One little flower? One pretty little flower?

'Who was that?' Hester Fairchild demanded, closing the kitchen door behind her, holding her hands to the fire. 'Who were you talking to, Poll?'

'Only Roz and Kath,' she replied without looking up. 'On their way to the game-cover. Just called, in passing.'

'The game-cover. Why on earth do we call it that? There's been no game in it since Martin died.'

'There's been partridge and a few wild pheasants and rabbits, too, though they'll be gone, now. The girls are fetching some wood, so go easy on the coal; there's bad weather ahead of us and you don't want to face it with an empty coalhouse, now do you?'

The mistress of Ridings did not, and though she had resented the tearing out of the game-cover she knew full well that next winter there would be logs enough to warm the whole house. It would be something to look forward to, with coal so hard to come by.

'They should ration coal,' she murmured, frowning. 'Ration it officially, that is, then we'd all know where we stood.'

'Happen they should, at that.' Polly was still upset about

the snowdrop but she had managed to throw it away and wash out the egg cup before Hester came downstairs. 'Happen they will. And I've seen to the water like Roz asked me. It's in the white bucket outside.'

'Water?'

'Rainwater,' Poll supplied. 'From the backyard tub. She wants to wash her hair tonight.'

'I see.' So tonight would be the last of her grand-daughter's evenings at home. Tomorrow, it seemed, the airman would be back from leave and the untruths and prevarications would start all over again.

She walked to the window that overlooked the orchard and gazed at the yellow carpet of aconites and the pale green sheen that covered the hedge bottoms; the green that promised snowdrops soon to flower.

Once – last year, even – the sight would have given her happiness, but not any longer. To see the first stirrings of spring left an emptiness inside her because now it meant only another year to be endured. She was, Hester admitted, getting tired. Her love of living had ended with Martin's death, but there had been a daughter to rear and a granddaughter, too; a grand-daughter who had changed overnight, almost, from child to woman.

'I'm lonely, Poll,' she whispered. 'Suddenly I'm so very lonely.'

'Nay, ma'am, you're weary. We all are. Sick and tired of this war and us never winning anything. There's nothing the matter with any of us that some good news and a day free from worrying wouldn't put right, and that's a fact. So let's make ourselves a pot of tea and be blowed to the rationing! Go on, ma'am. Put that old kettle on to boil, won't you?'

'Have you ever once wondered,' Hester smiled, 'what would happen if suddenly there was no tea?'

'That I have. Many a time. And I came to the conclusion

that if our tea ration dried up we'd just have to throw up our hands and give in.'

'But we won't, Poll?'

'We won't, Mrs Fairchild, ma'am. We won't.'

Tuesday, beautiful Tuesday and only five minutes more until he came. Five long, lovely minutes, then he'd be here.

Roz waited, hands in pockets, coat collar upturned. Today was cold, yesterday's little April forgotten. But the days were lengthening. Soon they would have to find some other place to meet. Soon, it would no longer be possible to wait, hidden by darkness, until she heard his footstep, his whistle.

Today she had seen catkins; not yet fat and fluffy and golden with pollen but her heart had beaten more quickly at the sight of them nevertheless. Today, everything was beautiful and precious, touched with their love; the gentle-eyed calves, fat little Daisy, the rooks, lazy wings flapping on the wind, and the daffodil tips, pushing out of the cold, wet earth.

She heard his footstep, then saw him as he turned into the yard. The sight of him set her pulses racing and she ran, not caring who might see them, into his arms, closing her eyes against the sweet, silly tears that sprang to them, lifting her face for his kiss.

'Darling, I've missed you so.' His voice was deep, husky with love.

'Hey!' She pulled away from him. 'That's what I always say!' She reached for his lips with her own, wishing she didn't feel so dizzy, so giddily happy. 'I love you, love you, and I've missed you, too.'

'I'm mad, aren't I?' His laugh was deep, and indulgent. 'Why did I go? Why did you let me?'

'Because I'm mad, too. Did you tell your parents about us?'

'No, Roz. Mum would have gone into a dither about it and Dad would have given me a lecture on why a fighting man shouldn't get serious about girls till the war's over. I told Pippa, though. She was glad for us, though she gave me a stern, sisterly warning.'

'It's all right. I'm not pregnant. I told you so, when you rang.' She was glad Paul's sister knew about them; that someone knew they'd been lovers. 'And did I tell you I love you?'

'You did, but say it again. Don't ever stop saying it, Roz.'

'I won't. Not ever. Fifty years from now I'll still be telling you.'

He held her tightly. Fifty years from now. She said it often, tilting at Fate, defying it to part them. Fifty years, my lovely love? Fifty weeks, fifty *days* he'd be grateful for. He closed his eyes, resting his cheek on her hair, grateful to a war that had brought them together, hating a war that could snatch them apart without a goodbye.

'I want you, Roz.'

'I want you, too. I can't think about anything else but wanting you.'

'Where shall we go?'

'To the haystack, again.' Every day for the last week she and Kath had cut deep into that stack, carrying hay to the cows wintering in the foldyard. Soon, it would all be gone, but soon it would be summer and the earth warm beneath them, freezing rain and biting winds forgotten. Soon, they would have no need of it.

They walked, not speaking now, fingers entwined, thighs touching, pausing only to kiss. Now fear was forgotten, caution flung to the sky. Need was all they knew and all else mattered little. The world was them, and only them; only this moment was real.

They sank into the hay and he unbuttoned his greatcoat, wrapped her to him inside it.

'Do you know something?' she whispered, her lips on his. 'Last time, when I got home, there was hay on the back of my coat. I saw it when I took it off and I thought, "Oh, my God!"'

'I'll brush you down this time.'

'Mmm.' He unfastened her coat and blouse, reached gently to slip the hook of her bra. She wanted him to kiss her until she was desperate with need for him; wanted this night never to end. She didn't care. She wouldn't care if the whole of Alderby knew. She wanted them to know.

'I love you,' she whispered, as he took her.

It was late when they left the shelter of the haystack. The wind had scattered the clouds and a half moon glinted down on them. Suddenly he said, 'There was a buzz, when we got back, that our replacement came.' They must talk, now, of real things, of the world they lived in. 'It's brand new, I believe. A woman ferry-pilot flew it up from the makers, they told us, and they diverted her to Linforth – told her to land it there. We'll have to go over and pick it up, I suppose, when the runway's in use again. Imagine – a woman, all alone in a plane that size?'

There would be no death on the new Lancaster bomber. A clean slate, another rear-gunner.

'You won't be collecting it yet,' she whispered confidently.

'No. Not for about a week. Two great holes in the runway to be seen to. We can meet every night.'

Every night, for a week. Seven tomorrows, sweet and safe. She didn't care about the replacement. It was ten miles away, at another aerodrome. The whole world was ten miles away.

'I don't want you to leave me,' he said as they stood close together at the orchard gate.

'I don't want to. I want you to stay with me all night. Could we make it, do you think – a night together?'

'I can manage it, sweetheart, but what about you?'

'I don't know. I'll talk to Kath about it. Kath can get sleeping-out passes so I could say I was with her. She'll help me, I know she will.'

'York? We could hide ourselves in York.'

'Anywhere. Anywhere they'll let us be together.'

'You're sure?' He cupped her face in his hands, touching her mouth gently, kissing away her doubts, if doubts she had.

'I'm sure.' She had never been so sure of anything in the whole of her life – except perhaps of how much she loved him. 'Let's try to make it soon, Paul; as soon as we can?'

There were sixteen more operations to fly; fifteen, and the last one. It had to be soon.

Kath stood in the darkness at the attic window, Barney's letter clenched in her hand. The reply to her Christmas Day letter, the one she had filled with love and concern, had come.

Well Kath, no need for me to say I'm still hurt by your behaviour but I hope you will give me no more cause for complaint. It is very hot here, sand everywhere. I would give a lot for a pint of good English bitter, pulled of course, in an English pub.

I'm glad you are looking to the future and saving all the Army allowance. More than a hundred pounds a year. Not bad, eh? I can see I shall have that car I've always wanted when I get back.

No more cause for complaint? Well, thanks, Barney!

Hot, is it? Well, it's so damn cold here you wouldn't believe it. Some of the girls at the hostel were picking sprouts today. You should have seen their hands, Barney. Blue and swollen, numb with frost. I'll send you some frozen sprouts, shall I, to cool you down?

That car you've always wanted? But when rugs and curtains and wallpaper are back in the shops again, I'd thought my savings could be spent on things for our home and some nice easy chairs.

She stuffed the letter into the pocket of her coat, breathing hard in her dismay. Chin on hand, she gazed into the night.

The stillness was touched with moonglow, but it did nothing to soothe her. She pulled her coat to her, shivering not with cold but with an unexplained apprehension.

Was it that strange, just-around-the-corner feeling, the certainty that something was about to happen or was she ashamed, still, of confiding in a stranger in a way no married woman should talk to any man – except her husband. But Marco was her friend, had saved her life, though saving her life should not have made him the keeper of her conscience. What, then, was this feeling of malcontent? Was she, for the first time, finding fault with her marriage or could it be that she missed not her husband, but being a wife?

Quickly she closed the window, drawing the blackout curtains, walking slowly across the room, hand outstretched, seeking the light switch.

Being a wife? She did not miss Barney *that* way. She never could, never would, for making love with Barney had been nothing more than an embarrassed giving, a closing of her ears to the rhythmic drumming of the bedsprings and closing her eyes to shut out the woman who listened on the other side of the partition wall.

She had known little about making love, save what she had heard whispered by kitchenmaids, so she had expected little from her wedding night. A duty, that's what being a wife was; something necessary to compensate for her marital status and for the making of the children she wanted and which Barney said they would have one day.

She snapped on the light, blinking in the sudden brightness, then throwing off her coat she undressed quickly and slithered into the pyjamas she had wrapped around her hot-water bottle.

It had been a lot more fun when they were courting, when Barney's kisses excited her. But even then she had been able to tell him 'No!' she thought miserably. And the kissing and cuddling had come to an end on their wedding night. From that night on he had merely taken her, grunting into a darkness for which she had been grateful.

Then why, suddenly, did she feel this way? Did she feel cheated or was this emotion one of envy? Was she jealous of Roz out there in Paul's arms? Did she, Kathleen Allen, want to snatch at love as Roz did; snatch carelessly, knowing only the need to belong? And why didn't she ache for Barney as Roz ached for Paul? Was gratitude a poor substitute for love, or did it outlast passion? She folded her clothes with deliberate care, angry with herself for harbouring such thoughts, shocked she could even think them.

Take a long, smug look in a mirror. You could have married any man you wanted . . .

Mouth set tightly she walked past the wall mirror and taking her husband's photograph from the chest of drawers she held it to her.

I'm sorry. Lord only knows what nonsense is in my head or where it came from. It's this war, Barney; this terrible war . . .

She shrugged into her dressing gown, hugging it around her. There would be a bedtime pot of tea on the kitchen table, and bread and jam. A cup of tea was what she needed, and a comforting jam sandwich.

I didn't mean to find fault with you, Barney. And I'm sorry I said those things to Marco – but you don't know Marco Roselli, do you?

Oh, damn, damn, *damn*! She wasn't going to that dance on Friday, even if she'd promised she would. Asking for trouble, it would be, with herself in this silly mood.

A pretty dress and gold dancing slippers, indeed! Oh, my word *no*!

For the first time since that mid-December morning, they delivered milk in daylight.

'Paul all right?' Kath asked. 'Had a good leave, did he?'

'Great. His sister managed to get home, too. Kath, I want you to help me – *need* you to help me.'

'What's the matter?' Kath glanced up sharply from the delivery book.

'Nothing's the matter. We're going to York for the night, and I'll need an alibi.'

'Roz! Good grief!' Her cheeks flushed pink. '*All* night?'

'All night. I don't know how to fix it at home, though. What do I tell Gran?'

'You tell *me*!' Kath gasped. 'Now see here, there's no way I'm going to help you, but I won't snitch on you, either. You work it out for yourself, then tell me about it. If I've got to tell lies, I might as well tell the same lies as you.'

'Oh, don't go all prissy on me. I thought you'd understand,' Roz pouted.

'I do understand, only I'll not be a party to deceit; not deceiving your gran, that is. What did you have in mind?' she asked grudgingly.

'I thought I could say I was with you; that you'd got a sleeping-out pass and we were going to the last-house flicks.'

'So we'd be too late to catch the last bus back and have to stay the night?'

'Something like that. Or we could be going to a dance, maybe? The girls at the hostel sometimes go to a big dance in York, don't they?'

'I believe they do – a couple of times a year – but they organize transport to bring them back when it's over.'

132

'Damn!' It wouldn't be easy, Roz brooded; she'd never thought it would, but somehow she would make it happen, even if she waited until April to do it.

'We might have to hold it back till my birthday. I don't want to, but it might be our only chance.'

'But wouldn't you want to have your birthday at Ridings?'

'Don't see why. I suppose we'll push the boat out for my twenty-first and have a good do, then – it'll depend on the way things are. But I don't think Gran would worry over much if I said one or two of us were making a night of it, on the twenty-fourth.

'By the way, have you heard if *Gone with the Wind* has come up north, yet? I'm longing to see it. It's been on in London for over a year. They get all the fun in London.'

'Yes, Roz, and a lot of the bombs.'

'What's the matter? You *are* going to help me, aren't you?' Roz demanded.

'I said I would, and I will. I won't connive, though.'

'Because you happen to be wearing your moody hat, this morning? Is that it?'

'Moody?' Kath snapped. 'Who's moody?' Roz could be a bit much sometimes!

'You are. You're not still worrying about Marco, are you – about what you said to him? Marco's all right. I like him. I just hope Gran won't want Mat to get rid of him once the ploughing's finished.'

'But she couldn't do that!' Not after the way Marco had worked, and on Ridings land, too.

'She could, she would and she probably will. I'd bet on it.'

'But that wouldn't be fair, Roz.' Surely she wouldn't do anything as underhanded as that? Marco had fitted in well – he even spoke good English. 'Surely she wouldn't be so petty?'

133

'All right, all right! Don't look so pained, Kath. I'm on your side.'

'*Pained? On my side?* What on earth do you mean?'

'I mean that I think you like him. You always stick up for him.'

'Of course I like him. I like Jonty and Mr Ramsden, too. Don't try to read meanings into things that aren't there. That's how gossip starts.'

'My, but we're prickly, this morning. Got a headache?'

'No, I haven't. You can be so infuriating, Roz Fairchild. You're so darned smug and happy that you make me want to – to *weep*!'

And the worst of it was, she thought dejectedly, Roz was right. Something *was* irritating her. Last night she had carried her thoughts to bed with her and lain awake, brooding on them and the *selfish* letter Barney had written.

'It's Barney, then,' Roz pronounced. 'He's written you another snotty letter. If I were you –'

'Well, you're *not* me, so you can –' Oh, it wasn't any use. 'You're right, Roz. Not a nasty letter, but not a nice one. And selfish, too.'

'Well, I've told you what to do, haven't I? Stick up for yourself.'

Roz pushed wide the creaking lodge gates then picked up Polly's milk. 'I told you ages ago,' she called smugly, over her shoulder.

Oh, Roz; moody and counting bombers you take some living with, Kath directed her thoughts at the jaunty back that disappeared behind Polly's woodshed. But happy and cheerfully planning a night in York with Paul, you're *impossible*!

And dammit, Kath decided, all at once having a try at sticking up for herself, she *would* go to the Friday-night dance, and more would be the pity if she didn't bring herself to go the whole hog, and flirt like mad.

'Y'know,' she murmured, watching her friend close the

134

gates behind the milk-float, 'I think I will write to Aunt Min and ask her to send me a nice dress.' *And* her gold dancing shoes!

Kath Allen could drive a tractor, harness a pony and milk a cow – by machine, anyway – and she had almost learned to cope with rats, too. So if she wanted to go to a dance with the rest of the girls, then go she would! And for two pins she'd write and tell Barney about it. After all, she might just as well be hanged for a sheep as a lamb.

'Come on, Daisy.' She clicked her tongue crisply. 'Let's get you home, old girl.'

7

She had enjoyed the Friday-night dance more than she should have, Kath admitted reluctantly, thinking of Skip with whom she'd danced almost every dance.

'You're looking very pleased with yourself, Mrs Allen,' Roz teased, rolling a milk churn to be filled.

'I was thinking about last night . . .'

'I said you'd enjoy it, didn't I? Thought you'd get on with Skip. He's nice. I'm glad he's Paul's pilot. They don't come any safer.'

Safe. That was exactly how she had felt, Kath thought, but in a different way. Two marrieds together, and Skip talking about his wife back home and the baby they expected in June. Easy together, they had been.

'I'm glad I met him – and Paul, too.' She knew now why Roz was so deeply in love. Paul Rennie was head-turning handsome, no two ways about it, and equally besotted. They had danced in a world of their own, the two of them; so right together, so young, so very beautiful. The kind of beauty, Kath thought sadly, that made the gods jealous.

'Had you ever thought, Roz, how much time it would save,' she murmured, directing her attention to the task in hand, 'if we used waxed cartons for the milk – it would cut out hours of bottle washing.' She frowned, arranging milk bottles in the sterilizer.

'I know. Mat did think about it though I imagine he's glad now that he didn't get rid of the bottles. Think how difficult it is to get paper; cartons will be hard to come by. They say the paper situation is really serious, and getting worse.'

Paper was certainly in very short supply. Thin, four-page

136

newspapers; little if any wrapping paper in shops – even food shops. It had become common practice to take along your own dish when buying fish and chips and newspaper to carry it home in.

'Roz – I've just thought! It's ages since I had any fish and chips.'

Fried fish and chips had never been placed on official ration – people said that no government could ever be that stupid, not even the one we were stuck with for the duration that didn't seem able to win one battle or give out one piece of news worth listening to. Even they weren't so stupid as to ration fish and chips. It was to the chip shop that a housewife turned when her meat ration was used up and she hadn't been lucky in the sausage queue nor the offal queue, hadn't been able to get even the smallest piece of off-the-ration suet to make into a pastry top for a vegetable pie. Queues at chip shops were half-an-hour long and worth every minute of the wait.

'There's a chip shop in Helpsley; we'll bike over there when the nights get lighter, if you'd like.'

Kath *would* like, she said. And wouldn't it be bliss to eat them with her fingers, the only way to eat fish and chips; well-salted, with vinegar oozing through the newspaper wrapping.

'It's a date, then. But how on earth did we get on to the subject of fish and chips? I was talking about the dance, and how well you and Skip got on together.'

'And I, Roz, was talking about milk in cartons.'

'Okay. Point taken. But you'll come again next week, won't you – if they're not flying, that is.'

'I might.' *Might?* She'd be there all right and in a pretty dress, too, if Aunt Min didn't turn funny. 'It's a long time since I had so much fun – oh, Roz, *look*.'

They ran to the door, surprised by the suddenness of the snow. It fell in shilling-sized flakes and was so fast-falling they could hardly see across the yard to the kitchen door.

'Might have known it – Polly said the weather was too good to last.'

'More winter to come, you mean?'

'Right. There's always a grain of truth in Polly's prophecies. Sometimes she frightens me.'

'For goodness' sake, it's only a spot of snow.'

It was not a spot of snow. Indeed, it looked like being the heaviest fall of winter, with everything covered white, even as they watched.

'It'll put paid to the ploughing if it carries on like this,' Roz said gloomily. 'My, but it's coming down thick . . .'

Polly Appleby saw the first of the snowflakes and ran to the washing line to gather in the shirts.

Drat the snow. Just when she was beginning to think the bite had gone out of winter, with snowdrops flowering and the buds on the wild daffodils beginning to swell. Now she would have to dry the shirts indoors which was never as satisfactory.

Shirt washing was another of Polly's sidelines and it was her habit, each and every Saturday, to collect six white shirts from the bay-windowed house standing back from Alderby Green. They were boiled, starched and ironed and delivered, carefully folded, at about three in the afternoon each Wednesday following.

The shirts, a clean one for each day of the working week, were worn by Mr Murgatroyd, a solicitor's clerk who travelled by train to his work in York. Each and every Wednesday afternoon his wife would nod her thanks and hand Polly the two half-crowns placed in readiness on the window sill and murmur that she would see her again on Saturday, all being well.

She was particular about her husband's shirts. At less than a shilling a garment she considered she was getting the best of the bargain and to show her appreciation it was her custom to allow Polly first pick of the jumble-sale pile each spring and autumn.

They were good quality shirts, Polly considered, arranging them on the clothes horse to finish drying. It was a fortunate man, she grudgingly acknowledged, whose wife had had the foresight to buy a dozen white shirts one week before the announcement of clothes rationing. It made a body wonder if solicitors' clerks knew things that lesser folk did not, though good luck to them, if they did. Polly believed in live and let live. Five shillings a week and a good sort through Mrs M's jumble suited her nicely, and when drying outdoors was possible again six shirts would be little trouble. And happen the dratted snow would be gone by morning.

The snow was not gone by morning. It had continued to fall throughout most of the night and high as the hedgetops it had drifted, with Kath and twenty more landgirls cut off at Peacock Hey, waiting for the snow-plough to reach them.

Jonty had done the milk-round by tractor that morning, for the depth of it had proved too much for Daisy. The snow had frozen into nasty ruts, making farm work ten times more difficult, with the milk cows slithering and sliding in the icy foldyard and beef cattle huddled in the shelter of the hedge, waiting for hay that would be a long time coming.

'What price working on a farm, now.' Roz grinned, for frozen snow meant frozen runways and she was not complaining.

'I suppose Paul couldn't get out, last night?' Kath asked. 'The weather, I mean. We were ages this morning, waiting till the snow-plough got through to us.'

'He didn't. It was bad at Peddlesbury, too. He managed to phone me, though. I was lucky – Gran was upstairs when he rang. It's all wrong, you know, this grabbing at phones and looking over my shoulder. And it's just as bad for Paul, having to keep it from his parents. I sometimes wonder what would happen if I got pregnant and we had to get married.'

'Don't, Roz! What ever you do, *don't* get pregnant. You said you'd talk to Paul about it; you promised you would.'

'And I did, and it's all right. But supposing something *did* happen? They'd die of shock. It's crazy. I'm old enough to get called up and Paul's old enough to fight, yet still we've got to act like it's wrong for us to be in love.'

'I know. It isn't a lot of fun being young these days. But be careful, Roz. You said the Alderby folk could be funny – think of the gossip and what it would do to your gran.'

'I *will*, I *do*, so stop your worrying. We're not entirely stupid. We both know the way it is for us, that my getting pregnant isn't on. I want Paul's babies but not yet; not in this mad world. I wouldn't be Skip's wife for anything – wondering when she'll see him again, *if* she'll see him again; wondering if she'll have to face life without him. Don't worry, Kath. And for goodness' sake let's talk about something else – and not the weather, either. There's been enough weather-talk since this snow came to last us for the duration. And don't ask about York, because the more I think about it the more I think we'll never be able to make it, not even for a night.'

'Then let's talk about tinned peaches, all thick with syrup and smothered in cream, and chocolate biscuits and big, thick steaks with onions fried in butter and boxes and boxes of chocolates. Let's remember when we could buy silk stockings and all the clothes we wanted without coupons, and lipsticks and scent? Where did all the lovely scent go?'

'Yes, and what about ice-cream? Think about strawberry ice-cream, Kath. Remember when the man came round, ringing his bell, and big cornets for a penny?'

Remember-when was a game, a nostalgic wallowing, a calling back of things almost forgotten.

'And banana sandwiches, all crunchy with sugar and bread thick with butter – *white* bread . . .'

'Oh, Kath, how long is this war going to last? How long, will you tell me?'

The snow that lay grey and frozen for almost a week gave way to a warm wind that thawed it overnight. Almost at once Peddlesbury's bombers were airborne again and the ploughing of Ridings' acres was resumed.

They cut the last furrow on the fourth day of March, three days late yet still a jump ahead of the man from the War Ag. who had not yet come to inspect it.

Mat Ramsden was pleased and relieved. Between them the young men had ploughed close on six acres a day and for more than eight weeks, too. They'd done a grand job. He said as much to Hester Fairchild and she had acknowledged the fact and said she was grateful.

'So what now, Mat?'

'So now we get the harrow over it to break up the clods, aye, and some good manure on it, too. Still plenty to be done yet,' he'd stressed.

'So you intend keeping the prisoner? There's no chance of finding a local man – well, they're so lazy, the Italians . . .'

'Not this one, ma'am. He's worked like a good 'un. Wouldn't find better, nor cheaper,' he added in final mitigation.

'Potatoes, you said, and sugarbeet?' She knew when enough was enough; she could wait. 'The War Ag. pay a subsidy on potatoes, didn't you say?'

'They do. It'll nicely cover the cost of the seed. Those old acres of yours'll be paying you back, come Michaelmas.' Mat smiled as he took his leave. 'It'll be right grand to see things growing again at Ridings.'

* * *

'I hope you won't make it difficult for the prisoner, Gran, now that the ploughing's finished,' Roz said later, careful not to use his name.

'Difficult? Has anything been said then, at Home Farm?'

'Not that I've heard, but I do know Mat wants to keep him.'

'I still say they're lazy,' Hester sniffed. 'Used to siestas, no doubt.'

'This one isn't – lazy, I mean.'

'I shall not speak to him,' Hester said with finality. 'I think, now that we'll be getting some money from the War Ag. for the ploughing, we ought to be paying you some wages, Roz. I understand that Kathleen gets about two pounds a week?'

'Can we afford it? Mat's got to be paid, remember, and I've got the rents; I can manage. Anyway, what is there to buy? No make-up, no clothes – well, only twenty coupons' worth. I'll be fine, Gran, till we've got crops to sell. I wouldn't mind a couple of pigs, though.' She smiled. 'I'd far rather we invested in some livestock of our own. The rents are all I need at the moment.'

The rents. They came from the three cottages given to Janet, her mother, as a wedding gift, and the seventeen shillings they yielded each week had once seemed like a fortune to Roz, though now she was more inclined to wonder where the money would come from should any one of them be in need of urgent repair.

'We'll see what can be done,' Hester said comfortably. 'Mat says I should keep proper accounts – I think Potter might help, don't you?' Mr Potter at the bank usually did. He saw to most things, moneywise, for the mistress of Ridings. He'd be extremely relieved to see a little more money on the credit side, now. 'Mat feels it might be a good thing to have a separate farm account, and he's right, of course.'

A farm account. That would really make them farmers.

It sounded good to Roz. Far better than *landowner* which her grandfather had been.

'We really should get a couple of pigs, Gran, and a few hens. They'd be no trouble.'

'But where on earth would we keep pigs?'

'Why not in one of the doghouses? They'd do nicely in there.'

'So near to the house, dear?'

'They'll be all right. Pigs don't like being dirty, you know. They only smell if you let them,' Roz defended, determined to have her way. 'We could keep one and sell one. A pig of our own would mean bacon and ham and lard – manure, too.'

'I'll see. Perhaps I'll have a word with Mat about it first.'

'I've already spoken to Jonty. He says we can have a couple from their last litter if I want, and I *do* want, Gran.'

'I'll see, I said.'

'Fine,' Roz smiled. When Gran said *no* it meant just that. When she said 'I'll see', it was almost a yes. 'I can get a form for pigmeal. Forms, forms, forms. Mat says it's forms for everything these days. Farmers are turning into clerks.'

'You'll be going to the dance on Friday?' Adroitly Hester sidestepped the pigs in the doghouse question.

'Yes. And Kath's coming, too. I said she could borrow one of my frocks; better than wearing breeches. And some shoes, too. Lucky we take the same size. It gets hot in the dance with the windows closed and the blackouts drawn. Gets a bit uncomfortable for the girls in uniform – collars and ties, you know,' Roz prattled. Ships and shoes and sealing-wax; talk about anything but Peddlesbury. 'Must fly, Gran. They're burning the rubbish from the game-cover this afternoon and it's all hands to the pumps.' She placed a kiss on her grandmother's cheek. 'Bye, darling. See you.'

'Yes, dear.' Another opportunity missed, and she so desperately wanted to know about the airman; hear it from Roz, that was. But Roz had the ability to block a question before it had even been asked which perhaps was as well. Unanswered questions were less hurtful than lies, and maybe some questions were best left unasked.

Letters for the gate lodges and farms around Alderby St Mary were not delivered by the post-lady but by the man who delivered parcels in the red Post Office van, and war or no war he prided himself on his timekeeping. So when Polly heard the crack of the letterbox flap she knew it was half past nine, give or take a minute, and time to be leaving for Ridings.

The envelope lay on the mat at the front door. It was slim and pink and when she picked it up it gave off a whiff of cheap scent. Reluctantly she turned it over. It bore all the signs of trouble, for not only did it carry a Hull postmark, but it was addressed to herself and not to Arnie as pink envelopes had hitherto been.

Her mouth formed a button of disapproval. She could smell trouble a mile off and the more so when it came in pale pink envelopes. She slit it open; frowning, she read its contents.

'So that's your game, my lady,' she whispered, folding the sheet carefully, slipping it back. 'Well, we'll have to see about that.' Oh, my word yes. And thank the good Lord that today was Wednesday, for something had to be done about Arnie's mother, and done before very much longer. Nowt but trouble, that one.

Dungarees tucked into her boots, hair tied in a turban, Kath walked with Jonty and Marco to the game-cover – or what, until two months ago, had been the game-cover. And they would always know that particular corner of Ridings parkland by that name; long after the war was over and she had gone back to Birmingham it would still be the old game-cover to the people she had left behind her. Now, that corner looked just like the rest of the ploughing save for the pile of uprooted hedges and brambles and tree-toppings that stood thick and high, ready to be set alight.

They would enjoy this afternoon. The burning of all that remained of the spinney would make a pleasant diversion; a celebration, almost, of the finishing of the ploughing.

'Roz said she'd meet us there after dinner,' Kath said. 'Asked me to take along a pitchfork for her. I think she's quite looking forward to this afternoon.'

'Aren't we all?' Jonty grinned. 'My backside's still numb from that tractor seat. By the way – about Roz's birthday. I don't suppose you've heard her mention anything she wants?'

'Like a dozen pairs of silk stockings or a box of chocolates; a bottle of Chanel, maybe?'

'Like something I can *give* her – but what?'

'Well, flowers are about the only thing that aren't rationed, but they'll have heaps of flowers by then at Ridings. Apart from that, most things a girl would like are under the counter or unavailable for the duration. There's the black market, of course. Know any spivs, Jonty?'

'No, so we're back to square one.'

'Afraid so. Mind, there's something I've heard her mention. Only yesterday, in fact, she said she'd like a couple of young pigs.'

'But of course! She said something about it the other day.'

'Pigs!' Marco gasped. 'You give a lady *pigs* for her birthday?'

'Talk of angels,' Kath warned, nodding in the direction from which Roz ran, calling to them to wait for her.

'Good. You remembered my fork, Kath. Be like the old days, won't it? Haven't been to a decent bonfire since Guy Fawkes night was banned.' Roz beamed.

'Who is this Guy Fawkes?' Marco frowned. 'Why is he banned?'

'I suppose you could say he's the patron saint of bonfires, sort of,' Roz teased. 'And bonfires aren't allowed now – not after blackout time, that is.'

'Guy Fawkes tried to blow up the king and parliament, a long time ago. Until the war came,' Kath explained gently, 'we lit bonfires every fifth of November.'

'To remember him by?'

'Not exactly. More because we like bonfires, I think.'

'He was one of us,' Roz offered. 'The only Yorkshireman with any sense, some say.'

'So the English were proud of him, Kat?'

'No. They hanged him.'

'Ah, *si*.' Marco nodded, mystified.

'We'll have to make sure it's properly put out,' Jonty warned, 'or there'll be every air-raid warden from here to York yelling blue murder. Fires can easily start burning again; only needs a wind to get up and we could be in trouble.'

'I'll keep an eye on it. We can see it from the house.' It had seemed strange, at first, looking out of her bedroom window and seeing sky where trees had been. Roz had missed them, just a little, even though they'd mostly been self-seeded, spindly things and choked by undergrowth left to run wild. But by the autumn, they'd be lifting potatoes from the game-cover, and beet for sugar. It would take a bit of getting used to, but if it helped to shorten the war, even by only a day, then all the upheaval would be worth it. 'Don't worry, Jonty,' she smiled, shouldering her pitchfork, matching her step to his, 'I'll take a look at it.'

'Jonty and Roz – they are lovers?' Marco whispered.

'No, more's the pity,' Kath shrugged.

'*No?*'

'No,' Kath said, flatly and finally. 'Roz is in love with someone else, but don't say anything?'

'Okay,' he shrugged. 'So would I be if I were a girl and a man gave me pigs for my birthday.'

'Oh, Marco,' Kath laughed. 'You say such funny things.'

'Funny? What is funny?'

'I'll tell you – one day. Now hurry up, will you? Hey, you two!' she called. 'Wait for us!'

Polly buttoned her best maroon coat and pulled on her maroon hat. She always wore her Sunday coat when calling at the house with the bay windows, a dignified arrangement which not even the rationing of soap the previous month had been allowed to upset.

'Take it or leave it, Arnie. It's a choice of soap or soap powder, for there'll only be eight ounces a week between the two of us, now,' she had mourned. 'I never thought I'd see the day when they rationed cleanliness. Don't you dare go leaving the soap in the water, now.'

And Arnie had promised he would not; he even considered giving up his soap ration for the duration if it would help the war effort, though he'd had the good sense not to say so.

On this particular Wednesday afternoon, however, dignity was the last thing on Polly's mind. If anyone could help her, Mrs Murgatroyd could, and Mrs Murgatroyd, because of the delicacy of her husband's position, was known never to gossip. To listen, maybe, but never to pass it on. And Polly hoped, lifting her eyes heavenwards, that Mrs Murgatroyd would be in a listening mood.

'Ah, thank you, Miss Appleby,' the lady nodded, handing over two half-crowns. 'I'm most obliged. See you on Saturday, all being well?' To which Polly should have nodded and murmured that all being well she would, and taken her leave. But this afternoon she stood her ground. Clearing her throat, she murmured, 'I wonder if I could have a word?' She glanced to her left and her right. 'Private and confidential.'

147

'Indeed?' Mrs Murgatroyd had heard nothing lately, of a private and confidential nature. Her husband never spoke about his work, and a little private confidentiality would go down very nicely since she had nothing better to do with the remainder of the afternoon. 'Come in, do, Miss Appleby. I was about to make a small pot of tea. Perhaps you would join me?'

Gravely, Polly nodded her thanks. She had seen the kitchen from the doorway, of course – a cosy room with upholstered chairs on either side of the cooking range, plants in pots on the dresser and the window sill – but she had never taken tea there.

The kettle was already on the hob; the tea was quickly made and set aside to infuse, to *mash*, as they said in Alderby.

Mrs Murgatroyd drew out a chair. 'Sit down, do. I hope nothing is troubling you, my dear?' Nothing too trivial, that was. 'I do hope,' she added, suddenly alarmed, 'that the shirts aren't proving too much for you?'

'Nay.' Polly removed her gloves and set them, with her handbag, at her feet. 'Shirts is no bother at all.'

'Then you may speak freely in this kitchen, Miss Appleby.' She lifted the teapot. 'Milk in first?'

'As it comes, thanks.' Polly took the pale pink envelope from her handbag. 'I'd be obliged if you'd read this. It's got me fair worried, and I'd be grateful for your advice.'

'Ah.' She took the envelope delicately. Mrs Murgatroyd did not care for pink envelopes that smelled of scent. A gentle blue-grey, maybe, but white for good taste; always white. Carefully she read the page of back-sloping, irregular writing, then read it again. 'From Arnold's mother, I take it?'

'From her.'

'I see. You know, I'm at a loss,' she frowned, removing her reading glasses, 'to find much fault with it – the contents, that is. She asks about her son, encloses a

148

postal order for five shillings and expresses a wish to visit him. Perfectly normal, I would say, for a caring mother.'

'Aye, and there I won't disagree. But that woman isn't normal and she isn't a caring mother. Since I took Arnie in she's been twice to see him, and that in the first six months I had him. For close on two years we've heard neither sight nor sound from her – till last Christmas, that was.'

'And?'

'And last Christmas there was a card for Arnie. Out of the blue it came, and a ten-shilling note inside it. Now why, will you tell me, should she take a sudden interest?'

'Conscience, perhaps?'

'Oh, no.' Mrs Murgatroyd did not offer sugar so Polly stirred her cup then took a sip. 'That one wants my lad back.'

'*Her* boy, Miss Appleby. *Her* son, remember. And in law she has a mother's rights. Mind, Hull is still getting air-raids which doesn't make it the safest place for a young boy to be, and I'll allow he's done well with you; vastly different from the scrawny little beggar they brought to your door. But for all that, I can't see one reason why she can't ask for him back. I'm sorry . . .'

'I can,' Polly frowned. 'Think of a reason, I mean. I don't think she's a right and proper person to have the rearing of a young lad.'

'Oh?' Mrs Murgatroyd leaned closer, eyebrows raised expectantly.

'Yes, indeed.' Polly looked left and right again. 'It's all a question of morals, see.'

'Morals? Oh, my word.' Mrs Murgatroyd pushed the sugar bowl across the table.

Nodding gravely, Polly returned the letter to the envelope then placed it in her handbag. '*Morals*,' she confirmed, closing her handbag with a snap, leaning across the table until they were head to head. 'She works nights, you see, and how is a woman who works nights to care for a lad that can find mischief without even looking for it?'

'You have a point, there. But perhaps Mrs Bagley has some relative who can step in and help?'

'*Miss* Bagley has not and I know it for a fact; no relation that acknowledges her, it would seem. And I'm talking about *night* work, Mrs Murgatroyd,' she said tersely, pausing for effect.

'You mean *that* kind of night work?' Mrs Murgatroyd's eyes gleamed. 'Oh, surely not?'

'*That* kind, and daytime too, if she can get it, I wouldn't be at all surprised.'

'You mean –' It was Mrs Murgatroyd's turn to glance uneasily around. 'You mean –' Her lips formed the word *prostitution*, though no sound came.

'On the game, it's my belief.'

'For money, Miss Appleby? You're sure?'

'As sure as a body can be – else where do ten-shilling notes and five-shilling postal orders come from, all of a sudden?' And pale pink envelopes and scent and lipstick and peroxide for her hair. '*You* tell *me* ma'am.'

'Oh, deary me. That puts a different light on things. Yes indeed.' She mouthed the word again. '. . . puts a very different light on it. Now do you have proof, Miss Appleby?' Proof, like possession, was something it was as well to have. 'Could you swear, in a court of law –'

'I'd swear it with my right hand on a stack of Bibles and that's a fact. But prove it – no. It's intuition, you see.'

'Intuition doesn't stand up in a court of law.'

'No, but if there was something I could throw at her – something special I could use . . .'

'Bluff, you mean?' Mrs Murgatroyd's tea had gone cold in the cup, but it was of no account when balanced against prostitution. 'Blackmail, even?'

'That as well.' Anything to keep Arnie with her. 'But

150

how does a woman like me go about it, will you tell me?'

Mrs Murgatroyd sat bolt upright in her chair and placed her hands together. Then she tilted her chin and said softly, 'I think this is a matter upon which we should take legal advice. A matter concerning the welfare of an innocent boy is not to be trifled with.'

'Aaah.' Legal advice. Exactly what she had been hoping for. Polly closed her eyes with relief.

'I take it, Miss Appleby, that you haven't yet replied to Arnold's mother?'

'Nay. I was so bothered at first, that I couldn't have put pen to paper. And then I thought I might ignore it. After all, proof of posting isn't always proof of receipt, as they do say.'

'And very wise, I'm sure. It doesn't hurt to sleep on so serious a matter. And before very long I might well be able to advise you further.' When she had taken legal advice, that was. When Mr Murgatroyd's slippers had been set before him and his supper eaten and his pipe filled. 'Could you leave it with me, then, until Saturday when you call to collect?'

Polly said she could; she would. Polly took her leave of the lady who lived in the bay-windowed house, thanking her profusely. Legal advice. That was what a body needed. Mrs Murgatroyd would come up with something, even if it was little better than bluff and blackmail. That one in Hull wasn't going to get it all her own way.

Polly straightened her shoulders, lifted her chin and made for home. Smiling all the way.

'Hullo?' Kath called, kicking off her boots at the door, padding across the kitchen in stockinged feet. 'They've sent me for the drinkings, Mrs Ramsden. They always pick on the littlest.'

'Goodness. Is it time already?' Grace looked at the

151

clock. 'Sit you down for five minutes while the kettle boils and tell me what they're up to. Got it lit, have they?'

'It's well ablaze. They're having the time of their lives.'

'Hmm. It'll be all nice and tidy, once the rubbish is burned, and the wood-ash will do the land good. Mat's impatient to get on with it. I'm glad to see it all turned over. Used to make my blood run cold, just to think of all those acres. You'll warn Jonty to watch that fire? It's a big pile; don't want it to topple over.'

'I'll tell him.' Kath leaned back in the fireside rocker. 'And don't worry – I'm a quick learner.'

'Threshing day, you mean? Ah well, farms are terrible places for accidents. Can't be too careful. But tell me about the dances. Roz says you have a fine time.'

'Well yes, I do, but –' She stopped, pink-cheeked. 'But I don't, what I mean is – I don't *do* anything.'

'Of course you don't,' Grace laughed. 'I wasn't meaning that you do. Why shouldn't you have a bit of fun? It's a queer old war and no mistake. Husbands and wives parted, and some of them not long married.'

'I know. Sometimes I don't know what I am, really; whether I'm married or single. I feel a bit guilty about going to the dances; daren't even write to Aunt Min and ask her to send me a frock.'

'But why ever not? Why shouldn't you wear something nice? A young woman can't go into purdah; it isn't natural. Your aunt ought not –'

'She isn't my aunt. I don't have one. I don't have anybody, Mrs Ramsden. Didn't you know that? Didn't Roz tell you?'

'Tell me what, lass?' Grace stopped, teapot in hand.

'That I'm – oh, you'll have to know, I suppose.' Kath looked down at her fingertips. 'I was brought up in an orphanage, you see.'

'Oh, deary me. Mum and Dad dead, are they?' Grace whispered, eyes bright with concern.

'Yes – oh, I don't know. They might be alive. What I do know is that they didn't want me. I was abandoned, you see, when I was two weeks old.'

'Well, I never! What a thing to do to a bairn! Kath lass, I'm sorry.' Her eyes filled with tears. 'How ever did we get on to such a subject?'

'I don't know, Mrs Ramsden, but we had to, sooner or later. It still hurts, you see, not being wanted, not knowing who I am, not knowing anything about myself. Best you should know. There might even be bad blood in me.'

'Bad *what*? Now see here, Kath Allen, that day I knew Roz was coming to work here was the same day we heard we'd got a landgirl: *you*. And I was real pleased that there'd be two young lasses here at Home Farm. Mat and me never had a daughter, then all of a sudden I get the two of you. Look at me, Kath. I'm trying to say that *I* want you. I feel sorry for your mother, whoever she is, because she gave away a baby that grew up into a beautiful girl with a lovely nature. I'd have been pleased and proud if Jonty had brought you home and told me you were the girl he was set on marrying. Now, does that help put your mind at rest?' she demanded, breathless.

'Bless you yes, Mrs Ramsden. Only one thing wrong, though. I'm married, and Jonty wants Roz – but you knew that, didn't you?'

'Aye. I've known it since he was a little lad no more than six years old. She came to Ridings, Roz did, a bairn of not much more than two, and he loved her then as if she was his little sister. Mrs Fairchild was badly upset over her daughter's death, you see, and I'd go over there and bring Roz here – give the poor soul a bit of time to herself. Jonty fussed over the little thing and watched her like an old sheepdog watches a wayward young lamb. He still loves her, Kath, only now it's a man's love, not calf-love, like it used to be. She still treats him like a big brother, though, and I know she's going out with an airman from

Peddlesbury. The whole village knows it, 'cept her gran. And I think Jonty knows it, too. Like I said, lass, it's a funny old war, which brings us back to you, and the dances. Why did you feel bad about going?'

'Because I wanted to go so much that I shouldn't have; because somehow I feel Barney might find out.'

'But he's abroad. How's he likely to find out unless you tell him?' Grace took mugs from the mantelpiece and placed them on a tray. 'Anything else you've got on your mind, while we're in the mood for it?'

'Not really. Just that – well, things haven't been very good between Barney and me lately – in our letters, I mean. I joined the Land Army without asking him and knowing he wouldn't like it. Then I sprung it on him just before I came here. He doesn't like women in uniform.'

'And he's annoyed about it – doing a bit of a sulk, is he? Hmm. Jealous, I shouldn't wonder,' Grace supplied, matter-of-factly. 'Stands to reason.'

'He needn't be, Mrs Ramsden. I've said I'm sorry. I write him loving letters and I'm saving up hard for our home. I know I shouldn't go to the dances, but I do, so there it is.'

'Yes, and you enjoy them. But I thought we'd decided there was nothing wrong in your going out once in a while, so stop worrying about your Barney. Just keep sending him nice, loving letters as if nothing's happened and he'll soon see he was wrong and give up hurting you. Men can be like that, you know – spoiled. Happen his mother is a bit possessive.'

'She was.' Possessive, that was Mrs Allen, all right. She'd disliked having to share her son. Barney's mother would have resented any girl he brought home. 'But I'll do what you said, about the letters.'

Keep writing loving, dutiful, forgiving letters. But for how long would Barney keep up his hurt? And for how long could she endure it?

'That's right, Kath. Bear with him. He's bound to take it badly, being parted from you; maybe makes him think things he shouldn't. But don't take all the blame on yourself. You've done nothing wrong, and don't you forget it.'

'I'll try not.' She would even try to stop being grateful for the ring he'd placed on her finger, because it didn't seem to matter here who she was or what she was. At Home Farm she was Kath, the landgirl. She was accepted – yes, and liked.

'Right, then. Off you go with that tea.' Grace stood at the door, tray in hands, while Kath pulled on her boots. 'And, lass –'

'Yes, Mrs Ramsden?'

'I think you and me have known each other long enough for you to call me Grace. Roz does, and I'd like it if you would.'

'And I'd like it, too,' Kath said, the tremble of tears on her whispered words. 'I'd like it very much.' Diffidently she took a step nearer, then gently kissed the older woman's cheek. 'And thanks. Thanks for – for *everything*.'

Sighing deeply, Grace closed the kitchen door. So that was young Kath sorted out; that was Kath's barrier down, she thought, well pleased with the turn their little chat had taken. If only she could sort Jonty's life so easily.

Clucking irritably she filled another mug. Best take Mat a drink, stay and chat with him a moment, take his mind off all that form-filling.

Her eyes misted over. She loved that great, soft Mat; loved him as Jonty loved Roz. And she'd had such hopes. In her silly daydreams she had sat in St Mary's and heard the words so often.

I publish the banns of marriage between Jonathan Ramsden, bachelor, and Rosalind Fairchild-Jarvis, spinster, both of this parish . . .

Once, there had been such substance to her dreams. And then the war had come . . .

'Just think, Mat – it costs a man his life for listening to the BBC, yet here we take it for granted.' Grace snapped off the late-night news, her face grave. 'I wish, though, that sometimes they could find something good to tell us.'

Mind, a convoy had got through to Malta; that was good, but at what cost in young lives? And on the Russian front, fighting was fierce, still, and neither side getting anywhere; only dead lads to show for it, and scorched earth; the burning of Russia, so the invader should not have it. And still fighting in Burma, our army was; men at war in a distant country some of them had hardly heard of, till all this started.

But most distressing of all, Grace fretted, was the newspaper editor in Poland who had tuned-in to our news broadcasts, and died for it.

'Something good? Aye, love.' Mat kissed his wife tenderly, lovingly. 'Think I'll turn in. Want to make an early start on Mrs Fairchild's land, get the harrow on to it. Fire all right?'

'I'll take a look at it.' Jonty reached for his jacket. 'I'll take a look at the sky, as well, while I'm out.'

A farmer always checked on the weather to come, studied the sky and the clouds, the rising and the setting of the sun, the more so since weather forecasts on the wireless were a thing of the past. Stood to reason, didn't it? We weren't going to broadcast the weather to the enemy so they'd know when to come and bomb us.

Jonty pulled up the collar of his jacket and walked out into the night, blinking his eyes until they adapted to the darkness, standing quite still until he could pick out the vague, darker shapes of stables, stacks and barns. A cloud drifted over the half moon and the outlines were gone.

Carefully he walked through the foldyard and the

stackyard, his eyes more accustomed now to the night. It was distinctly warmer; soon sowing and planting could begin. Only today he had noticed the pale, pinky light around the sycamore trees; the haze that told a countryman that buds were swelling and spring not far away.

The days were lengthening, too. Tonight there had been good light until well past seven. Winter was almost gone and like all men who worked the land, he would be grateful to see the back of it.

Quietly he closed the orchard gate. It was Ridings' orchard, really; the point at which Home Farm acres met those of the big house. It was land standing idle save for almost a hundred fruit trees, and most of them past their best.

Roz wanted pigs. They'd do well in this orchard when the fruit began to fall; could run-on into autumn and forage for themselves, save on precious feed.

But Marco had been right, Jonty shrugged; war or no war, you couldn't give a girl a present of pigs and he wouldn't be making such a gift to Roz. He would give her the piglets of course, but later, when they were ready to leave the sow.

He stopped at the far fence, leaning his elbows on it, taking in the quietness of the night. Roz was all woman, now. Without his ever being aware of it she had left girlhood behind her and with it the easiness between them had gone.

Roz had been a love of a child; pert, bossy, easily upset – that red hair, of course – and he had adored her with dog-like devotion. Had it been the Christmas after her seventeenth birthday when caring had been replaced by love, when he had been shocked that suddenly he had thought of her as desirable, had looked at the curve of her breasts and longed to cup them in his hands?

That was the time the Air Ministry had commandeered Peddlesbury, torn out hedges, felled trees and trailed two concrete runways across good farmland. That was about the time the uniforms came to Alderby and he began to be ashamed that he wasn't wearing one.

And now his Roz was a beautiful woman and the pain of wanting her was sometimes near-unbearable. Green-eyed Roz, who could send a man's senses into turmoil with the smile of a coquette or the wrinkling of that absurd, tip-tilted nose. Roz, who dated young men with the wings of aircrew on their glamorous uniforms; who were infinitely more desirable than farmers who worked all the daylight hours God sent, yes, and half the night if needs be.

Yet still he was called *conchie*, told to get some in, reminded that now women were being called-up into the fighting forces, and why should the likes of him evade call-up?

A hunting owl ghosted silently past; distantly, a dog barked. This was a night undisturbed by the roar of bombers. The Lancasters were grounded; tonight she would be with him, the nameless, faceless airman.

A faint, fresh breeze touched his face and reminded him of his reason for being there. Climbing the fence he walked to the old game-cover and all that remained of their fire, sniffing the scent of burnt wood, kicking the ashes with the toe of his boot, knowing they would not ignite again.

He heard the crunch of their feet as he stood there and the murmur of low, indulgent voices, lovers' voices. He heard a laugh that was easy to recognize and he moved into the shelter of the hedge as they drew near; so near that in the moon-haze he was able to recognize the outline of the woman and know that the man who walked with her hand in his own was an airman.

They did not see him. Pulling in his breath he saw them stop, watched as she took his face in her hands and lifted her mouth to his. The man took her thighs in possessive hands, pulled her closer, and they merged into one shape and one body.

Anger took him silently. Damn the man in his fancy uniform and damn the war that had brought him to Peddlesbury!

Fists clenched in his jacket pockets he stood unmoving as they moved past him and into the orchard, to the gap in the hedge that led to Ridings' kitchen yard. Jonty Ramsden did not wish any man dead, but he wished some great, godly hand would snatch up the aerodrome and fling it into oblivion; wished every bomber would take off and never return to Peddlesbury. But mostly he wished he could be free of his love for Roz and his tearing need of her; be free of the sight and the sound of her, the knowledge that she belonged, almost certainly, to another man.

'Everything all right?' Grace asked of her son as he closed the door and slid home the bolts.

'Everything's fine. The fire's dead. No trouble,' he replied, tersely. 'It's a good sky. No rain tomorrow.'

Roz. He would never get her out of his mind or out of his heart; it was as impossible to stop loving her as it was to stop breathing in and breathing out. And everything *was* fine – if you liked red-hot knives thrusting into your guts and turning till the pain made you want to cry out.

'Want a drink? Won't take a minute.'

'Thanks, Mum, no. I'll be off upstairs. Had enough for one day.' He bent to kiss her cheek. 'Say goodnight to Dad for me.'

No, he would never be free of her. He pulled off his clothes and let them slide to the floor. She had his heart and that was the way it would always be. There'd be no one else for him. Only Roz, for all time. Christ, how he needed her, hated any man who touched her.

He banged the pillow with his fist, then buried his face in it. What in God's name was he to do?

159

8

Spring came suddenly to Alderby St Mary with primroses at her heels and a gentle, south-west wind at her skirts, for spring is a woman called April.

Kath closed her eyes briefly and breathed in the sharp morning air that smelled of moist earth and green things growing. To her left hand gorse blazed golden; to her right, if she were to part the leaves gently, she knew she would find violets, purple and white, and smelling so sweetly it would make her heart ache with happiness.

Now, a little before six, it was daylight and by the end of the month, when clocks had been put forward an unnatural two hours, it would still be light at ten o'clock at night. Double Summer Time it was called and necessary, it was said, for the war effort and the saving of electricity. She wasn't at all sure that animals liked the strange, long days but she supposed it didn't really matter to a creature whose life could never be regulated by the hands of a clock. But extra daylight enabled farmers to work longer hours and grow still more food which pleased everyone, save those who worked on the land from dawn to dusk.

She looked up at the flock of rooks that rose cawing from the treetops, making for the fields and food. Kath liked rooks. They never seemed to panic. Unhurried birds they were, their call lazy and slow, the beat of their wings the same. She knew the difference, now, between rook and crow, was learning to identify a bird by its song; knew the warm, bubbling notes of a blackbird, the clear sweet piping of a thrush. Mornings were a din of birdsong; the dawn chorus that awakened the soundest sleeper. No need now for five o'clock alarms at Peacock Hey.

'I am so lucky,' she whispered to the morning. Lucky to be here, where she knew she belonged, doing what she wanted to do and doing it amongst friends. Soon, she would lean her cycle against the stackyard wall and if Mat and Jonty had finished the milking she would loose the cows from their stalls and herd them slowly to the pasture.

The milk-cows had left their winter quarters in the foldyard. With young grass growing thick and plentiful once more, they spent the day out at pasture and soon it would be warm enough, Jonty said, for the herd to spend nights, too, outdoors. That would save time and fodder, and the milk would be richer, more plentiful.

She wanted never to leave Alderby, there was no denying it. She wanted to stay here when the war was over, if some small miracle could make it possible. Barney was a lorry-driver, could take a job wherever he pleased – if jobs there would be when the war ended, of course. After the last one there had been terrible poverty, people said, with heroes begging in the streets, medals pinned to their chests; brave unwanted men, selling bootlaces.

She lifted her chin. The war was *not* over. This war, Kath Allen's war, had a long way to go. Only *now* mattered. One day, one distant tomorrow, there'd be an end to it but now there were cows to be pastured and milk delivered and the dairywork to be done. Done with Roz. With temperamental, bothersome, lovely Roz.

Life was good. She was ashamed it should be so in wartime, but there it was. She was happy – give or take a letter or two from Barney and even those petulant outpourings had begun to worry her less and less. North Africa was a long way away; no sense in looking for trouble. She would worry about Barney when Barney came home.

'Morning!' she called to Mat. 'Take this lot down to the field, shall I?'

*   *   *

'There'll have to be a proper going-on I tell you, or there's going to be such a muddle that we won't know where we are. You'll have to talk to Mrs Fairchild. There's the settling-up to be done for the ploughing and young Roz hasn't had a penny-piece in wages since the day she started here.'

Grace paused for breath, eyeing her husband. He needed telling, great soft thing that he was; needed a prod from time to time.

'Aye, love. I think we'll have to pay Roz the same as we pay Kath. She's a game little worker; don't hide behind her grandmother's skirts when it suits her to.'

'And the ploughing?' The ploughing had been the bane of Grace Ramsden's life and she wanted things straight. 'One egg, or two?'

'A couple, if you can spare them. I think we should charge the going rate for the ploughing. Mrs Fairchild wouldn't want it any other way, and she'll still have a bit left in the bank from the War Ag. money. And talking of banks, she reckons her and me should have a talk to Mr Potter, have him see to things for us. We'll both know where we stand, then. She's going to ring him up and fix a time.'

'Trouble with Mrs Fairchild,' Grace frowned at the spitting fat, 'is that she don't like talking money. Her sort never do.'

'Well, she's been a long time without it, so she'll just have to learn, won't she?'

'She will. And you should give Roz her wages into her hand, Mat. Don't let that man at the bank juggle them against what her gran owes us. The lass has worked for them; she should have them every Friday, same as Kath does. Happen you could see to that, an' all, whilst you're about it?'

'I will, Grace. I will.' They should have had things seen to by Lady Day, it being a proper settling-day for farm

162

matters, but they'd have everything set to rights before long, Mat thought comfortably. The back of the hard work had been broken and most of the seed potatoes set. With a bit of luck and a lot of fair weather they'd catch up with themselves before so very much longer. They would manage. 'And come on, our lass. When's a man to get his breakfast, then?'

Kath opened the field gate wide then leaned on it comfortably, calling the cows from the far pasture for afternoon milking. The herd of shorthorns looked up, eyes enquiring, then went on, tails flicking, with the business of cropping grass.

'Come. We give them a push,' Marco said impatiently. 'We'll be waiting too much.'

'Leave them,' Kath murmured, eyes closed, face lifted to the April sun. 'They'll come. You can't hurry them.'

You couldn't, she had learned. Cows had their own way of doing things, a pecking-order that was to be respected, with the oldest, longest-standing member of the herd taking precedence over the younger, newer beasts. They would wander slowly to the open gate when called, then stand there waiting their rightful turn, waiting for the cow who always led the way into the milking parlour, her bag so full that her udders stood out at angles, like the four short legs of a fireside stool. Only then would they follow her in, the newest amongst them being placed in order by the well-aimed toss of a head, the sharp, reprimanding jab of a horn. Cows were not, she had discovered, the gentle, mild-eyed creatures they were made out to be. A cow could be vicious when the mood took her; already Kath knew that a milk-cow with a sore udder had a kick like a mule.

'Have a cigarette whilst we're waiting. Go on,' she urged, at Marco's reluctance. 'I can spare it.'

He would smoke only half of it; the remainder, she knew, would be carefully saved and enjoyed later that evening in some quiet corner, if prisoner-of-war camps contained such a luxury.

'You smile, Kat. You go dancing tonight? Your husband will be angry.'

'Can't I smile, then? And I'm not going dancing but if I were it wouldn't be any of your business, Marco Roselli, nor Barney's either. If you must know, it's because Grace is planning a birthday surprise for Roz, that's all. And don't think I like keeping things from my husband,' she added sharply, 'because I don't.'

'Kat, I only tease. But there should not be things hidden between a man and his wife. If you were my wife, I would not –'

'But I'm *not* your wife! I'm Barney's – if wife you can call me,' Kath flung testily. 'I'm a married woman who *isn't* married. I don't know what the heck I am!'

'I think a woman needs always to be loved, Kat. I am sad you must be parted from love.'

'Then don't be. I'm just fine.' Of course she was. She didn't need to be loved. Kath Allen needed to be understood and Barney refused to understand her great need to once, just once, do something she wanted to do. 'I can manage very well without being loved. These days women have had to learn to, you know.'

'*Si*, Kat. I know it. It is the same in my country. Men go to war; women suffer.'

'Then you shouldn't have gone to war, should you?' Suddenly she was angry. 'Clever of that fat Mussolini of yours to sneak into the war after Dunkirk when he thought his German pal had got it all sewn up. The Brits were finished, weren't they, so why not kick them when they're down? But we aren't finished, Marco, and you're a prisoner and –'

She stopped, shocked by her outburst, at each waspish

word that tore from her tongue. Marco had done nothing to deserve her fury, wasn't the cause of the turmoil inside her. It always happened, didn't it, when she thought she was doing something wrong – like standing easily beside an Italian who was Barney's enemy, who would have killed him and thought nothing of it, had they met in combat in North Africa. But Marco had not killed Barney. Marco had saved her life and been kind to her afterwards, held her tightly and told her it was all right.

'I'm sorry,' she whispered. 'That was cruel of me. I shouldn't have said that. I didn't mean it. Please, Marco, I didn't.'

'Of course you not mean it. You have a bad day. Is okay, Kat. I too have bad days. Like you, I not know what I am. I think I am a man, but I am prisoner. I am nothing. I do as I am told. I must not speak to girls. You think I like it? You think I say to myself, "Hey soldier, is good you can't fraternize!"'

'I said I'm sorry, Marco, and I am. I felt fed up, all of a sudden. I took it out on you.'

'Took it out?' He frowned. 'What is took it out?'

'Something annoyed me, I suppose,' she shrugged, eyes downcast, 'and I took it out – it means that I –' She stopped, choosing her words carefully. 'It means that I threw my sadness, my annoyance, at you and for no reason at all except that you happened to be there. How do I say I'm sorry – in your language?'

'You would say *mi scusi*, but there is no need.'

'There is,' she said softly. '*Mi scusi*, Marco? Forgive me?'

'You are forgiven, and hey! You have your first lesson in Italian.'

Her first lesson? Sad that it should have been the words of an apology.

She threw down her cigarette and ground it into the grass as the first cow lurched toward them, walking awkwardly, impeded by the weight of her milk. 'Think you better had go and hurry them up a bit. They don't seem to want to come in this afternoon.'

Roz would be impatient for them to begin the milking, be finished in good time. Roz was meeting Paul tonight. Tonight they would touch and kiss, and stand close, arms clasped tightly. Make love.

Was she jealous, Kath brooded, or was she ashamed she could recall the safeness of Marco's arms so vividly, the way he had held her, touched her hair and told her she was safe? Did she want Marco's arms around her, or would any man's arms do? Was she, underneath, the same as any other woman? Was she lonely and in need of love?

She closed her eyes to shut out the shame. She was not lonely; she was not in need of love and Marco Roselli's nearness meant nothing at all to her.

'Come on, then!' Peevishly she slapped the dark red rump of a cow that had stopped in the gateway to eye her with curiosity. 'Shift yourself, you silly creature!'

Oh, damn, damn, *damn*. And this morning she had been so very happy.

The leisurely walk back to Home Farm behind a plodding Daisy was such a delight these mornings, Kath thought. Milk delivered, the time could be given to gossip and small-talk and *don't-tell-anyone-buts*.

On either side of the long straight drive that led to Ridings, oaks and beech trees were coming into leaf; the beeches first, the oaks more reluctant to show their green-brown foliage. And beneath them, in the parts left unploughed, drifts of bluebells grew on thick carpets of leaves, a shimmer of sapphire, slow-moving in the breeze.

'Listen, Roz – and don't tell anyone I've mentioned it – but you won't be planning to take the day off on your birthday, will you? I can't tell you why, but –'

'But do I plan to be in York with Paul, you mean?'

'No. I don't want to know about York. I've told you that already. What I'd like you to tell me is whether you'll be around for afternoon drinkings, that's all.'

'I suppose I will. I'm not planning to ask for time off that day. I'd rather have it when we've got something arranged and so far we haven't. Even when we can get around to it, it'll still depend on whether Paul is on ops. I won't know for certain till the last minute. But what's happening on my birthday? Come on – tell.'

'Sorry.' Kath smiled primly. 'Just be there, that's all. And you never got around to telling me about St Mark's Eve.' She changed the subject with a firmness that would have done credit to Hester Fairchild. 'Remember you once said something about Polly, and it all being a load of superstition. You got me curious.'

'It's just that, Kath. Nonsense. And Gran's as bad as Polly for believing it. You'd be surprised the lengths she goes to, even now, to keep people out of the churchyard that night.'

'On St Mark's Eve? But why?'

'Because that's supposed to be the time,' Roz shrugged, pink-cheeked, 'when people see the ghosts – images, if you like – of those who are going to die.'

'To *what*?'

'All nonsense. I told you so, didn't I?'

'I don't care what you say it is, I want to know, Roz.' All at once she was curious – yes, and uneasy, too. If Mrs Fairchild believed it and Polly believed it . . .

'Oh, I suppose it all started ages ago. It had been going on for quite some time before Gran found out about it. There was this old woman in the village, used to live in one of the almshouses. Daft Molly, people called her. Mad as a hatter, she was. She believed she was some kind of wise-woman, or something. She had a black cat and she swept her path with a besom – you know, made of twigs like a witch's broomstick. All part of the act, I shouldn't wonder.

'Anyway, Molly was in the habit of keeping the grave-yard watch on St Mark's Eve. People believed, you see, that at some time during the night – after midnight – the images of the people in the parish who were to die during the following year would pass the church porch.'

'Roz! That's terrible!'

'Like I keep saying – just nonsense.'

'But nonsense Polly believes in, and your grandmother?'

'We-e-ll, I suppose they just might have had reason to. It was during the last war, you see. Molly had kept the watch and at first she said there'd been nothing. But then she let it out; there'd be three, she said, in the year to come. A man of gentlemanly bearing, a soldier with two stripes on his arm, and a girl-child.'

'And she was right?' Kath ran her tongue round uneasy lips.

'She was right. A little girl – a toddler – ran under the wheels of a heavy cart and my grandfather and Polly's young man were killed in France.'

'And Polly's boyfriend was –'

'A corporal,' Roz finished.

'It's uncanny. I don't wonder your gran was upset. If I'd been in her shoes, I'd have put a lock and chain on the churchyard gates.'

'She did, eventually. At first she said it was all silly superstition and got the vicar to have a word with old Molly; warn her to stop messing about. But Molly was at it again the next year, sitting all night in the porch.

'There were no parish ghosts that following year, she's supposed to have said, but something awful was going to happen in the dead month – that's what country people sometimes call December, you know. "Beware the flames," was all they could get out of her. Alderby people thought

168

the church was going to catch fire, but you know where the flames were?'

'Ridings? She foretold that?'

'Yes; the second of Gran's December tragedies. And then there was my mother and father – they died in December, too.'

'But I thought Polly blamed that on a snowdrop?'

'She did – *does*. Anyway, now you know about St Mark's Eve.'

'Yes, and I'm sorry I brought it up.' Kath tried not to believe in anything she could not see, smell, or touch – apart from God, that was. 'And you're right. It's a load of rubbish.'

'Of course it is. Anyway, after the fire the vicar put a lock on the churchyard gates every St Mark's Eve and Molly went to Helpsley to live with her son and his wife.'

'And the gates are still locked on the twenty-fourth?' Kath demanded, cautiously.

'Yes. I think Gran likes the custom kept up. And you can't be too sure, I suppose. After the fire she was really upset by it – according to Polly, that is. I don't really know. I wasn't even born, then. Oh, look, Kath! Did you see it? Did you see the swallow? There now, that's made it all right. A first swallow is special. You can wish on it, and it'll come true. Swallows are lucky.'

'Roz! What next? Graveyard watches and first swallows? What a peculiar lot you country people are.' Wouldn't hurt to make a wish, though, even if she didn't believe in such things. 'Any more of your quaint old superstitions, whilst we're on about it?'

'Not that I can remember off-hand. Only the first cuckoo-call.'

'And what's that supposed to be? Lucky or unlucky?'

'It varies. There's a lot said about hearing your first cuckoo of the year, Kath. Even the direction it comes from is important. Mind, it's *very* lucky to hear it first on the

169

twenty-eighth of April. Pity I was born on St Mark's Eve. Better if I'd waited four days, and been a cuckoo-child. Polly says that when you hear your first cuckoo, you stand very still – after you've turned your money in your pocket, that is – and you count the number of calls it makes. That's supposed to be the number of years you still have to live.'

'And you believe it?' Kath gasped.

'Well, not about the number of years, that's for sure. Last year I counted and the blessed thing only called once, so I suppose if I can manage to stay alive till I hear a cuckoo again, that's one superstition gone for a burton.'

'Don't talk like that, for goodness' sake! I thought you were reasonably normal, but if you keep on about such things you'll have me wondering. Whatever next?' Kath clucked indignantly, taking Daisy's head, leading her into the yard.

'Well, there's the one about the tongue of a toad and the eye of a newt. Or I can give you a good love-potion to slip into your beloved's ale.' Roz laughed.

'Love potion! You've been having me on, haven't you?'

'Not about St Mark's Eve, Kath.' All at once, the sparkle left her eyes. 'Not about that. It happened, just like I said.'

'But it couldn't happen now? It would be too cruel – with the war on, I mean.'

'There was a war on then; Gran's war, and Polly's. But don't worry. There'll be no watcher in the church porch this St Mark's Eve, thank God. If there are any ghosts, no one will see them.'

'You *do* believe it,' Kath whispered. 'I thought it was because I was a towny, and you were pulling my leg.'

'Maybe I was. Maybe I wasn't. I don't know what I believe any more. I was brought up with superstition and such things. You believe what suits you, I suppose. So if I were you, I'd keep an eye open for that first swallow, Kath,

170

and make your wish. And don't forget to turn your money over when you hear your first cuckoo,' Roz called over her shoulder as she opened the dairy door. 'And you're *not* a towny. Not any more, so don't you forget it!'

'There now.' Grace fastened the ties of her clean pinafore and looked with pleasure at the kitchen table. Her best rosebud china stood on a white, starched cloth, her little-used cake forks lay beside the silver sugar bowl and milk jug.

She thought back with joy to the subterfuge; to the taking of a can of the Jersey cow's milk and putting it through the forbidden separator; to the grinding down of sugar with the pestle, for cake-making sugar had long disappeared from the shops. And the bother with the flour! But she had managed a birthday cake for Roz, had set it on a crocheted doyley on a large rosebud plate and put it on the cold slab in the pantry, behind a closed door.

'They'll be here any minute, Mat.' She smiled, setting the kettle to boil. 'And I told Kath she was to bring Marco in, too. We couldn't have left him out of it, could we?'

'We couldn't, love, though what the Ministry of Food'll say when they find out what you've been up to, I don't like to think. Land us all in prison, you will.'

'Up to?' Grace rose, pink-cheeked, to her husband's teasing. 'We produce gallons and gallons of milk on this farm and if I'm not entitled to take just a little of it, just once, for a drop of cream for a special occasion, then it's a poor do. And what else did I do that's illegal?' she demanded.

'What about that flour you sieved? Wouldn't like that either, would they?'

'Happen they wouldn't, Mat Ramsden, but folk can't abide that nasty brown stuff they're making us use. And who can make a sponge with it, will you tell me? Only fit for pigs. Lord alone knows what all those brown bits in it are doing to our insides.' She had sieved the detested flour through an old silk stocking to get the white flour she needed for Roz's cake then thrown the residue into the pig-swill bucket. She'd done nothing wrong, she thought defiantly; nothing *really* wrong. And was a drop of cream such a sin once in a while, even though the making of cream was absolutely forbidden. 'Anyway, who's to know, if you don't tell them?' she sniffed.

'I'll not tell on you, lass.' He placed an arm around his wife's shoulders. 'Did you find anything to give to Roz?'

'I didn't. It's a terrible thing, not being able to give presents. Nothing at all in the shops, not even a bottle of scent. Mind, I did think about Grandma Ramsden's jewel box – just something small – but it wouldn't have been right, would it?'

Grandma Ramsden's jewels had been left to Jonty, to be given to his wife. That box of trinkets was like the calling of the wedding banns in St Mary's; part of a lovely, indulgent dream that one day Roz would wear them. Now, Grace wasn't so sure.

'No, love. Not right. But the lass won't be expecting presents. And she'll be pleased as Punch with the cake.'

They came laughing into the kitchen; Roz and Jonty, Marco and Kath, demanding to know what the fuss was about and why the best cups and saucers and the silver teapot?

'It's for Roz's birthday, that's what. Come on now, the lot of you. Get your hands washed.'

Excitedly she ducked into the pantry; triumphantly she bore in the cream-filled sponge cake. 'Happy birthday, Roz!'

'Grace! A *cream* cake! Oh, you lovely, wicked lady!'

'Just this once,' Grace murmured, smiling at Kath, the fellow conspirator who had secreted away the milk and helped separate it into cream. And had kept Roz away from the kitchen when the sieving and grinding and baking

172

were being done. 'And it's to celebrate the finishing of the ploughing, and because we're all here together.'

'Grace, Mat, *all* of you,' Roz whispered. 'Thank you. Thank you so much.'

'Happy birthday.' Kath hugged her friend. 'And get that cake cut, do. Just to look at that cream is making me giddy.' She had forgotten, really forgotten, what a cream cake tasted like.

Happiness flooded Kath in great, warm waves. This kitchen, this farm, was where she felt at home. And just a few days ago Roz had claimed her as one of their own. *You're not a towny. Not any more* . . . On this day, this beautiful April day, Kath Allen at last knew where she belonged.

'You don't have to walk any farther with me,' Kath said as they walked through the lodge gates.

'No, but I want to. Paul phoned at dinnertime. He's almost sure it'll be all right for Tuesday. I wanted to tell you, that's all.'

'I see.' Gravely Kath regarded the bell of her bicycle. 'And what are you going to say – about being away all night, I mean?'

'That I'm going to York, for shoes. I do need some, Kath.'

'The shops'll be shut by the time you get there.'

'Not if I ask Mat for half a day off. He'll let me have it. I'll go by train – pick it up at Helpsley Halt.'

'And Paul will already be on it, I suppose?' Kath demanded, wishing this conversation hadn't been forced upon her.

'No. Paul will hitch a lift. There are Peddlesbury transports going to York all the time. We're meeting outside the station and don't worry, Kath, I'm not involving anyone. I won't say I'm with you, so you won't have to tell any lies for me. I'll just ring up and tell Gran I've missed the last

173

bus and I'm finding somewhere to stay. Best I don't say where. Don't want her looking it up in the phone book.'

'And the more lies you tell, the more you'll have to tell,' Kath clucked impatiently. 'Is it really worth it? Won't you be looking over your shoulder all the time?'

'Why? York's a big place. Who's to see us?' Of course it would be worth it. She wanted to be with Paul, just once. He'd flown twenty ops, now. Their new Lancaster had come to them with luck all over it, but for ten more times she would be counting them out from Peddlesbury and counting them back. Nine more ops and the thirtieth. And after the thirtieth, when they could hope to be stood-down for a while, she would take him to Ridings and introduce him to Gran.

'We'll be all right. It *will* be worth it, Kath. They say you can do what you want, take what you want, if you're willing to pay for it. Well, I want Paul and I love him so much that I can't begin to tell you. And I'll pay for loving him, if I have to.'

'That's fine, then. But it won't only be you, if you're found out. What about your gran?' Kath urged. 'Think how she'd feel if it got around the village that you'd signed into a York hotel with –'

'But why should it get around?' Roz demanded, impatiently. 'I'm not going to proclaim it from the pulpit next Sunday, am I? And York isn't Alderby. It's a big place. Nobody's going to see us.'

'But have you thought about it – *really* thought?' Kath leaned her cycle against a field gate for one last try. She wasn't going to talk Roz out of it; she knew already that the battle for reason was lost. Roz was so obsessed with Paul, so completely in love that reason didn't enter into it. 'Had you thought you mightn't be able to find anywhere?'

'No I hadn't, because we *will*. Skip's wife comes up often to be with him and nobody demands to know if they're married when they ask for a bed for the night.'

'Of course nobody asks them. Skip and his wife probably *look* married. They won't look all furtive and guilty when they sign the hotel register.'

'Neither will we, because we won't feel guilty. Paul and I are lovers, Kath. We're married already. We just haven't had it blessed in church, that's all.'

'Oh, you won't listen, will you? You're so stubborn and pig-headed! You haven't got a wedding ring have you, Roz, and do you think they're going to let you have a room if you march up to the desk without luggage, without at least one small case between you?'

'All right – so I'll remember to take a case with me. Thanks for reminding me.'

'Great! You'll walk out of the house on Tuesday afternoon with a suitcase in your hand? Your Gran is going to ask you how many pairs of shoes you intend bringing back with you!'

Kath shook her head despairingly, looking up at the sky as though she could expect to find the solution written there.

'All right, then, Paul can take a case. And I'll put my signet ring on my left hand, and turn it round.'

'You've got an answer for everything, Roz Fairchild. But think on this, will you,' Kath demanded. 'Skip and his wife probably started that baby she's carrying in a York hotel. It could happen to you, and then where would you be? Just imagine the gossip in Alderby – stop to think, will you, what tattle like that would do to your Gran, and to Mat and Grace and yes, to Jonty, too.'

'I won't get pregnant.' Roz leaned against the gate, arms folded, her stance defiant.

'Ha! Famous last words.'

'No, Kath. You said your piece, told me to be careful and to talk to Paul about it, and I did. Do you think Paul's completely irresponsible? Don't spoil it for us. And don't let's you and me fall out? If you go on and

175

on about it much more I'll be thinking you're jealous or something.'

'Jealous? Of course I'm not! It's just that I want you to be sure. Somebody's got to talk to you, Roz, but if you're set on it . . .'

'I am, Kath.' Her voice was calm. 'We both are.'

'All right, then. If that's what you really want, then good luck and God bless you both. And I'm truly not jealous – just a little envious, maybe. I suppose,' she said gently, 'I'd do exactly the same, if I were in your shoes.'

If she weren't Kath Allen and married to Barney; if ever she should love someone as deeply and dangerously as Roz loved Paul. If ever she should be so lucky.

9

Tuesday was not a good day for Arnie, but he knew he would accept it with the stoicism that had carried him this far in his nine-and-a-bit years and tomorrow, he reasoned, it would be all over for another year.

But today, this last Tuesday in April, the school dentist was coming to Alderby. His name was Mr Brown; a name spoken in a whisper. Two weeks ago, Mr Brown's visit had been a fleeting one. That day he had merely said, 'Open wide,' murmured to the lady who wrote things on a card, then said, 'Next one please, nurse.' And Arnie's keen ear had translated the murmurings into *one extraction* which was a relief, really, when it might well have been The Drill.

The Drill was an instrument of torture and this morning the dentist would bring it with him, and The Chair, and set up his surgery in the front parlour of the school house. And The Drill would stand beside The Chair like a thin, menacing stork which came to horrible, whizzing life when the pedal at its base was pumped up and down by foot; up and down without stopping as if the dentist were pedalling the organ in church, or Aunty Poll's sewing machine. That pedalling, Arnie considered, was bad enough at half-past nine in the morning, but by three in the afternoon, when the dentist's foot was tired, The Drill whizzed more slowly, more erratically, and fillings then were only for the stout-hearted; for those boys amongst them who would be Paratroopers or spies or maybe even pilot a Lancaster, should the war last long enough.

Arnie walked reluctantly to school, a clean white handkerchief – for the blood – folded carefully in his pocket.

He wished he were grown-up enough to be able to make up his own mind about visits to the dentist; wished people could be born complete with teeth which would stay there, undecaying, until they grew old like Aunty Poll and could choose to have the sort of teeth they could put in and take out and leave all night in a cup on the window sill. But mostly this morning he wished that God would drop a brick on Mr Brown's pedalling foot, or something equally miraculous and sneaky.

He stuck his hands in his pockets, thinking how it would be. He would be brave, of course, even though Aunty Poll had said it was only a baby tooth that was getting in the way of the new one growing beneath it; a tooth she said he could have wiggled out himself if he'd had the sense, and saved her a shilling. But even the comparatively painless loss of a milk tooth was nothing compared to The Waiting.

The Waiting was almost as awful as The Drill and The Chair. The Waiting began when the footsteps of the nurse could be heard in the corridor outside, causing the entire class to hold its breath and eyes to swivel to the door.

Sometimes the footsteps tapped past and the dreaded knock was heard on the door of the other classroom and they knew it was all right again for fifteen more minutes.

The dentist's nurse was little and plump and walked like a pigeon with short, jerky steps. She wore a white coat and a blue hat with a silver badge pinned at the front of it. She was always cheerful, always smiling. That was why Arnie disliked her almost as much as he disliked Mr Brown, for she had no right at all to smile or be cheerful whilst leading boys and girls to the horrors of The Chair and The Drill.

But it was lovely, he acknowledged, when a patient was led groggily to a low stool outside and given a white enamelled mug, half filled with rosy-pink liquid.

'Rinse and spit out.' They were words of magic, Arnie sighed. They meant it was all over and he could sit there, swooshing the liquid around his mouth and spitting noisily and splashily into the bowl on his knees. With luck it was possible to make the half-mug last until the next victim was led in, eyes wide with terror, as you grinned at him shamelessly.

Arnie also liked it because it was the one day on which spitting was allowed; the one day in the whole year when you could do it and not get a cuff around the ear.

He closed his eyes and thought not of the smiling nurse who would stand at the classroom door and cheerfully say, 'Arnold Bagley, please,' but of the delights of rinsing and spitting. If he hadn't, he would have run away to Hull, and never come back.

Had Kath known what awaited her at Home Farm that same morning, she too would have run away.

She had arrived to find a scowling Mat, an indignant, pink-cheeked Grace, and Jonty, who told her apologetically, almost, that the milking machine had broken down. Could she and Roz get milking-stools and caps from the dairy?

'Milking-stools?' This was the day she had so dreaded, the day on which she would be exposed for what she was: a towny who was unable to milk a cow by hand. 'Jonty, I'm afraid I –'

'Damn! I'd forgotten. Come on. I'll show you how. Best you should learn.'

This, thought Kath unhappily, was the moment of her undoing; when the silly cow kicked out or refused to let her milk down. This was when she would fail miserably and all she had learned these past four months would count for nothing. This was when Aunt Min would say, 'I told you it wasn't all collectin' eggs.'

'Chin up, now. Don't look so badly-done-to.' Jonty smiled. 'You can try your hand on the old girl. Placid as a worn-out boot, that one. You'll be all right with her.'

'I won't be able to do it.' Kath pulled the milking-cap over her hair. 'Your dad's going to hit the roof when he finds out I've never hand-milked before.'

'No he isn't. He's only looking annoyed because Mum's just said her piece. She never wanted a milking machine in the first place. New-fangled, she thinks they are and a waste of good money. Dad can't stand it when she does her I-told-you-so bit. But he'll get over it. Milking machines are here to stay and even Mum will have to admit it, sooner or later. Trouble is they sometimes break down and spare parts are hard to come by these days.'

'So how long is it going to be out of action?' Kath demanded anxiously, setting her stool beside the oldest cow in the herd.

'As long as it takes, I suppose. It's the pump this time, but I've been on to York and they're seeing what they can do to help. Now get yourself settled. Open your knees and hold the bucket between them. If you don't it'll most likely get kicked over. Relax, now. Wrap your fingers round her udder like it's a calf's tongue, and squeeze. Gently. *Squeeeeze* . . .'

Kath wrapped and squeezed and an amazing squirt of milk hit her knee.

'Good. Now just direct it into the bucket, and you're away.'

She squeezed again, tilting the udder. From her right hand came a ping as the milk hit the bucket; from her left hand a similar sound.

'Great. Gently does it, now. Relax, Kath. Rest your head on her side, find your rhythm . . .'

She glanced down at the froth of white in the bucket. The elderly beast munched contentedly on the cow-cake in front of her, lazily flicking her tail. The bucket began to fill; Kath's hands relaxed. She was doing it. She was getting milk out and why oh *why* wasn't Aunt Min here to witness this triumph?

'All right?' Roz called from two stalls down.

'I think so.' Her cheeks were burning and she was still shaking inside but she was milking a cow by hand, she really was. At last that fearful December morning when she had set out for faraway Peacock Hey could be forgotten for all time.

'Great, Kath. You've got it. Milk those two quarters out, then do the other two. You're doing fine,' Jonty said approvingly, picking up his stool, walking away.

Great. Doing fine. Such heady words. The milk hissed frothing into the bucket. It was all right. She could do it; she could hand-milk. Softly, contentedly, she began to hum. What a wonderful day this was turning out to be.

This lovely day had come, Roz exulted. Even though they'd be making a late start on the milk-round, Mat had given her the afternoon off and he wouldn't go back on his word – Mat was like that. Things were upside-down because of the milking, but she would still have time to bathe away the smell of cows and wash her hair before catching the three o'clock train from Helpsley Halt.

She kept one ear on the sounds around her, the other alerted for sounds of Lancasters taking-off. The constant noise of aircraft was a part of life now, and Alderby St Mary people became aware of Peddlesbury's bombers only when they weren't flying; it was the silence they noticed. If there was no activity at the aerodrome this morning, no aircraft taking off and circuiting the village on short test flights, it was almost certain that tonight the squadron would not be operational and that Paul would be waiting for her at York station, as they had planned.

Please, no circuits and bumps this morning. Let him be there when I get off the train.

And that was pretty silly, come to think of it; to ask such a thing of God when she knew she was about to break two of His commandments and feel nothing but happiness doing it.

Already she had pushed her nightdress into the bottom of her handbag and this afternoon she would leave the house with a nonchalant 'Bye. See you!' aware that her grandmother would expect her to catch the last bus or train back to Helpsley, knowing she would be on neither.

She wished she need not be wearing her blue cotton nightdress tonight; wished it could have been flimsy and clinging and that she had scent to dab at her wrists and ears. But there was a war on, and even brides must make do with ordinary nightgowns and very little else in the way of a trousseau.

But only Paul mattered; being with Paul, falling asleep in his arms, awakening to find him beside her, still. That would be worth all the lies and deceit. She would be grateful for tonight, remember it fifty years from now when her grandchildren demanded to know what her war was like – *really* like.

'Pretty awful,' she would tell them, 'but we survived – and there were the good bits to help us bear it, of course.'

And she would glance across the room at a still-handsome Paul, and he would return her smile because he too remembered a long-ago April night.

This would be the first of their many lovely days. It would all come right for them. She knew it.

She lifted her head to hear Kath singing. Softly, she began to sing with her.

'Time for drinkings, Marco.'

Cleaning out poultry arks and moving them to fresh ground was hard, thirsty work and Kath felt the need for a drink from the bottle of water that lay in the cool of the hedge.

She sat down on the grass, wriggling herself comfortable

182

against one of the arks, tilting the bottle, swallowing in noisy gulps.

'Want a cigarette?' She handed over the bottle. 'Go on! You can give me one of yours when your Red Cross parcel comes.'

'You always give me yours.' Marco frowned as she struck a match and cupped the flame with her hands. 'Why are you so kind, Kat, when you should hate me?'

'Hating is a waste of time.' She shrugged, inhaling deeply.

'Mrs Fairchild does not think like you.'

'No, and that's her business, I suppose. But Roz is all right – you know that, don't you, Marco?'

'*Si*. It is strange when Roz is not here. She goes to York?'

'To buy shoes.' Lie number one. 'And maybe she'll go to the flicks.'

'What is *flicks*?'

'The pictures. Films. Movies.' Kath laughed. 'And how about *my* Italian lesson today?'

'Ah, *si. La lezione*. Today, the word is *grazie* – thank you. And for the cigarette I say *molto grazie*, which is much thanks.'

'*Grazie. Molto grazie*,' Kath repeated.

'Good. And it is good also that you smile. You are happy today, Kat?'

'Very happy.'

She closed her eyes and tilted her face to the spring sunshine. She felt almost at peace. It was good to be Kath; *our* Kath, who was needed here. This morning she had milked her first cow, filled buckets with warm, frothing milk. She was relieved that the new-fangled machine would be working again for afternoon milking, but glad that this morning it had broken down. Milk a cow – of course she could, and Aunt Min would be the first to hear of it!

She leaned a little to her right and her arm brushed

Marco's. It felt good to touch another human being, feel the warmth of his skin against her, the comfort of it. Her hand lay relaxed beside his. Gently he covered it with his own.

'Why are you happy, Kat? You get a letter?'

'No. No letters.' Not for more than two weeks. 'Don't laugh at me, but this morning I learned to milk.'

'And this is being happy?'

'For me it is.'

'Ah,' he said softly, and she knew that if she opened her eyes she would see his forehead puckered into a frown of bewilderment.

But she did not open her eyes. She thought instead of Roz and Paul, that tonight they would be close, lips whispering against lips in the darkness whilst she, Kath, would be alone, a married woman who wasn't married. The wedding ring she wore warned other men she was not for the taking, that she must live out this war unloved and unloving. That was why this brief nearness, this unexpected touching was special and innocent and why life owed it to her. Gently she removed her hand from where it lay, then entwining her fingers in his she murmured, 'For me it is *very* happy.'

The engine pulled into York station, hissing steam, braking with a suddenness that sent bumper clanking against bumper the length of the train and caused passengers already standing to sit down again.

Roz let down the window, then pulling off her glove turned the soot-stained door handle and stepped on to the platform. Her heart thumped the way it always did when she and Paul were to meet; the will-he-be-there, won't-he-be-there thumping.

'At the barrier nearest the footbridge stairs' were the last words he had spoken to her and she'd whispered that she would be there, then reached on tiptoe for one last kiss before she ran through the ruins and across the cobbled kitchen-yard to feel in the darkness for the back-door keyhole.

Now she slammed shut the compartment door and walked with eyes lowered because she didn't want to know that no tall young airman waited beside the barrier nearest the footbridge stairs; didn't want to know that he wouldn't be coming because this morning *They* had told pilots and navigators to report at noon for first briefing which would mean that tonight S-Sugar would be operational again.

She heard a familiar cough and lifted her eyes. He had come! Paul was walking towards her, smiling the way he always smiled. He wasn't flying tonight. Thank you, God, thank you!

'Paul,' she whispered, then ran into his arms; his dear, waiting arms.

For a while he held her tightly then she pushed him a little way from her and whispered, 'I love you. Did you know?' and lifted her face for his kiss.

Linking hands, he picked up the small suitcase he said he'd remember to bring. 'You're sure about tonight, Roz?'

'Very sure. It was my idea, remember? And I just said I love you.'

'I love you, too.' His smile was indulgent. 'Right, then. Where to?'

'Let's find somewhere to stay, shall we, then the worst bit will be over.'

'I did hear –' He stopped, frowning. 'This chap told me about it – a little bed-and-breakfast place near Micklegate Bar. Small, but –'

'Discreet? Somewhere we'll not meet up with half of Alderby?'

'Well – yes. I was thinking about you, that's all – how it would be if someone from the village saw us.'

'They won't see us. York is a big place, and who knows about us but Kath? Don't have doubts, Paul. Not now.'

'I won't. I haven't.' How could he, when this was a day-to-day life and all that mattered was here on this street, and now, with Roz beside him. For just one night there would be no war; no fear-filled yesterdays, no uncertain tomorrows. Sugar was a lucky old bitch; it had been all right since they'd got her. They'd finish their tour, do their thirtieth. They'd make it. 'No doubts at all. And did I ever tell you I love you – at Micklegate Bar, I mean?'

He looked up at the great, towering gateway that stood guard over the city.

'Not at Micklegate Bar, you didn't,' she told him gravely. 'And never at four in the afternoon.'

'Then will you remember this time and this place? And fifty years from now, Roz, will you remember that it was here I asked you to marry me?'

Five past four on St Mary's church clock and all over for another year. Now the dentist would take away The Chair and The Drill and go to plague another school.

It hadn't been all that bad, Arnie considered. The worst bit had been when the nurse stood smiling at the classroom door and said, 'Arnold William Bagley, please.'

He had forced himself to smile back, just to show her he didn't care and so she wouldn't look down at his knees which were shaking something awful. He'd closed his eyes tightly so he couldn't see what was going on and he hadn't opened them until he heard the ping of the tooth dropping into the dish.

That beautiful sound caused his eyes to fly open, and the dentist was saying, 'All over, sonny. Off you go with nurse.'

All over, and the best bit still to come. He'd sat on the stool and held out an eager hand for the white enamel mug of rosy-pink liquid.

The memory of it caused him to whistle cheerfully and he kicked out at a stone, even though Aunty Poll said he mustn't kick stones because it did his boots no good at all and boots cost money and coupons.

He took a backward glance at the clock. It didn't chime, now. They'd had to stop the chimes because they sounded too much like church bells and church bells ringing would mean that the Germans had invaded us though it was very doubtful now because Aunty Poll said they'd bitten off more than they could chew, in Russia.

It was a pity they hadn't had a try. He'd always fancied fighting on the beaches and never surrendering; wanted desperately to throw Molotov cocktails or have a go with a machine gun in defence of the gate lodges. But his turn would come. The dratted war would never be over; Aunty Poll was always saying it, so with luck he'd be able to be aircrew, like Roz's young man.

He was almost home now, and he slowed his pace to a sad, foot-dragging trudge. Remembering the handkerchief in his pocket he unfolded it and held it to his mouth. Eyelids drooping dramatically he pushed open the kitchen door.

'Now then, lovey.' Polly gathered him to her and hugged him tightly. 'Didn't hurt much, did it?'

'It *did*!' he choked. Then, nose twitching, he demanded to know what was for supper.

'Supper? You won't be wanting supper!' Polly held back a smile.

Frowning, Arnie gazed up over the folds of the handkerchief. The smell from the oven was tantalizing and unmistakable. Meat and potato pie, that's what, and rhubarb and custard, he shouldn't wonder.

'It was only a baby tooth,' he said airily.

'So you weren't frightened, Arnie? Not even a little bit?'

'Nah,' he retorted scathingly, pushing the handkerchief back into his pocket. 'Hey, Aunty Polly,' he grinned, opening his mouth wide. 'Want to see the hole?'

*   *   *

After they had found a room, they spent the remainder of the afternoon walking the walls that circled the old part of the city.

Roz had held her breath as the door was opened to Paul's knock and she had forced her head high, returning the smile of the young woman who wished them a good afternoon and asked them to come inside.

She had only two rooms for letting, she apologized, and one was already spoken for; would they mind the smaller one, at the top? They could take a look at it first, if they wished?

Paul had said that wouldn't be necessary, that he was sure it would be fine – without asking how much it was, even.

He'd signed the little book that served as a register, then; *Mr and Mrs Paul Rennie. Bath*. He'd signed it firmly and surely; smiling at her gently as he laid down the pen.

She sighed, remembering, leaning her elbows on the walls; loving him, loving this day.

'Do you suppose they ever envisaged our war – those men, I mean, who once stood guard on these walls?' She frowned. 'What would they have thought, those bowmen, if they'd seen your Lancaster flying over, Paul?'

'That the end of the world had come, I shouldn't wonder.' He laughed, taking her hand.

She leaned closer. She would remember today; would remember sights and sounds and scents. Every smallest thing she would photograph mentally; the blueness of the sky, the blossom in the gardens below them, the chestnut trees breaking into bright green leaf. And ahead of them the Minster, standing uncaring like a great, ages-old watch-dog keeping guard over the city.

'Shall we come back here when we're very old, and remember today?'

'Fifty years from now, you mean?' He laughed at his use

of her own favourite phrase. 'It'll be almost the year two thousand. So many years ahead, will you still love me?'

'You know I will. What shall we do tonight, Paul – *before*, I mean . . .'

She would like to dance, if they could find somewhere. She liked dancing with Paul; the tallness of him and the delight of their closeness. Or would they just walk? She didn't really care what they did as long as she didn't have to leave him. But tonight there would be no last kiss, no parting. She closed her eyes, sighing. Even tomorrow morning he would still be there.

'Why the sigh?'

'Not a sigh; not really.' She smiled up at him, eyes bright with love. 'I was just letting a little of the happiness out of me, that's all. I'd have gone off pop! if I hadn't.'

'I love you. Did I ever tell you?'

'Often. And I'll never love you more than I do now, Paul Rennie, though I'll try. I promise I'll always try.' She closed her eyes to hold back the tears; the lovely, silly, happy tears, and begged her god not to ask too high a price for this wonderful, shining happiness. 'Fifty years from now, I'll still be trying. And did you mean it at Micklegate Bar when you asked me to marry you?'

'Did you mean it when you said you would?'

'You know I did and oh, Paul, wouldn't it be wonderful if we could announce it in the paper? Something like, on the twenty-eighth of April, 1942, at Micklegate Bar at about four in the afternoon, Paul Rennie, RAFVR to Rosalind Fairchild. But we can't. Not yet.'

'We'll tell them, soon. When I've got the last one behind me; when we've finished our tour.'

'Yes. I'll take you home then to meet Gran. And we'll tell her we want to be married. It's all right for you, Paul; you're over twenty-one. But I've still got two years to go. She'll understand, though. She'll let me.'

It was growing dark as they crossed the Ouse Bridge,

walking hands clasped to Micklegate and the bed-and-breakfast place. When the clouds parted they saw the moon, full and bright, all at once lighting hidden corners, giving shape to old buildings, towers and churches.

'I'd forgotten the moon, Paul. Moonlight sort of hides the war, doesn't it; makes everywhere look mediaeval again.'

'I hadn't – forgotten it, I mean. It's a bomber's moon.'

'Not tonight. Not for you, it isn't. And tell me why you're smiling?'

'I was thinking about when I was signing the register. You pulled your gloves off and I nearly yelled, "*Don't!*" I thought she'd see your left hand, but you'd swapped your ring over. And I do love you, Roz. I keep wanting to tell you. Crazy, aren't I?'

'No. Never that.' They had come to a phone-box. 'Look – can you walk on a little?' There was a call she must make and she didn't want him to hear her when she said she was stranded in York. Lying was bad enough; to have Paul hear would cheapen tonight, and that was far worse. 'Just want to ring home.'

'You'll be all right, Roz?' He understood and his face showed concern.

'I'll be all right. Just wait for me at the corner.'

Turning her back on him she reached into her pocket for the two sixpenny pieces she had put there especially, then lifting the receiver she asked for the Alderby St Mary number.

'Have one shilling ready, please,' the operator said. 'I'm ringing the number now.'

'I'm sorry, Gran,' she whispered inside her as she waited, breath indrawn, for the phone to be answered. 'So very sorry to do this to you . . .'

The room at the top of the tall, narrow house in Micklegate was small and the big old-fashioned bed took up most of it making it seem even smaller. At the window, the blackout curtains had already been drawn and the rose-patterned curtains that matched the bedspread pulled over them. On the wall opposite stood a washstand with a bowl and jug, a white, fluffy towel on the rail at its side. But because of rationing, there was no soap in the rosebud china dish.

'Paul – I haven't brought any soap with me.'

There had been a half-used tablet in the bathroom but she couldn't have taken it. Gran would have known then, wouldn't she?

'It's all right.' He opened the small case and took out his toilet bag. 'I've got some. And it'll be all right. Don't worry, sweetheart.'

'I'm not. I won't. Gran didn't believe me, though, when I rang. I told her I'd missed the last bus and the last train as well. She didn't *say* she didn't, but I knew. She sounded surprised, and hurt.'

'She must have been, and I'm sorry,' he said softly. 'I wish it could have been different. If there hadn't been a war; if I wasn't flying, we'd have all the time in the world.'

'But there *is* a war, Paul, and we might not have time.'

'I know. But it *will* come right for us. That Lancaster is a lucky old kite. When we've done our thirtieth we'll be taken off operational flying – maybe they'll send us somewhere as instructors. Could be we'll have a whole year away from ops.'

'Mm.' A year was a long, long time. When you lived each day as it came, a year was forever, almost. 'And, darling, I know that tonight isn't our first time, but it's the first time we'll be properly together and I feel just a little – well, edgy. I want it to be perfect, you see.'

'It will be. No snatching tonight. And no picking bits of hay off your coat.'

'There'll be tomorrow morning, too.' She smiled. 'That's what's going to be so wonderful – opening my eyes and finding you still there.' She took his face, his dear, tired face in her hands. 'Fifty years from now we'll come back to this place and fifty years from now I'll still be loving you. But till then, we'll always have tonight and this lovely, lovely room. Just you and me.'

She wouldn't think about tomorrow; wouldn't think of the hurt in Gran's eyes nor Polly's button-round, indignant mouth. Tomorrow was a lifetime away. All that mattered was here and now when her name, just for tonight, was Rosalind Rennie.

Hester Fairchild lay in the pink-eiderdowned bed, worrying about the phone-call from York. Roz hadn't missed the last train, except by choice. Roz had known, when she left the house that afternoon, she'd thought as she replaced the receiver, that she wouldn't be home tonight.

After the phone-call, a suddenly-old woman had gone to her granddaughter's room, opening drawers and cupboards, doing things she would never before have dreamed of. And everything had been there; her dressing gown hanging behind the door, her slippers beside the bed where she always kept them, and beneath the pillow – and she had blushed as her hand searched there – Roz's pyjamas lay, folded neatly.

Could it be, she frowned, that Roz had *not* gone to York prepared to stay the night? Perhaps it was as she had said – her watch had stopped and she really was stranded there. She had been glad that her suspicions were without foundation. Then she opened the bathroom door and her eyes were drawn to the tumbler beside the wash-basin and the white toothbrush that should have been there, and wasn't.

'Why couldn't you have told me, Roz?' she had whispered. 'Why must it have come to this?'

Now she tossed unsleeping, the moonlight making patterns through the uncurtained window, shining mockingly on the loneliness of the woman who lay there. Take care, Roz. She sent her anguish winging. If you are with him, with the airman from Peddlesbury, tell me about him when you come home. Don't lie to me. Trust me? Believe me when I say I know what it's like to love a man until it hurts – and to love and want him still.

A tear slipped from the corner of her eye and she let it slide unhindered, down her cheek. For the life of her she didn't know who that tear was for. For Roz? For herself? Either way it was wrung from the very deeps of sadness, and tasted bitter on her lips.

That same moonlight touched the house in Micklegate and lit the little top room. Roz had pulled back the curtains so it should light their nakedness and stand witness to their love, make it special. She had wanted to see him, too; to remember the need and love in his eyes.

'What time is it?'

'Nearly two, I think.'

'Don't go to sleep yet, Paul.' They mustn't waste a moment of this night in sleep.

'I love you.' He raised himself above her, chin on hand, looking at her shoulders, her mouth, sensuous now; her small, round breasts, the nipples hard from wanting him and red like cherries, after their loving.

'I wonder what the world is doing out there,' she murmured. 'I want it to be written in the sky for everyone to see. *Paul and Roz. They love, they have loved, they will love . . .*'

'Get out of bed and look.'

'No. I don't want to leave you.' She wanted him again.

'Was it good?'

'It was good, Paul. Tonight, we should make a love-child.' All babies should be made in moments this good, this perfect.

'No. Not yet. I love you too much.'

'But we will have children, Paul?'

'We'll have children. When there's no more war.'

'Everything's so quiet.' She reached up to kiss the hollow at his throat. 'The world's holding its breath, for us.'

She traced the outline of his jaw with her fingertips, ran her fingers through tousled hair that made him look like a boy awakened from sleep.

'The moon's watching us, though. It's a lovers' moon tonight, not a bomber's moon.'

'It's going to be all right for us, you know that, don't you, Roz? That night when Jock bought it – thank God I had you, darling. I thought I'd never fly again but I'm sure, now. Every time we get back it's thumbs up for another one behind us.'

'We were lovers that night. The first time, remember? It was so cold. Not like now, in this beautiful room.'

'It's a very ordinary room, woman. When we're married we'll have a bridal suite – do it properly.'

'When we're married we'll come back here. There'll have to be a moon and we'll arrange for the world to stand still, like it is now . . .'

The world outside was not standing still. In other, more ordinary rooms, children cried in the night and were comforted. In the sleeping streets of that old, old city, policemen walked their beats and women on switchboards blinked sleepy eyes, waiting for morning and the end of their watch, another blessedly quiet watch, thanks be. And air-raid wardens wondered if the ration would run to another pot of tea, for this was the ungodly hour when eyes longed to close and bodies were cold from fatigue. A hot, reviving mug of tea would help keep them awake until morning came.

The air-raid warden was stirring his tea, wishing there

was sugar to spare to spoon into it when the telephone at his side began to ring.

''Allo. ARP Priory Street.'

'Purple alert,' said the voice. 'Repeat. Purple alert.'

The air-raid warden said 'Ta', picked up his pen, dipping it ponderously in the ink bottle, then wrote *Purple alert. 0236. 29th April* in the log book.

Hostile aircraft, and a purple alert meant they were only minutes away. Mind, it'd probably be Hull again, poor sods. There was nothing here for Jerry to waste his bombs on.

'If you want a sup of tea you'd best come quick and get it,' he called to no one in particular. 'That was a purple . . .'

They came in over Flamborough Head. Twenty-four Junkers-88 bombers, their mission aided by a moon that shone on the waters of the Humber estuary. Navigation was easier on moonlit nights; easy to follow the Humber waters to where they were joined by the River Ouse. Straight and steady flying, then, to York. And all of that city laid out beneath them, easily visible. The Luftwaffe crews were on to a good number in the small hours of that late April morning.

The ten-fifteen express from King's Cross to Edinburgh approached York station almost on time and the fireman put down his shovel, wiping his face with a rag. The driver peered out into the half-light, recognizing the blacked-out signalbox that was just about a mile away from York. He could do with a five-minute break; trains were easy targets for hunting German fighters on moon-bright nights like this. You couldn't entirely black out a train; not when its red glowing firebox had to be regularly stoked. But it had been a good run north, for all that . . .

*　　*　　*

The telephone in the ARP post in Priory Street jangled again and automatically the air-raid warden reached for his steel helmet. Only four minutes since the purple alert . . .

"Allo!'

'Air-raid warning red.' That voice again. 'Repeat. Air-raid warning red.'

'It's a red!' he called, jamming on his helmet, reaching to throw the switch of the siren that sat atop the building. A flaming rotten red, and him not had his second cup yet. But those swines always knew when you'd brewed up, didn't they?

The Priory Street siren and those around it began their undulating wail; like souls trapped in torment thought those whose sleep it disturbed. For ninety seconds that seemed to stretch into forever the lamentations went on, chilling some into immobility, others to stark panic. There'd been alerts before and it had been all right. There'd be alerts again, like tonight, but best be sure. Best go to the shelter.

'Roz,' Paul said urgently, pulling his arm from beneath her shoulders, flinging off the sheet. 'Get dressed. Now!'

'No,' she pouted. '*Damn* it. Oh, let's not get up?' They were always having alerts, always getting up, going into shelters and then what? Nothing.

'*Now*, I said.' He was taking no chances with her safety. He wanted her downstairs – under a table or under the stairs, if that's all the shelter there was. 'Get something on. Quick!'

'Bloody hell,' said the air-raid warden, 'it's *us*!' Not Hull, again; not Manchester or Newcastle; tonight they'd come for York. And with fire-bombs, that's what. Incendiaries, raining down. They'd come to burn the place out.

He hammered on the door of a house showing a light. Only a small window, but big enough for those sods up

196

there to see. A lavatory window. It was always the lavatory windows, the minute the sirens sounded.

'Get that light out! Get it *out*!'

The ten-fifteen King's Cross to Edinburgh express pulled into the London and North Eastern station at York just as the sirens had done with their wailing; just as the first high-explosive bomb crashed through the glass, dome-shaped roof and exploded with a sickening, shaking roar. It shattered the platform, sent glass flying in sharp, lethal daggers. Carriage doors sagged; travellers lay where they had been flung, stood stupefied or ran toward the ARP warden who blew on his whistle and pointed them in the direction of the nearest shelter.

More bombs hurled down, and more; fire-bombs crashed into roof spaces and lofts, began their hideous blazing. York, once guardian of the north, ringed round by stout walls and defended by bows and arrows, had no answer to this.

The first, furious explosion wiped all protest from Roz's lips. Shocked into mobility she slithered into her nightdress then flung on her jacket.

'Paul!' She felt her hand grasped and followed him, stumbling in the darkness to the dim light that shone two floors below them.

'Come down. Careful of the stairs,' the bed-and-breakfast lady called from the cellar door. A sleeping baby lay over her shoulder, her hair hung loose down her back. 'Hurry. We'll be all right down here.'

A candle burned at the turn in the worn stone steps, lighting a small, damp-smelling cellar, its floor covered by old, worn rugs. Beneath a wooden table, its legs shortened so that it stood little more than a foot and a half from the floor, another child lay on a mattress, wide-eyed, thumb in mouth.

In the centre of the cellar, set six feet apart, two thick wooden joists gave support to the ceiling above and, catching Paul's eye, the woman whispered, 'My husband put them there. Safer for us, he said, if the house got a hit . . .'

She was on her own, Roz thought dully. Her man was gone to war and she managed as best she could, rearing her children alone, renting out rooms to eke out the Army pay she drew each Thursday from the Post Office. She was young; too young to have this existence thrust upon her.

On a bench opposite sat a middle-aged man. He looked like a commercial traveller and he'd pulled on trousers and shirt, though his feet were bare and he held a handkerchief to his mouth. He'd forgotten his dentures, Roz thought. In his haste to get down here he'd left them behind and it wasn't funny. It wasn't remotely funny.

She reached for Paul's hand and held it tightly. She was afraid. Those first bombs had been too near – the station, was it?

The bed-and-breakfast lady laid the sleeping baby beneath the table-shelter then drew a blanket over her children. Her face was young and fresh; her eyes old and fear-filled.

'All right, sweetheart?' Paul whispered.

'Fine. Just fine.'

The air-raid still raged and though the explosions seemed farther away now, the noise was horrendous. Why York? Had they mistaken it for some other city? Roz swallowed hard and it sounded loud in the trembling silence.

The commercial traveller pushed his handkerchief into his trouser pocket. Perhaps he had fought in the last war and was suddenly ashamed of his embarrassment. Perhaps all at once he thought damn it, and to hell with his teeth, sitting two floors up. Perhaps things like that didn't worry old soldiers.

Placing a hand over his mouth he said, 'Bad do, this. Who'd have thought they'd have a go at York?'

'We've had a lot of alerts but no bombs, till now.' The woman placed an arm protectively over her children. 'My husband'll be out of his mind when he reads about this in the papers. He's with an ack-ack battery, near Scapa Flow. Wish he were here now.'

'It'll be all right,' Paul comforted. 'These old houses are solid.' He looked to the window at ceiling height; a long, narrow window that opened out at street level. Useful that could be. 'You're safe as houses down here.'

'You fly, don't you?' she whispered, gazing at the wing on his tunic. 'Give 'em a bashing tomorrow night? For York?'

'I'll do that.' He felt Roz stiffen beside him, knowing that even though there was a lull in the bombing and the only sound that of anti-aircraft shells screaming up into the sky, this could well be only the start of it. There could have been incendiaries amongst the HEs. There almost always were. Fire-bombs started a blaze that could be seen for miles, provided a target for the next wave to bomb on.

He pulled Roz closer. Her hand clasped his tightly, her body rigid with fear and shock.

Was this then, she thought, how it always was? Tomorrow night would it be S-Sugar's bombs, falling on men too old to fight and children too young to understand. And on frightened, lonely women.

She smiled up at him and he bent his head to rest it on hers.

'I think it's stopping now,' the bed-and-breakfast lady said. 'It seems farther off, don't you think?'

She drew her tongue round her lips. She longed for a cup of strong, sweet tea. She needed her husband beside her, not in khaki; not called up to fire an ack-ack gun miles and miles away from her and the kids. She *wanted* him, the comfort of his closeness in the night and him kissing and touching her, as it once had been.

'I think you're right,' Paul said softly, knowing that was what she wanted to hear. 'I think the worst's over . . .'

The all-clear sounded a little before five in the morning; the sweetest of sounds in a shocked city.

'Right, then.' The commercial traveller made for the stairs. 'Back to bed, I suppose.'

He wouldn't go back to bed, though. He'd get a shave and finish dressing, then be off to the station as fast as he could, home to Manchester on the first train out.

'I'll be making a pot of tea, if you'd like to come up to the kitchen.' The woman looked at her children, sleeping still. 'They'll be all right here. Think I'll leave them. Let's put the kettle on.'

'It's kind of you,' Paul smiled, 'but we'll have to be away. Best I get back to camp.'

'Did you have to say that?' Roz sighed when they were alone. 'I'd have loved a cup of tea, I really would.'

'I know, sweetheart, but I want to get you out of here. Just look out there.' He drew aside the curtain to reveal a sky that was red with fires. 'We'd best get weaving. They could be back before long to bomb on those fires; it's the way it is. Believe me, I know.'

'But what will we do – get the milk-train?'

'Train? I suppose we just might be lucky. But I don't care how; all I want is to get you out of this. Just *out*, all right?'

The air was foul with the stench of destruction; of water-drenched buildings and blazing timber. Thick, dark smoke shifted in billowing drifts and ages-old dust floated around them, mixing with minute pieces of fire-blackened paper. Voices called urgently, men dug in rubble and those without spades used their hands. A fire engine sped past, bell clanging.

'That bomb, Paul; the one that sounded so near . . .' Her fingers tightened within the grasp of his hand. 'It hit the Convent. They're carrying people out.' Eyes wide with disbelief she gazed at the waiting ambulances, at a stretcher and the scorched, stained habit of the nun it bore away, a cloth covering her face.

'Come away, Roz. Let's get to the station. Maybe they've been luckier there.'

Maybe by some small miracle they'd get a train out – perhaps the early milk-train to Helpsley. There might even be transport waiting outside. The station was the likeliest place.

They had not expected the devastation that confronted them.

'Sorry, lad. No trains,' the elderly policeman who stood at the station approaches said. 'No station. Direct hit . . .'

'God, what a mess!' Paul jerked. 'Many hurt?'

'Aye. Hurt *and* killed. Got the London train, see. Most of it just gutted. If you're looking for someone, try the Butter Market. In Kent Street. That's where they've all been taken.'

'No. There's no one. Just wanted to get back to camp. Hadn't realized . . .'

'Then you'd best try shanks's. Only way out of here, this morning. Or you might be lucky with a lift . . .'

He turned and walked away. He had better things to do with his time than talk to airmen who were well able to take care of themselves. And besides, they were still digging in the rubble in there. Nasty business it was, finding bodies.

'He's right. Let's start walking.' He took her arm in his. 'We'll get a lift, no bother.'

'It – it's *terrible*. Such a mess. So many killed.' Her lips were stiff and she shook with fresh fear. It could have been them; could have been the tall, narrow house in Micklegate and the sleeping children whose father was miles away. And what about Gran, alone? They'd have had an alert at Alderby, too. She'd have known York was being bombed.

201

'Sir?' A hand pulled at Paul's sleeve. 'Sir, can you help us, please?'

Two young women stood there, faces dirty and tear-stained. Two young aircraftwomen, shocked and bewildered. 'We don't know what to do. Just getting off the train, we were. Lost all our kit. Burned. Don't know how we're to get there and there's no one to ask . . .'

'Where do you want to be?' Paul's voice was gentle.

'RAF Peddlesbury, sir. Don't even know where Peddlesbury is.'

'Your first posting, is it?'

'Yes, sir.' The second, the younger one spoke. 'But our kit? We'll be in trouble. Left it on the train. We just ran . . .'

'I wouldn't worry about it, if I were you. You're both in one piece – that's all that matters. And I'm going to Peddlesbury. You'd better come along with us.'

'Can we? Oh, thanks. It's awful in there . . .' Fresh tears, then, to be brushed away with the back of her hand.

'Would a cigarette help?' Paul offered his packet. 'There'll be no transport here yet awhile. Think we'd all best try to thumb a lift. And stop worrying about your kit. Enemy action. Nothing at all you could have done.'

Roz held Paul's hand as he struck another match, and held it out for her. His hands were steady. He'd look after her, look after them all. Paul would get them out of this nightmare. She smiled her thanks, her hand lingering on his.

'Come on then, ladies. Let's try to make it to the Helpsley road. Could be we'll pick something up there.'

They set off together; Paul scanning the sky, ears alert for sounds of aircraft, for a second wailing of the sirens that would confirm the worst of his fears.

He wanted Roz out of this, and the two Waafs. Just frightened kids, the pair of them. Ought to have been at home with their mothers.

Hell, but this was a damn awful war.

The fingers of St Mary's church clock pointed to seven-thirty as the Army lorry came to a stop at the top end of Alderby Green.

'Right, then,' the driver called. 'This is where I turn off. You'll be okay from here?'

Paul thanked him and said they would, helping the aircraftwomen down, holding up his arms to Roz.

'Tonight?' he whispered as he swung her to the ground.

'Yes. Same time?'

'Same time – unless . . .' He didn't have to say it.

'See you, then.' She knew he wouldn't kiss her; not in front of the Waafs; not here, right in the middle of Alderby.

''Bye.' His eyes said 'I love you', then he turned and walked away, the young girls beside him.

She waited until they had rounded the bend in the lane, then looked around her in amazement. There had been no bombs here, no fires, no killing. Nothing had changed in Alderby. Nothing ever would except that maybe this morning the milk delivery was late.

'Kath!' Just to see Daisy and the milk-cart, the normality of it, sent relief rushing through her. 'Oh, Kath!'

'You're all right? Oh, thank God! They're all frantic at the farm and I couldn't say a word. They know, though.'

'How? Who told them?'

'Jonty. He went to Ridings when the siren went; wanted to know if you were both all right.'

'And I wasn't there,' Roz whispered flatly.

'That's it. He stayed with your gran till the all-clear went. When I got there this morning he had a face like thunder on him.'

'Had he just? Well, it's none of his business, is it?'

'It is if he loves you. But you'll want to be getting home and I'm late enough as it is. The Warden made us all get out of bed when the bombing started; we were in the shelter most of the night and I slept through the alarm. Last up gets the worst bike. By the time I got there, there were only two left in the bike shed, and both of them with a flat tyre. Had to blow the damn thing up three times on the way.'

'Panic all round, eh?' Roz shrugged. 'Look, Kath – I'll tell you about York later. It was pretty bad; I was really afraid. Tell Mat I'll be over just as soon as I've got into my working togs and had a cup of tea. And Kath – thanks.'

'What for?'

'For not going on and on about it; for not saying you told me so.'

'Was it worth it, Roz?'

'Like I said, the raid was awful, but yes, it was worth it.'

'That's all right then, isn't it?'

She stood, frowning, as Roz hurried away, then clicking her tongue, she took the pony's head, leading it on.

My, but she wouldn't be in Roz's shoes for anything this morning. Facing her grandmother would be one thing; facing Jonty's rage would be altogether another.

Sorry love, but I did tell you so . . .

The kitchen door opened the minute Roz set foot on the cobbled yard and she was gathered into her grandmother's arms, and hugged until it hurt.

'Roz! Darling, you're all right!'

'I'm fine, Gran, and I'm sorry to have been a worry to you, but don't go on about it – not just yet. *Please?*'

'I won't. But, Roz, whatever possessed you to miss that train? What were you thinking about?' *Tell me? I'll try to understand, truly I will. Only tell me about him. No more lies between us.*

'But that's just it. I *didn't* think. My watch, you see. And I was all right. There was a shelter. York's in a terrible

204

mess, though. There were two Waafs in the YWCA with me and we all hitched a lift back together.' *Lies. Lies.* 'The army driver told us he thought the Minster is all right, but they got the Guildhall and the station's gutted and the Edinburgh express. The Convent got a direct hit, Gran. We saw nuns being carried out.'

Her face crumpled and she closed her eyes tightly against the tears she had been longing to cry since that first, frightening bomb; closed them against the lies she was telling and must tell, for Paul.

'There now. It's all over. You're back home and that's all that matters. Come inside and I'll put the kettle on. A cup of tea is what we're both in need of.'

'I'm sorry, Gran.' The tears came, then. 'I'm sorry you were worried and sorry you were alone last night.'

'But I was all right. Jonty came.'

'Yes. Kath said.' She should have remembered. 'And, Gran – I – I . . .'

'Yes?' *Tell me. Tell me about your airman.*

'Nothing. Just that I – I was afraid last night, that's all.' *I want to tell you about Paul, but I can't. I love you, but I can't tell you about how it is between us. Not just yet.* 'And I need that cup of tea. I really do.' *Some day soon, I'll tell you, Gran. When Paul has done his tour and we know he'll be safe for a while. I'll bring him home, then.* 'And I'm truly sorry – for missing the train.' *For lying about Paul and me when all I want is for you both to meet and like each other and for you to let me marry him.*

But you won't let me. You'll say I'm too young and that I'll understand, some day, that you were right. You'll say it because you've forgotten what it's like to be young and in love; desperately, hurtingly in love. 'Forgiven, Gran?'

Kath was still not back from the milk-round when Roz hung her coat behind the dairy door and rolled up her sleeves. But there was plenty to do and she was glad of the quiet; glad to be here, where there'd been no bombs. Paul would be back by now, and the two Waafs. She hoped it would be all right about their kit.

Fear ran through her again just thinking of it and she took a deep breath, willing herself to be calm. It wasn't only the air-raid; it was being found out. Gran knew, and Jonty, and there'd have to be more lies. It wasn't fair, which was stupid, wasn't it, when people were always saying that all was fair in love and war. Plain stupid. She flung round as the door opened, already on the defensive.

'Well, Roz, I hope it was worth it?' Jonty stood there, his face a mask of anger. 'I hope it was worth all the worry you caused? And how did you get back so early?'

'I hitched a lift, if it's any of your business. As soon as the all-clear went, we –'

'*We?*' His face flushed darkly.

'Yes! *We*. Me and two Waafs. An army lorry stopped for us.'

'Then why didn't you do that last night? Why didn't you hitch a lift then?'

'I would have, if I'd known what was going to happen. If I'd known about the air-raid, I'd never have gone to York, would I?' She breathed in deeply, trying to be calm, to bite hard on the anger that made her want to fling the truth at him. But he knew already, didn't he? And maybe Kath was right; maybe he *was* in love with her. 'But don't say you're glad to see me; glad I'm all right!'

'Glad to see you?' His hands reached for her shoulders, his fury erupting as he shook her violently. 'All right? God, you don't deserve to be all right! You were with the airman, weren't you? You were with him! *All night*. You're a tramp, Roz; a *tart*!'

Her hand flew high and wide then she slammed it into his face with all the force she could muster. White-faced, wild-eyed she spat, 'Don't ever do that again! Don't *ever* touch me again! You are not my keeper; you are not my lover; you are – you are *nothing*!' She pushed into him, and bewildered by the fury of her attack he stood aside to let her pass. 'Never – ever – touch me again!'

Head down, she ran blindly. Across the yard, across the orchard and up the lane that led to the village. Climbing the field gate she made blindly for the haystack, almost gone now, and throwing herself face down on it she began to weep with great, tearing sobs.

'I *hate* you, Jonty!'

Her fists beat her fury into the ground. She hated him for knowing about last night; hated him for dirtying it for her. But most of all she hated him because he'd made her hate herself.

She wept until there were no tears left; sobbed out the terror that had been York, their lovely night spoiled. And she cried shame for her lies and because Jonty had called her a tramp and a tart, and that had hurt.

She sat hugging her knees, fighting fresh tears. How long she had been there she didn't know.

'So this is where you've got to?' It was Kath. 'Jonty sent me to look for you. Trouble, was there?'

'I hit him.'

She wondered how Kath could be so calm, so matter-of-fact about it all. But Kath was like that. There was a quietness in her that made her that way. She had survived a lot of air-raids, hadn't she, though she never talked about it and she hardly cried at all that day she'd fallen from the stack. But then, it wouldn't do if everyone in the world were the same; if everyone had red hair, and a temper to match it.

'Hit him? Silly thing to do, wasn't it?'

'He asked for it. He shook me, then he called me a tramp, and a tart!'

'He'd been worried about you. And jealous, too, I shouldn't wonder. You aren't helping yourself any by getting into a state about it. What's done is done. It was just bad luck about the air-raid, that's all.' She offered a handkerchief. 'Here. Dry your eyes and blow your nose and let's be having you. We're behind with the work as it is, and I've still got a flat tyre to see to.'

Roz did as she was told, fear, anger, guilt all gone. Now she was drained of all emotion. She couldn't even feel shame.

'God, Kath, who'd be young? Just who, will you tell me? Right now I wish I were old, *really* old – or that I'd never been born. I just feel numb.'

'I know, love.' Kath laid an arm across the dejected, drooping shoulders. 'But things'll be better tomorrow. You need a good night's sleep. We all do. And just to help you feel a little bit better, there's the milking parlour to be mucked-out.'

Her mouth tilted into a smile, then she began to laugh and Roz laughed with her. There wasn't anything else to do.

10

There was a new word; a word to add to blitz and gone for a burton and civvy and conchie and prang. *Baedeker*. One more for the vocabulary of wartime slang: the German word for reprisal.

'Another Baedeker raid. It was on the lunchtime news. Did you hear it, Kath?'

'No. I ate my sandwiches outside. Reprisal for what? They've already had a go at Exeter and Bath and Norwich. Now York. *Why?*'

'Because they're all precious old places; mediaeval, or with beautiful architecture. It's senseless. Seems it's because of that thousand-bomber raid of ours on Cologne.'

'Did Paul's family have any bomb damage?'

'No. He lives in a little place outside Bath.' Roz pushed wide the gate. 'Wouldn't you know it? Those stupid things always take themselves off to the bottom end of the field just before milking. I swear they can tell the time. We'd better hurry them up. No use calling them.' They set off for the far corner of the pasture where the herd cropped steadily at the grass, swinging irritated tails at flies. 'It was as if that raid had never happened when I got back to Alderby this morning.'

'Bad, was it?' Kath sensed her need to talk.

'Awful. It was a lovely afternoon when I met Paul. The station was a happy place then, yet next morning it was bombed and blazing and people still buried under the rubble. It was like a warning not to get too smug.'

'I know, love. Air-raids we can all do without. But try not to think about it. You and Paul were lucky.'

'I suppose we were. Seems neither of us could have ghosted through the graveyard last Friday night.'

'Oh, for heaven's sake! You're not still on about that St Mark's Eve thing?'

'Not really. Just a bit edgy. I need to see Paul. It seemed wrong this morning, not kissing him. He just said, "See you" and walked off with the Waafs, as if we didn't know each other. I wish it didn't have to be that way.'

'It needn't be. I still think you should tell your gran. She'd understand. I know she would.'

'And I know she *wouldn't*. Oh, don't let's talk about it. Let's get this lot seen to. The sooner milking's over, the sooner I can go home. And listen! There it is – a cuckoo at last! Turn your money. Make a wish.'

'*You* turn your money. I heard my cuckoo yesterday, after you'd gone. Only had a few coppers in my pocket, though. Does it matter?'

'Matter? Yesterday was the twenty-eighth, you jammy beggar. That's the lucky day for hearing your first cuckoo. Hope you wished for something really good, Kath.'

'No. I just turned my money over, and left it at that.'

She'd heard that first cuckoo loud and clear as she walked across the stackyard to the poultry arks in the two-acre field and had gasped with pleasure and jingled the pennies in her pocket. But she hadn't wished. She hadn't dared. When you want something you know is wrong, you don't push your luck. So she had shaken that almost-wish from her mind and counted the cuckoo calls instead. One for every year of life still to come, hadn't Roz said? And it had called and called. It was still calling when she got to the poultry field and Marco had beckoned her over to the hazel hedge to show her a blackbird's nest with five blue eggs in it.

That cuckoo had gone on calling till she thought she must surely live for ever. But it was only superstition. She was getting as bad as Roz and Polly. Even if she had made that wish, nothing could have come of it.

'I was talking to Arnie the other day. He said he's seen fox cubs playing on the outcrop on Tuckets Hill. Come on, you stupid creature!' Roz slapped the rump of the old lead-cow. 'I thought I might take Paul up there to see them tonight. Why didn't you make a wish?'

'I thought we were talking about fox cubs.' Butterfly-minded; that's what Roz was. Flitted from one thing to the next like the pretty, fey creature she was. 'And I don't know why I didn't wish.'

'Well, you should have. And where's Marco this afternoon?'

'Haven't a clue.' Not all that long ago she'd wondered exactly the same thing. 'Last time I saw him he was talking to Mat. Why do you ask?'

'No reason. Just that he ought to be giving a hand with the milking, that's all.'

'My, but you *are* in a hurry to be off home.'

'Yes, I am. I could do with a bath and, as I said, I need to see Paul.' Get as far from Home Farm as she could; away from Jonty so that she need neither speak to him nor look at him. Not after what he'd said this morning. 'So tell me why you wasted such a lucky wish, though I bet you had a sly one and you're not letting on. You went as red as a beetroot when I mentioned it. Tell me. Your secrets are safe with me.'

'Secrets? What on earth do you mean?' The reply came too quickly.

'There you are! You're doing it again. You're blush-ing!'

'All right – so I'm blushing. And it isn't funny, Roz, so you can wipe that silly smirk off your face right now!'

'Sorry, love. Just teasing. Forget it.'

'All right. And you forget it, too – okay?'

Just teasing, Kath brooded, tight-lipped. She hadn't

been blushing though she should have been, just to think of the things that kept coming into her head lately. And it was as well she hadn't made that cuckoo-wish, because if she had and if it had come true, she'd surely have regretted it.

It was just that all at once she felt lonely and alone. Lately there'd been this awful thing that wouldn't go away; a longing, almost, to be near to someone. Not to have an affair, but just sometimes to have someone to care for her. Not to be in love like Roz; not wildly and dangerously, without thought for tomorrow, but to have a gentle loving – a cherishing, maybe, to help take the edge off her aloneness.

All right – so there was Barney. But Barney was miles away and his letters – when they came – gave her no comfort at all. They made her feel worse, in fact – rebellious, almost, and she had longed to wish for someone to share things with. Even though she had Barney, she was still alone, had been all her life, come to think of it. Marrying Barney hadn't changed a thing.

They walked in silence, back to the milking parlour, neither speaking until they drew near to the farmhouse. Then Roz pointed to Marco, busy outside the kitchen door.

'Look! That's where he is. He's mending your puncture.'

'It – it's good of him.' Marco mending her puncture? She dropped her eyes as he looked up and waved, forcing her thoughts to the bicycle she had left behind in Birmingham. Tin Lizzie. Old and black-painted, the first thing she had ever owned. And she remembered the cheeky young lorry driver who had mended another puncture in another life; another faraway life she seemed not to want to remember.

'By the way – I forgot to tell you, Roz. There was a letter for me when I got back to the hostel last night.'

'Good. Been a long time since you heard, hasn't it?'

'Yes. More than three weeks. Said he'd been away on a

long convoy, whatever that is, but he didn't say where. But I suppose he couldn't, though, because of the Censor.'

'Suppose not,' Roz offered uneasily, wondering why, suddenly, Kath looked as if she were about to burst into tears. But it was turning out to be that kind of day, wasn't it, with everyone snappy and tired because of last night.

Paul, I miss you. And I want you so much. Be there, tonight; please be there.

Polly walked purposefully to Alderby and the bay-windowed house set back off the Green, six newly-laundered shirts in her basket. This was Wednesday and not even last night could be allowed to interfere with delivery day.

My, but they'd sounded near, those bombs. It was as the Manchester lady had remarked in one of her rare moments of communication: one small error from the one who let the bombs go: one second earlier or later and they could have landed slap bang on Alderby.

The postman had been late this morning, partly because of York sorting office being inconvenienced by it all and partly because every isolated farmhouse and cottage had expected him to tell them all about it. But he'd brought no pink-enveloped letters, and for that she was grateful.

It had been terrible, though, to hear about the railway station and the carriage works – and as for those poor nuns! But the bombs had missed the Minster, thanks be, though that must surely be what the Luftwaffe had come for. Doing no harm to a soul that old place wasn't; stood there for hundreds of years and the pride of the three Ridings. But those Nazis had no respect for history and tradition. Be just like them to come back tonight, Polly brooded, and have another try at getting it.

Indignantly she opened the gate and took the path to the back door. Then straightening her shoulders, she lifted the knocker.

'Ah, Miss Appleby. Terrible last night, wasn't it just?'

Mrs Murgatroyd handed over two half-crowns. 'Would you have a moment to step inside? The kettle's just on the boil – thought you'd be here before very much longer. Sit down, my dear, do.' She laid the shirts on the dresser with care, indicating a chair with a nod of her head. Having already exhausted the subject of the air-raid, she was eager to talk of other things. Clearing her throat delicately, she murmured, 'The business about which we spoke, Miss Appleby . . .'

'Ah, yes.' The legal advice. Mr Murgatroyd's considered opinion on Arnie's mother and her goings on.

'My husband has come to the conclusion that most things considered, you have a good case for keeping the lad. There's a but, though, and a big one. Proof, Mr Murgatroyd says.

'Now the good God gave us ladies one thing he chose not to give to men. He gave us instinct and *we* know, don't we, what Arnold's mother is up to. But the law demands proof and that, sadly, we do not have.'

'We do not,' Polly echoed mournfully.

'But the welfare of a young boy is most important and there is one way left open to us. Bluff, Miss Appleby, a little bluff and deception. It just might work, though you'll have to be mightily careful how you go about it.'

She paused for the effect of her words to be fully considered, pouring the tea carefully into her second-best china cups. Then, pushing the sugar bowl across the table as if rationing had ceased to exist, she looked to left and right and murmured, 'Mr Murgatroyd is of the opinion that you should write to Hull without delay. Make it a brief but friendly letter telling Arnold's mother that he is well and that she'll be welcome to visit him whenever she has the mind to – though a postcard first would be appreciated.

'Then if your suspicions are correct – that for some reason she wants the boy back – you can be sure that

214

before many weeks have passed she'll be paying you a call. That will be the time when bluff and deception might prove to be the saving of young Arnold. Not that Mr Murgatroyd agrees with deceit and deception – in his position he can't, you know. Ah, no. This is something I have worked out for myself. When you have heard what I have to say, then I'm sure – given luck – that you'll have nothing more to fear in *that* direction. Tea all right for you, my dear? Well then.' She looked round again, then, leaning across the table, lowering her voice and raising her eyebrows, she whispered, 'And this is what I think you must do . . .'

Arnie was waiting at the back gate when Polly puffed up Ridings' carriage drive. Rarely was she out when school was over, but today she had stayed overlong at the bay-windowed house though, goodness, it had been worth it. It only went to show that it wasn't what a body knew, but who. Now her eyes gleamed with the spirit of conflict, and if that one from Hull tried any of her tricks, Polly Appleby would be ready and waiting for her.

'Now then, lovey. Been waiting long, have you? Got kept at Mrs Murgatroyd's, see. You should have got the key from the shed.'

'Didn't want to. I've been watching things.'

'Oh?'

'When will it be summer, Aunty Poll?'

'Not till the swallows come, and the old cuckoo gets here.'

'Then it *is* summer. I've heard a cuckoo and I've seen a swallow, so can I go into my short socks now?'

'*One* swallow, was it?'

'Yes, but it *was* a swallow.'

'Ah, then maybe you'll have to wait a while yet, 'cause it's a well-known saying around these parts that one swallow don't make a summer, Arnie. You'll have to wait till you've seen one or two more. That one little bird on his own might have been sent on ahead to see how the land lies. Can't rely on *one*. One doesn't count. Now out you go for five minutes while I make us a pot of tea.' She deserved a sup of tea after all the conspiring and plotting that had gone on. 'Supper won't be long.'

'I'm starving. What are we having?'

'Egg salad and baked apples. Now shift yourself out of my way while I get the kettle on. And while you're about it, fetch a few logs from the back, there's a good lad.' The day had been warm. Arnie might be forgiven for thinking that summer had come, but tonight could be sharp with cold as could all April evenings and a nice wood fire would be pleasant to sit over; to sit over, and think.

Arnie filled the log basket and set it at the back door, then leaning chin on hand at the gate he gazed into the sky. One or two more swallows, that's all it needed, and summer would really be here. Then he could do without his long, scratchy stockings, take off his pullover and paddle in the beck, go bird-nesting and look for tadpoles; all the lovely summer things that made being at Aunty Poll's so smashing.

Anxiously, he scanned the sky.

'I think,' Roz murmured, sitting hands round knees, 'that we aren't going to see the cubs tonight. The vixen must've got scent of us and holed them up somewhere.'

'There'll be other nights. Want one?' He offered his cigarette packet.

'Please, love. Light it for me?'

It was quiet and deserted on Tuckets Hill and from here they could see over to Peddlesbury and Alderby and, to the left, chimneys showing over the treetops, the house she lived in.

'Foxes are vermin, aren't they?' He placed the cigarette between her lips.

'Most farmers think so, but fox cubs are pretty little creatures even baby pigs are nice – all pink and squeaky. Isn't it peaceful here? Can you believe that last night happened when there's all this?' She waved an expansive arm. 'Can you?'

This beauty that was April. The freshness, the newness of everything. April was winter gone, green things growing and the promise of warm, sunny days. April was drifts of blossom, pale, delicate leaves, cuckoos and butterflies. It was young, as she and Paul were young. These were their green years and their love was April love.

'I'd like to make a picture of all this,' she said softly, 'to store inside me so I'd have it always.'

'And last night, too? The raid?'

'That as well, I suppose, because of us being together, though it's this time and this place I'd want most to remember fifty years from now, and you and me being young. When I'm old and wise, darling, I shall wonder why I ever worried about now.'

'You're so sure, aren't you, Roz?' He laid his cheek on her head, loving the softness of her hair, its newly-washed scent.

'Very sure. It's going to come right for us. You'll finish your tour and Gran will let us get married – well, engaged at least – and I'll meet your parents, and Pippa. And that'll only be the start of it. But I *am* sure.'

'Always love me? Always be my luck, Roz?'

'I will, my darling.'

They sat, hands clasped, lapsing into silence, wondering if the terror of last night had happened and grateful that they were here together.

'I don't think we're going to see the cubs,' he said, sending his cigarette end spinning.

'Not tonight.'

'It's so tranquil up here – so apart, isn't it?'

'Just you and me, Paul.'

'Want to go?'

'No, darling. Let's stay.' She searched with her lips for his own. 'Love me?'

'Hullo, lass. Still parky outside, is it?'

'Just a bit, but it's going to be another warm day.' Kath had poked her head round the kitchen door to say good morning and let Grace know she was here. 'Want anything doing before I start on the milk?'

'No, but spare me a minute, will you? Tell me what's going on between Roz and our Jonty.'

'Sorry?' Kath hoped her frown was convincing because not for anything would she admit to knowing of the harsh words there'd been about York. 'Hadn't noticed anything.'

'Oh, happen it's only me poking my nose into what doesn't concern me, and it isn't anything I can put a finger on, but –'

'Sure you aren't imagining it?'

'Maybe I am.' Grace took off her reading glasses and laid them on the kitchen table. 'I hope so. And it's no business of mine, is it?'

'What are you doing?' Kath had not meant to change tack so obviously, but there seemed no alternative if she wasn't to pile lie upon lie.

'You might well ask. It's counterfoil time again and I can't abide it. Surname, Christian name and address. Wish we lived in a place that didn't take so much writing out.'

Soon it would be time to exchange old, used-up ration books for new ones, but before that could be done counterfoils for all the basic commodities, even for clothing coupons, must be laboriously completed in neat block letters. Such a lot of bother for so little food.

'Leave them. I'll do a bit of filling-in for you at

lunchtime.' Kath picked up one of the books. 'Ramsden J. J.? That's Jonty, isn't it?'

'Aye. Jonathan James. Called for Mat's father, and mine.'

'He's lucky. Wish I knew who I'm called for.'

'Now then, our Kath. Thought we'd got that business settled long ago,' Grace admonished. 'Thought we'd decided it wasn't who you are, but what you are. And yes, happen there is something you can do for me. Fill yon kettle and put it on to boil. We'll have a cup of tea and be hanged to the dairy for ten minutes! Then pop over to the milking parlour and ask Jonty if he wants a cup, will you?'

'And Mat?'

'No. Mat's over at Ridings looking at the potatoes. Fuss, fuss, fuss. Worrying about frost getting at them, though I told him there'd be no frost, now that May's here.'

'There was no frost this morning.' Kath could understand Mat's worrying, for all that. Tender, newly-sprouted potato tops could be blighted by one late frost and all the work of ploughing, and harrowing and planting would count for nothing. 'Cold and sharp and a heavy dew, but no frost.'

'I know. I told him, but when that man's got a bee in his bonnet he'll listen to no one. And he wants me to have a word with you.'

'What about?' Kath took mugs from the mantel. 'Something I've done?'

'No. It's about your leave – your time off. Had you thought about when you'd like to go?'

Go on leave? Dismayed, Kath shook her head. She hadn't even thought about it. Time off would be nice, she supposed, but where was she to spend it? Only at Birmingham. Imagine? A week of Aunt Min's troubles and woes; seven long days of queues for this and queues for that and the risk of air-raids, like as not.

'Does Mat want me to go now?'

'Towards the end of the month would be as good a time as any, Kath. Before much longer there'll be work to be done on the root crops and after that there'll be the hay to be got in, then the wheat and barley . . .'

'I hadn't given it a lot of thought, truth known.' She really hadn't. But perhaps she hadn't wanted to think about that other life and the house she'd lived in with Barney; a week of being reminded of him and feeling guilty, and Aunt Min doing nothing to help relieve that guilt.

'Well, put your mind to it and let us know as soon as you can.'

'Okay. I will. I'll have a word with Flora or the Warden about it.' She stirred her tea, frowning. 'I – I'm sure it'll be all right.'

'You don't sound over sure. Anything wrong?' Grace demanded, bluntly. 'You *are* settled with us? You're happy here, lass?'

'Nothing's wrong.' Kath looked up, smiling. 'And I'm happy here, Grace. Wouldn't mind settling in for the duration – if you want me, that is.'

Happy? Too happy, that's what. Too happy for her own good.

It was a little after noon as Roz crossed the orchard that Jonty called to her to stop.

'Look, Roz, this thing has gone on long enough.' His face wore the worried expression that once would have caused her to laugh and say that of course it had; that she'd been going to say she was sorry, anyway. In the past they had quarrelled often then made up with a kiss and a hug, but not now. The old, easy ways were over.

'Has it? Well, it can go on a whole lot longer, as far as I'm concerned.' She made to climb the fence but he moved quickly, barring her way.

'Don't, Roz. We've got to work together – can't we at

220

least try to be civil, if only for Mum's sake? She knows something's wrong between us.'

'Then you should have thought about that when you stuck your nose in and presumed to become keeper of my morals. I'm sorry Grace is upset, but why don't you tell her what it's all about? Why don't you tell her you called me a tart? Go on. Tell her!'

Her chin jutted defiance though she was afraid inside. Jonty had the right to be angry – the Jonty she had looked on as a brother, that was. But everything had changed now. The easiness between them was gone and she didn't know how to cope with a Jonty who loved and wanted her.

'I'm sorry. I'd no right to say what I did. I overstepped the mark, didn't I?'

'You did, Jonty, so let's leave it at that, shall we?'

'And we're speaking again?'

'I suppose so. If we must. Only as long as you stop treating me like your kid sister and stop thinking that anything I do is any business of yours.'

'Point taken.' She was offering crumbs, but he'd settle for that. He looked at her with sadness, acknowledging that the time for hoping was over. He would never have her. She belonged to someone else; to a man who wore a glamorous uniform and lived life on a knife edge. 'And okay – you've grown up. I admit it.'

Hesitantly he held out his hand but she would not take it. She couldn't let him touch her; not now that everything was out in the open. He mustn't love her. She belonged to Paul.

'Then don't ever forget it, Jonty.'

'I won't.' His face was grave and pale with misery.

She turned abruptly then, and walked away, head high, shoulders taut, with an ache inside her for an innocence lost.

Sorry, Jonty. So sorry . . .

11

Kath set down the basket of eggs then leaned on the gate that connected Two-acre field to the larger of the cow pastures, watching Marco and Roz as they coaxed the slow-moving herd for afternoon milking.

Egg collecting was pure pleasure now that the flock was laying well again, remembering the sad sight of the near-featherless hens in their winter moult. It was good to see them in full feather once more, their fat, fluffy bottoms wobbling from side to side as they scratched for food. Now she must sort the day's gathering of eggs and pack them ready for collection, a task that made a change, she supposed, from milking.

Chin on hand she watched the lazy progress of the clumsy cows and the two who chatted so easily together. They were so different. Roz with her pale, freckle-dotted face, her hair a flame of red; Marco lean and muscled, stripped to the waist, his skin flushed to a warm apricot, his black hair tousled.

She gazed, squinting against the brightness of the sun as Roz leaned nearer, saw the mischief in her face as she whispered in his ear. Then Marco's shout of laughter and his smile. Such a ready, happy smile had this Italian with whom they must not fraternize; this enemy liked by everyone here – apart from Mrs Fairchild, of course. And how would she react to see them now, laughing together. Such bitterness inside her, and Marco the whipping-boy for a long-ago sniper's bullet.

Kath held up her hand, calling 'Marco! Over here!' and he looked up then hurried to where she stood.

'*Ciao*, Kat.' Again that special smile. 'I carry the eggs for you?'

'Thanks. And Marco – where is your jacket?'

He took off his jacket as often as he could. Maybe because he liked the touch of the sun on his body, maybe because he disliked the bright yellow patch sewn on the back – the symbol of his captivity. Did removing that jacket make him feel less a prisoner and more an ordinary young soldier who might not see his home for many years?

'Why you ask, Kat? Is in the same place like always: behind the barn door.'

'Well, be careful when you put it on. I'll slip a few eggs in the pocket for you. Is there somewhere you can cook them in the camp?'

He said there was, murmuring '*Grazie*', taking her hand, holding it briefly. 'You come now and help with the milking?'

'Not tonight. There's the eggs to see to and I – I won't be seeing you for a while. Tomorrow I'm going home, you see –' She stopped abruptly, wishing she had not said the one word that brought pain and longing to his eyes.

'Ah, home. I shall miss you, Kat.'

'Only for a week.' She wanted to explain that she wasn't really going home; that Peacock Hey and this farm were home to her now but instead she said, 'The eggs will be a little going-away present – but don't tell Grace.'

They walked unspeaking to the foldyard gate, with Roz already through it and urging the unwilling cows into their stalls. For just a second Kath hesitated, knowing she should not have; knowing she should have taken the basket and walked away from him. But she stood there, uncertain, knowing he would kiss her, wanting him to, closing her eyes as his forefinger tilted her chin.

It was a gentle kiss, without passion. They stood on opposite sides of the gate so they hadn't even touched. A kiss between friends, that's all it was, she insisted silently. Brief, though warm and firm, a parting kiss she had begged for with her eyes.

'*Arrivederci*, Kat. Come back soon. Take care.'

'And you, Marco. See you . . .'

Eyes down, cheeks flaming she walked quickly away. A kiss between friends, nothing more. Yet it had been good. She had wanted it, needed it, and he had recognized that need; answered the asking in her eyes.

So it was best she should be going away. By the time she returned that kiss would be forgotten – by both of them. It must be. Marco was her enemy, Barney's enemy; a prisoner of war with whom there should be no contact. It was as simple as that, and she should be ashamed of what she had just done.

So why then wasn't she?

Roz skirted the old game-cover, green now with young, growing potatoes, and climbed the stile that led to Ridings' garden and the red-brick ruins, covered now with a flush of clematis and wisteria. Warm from the sun they stood, their winter starkness banished in a disorder of pink, purple and white. This was the way she liked to see the old walls. Soon they would be even more beautiful, with climbing roses nodding through empty stone windows and the honeysuckle soon to flower, throwing its scent on the evening air.

She didn't resent the bespoiling as Gran did. This was the only way she had known this part of the house, so she could never dip into the past and remember tapestry-hung walls nor furniture that smelled of beeswax nor fires that burned in old, wide grates no longer there.

Through the empty, yawning door-arch she glimpsed the flagged courtyard laid down by the father she could not remember and the black-painted iron seat so pleasant to sit upon on summer afternoons. That seat, Gran said, stood where once the foot of the stairs had been; where a grand staircase made from holly wood had been polished twice a day.

Dear, remembering old house. Roz loved it in its poverty as her grandmother had loved it in its grandness. To Hester Fairchild, Ridings was no more now than a servants' wing and a ruin of flower-covered walls; to Roz it was the home she loved.

Skirting the mounting-block she hurried across the kitchen yard, pushing open the door, calling 'Hullo? Only me!'

'Roz?' Hester laid down the printed form she had been frowning over.

'Can't stay, Gran. Only popped in to change my shoes. And I might be a bit late for supper, with Kath gone on leave.'

'Spare me a minute, Roz. Can we have a talk? You've *got* to tell me about –'

But Roz was already away, boots in hand, calling ''Bye!' defences up against the probing.

Hester sighed. She was to be told nothing; certainly nothing about York. It was beginning to alarm her. Roz had always been so frank and open.

'Deary me – why the sigh?' Polly demanded from the doorway. 'And where's she tearing off to now?'

'She just called in for something. Didn't even give me time to ask her if she wanted a cup of tea.' Hester held up the pot. 'Want one? I can't drink all this myself.'

Polly looked at the kitchen clock. Five more minutes was neither here nor there and the blanket washing had been warm work.

'Best keep an eye on the clothes line,' she warned. 'Looks as if we're in for a drop of rain.'

'I will. It was good of you to help, Polly – even though something's been worrying you for days. And don't say it hasn't,' she hastened, 'because you always chew on your lip when you're worried.'

'Aye. There *is* something.' Polly was glad to talk. 'It's Arnie, see – or rather that dratted mam of his.'

225

'Mrs Bagley? I was beginning to think she'd ceased to exist.'

'And so was I. Hoped we'd never have sight nor sound of her again. But lately I've had my doubts. It's my opinion she's of a mind to have him back with her.'

'Take him back? Surely not, when he's doing so well with you? And Hull is still getting air-raids. She'd be mad even to think of it, no matter how much she misses him.'

'Ha! That one don't miss him at all. Was glad for him to be evacuated out of her way, if I'm any judge. So why's she all of a sudden taking an interest, will you tell me? Twice since Christmas she's sent money and it ain't like her. She's up to something. But best be getting back or the lad'll be home before me. Now don't forget what I told you. Keep an eye on those blankets.'

'I will. And don't worry too much about Arnie's mother – not until it happens. When I get myself into a state I think about something Martin used to say. "Hester, my love," he'd tell me, "when will you get it into your head that nothing ever matters half so much as we think it does – *nothing*." And you know, Polly, he was right – well, almost always.'

'Aye.' Polly smiled, remembering him handsome in his uniform as if it were only yesterday; remembering her own young man, too. 'And come to think of it, there's some lying in foreign fields as would like nothing more than to have our problems to worry them. We should think on about that, when we imagine we're being badly done to.' She pushed back her chair and unfastened her pinafore. 'And happen the Master was right. When you look back, most of what we worried about didn't happen, only we never seem to realize it at the time.'

'I think you may be right. See you in the morning, Polly. Take care.'

'I will. And when you're getting yourself all worried,

remember that nothing is half as bad as we think it's going to be.'

Nothing, Polly? Hester demanded silently. Not having your husband killed, nor your home burned down, nor losing your daughter and your unborn son; the boy Martin so longed for? And most cruel of all, knowing you should never have –

But she wouldn't think about that. Not once had Martin blamed or reproached her for it, nor Toby either, come to that. And she still had Roz, even though they seemed to be growing apart when they ought to be closer than ever now that Roz was a woman, and in love.

Martin, I miss you so, she yearned inside her. *Why did they take you from me?*

Arnie reached the gate lodge as Polly turned into the drive and he stood, shoulders heaving, taking deep gulps of air so she wouldn't know he'd been running; running like the wind to get home before she did so she wouldn't know he'd heard.

They hadn't known he'd been there outside the door, listening to what they were saying about him and Mam. He'd thought to go home by way of Ridings and call for Aunty Poll who'd gone there to oblige with the blanket wash; thought it would be nice to have a chat with Mrs Fairchild and tell her about the swans that were nesting on the riverbank. Then, just as he'd been going to push open the door he'd heard them talking about him and he'd stood there, listening like Aunty Poll said he never should and oh, how he wished now that he hadn't.

But he wasn't going back to Hull. Not ever. Mam could take him if she wanted, but he'd run away. And he'd keep running away till she got sick of it. It wasn't as if he could remember what Mam looked like. He'd tried to, a lot of times, but it hadn't been any use. All he could remember was being alone and afraid sometimes, and the good hidings. There'd been plenty of those hidings and him being told he was a nuisance and a naughty boy and that if he didn't behave himself they'd come from the Workhouse to take him away. He could remember that, too.

But just let her try to get him back. It wouldn't be as easy as she thought because she didn't know about the secret place; didn't know about the big oak tree at the end of Beck Lane. He hadn't told anybody about it, not even Aunty Poll, and none of them knew what a good climber he was or how he often sat there, high up at the forking of the branch. Safe as houses it was and he could see for miles and miles; see everyone who got off the bus, everyone who came anywhere near. They'd never find him up there, not if they looked all day. Mam would have to give up and go back to Hull without him, because he wasn't going. He wasn't!

Kath took a deep, sighing breath and straightened her shoulders. She was back; back in Birmingham almost glad that it was raining and if – just *if* – she'd forgotten the number of the house after so long away, then surely she must know that the one outside which she stood was the one she had left almost five months ago. There could be no mistaking it. This was the house with the whitest lace curtains in the street, the most brilliantly polished door knocker, the shiniest of windows. Barney's aunt had claimed this house for her own and loved it now, Kath frowned, almost as much as the London house the Luftwaffe had left in a pile of rubble. Housework was her religion; her home was her joy and wherever Min Jepson lived was home.

Kath stood outside the house she had come to as a bride, feeling like a stranger, an intruder. It seemed smaller than she remembered after the spaciousness of Ridings and Peacock Hey and you could, she supposed, fit the whole of its downstairs area into Home Farm kitchen.

Turning her key in the lock she pushed open the door, setting down her case, calling 'Hullo, there? It's Kath.'

The room had not changed. Barney's photographs still stood on the piano top and she turned her head from the smile of Barney in uniform and eyes she would rather not meet.

'Kath, for Gawd's sake!' The kitchen door opened. 'Why on earth didn't you knock, girl?'

'Sorry, Aunt Min.' Knock? On her own front door? 'Having a little nap? Did I wake you?' She bent to brush the lined cheek with her lips.

'No, I wasn't,' came the sharp reply. 'But why didn't you think to write and tell me you was coming?'

'I didn't know for certain till a couple of days ago.' And had she known she'd be so unwelcome she wouldn't have come, because she hadn't wanted to; she really hadn't.

'Not at all sure the spare bed's aired . . .'

'Not to worry. A hot-water bottle, perhaps?'

'Ar,' the older woman grudgingly conceded. 'I suppose so, though you should have asked, Kath. It might not have been convenient to have you. I might've been spring-cleaning and where would we have been, then? But you'd better take your coat off, now that you're here. Have you got your rations with you?'

'No, but they gave me a ration card at the hostel. And I've brought you a soap coupon, too.'

Soap. That would please her. If there was anything Aunt Min liked more than washing and scrubbing her home it was washing and scrubbing herself.

'I suppose you'll be wanting a cup of tea?'

'I'd love one – if you're putting the kettle on.'

'Always do, round about this time. You're losing weight, Kath Allen. Not feeding you at that hostel?'

'I'm eating well. The food is good and we don't go hungry. But I do a man's work now. You don't get fat,

229

labouring on a farm. I feel very fit, though. I'm really enjoying it.'

'Must admit you've got a bit more colour in your face, girl. Too pale you was. Barney won't know his own wife when he comes home. Must be terrible for him out there. All that sand and heat and you enjoying yourself, living off the fat of the land. You shouldn't have gone, Kath. Barney's still upset at what you did.'

'Upset? Why d'you say that?'

''Cause he told me. In his letters. Says it all the time.'

Kath met the blank gaze, wishing that sometimes Aunt Min would smile. But her face always wore the same pained expression, as if she'd just sucked on a lemon.

'So you hear from Barney?' she murmured, keeping her voice even.

'Lor' bless you, yes.' Minnie Jepson stirred the contents of the teapot with relish. 'Writes regular. Every week there's a letter. Last time I heard he'd just been on convoy duty.'

'Yes. A long convoy, he said. What does he mean,' Kath frowned, 'a *long* convoy?'

'Don't rightly know, girl. Maybe he meant he was away from base a long time or maybe he meant there was a lot of ambulances – you know – stretching a long way back. Make a nice change from the desert, though, those few nights in Alexandria – or was it Cairo?'

'Cairo? But how can you know that?' Kath felt uneasy. Or was it angry? Nowhere in his letters to her had Barney mentioned driving ambulances. 'Telling you where he'd been just wouldn't get past the Censor. Place-names are always blue-pencilled.'

'No, and he didn't tell me – not exactly.' Taking a clean tea-towel, Minnie Jepson polished two already-clean cups and saucers. 'But where else would he find a good billet for a few nights and have a night out with the lads except in one of them two places? Where else would he be able to get a few pints of decent beer, will you tell me?'

Kath could not tell her. Barney hadn't mentioned staying anywhere in the letter he'd sent to her nor of getting a pint of the beer he so missed. But Barney, it seemed, told his aunt much more than he told his wife.

'And there's something else.' The dull, gruff voice broke in on Kath's thoughts. 'Ain't got a thing for us to eat tonight.'

'Fish and chips?' Kath ventured, hopefully.

'Nah. They aren't frying tonight. Be open tomorrow night, the notice said, but where's the use in that?'

'I suppose the food queues are over for today?'

'Over and done with long ago. Didn't get so much as a couple of sausages,' Min sniffed gloomily.

'Then we'll get out early tomorrow,' Kath smiled, acknowledging how difficult it must be for a woman alone to live on such tight rations, 'and I'll stand behind you so I get some as well. There'll be enough meat on my ration card to make a dinner for the two of us. We'll manage. Tonight I'll treat you to a meal at the British Restaurant.'

Good old British Restaurants. Government sponsored and subsidized. Clean, bare, unfussy little cafés where the cook worked miracles with her meagre food allocation and could offer a meal for an unbelievable shilling. Soup, meatless pie made palatable with Oxo gravy, and saccharin-sweet stewed fruit and custard, too, if the milk ration held up.

'It'll set you back a couple of bob, girl; maybe half a crown,' the elder woman prevaricated. 'You got money, then?'

'Think I can manage two-and-six, Aunt Min. Tomorrow night I'll queue at the chip shop and that'll be another meal for us.' It was a long time since she'd eaten fish and chips and already the thought cheered her, even though the queue would be a long one. 'Don't worry. We'll manage all right between us. Wait till you see what I've brought you – a present, from Mrs Ramsden.'

She reached for her case, telling herself she must remember at all times never to mention Jonty, or Marco, or news of the civilian who hadn't joined up and an Italian prisoner of war would be winging by airmail to North Africa before there was time to blink.

She mustn't, Kath stressed, even *think* of Jonty or Marco – especially of Marco – because Aunt Min's pale blue eyes could look into your soul. There was something distinctly peculiar about her, of that Kath was sure. Min Jepson was the kind of woman who'd feel at home in the graveyard at Alderby St Mary, on St Mark's Eve.

'That's a posh case, Kath Allen. All covered with foreign labels, an' all. Where did you light on that, then?'

'It isn't mine. I wanted something smaller so Roz lent it to me. I've told you about Roz, Aunt Min – the girl I work with? I've brought both pairs of dungarees and my working shirts with me. Thought I'd wash them while I'm here.'

'That case is real leather. Rich, is she?'

'I don't think so. Maybe they once were, but not now.'

'Aah.' The pleasure in her face was unmistakable. She liked to hear of the gentry getting their comeuppance. Minnie Jepson didn't like toffs. Never had.

'Here you are.' Deftly Kath withdrew a package wrapped round with a towel. 'From Home Farm, for you.' She smiled. 'Careful how you open it.'

Inside the towel were six small, newspaper-wrapped parcels; inside each parcel lay a brown egg.

'For me, Kath? All of them?' Then quickly she recovered her composure. 'Told you they lived like lords, them farmers.'

'Aunt Min, that just isn't true. As a matter of fact, hens go into a moult in the autumn and winter. They lose their feathers and stop laying; they're a dead loss,

232

really. But by spring they've feathered-up again and they lay like mad. In April and May even old hens lay well. So Mrs Ramsden – Grace – said you were to have a nice boiled egg for your breakfast every morning that I'm here. I had strict instructions to make sure you did. No trying to hoard them. And be sure you don't tell anyone. Those eggs, Aunt Min, are strictly under the counter.'

'Black market, more like. End up in prison, we will.' Grumbling she placed them tenderly in a dish, whisking them away to the pantry. Six eggs, and all of them hers, was something she had not expected to see again until the war was well over; six large, country-fresh eggs could give a woman of her age a nasty hot flush, just to think of it. 'But don't worry. Nobody'll hear of it from me.'

She did not voice her thanks, but thanks had not been expected. The sudden pinking of her cheeks was as near as Aunt Min would ever come to a thank you.

'I collected them myself yesterday.'

Yesterday afternoon. She and Marco had stood at the foldyard gate and he'd kissed her goodbye. A goodbye kiss between friends, that was all. It wouldn't happen again. It must not. Another time they might not be so lucky. Next time, someone might see them and then what would happen?

'Well now; since there's no cooking to be done we can have a nice sit and listen to Music While You Work.' Aunt Min took up her knitting. 'So what does it feel like to be back? Do you *really* like bein' on a farm with all that cow muck and flies and nasty smells? Come on, girl, tell the truth. Deep down there must be times you wish you hadn't joined . . .'

'Oh, *no*, Aunt Min! It's fine, it really is. There are even times it's just – well, *marvellous*.'

'It's *what*?' Marvellous, did she say? The girl was enjoying it when no one should decently enjoy even a minute of this war. 'You surprise me, Kath Allen; you really do!'

'Oh, I didn't mean marvellous – not *that* way.' She felt her cheeks redden. 'What I really meant was how much I've learned. I drive the small tractor, now, and I can harness a horse *and* milk a cow. By hand, Aunt Min. The milking machine broke down so we all set-to and hand-milked the whole herd. It didn't take me long to learn.

'And it's all so lovely, now. You wouldn't believe how green everything is, and the hedges are white-over with May blossom. The beauty of it just takes your breath away.' She stopped, realizing she had said too much and suddenly not caring.

'Does it, now?' Lips pursed, forehead creased, the older woman concentrated on the counting of the stitches on her needle.

'Oh, *yes*. And everybody in the village is so nice; I know them all, now. Roz and I deliver the milk, you see, and Alderby is such a little place that everyone knows everyone else.'

'Do they, now?' The counting was finished. Time to dwell on a place so small that everybody knew everybody else's business. My, but that wouldn't do for Minnie Jepson. It wouldn't do at all.

She lifted her head to meet the blue eyes of her nephew's wife, gazing at her unblinking, wondering what had come over the usually pale, quiet girl Barney had married. Sitting on the chair opposite – and there was no denying it – was a very different young woman from the one who'd crept away wearing breeches, a daft hat and a worried expression. Here was a slimmer, bonnier, more confident woman; one who answered back sometimes, and seemed to be managing very nicely up there in the wilds of Yorkshire. It wouldn't do; it wouldn't do at all, and what was more she'd be failing in her duty to the soldier serving King and Country if she didn't tell him about it in her very next letter.

'Anything wrong, Aunt Min?'

'N-no. Nothing wrong, exactly, 'cept that you've changed, Kath Allen. My word, but you've changed.'

And in Minnie Jepson's considered opinion, not for the better, either!

Afternoon milking was over and Roz had almost finished cleaning out when a step in the doorway caused her to turn.

'Jonty – hullo,' she offered, cheeks flushing.

'Just wanted a quick word about the pigs.' He smiled. 'The litter is going to market on Monday – want to pick a couple out?'

Pigs. She had so much wanted two of her own, yet now –

'Oh, yes – well – I've been thinking about it as a matter of fact, and – '

'Don't worry about paying, Roz. I didn't give you anything for your birthday so they'll be a present – a sort of friends-again present.'

'But that's just it.' He was smiling at her; smiling indulgently as if nothing had changed between them and he mustn't do that. Jonty must accept the way things were, now. 'I don't think Gran was all that keen, really. The doghouses are a bit near the kitchen, come to think of it . . .'

Jonty – please understand. It's different, now. It's Paul I love. Only Paul – ever . . .

'Okay. Keep them at Home Farm with our bacon pigs. I'll mark them so you'll know which are yours.'

He took off his glasses, wiping away the insect that had settled there. Kath had been right, Roz fretted; without those heavy, dark frames he was almost handsome – if you liked tall men with weather-bronzed faces and blue eyes you just had to notice.

'No, Jonty,' she whispered to her shoes. 'Thanks all the same, but I'm off pigs for the moment. I really am. Oh,

235

you know me – mad keen one minute and the next it's something else.'

'You're sure?' Oh, yes, he knew her. He'd always thought he knew her better than she knew herself. Until she met the airman. 'You can always think about it and have a couple out of the next litter, if you change your mind.'

'No. I'm sure. They'd only be a – a *fad*.'

She had to say no. If she accepted them now she just might have to ask his help with them, his advice, sometimes. They'd always give him the excuse to come over to take a look at them and she didn't want that, either. The nearness she had taken for granted was an embarrassment now. Kath had been right. If she'd listened to Kath, hadn't dismissed her advice, maybe she wouldn't be standing here now, uneasy and apprehensive, yes, and worried, too. Because she had hurt Jonty; nothing was more certain.

But only Paul mattered. Soon he would finish his tour. By the end of June, by haytime, perhaps, S-Sugar's crew would have flown their thirtieth operation and all would come right. She would take Paul to Ridings, then, and everything could be open and above-board. Gran couldn't say that loving someone who was aircrew was asking for heartbreak because Paul would be away from flying for a time. Maybe for a whole year there would be a tomorrow for him and for Skip and the rest of the crew.

'All right, then.' He was still looking at her as if she were his kid sister; still indulging her as though he'd every right to. 'If you change your mind, you've only got to say so – or anything else you might want . . .'

'Thanks, Jonty.' She made great play of coiling the hose and hanging it on the wall. 'I'll remember. I've just about finished for tonight so I'll be off, if you don't mind. But thanks. Thanks a lot.'

She had tried to make her words impersonal and easy,

236

but she'd sounded awkward and unnatural. Imagine feeling that way with Jonty.

'Goodnight,' she whispered, kicking off her gum-boots, taking her jacket from the doornail. 'See you, then.'

Her face flamed red as she passed him, upset that she had let him make her feel this guilty, especially at a time she was already jumpy and on edge with Paul operational tonight. After four nights on stand-down, tonight was almost a certainty.

Shoulders hunched, hands in pockets, she hurried back to Ridings. If Gran said one word – just *one* word – about anything, she would blow her top. Why wasn't Kath here when she needed someone to talk to? All right – so maybe she deserved a week off, but couldn't it have waited? Did Mat have to insist that it be *now*?

She turned to look at the church clock. Nearly six. Kath would be well home by now, being fussed over, like as not, by Barney's aunt and boasting how easy it was to hand-milk a cow.

'Oh, Kath . . .' Only one day gone and already she missed her. Selfish though it was, Roz wished for the week to fly past and for Kath to be back at Home Farm again.

'*Damn!*' She jerked as rain began to fall in large, cold drops. Well, at least Mat would be happy. Mat had been grumbling for days now, saying they were in need of it – but was there ever a farmer who didn't grumble about rain, one way or another? But rain Roz Fairchild could do without; waiting in the rain for Paul who wouldn't come, anyway; trudging back home in the rain, missing him, wanting him, avoiding Gran's raised eyebrows. Then awakening to the sound of rain on her window, ears straining for the first sounds of homecoming bombers and no Kath to share the waiting and the counting with.

Oh, but this was going to be one hell of a week!

This, Kath thought miserably, would be the longest week

of her life. Rain spattered against the window from a leaking gutter; rain that hadn't stopped since the moment she stepped off the train and, to make matters worse than awful, the room was cold and the bed lumpy.

She had been mildly surprised to find she had been given the small, single room to sleep in, wondering by what right Aunt Min had moved into the bed next door. They had splashed out on that bed, Kath frowned. It had been the only concession that, come to think of it, Barney had made to married life. Now Aunt Min had taken it over just as she seemed to have taken over the rest of the house.

Without a doubt, this week would drag. Already the sight of streets and rooftops and row upon straight row of chimney stacks was beginning to make her feel hemmed in. She wanted, *needed*, the wide sky above her and to awaken to a May morning so sweet that it brought grateful tears to her eyes. She needed to be with Mat and Grace who loved each other, still; to be with the people who, in less than half a year, had become the whole of her life.

The truth must be faced. She no longer belonged in this little house. She had never belonged here. It had been a mistake to believe she ever could.

Turning restlessly, she wriggled into the depression in the middle of the mattress, wanting to be in her attic at Peacock Hey. How on earth was she to sleep when from the other side of the partition wall came the irritating sound of Aunt Min's rhythmic, contented snores?

Kath closed her eyes tightly, her cheeks flushing red. Every smallest sound could be clearly heard through the thinness of that wall. In this very bed Barney's mother had once lain, interpreting every movement, straining her ears for every word. And it wasn't as if, Kath thought, she had particularly enjoyed the sharing of that bed with Barney, so why should she care who slept in it now? She only knew she was homesick already for the noise and chatter that was Peacock Hey; wished with all her heart that tomorrow her alarm would jangle her awake and she could set out for Home Farm and Roz and Jonty. She wanted to be with them and she hoped they missed her, too.

Not Marco. She did not, must not, miss Marco. When she returned to Alderby she must see to it that never again must she find herself in a position of such nearness that a lifting of her head, a tilting upward of her chin, even, placed her lips even remotely near his own.

But you enjoyed that kiss, taunted her conscience.

All right – she'd enjoyed it. So what was she? A block of stone?

You're a married woman, Kath Allen.

'I'm lonely,' she flung back silently, resentfully. 'Barney didn't ask to be sent away . . .'

Nor did a great many husbands, but their wives don't find other men attractive; especially men who are their husbands' enemies.

All right! So Marco just happened to find himself fighting on the wrong side.

Marco Roselli is taboo. You shouldn't like him. You shouldn't want him to touch you, hold you . . .

Damn, damn, *damn*! Taking her pillow she shook it violently. All right – so for once she couldn't argue with Barney's aunt. She had changed, she wouldn't deny it. But her whole world, her whole life had changed with the coming of a war she'd been powerless to prevent. That war had taken her man and sent him to another country; sent him there without a by-your-leave and God only knew when he was coming back. And that, if it was any of Aunt Min's business, was why she had changed; because there had been no use sitting in this house counting the days and nights until she could be a wife again. That was why one day she had gone out in a flush of defiance and joined the Land Army; that and because she knew the war was offering her one brief flight into freedom; into a life she had dreamed of and longed for, thought could never be hers.

239

Well, now the dream was reality. For the first time in her life she was truly happy. She was where she belonged; where she had always known she belonged and if it had changed her then she was glad, because now she knew who she *really* was. She was Kath who was needed at Home Farm. She had thrown off her past and was her own woman for the duration of this war. There were only six more nights to spend in this uncomfortable, inhospitable bed and then she could go back to where she belonged. Only six more days of Aunt Min, then she could pack her case and go back to Peacock Hey; go *home*.

How it would be when she got there she had no idea. Yes, she *did* find Marco attractive and yes, his lips had been warm, had felt good on her own. That kiss had been her first fall from grace and it would be her last. That kiss, should she let it, could be the spark that would set her heart alight and that must not be allowed to happen. She was Barney's wife. For better for worse, till death did them part she belonged to Barney. There was no escaping it.

Viciously she slammed the flat of her hand against the wall and the rounded snorings on the other side ceased abruptly in a snort, giving way to a silence so complete that it was almost comical.

Kath closed her eyes. 'Please God,' she whispered, 'let it stop raining, no matter how much Mat needs it for the potatoes. And take care of Barney, wherever he is, whatever he's doing. And can you let this week pass quickly – *please*.'

12

Chin on hand Kath looked out at fields and hedges slipping past the compartment window, trying not to count the telegraph poles at the side of the track, still a little disbelieving of what she had done.

'The overnight train, Aunt Min? No – I think it's better to travel in the day.' Night trains were always so crowded; best she should leave a little earlier, she said.

'A *day* earlier, does it have to be?'

'Afraid so. If I miss just one connection I'd be late back. Don't want to land myself in trouble with the Forewoman.'

'Seems to me, Kath Allen, you're in too much of a hurry to be on your way. Your own home not good enough for you now – is that it?'

Her own home? It would never be her home. If she'd had doubts before, these past few days had done nothing at all to dispel them. Aunt Min was there to stay, for how could they ask her to leave when the war was over? Where could she go?

Kath had thought a lot about that, lying awake in the little room. Aunt Min was a fixture – why not accept it, and she and Barney find another house? There might even be a cottage at Alderby. Didn't Roz have houses of her own in the village? Suppose one of them became vacant? Couldn't Barney find work around Helpsley when the Army no longer needed him?

A train crashed past, travelling in the opposite direction, making her start, reminding her that soon she would be in York and only half an hour away, then, from Home Farm.

She frowned, wondering if she should have tried harder to stick it out. One more day of Aunt Min, grey, cold skies

241

and Barney's photographs on the piano top, that was all. But one more day had proved too much even to think about and she had hurried to pack her best summer dress and the gold dancing slippers, hoping Aunt Min would not discover they were gone, knowing she would; knowing she would wonder why a woman whose husband was fighting in North Africa should be in need of dancing shoes.

But her bridges were burned; she *had* packed her dancing shoes, she *had* left a day before she need and Barney would hear of it, nothing was more certain. Aunt Min and Barney were close and the day her husband came back to Birmingham was the day her troubles would really start, Kath acknowledged soberly.

But Barney wasn't coming back yet. It was a fact of life that it could be two years, three years – even longer before they were together again. How their marriage would stand up to a separation that long, she refused even to think about. And not just themselves. There were so many couples exactly like them – not long married, too soon parted. This war would have a lot to answer for before its time was run.

It had rained on and off for a week and enough to satisfy even Mat Ramsden. Now he declared it was sun the farmers needed; sun from daybreak to dusk, till the hay was cut and the corn harvested. He reached up to fondle the great grey horse that tossed its head at the stable door, impatient to be out.

'Stop your fretting, lad. There'll be work enough for you afore so very much longer.' Hay to be mowed and dried in the sun, then carted away to the barns; after that, the corn harvest. But Duke was up to it all. A superior creature; one of the Lord's finer creations and the equal of two tractors.

Mat wished he had passed on his love of horses to his son, but Jonty was one of the new breed who wanted more and more machines now that farmers suddenly had the money to buy them. Jonty was impatient, though for what his father had yet to discover. Time the lad was settling down, in his opinion; time he was doing a bit of serious courting, war or no war.

He smiled to remember himself at Jonty's age, walking the three miles to Helpsley to court the daughter of a farmer there. My, but Grace had been a beauty and worth every step of that six-mile trip. Grace was still a beauty and he loved her every bit as much as the day he'd wed her. Pity her hopes for Roz and Jonty seemed to have come to nothing, but there was time enough, Mat supposed – unless Alderby gossip was to be believed.

But Roz was a grand little lass. She'd taken to farm work like a good 'un in spite of her being a Fairchild and proudly reared. There were the makings of a farmer's wife in her, did she but know it. Sad that Jonty had let the grass grow under his feet . . .

Roz gave a shout of delight and held wide her arms.

'Kath! You're back! I've missed you. But have *I* got it wrong, or have *you*?'

'A day early, you mean?' Kath set down her case. 'I feel such a fool, but I couldn't have taken any more. They'll all think I'm mad when I get back to the hostel.'

'Then why go back there till you're due? Why not stay the night at Ridings? You know Gran would love it.'

'Could I? But what about food? I couldn't eat your rations.'

'We'll manage. It'd only be supper tonight, and surely we can wheedle an egg out of Grace for your breakfast. And don't worry about supper, come to think of it. Haven't we been promising for ages to bike over to Helpsley for fish and chips? Why don't we do that, then look in at the dance?'

'Great!' Kath's cheeks pinked with pleasure. 'I've brought a dress back with me and my gold shoes. Might be nice to go to a dance looking like a girl. But won't you be meeting Paul?'

'Afraid not. One of the reasons why I'm so glad you're back. Paul's gone on leave – a seventy-two-hour pass, so you'll keep me from moping. It'll be the last leave they get for a while. The next one will be when they've finished their tour. Only six more to go, Kath. But I've got to fly. I'm doing the afternoon milking with Marco. Mat's gone to see a bod at the War Ag. and Jonty's at the dentist's. Off you go and tell Gran you're staying. And Marco'll be glad to hear you're back. I think he's missed you, Kath. 'Bye. See you.'

Shaking her head, Kath watched her go. Quicksilver Roz. So full of life, so in love; wanting everyone to share her happiness. And six months ago, she thought, she hadn't known Roz existed.

She closed her eyes, contentment washing over her. She was home and she had been missed. Here was where she was happiest and she wasn't going back to Birmingham to live when the war was over, though how she would convince Barney, she thought, suddenly sober, was altogether another matter.

In the guest bedroom at Ridings, Kath regarded her mirror image.

'I *have* lost weight, Roz. Aunt Min was right.'

'You look fine. Do a turn? Let me look at your dress. Oh, by the way, Gran says you're welcome to use her bike tonight, and I forgot to tell you – when I went on the cadge for eggs I told Grace you'd come back a day early because your Aunt Min wanted your room tonight for a friend from London. And Grace said, "Oh, dear. Poor Kath," and I said you were glad, really, because you'd been promising to stay at Ridings for a long time and hadn't got round to it. So don't forget, will you? But is Birmingham really so awful?'

'Nothing wrong with Birmingham.' Kath turned, eyes grave. 'It's Aunt Min, truth known. She's taken over the house and she'll not easily let go, though I ought to be glad she's there, looking after it. But she and Barney seem really close. She's taken over where his mother left off.'

'Looks like you've got problems, old love.'

'You could be right. Do you know, Roz, Barney writes to Aunt Min more than he writes to me? And he's told her things in his letters he hasn't told me. It's hurtful.'

'I suppose it must be.' Roz brushed her hair vigorously, wondering how someone as nice as Kath could have married someone as awful as Barney. Or as awful as he sounded. 'But he can't still be holding a grudge about the Land Army? It's nearly six months ago. He's had time to get over it by now. Quite sure you haven't let anything drop in your letters?'

'Like what?' Of course she hadn't. What was there to let drop?

'Sure you've never mentioned Marco?'

'Certain.' She'd been careful not to. 'Nor Jonty, either. I'm not entirely stupid. Barney's got a thing about men who aren't in uniform. I'm careful what I write.'

'Then do you think he could feel insecure, being so far away? You're very attractive, Kath. Do you think he could be jealous?'

'I don't see why. I've never given him cause in the past and as far as Marco's concerned it was only a –' She stopped, eyes wide, cheeks flushing.

'Marco?' All at once Roz was alert, her head tilted expectantly. 'How does Marco fit into it?'

'He doesn't. I mean – well – it's just that when I told him I was going away for a week he – he kissed me. Just a goodbye kiss. That's all it was – honestly.'

'Of course.' Airily, Roz regarded her fingernails. 'All it was. Nothing at all to stammer and stutter and get all steamed up about. I kiss all sorts of people, but I don't

245

go hot around the collar over it. Come on, Kath – you enjoyed it, admit it.'

'I did *not*! And don't dare say I did!'

'Then you should have done. I think Marco's gorgeous. I bet he's a smashing kisser.'

'Roz! Do you realize what you're saying? Marco's an enemy alien and I'm a married woman, or had you forgotten?'

'No, I hadn't. Had you, Kath? And if you had; if you forgot for just long enough to let him kiss you – does that make you a fallen woman?'

'Of course it doesn't.' Why hadn't she been more careful? Why hadn't she watched her tongue? Yet didn't she want to talk about it; tell Roz what a mess and muddle her life seemed to be in? 'All I know for sure, though, is that I had to get out of that house – Barney's mother's house. It's full of her things and Aunt Min polishes and dusts them. She loves it but she's looking after it for Barney, not for me.

'I can't stand it. I can't stand Barney's photographs. They're all along the top of the piano and in one of them especially he looks so smug; it's as if he knows.' There now, she'd said it. Or as good as said it. And she didn't care, either.

'As if he knows that it all began when you slipped off the stack on threshing day and Marco was there when you needed someone? As if he knows you're flesh and blood and lonely, sometimes? And mightn't he be lonely, Kath? Mightn't Barney feel guilty, too?'

'*Guilty*? What can Barney have done to feel guilty about? For Pete's sake, he's in the desert. It's all sand and flies and hot days and cold nights. There's no distractions where he is. No barmaids; no dancing girls . . .'

'Sorry, love. Forget it. Just trying to help ease your conscience, that's all.'

'Well, I like that!' Angry, she walked to the window and

stood, arms folded, gazing out and seeing nothing. Then turning she said, as evenly as she could, 'My conscience is all right – okay?'

'Is it?' Roz smiled tantalizingly. 'Oh, dear. What a pity.'

By the time they were pedalling along the Helpsley road they had come to an understanding. Roz had promised not to tease any more and to forget every word Kath had said and Kath had determined, silently, of course, to try to understand how Barney must feel all those miles away from home. She had promised Roz, openly with hand on heart, not to be so hard on herself and accept that one kiss of friendship did not constitute a fall from grace. She would allow that women whose husbands were overseas had every right to feel lonely and that they in turn had no right at all to expect their wives to go into purdah for the duration of hostilities.

Now the sky was clear and bright, the rainclouds all gone and Roz was insisting that Kath had brought the sun back with her. They were going to eat fish and chips, well-salted, vinegared and wrapped round in newspaper; eat them with their fingers which was the only way, of course, then go to the hop in the parish hall, dance every dance and have a marvellous time.

Afterwards, Kath thought happily, she would sleep in the pretty guest bedroom at Ridings and when they had eaten boiled brown eggs for breakfast she would leave for Peacock Hey and tell Flora she was back.

She breathed in deeply. The air was thick with the scent of lilacs, the grass verges bright with dandelions and cow parsley; nowhere was there as much as the sound of an aircraft nor a sign of war. Tonight was special. Tomorrow she would worry about the muddle her life was in; tomorrow was always the best time.

'Oh, Roz.' She smiled tremulously. 'Isn't this the most beautiful evening?'

* * *

247

'We can leave the bikes at Polly's cousin Willie's.' Roz directed Kath to the rear of the shop bearing the name *William Appleby. Boot & Shoe Repairs & Leather Goods*. 'It's near the chip shop, so we'll be handy for the queue.'

They had checked on the notice which announced 'Frying Tonight' and noted that the head of the line had already been established by three ladies carrying newspapers.

'It's ages since I've had fish and chips.' Sniffing, Roz wrinkled her nose as they joined a queue now grown to seven. 'We can walk along the riverbank to eat them, if you like. Nobody'll see us there.' Even in wartime, fish and chips were not eaten in public view. 'And I'll show you where Marco's camp is; not far from the dance hall, actually. Poor Marco. He was upset the other day. A lot of Helpsley people don't like having prisoners here, and one woman yelled at them to clear off back to Italy; called them Wops and shook her fist at them, he said. There's been quite a bit of resentment; the women are the worst. They feel it, I suppose, having their men abroad and seeing prisoners doing nothing, and getting fed on our rations.'

'Marco works,' Kath defended.

'Marco's in a minority. He hates being cooped up, he told me. We talked quite a lot while you were away.'

'Hope your gran didn't see you.'

'Gran's like the Helpsley women, I suppose, though I can't see her cat-calling and shaking her fist. Gran's protest comes in the form of icy aloofness – far more effective, actually. Anyway, I told Marco not to worry because it's the same for Jonty, come to think of it. Jonty comes in for more than his fair share of flack and it's almost always from women.'

The doors of the chip shop were opened with a flourish; the queue moved slowly inside and the smell of hot fat and crispy batter set empty stomachs rumbling.

'Aaaah.' Roz closed her eyes blissfully.

Kath smiled. Tonight Roz was relaxed and full of chatter, but she always was when Paul wasn't flying. Six more to go, hadn't she said? Six more times waiting and worrying, then counting them home.

Fish – 4d. Chips – 2d. said the notice on the counter. 'My treat tonight.' Kath took out a shilling. A celebration, a thanksgiving for her homecoming. And of being happy again.

'Fish and chips,' Roz said as she screwed the vinegar-soaked newspaper into a tight ball and tossed it in the river, 'have only one drawback. They smell. All fatty and fishy and vinegary, especially when you eat them with your fingers. Bet we smell so awful we won't get any partners at all tonight. And where are your dancing shoes?'

'In here.' Kath held up a brown paper carrier-bag. 'What time does it begin?'

'At half-past seven, usually, though the men don't start arriving till after eight. But we might as well make our way there and grab ourselves a couple of chairs. There isn't a band, by the way, but they've managed to get hold of an electric gramophone and they play Victor Sylvester records. It's quite good, really, for a shilling.'

The parish hall was at the end of Church Lane, beside the vicarage. It had once been the church school and, being stone built and sturdy, had survived with no ill-effects its conversion into a small kitchen, two cloakrooms and a fair-sized dance floor. Lavatories, still marked Boys and Girls, remained outside, at the far end of the schoolyard.

'Over there.' Roz pointed as they reached Church Lane. 'Behind that clump of trees. You can't see much of it because of the vicarage hedge. Marco's camp, I'm talking about . . .'

'Don't know why people are upset by it. It's well away from the village,' Kath shrugged.

'Yes, but it's *there*, and some people don't want it.'

'Then we shouldn't take prisoners, should we?'

'You've got a point. Bet Marco would agree with you on that. Come on. You bought the chips – I'll pay for the dance.'

The hand-printed notice said, *Entrance 1/0d. Servicemen & Women 6d.*

'If you must.' Kath smiled. 'And I'm – ssssh!' Urgently she grasped Roz's arm. 'What was that? Sounded like –'

'Kat! Over here!'

'Marco!' Roz gasped. '*Marco*?'

There was a movement in the tall, unclipped privets opposite the door, then they parted to show the prisoner of war, smiling gently, saying softly, 'You are back, Kat.'

'Marco, you fool, what in heaven's name are you thinking about!' Roz was the first to find her tongue. 'You know you shouldn't be here!'

'*Si*. I know. But you told me Kat is too soon back and that you come here tonight –'

'She's right.' Kath's voice was low and anxious. 'You'll be in terrible trouble if anyone sees you.'

'Yes, they'll take away your yellow patches and make you stay in the camp, then there'll be no more Home Farm,' Roz urged. 'How did you get past the guards?'

'To get out is easy. I do it because I want to say hullo to Kat.'

'Then you'd better say it, and be on your way. And you'd both best get yourselves out of sight. I'll stay here, in case anyone comes.' Roz herded them round the corner of the building. 'Get round the back and be quick about it. And keep your voices down, for heaven's sake!'

'Marco, *why*?' Kath whispered when they were alone. 'Whatever possessed you to take such a risk? Couldn't it have waited until tomorrow? Why the tearing need to see me?'

'You know why.' He stepped closer, taking her hand in his, lingering his lips on it as his eyes held hers. 'A week without you is too long, Kat – and I was bored.' He shrugged eloquently then dropped her hand abruptly. 'I don't like being shut in. I don't like barbed wire and I don't like yellow patches.'

'I know, and I understand. But those patches mean you are a trusty. You couldn't go out to work if you didn't wear them.' Yet oh, how she understood his loneliness, his need to be near someone, his need to touch, to love. 'But if we're caught we'll both be in trouble.' He mustn't look at her like that; mustn't try to kiss her. She wanted him to, but he mustn't. 'Go back. Please go, Marco.'

'If you say you miss me.'

'Of course I've missed you. I've missed you all – Roz and Jonty and Grace and – oh, just *go*!'

She took a backward step; a step away from a kiss that could be the start of something they couldn't control. She was shaking as if she were cold, yet her cheeks burned and she fixed her gaze on her shoes, not trusting herself to look into his eyes.

'Don't worry. I go back, now.' His fingertip found her chin and she pulled in her breath. 'Kat?'

She looked up and he smiled gently, shaking his head. Then he laid his finger to his lips and kissing it, placed it on her own. 'Goodnight, Katarina.'

He turned, then, and walked quickly away, parting the bushes in which he had hidden, leaving her alone and dismayed. She let go her breath in a sigh of relief and hurried to where Roz leaned on the wall, arms folded.

'He's gone, then? Got it all sorted, did you?'

'There was nothing to sort, but oh, what a damn fool thing to do. What if someone had seen him – seen *us*? And how will he get back in?'

'Same way as he got out, I suppose.' Roz had had time to recover from her surprise; now she was enjoying Kath's wide-eyed consternation. 'And don't look so worried – no one saw you. Did he kiss you again?'

'No, he did *not*! And he didn't really come to see me; he did it, I think, because he was bored. Just a lark, that's all it was. So you can wipe that smirk off your face, Roz. Now!'

'Yes, Miss. And, Kath – don't take it so seriously. Like you just said, it was probably only a bit of bravado.'

'Exactly.' She shouldn't be making such a fuss about it. 'A bit of fun. Getting one over on the guards. And I'll tell him when I see him tomorrow that he'd better not do anything so stupid again.' Nor kiss her hand so exquisitely that a shock ran the length of her arm; nor ever again look at her as he'd done tonight, because she knew what a look like that said, and where it could lead. And wasn't she to blame, really? Wasn't it her own fault that she had allowed it to start, let alone get this far?

'I'm sick of men, Roz. Sick of them all!'

They left the dance early. Roz missed Paul and every melody they had played tonight was one she had danced to with him – no other man but Paul must touch her, nor smile at her, nor hold her as he did.

'Getting a bit crowded,' she said. 'Had enough, Kath?'

'Yes. It's been a long day, come to think of it.' Her heart hadn't been in it tonight. Her feet hadn't kept time to the music, she'd been thinking so much about Marco and worrying in case he got caught. And she *shouldn't* worry about him. Marco was her enemy; Barney's enemy. Marco's country had declared war on her country and tomorrow she must be cool and calm and off-hand so he wouldn't know how attractive she found him. Because she did. She liked the tallness and the leanness of him, the way he smiled suddenly and threw back his head when he laughed. And worse than that, she liked the way he looked at her as if she were the most beautiful, the most desirable woman he'd ever known.

'I'm a fool,' she said as she shrugged into her jacket. 'Why on earth am I worrying about Marco Roselli?'

'I don't know, lovey. Suppose *you* tell *me*?'

But for the life of her, Kath could not. Or dare not.

They pedalled slowly back to Alderby, wobbling and weaving from side to side of the road, knowing there would be little traffic to bother them – the rationing of petrol had seen to that.

Behind them, a big orange sun lay low in the sky, the night gone suddenly cold, reminding them that high summer was not yet here. And when it came, Roz considered, when days were hot and long, nights short and soft with half-light, how would it be? How would it feel to know that Paul had made it; that Skip and Sugar between them had touched down safely with that magical number reached?

Enjoy being home, Paul, but hurry back, my darling, because you're only a day away and already I miss you so much that it's like an ache inside me that won't go away. Take care of your dear self . . .

Kath drew the rose-chintz curtains then switched on the bedside light, looking about her with pleasure. In the soft shaded light, the room was even more beautiful. So understated the palest green walls, the white paintwork of windows and doors, the sheen of ages-old furniture. Roz was lucky; not in having all this, but in belonging to it, being a part of a family who had been here for hundreds of years. A Fairchild had felled his tallest oaks to help build Drake's little ships and a Fairchild had fought for his king against Cromwell, Roz told her, that first time she came here. Lucky, she insisted, picking up her comb, searching for her little box of hairpins.

'Can I come in?' The door closed behind Roz. 'What were you brooding into the mirror about?'

'Not brooding. Thinking, perhaps . . .'

'Tell me?' Roz flopped on to the bed, drawing her legs beneath her. 'Unless you're too tired, that is.'

'No.' The tiredness had left her. Now her head was busy with thoughts that wouldn't go away. Eyes wide, she spoke into the mirror. 'I don't want to go back there, Roz. When the war is over, I want us to live in Alderby and I want Barney to get a job round here. Does that sound selfish – or completely crazy?'

'What brought all this on? Did something happen when you were home?'

'Not *home*. Don't call it that.' It wouldn't ever be home. 'Nothing happened; nothing I could put a finger on. It's just that Aunt Min won't ever leave there so I suppose it's best to accept it and try to find somewhere else.'

'You and Barney?'

'Of course me and Barney. Oh, I know things are in a bit of a mess between us and for the life of me I don't know why. It's partly my own fault, I'll admit that much, for doing what I did. But Barney's got to get over it. My joining the Land Army shouldn't be the end of the world, like he's trying to make out.

'But it's really because we can't talk, you see. It's the war to blame. Barney and I aren't the only ones, either. There are plenty more like us who are going to have to get to know each other again. But we'll be all right, I suppose. We'll have to be. We're married.'

'Don't say it like that, Kath. Don't say *we're married* as if it's a prison sentence. Or is it? Are you thinking now that you might have made a mistake?'

'No! Of course I –' She stopped, shaking her head, swivelling round to face her friend. 'I just don't know, Roz. I honestly don't know. There are such feelings inside me; feelings I should be ashamed of.'

'Like what?'

'Like me wondering what it would be like with someone else.' There now, she'd said it.

'With Marco?'

'No, though I think Marco started it all off.' She jumped to her feet, hugging herself tightly, pacing the floor. 'What it would be like with *any* man. There was only ever Barney, you see. I wonder now if I've missed out on something. I wish we'd gone the whole way before we were married. I'd have known, then . . .'

'Paul and I have gone the whole way a lot of times and I'm glad we have, because we're so right together. When we're married we'll know it can only get better.' She uncoiled her long, coltish legs and walked over to the dressing table. 'Hand me the comb and pins. I'll roll up your hair. And you aren't keeping anything back, are you? Marco only kissed you? He didn't try anything on?'

'Of course he didn't! He wouldn't.'

'He would, you know, if you wanted him to. Men know these things. A come-on is the same in any language. It doesn't need words, Kath. I knew Paul was right for me the minute I saw him; before we even spoke or touched, I knew. He was standing there and I looked at him and he crossed the floor to me and that was it.'

'So you think I've been giving Marco the eye, do you? Well, I haven't – at least I don't think I have. Oh, for Pete's sake let's talk about something else. D'you know, if there was someone on the other side of the wall with a glass to it, they'd think the pair of us were man mad.'

'But I am. I'm mad about Paul. Crazy about the guy.'

'Well, *I'm* not crazy about Marco.'

'Nor Barney, either, it seems. You've got problems, Kath Allen. More pins,' she demanded, holding out her hand. 'But do you really want to live here – permanently, I mean, because I'd like it if you did. There are no cottages empty at the moment, though you could have one of mine like a shot if ever it came vacant.

'In Grandpa's time, I think we owned every house in Alderby, except the pub, but now they've mostly all been sold off. I think we only have half a dozen between us. Once, everyone who worked at Ridings had a house, if he was married. It came with the job, and when they retired, they went into one of the almshouses, or a gate lodge, or something smaller.

'But those days ended when Grandpa was killed. We can't afford servants, now. There's only Polly and she's more of a friend, really. Might be a good idea to keep an eye on the Manchester lady, though. She'll be away as soon as the war's over, I wouldn't mind betting. And I'd forgotten – what I came in for was to ask if you'd like a glass of milk. Grace let me have an extra pint when she gave me the eggs, bless her. Fancy a glass?'

'Please.' Kath smiled. She felt more relaxed, now; better for letting it all out, and having Roz pin-curl her hair had helped soothe her. 'And thanks for listening. Okay – I've got problems, but I'll sort them; I really will.'

The war wouldn't be over for ages; she didn't have to be very bright to know that. Barney wouldn't be home, just yet. There'd be time. She would work it all out. If Barney could only meet her half way, try to understand the way she felt. And if Marco were to go out of her life, perhaps? If they stopped letting prisoners work; if they sent him to another farm, wouldn't that help?

But she didn't want Marco out of her life. She liked him; liked him more than she should. And there, she acknowledged, lay the whole of her trouble.

Kath Allen wanted it both ways, it seemed.

At weekends, Polly did not oblige at Ridings. Saturdays and Sundays she considered to be her own; Saturday for shopping and shirt-collecting, Sunday for church and the *News of the World*. But this last Saturday in May would be different; she had sensed it with the snapping of the letterbox flap. Few letters came to the gate lodge since most of Polly's business, family and otherwise, could be conducted by word of mouth, so it followed that anything delivered by the Post Office aroused curiosity and consternation, the more so if the envelope lying on the doormat was pale pink and scented.

Suddenly stiff, she bent to pick it up. Carefully, because she liked to do things tidily, she slit it open.

'Your Mam's coming,' she announced, shocked, to the back of Arnie's head. 'This morning. At eleven.'

Arnie looked up from his comic. What they'd said at Ridings was true, then? She *was* taking him back to Hull.

'Why's she coming?' he grunted.

'Coming? To see you, that's what. Says she's sorry she didn't let me have more notice, but she got the chance of a lift with a – a gentleman friend.'

'In a car?' Arnie hoped it wouldn't be with Kellygodrottim. Any mention of that name made Mam's face go red, if memory served him rightly.

'Of course in a car. There's no bus at eleven, you should know that by now.'

Arnie brightened considerably. Kellygodrottim was an idle good-for-nothing without a penny to his name, Mam always said, let alone a motor car. She couldn't be coming with him.

'Where are they getting the petrol?' he demanded.

'That's something I wish *you'd* tell *me*. Shift yourself and get your best boots blacked and polished, and make sure you scrub your fingernails. And for goodness' sake lad, get a comb through that hair!'

Arnie folded his comic at once. He always did things immediately when Aunty Poll showed signs of agitation.

'I'm not going back to Hull,' he muttered. 'I'm not, Aunty Poll.' Not even in a car, he wasn't!

'Course you're not! Whoever put such a notion into your head?' Drat the lad. Too sharp for his own good, that's what.

'I heard.' His toe traced the patterns on the hearthrug. 'I heard you tell Mrs Fairchild you thought Mam wanted me back.'

'Oh? Listening at keyholes, were you? You know what happens to boys who do that, then? Never hear any good of themselves, they don't.'

'I won't go.' He didn't care what happened to boys who heard things at back doors; he *did* care about going back to Hull. 'You'll not let her take me?'

'Bless your life no, lad. Not if I can help it. Now get your boots seen to like I told you and don't bother me with your chatter. I've got a bit of thinking-out to do.

'And don't go sneaking off when your Mam arrives. You'll stay and greet her civilized – let her see how you've growed these last two years. Wait till I say you can go – is that understood?'

'Yes, Aunty Poll.' Already he was making plans for Beck Lane. The oak tree was in full leaf again; no one would ever see him up there. He'd stay there for a week if he had to and when they found him they'd all be sorry, when it was too late.

Visions of an Arnie lying palely dead brought tears to his eyes. Polly saw them and hugged him to her, planting a rare kiss on the top of his head.

'Now then, lovey, don't take on so. I don't want her to take you any more 'n you want to go, so leave it to me, why don't you? Your old Aunty Poll isn't as green as she's cabbage-looking.' Oh my word, no!

Mrs Bagley arrived a little before noon. She was sorry for being so late, but they'd had trouble finding the place, she explained, waving from the doorstep to the driver of a small black car.

'My friend has business in the area, Miss Appleby. He'll be back later to pick me up. And is this my boy, then?'

She patted Arnie's head and he took a step away from her in case she tried to kiss him.

'Hullo, Mam.'

'This is Arnie,' Polly confirmed, marvelling how easy her voice sounded when her inside was churning something awful. 'He's growed, don't you think?'

'Goodness me, yes. Nearly as tall as your Mammy, aren't you?'

Arnie regarded her dispassionately, forced to admit that she looked nice in her flowered dress, and the furs looked posh, too. And she was smiling at him as if she really liked him, he supposed, though she didn't smile like Aunty Poll did; not with all her face.

Polly took stock of the fancy frock and the double fox furs, worn as if she'd been brought up to them, which she hadn't, or she'd have known that no lady wore furs when there wasn't an R in the month. Mrs Fairchild's fur coat was put away at the end of April and never taken out until the beginning of September. Nor did Mrs Fairchild paint her nails or pluck her eyebrows to a thin, surprised line. And where had that nail polish come from except from the black market?

'You'll take a cup of tea, Mrs Bagley?' Polly indicated the rocking chair at the hearth. 'Afraid it's all I can offer you, rationing being what it is.'

'Deary me, yes. Wouldn't dream of taking your food, Miss Appleby. As a matter of fact, my friend was able to get a little boiled ham so I've brought sandwiches with me. They're in the car. To eat later. Now, Arnie, tell me how you're getting on at school?'

'All right.' He scowled, wishing he could go, wondering how long a civilized greeting was expected to last.

'He's doing very well.' Polly nodded. 'They're expecting him to win a scholarship to the Grammar School next year.'

'Well fancy that, now. What a clever boy I've got. I think that deserves some sweeties.' Tantalizingly she opened her handbag, peeping inside; slowly she drew out a paper bag. 'There you are. Don't eat them all at once and say thank you to your Mammy.'

Red-faced, Arnie obliged then opened the bag to release the heady whiff of mint humbugs. His smile of pure joy so pleased his mother that she opened her handbag again and gave him a shilling for doing well at school.

Polly shook with indignation. Bribery, that's what, and Arnie falling for it, an' all. Mind, you couldn't blame the lad – not when quarter-pound bags of sweeties were as rare as hens' teeth, though it wasn't fighting fair if she thought to entice him back to Hull with humbugs.

'Will you take a saccharin in your tea, Mrs Bagley?'

'Thank you, no. I take my tea without. All sweetness is bad for the complexion.'

Polly glared at her visitor's handbag. New it was, and pigskin, if she was any judge. *Real* pigskin like her gloves which only went to show she'd been right all along. Petrol, nail polish and expensive handbags, not to mention boiled ham and bags of humbugs had ceased to exist for ordinary folk. Only money could buy such luxuries, and since Arnie's mother had been on the bones of her backside not two years ago, Polly considered, it stood to reason that her new-found prosperity could only spring from one source.

She closed her eyes as a sharp crunching caused a shudder to run through her. Glowering at Arnie she demanded he hand over his bounty before he made himself sick.

'You ration them sweeties out, lad. Make 'em last,' she admonished, placing them in the dresser drawer, closing it firmly.

'Can I go out, now?' All at once he was bored.

'Of course you can go out, lovey,' the visitor beamed, asserting her mother's rights. 'Miss Appleby and me have important things to chat about, haven't we?'

'I reckon we have. Off you go, lad.'

Things to chat about. *Important* things. She really had come to take him back?

All at once Arnie was afraid, sorry he'd taken the humbugs, realizing that not if Mam gave him sweeties every day would it make up for leaving the gate lodge and his warm, soft bed, Aunty Poll's suppers and all the lovely things a boy could do at Alderby. And nothing in the world could make up for leaving Aunty Poll. As if the man from the Workhouse was on his tail, he made for Beck Lane, and sanctuary.

Some folk, Polly seemed to remember as she listened to Arnie's fast-fading footsteps, considered that attack was the best form of defence and attack was exactly what she intended; a head-on, no holds barred confrontation. Taking a seat at the kitchen table, folding her arms belligerently she flung:

'You want the lad back, don't you?'

'I – er – oh!' Mrs Bagley sat bolt upright. 'He – he's my son,' she defended. 'A mother gets lonely for her child . . .'

'You've come to take him back,' Polly insisted.

'Well, I – yes. Since you ask, Miss Appleby, I have.' Her head tilted defiantly.

'Back to where there's bombing, and you on war work, I shouldn't wonder? How's a lad not yet ten to be looked after properly, will you tell me, with his mam on war work and no father to guide him?'

'Same as he was looked after before he was taken from me.'

'*Taken* from you?'

'You know what I mean.' The thin eyebrows met in a frown. 'We didn't know what to expect, when war broke out. We panicked, let our children go . . .'

'Happen so, but now we know, don't we? Air-raids and rationing. How's a mother on war work to find the time for food queues, will you tell me?' She didn't, Polly thought, know why she was going on so about war work, but instinct seemed to have put the words there. 'And what about if you had to work nights?'

'Arnie would be all right.' The red lips formed a sulky pout. 'I wouldn't be far away . . .'

'You mean to tell me you'd take him to live near a factory?' Factories got bombed, were prime targets for German planes.

'I didn't say that. But it doesn't matter where I take him to live, if you'll forgive me for saying so,' she threw haughtily, suddenly recovered from the speed of Polly's assault. 'It isn't any of your business. *I'm* his mother. *I'm* the one with rights.'

'The right to take him away from where he's happy, and wanted?'

'He'd be happy enough with me, Miss Appleby, because *I* want him, too.'

She jumped to her feet and strode to the table, glaring down angrily.

At once, chair legs scraping, Polly stood to face her. You couldn't win an argument when you were being looked down on. Folding her arms again, chin jutting, she met her protagonist eye to eye.

'And why,' she said slowly, 'do you all of a sudden want him? Or is it that you *need* him? Could it be that your age-group has come up, Mrs Bagley? Have they sent for you to register for war work? Do you *need* to have a child under fourteen – is that it?'

'I'm sure I don't know what you mean.' She took a step backward, repulsed by Polly's gimlet gaze and the blaze of anger that flushed her cheeks.

'Then I'll tell *you*. I'll say it in words so simple, Miss, that even you can understand.' Polly's chin jutted farther and higher. She was winning, had touched the raw nerve she'd been probing for. '*Miss*, I said, for you're no more wed than I am and single women your age have to do war work. No getting out of it.

'Except, of course, if you happen to be a woman with a bairn under fourteen years old; then you don't have to work anywhere, can stay at home and look after him. That's why you want Arnie back – so you needn't go out to work. Suit you down to the ground, wouldn't it?'

Polly stopped, amazed at her own eloquence, taking a deep, calming breath, wishing she knew all the big words Mrs Murgatroyd knew; wishing her inside would stop its churning.

'So is it wrong to want my boy with me? And why am I making excuses to you? He's coming back with me.' Mrs Bagley curled a fist, banging it on the table-top.

'Then I'll have the law on you if you so much as take one step outside that gate with him!' Polly countered with a harder, noisier fist. 'I'll have the Billeting Officer here so fast you'll wonder what hit you, my lady!' Jamming her hands on her hips, she stood with feet apart, eyes narrowed, challenging. 'And you're *not* taking him because –'

And that had been where she played her trump card she had recounted later to Mrs Murgatroyd. That, she said as she stirred her tea in the kitchen of the bay-windowed house, had been where the benefit of legal advice had proved its golden worth.

'". . . *because*," I said to her, "you're having men at your house, Mrs Bagley. You've no need to do war work. You're doing very nicely without it and doing honest war work would put paid to your little game, wouldn't it? Put paid to pigskin handbags and black market petrol for your friend's car, wouldn't it?"'

This, Polly paused to explain, had been the point at which Mrs Bagley had gasped and collapsed into the rocking chair.

'"And what's more," says I, "there's something you

should know; something it's my duty to tell you because I don't want you landing up in prison. Did you know," I says, "that it's an offence in law" – oh, how she flinched at that, Mrs Murgatroyd – "an offence *in law* to have a child under fourteen living in a – a house of ill-repute. 'Cause that's what your house is," I says. "A *brothel*! That's what you're up to," and she told me to prove it. I said I wouldn't have mentioned one word of what I had if I hadn't had proof, because since the matter of Arnie's welfare had forced me to take legal advice . . .

'*Legal advice*, Mrs Murgatroyd. It stopped her in her tracks. Said I'd had no call to go to those lengths, but I said my concern for Arnie had forced me to do it.'

Polly accepted a second cup of tea, still shaking from her encounter with the lady from Hull; still flushed and triumphant, not a little disbelieving in victory.

'Yes?' Mrs Murgatroyd offered the sugar bowl. 'What happened then?'

'You might well ask.' Polly stirred her tea slowly, savouring the moment. 'I'd got her with her back to the wall by that time, and she knew it.'

'"Then what'll I *do*?" she wailed. "Try to see it my way, Miss Appleby? All right – so maybe I do have gentlemen friends?"

'"And do very nicely out of it," says I, "if I'm any judge," and she says to me, cheeky as you like, that it was better than working in a factory and could I blame her for doing what she was good at?

'"Kelly," she said, "may God rot him," she said, had left her as soon as the morning sickness started. What else was she to do, with the Workhouse no more 'n a step away?'

'The Workhouse . . .' Mrs Murgatroyd breathed.

'Have to give it up, she said, and go on war work if I wouldn't let her have Arnie back. So I asked her why bother? She was doing very nicely, and since I wanted

Arnie more than she ever did, why not carry on with what she was doing? Why not tell them at the Labour Exchange when she went to register that she had a young boy? No need to tell them where he was.

'Did she suppose, I asked her, that a man from the Government was going to come knocking on her door to check up if the lad was there? Far too busy, I said, with a war on. Got better things to do, I told her.

'"But supposing – just *supposing* they did," she says to me, and I told her to tell them – hand on heart – that her boy just happened to be at his Aunty Poll's on a few days' holiday. But they'll never check up on her, Mrs Murgatroyd. Nor on me.'

'Very unlikely.'

'Exactly. And that was where the blackmail came in – or is it called extortion? Anyway, I told her that since she was doing so nicely I wouldn't say no to a bit of something occasionally towards Arnie's keep and so's I could save some for the Grammar School uniform he's going to need, and she was only too ready to promise it. It's the last we've seen of her, I'm sure of it, but whether she'll send any money remains to be seen.'

'She'll send it.' Mrs Murgatroyd permitted herself a small, self-satisfied smile. 'Legal jargon can be very intimidating to the likes of Arnie's mother. She'll send it, though I'd like to have thought it would be of her own free will.' Blackmail *or* extortion – either word made the wife of a legal gentleman extremely uneasy.

'Well, only time will tell.' Polly lifted her hands to her throbbing cheeks. 'I'm keeping the lad and that's all that matters. And if I don't get myself back he'll be wondering what's become of me.'

'All right, is he?' Mrs Murgatroyd handed over six shirts and Polly placed them in her basket.

'Safe as houses.' She nodded. 'Best be off, though, and collect him. See you Wednesday, then.'

'Wednesday. All being well. And thank you, Miss Appleby.'

'Nay. Thank *you*.' And thanks to Mr Murgatroyd, too, for his masterly piece of legal advice – that the lady in question should be acquainted with the fact that it was an offence in law to permit a child to live in a house of prostitution. My word, who'd have thought of that one? But it only went to show that legal advice was a wonderful thing to have. That, and a measure of bluff and cunning.

At the top of Beck Lane Polly paused, then walking quietly to the oak tree she looked up into the branches and called, 'It's all right, Arnie. You can come down now.'

There was a movement above her, a rustling of leaves, then a small red face looked down.

'Has Mam gone?'

'She's gone. More 'n an hour ago. Been to Mrs Murgatroyd's for the shirts. You hungry then, lad?'

'Is she coming again to take me back?'

'Take you back? Oh my word, no. Your Mam's far too busy on war work.'

'But you said you thought she wanted to take me back to –'

'Then I was wrong, for once.' Polly was becoming impatient. 'Reckon you're stuck with your Aunty Poll for the duration, so best get used to the idea. Now are you coming down *this minute*, or do you want a slap on your backside?'

'What's for dinner?' With the agility of a small, cheeky monkey Arnie dropped to the ground at her feet. 'I'm starving.' Then, slipping his hand in hers he looked up enquiringly. 'Aunty Poll – how did you know about my tree?'

'Ah, now. If I told you that you'd know as much as I do, wouldn't you? Now for goodness' sake let's be having you home, lad. *Home*, I said . . .'

13

'Grace! I'm back!' Kath closed the door quietly, gazing around the kitchen, anxious that nothing at Home Farm should have changed.

And nothing had. The mugs still stood atop the mantelshelf, the soup pan still swung from the hook above the fire and the smell, the warm, Home-Farm smell of baking bread told her she was truly back; that she was home again.

'Kath, lass. We didn't expect you in till Monday.' She turned, sighing softly. 'I'm right glad to see you, though, for all that.'

'Grace?' At once Kath was at her side, forehead creased with concern, for the eyes that met hers brimmed with tears beneath eyelids red from weeping. 'What is it? Tell me?'

'It's this war; this *awful* war.' The voice choked to a near-whisper. 'A body can only take so much . . .'

'I know, love. I know. Here –' Kath offered her handkerchief.

'Sorry. So sorry . . .' She dabbed at her eyes. 'But hearing about it this morning and me with my son at home . . . Such a terrible shock. Poor Peggy – but you'll not know Peg Bailey?'

'Holly Tree cottage? Next to the pub?' Kath knew every house in Alderby, now.

'That's them. The telegram came last night. Killed on active service, it said. On a gun-site down south and her only a bit of a lass; Jonty's age to the very day. And her mam and dad, Kath? What'll they do? How are they going to bear it, will you tell me? Alderby's only a little place, yet the war's taken two of our lads already. Now it's taken Peg. It isn't right. It *isn't* . . .'

'Don't, Grace. Don't get upset. It's the war and there's nothing any of us can do about it except try to be kind to her parents.'

'I know, but I watched Peg grow up, you see. Right from her being born. She was special. Such a day, that was. The district nurse said she'd never forget it. Me and Peggy's mother both in labour and the poor nurse backward and forward between Holly Tree and Home Farm all day. Said she was lucky if she had two bairns in a year in Alderby and wasn't there two, now, deciding to be born on the same day!'

'So tell me – which of you made it first?'

'I did, and Peggy born about two hours after. And her and Jonty christened on the same Sunday, both confirmed the same Easter. Engaged to a Helpsley lad, Peg was. Had the wedding arranged for his next leave, but he was killed at Dunkirk. So she made no more to-do; volunteered like a good 'un for the army; said she'd be a soldier, in his place. Stationed near Dover. Hell-fire corner they called it with all the bombing and shelling they got. And now she's dead and how I'll ever look her poor mother in the face again, I don't know.'

'Ssssh, now. Try not to take it so badly, Grace. It was nothing you did that killed her . . .'

'But don't you see, Kath, I *do* feel badly. Wouldn't you, with most of the young ones gone to the war and my own son still at home? I don't want him to go, mind. He's all we've got. But you'd feel it, when a slip of a girl who was like his twin gets taken . . .'

'I know. I do understand. But there's no blame attached to Jonty. People like us don't make the rules. We just do as we're told and hope for the best. C'mon, now? Dry your eyes and give your face a good splash with cold water. I'll stay with you till you're feeling better – unless Mat needs me, that is.'

'No. Like I said we hadn't thought to expect you back

today. They're all of them working over on Ridings' land, thinning out the sugar-beet. And here's me with my face a mess from weeping and the new ration books to be collected from Helpsley today.'

'Then I'll get them for you. Won't take me long on the bike.'

'Would you, Kath? Wouldn't want to bump into anyone I knew looking like this.' She let go a long, shuddering sigh. 'Don't usually give way, but when I heard about Peg this morning, it seemed there was no end to the madness.

'You know where to go, Kath? There'll be people from the Ministry of Food at the parish hall, it said in the papers, giving out the books. Don't want to miss them or it'll be an afternoon wasted going to York to get them there. Be glad you didn't marry a farmer, lass. There's never enough hours in the day, if you do.'

She smiled a sad, small smile then walked wearily to the sink, filling her cupped hands with water, splashing her face.

Kath stood beside her, towel in hand, waiting, not knowing what to do or say. But it was like that, now. So much grief and words the only comfort. And being there, listening, and taking someone's hand in your own.

'And lass,' Grace whispered from the deeps of the towel, 'I shouldn't have gone on so about it to you; not when your man's fighting in North Africa. You've got worries of your own and I'm sorry.'

'You didn't upset me. Barney's all right.' Or was, last time she'd heard. There hadn't been a letter at Peacock Hey when she got back, though she hadn't really expected one, because up until two days ago she knew that Aunt Min hadn't had one, either. But Barney was all right, she was sure of it. Probably away on another long convoy – whatever a long convoy was – and looking forward to a pint of beer at the end of it. 'Barney's just fine,' she smiled.

Of course he was. Barney was a survivor. There'd be a letter on Monday or the next day; maybe even a kind and caring letter like the ones he used to write.

'I'll be off now for the books.' Tenderly she cupped the tear-stained face in her hands. 'Don't cry any more, Grace. Please don't cry.'

Kath saw Jonty as he climbed the orchard fence and she stopped to wave, waiting until he was in earshot.

'I'm going to Helpsley – anything you want?'

'No, Kath, thanks. And it's good to see you back. Mum missed having you around. Is she all right, by the way? I'm going for the drinkings, but really it's to see how she is. She's been upset all morning. Did she tell you about it?'

Kath nodded, propped her cycle against the hedge then leaned on the gate, chin on hand.

'Poor Peggy. I never met her, yet it hurts. It's frightening, too.'

And hard to accept that any young life should be ended on a day such as this; on a day bright with sunlight, alive with cuckoo-calls, sweet with the scent of elder blossom.

'Frightening? It – it's *obscene*. A girl, born on the same day as I was, killed because she wore a uniform, and I'm here, Kath, safe. I'm a civvy. I stay at home and let women fight my war. Christ! It's degrading.'

'Your war is here, Jonty. This farm and Ridings is where you can do most good; you've just got to accept it.'

'Then I can't.' He slammed a fist on the gate-top. 'Don't you think I'm sick of the innuendoes and the sly digs? I get it all the time and from women it's even worse. They don't wrap it up when their sons are away fighting. Right now, Kath, farmers aren't popular. Living off the fat of the land, we're supposed to be; sitting on our behinds, counting all the subsidies the government pay us for getting out of military service. Soldiers are paid about two bob a day for getting shot at, yet we're being paid good money for leaning on gates, according to some, and chewing grass!'

'Like we're doing now?' Kath reached for a blade of grass, offering it obligingly, waiting, head tilted for his smile. 'There now – didn't crack your face, did it? And, Jonty, you're very nice when you smile.'

'You're not listening to a word I'm saying.'

'I am. Truly I am . . .' And I'm looking at you, thinking how different you and Paul are; Paul who is tall and fair, perfect as a young god; you whose shoulders are broad, whose hands are big and safe, whose hair is thick and in need of cutting. Both of you love Roz, yet she's Paul's, his completely. 'I think I know how you feel.'

'Do you, Kath? Then you'll know that this morning I felt like going to York, walking into the first recruiting office I came to and joining up.'

'Then more fool you, Jonty Ramsden! How much good would it have done once they'd found you were reserved? And anyway, men who wear glasses are no use for aircrew and that's what you want to be, isn't it? You want Roz to worry herself sick about you every time you take off with a bomb load, is that it? Because that's what she's doing now. Well, thank heaven they don't take short-sighted pilots!'

'Hey! That hurt, Kath!'

'Sorry. It wasn't meant to and I'd no right to say it. But you're a farmer, and farming is important. You do as many Home Guard parades as the farm'll let you; you work all the hours God sends – isn't that enough?'

'I'm a civilian; a *bloody* civvy, I think the term is. If some people had their way I'd go round like a leper, ringing my bell, shouting "Unclean! Unclean!"'

'Don't, Jonty. You can't change things. You can't volunteer and that's all there is to it.'

'You joined up, Kath. Married women don't have to volunteer. *You* didn't have to.'

271

'Oh, but I did; I damn-well did. It was something I had to do.'

'There you are, then! So why shouldn't I?'

'Now it's you who isn't listening.' Kath shook her head, dismissing his argument. 'Listen – I didn't do it for King and Country, I did it for *me*! I did it for Kath Allen because it was the only chance she'd ever get to do what *she* wanted.

'And I'm so happy doing it that I'm scared stupid sometimes and wonder when the reckoning day will be. So don't try to make out I did something noble and patriotic, because I didn't. One day I thought that it was now or never. I think joining up was the bravest thing I'll ever do, and I know it's nothing to do with me but I'm going to say it just the same. Don't go making any marvellous gestures, Jonty. Not for Roz, I mean . . .'

He didn't answer her. Instead he made a sign of surrender with his shoulders; a sad shrugging that acknowledged all.

Strange, Kath thought, gazing across the field. When she had come here that field had been dark, cold and wet, the wheat in it sown in the short grey days of winter. Yet now it stood knee high almost, its pale green ears ready to swell and turn to summer gold. She hadn't known Jonty and Roz, then. Nor Marco. In six months a small grain of wheat had grown almost to fruition. And her own life had completely changed.

'What's his name, Kath?' he asked without turning his head, without moving his gaze from the far end of the field.

'Paul. Paul Rennie.'

'I saw him once. With Roz. I'd gone to the game-cover to make sure the fire was properly out. It was dark. They didn't see me but they were so close I could have touched them. And you don't have to rub my face in it, Kath. I know she's mad about him.'

'She's besotted, Jonty; best get it straight, since we're

on about it. And whilst you're binding about not having a glamorous uniform and I'm feeling guilty for volunteering and actually enjoying it, let's both of us think about Peggy Bailey, shall we?'

'Think we better had. Thanks for straightening me out. It had to be said, I suppose. Reckon Peggy wouldn't mind being called a bloody civvy, right now . . .'

'Reckon she wouldn't at that. You know what they say – it'll all be the same in a hundred years. In fifty years, even, most of this'll be water under the bridge – fifty years from now, as Roz is so fond of saying.'

'Lord! Fifty years from now Roz'll be nearly seventy. And I'll be seventy-*four*!'

'Hmm. Sobering thought, isn't it? And Jonty – since you care for her so much –'

'Yes.' He trailed his fingers through his hair. Just as Mat did, Kath realized. 'And since I suppose I always will . . .'

'Then don't turn your back on her, will you, if ever she needs you?' She touched his cheek gently, affectionately, but his gaze was still a million miles away. 'Best be getting off to Helpsley, then. So-long, Jonty. See you.'

Without speaking, he nodded his head. He was still there, leaning on the gate, when she turned at the end of the lane to look back.

What a mess it all was. And there couldn't be a happy ending to this story. What ever happened, someone was going to get hurt. When there was a war on, it was all you could expect . . .

June came in with an early sunrise that touched the blowsy red roses on the walls at Ridings; a bright sun that threw gold on the little twisting river and the tiny, peeping ducklings that swam there.

Roz quickened her step. No time to waste counting ducklings. Soon Paul would be back; even now his train should be somewhere north of Birmingham and by noon he'd be at Peddlesbury, only a step away from a telephone. If she could slip away, if they were still working on Ridings' land, she could call him to say 'I love you', and beg him please, *please* to be there tonight.

Days were long and the nights short now. Because of Double Summer Time, which was really the stealing of an extra hour of daylight to help the war effort, it was light until almost midnight and blackout curtains drawn late. No longer could darkness wrap round their secret meetings. Now they met in Peddlesbury Lane, beside the wood of oaks and elms that grew thick and dark with undergrowth.

He's on his way. He's on his way. She said it to the rhythm of the train wheels that brought him nearer with every ticked-away second. She had missed him unbearably. Three days without him had been an agony. She had wanted him until it became an ache inside her; wanted the nearness of him, his mouth hard on hers. Now her body screamed its need to be roused and loved.

What would she do she thought, suddenly cold with fear, if one morning – a golden morning such as this one – she were to awaken to the certain knowledge that she would never again see him nor hear his voice nor close her eyes and lift her face for his kiss? How could she tolerate a life of which he was no longer a part? How would her heart, her mind, her aching, unloved body endure without him?

Six more flights into an alien sky. Six more green lights flashing him on his way; six more touch-downs, that was all. They would make it. Somewhere in England a bomber crew completed its tour of ops every day of the week and soon it would be Sugar's turn.

She cleared her head of anxious thoughts, recalling instead the early morning news bulletin. Over Cologne again; a thousand of our bombers in a massive raid. A *thousand.* Who would have thought we had so many? She tried to envisage a sky filled with aircraft. Ten Lancasters took off from Peddlesbury; imagine a hundred times that number?

But we were getting stronger all the time; not winning battles yet, but getting over the mauling that had been Dunkirk. We were no longer alone. America and Russia had joined the fight and one day we would win; a day dim and distant, but certain. There would be peace and no one need ever know fear or parting or heartbreak again.

She looked at her watch. Six more hours before she could ring him. Already she could hear the low, slow clunk of the milking machine. Another day had already begun at Home Farm.

I have missed you so and I love you so. Be there tonight, Paul. Please don't be flying.

She had not seen Marco since Friday night which was just as well, Kath thought soberly, since he'd hardly been out of her thoughts since the night of the Helpsley dance. How completely stupid he had been, yet she understood his impatience with the indignity of imprisonment.

She clicked her tongue, backing the little pony into the shafts of the milk-cart, smiling at Roz who crossed the yard at a run.

'I'm late. Sorry, Kath. Did a bit of day-dreaming along the way.'

'Heavy date tonight?'

'Hope so. Shouldn't think there'll be much going on at Peddlesbury; not after last night's shindig. A thousand bombers! Imagine it!'

And thirty-one of them missing. Roz had blanked that bit out of her mind. More than two hundred airmen unaccounted for, though the announcer who read the news hadn't put it quite like that. The announcer never did, Kath brooded. '. . . *and thirty-one of our aircraft*

275

failed to return.' That was all, just a few trite words. Thirty-one bombers out of a thousand wasn't bad; not bad at all decided the man in the street. Only those who might have a son or lover on that massive raid closed their eyes this morning and prayed that it wouldn't be to them that one of the small yellow envelopes came. Someone once told her they asked you to sign for that telegram. *Sign* for it. *The next of kin have been informed . . .* So who would inform Roz, who wasn't next of kin, if one night Paul's plane did not return?

Stop it, Kath Allen! Paul would make it. Skip was an experienced pilot. Skip had a wife and a soon-to-be-born child to come home to. Sugar was a lucky old bitch; all the crew said she was.

'What am I going to do about Marco?' she asked suddenly.

'Marco? You're asking *me*, Kath? I've got problems enough of my own.'

'Like telling your gran the truth about Paul?'

'Well – no, not really. I *will* tell her, though, when he's –' She stopped, frowning. 'Of course I'll tell her when they've done their thirty. It's just getting the thirty over with that sometimes has me worried.'

'You're worried about it, Roz? But I thought you were so sure?'

'I am sure – most of the time. It *will* come right for me and Paul, I know it. But just sometimes I get afraid; times when I love him so much it's as if I'm a part of him and if he died, then so would I . . .'

'Hey! That's enough!'

They had reached the village and Kath picked up the first two milk bottles. One for the Black Horse, the other for Holly Tree cottage. God, they knew all about telegrams there.

'Here, do the pub; I'll take this one.'

Gently she pushed open the gate of Holly Tree cottage,

walked quietly up the path. In all other houses, curtains were drawn back and doors opened to the morning; here the door was shut against the world, the curtains at every window still resolutely closed. And they would remain closed, until Peggy had come home and been carried to the little graveyard across the green. It was like that, in the country, when a house was in mourning.

Carefully Kath set down the bottle; not even the slightest clink against the step this morning. Briefly she gazed at the door.

I didn't know your daughter, but I'm sorry; so very sorry . . .

They didn't speak until well away from the house that grieved. It wouldn't have seemed right, somehow, for the man and woman who lived there to have heard young voices.

'Will you be going to the funeral, Roz?'

'I don't know. I'd like to. Gran'll be there, of course, and Grace and Mat, so someone will have to stay behind at the farm. I don't know if Jonty will go. I think he'll want to, but suppose Mrs Bailey sees him? It wouldn't help her any. Oh, damn this war!'

Damn it, Kath silently agreed. *This* war as opposed to the last war, as the Great War was now called; the one they said was the war to end all wars. But they had let it happen again, those people who should have known better, then left it to the young ones to fight.

'Yes, dammit,' she said out loud. 'But let's try not to think about it, Roz. Let's only bother about the war when the war bothers us?'

And Roz agreed that it was the only thing to do. After all, only fools looked for trouble.

'Kat,' said Marco when she and Roz joined the men working on Ridings' land, 'you have been avoiding me. I haven't seen you since three days.'

'*For* three days,' Kath corrected automatically, 'because on Saturday I went to Helpsley and Sunday was your rest-day and mine, too, and this morning –'

'Okay. Okay. I only tease you. But bring your sandwiches outside, Kat? Today is too good for eating in the kitchen. And I have something to tell you, and something to give you.'

She should have told him no; that she wanted to eat her lunch in Grace's kitchen, but when Marco smiled as he was smiling now, when his eyes challenged her and her own stupid heart joined in the clamour, should-haves became why-nots and made it easier to say that yes, she would like that.

'We can have a talk,' she said with studied ease as she moved away from him down the row, eyes down, hoe working rhythmically.

Talk. Why shouldn't they? Marco was her friend like Jonty was her friend; two men Barney knew nothing about and heaven only knew the fuss he'd make if he did.

But all this was Barney's fault, Kath thought irritably. Barney should write more often; write warm, loving letters like Flora's husband wrote – letters to pink her cheeks when she read them as Flora's did.

Yet maybe it always got like this after so long apart. She frowned petulantly, jabbing her hoe deep. Just five months of being a wife, then the Army had sent Barney to North Africa. Not France, thank God, his mother had said. If he'd gone to France he'd have been killed on the Dunkirk beaches; nothing was more certain. But Barney's mother had been like that.

Now they had been apart for more than two years. Once, when she read his letters she had been able to hear his voice, saying the words to her. Now, she could not.

She forced her mind back to a July wedding, just before the war started. There had been a lot of weddings in the summer of thirty-nine. Soon, on her twenty-fourth birthday, it would be their third anniversary. Would Barney remember? Did she want him to?

'Kath! You haven't heard a word I said,' Roz pouted. 'You were miles away.'

'Mm. Birmingham.' At a Register Office, getting married to Barney – and Barney's weeping mother, had she but known it. 'Sorry – what did you say?'

'I said I was going to slip away in about an hour. Down the lane, to the Black Horse . . .'

'To the phone?'

'Right in one.' Her smile was brilliant. 'If I ring a little after noon I'll be almost sure of getting him. If anyone notices I'm gone, be a love and tell them I had to go home for something. *Please*.'

'Oh, all right.' Roz was on one of her highs and her joy was catching. See-saw Roz, who was up in the air or down in the deeps; never with two feet planted firmly on the ground. Today she floated high on a fluffy pink cloud, scattering down rose petals on a world filled with love.

Kath took her sandwiches to Two-acre field. The grass on which she sat was warm from the sun and kicking off her shoes, she wiggled her toes gratefully. Heavy shoes, shirts and dungarees were not the coolest of dress for a blazing June day, but she admitted they were the most sensible.

She wondered if Marco would find her here. Most days he took his midday rations to the Dutch barn at the far end of the yard and it wouldn't be right, she had decided truculently, to go there to him. Let him find her here, she thought in a last, defiant effort at conscience-easing. Why was she so bothered? They had only agreed to eat their sandwiches together and exchange news. This meeting wasn't a date or anything vaguely resembling it so why she should feel so uneasy about it she didn't know.

He came striding through the poultry arks toward her, smiling, tunic over his arm. He disliked that tunic and the big, square, yellow patch on the back of it. Marco liked to work stripped to the waist, the sun on his body, and if he knew how good he looked, then for sure he wouldn't do it.

'*Ciao*, Kat.' He sat down beside her, still smiling. 'I think you will be here. You want one of my sandwiches?'

'No, thanks. I've got plenty. Have one of mine. Spam, I think they are.'

'You're sure?' Marco had never tasted Spam, though he'd heard about it. Grew on trees in America, they said in the camp; had so much of it they sent it in ship-loads to the British. 'Ah, this is a good day. You are back, Kat, and this morning I have two letters from home. Good letters. Good news. *Zia Rosa* – my aunt Rosa – writes that my cousin is no more missing. Toni is a prisoner of war now, like me.'

'Marco – that's great! Where is he?'

'Toni was a soldier in the desert; now he is wounded and in a prison hospital. I think near Cairo, but he couldn't say. Maybe some day they'll send him to England – I don't know. But he's okay. That's good, eh? Maybe now *Zia Rosa* can stop her weeping . . .'

Aunt Rosa. Cousin Toni. Marco had a family. Almost everyone but Kath Allen had a family.

'And Kat, I have something for you.' Reaching for his jacket, he dipped into a pocket, triumphantly holding up a twist of paper. 'Today we smoke *my* cigarettes. Yesterday, I have my special issue and now I can give one to you.'

'But you can't. You worked hard for those.' For every hour of overtime a prisoner of war worked, the payment was two cigarettes, he'd told her. Two *large* cigarettes.

'No? But I want to. Last month I earn twelve and this morning they gave them to me.' Carefully he unfolded the paper; proudly he offered a cigarette. 'Please, Kat? Being a prisoner is not good. We have nothing; we *are* nothing. But I would like it if I give a lady a cigarette that is mine, and not every day smoke hers.'

His eyes asked that she take one, and she knew that on that taking depended his pride.

'Then I'd like one. Thank you very much.'

Gravely she took it, offering her matches, and when he struck one and held it for her she took his hand to steady it as she bent her head to the flame. Then smiling up at him she said, 'And you are right. This is a good day. Roz is happy, too. Paul comes back today.'

'And you, Kat? You have something to be happy about? You get a letter?'

'No letters. But can't I just be glad I'm back again, with my friends?'

'And with Marco? Am I your friend?'

'Of course you are, though you shouldn't do stupid things like breaking out of camp. Don't do it again, Marco?'

'Okay. It's good, though, getting past the guards. The guards are *stupidi*. It's easy to get out.'

'And big trouble if you'd been caught or there'd been a roll-call. And it can't be so bad. They don't ill-treat you? You get good food?'

'Not good food; not Italian food, but we don't starve. And Mrs Ramsden helps. Her soup is good. But being a prisoner is bad for a man.' He pulled hard on his cigarette, then drew the smoke deep into his lungs. 'Not good at all.'

'Tell me what it's like in the camp. Is it cold there in winter? Do they let you have a fire?'

'*Si*. In winter. We have a fuel ration and we find wood to burn, too. We save our coal for the cold weather. There is a stove in each hut, for twenty of us.'

'And the camp?' She was trying hard to envisage what it was like. Suddenly, it seemed important that she should know.

'There is a high fence – I don't like that fence – and guard-towers all round it and the guards have guns.

Always, they are watching us, but I know how to get out. There are ten huts – old huts, but the rain does not come in. And there are places to wash and somewhere we can wash our clothes . . .' His voice trailed to a whisper. 'Look at it. Such a little creature; such noise.'

His eyes narrowed, following the lark that rose singing into a blaze of blue; higher and higher until it was lost to their eyes and became no more than a disembodied song above them. A small, soaring bird that was free.

'And your beds?' To know where and how he slept was all at once important, too.

'There are no beds. We sleep in bunks. They are hard, just pieces of wood. Our mattresses are filled with straw and our blankets are grey, very rough.

'But it's okay. Toni's mamma is glad he's a prisoner. Being a prisoner is better than being missing – or dead.'

'Marco – I'm sorry. I shouldn't have asked you.' Impulsively she laid a hand on his arm. 'And I'm sorry that you miss your family, because I know you do.'

'*Si*. In my country families are big – and noisy, too. I have four brothers and many cousins.'

'No sisters?'

'No sisters, but who needs sisters? Only mamma cares that she doesn't have a daughter. A woman should have a daughter, I think. You have sisters, Kat?'

'No. I – I don't know.' *A woman should have a daughter*. Her eyes filled with sudden tears. 'I don't honestly know . . .'

'Kat. You weep. What is it? What did I say? You once had a sister and you lose her? I'm sorry.' Gently he gathered her to him, holding her close, stroking her hair; just as he'd done the day she had fallen from the stack. Held her safely as if his arms could keep away all harm. 'Not to cry? Please not to cry?'

'I'm not.' She pulled a hand across her eyes. 'I'm all right.' She relaxed against him; against his warm, bare chest, feeling the beating of his heart against her cheek. 'I never had sisters or brothers. I'm an orphan, Marco. Or maybe that's not strictly true. Maybe I'm not an orphan. My parents didn't want me, you see.'

'Kat, I am sad for you. In Italy every woman wants children.' He laid a cheek on her hair. 'My mamma would not have given you away.'

'Mine didn't, either – give me away, I mean. She just dumped me. All I really know about myself is when I was born – the first of July. So now you know.'

'What do I know, Katarina?' His voice was gentle. 'And what do *you* know? That some woman – some young girl, perhaps, had you and couldn't keep you?'

'Maybe. Do you think I haven't wondered about it? One thing I'm certain of is that I was a war baby; conceived in the last war. Perhaps I'm the child of a soldier going to the trenches. And maybe he was killed and couldn't come back to marry my mother. Or perhaps my mother just got into trouble. It happened, and it was a terrible thing – it still is, even now.' She stirred irritably in his arms and made to push him away but he held her, making little hushing sounds against her ear. 'And why I'm telling you all this, I just don't know, Marco. Maybe it's good to get it off my chest. I suppose I still feel that I've got to tell people about it before they find out for themselves. But I've never gone on about it like this before – not the wondering who I am bit . . .'

'Not even to your husband?'

'Not even to him. When he met me he thought I was an orphan, so I let him go on thinking it, though his aunt is always probing. She's got it into her head that I'm Irish.'

'And I think – shall I tell you what I think, Kat?' He pulled her closer and rested his cheek on her hair again. She relaxed against him, closing her eyes. It was what she wanted, to be held; to be close to someone and, for just a little while, not to feel alone. 'I think you are a very

283

dear person, and I don't care who you are or what you are because you are my friend. There now – does that make you feel happier?'

'Mmm.'

'And shall I tell you something else?' He pushed her a little way from him, tilting her chin with his forefinger, just as he'd done that first time they kissed, and she closed her eyes because she was unable to look into his face. 'You are a very beautiful woman; do you know how that makes me feel – me, who should not tell you so; me, a prisoner who should not like you nor speak to you? Do you know, Kat?'

'No,' she whispered. It was the only word her lips could say. She knew how it was for him, how it was for herself, and if she didn't escape from his overwhelming nearness she knew with absolute certainty she might be sorry about it for the rest of her life.

'I think you do, but you will not say it. And you are right not to say it, but oh, Kat, *ti amo*. *Ti amo*, Katarina-mia.'

'What is that?' She smiled, opening her eyes, looking into his. 'My lesson for today? What does it mean?'

'It means that – that we are friends.'

'Then *io ti amo*, Marco. We are friends . . .'

'I am glad. And I am glad you say it to me. But, Kat – only say it when we are alone?'

'All right. If that's what you want – but why?'

'Because we should not be friends. No fraternization. It is not allowed we be friends.'

'I know, and I'll be careful. But because we *are* friends, will you –' She cupped his face with her hands and her eyes looked into his and what she saw there helped her to say, 'Will you kiss me?'

Her words hung on the air above them, lingering, waiting querulously to be called back but she could not, would not deny them.

284

'Please, Marco?'

His kiss was gentle and a little unbelieving, but warm like that first time; the kiss of a friend.

Her fingertips trailed his cheek softly, then timidly, almost, her arms moved to his shoulders, then circled his neck. She closed her eyes and pulled him to her, lips parted, searching for his.

His mouth was hard on hers then, fierce with wanting, and her heart pounded in her ears as she clung to him. Suddenly she was floating on a breathless, beautiful cloud and she didn't care. Tonight she would care. Tonight in her small, half-dark attic she would lie sleepless and ashamed, but now, wonderful, warm, sunkissed now, she was loving desperately and dangerously, wanting him and –

'*No!*' Her cry was harsh as she flung herself away, falling backward, rolling over, scrambling and stumbling to her feet. 'No, Marco! Oh God, *no . . .*'

She was shaking and afraid. She was a fool for wanting him, a fool for denying him, but for one mad, unguarded moment she had needed him; every small, sinful pulse in her body had beat for him and every woman's instinct in her cried out desperately for love.

She had wanted him to make love to her; make love as she knew loving could be, should be. She had almost begged it of him and then the voice came, filling her head. Aunt Min's voice, telling her she was married. To Barney.

'Marco, I'm sorry.' Her lips were dry and it was hard to speak. 'I shouldn't have done that; shouldn't have asked. It wasn't fair of me and I won't do it again to you – I promise I won't.'

On the grass at her feet lay the cigarette that had slipped, unnoticed from her fingers. Slowly it had smouldered to ash. Now it was dead.

'No, Kat, you will not do it again. If you do, there'll be no going back,' he said slowly, quietly. 'Like you want me to, next time I'll take you.'

Distantly, from the far field, came the sound of a tractor being started.

'I'd better go. They'll wonder where I am.' Go, fool. Just go!

'*Si*. And it would not do for them to think the worst, would it?' His mouth was set traplike, his eyes narrow and bright with anger. He opened the field gate and she walked through it, head down.

He was right; it wouldn't do. And, oh, get out of my thoughts, Aunt Min, out of my head. Leave my conscience alone, won't you? Just leave it alone? Aunt Min, who knew things without being told, whose small, unblinking eyes could read thoughts still unspoken. What would she have made of this, Kath demanded silently, breaking into a run, leaving Marco to shut and latch the gate. Would it have pleased her that her nephew's faithless, wanton wife –

Wanton? Was that what she had become or had it always been there, bred into her along with her bad blood? Had her mother been a wanton? Was that, she wondered, how that unknown woman had made her? Had she been carelessly conceived, and just as easily abandoned?

Ti amo. You are my friend.

Oh, Marco, we aren't friends, now. This wanting will scream out between us whenever we touch or speak or smile. Next time, if they were not careful to watch every word, every smile and gesture, that smouldering want would leap into sudden fire, and then what?

Why had she asked for his kiss and why, after, had she said no whilst her heart cried out *yes*! Barney thought the worst of her already; she might just as well have been hanged for a sheep as a lamb, so why hadn't she?

God, what a mess it all was – and Roz thought *she* had problems?

14

Roz awakened to the clamouring of the alarm, reaching out, making small grunts of protest, finally finding it, silencing it.

'Aaaaah . . .' She blinked open her eyes, focusing them on the ceiling, willing them not to close again.

Tuesday, and last night had been wonderful. She raised her arms above her head and stretched her body awake from fingertips to toes, then curling herself into a ball she lay, hugging herself tightly, remembering.

Last night they had come together as if they'd been parted for weeks, not days; as if only last night was left to them, then after that – nothing. And that was mad, she knew it, because soon they would have a tomorrow; maybe a whole year of tomorrows. *Soon*, it would be; not *if*.

She smiled, calling back last night; calling back Paul's lips, his fingertips, his hard, lean body. Once, when first they were lovers, she had been a little surprised, afterwards, had not wanted to move from the circle of his arms. She had even found it difficult to speak, except to say his name, because the newness, the enormity of it, had left her strangely shy, once the pulsating need for him had left her.

But their couplings now were passionate and wild; a defiant, delirious snatching from life, just as it had been last night in the cool green deeps of the wood. Now she wanted to reach out and touch him as if he were beside her in the big bed in York, yet now she must get up and deliver milk, clean the dairy and hose down the milking parlour. Oh, *why* was life away from Paul so ordinary and colourless? Why did she only exist between their meetings; only come alive when she was with him?

She shrugged into trousers and shirt, running downstairs on stockinged feet and it was only when she lifted the kettle and realized it was already hot and full, that she turned to see her grandmother sitting at the table.

'Gran! Morning, love.' She bent to kiss her. 'You're up early. Birds, was it?'

'No.' Briefly her fingertips lingered on the warm young cheek. 'It was Peggy, I suppose. I awoke at three and couldn't get back to sleep.'

'So you spent the rest of the night thinking and brooding? Have another cup with me, and a piece of toast? Nothing will make it better, I know, but –'

'Nothing ever makes losing a daughter better.'

'I know, Gran, and I'm sorry. But I never knew my mother. I've tried to remember something – anything – about her, but there's nothing there; not the sound of her voice, nor the scent of her nor even her holding me . . .'

'You were only two.'

'Yes. It was different for you. You had her, Gran, and she was with you for a long time. I realize she was your comfort for losing Grandpa and your little boy. And now all you've got is me; red-haired Roz – with a temper to match.' She smiled. Then, almost in a whisper she added, 'And who isn't always as good as she ought to be.'

She looked at the woman whose fingers fussed nervously with a teaspoon. Hester Fairchild, her grandmother, mother and father – yes, and friend, too. Always there. Safe and gentle and unchanging, though inside her she must have wept more tears than most.

'You know I love you, Gran, even though sometimes you mightn't think I do. It's just –' She shrugged, spreading her hands in a gesture of bewilderment.

'It's just,' Hester said softly, willing herself to tread carefully, 'that there's a war on, and no one understands your war but *you*. Well, *I* understand. I have loved someone with all my heart and this old woman I've become loves him still. I know what it's like to stand there as he walks away from you and all the time trying to be brave. I know how it is for you, Roz.'

'We've run out of saccharin. Can you drink it without?' Roz set the cup on the table then hurried back to the stove to turn over the toast.

'Gran – I know what you're going to say and yes, I will bring him home, very soon now.' She closed her eyes as she said it, mentally crossing her fingers. 'Very soon you'll meet him; when haytime's over, perhaps . . .'

'Your young man? You promise, Roz?' Her head had jerked up, eyes suddenly alert.

'I promise.'

Hester sighed deeply, thankfully. She had never got this far before and elated she was tempted to ask why soon; why not tonight, tomorrow? But she did not. Instead she whispered, 'Will you tell me his name?'

'It's Paul.' Smiling, Roz turned from the stove. Paul. It was good to say his name in this kitchen; in this house. 'Paul Rennie. And there's only a scraping of marge I'm afraid, and the marmalade's all gone.'

'Never mind. There's another jar due on Friday.' All at once the marmalade ration didn't matter. Weren't there more important things in life – that suddenly Roz's young man had a name and that soon he'd be coming to Ridings.

They ate in silence, Hester accepting that no more must be asked, that all she could do now was wait; Roz knowing she could not, dare not, make any promises that Fate might hear and fling back in her face. *Soon*. That was all it could be for just a little while longer.

'Will you wear black this afternoon, Roz, or your grey costume?'

'Neither. I shall go ordinary, as Peggy knew me. It

doesn't seem right to wear mourning for her; she was always so full of fun. Even after –'

She couldn't say it; couldn't say 'even after Dunkirk'. It would have been like saying, 'even after Paul was killed'.

'You'll wear a hat to church, though?'

'I'll wear a hat, Gran.' Her summer straw. She would say her goodbye in a hat with little pink roses around the crown. That's what Peg Bailey would have wanted.

And there would be no tears. Her tears would all be inside her. She was a Fairchild; later, privately, she would weep.

Tuesday morning, and Kath had set her alarm half an hour earlier. Today there would be a lot to do at Home Farm and half an hour on a June morning was no privation, really, especially when Grace was so dreading what was to come.

'Hullo, lovey,' she said when Kath walked through the open kitchen door. 'You're early, or is that clock wrong?'

'The clock is fine. I must've smelled the teapot. Will it take a drop more water?'

'It will, lass. And Mat and me were wondering –'

'We were wondering,' Mat said, 'if you and Marco could manage on your own for a couple of hours?'

'Of course we can.' Kath took in the great size of him; tall and broad he was, just like Jonty, yet with a leanness that made him seem younger than his fifty years. 'No bother at all.' His face was still young, when he smiled, which wasn't often these days; when he ran his fingers through his still-thick hair.

'I knew you'd say that. Not so long ago me and Mat were faced with the worry of the Ridings acres and wondering how we were to manage, yet now we've got you and Marco and we're as straight as we'll ever be. Thanks, lass, though

290

I'd rather be here, this afternoon; rather be anywhere,' Grace whispered.

Tears that had never been far away since the night the telegram came sprang again to her eyes, and Kath reached for her hand, held it tightly.

'I'm all right, now.' Grace took a deep breath then let it go with a shuddering sigh. 'Off you go to Jonty, Mat. And try not to say over much to him. He was close to Peggy and he's got things on his mind.'

'You're sure, love?' Mat bent to kiss her cheek, still moist with tears.

'I'm sure, Mat. I'll be all right now Kath's come. Away you go to the milking.'

'There now.' Kath placed mugs of tea on the table. 'Just tell me what's to be done?'

'Well, Jonty'll want to go this afternoon – nay, not *want* to go; I think he'd give a lot for it not to be so. But we all want – *need* – to be there. Peg was like our own, you see.'

Like their own. Precious words, Kath thought. Belonging words.

'But what's to be done, Kath? Well, best you leave the Ridings acres alone this afternoon; better if there's someone here, around the house. The man from the egg-packers should be coming – you'll have to see he gets them all right. And he'll be leaving last week's egg money . . .'

'Yes. About half-past three, I should think. Marco can get the cows in, then we'll start the milking. Don't worry yourself, Grace. We'll manage.'

'Thanks, our Kath.' She was rewarded with a small, uncertain smile. 'And, lass – Mat thinks it's best to keep Marco off Ridings land for a day or two; just in case. We don't want anything to happen; not when he's settled in so well . . .

'It's Mrs Fairchild, you see. She'll be there at the

funeral, proud as Lucifer, breaking her heart like anyone would who knows what it's like to lose a daughter, but not a tear nor a sigh about her. She'll be remembering Miss Janet, though, and maybe thinking as how it was a German shell killed Peggy like it was a German sniper that took her man and she'll be bitter. It's always hardest when you can't weep and her sort don't weep in public . . .

'So mind what I said about Marco and watch what you say up at the big house for a day or two? Just a word to the wise, Kath. I think I'll put Mat's suit outside on the line to sweeten. I call it his sad suit; the only dark suit he's got, so it only sees the light of day at funerals. Smelled something terrible of mothballs when I got it out yesterday.'

The whole village would be there in their black this afternoon, and all of them smelling the same. Mothballs at a young girl's funeral. It didn't seem right, somehow.

'Now then,' said Polly, setting the kettle to boil before she had even taken her pinafore from the brown paper carrier-bag. 'A cup of tea, I think.'

Tea comforted, and healed. When all else failed, only tea stood alone. And this day had to be lived through. It wouldn't go away, so be blowed to tea-rationing – today, at any rate.

'So everything's ready, is it, ma'am? You'll be wearing your comfortable black shoes – I'll give them a polish. And it'll be the usual hat and the pearl hat-pin, though I wouldn't recommend black stockings; not when you're not family.'

Not family? No. Maybe not. She would not intrude this afternoon, nor sit in the Fairchild pew, opposite the choir stalls. Today she would slip in at the back, try to keep her thoughts in check and send her love and understanding to the couple who must live through the pain of this afternoon.

'Will you walk there with me, Polly?'

'Aye. If that's what you think best. There's to be no flowers; only family's. A silver collection, though, for the Red Cross.'

'Yes. Sensible. Do more good than flowers.' Such a sin; flowers left there to die and wither.

'I did hear it said,' Polly stirred the teapot round, 'as how the Army brought her home last night. Two of her friends from the gun-site came up with her coffin, but they had to go straight back. Couldn't stay overnight. Seems the war don't stop for funerals.

'So how about a spoonful of sugar in your tea this morning? Set you up nicely, a spoonful of sugar will.'

Polly Appleby knew when enough was enough and they sat in silence until Hester said, 'I try to be grateful, Polly, that I still have Roz.'

'Aye.'

'Do you know – right out of the blue – Roz told me she was bringing her airman to meet me. Soon, I think. Maybe after haytime, she said.'

'Why after haytime? Why not tonight?'

'I don't know. But he's called Paul Rennie – she told me that, too.'

'Well, I suppose the lass has her reasons, and I suppose you'll know them in good time. And it'll soon be haytime. Hay's getting good and thick; two or three weeks more sun, and it'll be ready for cutting.'

'It will, though there's none here at Ridings, nor wheat, either.'

'Happen not. But your land'll be growing wheat next year. And come autumn your potatoes and sugar-beet'll be ready for lifting. Are we all right for milk?' she demanded, in desperate need of another cup. 'Just think, ma'am. Those acres will be paying you back something at last. The Master would've been pleased about that.'

The Master. Hester stirred her tea, eyes gazing out over the treetops and back across the years. Strange that lately she had thought about Martin so much; had heard the deep, rich timbre of his voice, heard his laugh. He had been so close that sometimes she had thought that if she walked quietly to the ruins, she would see him there in his uniform, coming down the staircase toward her as he'd done only minutes before he left.

But he had never been there; only an empty shell to remind of what was gone. For all time. All she had now was Janet's child.

Kath watched them go, Mat, Grace and Jonty, straight-backed and unwilling to Alderby church. She had told them not to worry, that she would look after things; have the kettle on the boil, and the teapot warming, for when they got back.

Once, Grace said only that morning, hospitality following a funeral had been lavish in these parts. It had stemmed from necessity, she supposed, for in the old days men and women had walked miles to a burial and been in need of sustenance before they walked back.

Old-fashioned Yorkshire hospitality, she said, and the custom still kept – until the war, that was. Ham cooked on the bone, ribs of beef and plates of bread and best butter. And maybe a glass of port wine, afterwards, with a slice of good, rich fruit cake. But the rationing of food had put paid to all that; not even a cup of tea could be offered, now. There were some, even, who said that funeral feasts would be a thing of the past by the time the war was over, and maybe it would be a good thing.

Kath sighed as she set a tray with cups and saucers in readiness for their return. She was glad Marco was working in the far cow pasture, checking the fences. Faintly she could hear the sound of the hammer as he beat a post secure. She didn't want to be alone with him, today especially. She had lain awake last night as she had known she would and told herself it must never happen again. She had married Barney for better or for worse; been glad of his name and the respectability marriage gave her. She had made her bed, she would lie on it and anyway, only a fool expected marriage to be one long honeymoon.

It had all been fine, last night. She had accepted that from here on she would behave as a married woman was expected to behave; that loneliness and separation was no excuse for what she had done. But her resolve was gone by morning and her good intentions flew high and wide when Marco smiled his lovely smile and said, '*Ciao*, Kat.' The churning was back inside her, and the longing she felt to touch him made it hard to remember all she had vowed that July Saturday almost three years ago. But when this day was over, she would tell Roz about it. Maybe talking would help, though knowing the state of mind Roz was in these days, maybe it wouldn't.

She hoped Marco wouldn't come to the house; that he'd have the sense not to. With luck he would stay in the field until it was time to bring the herd in for milking and by then Grace and Mat and Jonty would be back.

Lord! It was all such a mess and the war to blame for it all; the fault entirely of this war that women were alone, and men were prisoners and that people gathered now in sadness in Alderby.

Coldly, deliberately, she cleared her mind of such thoughts and made herself think instead of the little greystone church and a young woman called Peggy who wore the uniform of a soldier.

'I'm so sorry,' she whispered.

Hester was glad that the ringing of church bells had been forbidden for the duration of hostilities; grateful that today there could be no slow, mournful intoning of the calling bell. And it was good, too, that the passing bell could no longer be rung; the death bell, as they called it around Alderby.

They had rung the death bell in the last war for Martin; one sombre peal for each year of his life. She could hear it still; feel the cold, even yet, of that December day. At least Peggy's parents had been spared that terrible tolling; could give back their daughter on a day bright with sunlight.

She lifted the latch of the church door and it sounded like the snapping of a whip in the hollowness inside. Heads turned automatically then turned back again to the altar and the studying of the Elizabethan glass window of Christ rising, illuminated to near-splendour by the brightness of the day outside.

Hester sank stiffly to her knees. She did not pray. Today there was too much hatred in her for that. Clasping her hands together she stared ahead to the coffin that lay at the foot of the altar. Peggy had come home to Alderby and had rested all night in the little church, covered by the flag of her country. On that coffin lay the khaki cap of a woman soldier, its brass badge brightly polished, and with it a rose; one pale pink rose, picked tenderly from a cottage garden and placed there with love. It was the kind of thing only a woman would do.

Martin. Hester said his name in her heart. She had not seen his grave, nor picked a flower for him. His memorial stone was here, in St Mary's churchyard and when the time came, Roz knew it was her wish to be laid there, beneath Martin's stone.

But not just yet. Not until Roz was happily settled. *Oh, Roz, my dear, it's a dreadful world we've wished upon you young things.*

Roz closed her eyes, bowed her head and whispered the Lord's prayer. She didn't know what else to pray for, except that Peggy was at peace, now.

Were you in Alderby, Peg, on St Mark's Eve? Did you wraith past the church porch when the rest of us were asleep, and if you did, was anyone there with you?

She lifted her head to gaze at the flag-covered coffin,

wondering where Peg was now. With her young man, she hoped. She ought to be with him; they deserved to be together. Closing her eyes again, she clasped her hands tightly together.

Please let there be a heaven? Like it says in the Bible, let there be one?

There'd be no sense to all this killing, if there wasn't. No sense at all . . .

Jonty Ramsden sat with his parents in the pew they usually occupied at the front of the church. He'd rather have been at the back, where no one could have seen him. It hurt to see that coffin, there. It didn't seem right – her so still, now.

Peg Bailey. Margaret, really. They'd come in for their fair share of teasing over the years.

'Now think what might have happened if that old stork had dropped his girl-bundle on Home Farm, eh? You'd have been Jonty Bailey, wouldn't you, and our Peg'd have been called Ramsden.'

And they'd laughed and gone along with it, he and Peg, for country children learned soon about begettings and birthings and that storks had nothing at all to do with them.

I'm sorry, Peg, and ashamed. It's awful being young, and a civvy – bloody awful . . .

Grace reached for Mat's hand. She wasn't a bit brave. If they didn't come soon, Peg's parents, she'd be weeping again and making a fool of herself in front of the whole of Alderby. And they'd think, 'Look at Grace Ramsden taking on so, and her with her son safe at home . . .'

Poor Jonty. He'd miss her, too. They'd shared a christening, with Peg making most of the noise; bawling the devil out of her like the good 'un she was. And Jonty and Peg at their confirmation; Jonty in his first long trousers and Peg in her white dress and pretty little veil. Not so very long ago, the vicar had read the banns of marriage for Margaret Bailey, spinster of this parish, and the lass had planned a wedding that the war hadn't allowed. Peg had not come here as a bride . . .

She felt Mat's hand tighten on hers, saw Jonty turn, heard the small rustlings at the back of the church.

Peg's family had come, were walking stiff and straight to the reserved pews at the front of the church; walking to where their daughter waited.

Please, Grace prayed, *let me hold my head high and not make a fool of myself? I loved that lass. She was like my own* . . .

She took a deep breath, closing her eyes, grateful that the war had spared Jonty; angered that it had taken Peg. Either way, she couldn't win.

Tears spilled from her eyes and she let them fall unchecked. You couldn't fight grief. You had to let it take you, wring you dry and leave you spent.

God – be gentle with her parents?

Roz waited beside the church gate as the congregation filed slowly away. Her grandmother had already left, slipping out by the side gate, making for Ridings where she might weep for all grieving mothers.

Roz waited until Grace and Mat had passed, then falling into step with Jonty she touched his arm briefly, smiling up at him.

'Shall we walk home together – the back way?'

'Thanks, Roz. I'd like that . . .'

'Sure you didn't want to go to the graveside?' she asked as they passed the Black Horse and turned into Home Farm lane.

'No. Mum's staying, but I –' His voice thickened and he looked down, unable to go on.

'It's all right. I know you cared for Peg and I know how you feel.'

'Do you? Do you, Roz? How can you know what I'm feeling right now?'

'Because I know *you*, Jonty Ramsden.' Reaching for his hand she circled it in her own, holding it tightly. 'Come on, you old dope, let's get back. Bet you anything you like Kath'll have the kettle on . . .'

Hands clasped, they walked away from the sadness. For a little while, the war that had separated them had never happened and he loved her still, as a boy loves his sister; young and innocent again.

'Are you going out tonight?' Kath asked of Roz after they had called a goodnight to Grace.

'I'm going, but I don't think he'll come. They were stood down last night, so it's almost certain they'll be on tonight.'

'You'll be home then, later, if –'

'No. Think I'll go up to Tuckets Hill if Paul doesn't show. You can see Peddlesbury from up there. Might watch the take-off, if they go early. Why do you ask?'

'Because I want to talk to you. About *me*.'

'You and who else, Kath?'

'I'll come to Tuckets about half-past eight – just in case?' Kath begged the question.

'If you want to. Sounds important.'

'Not really – oh, I don't know! I just need to talk, I suppose. Well – best be away,' she murmured, eyes averted, as they reached the orchard gate. 'It's been a pig of a day. I'm glad to see the end of it. See you, then?'

'Hope you don't, but I've a feeling you will.' Roz shrugged. 'And if they're operational, at least it'll be –'

'One less to go,' Kath finished gravely.

'One less.' Nearly there, and it *was* going to be all right. She was certain of it, now.

Roz sat, arms hugging her knees, looking beyond the cluster of trees and rooftops that was Alderby to the little river, smudged yellow with wild irises and bordered by elders.

Roz had waited in Peddlesbury Lane until eight o'clock, but Paul had not come, so she had gone to Tuckets Hill to watch the Lancasters taking off. If by chance the bombers should be stood down and Paul could leave camp, he would know where to find her.

She would wait for a little while longer. It was pleasant here, and quiet. If she went home there would only be questions and she didn't want to talk about Paul until that last op was over. She'd tell all, then; insist that maybe for a whole year Paul would be away from flying and time enough for them to marry, even though the law said she wasn't old enough.

It would be wonderful, though, when it was all out in the open; when she and Paul need never again worry about being seen together. They were engaged, of course. He'd asked her to marry him that afternoon in York, but Gran's permission would make it official and then she could call him her fiancé. Openly.

Paul. The man she would marry. He was down there now, probably eating a supper of bacon and eggs washed down with hot, sweet tea. It was almost always bacon and eggs before an op. Then he would put on his flying kit and draw his parachute; there would be the inevitable joke about him bringing it back and changing it for another one, if it didn't open when he bailed out.

And after that they'd be driven to Sugar, out there beside the perimeter track; driven by an aircraftwoman called June who was lucky for them, Skip said. Some women drivers were chop-girls, bad to have around, but little Juney was okay and went through the rituals with them; the silly, childish things most crews did before take-off. Roz smiled. Paul had told her about the crew who always had a pee on the tail-wheel before take-off, another who wouldn't fly without a copy of the New Testament stuffed into each left-hand top pocket, and one who flew with a one-eared teddy bear called Wilfred in the cockpit.

Wouldn't have dreamed of taking-off without Wilfred . . .
But with Sugar's crew it had to be the counting ritual.
June would walk the full span of Sugar's wings, solemnly
counting, 'One, two, three, four. They're all there, Skip.
Nobody's nicked one of yer engines. The old crate'll fly
. . .' Then she always stuck up a thumb and said, 'So-long,
lads. See you.' Good old Juney.

People could be so amazing, Roz pondered. War brought
out the best in some, the worst in others. Some people –
just a few – were unkind. Jonty knew about people like
that. Jonty had been hurt and upset today, in church.
She was glad they had walked home together. They were
friends again, now. Friends. That was all.

She saw Kath as she skirted the clump of rowan trees
at the bottom of the rise. She had forgotten Kath was
coming, and who she needed to talk about she had no
idea. She hoped it would be about Marco. Barney was
dull and pompous. What on earth had she been thinking about to marry a pudding like him? She raised her
hand so Kath would see her, then rose to her feet to
wait.

'Hi,' she said, sitting down again, patting the grass at
her side. 'He didn't come, you see.'

'No. There's plenty going on, though.' They studied the
activity below them. 'What are they doing?'

'Looks as if the armourers are fitting the guns. They'll
be flying tonight. Nothing's more certain.'

'And those tractors, Roz? Is it bombs they're pulling
behind them?'

'It is. They'll be loading them into the planes. Bombing-
up, it's called. It'll be a while yet before take-off, but best
if it's dark when they cross the coast. These light nights
aren't a lot of good to air-crews. But you haven't come up
here just to count them out . . .'

'No, though I'll stay with you, till they've gone.'

'Tell me about Marco. What happened this afternoon

when you were alone?' It was Marco Kath wanted to talk about; Roz knew it.

'*Nothing* happened! He was in the far field all the time – never came near.' She had been glad he hadn't; sad he hadn't. 'This was waiting for me when I got back. Take a look at it.' She took an airmail envelope from her trouser pocket. 'Where has he been, do you think?'

There was a postcard in the envelope; a picture of a river with a garish sunset reflected on its waters and palm trees beside it. *Sunset on the Nile*.

'Want me to read it, Kath?'

'Be my guest. Nothing there the vicar couldn't see.'

'"*Managed to get a look at the Pyramids. They are big. Yrs.* B." Nothing there the Censor couldn't see, either. But which pyramids, and where?' Roz frowned.

'Probably the Cairo ones. Maybe Barney's been on another of his long convoys.'

'And is that all? One postcard in over three weeks? He isn't exactly inviting writer's cramp, is he?'

'I don't know. I just don't know what to think, any more.'

'Neither do I, old love. But you didn't come all the way up here to show me *that*?'

'No. Want a cigarette?' Kath settled her back against the trunk of a silver birch tree and offered her packet. 'It – it's Marco. He kissed me.'

'My word!' Roz grinned.

'All right! If you think it's funny, there's no point in saying any more!' Kath drew deeply on her cigarette.

'Okay. So he kissed you – again? That makes it twice.'

'Yes, but this time I asked him to. Stupid of me, wasn't it?'

'Dunno, lovey. Depends how far you went.'

'What on earth do you mean!' Kath's cheeks blazed pink.

'I mean did he or didn't he – try it on? And if he didn't, what is there to get so het up about?'

'Of course he didn't try it on. Nothing happened – honestly. But it could have . . .'

'You reckon?' Roz watched the rising of a smoke ring with studied concentration. 'There you both were, in full view of Grace's kitchen window –'

'We were in the poultry field.'

'All right – there you were in the poultry field and you in your dungarees – not what you'd call quick-release gear, exactly. You'd have had plenty of time to count to ten, wriggling yourself out of *those* things. Nothing could have happened unless you wanted it to. Grow up, love.'

'Roz! Well! I must say you've a knack for being very – very *blunt* at times,' Kath gasped, embarrassed. 'I ask you for advice, and you –'

'Oh, come off it, Kath. I can't tell you what to do, and you know it. Just think it out for yourself, will you? Things aren't so good between you and Barney, then along comes Marco who's a decent bloke, in spite of the fact that he's one of *their* lot –'

'That's it! An *Italian*!' Kath threw down her cigarette then jumped to her feet to stamp it out. 'I ought to have my head examined. What could it lead to? And imagine the scandal? What would Grace think if she knew I liked him. And as for your Gran!'

'And Barney. Don't forget him. Don't think he'd be over-pleased about it.'

'Don't, Roz. I don't know what's got into me. I *don't* . . .'

'No more do I, Kath, but I understand. Marco's supposed to be a greasy Wop, and we shouldn't fraternize. But he's a nice guy, who'd have been at university reading law if this war hadn't happened; a man your mother would have been glad to make welcome if you'd taken him home – well, you know what I mean?' she finished, lamely.

'I know.' Kath sat down again, accepting with a shrugging of her shoulders that what had happened was her problem, and hers alone. 'It's just that all of a sudden, life's become so unreal.'

'You're right. And, Kath – you're not the only woman on her own who's finding it difficult, you know,' Roz murmured, eyes fixed on the activity below them. 'Oh, they give us our orders; do this – don't do that. *They*. The faceless ones. They should come out of their ivory castles once in a while and see what it's like in the real world!'

'Ha!'

'And I can't sort your love life for you, Kath – I wouldn't dare try. But I do sympathize and I think you'll have to take it one day at a time. I mean – tomorrow they could send you down to Devon or up to Scotland. Had you thought of that?'

Kath had not, and the thought dismayed her. 'They couldn't. They wouldn't – would they?'

'I doubt it.' Roz shrugged. 'They're more likely to move Marco on.'

'*Marco*?' Not once had she envisaged such a thing. She'd been so pleased with her new life, she thought it would go on for ever.

'Makes you think, doesn't it?' Roz said softly. 'Losing Marco, I mean . . .'

'It does. We'd never see him again, would we? We couldn't write to him; he couldn't write to us. That would be it, wouldn't it?' she said, flatly.

'Suppose it would. Just one thing, though. It isn't *we*, but *you*. Marco's *your* problem, not mine. Though what you could do about it, I don't know. There's a war on, isn't there?' A war on. A trite, useless phrase. Everybody said it these days. It explained a lot; it explained nothing. 'And, Kath – I don't think I'll wait for very much longer. Seems take-off won't be just yet. Wish I could ring Paul, but they wouldn't accept the call; not when they're flying.

'Think I'll go home and wash my hair. I can hear them go from home. Will you count them out, too, Kath – wish them luck? All of them?'

'I will. I'm nearer to Peddlesbury than you are. I'll count.'

'Has it helped – saying it out loud, I mean,' Roz asked as they stood at the top of Peddlesbury Lane.

'I think it has. That bit about Marco or me being moved on tomorrow. Put things into perspective all right.'

'Be my guest. Love lives sorted, confessions heard any time. Goodnight, Kath. Sleep well . . .'

Kath did not sleep well. She lay awake until the bombers began their take-off; roaring and thrashing overhead; a fearsome mixing of full fuel tanks, spiked guns and bombs, ready primed. And four great engines, at full throttle. All that, hurtling over the chimney pots at Peacock Hey once, twice, ten times. Ten crews whose average age was twenty-and-a-bit; all of them wanting to get there and get back. Get back safely.

Where would it be tonight? Skip knew. Already Paul would have begun his calculations. They'd be all right. Sugar would make it. They would all make it. They'd probably not be back until well into the morning, either. She and Roz could count them down together.

'Thanks, Roz,' she whispered to the ceiling. 'It helped. More than you know.'

Having to accept that They could part them – that had really clinched it; made her face the situation for what it really was; that in truth it would be near-unbearable to leave Home Farm and any of the people who lived or worked there. Marco most of all. She'd had to admit she would be devastated were he to leave.

Tomorrow they could send her down to Devon or up to Scotland, Roz had said. *Tomorrow*, that was, and everyone knew that tomorrow never came.

Oh, please, it didn't?

305

15

Last night Bomber Command had hit the Third Reich again, the early news bulletin gave out triumphantly. Yet another one-thousand bomber raid had dropped a massive bomb-load on Essen, inflicting heavy damage, leaving fires raging behind them that could be seen for miles. As yet, no indication of our own casualties had been released, the announcer said in his one-tone voice, but it was thought that our losses in men and aircraft had been light.

This morning, his words did not send fear tearing through Roz, for she knew already that Paul was safely back. The last of the Peddlesbury Lancasters had thundered overhead as she and Kath returned to Home Farm, walking either side of Daisy's head.

'That's him! That's Paul!'

The last aircraft home was always S-Sugar. It had to be because not until all had returned could she be certain that Paul was back. It was the same with take-off. When all were safely airborne, then Paul was safely airborne. It was the way her anxious mind worked and lately, Kath frowned, the strain was beginning to show in the tightness of her mouth, her paler than usual face.

'There was a queen,' Roz murmured, 'who said that when she died they would find Calais written on her heart, and when I die there'll be *thirty* written on mine.'

'Getting bad, is it?'

'Mm. I try to think how much worse it must be for Skip's wife but it doesn't help any. The baby's due in about a month, I believe.'

'Yes, but think how it'll be for her when Skip goes on leave; the baby there all safe and sound, Skip safe and

306

sound, too; well, for a year at least. And think how pleased your gran's going to be to meet Paul. Don't think about five more ops to go, Roz; think about the day you take Paul home. Your gran'll fall for him – she won't be able to help herself, bet you anything you like.'

'Kath?' Roz reached for a bottle from the crate. 'It's awful having a baby, isn't it – really bad?'

'Now how would I know, will you tell me? But I know women who've had babies.'

'And what did they say it was like?'

'They were all a bit apprehensive, I suppose, but every one of them said that the moment they held their baby they forgot every pain they'd ever had. And if having a baby is so awful, women would stop at one, now wouldn't they, so go and give Polly her milk and less of your worrying. Skip's wife is going to be just fine – and so is Skip, and Paul!'

'Bless you, Kath. What would I do without you?' Roz pushed open the gate, happy again. Mercurial Roz. In a state of bliss one minute and deep in despair the next.

'Do without me?' Kath whispered. 'But you won't have to. I'm not going anywhere – Scotland *or* Devon.'

She crossed her fingers, though, as she said it. Just to be sure.

Arnie Bagley walked slowly to school, thinking about life in general and its unfairness to one boy in particular.

He desperately needed sixpence, though fivepence would do, really. Fourpence for the card and a penny for the stamp, because birthday cards were better if the postman brought them.

Soon, it would be Aunty Poll's birthday. He had seen the very card for her in the paper shop in Helpsley and it was important that he should buy it as soon as possible. There'd be no more cards like that one, said the shopkeeper; no more cards with red roses and gold writing on them till the war was over. Pre-war stock that birthday card was, and a pre-war price, too. Soon you wouldn't be able to buy a card like that for love nor money, he said, never mind fourpence.

It wasn't, Arnie frowned, as if he were poor. He was good at adding up and Mam had sent two pounds since Christmas – could Aunty Poll let him have sixpence out of that, he'd enquired. But indeed she could *not*! The money from Hull was staying in the Penny Bank where she'd put it until such time as it was needed for Grammar School uniform.

There was nothing else for it, Arnie accepted. He could earn the money, though how he wasn't at all sure, or he could borrow it, but since Aunty Poll said never a lender nor a borrower be, it looked as if he would have to win it.

He waved to Mrs Fairchild who was picking roses in the ruins, then returned his thoughts to the matter of the money and the War Weapons Week, to be held on the fourth of July.

War Weapons Weeks had become a way of life in wartime Britain. Once a year, every hamlet, village and city held its money-raising week for the war effort, urging every man, woman and child to place every penny they could spare into national savings. It was amazing, Polly Appleby had said only last year, the amount of money Helpsley had saved, though it wasn't all that much of a nine-day wonder since no one could buy anything in the shops these days, and what they could was rationed to the point of severity.

This year, the people of Helpsley and those who lived in the villages around had voted unanimously to save enough money to purchase an armoured gun-carrier as their particular contribution to Victory – though the Savings Committee had no idea at all how much an armoured gun-carrier cost and some, though they declined to admit it, had never even seen one. So they had set their target at one thousand pounds and hoped for the best, trusting that local people would save enough money during War Weapons Week to buy this magnificent weapon of war.

'*Buy* it? What if the Germans drop a bomb on it – what happens to our money, then?' Arnie had demanded anxiously.

'Happens, lad? Nothing happens to our money. We don't actually *buy* the dratted thing; we buy saving stamps and saving certificates on the understanding that we'll leave the money where it is till the war's over, that's all.'

'So what about the armoured gun-carrier, Aunty Poll?'

'Well, the Government buys it on the *strength* of what we all save. It's too complicated to explain proper. High finance, it's called. The banks know more about it than I do.'

It was then, exactly, that Arnie began seriously to consider working in a bank. High finance sounded interesting. Buying something on a kind of understanding and not actually paying the money for it was *very* interesting. If he worked in a bank, fourpence for a birthday card would be no problem at all! But that wouldn't be until he was sixteen and Aunty Poll's birthday was next month, so it was the War Weapons Week, or nothing.

Not that he wasn't looking forward to it. There would be the roll-the-penny and the bran tub at a ha'penny a go, though last year nobody had found the prize till the very end and then it was only a bar of chocolate wrapped in fancy paper. Arnie was looking forward most to guessing the weight of the pig – especially if the pig got away like it did last year. The commotion that followed had been magnificent, with all the ladies screaming something awful and the vicar damning and blasting, not caring who heard him since the animal had made a terrible mess of his rose beds. The Air Force band from Peddlesbury would be playing for the parade and then they would give what the programme said was a selection of melodies throughout the afternoon, outside the committee tent.

But it was the races that would be the saving of him. This year, each winner would receive a silver threepenny piece; those coming second would get twopence whilst the third would get a penny and even a penny would be welcome in his present state of poverty, Arnie thought morosely. He would, he calculated, have to win two firsts; two seconds at the very least. Two seconds would cover the cost of the card, he supposed, and if the worst came to the worst he could always write OHMS on the envelope and put it through the letter-box himself. And what was more, this year the boy and girl who won most races would each be presented with a saving-stamp, though saving-stamps were only paper to be stuck on a card for the duration, he considered, and what he was in desperate need of was the clink of *real* pennies, dropping into his hand.

There was nothing else for it. He would have to enter every race for the under-tens and try like mad. It was the only way to get the money.

'Well now, Arnie. Putting the world to rights this morning, are you?'

Arnie looked up from his mental arithmetic to see a smiling Mrs Ramsden, bucket in hand, going to feed the hens in Two-acre field, like as not.

'Not really,' he sighed.

'Then what?' Arnie had a very engaging sigh. 'Tell your Aunty Grace?'

'I was thinking about fivepence, but fourpence would do, I suppose.'

'That's a lot of money, Arnie . . .'

'Yes.' Four weeks' pocket money. You didn't have to know a lot about high finance to work that one out.

'And what's this fourpence for, will you tell me?'

Grace was fond of Arnie. He reminded her of Jonty

at that age, though she liked small boys no matter what shapes and sizes they came in.

'It's for Aunty Poll; for her birthday card, and oh . . .' He told her all in a breath what the man in the paper shop had said and how that card would be gone, never to return for the duration, if he didn't get fourpence, soon.

'I could earn it,' he brooded, 'but there aren't many jobs for boys, so I'll have to try to win it at the War Weapons Week. If the card's still there, that is.'

'Well, there's fourpence-worth of jobs around my house, if you want them.' Grace did not hesitate. 'I know for a fact that Mr Ramsden's heavy boots need a good coat of dubbin before he puts them away for the summer and there's my brass candlesticks to polish. Shouldn't wonder if there wasn't a sixpence to be earned on Saturday, if you set your mind to it.' She smiled at the young boy who could be Jonty, all those years ago, fretting for twopence for a comic. 'Shall I expect you at nine o'clock, say?'

Arnie struck a deal there and then. Sixpence covered the card and the stamp and a penny left over for a gob-stopper. And until he learned a bit more about high finance, he supposed that working for money was the surest way out.

Good old Mrs Ramsden. Grown-ups – some of them – weren't all that bad, when you came to think about it. Not bad at all.

Grace watched him go, whistling. Bless the lad. Must see to it that he got his birthday card. She'd call in on Polly, later, to make it all right for Saturday.

My, but that boy had come on a treat since he'd lived at the gate lodge. A fair treat.

'Roz,' Kath ventured as they hoed their way steadily, monotonously through the last of the sugar-beet, 'remember what I once asked you – about somewhere to live after the war?'

Roz stopped, glad of a break, leaning on her hoe.

'What I'm trying to say is did you mean it, Roz? And you *will* remember, won't you?'

'Of course I will, but what's brought this on all of a sudden?'

'Just me, I suppose. Thinking. And it isn't any good; I've turned it over and over in my mind. I've told myself to be grateful for what Barney's done for me but –'

'*Done* for you? What's Barney ever done for you that would set the world alight? Apart from going all dog-in-the-manger like a great spoiled schoolboy and making you miserable for no reason at all that I can see. Go on, Kath. Tell me!'

'He married me. I had a name that was mine; really mine.'

'And what else?'

'He gave me a home of my own . . .'

'Kath – he took you home to his mother's house. And now his Aunty Minnie's in it. You said yourself that she'll never let go.'

'I know, and I really did try to be grateful. But I can't go back to things the way they were when the war's over. I can't go back to that house and that – that –'

'Bed?'

Shrugging, Kath gazed steadily down. She had said it now and she ought to have felt relief that it was out in the open, but she didn't. Because it was her own fault. She hadn't had to marry Barney, but she'd been sick and tired of being a nobody; of scrubbing and cleaning someone else's house. No one had ever paid her such attention before; she had fallen for his flattery and his blinkered determination to have her.

And then what? Just a few months of being a wife, then separation before either of them had learned to adjust; he to her dreams, she to his Victorian attitude to all women – except his mother and her sister Minnie.

'Sometimes I think I'll just clear off,' she choked, no longer able to keep the trembling inside her away from her voice. 'Sometimes I think I'll ask for a transfer – put Alderby and Marco behind me. They'd give me one, I suppose, if I asked . . .'

'Kath!' Roz jabbed her hoe deep into the earth so that it stood upright, swaying from side to side, then digging deep into her pocket she took out cigarettes and matches. 'Here – let's stop for a puff? And for heaven's sake don't do anything stupid. If you're determined to turn your life upside down, why do it amongst strangers? And besides, *I* need you. Had you forgotten that?'

'My life's upside-down already, only today is the first time I've said it out loud. And I'll never get things straight in my mind with Marco around because he's the cause of it, really.'

'No, he isn't! Marco just brought things to a head sooner than you expected, that's all.'

'Oh? What you're trying to say is that if it hadn't been Marco it would have been some other man?' Kath lifted her head, her glance defiant. 'So what does that make me, then? Some kind of mixed-up tart? And why don't you hate Marco Roselli? You ought to hate him just as I should. Why don't you?'

'Don't change the subject – but since you ask, I couldn't hate anybody – not as Gran does. If anything happened to Paul I'd just go to pieces, go numb I suppose, but I couldn't start hating the man who'd done it.

'Although sometimes I think there's more to it than that – Gran hating the Germans so, I mean, for killing Grandpa. I think there's another grief that no one knows about. I can't explain it, but it's there. Still, all this talking isn't getting the war won, is it?'

They began working again, steadily, automatically, thinning out the beet to a hoe's width, staying close enough to chat.

313

'What could Barney do if I told him I thought we'd made a mistake?' Eventually, reluctantly, Kath spoke.

'I don't know. I suppose he could demand that you went back to being his wife – you know what I mean? There's a legal phrase for it, but I'm not sure what.'

'And if I said no, I wouldn't go back?' She could not prevent the shudder that ran through her.

'Then I suppose he could divorce you for desertion or – or refusing him his rights.'

'Roz! Stop it! You make it sound so *awful*. And it isn't. It's only that I wanted – just *once* – to do something *I* wanted to do. And this is how it's ended up. You're right, Marco isn't to blame. He was nice to me, that was all, and I began comparing him to Barney and somehow it got out of hand. It could just as easily have been Jonty who sparked it all off, couldn't it?'

'I don't know.' Roz threw down her cigarette and stamped it out. 'Tastes awful, that thing! I know you like Jonty, but –'

'But I never wanted Jonty to kiss me, did I?'

'No, Kath, you didn't, so we're back to square one, aren't we; back to Marco? And that's a pity, because you'll never be able to have him – even if you weren't married – because how long is this war going to go on for? It isn't over in Europe yet, and still there'll be Japan. The Americans have come in on our war and we'll have to do the same for them, won't we?

'But you *are* married and Italy is a Catholic country. How do you think Marco's mother would like a divorced woman for a daughter-in-law? Divorce – even here – is a nasty thing. There's still a stigma attached to it. You being divorced would be almost as bad as me having an illegitimate child. It just isn't done . . .'

'It's done all right, but it doesn't half rock the boat when it happens, more like.'

'Exactly. So be very careful, old love?'

314

'Yes. You too . . .'

'Hmm. Reckon we've both got problems, Kath.'

'I reckon we have. But problems apart, it's pretty well all plain sailing, isn't it?'

Gravely they regarded each other, then suddenly the laughter came. It had to.

'Oh, *damn* this war,' Kath gasped.

'No!' Roz was instantly serious. 'It gave me Paul.'

'Yes. And I suppose it gave me what I've always longed for – to live in the country.'

'And it gave you Marco, Kath.'

'Back to Marco, again . . .'

'We are. And we always will be. He's in your life, whether you want to admit it or not.'

'I've made a mess of things,' Kath murmured, 'haven't I?'

'Maybe. But why not wait and see? Why not take it one day at a time? Fifty years from now, you and me both could be looking back wondering what all the agonizing was about.'

'You could be right. Maybe then, what's happening now won't seem all that important.'

'Exactly. So why don't we both wait and see?'

Roz stood very still in the shelter of the hedge. She liked to be early; to be there, when he arrived.

Sometimes he came swinging up the lane to meet her; other times a transport would slew to a stop and he'd jump down, smiling. Always smiling. Paul was confident, now, of finishing his tour of ops.

'Get that thirteenth op behind you,' he said, 'and it's a piece of cake, till the last one.'

They had survived that thirteenth op. All of them but Jock had walked from the shattered bomber. And then they'd got S-Sugar, the lucky one. They would be all right.

She heard his low, slow whistle; saw him walking up the

lane. She didn't run to him, or raise her hand. She just stood there, watching him, wanting him, loving him, the blue of his eyes, the brilliant fairness of his hair. Everything about him, she loved; the hands that touched her, caressed her, and his body that was hers and oh, dear sweet heaven, had anyone ever loved as they loved?

She lifted her face as his arms claimed her and closed her eyes as she always did when he kissed her.

'Hi.' His voice was low. 'Missed me?'

'I missed you,' she whispered, her lips on his. 'Can we walk a little? I want to talk to you. I told Gran about us, you see – well, that soon I want to take you home to meet her.'

'How did she take it?' He laced her fingers with his own then tucked her arm in his, drawing her closer. It was how they must be, now. Even walking, their bodies must touch.

'She was fine. We'll tell her we're engaged, won't we?'

'I'll tell her – *ask* her. It's only right that I do. Where are we going?'

'The riverbank. There won't be many there tonight.' Only lovers like themselves walking close, stopping, sometimes, to kiss. And being seen with him didn't matter so much, now that Gran knew.

Theirs was a slow-moving river that looped back on itself, encompassing the village, almost, then straightening out to flow on through flat, fertile fields, to York. Here at Alderby it was pretty, its banks thick with greenery and rich with flowers. Here ducks nested and lately swans had come. They could walk the loop of the riverbank, then return to where they had started; at the Peddlesbury Lane Wood and its secret places that only lovers knew.

'Darling – do you think she'd let us get married? If I tell her we'll be fine, once I've got university behind me? I'll be almost sure to get in – they're giving more places to ex-servicemen when the war's over. I'll be able to look after you all right, when I've got my degree.'

316

'Gran'll like that – you wanting to be an architect, I mean. My father was an architect. It was he who prettied up Ridings, after the fire.'

'He made a good job of it. I've seen it. You can get a good view flying over. From a height, you can see everything laid out and imagine how it used to be.

'I've always wanted to be an architect, but now I suppose I *ought* to be. I've helped knock so many buildings down I think I should do something when the war's over to make it good. But do you think she'll see it our way?'

'Yes, I do. She was only my age when she married Grandpa, though there wasn't a war on for them. But didn't you say your father was against you getting married, Paul? Doesn't he want you to concentrate on getting a good degree – no distractions?'

'He does. They both do.' He smiled down and small, wanton shivers sliced through her as they always did when he smiled like that. 'But, Roz – I'm nearly twenty-three and God alone knows how old I'll be by the time it's all over. They still treat me as if I'm their boy and I'm not. I've earned the right to marry. If your gran will let you we can start making plans as soon as the tour's over – if you don't want a big affair, that is.'

'Darling! Who has a big affair these days? But are you asking; *really* asking?'

She wanted him to say it again, here on the riverbank, where copper-beech trees rustled brown and the grass beneath them grew green and lush; like he'd said it, hesitantly almost, at Micklegate Bar, only this time it was *when*, not if.

'I'm asking, my lovely love. Marry me? Soon?'

'I'll marry you.' Gently she touched his cheek, her eyes wide with wonder. 'And as soon as we can. I do so love you, Paul. And I'll go on loving you, always.'

'Fifty years from now, will you?' he teased, tweaking her nose.

317

'Fifty years; a hundred years. On and on, into forever.'

'Come back to the wood?' he said thickly, sudden need in his eyes.

'Yes,' she whispered, her lips against his cheek.

And later she would lie still in his arms and he would tell her about that massive raid; about flying with a thousand bombers to Essen. He always told her, now; talked the killing out of himself.

But afterwards, that would be. When they had loved.

'Paul said,' Roz murmured, 'that it was really something, on Tuesday night.'

'The big raid on Essen, you mean? A thousand bombers – takes some imagining, doesn't it? The ten that took off from Peddlesbury made enough noise.'

'They all met up over the south coast, he said, then went in in waves.'

'Bet it wasn't very pleasant, being on the receiving end of that lot. You could almost feel sorry for them, couldn't you?'

'Yes, but never let Gran hear you being sorry for the Germans. Do you think we'll win this war, Kath?'

'Dear God, I hope so! Imagine being occupied? Trouble is, I just can't see an end to it – not yet. There's those Japs doing almost as they like in the Far East and as for the fighting in Russia . . .'

'The early news said there'd been heavy fighting in North Africa. Seems Rommel's trying to take Tobruk. If their lot get Tobruk it won't look so good for us there.' She stopped, a sudden flush on her cheeks. 'Sorry, Kath. I should have thought about Barney being there. Do you worry about him – like I worry about Paul, I mean?'

'I don't want him to get wounded,' Kath murmured. 'Just because things are a bit awkward between us doesn't mean that I don't care. Oh, I don't show my feelings like you do, Roz, but that's the way I am.' Of course she wanted Barney to come home safely but then, she'd always thought that he would.

'Maybe you don't, but it wouldn't do for everyone to be like me, would it? Or could it be that you haven't fallen in love yet – *really* in love. Wait till you do, and see how you feel, then.' Roz swirled the dregs of cold tea around the bottom of her mug then upended it, frowning at the pattern of the tea-leaves. 'Know anything about telling fortunes from teacups?'

'No, I don't. And don't change the subject.' Kath got to her feet, brushing grass from the seat of her overalls. 'And don't think I haven't wondered what it's like being crazy about a man. There's a war on. Anything could happen to any one of us. Civilians are in the war, too. Don't you think I haven't wanted to be in love like you are? And how long do you think women like me are going to be able to put up with it? There's a ring on my finger that's supposed to make me immune to feeling; to give out a warning. Keep off! Don't touch! She's married! Well, I'm flesh and blood and this war could last for years and years – all my young years gone!'

'I know, love. I know. It must be the very devil for you when I go on and on about Paul. Don't think I want Paul to be flying for years and years. I don't. One tour of ops – that's lucky. Two tours – hardly ever.' She shrugged her shoulders eloquently. 'That's why I'm going to ask Gran to let us get married. It's so stupid, having to be twenty-one before you can please yourself what you can do. They conveniently forget we're minors, though, when they want us to fire guns and fly bombers and drive tanks and get shot at.

'Hell, but I'm sick of this war! If Paul is flying tonight I think I'll go down to the Black Horse and get drunk!'

'Let me know if you do.' Kath's mouth quirked down at the corners. 'I just might join you. But right now there's these arks to shift and cows to milk and –'

'Kath – have you and Marco talked since – well –'

'Since I made a fool of myself, you mean? No. Well – nothing personal, that is. Suppose you can't blame him, though. I did offer it on a plate almost, then got cold feet. Maybe he thinks there's no future in it, and maybe he's right. Stupid of me, really, when probably all he wants is just to be friends. *Ti amo*. A friend.'

'A *what*?' Roz demanded, eyes wide. 'What was that you said? The bit in Italian, I mean.'

'Oh, just my *lezione*. I'm picking up quite a few words, now.'

'And *ti amo*? That's Italian for just good friends? You're sure, Kath?'

'Of course I'm sure. Marco said it was.'

'Then I've got two bob that says he's been having you on.' Roz laughed, eyes bright with teasing.

'*Roz?*' Having her on? How? And come to that – *why*? So they'd kissed? A kiss meant nothing. They were friends, weren't they? 'What do you mean – two bob?'

'Two shillings that says *ti amo* means I love you. I'm almost certain it does.'

'But it can't! Marco *wouldn't*!' She felt the heat of the flush that stained her cheeks. He'd said it to her and she, idiot that she was, had said it to him, too; had smiled into his eyes, and said it! 'Roz, he wouldn't . . .'

'Seems he has.'

'All right, so maybe – just maybe – you're right. But you'd better wipe that smirk off your face because I don't think it's one bit funny. And when I see him, I'll – I'll –'

'You'll what, lovey?'

'I'll give him a good telling-off, that's what!' She drew in a deep, indignant breath. 'Imagine if I'd said it – innocently, I mean – and someone heard me – someone who understood? We'd both be in big trouble.'

'Kath! Can't you take a joke? Think of it – it probably made his day having the best-looking landgirl for miles around tell him she loved him.'

'A joke? You're sure? You're certain it doesn't mean something well – *really* awful?'

'Something like how about us making mad, passionate love? No, Kath – I'm almost sure it means what I said, and I'm sure he was only having a bit of fun, truly I am.'

'Yes. Of course.' But fun? Oh, no, he'd meant it. Looking back to the way it had been, she knew he'd meant it. 'A joke, Roz; you're right. But he'll have to be told; he really will!' The minute she saw him, he'd be told!

Kath sighed loudly, impatiently, plumping up her pillow yet again, turning over for the umpteenth time. Another sleepless night, she shouldn't wonder – but there had been quite a few of those lately. Nights spent counting taking-off bombers; thinking about Roz and Paul; thinking about Marco and this afternoon that had given her reason for even more wide-awake nights. In the milking parlour, it had been. Not exactly the place, come to think of it, to have your entire life turned upside-down.

'Damn!' Roz had said. 'I've forgotten to give the cats their milk! Won't be long.' And she had disappeared without another word, leaving the two of them alone.

'It wasn't very kind of you, Marco . . .' She had been waiting, agitated, all afternoon for just this moment and the words came out as she had rehearsed them in her mind. 'Saying what you did, I mean, about being my friend.'

'*Si*, Kat? But I *am* your friend.'

'Then you told me the wrong words for it.' She turned to face him, eyes wary; unwilling to say those words, now that she knew their real meaning.

'*Ti amo?* Who told you?'

'Roz did.' She watched the jet of water from the hosepipe collect into a pool at her feet. 'Why did you do it?'

'Because I wanted to say it, Kat.' His eyes sought hers, begging for her understanding. 'And because I wanted to hear you say it to me.'

'Then you shouldn't have. It could have got us both into trouble. And you know the way things are with me.'

She turned to walk away from him, but he took her arm and turned her to face him again.

'I don't know how things are with you. I only know how *I* feel about you, about us. What else matters?'

'*Matters?*' Shaking, cheeks blazing, she stuck out her left hand, jabbing with her forefinger at the ring there. '*That's* what matters. Me, being married – or do you think a married woman on her own is fair game – is that it?'

'Fair game? I don't understand fair game. What I understand is that I love you. *Io ti amo*, Katarina,' he said softly. 'And I know you love me.'

'Marco! We are *not* in love; we can't be.' She closed her eyes, shaking her head, unwilling to look at him. 'We hardly know each other. It isn't love you're talking about; if it's anything it's – it's *attraction*. It's me being lonely and you being lonely, but it isn't love, it mustn't be.'

And please don't look at me like that. Don't want me, Marco. Please don't want me with your eyes . . .

'Why mustn't it be? I loved you the first time I saw you, Kat. You brought soup. "Mrs Ramsden sends soup," you say to me. I saw the ring on your finger then, and it make no difference.'

'Then it should have!'

She stood there, fighting back tears; fighting the urge to touch him, gather him to her, lift her mouth to his. She stood unspeaking, for words must be carefully spoken when her heart contradicted her head. Love *could* happen in one small second. Roz had loved Paul right from their first meeting; from the first naked glance, even. Call it love, call it attraction, call it needing or wanting – it happened. When love happened it didn't wait for moon and June, and soft lights and sensuous music, it was there, in the air, sometimes coming like a jabbing, flashing fork of lightning, taking no account of wedding rings or vows or if that man was your country's enemy.

'What's to be done, Marco?' She walked over to the tap and turned it off. The floor was awash, their long hessian aprons sodden at the hems. This couldn't be love; not in a shed that smelled of cows. 'It's got to stop. It's all so – so *hopeless*.'

'Stop? You turn love off, then, like you just turned off that tap?'

'I can try, Marco,' she whispered. 'I can try. And there must be no more kisses; no more saying I love you.'

'So how can that be? You want I should leave here – no more coming to Home Farm?'

'No! That wouldn't be fair to you nor to Mat, either. But think; we can't love each other. Even if the war ended tomorrow and suddenly you were free, it wouldn't be any use. I'm married, Marco. It's as simple as that.'

'Married! Only you don't love him. I know it. I see it in your eyes and I know it when you kiss me . . .'

'Don't! No more kisses, I said; no more touching, even.' She had closed her eyes tightly against the tears that threatened; closed them because the sight of the hurt in his face sent pain stabbing through her. 'Help me, Marco? Don't stop being my friend, but don't want me. Help me to try not to want you?' she had begged him.

Try? She stared unblinking at the ceiling. She could still see it, dimly. Soon it would be the longest day, the shortest night. Winter it had been when she and Marco met and now summer blazed and with it had come a longing between them that couldn't be denied, hopeless though it was.

Roz – I envied you; envied that dangerous loving of

yours, even though it made me afraid and glad it hadn't – couldn't – happen to me. But it has happened, and I don't know what to do about it, because I'm not like you. I'm not free to love.

The tears she had fought for so long came in a flood of self-pity and she buried her face in her pillow with a low cry of dismay.

How long she wept and when finally she slept, she had no idea. She only knew that as the alarm jangled her awake the first face she saw with her mind's eye was not Marco's nor Barney's but that of Aunt Min, lips set, eyes narrowly triumphant.

'What will I do?' she whispered out loud and Minnie Jepson's vinegared rasping voice answered, 'Do, Kath Allen? You do your duty to your husband, that's what!'

Duty. A cold word; cold, almost, as charity and she'd had enough of that in her life and enough of duty, too.

All at once a blaze of defiance took her, shaking away the melancholy that wrapped her round. She threw back the bedclothes and swung her feet to the floor.

Leave my conscience alone, Aunt Min! Get out of my life, won't you, and take your smug hypocrisy with you! And next time you write to Barney, tell him that Kath's up to the eyes in it, will you? You'll enjoy that, won't you, Aunt Min?

Up to the eyes, was she? Well, she'd see about that! Maybe soon they'd *all* see!

Snatching up spongebag and towel she hurried down to the washroom. She was in a hurry to get to Home Farm, and Roz. Roz must be the first to know. Roz would understand.

Kath was waiting, foot tapping, when Roz pushed open the dairy door. She had been eager to be out, snatching only a mug of tea, too impatient to be away to spare time for breakfast.

'Roz! I've been waiting ages! Listen – I spoke to Marco, after milking . . .'

'And?' Roz had known she would, given the opportunity – one which had necessitated giving the grateful farm cats a second ration of milk. 'Thought you might have told me about it, but then I saw you belting back to Peacock Hey like you'd got something on your mind.'

'I had. Believe me, I had! Marco knew what he'd said. He wasn't pulling my leg, either. He meant it. He said so.'

'Oh, my word! Seems I owe you –'

'Forget the bet – this is serious! I'm in a mess, Roz; a heck of a mess, but at least one thing's come out of it all.

'I worried myself sick last night – cried myself to sleep. But this morning it hit me. I don't have to put up with it, you see.' She paced the length of the dairy then turned, eyes wide in a chalk-white face. 'So I'm married? Well, I've had enough, so you'd better take it seriously about letting me have a cottage because I'm not going back to Barney when the war's over!'

'You're not *what*? Say that again? You're leaving him?'

'I mean I can't face it; can't face that house nor Aunt Min nor Barney touching me ever again. I couldn't let him. I couldn't!'

'Oh, lovey.' Roz shook her head, her expression one of blank disbelief. 'You've got yourself into a mess all right. And you can't have Marco, you know that, don't you? Not for years and years – if ever.'

'I know it, though how we're going to manage is beyond me. Marco said he wouldn't come to Home Farm any more – well, they can't make him work . . .'

'Best solution all round, I'd say, but you'd both be miserable, then; it'd be worse, I should think, than the two of you being here and having to pretend the other doesn't exist. But what do you intend doing? Will you ask Barney for a divorce?'

'No! How can I? It's me that's the guilty one, not him.'

'Guilty? But you haven't done anything – have you?'

'Of course I haven't. It just hasn't worked for me and Barney, that's all,' Kath whispered, tears trembling on her voice. 'Isn't it a pity when a marriage dies that you can't bury it decently? Why does there have to be a guilty party? Why does one of us have to go off the rails?'

'I wouldn't know. Divorce is something I don't know a lot about. But are you absolutely sure, Kath? Is walking out on Barney going to be worth all the bother and worry it's going to cause? He can make it difficult for you – he probably will.'

'I know, but my mind's made up.'

'So you'll write him a dear-John letter?'

'Of course I won't. I couldn't do that to a man overseas. I'll carry on with the letters. When he writes to me, I'll write back to him. And I'll tell him what I'm doing – around the farm, that is, and what's happening at Peacock Hey. I don't want to hurt him, but I can't go on being grateful to him for the rest of my life. I'll tell him, face to face, when he comes back, tell him I'm sorry and that if he wants it he can have all the Army allowance money I've saved.

'But this morning – all of a sudden – I thought I'm *me*! Not Kathleen Sykes, that was; not Mrs Barney Allen – I'm Kath. And I won't apologize any more for being left on a doorstep. I won't live the rest of my life being ashamed because I was abandoned. I can milk a cow and drive a tractor and if the worst comes to the worst, I can still go back to scrubbing and polishing when the war is over. I'll manage!'

'Without Marco?'

'I'll have to. Oh, I could love him with all my heart, but I won't let it happen. Maybe like you said, either of us could get moved on and that would be that, wouldn't it?

And heaven only knows what a mess I'm getting myself into, but I'm sick of being sorry about myself. The good Lord gave me a chin – think I'm just going to have to stick it out, and see what happens!'

'Atta girl!' Roz grinned. 'I take it you'll be coming to the dance, then?'

'I'll be coming.' Pretty summer dress, gold sandals and all! 'Oh, Roz, what on earth has got into me?'

'Search me – but whatever it is, it suits you. Now – are you going to harness Daisy, or am I? There's work to be done – don't forget there's still a war on!'

But fancy that, now? Roz frowned. Kath giving Barney his come-uppance? Talk about worms turning! Whatever next? Flying pigs dropping bombs on Berlin?

16

The RAF transport driven by a woman corporal came to a stop at Peddlesbury guardroom gates. Leaning out of the window she called, 'Dance!' and the red and white striped pole that barred their way rose slowly to let them through.

The transport had started from Helpsley, made a stop at the Black Horse in Alderby then gone on to Peacock Hey to pick up landgirls there. Women partners were in short supply at the Friday dances at RAF Peddlesbury and the Air Force obliged by taking them there and taking them back when the dance was over.

'Hi,' said Roz as Kath took the wooden seat at her side. 'Everything okay?'

'If you mean were there any letters – no.' At least tonight she could enjoy herself without being reminded too much about the decision she had made. Not that she had changed her mind – she hadn't, but that first flush of heady defiance was taking a bit of getting used to and Kath Allen's conscience had always plagued her, ever since she could remember. 'Everything's fine. I'll enjoy myself tonight if it's the last thing I do, so –'

'Point taken.' Roz smiled. A decidedly self-satisfied smile, Kath thought, but then very soon Roz would be with Paul, dancing close. Soon, the whole of her world would be enclosed by Paul's arms and nothing and no one would exist but themselves. Lucky Roz, who lived her life on a knife-edge and loved wildly; Roz, who counted the days, now, as a child counted the days to Christmas. For Roz, the next few weeks would be agonies of apprehension and fear intermingled with frenzies of joy and relief. There would be no in-betweens. Life with Roz would be tumultuous until it was all over.

The transport drove slowly, past Nissen huts with roofs of curved metal sheeting; past camouflaged buildings and tall, wide-doored hangars. In the distance, at the far end of the runway, stood the control tower, angular and many-windowed, painted like the rest in the camouflage colours of black, green and khaki. Every building was utilitarian and unpretty, standing out with something akin to vulgarity against so beautiful a landscape. It would be good when it was all over and they were pulled down, the concrete runways broken up, ripped out and carted away. Or would the aerodrome be abandoned to rot and crumble? Kath frowned. Would elderly men and women come here to stand remembering their fear-filled youth and say, with just a little pride, 'I was here at Peddlesbury in forty-two. My, but you should have seen it then. Lancasters all over the place, taking off every night,' – with the passing of the years it would *seem* like every night – 'and knocking hell out of the Krauts. Bloody marvellous, it was. Made you feel proud. You young 'uns haven't a clue; haven't lived . . .'

Looking back, it would seem marvellous, Kath supposed, all the bad times forgotten. Fifty years from now . . .

'You're quiet.' Kath felt the jab of an elbow.

'Mm. Just thinking about this and that. I'm looking forward to tonight.'

She was. She would forget Barney and Aunt Min – forget Marco, even – she would dance every dance in her gold slippers and have the time of her life. Tomorrow was another day. Tomorrow there might be a letter – from North Africa.

The truck braked to a stop and the driver let down the tail-board.

'Right, girls. This is it. Straight ahead to the dance.'

She smiled as she recognized Kath, a smile that was returned.

'Hi! I remember you. York station . . .'

'York station.' A cold, December night and no bus for two hours to take her to Peacock Hey. She had come a long way. 'Nice to see you again, mate!' Kath Allen was one of the crowd, now; a landgirl with six months' service in. She'd changed some, since York station. She lifted her hand, smiled a goodbye.

Oh my word, changed? But she wouldn't think about that. Not tonight.

With the exception of the flight-engineer, the whole of S-Sugar's airmen had come to the dance. The flight-engineer, a valued member of the crew because he was a failed pilot who could land the Lancaster in an emergency, waited at York station for a fiancée who was booked in for six nights at the Black Horse, Alderby. And the very best of British! said the remainder of the crew, saucily.

Paul and Roz found seats in a quiet corner; Skip smiled at Kath, holding out his hand as the first dance was called, and the tail-gunner who had come to them as Jock's replacement, went in search of little Juney, the driver who brought them all luck.

The dance hall – the gymnasium, really – was pleasantly cool. Tonight, blackout curtains need not be drawn until nearly eleven o'clock and open windows let in cooler air and let out cigarette smoke that in winter would have hung in shifting clouds at the ceiling.

'Everything okay?' Skip smiled, taking her in his arms. They took it for granted, now, that they were partners.

'No complaints.' Not tonight. 'And Julia?'

Julia, Skip's wife, at home with her mother in rural Derbyshire.

'She's doing great – finding it a bit difficult to sleep nights, now. Bump does his daily dozen the minute she lies down, she says. She's sure we'll have a boy. Got the kick of a footballer, she says – boots and all. And how's your better half?'

'Fine. Just fine.' Kath smiled. 'Not a lot of letters lately, but there *is* a war on.'

'Mm.' Skip pulled her closer and rested his cheek on her head. Kath knew the way things were. Both of them married, their weekly liaison was safe and uncomplicated. 'Julia wanted to know how my landgirl was getting on last time she phoned and I told her you were still madly in love with me.' He grinned. 'A very understanding lady, my Julia. Doesn't mind me going to dances. Expect your bloke's the same?'

'Oh, yes. Barney's very understanding.' She closed her eyes, begging forgiveness for so blatant a lie. 'Last time I heard he'd been on a long convoy, had a look at some pyramids and managed to find a pint or two of decent beer.' All of it true, really, though there were many shades of grey between black and white. 'You'll tell Julia I asked about her, won't you? Y'know, it's funny; we know each other so well, you and me, Skip, but I don't know your name – except that it's Johnny.'

'That's life, girl, when there's a war on. It's John Wright, as a matter of fact, though I answer better to Skip these days.'

John Wright, from somewhere in Cheshire. Captain of a massive bomber with a crew of seven; a father-to-be at twenty-four and well above the average age for aircrew. Life was a bit unfair, Kath frowned, if you let yourself dwell overmuch on the whys and wherefores. Life was two-faced, as well; like the talk they'd had in the sugar-beet field.

'. . . *a nasty thing, divorce – still a stigma attached to it. Almost as bad as having an illegitimate child. Just not done . . .*'

Not done. Yet They, the faceless ones, separated husbands and wives without a second thought, then threw men

and women – *lonely* men and women – together regardless
of what might and often did happen. Yet still They clung
to their dogma. *Thou shalt not . . .*

Life wasn't a bit unfair, Kath brooded; it was bloody
unfair, sometimes.

'Sorry, Skip,' she murmured, stumbling. 'Got two left
feet tonight. Be an old love, and buy me a beer?'

They left the floor, smiling at Paul and Roz as they made
for the end of the room where beer was being sold.

Paul and Roz, dancing now, she with her arms clasped
tightly around his neck, he with his hands laid possessively
on her buttocks, their feet hardly moving. Lovers, their
actions proclaiming it and they not caring who knew it.

Lucky Roz. She who met life head on and who would
think about the consequences tomorrow. Roz who was
loved as she, Kath, wanted to be loved, *needed* to be
loved.

She wished she could get a little tipsy tonight. Not
drunk; just relaxed enough to help her forget this war,
this damn' awful war. But you could never get drunk
when you were miserable, and if you weren't miserable,
the need wouldn't arise.

Oh, yes; life could be very unfair – if you let it.

It had been pleasant this morning, picking the raspberries,
Hester thought. Getting up early and beating the black-
birds to it. Even so early, the sun had been bright and
the walled kitchen-garden, though in a sad state of neglect
these many years, had been warm and private and she had
found herself singing quietly as she picked.

This year, the fat red berries were ready long before
their time, due, no doubt, to an early spring followed
by a week of rain at just the right time, and the warm,
south-facing corner of the walled kitchen-garden in which
they grew. Hester always gave raspberries to Polly and
Grace; it was a custom that even a war couldn't break,

though what either would do with them when sugar was in such desperately short supply, she had no idea. But wars, she insisted stubbornly, could not be allowed to interfere with habit – not at Ridings.

She tapped on Home Farm kitchen door, then walked in. Walking-in was a country custom, just as it was the custom to enter a house by the back door, the front door being used only on important occasions, like a child being carried to its christening, a bride leaving for the church or, sadly, at times of bereavement. On all other occasions the back door sufficed, it being considered more neighbourly and better all round than depositing muck and mud in the hall.

'Good morning, Grace – and Arnie?' Hester regarded the small boy, scowling with concentration, tongue protruding. On the newspaper-covered table top stood ornaments of copper or brass, several pieces of rag for putting-on and a bright, fluffy yellow duster. 'My word, but you're busy.'

Arnie glanced up, smiled broadly at his grown-up friend, then returned to his rubbing.

'Arnie is earning himself a sixpence,' Grace supplied, 'on account of it soon being Poll's birthday, aren't you, lad?'

'Mm. For a card. And a stamp.'

'A special card,' Grace confirmed. 'A card with roses on it and what else, Arnie?'

'A *pre-war* card, with real gold writing on it. I've got to buy it soon or somebody else'll get it and I want Aunty Poll to have it. Mrs Ramsden's going to get it for me when she goes to Helpsley on Monday.'

'That's a very nice thought, Arnie, and thank you for reminding me.' Hester smiled. 'I've brought the usual, Grace, though I wish I could have brought a bag of sugar, too. Raspberries aren't the same without sugar, are they?' Eight ounces of sugar a week went nowhere.

'Happen not, but Mat fair loves them and he's not all that much of a sweet-tooth, thanks be.' Grace smiled. 'You'll take a cup, Mrs Fairchild?'

'Thank you, no.' Hester made it her habit never to accept tea, rationing being what it was, though in the old days she had dearly loved to call in at Home Farm for a cup and a chat. 'Oh, dear. Such a state we're in. No sugar for raspberries; no sugar for *anything*.'

'No.' Grace cast her mind back to peaceful times, and the squirrelling of summer's goodness, learning to her cost that such ordinary things needed sugar and never would she take those precious white grains for granted again. 'Do you remember the pantry at Michaelmas? Such an array. Rows and rows of jams and chutneys, jars full of bottled fruit? Such a sight it was . . .'

'And now there's nothing in pantries, nor in the shops, Grace. It took a war to put paid to unemployment, yet there's nothing to be bought now with a man's wages. Birthdays aren't any fun at all.'

What should she give to Polly? What *could* she give? Not even a tablet of her favourite lavender-scented soap to be had.

'You're right.' Grace nodded mournfully. Being young was no fun these days. A man couldn't even buy his sweetheart a ring, except one with diamonds in it so small that they were no more than chippings. And as for wedding rings – now they had to be in nine-carat gold, if you please. Seemed wrong, somehow, starting out in marriage with a utility ring costing one pound, nine shillings and sixpence. And what about a bride's trousseau? One pair of fully-fashioned stockings, two pairs of knickers and a petticoat, with hardly enough clothing coupons left for a nightie. Twenty coupons gone; six months' allowance and nothing to show for it. And as for wedding dresses with yards and yards of satin in the skirt; well, wedding dresses were downright unpatriotic, now.

Mind, Jonty's young lady would be all right – if ever he got around to asking one to marry him. Grandma Ramsden's jewel box had a heavy gold wedding ring in it, aye, and one set with pearls and garnets that any lass would be proud to wear. Sad he'd not be giving it to Roz . . .

'Sad,' she murmured, hastily adding, 'about the young ones, I mean, and nothing for them to buy . . .'

'Sad,' Hester agreed, recalling Polly's indignation at having to queue for twenty minutes for a yard – *one* yard, mark you – of knicker-elastic only yesterday. 'You know, Grace, since the Japs came into the war, our supply of latex has practically dried up. Most of the rubber-producing countries overrun, now.' Knickers without elastic? It hardly bore thinking about.

'Aye.' It wasn't the Far East that Grace was so bothered about; it was no further than your own doorstep that you needed to look, she thought grimly. Shops empty and people who'd lost everything in the bombing having to beseech the Board of Trade for dockets just to replace a few essentials. 'It's coupons for this and dockets for that and permits for a few yards of curtaining, even, and them taking months and months to come through. My cousin's girl has a little one who's grown out of her cot, but can she get a bed for the bairn? Takes time, she's been told and small comfort that is, with the little one's feet sticking out at the end.'

'So we just go on counting our blessings, Grace.' Hester rose to her feet. 'And we are luckier than most in these parts. At least we're safe here, and can sleep nights. Ah, well – must be away.' She smiled down at the boy who was more interested in his polishing than in the seriousness of rationing and privation. 'Come and see me soon,' she whispered, her hand lingering on his untidy shock of hair.

It was lonely, now, at Ridings with Roz hardly ever in. She dreaded the winter with its short days and long, closed-in nights. Some mornings, even in the kindness of summer, she dreaded getting up to face the day. She missed Martin so much, now – perhaps because all at once she'd had to face facts and facts were that Roz was no longer hers. 'Don't forget now – if Polly can spare you.' Such a delight of a boy; such an inquisitive, active mind. A privilege, that's what a son was and her son – hers and Martin's – had died in her womb.

'Mat shall have the rasps for his pudding tonight.' Grace smiled, holding open the door. 'It was kind of you to spare the time picking them . . .'

Time. It was something she had plenty of, Hester thought as she opened the orchard gate. Time to brood, to think, to want Martin as she hadn't wanted him for years, now. Time to grow old without him, the husband they'd snatched from her.

'Oh, my dear, how I need you with me now . . .'

It was the wrong time to see him, that man she had so far avoided; to come face to face with Marco Roselli when she was aching so for Martin, could not have been more wrong. For just the passing of a second she hesitated, off balance, then taking a gasping, steadying breath she walked, stiff-backed, toward the man she would rather never have seen.

He was tall, but then she had known that, yet she was not prepared for his slimness, for the warm, golden-brown of a body stripped to the waist, the thick, dark hair. Nor was she prepared for the slight bow of his head, the smile that was genuine, the whispered, '*Buon giorno, Signora.*'

How could he; how *dare* he? She clamped her lips tightly, stared at him, through him, then turned her head away as if to shut him out, ignore him, make believe he were not there; not deserving of even a passing glance. One of Martin's enemies on Martin's land. She could not prevent him being there; she could not, even, demand that

Roz should not work with him, but she, Martin's wife, need not and would not acknowledge him.

She tilted her chin and, shaking inside, walked on, her breathing uneven. Since January, when he had been forced upon them, she had been careful to avoid him, to go nowhere he might be, yet this morning when she had been totally unprepared for this meeting, they had come face to face in her own orchard. She quickened her step, anxious to be at Ridings, feel the comfort of its walls around her. She needed to be in Martin's house, needed his nearness; to stand still and quiet so she might hear his voice. Because she did hear it. More and more, now, she felt his presence. All she need do was to stand beside the garden seat and he would walk down the staircase to her.

Her heart had slowed its erratic beating, had steadied to a dull thudding she could feel in her throat, and even as she placed her hand on the door knob she knew she had been wrong. A nod, no matter how slight, an acknowledging of his presence would have cost her nothing and left her with her dignity. Instead, she had over-reacted; had flounced past him like a teenaged girl so that he had had the better of the encounter.

She closed the door behind her, shutting out the morning. She felt calmer, now. She was in her own kitchen, in her own house – the house from which Martin had left the morning of his last leave. She was safe, again.

Filling the kettle, she placed it to boil, dismayed that today was Saturday and Polly would not be here; nothing to do but wait until Roz came home. She looked at the empty cigarette packet on the table, wishing that she smoked, that it hadn't been considered fast for a woman to be seen with a cigarette between her fingers when she was young. She would have liked to light one now; inhale its smoke deeply as the young ones did. Since the war, almost everyone smoked. It was good for stress, they said, and calming. The young ones needed them.

Taking the empty packet she threw it on the fire, watching the flames take it. When she had had a cup of tea, she would go back to the garden and pick raspberries for Polly, then walk down the drive to the lodge with them. It would help rid her of this unreasonable anger; help allay this awful loneliness.

The pain of Hester's encounter was still with her when Roz came home at midday. Sighing, she held her cheek for her granddaughter's kiss, fighting the indignation that struggled to be brought into the open.

'The prisoner,' she said much, much too quietly, 'was in the orchard and I think it has come to something that even on my own land I must put up with such – such *intrusions*.'

'Gran?'

'The Italian, I'm talking about. Impudent as you like he wishes me a good morning – in Italian – then smiles at me as if we're long-lost friends. I tell you, Roz –'

'Don't get upset, Gran – *please*? So Marco smiled at you? There's nothing wrong in that, surely? He's young, Gran, like Kath and Jonty and me. He isn't exactly enjoying this war and heaven only knows when he'll see his family again.'

'Then more fool him for coming here. But I never wanted him at Ridings; I said so at the time and I don't like to hear you defend him, Rosalind. Not here, in my own home.'

'All right. I'm sorry.' Walking over to the sinkstone she began to scrub her hands, eyes down. She didn't want Marco to be the cause of trouble; especially now when Kath was getting so fond of him. 'But don't go on, so. I don't suppose he wanted to be in the army any more than our own boys wanted to. Don't stoop to the level of those Helpsley women? It isn't like you to be so unfair. Marco works very hard, and we – well, we all like him,' she added, defiantly.

'You may please yourself, I suppose, though it hurts me to hear you talking like that.'

'Darling – sit down.' Gently Roz took her shoulders, guiding her to the table. 'I've only got half an hour and I don't want to waste it talking about the prisoner. Ready for your soup? Try to eat some – please?'

Carefully, she filled two bowls; without speaking she cut bread. She could do without this upset. She had worries enough of her own.

'You know, Roz, it's strange to me that you've talked more about the Italian than ever you've done about your own young man.' Hester said it softly, though her eyes were filled with reproach.

'Paul? But I told you about him.'

'You told me his name, Roz, and that you might bring him to meet me . . .'

'Gran – I *will* bring him and before much longer, I hope.' She hadn't wanted to talk about Paul; not until she brought him home, until she knew it was all right for them. But her grandmother was upset, so she had little choice. 'I want to bring Paul to meet you when he's finished his tour of ops – that's thirty raids *over Germany*.' Almost without thinking she had laid stress on those words. 'I think he'll be flying tonight or tomorrow, and if he is he'll only have four more to do and then he'll be taken off flying for a time.'

There, she'd said it, now. And she hadn't wanted to; hadn't meant to say anything about him until she was absolutely sure it was all right.

'But why wait? Can't he come soon – tomorrow, Roz? I'd so like it if you'd bring him. Why must it wait?'

'Because –' She was crumbling her bread, making a mess on the table top and she couldn't lift her eyes to face her grandmother fairly and squarely. 'Because – well, we want to get married when Paul comes off flying, but you won't let us, will you? You'll say I'm too young and you'll forget that you were my age when you and

Grandpa got married, that our war is just as awful as yours and –'

She took a deep, despairing breath then forced her head upwards to gaze clearly into her grandmother's eyes. She'd said it, now. She'd messed it up when she'd been so careful for so long. And all because of Gran's hatred for an unknown sniper who had waited at the window of a ruined house for the slightest of movements; had lifted his rifle and had squeezed the trigger, gently, gently. 'Oh, God, can't you forget your war? Can't you help me and Paul to fight ours?' She covered her face with her hands, fighting back tears of sadness and pity and frustration.

'Roz – darling child – don't cry.' Pushing back her chair she gathered her grandchild to her, making little hushing sounds, gently pushing back the hair that fell over her face. 'Please don't cry. Do you think me so awful? And how can you be so sure I won't say yes? Don't you think the sooner you bring your Paul home, the sooner you'll know?'

'Gran – you mean you'd let us?'

'I mean that I want to meet your young man – talk to him, see for myself what he's like. You don't expect me to say yes, until I've met him?'

'No. And I don't know a lot about him myself – only that I love him so very much. I haven't met his parents, either. They want him to go to university, you see, so he hasn't said anything to them about me.

'But Pippa knows about us. She's his twin – Philippa. She's a sergeant in the WAAF. They aren't a bit alike,' Paul says. Pippa's dark, like her father and Paul is fair – very fair – like his mother. He's nearly twenty-three and he wants to be an architect, like my father was . . .'

Oh, and Gran, there are things I can't tell you – not yet – but you must let us get married – you must.

'Roz, child, it's all right. All I want is for you to be happy. I only want you to be sure, that's all. Bring Paul home – soon. And let's eat our soup. If you don't fret about Paul, I'll forget about the – the prisoner and we'll both calm down and act like grown-up people, shall we?'

'Okay.' Roz blew her nose loudly. 'And you're right. Of course you must meet Paul, first . . .'

She picked up her spoon, staring down. She didn't want the soup; she didn't want anything. She felt churned up inside and ready to scream. When she wasn't with Paul she went to pieces, just thinking about things. Only when she was with him could she force herself to believe that things were normal and would turn out right. But for Paul, she would have done anything.

She lifted the spoon to her lips. The soup tasted awful. She wished she could be sick.

'It was good of you to come up here,' Roz murmured. 'Didn't much fancy waiting it out on my own.'

'No bother. Didn't fancy a night in the hostel; most of them have shoved off into York, to a show. Peacock is so quiet it isn't natural.'

They sat, arms round knees, looking to their left to Alderby, to their right to the aerodrome. The evening sky was bright and cloudless. From here on Tuckets Hill it seemed that if they tried hard they would pick out the spires and towers of the York churches.

'I knew Paul would be flying tonight. Doesn't seem right, somehow, going bombing on a Sunday night.'

'It's one less to go,' Kath countered, practically. 'And the sooner Paul's off flying the better, as far as I'm concerned.' The strain was telling, now, on Roz. That darting smile was seldom seen lately, and the mischief had gone from her eyes. 'And no, if you're about to ask, there wasn't a letter there when I got back last night, though I hope he's all right.'

There had been heavy fighting in North Africa, the BBC news broadcasts had given out soberly, to be followed by more graphic accounts in the daily papers. Rommel was attacking at Mersa Matruh. Mersa Matruh had surrendered. Rommel's tanks were pushing on to El Alamein. There had been heavy casualties.

She hoped he was all right. Her love for Barney was gone – if love there had ever been – but still she wished him well.

'Did you know,' Roz said softly, her eyes fixed on the control tower at the runway end, 'that Gran came face to face with Marco yesterday, and cut him dead. She was really upset. In the end I started talking about Paul, just to get her mind off the Germans and Italians. I didn't mean to, Kath. I've been playing it close to my chest; fingers crossed, sort of, and not meaning to say anything till Paul knew where he stood. But lately she's been talking more and more about Grandpa, though I don't know why. Maybe she's getting tired of the war.'

'Aren't we all – and this is your gran's second war, remember. But I knew about it – about her and Marco, I mean. Marco told me. He didn't say a lot; just that she was a formidable lady and he'd keep out of her way in future. I think he was a bit hurt, though.'

'So would I be.' Roz pulled a stem of grass then chewed it reflectively. 'How are things going, by the way, for you and him?'

'They aren't, and what's more they mustn't.' Kath narrowed her eyes, staring down at Peddlesbury. 'You know what we need up here, don't you? A pair of binoculars or a telescope, or something. We could see better, then. We might even be able to make out which one was Sugar. Mind, if anyone caught us at it we'd get carted off to prison as spies, I shouldn't wonder – but it's a thought.'

'Kath! You're brilliant! Why didn't I think of that? We've got a pair at home somewhere. Next time, I'll bring them. But we were talking about you and Marco. Are things really bad?'

'As bad as they can be, I'd say. D'you know, Roz, ever since I knew I didn't want to go on living with Barney I feel guilty every time I see Marco – as if it's because of him that it happened.'

'And it wasn't, of course? You're sure? Would you swear that if you'd never met Marco, things would have been all right between you and Barney?'

'They wouldn't. Things started going wrong when I joined the Land Army. If I'm truthful, I suppose it was when I got it into my head that if I didn't go out and volunteer there and then I'd be trapped for the rest of my life. Trapped? A young married woman shouldn't have been thinking like that.'

'Maybe it was Aunty Minnie who was getting you down?'

'I don't know. Maybe it was Barney and Barney's mother's house and Aunt Min, all rolled into one. All I know is that I wanted out; wanted to start again, in the country. I knew, even as I signed on the dotted line, that Barney wouldn't like it.'

'And you've been proved right. Do you think he'll let you go, Kath – willingly, I mean?'

'No, I don't. Not for one minute. But I wouldn't ask him for anything – only my clothes and they're mine, anyway. He could have all I've saved. There's quite a lot in the bank, now; enough to buy him that car he's always wanted. He'd like that, I know.'

'And he could take Aunty Minnie out for rides in it.' Roz laughed, mischief briefly lighting her eyes.

'He's welcome to her. Personally, I need Aunt Min like I need a rat up my trouser leg!'

'Now we're back to Marco again! Funny how the talk gets round to him, isn't it?'

Marco, and threshing day, and the rat. Marco holding her wrists, telling her to hang on, the thresher beneath her, banging and turning. Then Marco holding her close, hushing her, telling her it was all right. Even then it had felt good to be near him. Now, she could think of little else.

'Tell me what you told your gran about Paul?' she demanded, shutting down her thoughts.

'I told her we want to get married.'

'Great! I always said you should be open with her, didn't I?'

'I know. But she said she'd have to meet him first. She didn't say a downright no, though.'

'She'll love him, Roz. She'll fall for him – bet you anything you like she will. So don't look so miserable. And what's that, down there? Something's going on. There's a couple of little pick-ups on the perimeter track . . .'

'Yes. The crew-trucks. They'll be taking-off soon. Oh, dammit. Wish I'd got those field-glasses with me!'

'We'll bring them next time.' Kath reached for Roz's hand and it felt cold in her own. 'Come on, love. Let's count them out and wish every one of them well? He's going to be all right, I know he is. And tomorrow night, I think you should take him home. It's time he and your gran got to know each other – all right?'

'All right. Except that I forgot to tell you. By tomorrow night we could be on with the first cut of hay. Mat said that as soon as the grass was dry in the morning he was going to open up the Beck Lane field.'

'Open up? What's that?'

'They cut the first hay – and corn, too – by hand with a scythe, to make an opening so the mower can get in. I hope Mat won't want to go on working till it's dark – won't expect you and me to stay too late, Kath.'

'Wouldn't know, love. It'll be my first haytime. And listen! There's one of them starting up.'

They sat, breath indrawn, and thinly the sound came to them: four engines, warming up. Then there would be more and more until there were close on forty great roaring engines being revved into full-throttled life.

Kath crossed her fingers as the first bomber began its clumsy trundle to take-off point. 'Good luck,' she whispered. 'And next time we'll be able to see which one is Sugar, won't we?'

But Roz made no reply. Already her eyes were wide with apprehension, her world fear-filled until she knew Paul was back.

'He'll be all right.' Kath squeezed the hand that lay clenched in her own. 'He will be. I know it.'

'Yes, Kath. Funny, but I always had it in my mind that they'd get that tour of ops over with around haytime and it looks as if I'm going to be right.'

'It does. And didn't you tell me it was lucky to see a load of hay – that it was good for a wish? Think of all the loads of hay we'll be seeing – all the wishes?'

Wish on a load of hay. Like the first swallow and the first cuckoo-call, hay was lucky.

And she would be wishing, Roz thought as the first green light flashed out from the control tower. She wished a lot these days and always, *always* for the same thing.

'Take care, Paul,' she whispered. 'Come back safely.'

17

Last evening they had watched nine bombers heave reluctantly into the air; had silently blessed them on their way, wished them a safe return. Some had needed the full length of the runway, skimming the top of Peddlesbury Lane wood with little to spare.

'They're heavy. Seems they've got a full fuel load,' Roz had said. 'It's going to be a long one tonight.' Deep into Germany. Berlin, could it be?

They returned at first light, their engines making a different sound on the cool morning air, awakening those who still slept as they roared in low over Alderby. The last of them, the ninth, touched down as Kath reached Home Farm and she closed her eyes and whispered her thanks to the god who had brought them all back.

'Hi!' Roz called from the dairy, her voice light. Roz too had counted.

'You're early this morning. Couldn't you sleep?'

'When he's flying, do I ever?'

'I'll tell you something, Roz. When it's all over and done with, I shall feel as if I, in person, have flown all thirty. Don't do it to me again, there's a love. Where has everyone got to?'

'Mat's doing the milking and Jonty's gone to collect Marquis.'

'*Who?*'

'Another shire. The mower needs two horses; Mat and another farmer have an arrangement – they each borrow the other's. Marquis is Duke's half-brother. Same sire, different mares. They look alike, too. Mat'll be in his element, today.'

'They won't be using the tractor, then?'

'They will, but later. Mat always uses the horses for the first cut, though. Grace wants milk, by the way. Be a dear, and take her some?'

Kath took jug and ladle, stirring in cream risen thick to the top of the churn before filling the jug. 'Want a cup, if there's any tea going begging?'

'No, ta. You have one, though. Stay and have a chat with Grace.'

Roz was happy. Paul was back and tonight they would be together. And only four more to go . . .

'The gaffer outside says I'm to stay for a cup.' Kath smiled, taking a mug from the mantelshelf. 'She's in a good mood this morning.'

'Got a date tonight, has she?'

'Almost certain.' Kath settled herself at the table. 'Tell me about haytime, Grace?'

'What do you want to know, lass? That it's hot and dusty – that it always is? Got to have the sun. Can't make hay in the rain.'

'But how do you know when it's time – when it's ready for cutting?'

'Mat knows. When the hay's just coming into flower is the time, weather permitting, of course.' Grace pulled out a chair and propped her chin on her hands. 'A farmer knows his land, Kath; knows every field. Now's the time, Mat says, and the weather set fair for a day or two. It'll be a fair crop, this year.'

'How can hay flower? I thought it was just grass.'

'Oh, bless you no! There's herbs and suchlike in hay – in good hay, that is. You've got to catch it just right. Mat can.'

'And the weather?' Could Mat order that, too?

'No problem with the weather, this year. Didn't you notice those little swallows, last night – so high up in the sky you could hardly see them? Swallows live on

347

insects and when their food is high it means the pressure is high; don't need a weather-glass to tell the day that's to come. When swallows fly high, it's haymaking weather. Mind, when they swoop low to the ground,' Grace added, ever practical, 'you know not to hang the washing out. Low-flyers means rain to come, and soon. Mat came in last night and said the sky was good and the swallows high. Mat knows.'

Mat knows. Mat can. Mat said. She still loved him, and he her. He didn't notice the thickening at her waist, the grey hairs. Mat loved the girl he had married, for girl Grace still was, to him. Theirs was a quiet love, a sure love; a love it would take a thousand sonnets to describe. They were the lucky ones.

'Roz'll be eating here, today,' Grace remarked. 'I like to have us all together when there's something big on, though it's a worry, finding rations.'

'Rabbit pie, will it be?' Kath recalled threshing day. 'And rice pudding?'

'No. I'm getting low on rice and folks say it'll disappear for the duration before so very much longer – the Japs, you see – so it's baked custard and the last of the apples. You'll tell Marco he's to come in?'

'I'll tell him.' Grace didn't know about them. No one knew, but Roz. 'Well – best be getting on with the milk. See you, Grace.'

Hester sang softly to the tune on the wireless. This morning she felt almost happy. Though dramatic, her talk with her granddaughter had been the first hesitant step toward the openness between them she so wanted. In wartime especially, having someone to love was normal and natural, but she had been dismayed by Roz's evasions – yes, and lies, too. But soon it would come right; she was to meet this airman who had a name, now, and a twin sister and who wanted to be an architect, like Toby.

Yet married? Hester frowned. Roz had been a child at the outbreak of war; just sixteen and striving to keep up with Jonty. And she had looked on fondly, sure that love would grow between them. She had never worried when they were together. Roz was safe in Jonty's care. He was right for her. One day they would marry and Ridings would have a master again, and sons. Martin would have liked the young farmer – without a doubt, he would.

Then war had come to Alderby St Mary; came in the guise of an aerodrome and bombers. Acre upon acre of farm land laid waste to runways and ugly Nissen huts, buildings that grew overnight like mushrooms. In field corners, ringed round by fences of barbed-wire, stood guns to protect those bombers; camouflaged trucks and transports sped up and down lanes that had known nothing more startling than a horse and cart or a herd of slow-moving cows. Roz had fallen in love with one of those incomers: a young man, handsome in his uniform, with the wing of a flyer on his tunic. He and Roz were lovers. She knew it as surely as she knew her granddaughter and now nothing would do but that they be married and proclaim that belonging to the world.

Hester sighed; a sigh of regret and of surrender, too. She would wait and see; wait until Paul came. And she would do what was right for Janet's child – that at least she owed her daughter.

'Do you know what suddenly I've got a fancy for,' she demanded of Polly. 'For shortbread fingers, would you believe? Now isn't that unpatriotic of me?' She laughed.

'More like downright foolish, I'd say. One baking of shortbread would take your butter and sugar ration for a fortnight.' It was good, though, to hear Hester Fairchild laugh. There had been a sudden change in her mood, Polly's alert mind had noted that morning; a lifting of her spirits. 'And who might be coming to tea that's deserving of shortbread fingers?'

'Not to tea, but coming soon – Roz's airman. She's told me more about him. And Polly – this is strictly between the two of us – she wants to be married. Now what would you say to that, if you were me?'

'Married, is it? What's so wrong in that with a war on and them never knowing what tomorrow'll bring. You and me should know all about that – me especially, that never knew what it was to be a wife.' She reached for tray and cloth, smoothing it meticulously, setting out cups and saucers. 'You'll not deny her? The youngsters have to grow up before their time, these days. She's a bairn, by law, but she's a woman for all that. You'll let her?'

'I've wanted nothing less than her complete happiness since the day Janet died. I won't deny it to her now, Polly, be sure of that.'

The two grey shire horses were harnessed into the mowing machine and a fine sight, Mat exulted, wishing they were both his; knowing Marquis was every bit as good an animal as his own gradely Duke, though he'd never have admitted it openly.

He eased himself carefully on to the iron seat of the mower. He'd have an aching backside before the field was cut, but it was a small price to pay for sitting behind two magnificent shires; seeing the hay fall in swathes with every step they took. The cutting of Beck Lane field would take less than a day; Jonty and his tractor were welcome to Ten-acre, then. So long as the first cut belonged to him and the shires, Mat cared little. And later, Marquis would be watered and fed and returned to his owner who managed nicely without tractors; a man after Mat Ramsden's own heart. By the time the hay had been turned and dried, raked into cocks and carted into the barn smelling as sweet as anything on the face of this earth, old Duke would have worked like the thoroughbred he was and earned his keep for the year.

The morning sky was blue and cloudless, the hay thick and ready for cutting and he had two magnificent horses at his fingertips. This day, war or no war, Mat was a contented man.

Kath had loosed Daisy from the milk-float shafts and was standing beside the little animal at the water-trough when Marco crossed the yard.

'Kat.' He said it softly, eyes wide and warm with pleasure. 'Will you be working at the field? Will I see you?'

'I don't think so.' Her words came in a whisper, her face grave. 'Later, maybe, when the cutting is finished.' Why did she feel this way whenever he was near her? Why was it so easy to forget she was married? 'Grace says you're to eat with us. We can talk then, Marco.'

It would be easier when they were not alone; when there could be no reaching out to touch, no speaking with their eyes. Marco did it all the time, now – was good at it; good at looking at her and having his eyes say 'I want you'.

'*Si*. Already Jonty has told me. I like to sit with the family. I can think I am home, then, with my brothers and all of us talking and laughing and arguing. Our kitchen was a noisy place, but Mamma loved it. I am sad for her. They are alone now, she and Papa.'

Sad. The whole crazy war was sad. Families broken up and marriages placed on ice. She wished, sometimes, that she had never come to Alderby but that was a nonsense when she knew that not for anything would she have missed one day of all this; not even threshing day. Especially threshing day. Yet she ought to try harder to stop caring for Marco; stop it before the restlessness between them had its way. She was fooling herself if she thought anything could come of their affair, because affair it was. Love, attraction, wanting – by whichever name she let it be called, it was there. It snapped and crackled between them like summer lightning; was there in his eyes so she must look away lest he should know it was the same for her, too.

'Sad. Well – see you . . .' She made to walk away but he said softly:

'Katarina?'

Just her name, that was all, but she raised her head and saw the words there.

'I love you,' his eyes said and she wanted to look back at him; to hold his eyes with her own so he would know that she understood.

'Must go.' Quickly she looked away. 'Must feed Daisy . . .'

They ate a typical wartime farmhouse meal of rabbit stew. Rabbits were not a part of the meat ration but there for the catching and blessed by many a country housewife when she had nothing left with which to feed her family. The onions, potatoes and carrots they were cooked with were grown now in most gardens in place of flower-beds and lawns which were considered unpatriotic and must be dug up and given over to the growing of food. Digging for Victory, it was called.

Grace carried dishes of vegetables to the table, then served portions of stew on hot plates. She liked having people at her table and she must remember to pick out a large piece for the prisoner. Marco was a good lad who worked hard and deserved what little food she was able to give him. Marco had a mother, too, who must worry about him. Had Jonty been a prisoner, she, Grace, would have been grateful to the unknown woman who showed kindness to him. Sons were sons the whole world over, though some must be called enemies.

She placed an extra piece of meat on Marco's plate, just to give thanks that her own son was at home and not thousands of miles away, a prisoner in a foreign country. It was the least she could do and after all, she thought defiantly, this *was* Grace Ramsden's kitchen!

'When will you be finished in Beck Lane?' Jonty was eager to start on Ten-acre, though he didn't begrudge his father the pleasure of cutting the smaller field with his precious horses.

'By about two, I reckon, then Marquis can go back.'

'Can Marco take him? It'd save me a lot of time, if he could. You know the farm – the smallholding by the crossroads?'

'I know it, Jonty, but it is not possible. I am not allowed out alone. I must not leave the farm – it is the rule.' Even here he was still a prisoner, and Mat his gaoler. 'But I'll rub him down, and feed him.' Marco liked horses, too; would have liked nothing better than to walk the animal back to its owner. But such a freedom was denied a prisoner of war. Returning alone he might be mistaken for an escaper, his yellow patches would see to that, reminding him as they always did of what he was – disliked by most, and unwelcome. He'd have gone slowly mad but for Home Farm. Idling behind barbed wire was not for Marco Roselli. Carving wooden ornaments or making baskets, enduring every long-drawn-out hour of every day was not for a man whose body was young and pulsing with life.

'It's all right. I'll see to it.' After the jolting of the mower the walk would do him good, Mat considered, and Marco and the lasses could see to afternoon milking. The young ones wouldn't miss him for an hour.

He rubbed his empty plate round with bread and smiled his thanks to Grace. She was looking tired these days, but she always dismissed his enquiries for her health with 'Away with your bother, Mat Ramsden. It's only my age. Comes to all women. It'll pass . . .'

A woman's age. Those strange few years of her life that a man didn't rightly comprehend nor was encouraged to talk about for only, it seemed, could another woman truly understand what it meant.

'That stew was right good, lass,' he offered by way of sympathy.

'Aye. The Lord bless rabbits,' which was a strange thing for the wife of a farmer to say when rabbits were pests and did untold damage to most things that grew. And Lord bless the poor women who lived in towns and cities managing on bare rations and often went without so their families should not go hungry.

Almost guiltily she spooned apples and custard into blue-patterned dishes. Sometimes her good fortune made her afraid. Sometimes she thought that the little domain that was Ridings and Home Farm had shut itself off from the world outside and she wondered how long it would be before that ugly, warring world discovered their contentment and set about destroying it. She smiled across at Jonty and at Marco, too; gave that smile for an unknown woman in a faraway country.

It was the least she could do.

Polly had just left Ridings when the telephone rang – as it very often did at around noon.

'Hullo?' Hester announced the number to the clatter of falling pennies.

'I – oh – hullo? Might I speak to Roz?' Clearly he had expected Roz, for on any day but today Roz would have answered the midday ringing; would have run to get to it first. 'This is – it's Paul Rennie. I can ring back if –'

'Paul – no! Please don't hang up. Roz isn't home to lunch today. Haymaking, you see.' She spoke quickly, urgently, trying to get the words in before he found an excuse to put down the receiver. 'I'm Hester Fairchild. I'll give her a message, if you like?'

There was the smallest pause then warmly he said, 'Hullo, Mrs Fairchild – good afternoon. Can you tell Roz there's something on in the Mess tonight and I'll be a bit late – about eight . . .'

'About eight, Paul. I'll tell her. Does she know where?'

'Same place, will you tell her?'

'I will. I'm so glad to have spoken to you. I hope it won't be too long before we meet. And Paul – will you do something in return for me?'

'Gladly, if I can . . .'

His voice sounded more relaxed, now. There might even, Hester thought, have been the hint of a smile in it.

'Will you come to Ridings tonight – call for Roz? Not to stay,' she hastened, 'but just so I might meet you? Will you? I'd be so glad, if you would. It would make an old lady very happy.'

'Then what can I say, but yes? I'd like that very much. Eight o'clock, shall it be?'

'Eight would be fine – or a little before,' she said, breathlessly. 'Well, then – see you tonight . . .'

'Tonight. And thanks – for asking me, I mean.'

She stood for several seconds, the receiver in her hand, then gently she replaced it, amazed at her daring, hoping it would be all right, that Roz wouldn't flounce upstairs, red-cheeked, when she told her what she had done. She let go a sigh. Whether or not, it was done, now. She had asked Paul to come to Ridings. He'd sounded so nice; his voice deep and low and at first a little surprised. She'd been afraid she had gone too far, but he had agreed to come almost at once. She hoped she would like him; that he would like her. She would know the instant she saw him, if he was right for Roz.

She wanted him to be; wanted to say yes to their wedding, give Roz into his keeping for however short a time. Theirs wouldn't be the wedding she had hoped for, dreamed about, but there was a war on. Time was short, now, and immeasurable, and Hester Fairchild, she told herself firmly, did not have the right to play God.

*　　*　　*

'Now why,' said Mat to Grace who clucked impatiently at the crossroads at the lateness of the Helpsley bus, 'don't you make an afternoon of it, and have a look at the shops?'

'Shops?' With nothing in them to buy and no coupons to spare, even if there had been? 'Nay, Mat, I'll get the next bus back.'

She lifted her cheek for his kiss then watched him go, taking the lane to the smallholding with Marquis beside him, irritated at the loss of even an hour; chiding herself for letting her spectacles fall to the floor and a lens to shatter. But she was lost without her reading glasses and at least the trip to Helpsley gave her the chance to pick up Arnie's precious card.

Just to think of it made her smile. There would be two birthdays to remember, now; Kath's on the first of July and Polly's less than a week after. She was wondering if she dare make another cream cake, as the bus rounded the corner.

By the time she had paid her fare she had decided she very well might, for wasn't there a war on and wasn't life altogether too short to worry overmuch about a few pints of milk for the illicit separator? And mightn't it be a celebration, too, of the finishing of the hay harvest and as good a crop as they'd had in years? Oh my word, yes! Another birthday cake and be blowed to that daft lot in London! Kath was family, now; only right and proper the lass should have a cake, and who was to know about it, if she didn't tell them? She looked at her wrist-watch. A quarter-past two. She would be back by three. My, but it was hot inside this old bus . . .

In the Nissen hut that served as a barrack room and guard room and anything else the gunnery sergeant-major cared to call it, the duty army private picked up the telephone. She was very young and homesick and the day was much too hot to be wearing a thick khaki shirt and jacket. She

356

wished she were back in Greenock in the apartment that was home. She didn't like all these great open spaces and not for anything had she wanted to leave Scotland to be an ATS girl. *They* had said she had to.

'Air-raid warning purple,' she repeated, suddenly dry-mouthed!

'Message timed at fourteen-twenty hours.'

'Fourteen-twenty hours.' A purple alert meant they were coming! German aircraft, and only minutes away!

'Purple alert!' she called to the duty corporal, reaching automatically for her steel helmet. 'Message timed at fourteen-twenty hours,' she added, trying to keep her voice calm as the sound of running feet and barked orders jerked the gun emplacement into sudden, tingling alertness.

The young girl in the khaki uniform swallowed hard and noisily. She was afraid; very afraid. She closed her eyes and crossed her fingers, hoping to God they wouldn't come. It was a hoax, a false alarm – it had to be. At half-past two on a sunny afternoon that was all it *could* be. But for all that, she wanted her mother. Lord, how she wanted her.

Jonty connected the mowing machine to the tractor tow-bar. The sun was high and fierce; heat danced in the distant corner of Ten-acre field. He was eager to start. The blade was newly sharpened, the teeth freshly honed. Given luck, he could cut the lot before the light went. Marco and the old man could have their horses; this was the age of the machine and Jonty Ramsden was a tractor man.

He squinted into the distance at the slowly-rising barrage balloons, fat like white whales wallowing puffily in the sunlight, secure at their cable ends. They ringed the entire aerodrome, a recent addition to its defence; an extra deterrent to bombers that could come screaming out of the sun to hit and run before the gunners could get them within range.

He looked around a sky empty of aircraft. Only practising, today; a dummy run to keep bored balloon crews on their toes. He started up the tractor, inched forward slowly, then carefully lowered the blade.

From his seat he could see the church clock. Half-past two. He'd be twice round the field before Marco was back; just see if he wasn't. He wiped his face and arms with a red and white handkerchief. My, but today was a hot one, all right . . .

Hester would prevaricate no more. She had dithered on the edge of indecision for long enough. She would find Roz and give her Paul's message then tell her granddaughter what she had done.

So she had cheated. Hadn't Roz needed a push? After tonight it would be all right, she was sure of it, she smiled, all at once happy. Tonight they might even be wondering what all the fuss and bother and evasions had been about.

She skirted the ruins where a late-flowering clematis clung purple to the wall; where honeysuckle in its second flowering would throw out its sweetness when the light began to fade. It would be good to walk this evening in the scented cool. Tonight, she would know if Paul Rennie was right for Roz. Soon they might even be planning the calling of the banns in St Mary's. She closed her eyes briefly and imagined children at Ridings again. The noise of children – that's what the old place needed. She hoped she would find Roz in the Beck Lane field. She had seen the prisoner leading the shire back to the yard and there she hoped he would remain. Their first encounter was still fresh in her mind. It had angered and unnerved her and she had no wish for it to be repeated. Italian or German, he was still the enemy. It was monstrous that she must tolerate his presence on Martin's land; best she took care to avoid him this afternoon and who knew but that soon she could find a way to be rid of him?

Paul Rennie stood at the window of the small, bare room he shared with S-Sugar's flight-engineer. The room was abnormally quiet. These last few days Flight had been away a lot, spending his off-duty time and every free night, come to that, at the Black Horse.

He unfastened his battledress top, throwing it on the bed, loosening his tie. Today it was too hot for comfort; tonight, with luck, it would be cooler.

Tonight. A little before eight, at Roz's house. It had thrown him at first, hearing the unexpected voice, but now he was glad it had happened. He had never liked the lies and deceits, had wanted all along for their affair to be open and above-board. Tonight, if things went well for them, he would try to get through to Bath and tell his parents that he and Roz wanted to be married. He was old enough to fight; old enough to get shot at. They'd have to accept that he was a man, now; had suddenly hurtled into full maturity on that first, frightening raid over Germany. And he wouldn't ask; he'd *tell* them.

Roz, he thought fondly, staring out over the wide expanse of the airfield and the two crossing runways, almost white in the sun. Lovely, lovely Roz . . .

They were winching up the balloons out there. The one at the end of Peddlesbury Lane would be the first up, he wouldn't mind betting.

Peddlesbury Lane, where he and Roz met, close by the wood of beeches and oaks and green, dark places. Rosalind Fairchild-Jarvis; intense, moody, exquisitely beautiful Roz. The more they loved, the more he wanted her. He envied Skip his unborn child. When they were married he wouldn't care how soon Roz got pregnant – if she wanted to, of course. Children would be one of the things they must talk about, agree about, if Mrs Fairchild said yes.

He pulled off his shoes and lay down on the grey-blanketed bed, arms behind his head, staring at the familiar pattern of cracks in the ceiling paint. What are you doing, Roz, right now? Are you in the hayfield or are you starting the afternoon milking? He looked at his watch. Not quite half-past two. Too early, yet, for that.

Roz. Roz, his lovely love. Roz of the cheeky nose and eyes so green he'd never seen their like before. Red-haired, tempestuous, fun-loving Roz, who'd lately had lapses of quietness he hadn't been able to penetrate. But she was worried about that last op. He was worried, too. Skip was; they all were. But they'd make it! It was as certain as anything could be in this damn-awful war. The next one might well be tomorrow night and only three to go, then. Four more take-offs; four more times sighting those bloody wonderful cliffs of home, golden-white in the morning light.

Four more times, then two fingers up to flying. Freedom from it for as long as they could wangle and some nice cushy instructor's posting to Somewhere in England, Roz with him in civvy digs and every night – every *safe* night – together like it had been in the house in Micklegate.

Be good to us, Sugar.

Duke drank deeply from the pump trough in the yard, pausing to raise his head, splashing cold droplets of water against Marco's chest. The horse had worked well. One field was already cut; by nightfall perhaps two.

He would be staying late tonight. The camp truck would not call for him until ten o'clock and that was good; would be ten cigarettes to his credit at the end of the month.

He reached up for the bridle, clicking his tongue against his cheek, leading the animal back to its stable and a feed of hay and oats. His father's horses were of a different breed, yet still Duke reminded him of Italy and the farmhouse at the foot of the hills. What would they say at home if they knew that Marco who boasted that no woman would entice him into marriage had fallen in love with a foreigner; with a woman who was married to a man she had not seen for two years and whom, would she admit it, she no longer loved. Ah-ha! his brothers would laugh. A married one, was it? Okay, Marco – so have your fun, get the wildness out of you, then find yourself a good north-Italian girl to marry and father your children on; a girl still a virgin, eh?

But he wanted Katarina; her of the sad blue eyes and the too rare, so beautiful smile. Only Kat should have his children; Kat who belonged to a faraway soldier who should be writing daily, telling her of his love. The saints be thanked that he was not, though it made little difference. Kat was married and only a miracle would free her from it, and though he ached to have her he could not, would not, wish widowhood on her. He was coming to dislike Barney Allen more and more; it bordered on hatred, sometimes, when the wanting got bad, but he couldn't wish him dead.

He closed the stable door, then thrust his arms deep into the pump trough, scooping water in his hands, splashing his chest, his face, wetting his body all over. On the walk back to the field the water would dry on his skin and take the heat of the sun from it, briefly cooling him.

Kath; Kat; Katarina-mia. I wish I'd never met you; I'm glad that I did.

Mat saw them as he neared the smallholding on the Helpsley road. Daft young beggars, flying that low. Hedge-hopping, didn't they call it? They'd come a cropper one of these days if they weren't careful.

Automatically his hold tightened on the horse's bridle in case the young fools frightened the creature with their sudden noise; making hushing sounds, reaching up to stroke its neck. Fighters, weren't they? Not the big ones from Peddlesbury. Not bombers. He squinted into the sun as they climbed and wheeled.

'Hell! Bloody hell!' *Theirs*, not ours. Black crosses on them! Three hit and runners, out to get Peddlesbury again!

He pulled and pushed the shire close into the shelter of the hedge, stroking its nose, whispering, 'Steady, old lad. Hold still . . . still . . .'

Three of *theirs*, out for a sudden, swift strike. Machine gunning, strafing, out to get the bombers that sat like decoy ducks around the perimeter track.

The fighters wheeled again, snarling for position. They couldn't come in low; the balloons were stopping them and damn-well serve them right! Didn't know we've got balloons now, did you?

'Steady, there . . .' he soothed as the sudden hollow scream of shells caused the horse to whinny softly. The ack-ack guns were on to them now, blasting out from all sides! Let 'em have it, lads!

Messerschmitts, weren't they? Three ME109s. Mat took his forearm across his brow, wet with sudden sweat, all the time hushing and patting, passing on his calmness to the anxious animal. 'Be still, Marquis . . .'

A single fighter dived out of the sun, came in low, slipping with wings almost vertical through the balloons, its guns spitting bullets to smack and bounce along the edge of the runway in little puffs of dust.

Airmen and women ran, flattening themselves against anything solid, avoiding trucks and transports that could explode into a ball of fire with a single hit.

Then it swept up to join its fellows; up into the sun again for another dive.

Marco saw her standing there, eyes shielded, gazing bewildered into the sky.

'*Signora!*' Couldn't she hear them – hear the guns? What was she thinking about? '*Signora! Giù! Giù!*' Down, for God's sake! Get down!

He ran the length of the lane, heels pounding, making downward movements with his hands, but still she gazed up. Didn't she know whose they were?

'Down, *signora*! Into the hedge!'

He heard the sudden spat! of bullets. God! It wasn't the bombers they were after! Fear gave him more speed. '*Signora!*'

The roar of the engine blasted his ears; a dark shadow passed over him. He heard her small, bewildered gasp, saw her throw up her arms, spin round and fall, arms and legs straddled. Even as he threw his body over hers he knew it was too late. He clasped his hands around his head, closing his eyes tightly, pulling in his breath as another hail of bullets slammed into the hedgerow. *Bastards!*

'*Signora!*' He gathered her to him, whispering softly. 'It's all right. They've gone, now. They've gone . . .'

Her head rolled limply against his arm, her blood warm on his hand. In the back they'd hit her; they'd shot a woman in the back! Crying out with rage he held her closer, rocking her gently, whispering softly. Her lips were moving and he bent closer.

'Martin? Is that you?'

'I'm here.'

'It's dark, Martin. I can't see . . .'

'It's all right. I've got you.' He laid his lips on her forehead, on her eyelids. Her mouth moved in the sweetest of smiles, then she sighed softly. It was a gentle passing. She was still in his arms when Jonty found them.

'Marco! Oh, God, *God* . . .'

'The fighters, Jonty. She just stood there. I called out, but she stood there. I got to her too late . . .'

Carefully he eased his arm from beneath her; gently he lowered her to the grass. Her blood had stained his chest;

already the edges were drying brown. The smile was still on her lips.

'She's dead, Marco?'

'*Si.*' He was no stranger to violent death. Slowly, reluctantly, he crossed himself. 'Who is Martin?'

'He's her – *was* – her husband. Why?'

'She said his name. She thought I was him.'

Jaws clamped tight, Jonty looked down. Her face was white, her hair lay ruffled against her cheeks. On her blouse a dull red stain was spreading web-like. 'Let's get her home,' he said.

They lifted the gate of Ten-acre field from its hinges and laid her on it.

'We'll have to get the doctor, Marco – tell the police . . .' Death was death. Even in wartime the ritual must be observed. Jonty looked at Marco and the silent tears that slipped down his cheeks. Lucky Marco. Perhaps it was all right for him to cry. 'And we'd best get Polly over.'

Why wasn't his father here, and his mother? How was he to cope with Roz's grief? And what kind of a war was it that gunned down a helpless woman?

'Let's get her home,' he said again.

The back door at Ridings was low and wide and took the field gate easily. They laid her on the kitchen floor then Jonty took the cloth from the table and laid it over her.

'Go and tell Kath, will you, Marco? She'd best be here when I tell Roz. Can you go to Polly's? And see if Mum's home yet?'

He filled a glass with water and drank deeply, reluctant to look down. The world had gone mad and there was worse to come. He didn't know how he'd tell Roz. Every instinct rebelled against saying the words that would tear her world apart.

He walked to the back door and sat on the step, arms on knees, head bent, waiting.

The sound of running feet caused his head to jerk up. Roz and Kath, white-faced, in spite of their exertion. He jumped to his feet, running his tongue round suddenly-dry lips.

'Someone's been hurt? Who is it, Jonty?' Her eyes were wide, wild with fear. 'It isn't Gran. It *isn't*!'

He took her arm, unwilling to let her go inside, to come upon it so suddenly. She struggled to free herself, but he held her tightly.

'Let me *go*!' Fear gave her strength. She pushed him from her and ran into the kitchen.

'*Gran!*' Her cry was harsh, dragged disbelieving from her tight, terrified throat. Why was she so still? Impatiently, angrily, she threw aside the cloth that covered her then opened her mouth to an anguished, animal wail. She had not seen death before. Blindly she turned into the waiting arms. 'Jonty, she isn't, is she?' Soundless sobs shook her body. 'She *isn't* . . .'

'Hush, now.' He pulled her closer, his hand cradling her head, forcing it against his shoulder so she should not look down again. 'Roz, I'm sorry, so sorry . . .'

'Sorry, yes . . .' There was an ache in the pit of her abdomen; a gnawing pain. She wanted to be sick. The need was jerking about inside her with every frightened spasm.

'Ssssh . . .' He was patting her, hushing her, stroking her hair; afraid to let her go from his arms lest she slip away in a faint at his feet.

'Kath?' His eyes begged her help.

'Come away, Roz. Come outside till the ambulance comes?'

Her voice shook; it hurt her throat to speak. None of this was happening. On a June day that danced in the heat with a sky so clear, so blue it couldn't be. This wasn't a day for dying. Not Mrs Fairchild. Not anyone.

Jonty swallowed hard as if to rid his mouth of death and disgust. His eyes went with the stumbling figures, each supporting the other. He wished he could weep.

18

They had given it out on the six o'clock news bulletin that a
Royal Air Force fighter had buzzed enemy-occupied Paris,
flying in dangerously low, dropping the Tricolor near the
tomb of France's Unknown Warrior. An act of chivalry,
of defiant bravado, said some. All very fine, said others,
but wouldn't that fighter have been better employed in the
skies over Malta, or in North Africa? Those who lived in
Alderby St Mary thought much the same, except that it
might have been better still had that fighter of ours been
here, over Peddlesbury this afternoon. It need never have
happened, then. The war had taken three from Alderby
already. From a hamlet not worth a dot on a map, two
young men and a girl had been killed, now Mrs Fairchild,
and her doing no more harm than walking past one of her
own fields.

The last war had been terrible to a degree, they all
agreed on that, but it had been fought in another country.
This war was the people's war, brought to them from the
air. Soldier or civilian, woman or child, none felt safe. And
ill-luck had come again to the Fairchilds. Only young Roz
was left, now, they thought in their stunned disbelief. A
lass not yet of age had inherited their troubles.

Once, in the proud times, a Fairchild could look from
any upstairs window and know that all he saw was his.
Now, the last of them lived in a ruin and worked on the
land as if she were the same as anyone else. Who among
them would have thought when they got out of bed this
morning that the war would be back on their doorsteps
before nightfall? By the heck, but it made you think . . .

*   *   *

'How did you find her?'

'Stunned, Mat. White as a little ghost and not a tear to be seen. It's all wrong. She ought to cry. I didn't want to leave her.'

'She's in good hands.' Mat gathered his wife to him, patting her back with big, awkward hands. 'There's Polly with her, and Kath.'

'I know. It's awful that Roz is so alone now, and her not understanding rightly that it's happened to her. Yet this war goes on and the world hasn't stopped its turning . . .'

'Don't take on, lass.' He knew what she meant. Jonty was back in Ten-acre field with the hay, himself and Marco had seen to the cows and the dairy work, in spite of what had happened. But a farm couldn't stand still; not even for death. Cows must be milked twice a day, seven days a week, crops harvested and animals fed. Even on Christmas Day.

'I'm not taking on. I know the way it is.' With fingers still clumsy from shock, Grace set the kettle to boil. She had known something was wrong the minute she'd stepped off the bus, else why was Mat waiting there for her, grave-faced, when he should have been in Beck Lane? Jonty? An accident with the mower, she'd thought, cold with sudden fear. He'd taken her shopping bag from her then laid an arm on her shoulder and told her. She hadn't believed it; hadn't even known there'd been a raid. No siren had sounded in Helpsley – not that she had heard.

Near Ten-acre field, Mat said it had been, but they did that all the time now; our own fighters did the same over the Continent, shooting-up ammunition trains, gun emplacements. Daylight sweeps, we called them. Nuisance raids the Nazis said they were. But surely our own fighter pilots didn't shoot at civilians working in the fields, nor an elderly woman walking in a lane?

'I'll make us a cup of tea, Mat.' She was still shaking

inside, still fighting the tears she knew she must soon give in to. Just one kind word from Mat, and that would be it. She'd cry and cry until she was sick.

Damn this war! Damn it, and the madmen who'd started it!

'Here you are, then.' Polly placed cup and saucer, rattling in her agitated hand, at Roz's side. 'Drink it while it's hot.'

Polly had not wept. Mrs Fairchild would not have broken down – not in public – and nor would she. Later, when Arnie was asleep and the little lodge was quiet, she would give way to her grief. But not here, not yet, whilst Roz needed her; pale-faced, dry-eyed Roz who stared at the floor where the Mistress had lain before the ambulance men took her; stared at the smudge of blood on the floor tile that she, Polly, hadn't had the courage to wipe away.

Jonty and the prisoner had gone, taking the field gate with them – work never stopped on a farm.

'Sorry, Polly. I couldn't . . .' The terrible ache was still inside her and she still wanted to be sick. 'Sorry . . .'

'A cigarette?' Kath lit one then placed it between Roz's fingers.

'Thanks, Kath.' She drew on it, deep and long. 'What time is it?'

'Half-past six. Will I go and find Arnie, Polly – bring him in?'

'Thanks, Kath, but leave him. He's in the garden; said he didn't want to come in. Best I take him home, poor bairn; see if he wants any supper.' She walked wearily to the door, as if the happenings of the day had been too much for her. 'I'll be back, later on . . .'

There were things to be seen to, things to be arranged and all Roz had done was to sit there, staring and smoking, and wild-eyed as though any minute she'd break into terrible screaming.

'No. Stay at home with Arnie. Kath's here and Grace said she'd be back later. And thanks, Polly. Come tomorrow as usual, will you?'

'All right. Tomorrow, then. If you're sure?'

Kath followed Polly to the door then out into the yard. 'What'll I do?' she demanded, stiff-lipped.

'Stay by her. Don't let her go off on her own. She's not with us. In shock. A good weep, that's what she needs. I'll be back early tomorrow, but happen it might be best if someone's with her tonight. Could you stay, Kath?'

'I'll try. I'll ring the hostel and ask the Warden.'

'Aye. Do that.'

Polly walked into the garden, calling softly for Arnie. Her back was straight, her head high. No tears. Not in public. Later, though. Tonight she would cry and sob and rant until she made herself badly.

Roz took a sip from the cup then put it down, choking.

'Polly's put too much sugar in,' she offered in answer to Kath's raised eyebrows.

'You'll have to eat something, Roz. Grace left milk – won't you try a glass of milk?'

'No, thanks. Nothing. I want Paul, though. Oh, I know he shouldn't come here the minute Gran's –' She stopped, not able to say the word. 'I mean I –'

'I know, love. You just want to be with him,' Kath supplied gently. 'Shall I try to get him on the phone?'

'Would you? The switchboard mightn't accept the call, though. They don't, if the squadron's going to be on ops. Security . . .'

'Helpsley 217, isn't it?'

'Extension thirty-nine.' Roz nodded.

The switchboard at RAF Peddlesbury accepted the call. Kath gave Roz a thumbs-up sign then asked for the extension number.

'Sorry,' said the operator. 'I'm getting no reply from thirty-nine. Anywhere else I can try?'

'No – but thanks a lot.' She smiled, replacing the receiver. 'No reply, but I got through all right, so they shouldn't be operational tonight. What'll you do, Roz? Where are you meeting him?'

'Same time – half-past seven, Peddlesbury Lane. You couldn't go there, Kath? If we can't get hold of him, will you go?'

'Of course I will – if you'll drink some milk.'

'No. No, I *couldn't*.' She walked to the sink and filled a glass at the tap, drinking deeply. 'Kath – it's true, isn't it? It *did* happen?' She was gripping the sinkstone tightly as if she might fall if she let go her hold. 'It *was* Gran they took away . . .'

Unspeaking, Kath nodded then spun round, startled, at the knocking on the door. Almost with relief she opened it to Marco. His hair was tidily combed, his face sad; he was wearing his brown jacket.

'Kat – how is Roz? I worry for her. I think that maybe I can give her comfort, tell her that –'

'Who is it?' Roz stood behind them. 'Marco?' She held out a hand and he took it in his own, kissing it briefly, his eyes on hers.

'I come to tell you, Roz. I think it will help – is it right that I come in?'

'It's right, Marco, though I'm a bit bewildered. But come in.' Gran wouldn't have liked it; wouldn't have allowed it, but for all that she held open the door.

'Mrs Ramsden said I should come – tell you. She said it perhaps would help.'

'Help?' Kath queried.

'*Si*. Bring comfort. I was with the *signora* when it happened, Roz. I wasn't able to get to her in time – not to save her, but she was alive. For a little while she was alive and she spoke . . .'

'Marco!' Roz's head shot up. 'What did she say to you?'

'Not to me. Not to Marco. I put my arms around her and

370

held her and she think I am Martin. "Is that you, Martin?" she say and I tell her yes. I didn't know, then, who he was, but I kissed her for him and she smiled. She thought I was Martin.'

'Martin was her husband – my grandfather. She never stopped loving him. I'm glad she died in his arms. Thank you, Marco . . .'

'*Si*. She smiled. It was peaceful for her. I wanted you to know she was not alone.'

'Yes.' She touched his cheek with her fingertips. 'I'm grateful to you; I truly am.'

'And you are comforted, Roz?'

'I'm comforted.' Her smile was gentle. 'More than you'll know.'

'Aunty Poll – you won't let them hurt you? You won't go away and leave me?'

Arnie knew that big boys who were nearly ten should not cry but sometimes, when it was worse than going to the dentist, worse than going back to Hull, even, you had to. Mrs Fairchild had been his friend.

He reached up from his bed, clasping Polly tightly, burying his face in the folds of her pinafore. Life without Aunty Poll was unthinkable and unbearable and all at once he was afraid.

'Hurt me? Your Aunty Poll go away? And who's to see to things at Ridings if I was to do that? Now see you here, lad; old Kaiser Bill couldn't frighten me so I'll be blowed if a little pipsqueak like Hitler can do it. Anyway, lightning don't strike twice – not in the same place. Stop your fretting, lad. Your Aunty Poll isn't leaving you, and that's a promise. So get yourself off to sleep – try not to think; just close your eyes. Mrs Fairchild is with God now. Nothing can harm her any more.'

With her Martin, she was. Her loneliness was over. They were together again.

371

Don't you fret none, ma'am. I'll look after Roz like we always said. I'll do what's right, you know I will.

'What will you do, Roz?' Kath counted the cigarettes in her packet then resolutely pushed it back in her pocket. Only three left and Roz might have need of them tonight. 'I mean – how do you stand, now?'

It wasn't the thing to ask, when you thought about it, but the silences were becoming oppressive and the ticking of the kitchen clock too loud.

'Stand? I suppose it's mine, now,' she shrugged, 'or will be, when I'm old enough to inherit. Ridings, Home Farm, six cottages in Alderby and the watermeadow fields on Peddlesbury Lane. Gran said it would be . . .'

'No, love. I wasn't talking about – *things*. I meant you and Paul. Your gran would have said yes, I know she would. What'll happen, now?'

'Oh – I don't think anything will have changed.' The smallest of smiles briefly lifted the corners of her mouth. 'Gran told me how it would be, if ever – well, it was all taken care of, I mean. I've got three guardians until I'm twenty-one; I suppose I'll have to ask one of them, now.'

'But who are they, Roz?'

'There's my great-uncle – Gran's older brother. He never married. Went to Tasmania after the last war. They kept in touch, but things got a bit strained with the war – letters getting lost at sea, and all that. And Uncle John was never very strong, I believe; not strong enough to fight in the last war, Gran said.'

'And there's me thinking you hadn't any family – apart from your gran, I mean . . .'

'No. She seemed to cut herself off – to cut us both off. She had a sister, too; Mary, her name was. She was a year younger, but she died when I was little. Mary didn't have children, either, so there are no cousins on Gran's side and no Fairchild cousins.'

'And the other two, Roz? Your great-uncle in Tasmania wouldn't be a lot of use. It would take ages to get permission from him.'

'I know. But there's Gran's solicitor – Mr Dunston, in York. He's coming here tomorrow. His father was Grandpa's solicitor. Gran trusts – trusted – him implicitly. He sends me a card, on my birthday. Dutifully, sort of, and to let Gran know, I suppose, that he's still mindful of his obligations – and the third,' she paused, and for a moment the haunted look left her eyes and her face gentled. 'The third one is Polly . . .'

'Polly Appleby? I'd never have –'

'Never have thought it? But Kath, Polly is all that remained of Ridings – Gran's *real* Ridings when she had a husband and a little daughter and was carrying her second child. Polly was there in the good times – knew how things had been – and she was there in the bad times, too. Gran wouldn't have kept her sanity without Polly, she once told me. Polly knows everything. She'll have been told about Paul and that we want to be married, be sure of it. Polly is family. She'll say yes, I know she will. So don't worry about us. Just help me, Kath? Help me get over these next few days – to be a credit to Gran. And don't leave me. You'll have to be family, now. Apart from Paul, all I've got is here at Ridings and Home Farm. Will you stay tonight? Afterwards – when it's all over – the funeral, I mean, then Paul and me can be together, here. But not just yet. So will you ring the hostel and ask? And I think I'll have a bath and make myself look decent.' A bath might make her feel better; wash away some of the horror and disbelief.

'You'll be all right, Roz?'

'Sure I will. And I'll feel better when I've seen Paul.'

'Okay. But before you do anything you're going to get a glass of milk inside you or you'll be passing out on me, then what'll I do? No messing, now,' she called from the pantry, glass in hand. She was going to drink

373

it, Kath thought grimly, if she had to hold her nose and force it down.

She had tapped on the bathroom door and called, 'You all right, Roz?' and received a 'Fine, thanks,' before she asked the operator for Peacock Hey's number.

'Kath – is that you, hen?' Flora's lovely Scottish voice, safe and sane. 'Sorry, but the Warden's away tonight to a silver wedding party. Where are you? What can I do? And how's Roz taking things?'

'She's bearing up – I'm with her now at Ridings. But she shouldn't be alone, Flora. I want to stay with her, if I can. Will it be all right?'

'Of course it will.' She hesitated for only a second, then said, 'Do you need me to bring any of your things? Tell me where to find them and I'll pop over – just have a word . . .'

'Thanks, Flora, but I've got the bike. I can get them myself – no bother. I'm meeting Paul, you see; Roz wants me to tell him, so I might as well call in. I'll be there just after eight, if that's okay with you?'

The Forewoman said it was, though she'd rather have gone to Ridings to tell her about the message, she thought. Not that she knew all that much. The old lady had been agitated on the phone and the line bad, and anyway she'd never been able to understand the half of what those Londoners said. But she'd got the gist of its message, worse luck, and yes, she'd pass it on to Kath Allen, she'd said. That, she accepted reluctantly, was what a Forewoman was for.

But did it have to be today of all days? Wasn't there upset enough at Ridings without herself adding to it?

Yet trouble always came in threes, didn't it; just like death. Peggy Bailey, Mrs Fairchild – who next? Hear of one, they said; hear of three.

Flora Lyle sent her thoughts winging to a faraway soldier.

Take care of yourself, my love. For God's sake, take care.

Roz looked again at the kitchen clock, checked it against her wrist-watch then let go a long sigh of dismay. It was twenty minutes to eight and Paul wasn't coming.

Half-past seven, they'd said. Always half-past seven in Peddlesbury Lane. And Kath was there, waiting. Kath should have told him by now and he'd have come to her, run to her, concerned. It didn't take ten minutes to get here. Paul knew the way; in the dark, he knew it, and the short cut through the orchard.

But Kath would still be waiting because they were on ops again tonight, weren't they? Paul was flying when she wanted him so desperately. Not the need, tonight, for his lips and his fingertips arousing her, their bodies close. Tonight she needed the safeness of his arms and his cheek against hers. She needed to tell him; to say out loud that Gran was dead and for Paul to tell her it would be all right, that the pain and the misery would pass.

But he was flying. This night of all nights, he couldn't be with her. She closed her eyes and covered her face with her hands. It was called kicking you when you were down; rubbing it in.

Wrapping her arms around her waist she hugged herself tightly. A quarter to eight. He wasn't coming. He definitely wasn't coming.

She glared at the telephone standing smug and silent on the dresser. Paul was at the other end of that thing. All he had to do was lift it and tell her he loved her. He wouldn't, though. When the squadron was operational no one could get in to the aerodrome and no one could come out. And no one could ring in or ring out, no matter how much it mattered that someone should whisper 'I love you'.

She wanted to walk in the ruins; walk alone staring down at the grass and think it all out. She wanted to come to terms with what had happened – accept that Gran was dead.

Dead. That was the word for it. Not passed over nor passed away nor even gone to her rest. Gran was dead and she didn't want to think about tomorrow nor next week; she just wanted – needed – to think about today, about *now*, and she needed Paul beside her so she could find the strength to do it.

She couldn't go into the garden, though. She must stay here so that when Kath came back she would know where to find her. Anyway, she couldn't hear the phone from outside.

Why, Gran? Why did it have to be you? Why were you in Beck Lane? If you really had to be there, why wasn't it a minute before or a minute after? Why *then*?

She thought back to their parting this morning; to their last words. It had been the same as always – perhaps just a little bit better, because this morning Gran had known about Paul. And she had said, "Bye, darling. Take care," as she always did and then lifted her cheek to be kissed.

Why, Roz demanded angrily, hadn't she hugged her and told her she loved her? Why hadn't she told her she was sorry for all the silences there had been between them; sorry she hadn't told her sooner about Paul when she'd known all the time that Gran would have understood. And why, this morning, hadn't she thanked her for always being there; for being her mother and her gran and her friend? Darling Gran, I'm so sorry; I loved you, love you, will always love you. And I'm telling you too late.

There was a knock on the door and Roz wanted to leave it unanswered; couldn't bear to see anyone now. But Gran, no matter what her grief, would have opened that door and she must do the same.

She walked across the kitchen, listening to the echoing of her footsteps against the stone-flagged floor of the inner hall. She lifted the old, heavy latch, swung the door wide.

And Paul stood there. He was carrying flowers and lifting his shoulders in a little shrug as if to ask, 'What do I do next?' and she didn't believe it because he'd come, *he'd come*!

'Darling, oh darling, where have you been?' She closed her eyes, her mouth searching for his and he pulled her to him with his free arm. Why was he bringing flowers? He never gave her flowers. 'Oh, Paul, I need you so. Just hold me. Hold me tightly and say, "I love you, Roz Fairchild."'

'I love you, Roz.'

She heard the flowers fall to the floor, felt his arms around her, pulling her closer.

'And I love you, Paul.' There were tears in her eyes, spilling down her cheeks; it was good to weep.

'What is it, sweetheart?' He pushed her a little way from him, eyes wide with concern. 'You're shaking – what is it? What's wrong? It's all right, truly it is . . .'

'No, it's *not* all right. It won't ever be all right again. Didn't she tell you? Didn't Kath tell you?'

'Tell me what – and when? I haven't seen Kath since the dance.'

'But she's at Peddlesbury Lane, waiting. She's been there since half-past seven, to tell you about Gran and to tell you to come here.'

'I didn't see Kath. I came here over the fields.'

'We rang you – about half-past six. Where were you, Paul?'

'On my way back from Helpsley. I went for flowers for your gran.'

'For *Gran*?' He didn't know? But if he hadn't seen Kath, how was he to know? 'Darling – Kath came to meet you; tell you I couldn't come and that you were to come here so I could tell you; tell you that this afternoon –'

She laid her cheek on his chest and between anguished sobs she told him. She poured out her misery and all her regrets. 'Gran's dead.' She needed to say it again and again, to cry out the words to the four winds and for God to hear them. She longed to be forgiven for all the things she had said that she shouldn't have said and for all the words, the kind words, she had left unspoken; words like I love you, Gran. Her pain poured out in a torment of grief. 'Dead, Paul. Gran's dead and you never knew her.'

'But I did – I *did*. That's why I'm here. I phoned, but you were in the hayfield, she said, so I asked if she would give you a message, tell you I'd be a little late . . .'

'You *spoke* to her?' She jerked her head up sharply, her eyes disbelieving.

'Roz – can we walk? In the garden?' He was still a little reluctant to step inside the house. There was so much he didn't understand, things he must ask her when she was calmer. He had to tell her why he was here, explain about the phone call he'd made and who had answered it and asked him to come to Ridings. 'Let's go out – unless you want me to go and tell Kath I'm here?'

'No. She was only going to wait until eight. She'll be on her way to the hostel now, to pick up some things. She's staying with me tonight . . .'

'Good.' He smiled gently, to give her reassurance, then tilted her chin and wiped her tears away with his handkerchief, all the time kissing her softly. 'Let's walk outside, then you can tell me about it. And did I tell you I love you and that I missed you?'

Unspeaking, she shook her head, then linked her arm in his. He had come. He was here at her side and she was safe and loved. For just a little while, nothing else need matter.

'That's it, then!' Kath looked at her watch. He wasn't coming. Best, now, she should get back quickly. Roz was at breaking point. She mustn't be alone when it all got too much for her. Poor Roz. Tense as an overwound spring.

Kath pedalled quickly. She had come up and down this lane so often that she wouldn't mind betting she could do it blindfolded; it stood to reason that in winter, in the blackout, you might just as well have your eyes shut. Winter. So long ago, it seemed. She had lived in Alderby for six months; it could be a lifetime.

Peacock Hey was unusually quiet when she pushed open the back door and went in search of Flora Lyle. Most farmers around were haymaking and many of the landgirls who lived here would be working late. Automatically she scanned the letter-board. Nothing there for Kath Allen; no airmail envelope or pale blue letter-card with *Passed by Censor* stamped on the front and bearing Barney's name, rank and number on the back. So long since she had received a proper letter, but there must be some explanation. You could never be sure of mail in wartime; not even of letters posted here at home. Ones from abroad were always at risk, with ships being sunk all the time and planes carrying mailbags shot down every day of the week. She must give her husband the benefit of the doubt. He *could* have written; he most probably had. Letters went missing all the time.

'Hi, Kath. Thought I heard someone come in.' It was Flora in dressing gown and slippers, wet hair wrapped in a towel, her face grave with concern. 'How is it at Ridings? I can't believe it. Does it make them feel good to gun down a woman? How's Roz taking it?'

'Pretty badly. I wish she'd cry, but she won't. I was hoping Paul could be with her tonight. I waited to tell him, but he didn't turn up. He'll be flying again, I suppose.'

'You'll give Roz my love, Kath? And tell Mr Ramsden that if he wants any help for a few days, I'll do what I can for him. But be sure to tell Roz I'm sorry . . .'

'I will, and thanks. I don't suppose there's any food about?' Not that she was hungry, but she hadn't eaten since noon and her inside was making noises.

'Cook's left some plates on the cold slab for late workers. Cheese salad, I think it is. Help yourself. And Kath – I'll be in the kitchen. When you've got your things together, will you pop in? I'll put the kettle on. Could you do with a cup?'

'Thanks, but no. Best I should get back to Roz. Polly said not to leave her, the state she's in. Won't be long . . .'

She ran up the linoleum-covered stairs then up the narrow little staircase that led to her attic. Nothing had changed since she left it this morning. Her sheets and blankets lay folded on the black-painted bed; the window was still open wide; the vase of wild flowers was there on the sill.

Frowning, she closed the window then placed pyjamas and slippers and the clean clothes she needed in a carrier-bag. She loved this attic with its low, sloping ceiling and the little window in the gable end of the house. It was bare, hot in summer and cold in winter, but it was all hers; the first room she had been able to call her own.

Sighing, she hurried downstairs. A cup of tea would have been bliss, but there was no time tonight to sit and chat.

'There y'are, hen. I've sorted you a sandwich; lettuce and cheese. All right, is it?'

'Fine, thanks. Bless you, love. I'll eat it on the way back. Sorry I've got to dash, but I'll tell Roz what you said. I suppose it'll be all right if I stay at Ridings till after – well –'

'Stay as long as Roz needs you.' It wouldn't matter all that much, Flora considered. A lot of landgirls lived out – ate and slept on the farms they'd been allocated to. 'I'll make it all right with the Warden tomorrow and get you a temporary ration card. But sit down – I'll pour us a cup.'

'Sorry, Flora. I really must get back. I've left Roz alone too long already. I'll let you know how things go . . .'

'Sit down, Kath! *Now!* There's something I must tell you. There was a message – at half-past six. She'd been trying to get through all day, she said –'

'For me? A – a message?'

'Sugar?' Flora's face was grave.

'Y-yes. One. Flora – what is it?' All at once her mouth had gone dry. She reached for the mug, wincing as the too-hot liquid burned her tongue.

'I don't rightly know. She was in a bit of a state. Mrs Jepson. You know her?'

'Aunt Min? Oh, Flora – not an air-raid?'

'She's fine, as far as I know, and it was nothing to do with bombing. There was a letter, addressed to you. She opened it, she said, because it looked official.'

'Yes?' Kath drew in her breath sharply.

'From your husband's Commanding Officer. It was to tell you he's in hospital – wounded. Look, Kath, I'm sorry but I'm not one for beating about the bush. That's what she said, but she didn't have long. The pips went and the operator didn't give us any more time.'

'But was that all she said?' Kath reached for her mug then put it down again. 'I mean, she couldn't just –'

'No. She said she'd already posted the letter on to you but she thought you ought to know.'

'But wounded? Was that all it said? Surely there was more?'

Oh, God. Barney wounded! Dear, sweet heaven – she didn't love him but she hadn't wanted this. Not once had she wished him harm.

'Aye. He's in hospital at – oh, some Egyptian name – I couldn't make it out. But like I said, she was in a state, poor old body. And the letter said his condition was satisfactory, but she didn't get time to say any more. You know what long-distance calls are like these days?'

'I see.' Her lips were so stiff she had to make a conscious effort to speak. 'What'll I do, Flora?'

'Do, lassie? I'd wait for that letter, if I were you. It'll be here by morning – by the midday post at the very latest. I'll get it to you, somehow. And Kath – I'm sorry, really I am. And I'm sorry to be the one to have to tell you.'

'No. You've been kind. I – I haven't taken it in, yet. It'll be a military hospital, won't it? Are you sure she didn't say where?'

'Not that I could understand. But when the letter comes you'll likely make more sense out of it. I suppose you'll be getting told officially when the great war machine gets round to it. And, Kath – at least they didn't send you a telegram.'

'No.' That, she must be thankful for. When they sent a telegram first it meant only one thing.

'Cheer up then, lassie. It mightn't be as bad as it sounds. You'll know tomorrow. Now you're sure you're all right? I'll ring Ridings and tell Roz – if you don't feel like going back there.'

'No. She'll need someone with her. I don't think I'll tell her just yet. She'll have enough to worry about in the next few days. Maybe Aunt Min panicked a bit. Perhaps when I've read the letter for myself, it won't seem quite so bad.'

'Aye. And think on this – while you're worrying, your man's likely tucked up all snug being fussed over by a bonnie wee army nurse. He'll be fine, Kath; just see if he isn't. Now, will I wrap up that sandwich so you can eat it later? And stay a wee while longer,' she hastened when Kath got unsteadily to her feet. 'At least drink your tea.'

Thank the good Lord, the Forewoman thought, that it was Kath Allen sitting there and not others she could mention who'd have thrown a weeping fit and gone all to pieces to hear such news. But Kath was like that; Kath never showed her feelings. Quiet, she was, and private, somehow.

'Tea? Yes.' She sat down again; not because it was the most sensible thing to do but because her legs had suddenly gone weak and she really did need that tea.

Barney wounded? But how badly, she fretted, guilt flushing her cheeks. And how wrong could she have been because not once had she ever imagined that anything would happen to him. She hadn't worried, as Roz had, because Barney had always had the ability to take care of himself. 'Don't worry, girl,' he'd said. 'No heroics for Barney Allen. I'll be looking after number one – get myself a cushy number. I'll be back, Kath . . .' He'd been so sure.

The tea was cooler, now, and she drank gratefully. She hadn't wanted anything to happen to him; she really hadn't. Their marriage was over as far as she was concerned, but she hadn't, never once, she told herself again, wished him harm.

But this was a judgement on her. She had fallen in love with another man – a man she could never have – and she was being punished. There was no one to blame but herself.

Barney. I'm sorry. I'm sorry you've been hurt and that you're in hospital, but I can't love you. I can't. I don't think I really ever did . . .

'You'll be all right? You're sure, now?' Flora urged.

'I'm fine – or I will be, once I've seen that letter. And I'd best be getting back. I'll be better with something to take my mind off it. If you think of what Roz has got to face – well, I'll manage, once I've had time to take it all in.'

She rose to her feet, pushing back her chair, grasping the edge of the table. Tomorrow she would believe it. When the letter came, then she would know it was true. Tomorrow she would worry. Tomorrow was always the best time . . .

Slowly, suddenly very tired, she pedalled the familiar lane back to Ridings. Everything was so normal. The sky was blue, still; birds were singing as if nothing had happened, and in the ripening cornfields poppies grew red with white ox-eye daisies. Such incredible beauty, silently mocking the cruel world.

Peddlesbury was behind her, and if she didn't turn and look at it, she could almost believe there had been no war; that none of today's awful things had happened. The barrage balloons had been winched down again, the danger over, and nowhere in the sky was there sight or sound of any war plane. But Mrs Fairchild was dead. It had taken two startled minutes. Those fighters had screamed in, had circled and dived then hurtled out, skimming treetops and rooftops, flying low out to sea.

And in minutes, a phone call had consigned Barney to a hospital bed in a faraway country in some place Aunt Min hadn't been able to pronounce and this lovely world around her only served to remind them all how it once was and would never be again.

Yet tonight she must go back to Roz; tell her that Paul hadn't been there and that there'd be no awakening from this nightmare – for either of them.

She found them in the garden, sitting on the staircase seat. After running from room to room, calling Roz's name, she saw them from the bedroom window, Roz with her head on Paul's chest, he with his arms around her. Neither of them moved nor spoke. They did not need her. For Roz, the worst was over.

Slowly, dejectedly, she returned to the familiar, once-friendly kitchen and pulling out a chair she folded her arms on the table, laid down her head, and wept.

19

It was late when Roz came in. Her face was pale, and tear-stained, but she seemed calmer.

'How are you, love?' Kath's tears were over. She had washed her face and combed her hair, determined not to add to Roz's unhappiness. The news from Aunt Min, dreadful though it was, must wait.

'Better, now. I needed to say it out loud, make myself believe it. Paul just listened, most of the time.' He had held her tightly and safely, understanding the pain inside her and the terrible burden that was her conscience. 'I wanted him not to go; to stay with me. But it wouldn't have been right, would it? Not tonight, when she's – I mean, not until after . . .'

'After Thursday,' Kath supplied gravely. 'Until it's – over.'

'Thursday, yes. At two, it'll be. Until then this is still Gran's home and I must do things her way, keep to her rules – well, that's how I feel about it. I wanted him with me tonight, just to be beside me; to hold me if I awoke – nothing else, Kath, but –'

But Paul had understood. He had just kissed her gently, and whispered a goodnight, promising to ring in the morning, telling her she was to try to sleep. She had watched him go, wanting him to turn and wave, knowing he would not invite ill-luck by doing so.

'Tonight he was kind, Kath, gentle and safe, somehow, to be with. I love him so much.'

'I know. You're good for each other. It'll all come right, Roz, I know it will. I'm going to put the kettle on now and you're going to share my sandwich, that's an order. You'll never sleep if you don't eat something.'

'Yes. Think I'd better. I feel so – so *drained*. Did you see Flora?'

'I saw her. She sent her love and said I was to stay as long as you needed me. She's popping over some time tomorrow to bring me a – a ration card.' Mustn't mention the letter. On Thursday, when it was all over, she would tell Roz about Barney. 'I've put my things in the small spare room – the one I had before. Is that all right, Roz?'

In the little room with pale green walls. Last time she'd slept there Paul had been on leave and they'd gone to the Helpsley dance. And Marco had – But she mustn't think about Marco. Not tonight. Never again, if she had an iota of sense left in her.

'Of course it's all right. Paul might be flying tomorrow. The twenty-seventh, it'll be, Kath. He said I wasn't to wait by the wood. If they're not on ops he'll come here to me. Did you know Gran had asked him to Ridings tonight? He phoned me, like always, but I was at Home Farm. He had a little talk to Gran and she asked him to come and call for me. That was why he wasn't at Peddlesbury Lane. It's awful, isn't it? Gran might have been on her way to tell me . . .'

'Well, at least they met – if only over the phone; but you mustn't think things like that. Your gran was probably only out for a walk. It was a lovely afternoon. Maybe she wanted to see how the haymaking was going. We'll never know, Roz.'

'No. But it makes it all right for Paul to be here, now. She'd asked him to come, hadn't she, so I don't feel I'm sneaking him in the minute – well, you know . . .'

'Yes. She wanted him to come. She always did. Look, there's no need for you to get up for the milk-round, but if you wake up and find me gone you'll know where I am. You'll be all right for a couple of hours, won't you?'

'I'll be fine. Mr Dunston is coming and Paul will be ringing. Can you manage on your own?'

'Of course I can. It'll be funny without you, though.' She sliced the large, thick sandwich into two then poured tea into the dainty china cups Hester Fairchild had always used. 'Supper first, then straight into bed. You look all in. I'll check the blackouts and lock up. We'll both feel a whole lot better in the morning. Sleep. That's what we need.'

Sleep did not come easily. Kath lay unmoving in the unfamiliar bed, thinking about Barney; wondering how he was and where he was; how seriously he had been hurt. She could not envisage Barney in a hospital bed, maybe helpless and in pain. Was he thinking about her, wanting her beside him, his pique forgotten? Soon, perhaps, he'd be coming back to England. They did that, didn't they – brought wounded men home in hospital ships?

Then what would she do? How was she to tell a wounded soldier she was leaving him? How could she? She had intended to tell him when the war was over, when he came home. Squarely and honestly she would have asked him for her freedom, but things had changed, now. The distant day she had so dreaded was all at once very much nearer.

And what will you say to him? demanded her conscience.

Say? What was there to say? That she was desperately sorry, but –

'*But I've fallen in love with another man.*'

No! Yes! She *was* in love with Marco Roselli if wanting to be near him always, needing him to touch her, kiss her, make love to her, was falling in love – all right, that's the way it was. She was guilty.

Then what about your promises, Kath Allen? For better, for worse; in sickness and in health . . .

All right! So people made mistakes. She had made one and Barney, too, if he were honest – else why the long silences, the refusal to meet her half way, to even try to understand?

But it was all right until you met Marco Roselli. It was bearable.

It was *not* all right. It never really was. She had been so very tired of being a nobody, a foundling, a charity child that she had married the first man who asked her.

He gave you his name.

Yes, then mocked my dreams.

He gave you a home.

He took me to his mother's house. It was never mine; never a home.

They had bought a big, double bed and he claimed his rights in that bed. Every night. Clumsily and selfishly, until he tired of it. He had never made love to her; he *took* her – with his mother listening on the other side of the wall, hating her.

What did you expect – you, Kath Sykes, a nobody?

I expected kindness and tenderness and understanding. Even a nobody has feelings. And here at Home Farm I'm *our* Kath, and Marco loves me . . .

Marco Roselli is your husband's enemy; your country's enemy.

All right! But I'm a woman and I want him. I'm sorry with all my heart that Barney has been wounded and I'd give anything for it not to have happened. But Barney will fall on his feet. He always has; he always will. And when the time is right, I'll tell him. I *will* . . .

The moon was half-grown and rising pale; hardly to be noticed against a sky still vaguely light. Now, as the longest day approached, there seemed hardly any night; the sky was not fully dark until midnight and long before five in the morning birds sang a welcome to a new day. It was somehow unnatural, Roz thought as she thumped and turned her pillow yet again.

She wouldn't sleep; nothing was so certain. Her mind was a seethe of thoughts and doubts, regrets and sorrow.

It would help if she could weep again; if the knot of pain in her throat could dissolve into blessed tears. But her tears were spent and the pain must remain, a small part of her penance.

I love you, Gran. Are you here, still, or are you already with him, with the love you lost all those years ago? And did you know about this afternoon? Was a part of you there in April, on Mark's Eve – you and Peg together?

You wanted to go; I know it. Lately he's been beckoning, calling. You felt his nearness, didn't you, Gran? You did know. And who that we don't know about was there with you on Mark's Eve? Who else in this parish will die before the year has run?

Paul, take care of your dear self. I want you and need you. Fifty years from now I shall still want and need you. I couldn't live if you left me. Don't let them part us, Paul . . .

The milk delivery took longer than Kath had thought. Not only was she alone, but at every house doors opened immediately and she was asked for news; news of Mrs Fairchild's death, of the time of the funeral on Thursday and of how Roz, poor lass, was taking it. And wasn't it shameful? Her who'd never harmed a soul, killed by *them*, just as surely as they'd killed her husband.

Kath carried back many messages of sympathy and love, but then Roz *was* loved. She was one of their own; a Fairchild. Ridings was hers, now, and she would go on belonging like the beeches and oaks on either side of the carriage drive, deep-rooted and immovable.

She backed the milk-cart into the shed then loosed Daisy from the shafts, leading her to the drinking trough. She really must hurry back to Roz.

'Kath!' Flora was calling her, grave-faced. 'It came, hen; first post. Bad news travels fastest, doesn't it? Want me to stay around, till you've read it?'

'No, Flora, but thanks for bringing it.' She pushed the letter into the deep pocket of her dungarees. 'Later. I'll read it later. And is it all right for me to sleep out – did you ask the Warden?'

'I asked her. Can you call in, later on, and she'll give you some rations, she said; save messing about with a temporary card. How's Roz?'

'Bearing up. Her gran's solicitor is coming this morning. There'll be things to talk about, to arrange. I haven't seen her since last night, but I heard her go downstairs in the early hours. I don't think she slept, either.'

'Aye. It's a terrible war, so it is. Ah, well, I'll be away and have words with Mr Ramsden. I've a girl can be spared, if he's short-handed. My, but it couldn't have happened at a busier time . . .'

'Mat's in Ten-acre field, Flora. They're turning the hay this morning – the top end of Beck Lane.'

'Right, then. See you, Kath. And I hope things won't seem so bad once you've read the letter. Try not to worry too much?'

'That was Flora from the hostel,' Kath announced, sitting down at the kitchen table. 'She brought me a letter.'

She looked around the familiar kitchen, safe and unchanging, and let it wrap its comfort around her.

'Flora has a girl Mat can have, if he's pushed. She's gone to Ten-acre, to see him.'

'Aye. Everyone is good. Mat'll be grateful. Normally we'd have managed.' But yesterday and today and for the remainder of the week, things would not be normal. Come to think of it, things would never be normal again. 'From home, was it – the letter, I mean.'

'From Aunt Min.' Home? Where was home? 'Is there anything else you want me to do, Grace?'

'No. It was good of you to do the round. Get back to Roz. I'll do the dairy work, this morning. We'll all have to rally round till after the – the –'

Funeral. The word no one wanted to say. On Thursday, at two. By Thursday tea-time Mrs Fairchild would be gone and it would never be the same without her. But the world had gone mad and the madness had reached out even to little hidden-away Alderby. Nowhere was safe, now; nowhere at all.

Kath opened the letter the moment she was out of sight of Home Farm and removed the long, buff envelope Aunt Min had folded into three. It bore no stamp; only the words *On His Majesty's Service*, the red mark of the Censor and the date.

Inside was a single sheet of buff-coloured notepaper. It bore an address similar to the one Barney wrote at the top of his letters, and two sets of initials. Those of the officer who had dictated and signed the letter, perhaps, and the soldier who had typed it.

Allen B. T/157663. Royal Army Service Corps, the letter was headed, and it went on to tell her that Barney had been wounded in action and was now in hospital at Hafiif; that his condition was satisfactory and that she could continue to send letters to his battalion address.

Hafiif. Near Cairo, was it? Had Barney already driven an ambulance to that hospital on one of his long convoys? Why couldn't she write directly to the hospital and when would she be told officially by the War Office?

T/157663. Barney was a number, a statistic, now. How badly had he been wounded? Had there been so many casualties that his Commanding Officer had had neither the time nor the inclination to tell her more? *Allen B*. Why couldn't they call him Barney Allen? Why did the war take satisfaction from stripping men and women of their identities, making nameless numbers of them?

She thrust the letter back into her pocket. She wished Aunt Min had enclosed a note; a few lines, perhaps, to wish her well. But she'd probably been so agitated that the thought had never entered her head.

Barney wounded, and in hospital. She didn't love him but not in her bleakest moments would she have wished him ill.

Tears filled her eyes and she brushed them away with the back of her hand. Her life was in turmoil; the whole world was in turmoil, and there was nothing she could do about it.

From the small sitting-room came the murmur of voices. Mr Dunston was here already. He and Roz would be talking about what was going to happen on Thursday and what would happen after that; things which after a death must be discussed, however distressing.

Kath walked quietly across the kitchen and closed the door that led to the passage outside. What was being said in there was no business of hers; what Roz wanted her to know she could tell her in her own good time.

She lifted the kettle. It was cold, which meant that Roz hadn't made tea. Perhaps she should set it to boil anyway, Kath thought; she needed a cup herself. She'd had no breakfast, come to think of it. A slice of toast might take care of the muzzy feeling in her head and the strange ache in her stomach.

She sighed deeply. She didn't understand any of this. Two days ago she and Roz had been so happy; mixed up, perhaps, but happy. Then the fighters came, and Flora had told her that Barney was wounded and in hospital. Was it like that, then, if you dared to be happy? Did happiness make the Fates jealous? Did it have its price and were she and Roz being asked to pay?

Thursday, at two. On Thursday they would have to accept that they would never see Hester Fairchild again. And when it was all over she would tell Roz about Barney; pour out her bewilderment and guilt and hope that the telling would help to ease it. Would things be back to normal again, after Thursday? Would they pick up the threads and try to carry on as if none of it had happened? Could they?

'Now then, our Kath. Got the kettle on, I see.'

Polly had come; Polly, level-headed and unchanging. Kath had forgotten that ten o'clock was Polly's time, always would be, no matter what.

'I'm hungry, Polly. I don't seem to have eaten since – since it happened. And Mr Dunston's here, I think, in the little sitting-room.'

'Aye.' Polly nodded her approval. 'Best get it over with then the lass'll know where she stands. These things can't be put off. Got to be done and the sooner the better.'

She put on her pinafore, and tied the strings. Then she changed her shoes as she always did and hung up her brown paper carrier-bag on the peg behind the door as she had been doing for longer than she wanted to remember. Life must go on. No one had known that better than the Mistress and on life would go, Polly vowed. 'And if you're making a pot, I'll take a cup with you, a piece of toast, an' all. Set a tray, will you – the white china cups with the blue rim and a clean traycloth, from the top drawer. And what about this fire?' She wielded the poker vigorously. 'Almost out, it is. Turn your back for five minutes and the place goes to pieces. Well, what are you waiting for?' She turned abruptly away. She hadn't meant to be sharp with Kath, but coming here and her not being there – well, it was something she would have to face for the rest of her days, for nothing would bring her back. Not if Poll Appleby wept until the crack of doom would it. And why couldn't she weep? When would she be rid of the pain that raged something terrible inside her? Dry-eyed she turned round. 'Sorry, Kath. But you know I don't mean to snap. It's just that – that –'

393

'I know, Polly. Just that she isn't here any more. It's going to take a bit of getting used to.'

'A *lot* of getting used to.' She would never get used to it; not if she lived to be a hundred. 'We'll never see her like again, you know.' Her lips moved into a small, sad smile. 'She was a lady, you see. Ah, well . . .' She threw kindling on the dying fire then carefully placed coal on it. 'There, now. Another minute and it'd have been out. Not much milk in mine, lass, if you're pouring.'

Why did the hours drag so? Why did Thursday at two hang over them all like a great dark cloud full of tears? And would this dratted pain never go?

'Tea, is it? Mr Dunston wants a cup?' she demanded sharply as Roz came in through the passage doorway.

'No thanks, Polly. He's just gone – left by the front.' She pulled out a chair then sat down, chin on hands, at the table. 'Paul rang. He won't be coming. They're on standby.'

'Flying, do you suppose?'

'Just standby, which means they might go or they mightn't. And no tea for me, thanks. Just a glass of water.'

'You'll not get fat on water. A glass of milk, why don't you?' Polly was worried. The lass looked dreadful; pale and pinched, her eyes dark-smudged with not sleeping. 'And what did he have to say, then,' she demanded. 'Everything's all right – moneywise, I mean?'

'I think so, Polly. Seems there's still some of the ploughing subsidy left and I can draw on that, the bank told Mr Dunston, until everything is settled. Gran made a will, so it should be fairly straightforward. I'll be able to keep Ridings, if I want to, but only if it goes on being a farm and earning its keep.'

'So that's what you'll do? Stay here and try to make a go of it?'

'Isn't that what Gran would want?'

'Aye. She'd want you to, lass, but what do *you* want?'

'I want Ridings – and Paul.'

'Then that's all right, isn't it? Seems you'll have what you want. Not many of us get that.'

'I know, and I'm grateful. And Polly – Paul and I want to be married. Did Gran tell you?'

'She told me. She said she'd never wanted less than your complete happiness. Them was her exact words. Telling me, I reckon she was. Telling me – in case –' She bit hard on her lip to stop its trembling. 'So if that's what you want, you'd best tell your young man it's all right. Quiet, though, it'll have to be. If there hadn't been a war on you'd have had to keep to the mourning – you know that, don't you? If there hadn't been this war, you'd have to wait six months at least.'

'I know, Polly, and thanks for letting us.' And for understanding that time was so short; that six months could be six lifetimes, or six nevers. But it was going to be all right. Gran would have said yes, and Polly understood.

Relief washed over Roz like a blessing. Tonight, if she saw Paul, she could tell him. If she didn't see him, then there'd be only three more ops to go and after that they would have a whole year of lovely tomorrows and that was as far as she dare imagine. For the first time in two days she smiled; a tremulous, trembly little smile. 'Thanks, Polly love – and bless you . . .'

'Right, then. I'll be getting on with the bathroom.' Head high, lips set tightly, Polly picked up dusters and cloths, banged the door too loudly behind her and walked upstairs where nothing had changed except that *she* was gone. The soap she had used on Monday morning was still there; the bed she had slept on unruffled and untouched as though she would turn back the quilt and sleep in it tonight. But for all that, she was never coming back.

*   *   *

'Because I'm a minor, Kath, Mr Dunston is doing everything for me; you know – getting the death certificate, and
everything. I didn't know there was so much to be done. I
thought that death was death; that that was the end of it,
but it isn't. So many formalities . . .'

She sat, chin on knees, looking down over Peddlesbury.
Standby had become reality, now. Paul's squadron was
operational tonight, and this would be his twenty-seventh
flight over Germany. And it would be all right. It was the
last one, the thirtieth, that would be so awful; for herself,
for Skip and every one of Sugar's crew. The last op. of
the tour was every bit as fear-filled as the first and the
thirteenth.

She reached for the binoculars they had remembered
to bring and held them to her eyes. 'Do you think it's
terrible of me to come up here and watch the take-off
– disrespectful, I mean? Will people think I shouldn't
have?'

'Shouldn't show your face until Thursday, you mean?
Rubbish! Who's to see you, anyway, up here? And if they
do, what business is it of theirs?'

'Oh, but they'd make it their business. They're like that,
Kath, in villages. But I couldn't have stayed in. Okay – so
I could have sat in the garden and counted them out from
there, but I wanted to be here.'

'So it's all right, then.' Kath offered her cigarettes.
'Want one?'

'No, ta. Smoking on an empty stomach makes me feel
queasy.'

'Then for goodness' sake eat something!' Hardly a thing
inside her since Monday morning, Kath brooded. Drinks
of water and sips of milk. She'd be passing out soon, if she
wasn't careful. But the air tonight was cooler, and fresh;
it might sharpen her appetite. 'Can you make out who
is who?'

'Yes. When they start taxi-ing to take-off I'll be able to

see their markings. We'll know exactly which one is Paul, then. Wish we'd thought to bring these things sooner.

'And there's a couple of crew-trucks going along the runway. Amazing how clear these glasses make them. They could all be up and away within half an hour . . .'

'Good. Then we're going straight home and you'll eat something – or else! You can't go on like this. Are you trying to punish yourself? What's to be gained by starving yourself, will you tell me? You're going to be married, girl. Try thinking about that for a change.'

'I'm not starving myself. I just can't face food. I'm glad about us being married and I'll be all right, truly I will. It's just that it won't leave me, Kath – Monday, I mean. I keep telling myself it didn't happen. I close my eyes and will her to be there when I open them. And she isn't. I suppose that's why it hasn't sunk in that Polly said yes. I'm probably still waiting, inside me, for Gran to say it, too.'

'I know, love. I know.'

'And there's Thursday to be lived through and after that there's Paul's last three. Sometimes I want to go to sleep, Kath, and not wake up till it's all over, and all I have to worry about is getting to the church. You know I'd give anything – *anything* – to have Paul with me tonight. I need him so much – just to be near him; nothing else. Would you say that was selfish and heartless of me?'

'I'd say that it's your life,' Kath said slowly and carefully, all the time watching the wisp of smoke that rose, trembling, from her cigarette, 'and that it's up to you who sleeps in your house. It's nothing to do with what Alderby thinks. But you won't have Paul stay the night. Not yet. You'll do things *her* way for just a little while longer; you know you will. And give me the glasses, will you? There's one of them not revved up, yet. The others all seem to be moving, but one looks like its propellers haven't done a turn.'

'Where?' Roz held tightly to the binoculars, sweeping them the length of the runway.

'Focus on the control tower, then over to your left. Got them?'

'Yes! And it's Sugar – I know it is! The crew are all standing around. I can see them. Take a look.'

'Now how on earth can you tell who's who? All crews look alike in flying kit.'

'I know they do, but Paul and Skip are a head and shoulders taller than the rest of the crew; I just *know* it's them. There's some sort of trouble. They won't be going, Kath. They're not going to take off – bet you anything you like!'

'So what'll we do? Wait and see?'

'No! We'll get back home. Paul will ring me – let me know what happened. I've got to be there when he phones.'

She was on her feet and running down the steep slope of the hill, Kath slipping and sliding behind her, calling to her to be careful.

'Wait for me, Roz! And watch it! The grass is slippery. You'll break your neck!'

They waited for a long time, eyes on the telephone, willing it to ring, but it did not.

'It was probably some other crew,' Kath ventured, eventually. 'You didn't get a proper look at the markings, did you? You only saw that Lancaster head-on; it could have been any one of them.'

'It was Sugar, I know it.' Roz's chin tilted stubbornly. 'And it was Sugar's crew standing around. Think I don't know Paul when I see him?'

'I still say they all look alike in –'

'*It was them.*' She would endure no contradiction. 'And how many took off? How many did you count on the way back here?'

'Eight.'

'Yes, and so did I. And it's usually nine or ten. Paul won't be going, now.'

'All right. It was Paul's plane we saw – but he won't be able to ring. You know that. There'll be no calls in or out. And you're shattered. Go to bed, Roz. He'll ring in the morning just as soon as he can . . .'

She didn't like saying it; didn't like seeing the pain in Roz's face. It was like dashing the hopes of a small, eager child, Kath thought; like taking away a promised treat. And Roz looked dreadful. Her face was pale and tight with stress; if she didn't get some sleep soon she would make herself ill.

'I'll wait a little longer. You go to bed, Kath. You're doing the milk-round in the morning and you need your rest. I'll wait up, for the phone. I wouldn't sleep, anyway,' she added hastily, 'for fear I missed him. You go on up.'

Kath had been going to refuse; had almost countered with, 'No. If you stay up, I stay up,' when the knocking on the back door caused them both to start.

'It's him! It's Paul!' Roz flung wide the door and was in his arms in an instant, laughing, crying, searching with her mouth for his, whispering, 'I knew it was you, darling; I *knew* all the time it was Sugar . . .'

'Paul,' Kath whispered, relieved it had not been Grace, or Jonty who stood there. 'How did you manage to get out?'

'Oh, the luck of the Rennies.' He grinned. 'And how did you know we had gremlins in two engines?'

'We were watching take-off on Tuckets Hill,' Roz gasped, her eyes not leaving his face. 'Stay with me tonight, Paul? Don't go back to Peddlesbury?'

'Sorry, sweetheart.' Gently he kissed the tip of her nose. 'I shouldn't be here at all. I can't stay too long.'

'Stay long enough to make her eat something,' Kath entreated. 'If she doesn't eat soon, she'll be ill. She won't listen to me. And I'm sorry, but I'm off to bed. Got to be up early for the milk-round. You'll have to excuse me.

Goodnight, both.' She smiled, eager to leave them alone. 'God bless.'

'Well, now. What's this about not eating?' Paul demanded as the door closed.

'Oh – I just can't be bothered,' Roz countered, shrugging. 'It tastes so – so *awful* in my mouth. I suppose it's all to do with – well, with Gran. Shock, maybe. I'll pull myself together, soon.'

'How about a sandwich, and a glass of milk?' Paul took off his jacket and draped it over a chair-back. 'Where do you keep the bread? I'll go this minute, if you don't eat something,' he threatened, his eyes deep with concern. 'Kath's right. You'll be ill.'

Roz ate a slice of bread and drank the milk Paul poured for her then set the glass down triumphantly.

'There now – satisfied? Let's go outside. It's a lovely night. Let's sit on the staircase seat. There's something I want to tell you – something wonderful. How long have we got?'

'An hour. No longer than that. It's a half-hour's walk back. And if it's so wonderful, tell me now.'

'Do you still want to marry me?' She reached up, taking his face between gentle hands. 'Do you still feel the same – that we should get married as soon as we can?'

'At the end of the tour.' He took her hand in his and they walked out into the twilight. 'Is that soon enough?'

'How about next week? Before you finish the tour, even? Polly says I can. She's one of my legal guardians and today she said that Gran had told her it was all right, so she said yes. We could get a licence in less than a week. Marry me, Paul? Quietly, with just two witnesses? Please, darling?'

'They do say,' he said gravely, 'that a special licence only takes three days. Allowing for the weekend, we could even make it by Tuesday – if you think that's not too soon?'

'No. Gran would understand. I'll have to get Polly's official permission, I suppose. Wish I knew how it's done.'

'I know how it's done. I talked to the padre at Peddlesbury. It's the bishop who grants the licence, I believe, but your vicar'll tell you. A bloke in the Mess got married in York the same way only last week. Shall you and I be married in York, darling?'

'And stay at the house in Micklegate again?'

'Would you like that?' He draped his battledress top around her shoulders then sat down beside her, pulling her close. 'But didn't we once say we'd do it in style?'

'*You* said that. The house in Micklegate will suit me fine,' she smiled indulgently. 'But I won't speak to the vicar until – well, until after Thursday. Best not till then.'

'I can't believe it.' He laid his cheek on hers. 'We *are* talking about a wedding, aren't we?'

'We are. A quietly-in-York-by-special-licence wedding. And fifty years from now, my love, I'll bet you anything you like we wouldn't have done it any differently.'

'Fifty years from now,' he echoed, knowing that he'd settle for five years, for five weeks, even; knowing that all he wanted was to marry her for however long or little the Fates allowed. 'Do you want children, Roz?'

'Of course I do. I think we'd better have three.'

'Two boys and a girl?'

'No. I rather fancy two girls and a boy.'

'There you are! We're arguing already.' Laughing, he kissed her gently, all at once seeing her pregnant with his child. It was the sanest, most certain thing he could think of in an insane, uncertain world. 'We're going to make it, you and me, Roz. There *will* be a fifty years from now for us. I know it.'

'Mm. Remember the thirteenth op. – and Jock? Nothing still to come can ever be as bad as that, darling. Just remember that, won't you?'

'That I was ready to jack it in, Roz?'

'That it was normal and natural for you – for you *all* – to think that way after what happened. But you all went on, and soon you'll have made it.'

'I'd still rather forget that night.'

'I wouldn't. That night you said you'd always love me. We made love for the first time.'

'I still love you, Roz, only more. And I feel good about us; sure I'll make it. Shall we live here, at Ridings? Fifty years from now, shall we sit here and remember tonight – the night Sugar refused to take-off?'

'We will, Paul.' She lifted his hand, touching his upturned palm with her lips, closing his fingers around it. 'Keep that kiss for your next take-off, to bring you luck. Where should you have been going tonight – or can't you tell me?'

'I shouldn't, but tonight would have been a piece of cake; a milk run. We were going razzling, as a matter of fact.'

'Going *what*?'

'Razzling. Dropping nasty little strips that ignite when they've dried out – set fire to big areas of woodland and fields of almost-ripe corn. Right out in the German countryside, away from guns and night-fighters we'd have been. Like I said, an easy one, but it would have counted.'

'Never mind, darling. I think Someone up there knew I needed you with me tonight – and I did, Paul. I'm glad you're here. Just think – a week from now we might even be married.'

'We *will* be.' He rose to his feet, taking her hands, drawing her close. 'Walk with me through the orchard, Roz? Best I get back, just in case there's a flap about Sugar. I'll talk to the padre again, first thing tomorrow. And try to eat something. Promise me you'll take care.'

They said goodnight at the little gate, standing close, not wanting to part.

'I love you, Paul Rennie.'

'And I love you, my lovely girl. Fifty years from now, I'll still be loving you.'

She stood in the half light, watching him walk away from her, wrapping him round with her love.

Take care, my darling . . .

20

Arnie walked to school the long way round; along the
narrow road and around the big, sweeping bend that led to
the village. That way he didn't have to turn his face away as
he passed Ridings, and didn't have to walk past St Mary's
and see the deep, dark hole in the churchyard. He didn't
want to look at where they would put Mrs Fairchild, but
when it was all over and the flowers were there to keep
her company, he'd go and stand beside her, have a big,
long think about her. Not today, but soon . . .

Today, Aunty Poll had packed sandwiches for him to
eat at school at dinnertime and an orange she had stood
in a queue for at Helpsley. He usually came home for
his dinner, but not today because Aunty Poll would be
at Ridings and busy with the funeral and funerals were
no place for a little lad, she'd said.

It was funny, he frowned, that when he was expected
not to cry he was a big boy, nearly ten, and when Aunty
Poll wanted him *not* to do something he was no more than
a nine-year-old tiddler. He wished she would make up her
mind. And he wished Mrs Fairchild was still here. She'd
been his special friend and she'd promised to teach him
to play chess when he was ten. He missed her already.
Almost always in summer when he walked to school by
way of the farmyard and the apple orchard, he'd see her
there in the ruins. She'd always been pleased to see him
and always found time for a talk.

Last night, he'd gone to Home Farm because Aunty Poll
had said it would be a kindness to help Mrs Ramsden and
that maybe, if she had someone with her, she wouldn't
burst out crying so much. Very inclined to tears was

Grace Ramsden – at the weepy age, Aunty Poll said – and if she had a small boy to chat to, maybe it would take her mind off things and that would be doing something for Mrs Fairchild, in a roundabout way.

So they had spread a newspaper on the table at Home Farm and he'd cleaned all the horse brasses that Duke would wear to the funeral. He'd polished them really hard because Mrs Ramsden said they wanted old Duke to do Mrs Fairchild proud. When he'd made them shine so much that Mrs Ramsden said she'd never seen them looking better, he'd gone out to pick long trails of ivy and young, fresh sprays from the yew trees for the cart they'd be taking her to church on.

But he didn't want her to go and he didn't like what those Germans had done to her. All at once it didn't seem such fun to fly in a bomber or be a pilot; not when you had to kill people. Maybe after all, he'd set his mind on being a bank clerk; maybe a bank was the best place to be.

His bottom lip began to tremble again and the funny little croaky bit in his throat got worse, all the hurt he'd felt since it happened welled up inside him and burst out in tears – big, warm salty ones and not even to think about his orange would stop them.

This morning he was a nine-year-old tiddler and he didn't care if the whole village saw him crying.

Roz decided to wear her grey costume and white blouse because all black, Polly said, was too stark for so young a lass, though if Roz hadn't looked so peaky and frail she'd have dug her heels in over the business of the hat.

'But I don't have a black hat, Polly. The only one I've got is my summer straw.' And even with the rosebuds removed and a black ribbon sewn around the crown, it still wouldn't have looked right, she'd urged. Nor would she wear one of Gran's black hats, she said, fixing Polly with a Fairchild stare.

'I'll tie my hair back with a black ribbon,' she muttered mutinously, 'and if the vicar doesn't like it, then hard luck!'

'You may please yourself,' Polly retorted primly, conceding defeat, acknowledging that the lass had grown into a fine Fairchild. Once this dreadful day was over, she could turn her mind to her young man and to fixing a date for the wedding; she'd settle down and care for Ridings as she'd been reared to do. Aye, and do it well.

'Have you thought which way we'll all walk to the church?' she demanded of Roz, determined things should be done correctly. 'Will you walk alone, or shall Mr Dunston be with you?'

'I think it's best if someone is with me, Polly – one of you, anyway.'

'Nay.' Poll Appleby knew her place. 'I'll follow behind you.'

But in front of Grace and Jonty, mind, her being an official guardian. 'Mat will be leading the horse, then? You've got it all settled?'

'Mat and Duke will take her there, Polly.'

'Aye.' On a farm cart, the way she'd have wanted it. No fancy motor-hearse for Hester Fairchild. She'd made that plain more than once. A shire horse had more dignity than ten men in top hats and when her time came, she'd said, she hoped Polly would remember it. 'And Kath?'

'She'll be there, with Flora. She's gone to the hostel to pick up her best uniform. Marco will see to the farm. There's a relief landgirl there for a couple more days. He'll be all right.'

'Your young man isn't coming, then?'

'No. Gran never met him – well, not officially – and we haven't made our engagement public, yet, so it wouldn't be right. And anyway, he can't come. He was on standby last night and they didn't go, so it's almost certain he'll be flying tonight, he said.'

'That was him on the phone, I suppose?' As if she'd needed to ask, Polly sniffed.

'It was Paul,' Roz whispered and for the fleeting of a second the pain left her eyes and the corners of her mouth shaped themselves into a smile.

He'd phoned to tell her he loved her; phoned early because soon all outside lines would be dead.

'I love you,' he whispered as he put the phone down. 'Fifty years from now, I'll still love you.'

'Take care tonight, Paul. And I love you – so very much.'

No one but you, my darling. As long as I live, only you . . .

'I'm glad I kept these ribbons, Mat. Must've known, when I put them away that we'd be in need of them again.' And she must somehow have known, Grace frowned, that five years after they'd been used for Grandma Ramsden, there would be such a shortage of everything as to make black funeral ribbons non-existent.

'Didn't we use them for Mother?' Mat watched their careful ironing intently. 'Didn't I plait them into Duke's mane?'

'You did, love; and Duke not long broken-in to harness, then, and a bit mettlesome, still . . .'

'But he did the old lady proud.' And would do Mrs Fairchild proud, an' all. Duke knew what was expected of him.

'I'll be glad when this day is over, Mat. How I'm to get through the afternoon, I don't know.'

'You'll be all right, lass. There's no shame in honest tears. And I'll be beside you in the church.'

The farmer on the Helpsley road was to walk the Shire horse back to Home Farm and stable him. Once they had carried Mrs Fairchild into church, Duke's work would be done.

'I'm grateful, Mat. How you put up with my moods and tears, I don't know. I weep so easily, these days. Must be my age.'

'Whatever it is, I love you Grace. You know that, don't you?'

'I know it.' She'd wanted to tell him she loved him too, but he didn't often say such things and when he did it seemed to make her go all soft inside and tears fill her eyes. 'Don't ever leave me, love,' she whispered, dabbing her eyes, taking deep, steadying breaths. 'I couldn't abide it, if you did.'

'I won't leave you, and you know it,' he said softly, pulling her into the shelter of his arms, hushing her and kissing her tear-wet eyelids, just as he'd done when they were courting. 'Oh, you silly woman – just who would I leave you for, will you tell me? And whilst we're about it, don't you ever leave me, for neither could I abide it, if you did.'

She had smiled, blinked away her tears and was comforted, for a while.

At a little after one o'clock, Hester Fairchild returned briefly to Ridings. They brought her coffin in a Red Cross ambulance, driven by a wartime volunteer and accompanied by a nurse who looked younger, even, than Roz.

Mat Ramsden waited at the head of the great grey horse, proud in full harness, its mane and tail entwined with ribbons of black, the bright brasses glinting in the afternoon sun with every toss of its head.

With gentle, capable hands, four young men from farms around placed the oak coffin on the low waggon covered in greenery and trailed with loops of ivy. Mat, wearing his sad suit for the second time that month, fondled the horse's neck with slow, steady strokes. Then he clicked his tongue in his cheek and said softly, 'Walk on, lad. Take her proudly.'

Slowly they circuited the house then swung left to the carriage drive. It had to be the long, agonizing way, for hadn't she loved those trees of oak and beech and wasn't it right that she should leave by the great, ornate gates through which she had come as a bride, more than forty years ago?

Roz walked alone, a bunch of pink roses in her hands. Behind her, though she had not wanted it that way, walked the two people Hester had chosen to guide her grandchild through the remaining years of her youth: a middle-aged solicitor from York and a Helpsley-born servant.

At the gates of Home Farm, Jonty offered his arm to his pale-faced mother and her eyes sought those of her husband, needing the reassurance of his smile and the love that was never far from his gaze. Her hand clasped that of her son and she leaned against him for support then took her place in the procession, her chin tilted stubbornly.

The cart moved slowly on. From the stackyard gateway Flora and Kath moved to take their place and Marco held wide the gate, lowering his head, crossing himself as the woman who had died in his arms passed through it, asking his God that her soul might rest in peace.

By the gate lodges, where once estate workers had waited cap in hand for her coming and their wives in starched white pinafores had bobbed a curtsy to Hester Fairchild, the Manchester lady placed her tribute of flowers on the cart beside the coffin. From cottages along the way came men and women in sober suits, black coats and hats to join those who followed the mistress of Ridings to the little church in Alderby.

Roz walked dry-eyed, the roses picked that morning clasped tightly to hide the trembling of her hands. Yet she walked with the dignity her grandmother would have wished, shoulders straight, head high; walked in slow time to the clopping of the horse's hooves, to the jingle of harness, the clinking of brasses and the rotund grind of the wheels of the cart. Her eyes did not waver; her heart cried out to her lover to help each sad step that took her nearer to the place of parting.

At the churchyard she paused beside the newly-dug grave. She did it deliberately to accustom herself to it and not come on it later, with shock. Leaning against the hedge was Martin Fairchild's stone. When it was in place again it would bear two names and Gran would rest beneath his memory. They had taken down a span of the railings that encircled the Fairchild graves, that the gravediggers might work the more easily. Those railings must not be put back. As a small child they had saddened her and she had demanded to know why those who lay there should be set apart from the rest. Gran said that one day she would understand, but she did not understand. She only knew that the railings were wrong and that the verger should be told she did not want them replaced.

At the church porch, the bearers waited. She must go. She must listen to intonations and sad psalms; must join in the singing of hymns chosen long ago by her grandmother.

This day should be cold and grey, wet with December fog, but it was June and the sun high in a sky of brilliant blue. For that at least she was grateful.

Polly removed her pearl-ended hatpin, took off her hat and hung it on the door peg, sighing with relief that it was over.

'Tea?' she asked of no one in particular. 'Think we could all do with a cup.'

And thanks be that the war had put paid to funeral teas, she thought grimly. She didn't like funeral teas – she never had, with everyone standing about not knowing what to say and saying the wrong thing every time they opened their mouths, like as not. The rationing of food had settled the matter and with a bit of luck it would never return.

'Please,' said Kath.

'Right, then. Set a tray, Roz, there's a good lass, though I suppose I shouldn't be giving you orders, now.'

'You shouldn't,' Roz smiled, 'but you will, Poll Appleby.'

'Aye. And come to think of it, I'll be able to go on giving you orders till you're one-and-twenty,' she teased, glad of that smile, though brief, on the young girl's lips.

'Mind if I go upstairs and get out of these clothes?' Kath's walking-out uniform of breeches, knee-length stockings, pullover and shirt was much too hot for a day such as this. 'Won't be long.'

'Is your young man coming tonight?' Polly asked when they were alone. 'I think it's right that him and me should meet, don't you? Your Gran would have wanted it.'

'She would, and you shall – but tomorrow. I'm almost sure he'll be flying tonight. He hinted as much when he phoned me this morning. He said he'd had a talk with the padre – about us getting a special licence. It's still all right – the wedding, I mean?'

'I said as much, didn't I?' Polly Appleby did not go back on her word. 'But quiet, mind.'

'Just Paul and me and you and Kath as witnesses. How will that suit you?'

'It'll have to suit me, I suppose, though I'd have liked to see you in white and a decent honeymoon afterwards.' But the rationing of clothing had made proper weddings impossible, she sighed – unless a bride could borrow a white dress and shoes. And what about utility wedding rings? Her face flushed dully as she remembered.

'Roz – there's something you must know. When Mr Dunston went to the hospital about – *things*, they gave him your gran's wrist-watch and the pearls she was wearing, and her wedding ring. They're upstairs in her jewel box; they're yours, now.'

'And?' Roz whispered.

'And I'd like it if you'd wear her pearls on your wedding day, and –'

'Be married with her ring, Polly?'

'Be married with her ring,' she confirmed gravely. 'That way she'd be there, too, wouldn't she?'

'She would, Polly. I'll wear them for her – and thank you.'

'Nay. 'Twas but a thought.' Polly's mouth trembled and her eyes misted with tears but she blinked them away impatiently. 'Stands to reason you don't want one of them cheap little utility rings. Which lass would, given the choice? Ah well, I'll just sup this tea, then I'll be off. Don't want Arnie waiting for me at the gate.'

Arnie had had more than his fair share of neglect these last few days; he'd felt Mrs Fairchild's passing, too. Best make a bit of a fuss of the bairn tonight. A bit of love and attention once in a while never hurt anyone. Besides, she wanted to be out of this kitchen. Tomorrow she would start afresh. Tomorrow Roz would be mistress of Ridings, Polly reasoned, and by then she would have cried her long-overdue tears, cussed them Germans roundly and asked the good Lord to see to it that Mrs Fairchild was with her Martin again.

'Say so-long to Kath for me,' she whispered. 'I'll be here tomorrow, same time. I've got my own key, if you're out.'

She left quickly, for tears still threatened.

'Bless you, Polly,' Roz whispered to the empty room. 'Thank you. For everything.'

'Polly said,' Kath murmured, draining her cup gratefully, 'that there was great respect at the church today. Every house in Alderby represented and half of Helpsley, too.' Polly had watched and noted; had taken in every smallest detail of the afternoon. It had kept her mind off things; helped her maintain the dignity of Ridings. 'The church was packed.'

'Was it? I hardly saw a thing. I shut myself off; I had to. All I saw was the grave. It seemed so very sad. Until then I'd told myself no, it hadn't happened, that I was going to wake up from this gigantic nightmare and Gran would be there, pottering about in the ruins. But this afternoon, in the churchyard, I had to accept it. I'm on my own, now.'

'You've got Paul. And you'll soon be married.'

'Yes, I will. And I've got you, Kath. You won't ever think of moving on, will you?'

'I won't. Only if they insist and then not without protest. But how about tonight? Are we going to Tuckets Hill? I feel like notching up another op.'

Anything to steer the conversation away from the trauma of the afternoon. And she must learn, Kath resolved, to be a good listener, for there was so much more, she was sure of it, that Roz had yet to talk out of herself.

'You bet we're going up to Tuckets! And Kath – I *will* try to pull myself together. Just give me a little time.'

They were half way up the hill that overlooked Peddlesbury aerodrome, walking slowly in the early evening warmth, hands clasped companionably.

'Crazy, isn't it,' Roz muttered, 'them being so cagey about accepting phone calls when the squadron is operational? It's like confirming it; like giving advance warning. Any German agent need only lift the phone and ask for 217.'

'Oh, I doubt it, Roz. So our bombers are flying? How is Jerry to know how many – and where they'll be heading? I'll bet they've come to expect air-raids, somewhere or other, every night of the week, now. Those thousand-bomber raids must be getting Hitler really rattled.'

'You could be right. And don't take any notice of me. I won't be fit to live with till Paul's got these last four behind him. I thought, just *thought*, mind, that it might be nice to hold back the wedding till he's finished his tour. But we won't. I just want to be married to him; properly and openly married, and as soon as we can. And, Kath – thanks; for these last few days, I mean. I don't know how I'd have got through them if you hadn't been with me. They say no two women are really close until they've shared a grief, and wept together. Thank you for sharing mine, and putting up with my tears . . .'

'No bother.' Kath's reply was rough with emotion. Just to be needed was thanks enough. She had never been close to anyone; not before Roz. 'You'd have done the same for me. In fact there's something I've got to tell you. I've known since Monday, but I figured you'd got enough on your plate. Flora brought me the letter, telling me about it, and when I saw her this afternoon she gave me another; one that arrived this morning.

'Barney's been wounded, you see. His CO wrote to me first, to the Birmingham address. Barney's in hospital at a place called Hafiif – it's near Cairo – though they told me precious little else. But this morning's letter was from Barney – well, sort of. Actually, it was written by a nurse; she put a little note on the bottom.' She reached into her pocket for the envelopes, handing them over with a shrug of resignation. 'Read them, Roz. See what you make of it. I'd just about got used to it, and then the second letter came. Do you think it could mean he's too badly injured to write?'

'Oh, Kath – I'm sorry. I know Barney could have his moods, but I'm sorry he's been hurt. But his letter – well, the reason could be simple, couldn't it? It could just mean that his right hand – or arm – has been injured, or something. I mean, think back to a time when you might have cut your finger – fairly badly, that is – remember how awkward it was, writing with even one finger bandaged? Maybe Barney's arm is in a sling – of course a nurse would write a letter for him. Anyway, it's one way of looking at it.'

'I suppose it is. Oh, I know I'd decided that Barney and I were finished, but I didn't want this to happen; truly, I didn't.'

'I know. Don't you think Barney might have told you a bit more in the letter? He said he was fine; mightn't he have said *why* he couldn't write, or didn't it occur to him?'

'Don't think that. Let's face it, nurses are there to nurse, not write letters all day. There could be quite a few in that hospital not able to hold a pen and maybe the nurses don't have time for long letters. Or perhaps they aren't allowed to give out information like that?'

'You're always willing to give Barney best, aren't you? But you're going to have a bit of facing-up to do now, you know. Have you told Marco, by the way?'

'No. No one knows but you and Flora. I've been trying to keep away from Marco these last few days, but tomorrow I'll be getting back to normal working and it won't be easy.'

'It won't. Have you thought what's going to happen now between you and Barney?'

'Happen? How *can* I know?' Kath let go a sigh of exasperation. 'I won't change my mind, if that's what you mean, but I thought the day I asked him to let me go would be a long way off and suddenly it isn't. It's almost certain he'll be sent back to England, now. The wounded usually are.'

'You could be right.' Roz handed back the letters. 'But maybe he hasn't been seriously wounded; at any rate, that's the way you're going to have to think until you hear to the contrary. Just tell yourself that he can't write because his arm is in a sling – okay? And I think you should tell Marco, too, because it seems that decision time is going to be a whole lot sooner than you thought.'

'Decision time? But I already told you. I've made up my mind. Nothing has changed. I want to leave Barney. Does that make me sound like an unfeeling bitch, Roz? My husband is in hospital – maybe badly wounded – yet still I want him to let me go?'

'Not unfeeling. Just honest – so for goodness' sake stop agonizing. It'll give you wrinkles. Right now we're here to see Paul on his way – remember? After that we'll talk about you and Barney – and Marco.'

'No, Roz. There's one thing I *have* faced up to and that is that there's no future at all for Marco and me. Nothing is more certain, or more hopeless.'

Her eyes misted with tears and she covered her face with her hands, wishing she didn't feel so guilty, so heartless. But she'd be punished, wouldn't she? They, the Fates – or whoever it was up there who decided the way things should be – would make her pay for what she wanted to do. 'All right,' they'd say, 'let her be rid of Barney, if that's what she wants. But she shan't have Marco . . .'

'Don't say that, Kath. Think how hopeless it seemed for Paul and me; yet look at us now – almost married.'

'But *you* are single and I'm not.' Kath dabbed at her eyes then blew her nose, loudly. 'And you're right – we're here to wish Sugar good luck. Look down there, Roz. Something's happening. A couple of them have got their engines running already – and we forgot the binoculars!'

'Never mind. We'll just wish them all good luck, like always, then we'll know they'll all get back. And they will. They'll be all right, won't they, Kath?'

'They'll be fine. Paul has the best skipper in Bomber Command. He's got you to come home to and Skip has his baby to look forward to, so they'll make it. They'll do their thirty. Why don't I go back for the binoculars? It won't take me long and we'll be able to see a whole lot better.' She held out her hand. 'Give me the key and you just stay here and relax. Close your eyes and think about weddings – okay?'

'Mm. Weddings.' Smiling, Roz closed her eyes. 'Don't be long?'

'I won't.' It was good to see her smile again.

Once she reached the bottom of the hill, Kath began to run. Not so very far away she knew that Mat and Jonty and Marco would still be busy with the last of the hay. Since the first cut, the weather had been perfect, with a hot sun beating down from a clear sky and though she had missed her first haytime, Kath knew that hay needed sun to dry it. Now that hay, sweet with the scent of high summer, had been raked into cocks, ready for carting away and storing in the loft above the cowshed. In spite of time lost, just one more day would see them finished, Mat had told her. And another good day they would have, Kath thought, lifting her gaze to the sky. The swallows were still flying high. Mat's hay would be safely in before the weather broke.

She heard the slow, steady clopping of a horse's tread and knew that just around the bend in the lane she would meet up with Duke, the waggon behind him piled high with hay and Mat leading him companionably. Stepping on to the grass verge she waited, smiling, as they passed.

'Whoa-up, lad.' Mat brought the horse to a halt. 'Now then, our Kath. Out for a walk?'

'No, Mat. Just going to the house to pick up something we'd forgotten. Roz is up at Tuckets, watching the take-off. Thought we'd see it better with the binoculars . . .'

'Is Roz feeling a bit better? She looked badly this afternoon. Happen now it's over she'll pick up a bit.'

'I think she will. Mat, I don't know about Roz, but I'll be back to work in the morning. I can manage the milk-round alone; tell Grace I'll be seeing to the dairy work, too. It can't have been easy for you with the two of us off.'

'It wasn't. Didn't realize we'd come to rely so much on the pair of you. Grace has missed having you about the place, Kath. Will I tell her you'll be in for an early cup, like normal? She's been in a terrible state over Mrs Fairchild. Try to cheer her up a bit, there's a good lass.'

'I will.' Kath smiled up into his eyes, her affection real. Our Kath, they always called her and she wished she were indeed theirs. Could she have chosen her parents they would have been exactly like Mat and Grace. 'But I'll not keep you. You look tired, Mat.'

'I am. Shan't be sorry to hit the hay tonight,' and he threw back his head and laughed at his play on words. 'So-long, lass. Tell Roz I – *Good grief!* See that?' His face creased into disbelief as he reached for Duke's bridle. 'What's he playing at?'

Kath closed her eyes, flinching at the roar of a bomber flying low; too low. A Lancaster, its black underbelly so near she could almost have reached up and touched it.

'Ruddy-well hedge-hopping, that's what! Nearly took the top off the load!'

'He's in trouble, Mat,' Kath whispered. 'He's far too low.'

They watched, stunned, as the bomber disappeared behind the trees in Peddlesbury Lane, its engines spluttering.

'He isn't going to make it . . .'

They sensed and felt the impact as it hit the ground, heard the terrible roar, saw the blinding flash of the explosion high above the treetops.

'Oh, my Lord!'

There was silence, then; a second dragged out to a minute. Then smoke, mushrooming up; black and dense, flames licking through it.

'Mat! I must go!' Back to Tuckets, back to Roz. Oh, God, God, *God!* One of Peddlesbury's and with a bomb-load, too. The noise of the explosion still beat inside her head. She had never run so fast. *Roz, it's all right. It wasn't Sugar. It wasn't!*

They met at the foot of Tuckets Hill; Kath breathless, chest heaving, Roz white-faced, eyes round with fear.

'Kath! I saw it! Right at the very end of the runway – going like mad for take-off. Then it seemed to slew . . .'

'*Slew*? Then what?'

'He was going just fine. Another second and he'd have been airborne. Then something went wrong. I think it's just behind the wood. I'm going there!'

'No, Roz! You mustn't! You can't! They won't want people there. It could be dangerous.'

But she was running already, heels kicking the ground, hair flying.

'Wait for me!' She couldn't run any more. Already there was a pain in her chest. 'Roz – come back! That wasn't Skip; it *wasn't*!' Holding her heaving sides, Kath stumbled after her. Roz mustn't see that crash. It would haunt her, if she did, every time Paul took off. 'Wait for me . . .'

She caught up with her at the edge of the wood, arguing with the armed sentry who blocked her way.

'Sorry, girl – like I said, you can't go any further and that's an order.' There was damn-all to see, anyway. Just bits here, bits there and a hole so deep it could hide a hangar.

'Which one was it? Was it Skip Wright's?' Her voice was high and wild, bordering on hysteria. 'What are the markings on it? Surely you know that? It's all I want to know.'

'Markings? How the 'ell would I know?' He looked up sharply as a bomber roared overhead, climbing surely, its undercarriage already up.

'They're still going?' Roz gasped. 'After what just happened, they're still taking off?'

'There *is* a war on, or hasn't anybody told you?' The sentry's voice was surly. Today had been pay-day. He'd intended spending an hour or two at the pub tonight, not being ordered out to stand guard over a bloody great hole.

Because that's all there was to see. There'd be none of them walk away from *that* one, poor sods. 'A war on – all right? So why don't you go home, miss? There's nothing you can do and I don't want to have to call the sergeant, now do I?'

'But I want to know! I *must* know!'

'And I flippin' can't tell you.' She was beginning to annoy him. 'So ring the aerodrome – they'll know something. Ring the adjutant or the padre, but don't ask *me*.'

They flinched as another bomber roared into the sky above them. Two gone. Three, if you counted the first.

'Kath – what are we to do? He won't let me go any farther; said people would be all over the place, looking for bits of shrapnel, bits of the plane. I'm not after souvenirs – God knows I'm not. I just want to *know* . . .'

'Come home, Roz. He's right. He doesn't know anything. We'll ring the aerodrome – set your mind at rest . . .'

'But they might refuse the call. What'll we do if they won't accept it?'

'We'll keep on ringing till they do. And if we can't get any sense out of them tonight, then you'll have to wait until morning when Paul phones – all right?'

'Yes. It wasn't Sugar, was it?'

'Of course it wasn't.' She took Roz's shoulders, gripping them tightly. 'Listen to me, will you? You've had more than your fair share of trouble for one week and there's Skip's baby to think about, too. God wouldn't be *that* rotten, now would He?'

'No. You're right. It isn't Paul. Paul said he'd take care.'

'And he *will*. He's getting married next week. Now are we going home or are we going to stand here debating the issue all night? I could do with a cup of tea, I know that much. And as for you, Roz, you'll do exactly as you're told. When I've phoned Peddlesbury you'll go to bed with a cup of hot milk – all right?'

'All right. I'm sorry if I made a fool of myself, only it was such a shock; such a terrible explosion. I don't seem to have slept for so long. I feel like I want to close my eyes, shut it all out and not wake up till Paul phones.'

'That's my girl. Sleep – that's all you need. In no time at all it'll be morning and you'll be telling yourself what a fool you were to get so worried. It's ten to one *against* it being Paul – and odds like that are just fine by me.' Kath laid an arm across her shoulders, pulling her close. 'Come on, now. Home.'

And Paul? Kath sent her thoughts high and wide. *Wherever you are, whatever you are doing right now, for God's sake take care. She can't take much more. She really can't . . .*

21

'The key, Kath. I gave you the key . . .'

Kath dipped into her pocket, surprised she could have forgotten so heavy an object. Was it really only an hour ago she had set off, light-heartedly almost, for the binoculars?

Yet since then a bomber had crashed on take-off; had slammed into the earth behind Peddlesbury Lane wood. And they had run there, dry-mouthed, with thudding hearts only to be ordered away.

But it wasn't S-Sugar, Kath insisted silently as she slid the big iron key into the lock. Why should it be? Roz had had more than her fair share of grief. Tonight, it must be the turn of someone else to weep.

She pushed open the door. Nothing had changed since they left. Paul was all right – they were *all* all right – in the morning he would telephone Roz and she'd be starry-eyed with joy again, breathless with relief and everything would be marvellous until next time.

'I'm cold. This kitchen is like an ice-house.' Roz rubbed her arms, glaring at a firegrate laid with paper and kindling. 'I suppose we couldn't light it?'

'We can if you want to, but you're cold because you aren't eating. You'll make yourself ill if you carry on like this,' Kath grumbled. 'Polly is only trying to save coal for the winter. No one needs fires in June.' She didn't know why she was going on so about one shovel of coal when logs were stacked high in the stables across the yard; the tearing out of the game-cover had seen to that. Next winter, and the winter after that, Ridings would be warmer than it had been for years. 'But I suppose it mightn't be a bad idea.

We could get the water hot and have a decent bath,' Kath conceded. 'Shall I bring some logs in? They'll be good and dry, now.'

'Would you – and Kath . . .'

Kath turned in the doorway, knowing what was to come.

'It's all right, isn't it? It wasn't Sugar?'

'It *wasn't* Sugar. How many more times – oh, put the kettle on, will you. I need a cup of tea and a smoke.'

It wasn't Sugar, she insisted as she filled the log basket. Why should it be? Why, when they were nearly at the end of their tour should the best and most experienced pilot in the squadron crash on take-off? Though it was understandable that Roz should be anxious. Roz wasn't over the shock of her gran's death yet, and she was only a kid when all was said and done. Of course she was anxious.

But tea was what they needed. Tea with sugar in it and be blowed to rationing. And she was taking no more refusals. Roz would eat something before she went to bed – or else!

Roz spun round almost guiltily as Kath heaved the log basket through the kitchen door.

'I – the phone,' she murmured. 'No use . . .'

'You rang? You tried to get through to the aerodrome? But surely –'

'I got through, Kath. They accepted the call and I asked for the padre, only he wasn't there. So I left a message and my phone number. The girl who answered said she'd make sure he got it.'

'And that was all? Just that he'd ring back? The girl didn't tell you anything?'

'No.' Roz turned away from Kath's probing eyes, carefully piling wood on the fire. 'But I didn't ask because she wouldn't have told me, anyway. She couldn't have. But the padre – well, I thought that maybe, if there was anything to tell –'

'*If* there was anything to tell – but there won't be.' Kath picked up the kettle. 'And I thought we were going to have a cup of tea.'

'Sorry. I'm still a bit light-headed. I'll be all right, once I've had some sleep.'

'Too darn right you will. And you're going to eat something, too. When we've got the water hot you'll have a bath and get straight into bed! You're going to close your eyes and think about the wedding, what you'll wear and how wonderful everything is going to be.'

'The wedding.' She looked over to the dresser and the vase of flowers. Pale pink carnations and white gypsophila. Paul had brought them on Monday night. She wondered how he'd managed to get so large a bunch. Flowers were considered a luxury now, but Gran would have been so pleased to get them. They were still fresh and sweet-smelling. Paul's flowers. In this house. Reminding her of his love.

'Our wedding. I can't believe it, Kath. Roz Rennie. Sounds good, doesn't it?'

'It sounds great – so how about something to eat? I think we can run to toast and jam. In the morning I'll ask Grace if she can spare me a black market egg for your breakfast – okay?'

'Okay – and thanks. You're an old love.' Shyly, almost, she kissed Kath's cheek. 'I'm grateful – I truly am.'

'Oh, away with your bother. It works both ways, doesn't it? Only try to eat something or you'll look dreadful at the church and you don't want that, now do you?

'And, Roz – don't worry overmuch if the padre doesn't ring back. Chances are he'll be up to the eyes in it with – well – other things.'

'I won't. I've got myself in hand, now. I'll be all right, once I've had some sleep.'

Sleep. Blessed, beautiful sleep. She wished she could sleep for a week; sleep until Kath shook her awake, saying,

'This is your wedding day!' But she couldn't, of course, because tomorrow she must go back to work. Mat had been short-handed at a time when he could least afford to be and next week, maybe on Tuesday or Wednesday if all went well, she would be asking for more time off. Even a day could be ill afforded.

Such a quiet wedding it would be. No white satin slippers, no confetti. No trousseau, no honeymoon. No marquee on the lawn nor tiny bridesmaids stealing the show nor half the North Riding there in big, beautiful hats. And she didn't care. Only Paul mattered, and that they be married. Soon.

Kath was washing-up at the sink when the phone rang. Quickly she snatched it up.

'Good evening. Miss Fairchild?'

'Sorry, Roz is – well, she's in the bath, but I can get her down. Is it the padre?'

'It is. I got her message. Are you family – or a close friend, perhaps?'

'Her friend. Kath Allen. Is there anything I can do?'

A message she could take? That Sugar was all right, perhaps? It was all she wanted to know.

'There *is* a message, Miss Allen –'

'Yes?' Kath sucked sharply on her breath, wishing she could see his face, read what was there, in his eyes.

'Tell me – is it the same Rosalind Fairchild whose grandmother was recently killed? Is her young man aircrew here at Peddlesbury – Paul Rennie? And were they wanting to be married?'

'That's it. By special licence. I think Paul spoke to you about it.'

Her words sounded strained and strange. *Were* they wanting to be married . . .

'Then the news isn't good, I'm afraid. Are you up to it, Miss Allen? Will I come there, or can you tell her that the bomber that crashed tonight was –' He stopped, unsure, and the silence was terrible and menacing.

'It was Sugar, wasn't it?'

'The pilot's name was John Wright. Paul Rennie was the navigator . . .'

'And they're all –'

'There were no survivors. I'm sorry; so very sorry. Are you there, my dear? Are you all right?'

'Yes.' Yes, she was here but no, she wasn't all right! She damn-well *wasn't*!

'And can you manage?'

'I'll tell her.' Somehow, she would tell her. Tell her that her lovely world had come to an end; that there'd be no wedding, no Paul, ever again. Oh yes, she'd tell her, then hope Roz wouldn't hate her for the rest of her life.

'Thank you, my dear. Goodnight, then, and God bless you. I'm sorry to put such a burden on you . . .'

Kath stood for a long time, staring at the receiver, wondering if she had heard aright; wondering if it had been a tragic mistake.

'I can't do it,' she whispered. 'I *won't*.'

Carefully she opened the kitchen door. Holding her breath she stood there, listening.

There was no sound; no bathtub singing, no splashing of water. The bathroom door was shut. Roz hadn't heard.

Tomorrow, she would tell her. Tonight, Roz must sleep; why tell her tonight? Tomorrow would be soon enough and maybe by morning something could have happened; something wonderful and miraculous and Paul would ring and –

But it wasn't a mistake, she thought dully. It was true; tragically true. She clenched her hands to stop their shaking as anger took her. It blazed inside her and she wanted to open doors then slam them shut with all her strength; she wanted to hit out, to hurt someone, everyone.

The world had gone mad. She, Kath Allen, had gone

426

mad and she wanted to cry. She wanted to close her eyes, wail and scream; to go down on her knees and beat the floor with her fists in a fury.

What had Roz done that was so wicked? What awful thing from her past was she paying for? Had she been too happy, loved too much? And what was to become of her now?

Dear, sweet heaven – Paul dead and Skip and Flight. All of them dead. What went wrong, Juney? Didn't you count tonight? Why wasn't Grace here, and Polly? They would know what to do, what to say. And Jonty. Where was Jonty when Roz needed him so? Did nobody care?

The lifting of the kitchen door latch made such a noise that Kath spun round, startled.

'My, but I feel better for that.'

Roz stood there, her wet hair wrapped in a towel. She was wearing her pale green dressing gown and faded pink slippers. 'The water was lovely and hot. There's enough left for another bath. Why don't you have one? You can use my soap.'

'Yes. Think I will. Y-yes . . .'

'Kath – what is it? Are you all right?'

'All right? Well – no, I'm not. Got a bit of a headache and I suppose I'm missing sleep, too. Look, love – why don't you get into bed now whilst you're nice and relaxed? I'll check the blackouts before I run a bath.'

'Would you mind if I did, Kath – got into bed now, I mean? I *am* tired and I know I could sleep. I'll do the milk with you in the morning – give me a shout, will you, if I'm not awake?'

'Okay. Now off you go. Close your eyes and don't think about – about *anything*.'

'I won't. I think I could sleep the clock round.' Smiling she kissed Kath's cheek. 'Goodnight, love – and thanks.'

Thanks, Roz? For what? For knowing about Paul, and not telling you? For letting you go to bed knowing that in

*the morning I'm going to shatter your lovely world for ever?
Thanks? Oh, Roz, tomorrow you'll hate me . . .*

Kath did not sleep. Her mind was a turmoil of panic and bitterness. She would never, ever, forget this night; would never forget the slowness of its passing nor the worry of what the morning held and how she was to find the words and the courage to tell Roz.

She had tried counting sheep; she had spun splendid, brave fantasies about none of it having happened; that she was asleep, dreaming, and soon her alarm would awaken her and she could count the bombers home with Roz as they delivered the milk.

She thumped and turned her pillow yet again. She had tried to think about Barney and why a nurse had written his last letter. She had thought about Marco; that soon it would be her birthday and her third wedding anniversary and, poignantly, that Roz might have been married by then, too.

But now Roz and Paul would not be married and her own marriage was over because she was in love with Marco Roselli. Her eyes hurt. If only she could close them and sleep; block out this awful night.

Sleep had not come and she had been glad to open the curtains and draw aside the blackout; look out on to another bright morning, the clouds tipped gold from a rising sun. Tomorrow had become today and today she must tell Roz.

Carefully she dressed, then picking up her shoes, walking quietly past the door of Roz's bedroom, she went downstairs.

Half-past five. She checked her watch with the kitchen clock. Too early yet for work, but Jonty would be up. Maybe already he was bringing in the herd for milking. Jonty would know what to do; he would help her.

She found him as she'd hoped she would, at the gate of the cow pasture. He looked up as she called his name, then glanced down, smiling, pointing to his watch.

'You're early, Kath. Couldn't you sleep?'

'No, I couldn't. I lay there worrying and in the end I couldn't stand it. Last night, Jonty – the bomber . . .'

'Bad do, that. Is Roz worrying about it?'

'She was, but she went to bed and she's still asleep – or I hope she is. But Jonty – oh, God.' She gave a shuddering sigh, covering her face with her hands, holding back the words so awful to say.

'Kath! What is it? What happened?'

'Paul's dead.' There was no other way to say it. 'The bomber that crashed was his. The padre rang last night, but Roz was in the bath and I said I'd tell her, but I couldn't. I just let her go to bed thinking it was all right, that it had happened to some other crew. And I can't face it. I can't. Not without you, Jonty. Be there, when I tell her?'

'Oh, God – you're sure?'

'I'm sure. I wish I'd dreamed it, but I haven't. The padre wouldn't get it wrong. I don't know what to do. What's going to happen to her? Monday her gran; today, Paul. Two terrible shocks, one after the other. It's too much.'

'Let me think, Kath.' Jonty ran his fingers through his hair. 'Look – give me a hand with this lot. Help me get the milking started and when Dad comes out I'll tell him. He'll be here in a minute, then I'll do the milk-round and you can get back to her. Best be there, Kath, when she wakes up . . .'

'No, Jonty. Not without you.' She set her mouth stubbornly. She wasn't brave enough to do it on her own; wouldn't know how to cope with Roz's grief. 'Please? I'll make it up to you, Jonty – only I can't do it. Not alone.'

'All right – but give me a minute? Can't think straight. Does Polly know?'

'No one knows but you and me. Polly will be there about ten; she'll know soon enough – unless you think she should be told . . .'

'I don't know, Kath. I just don't know. But it seems to me that no matter who's there it isn't going to make any difference to Roz. And she's the one who matters. It's Roz we must think about.'

'Right. So let's get the milking started and maybe Mat will think of something. I'm sorry about all this. I know I'm asking a lot and I know that farms don't run themselves, but all I can think about is how I'm to tell Roz. How am I to stand by and see her misery and not be able to do anything about it?'

'You won't be on your own, Kath. There'll be Polly and Mum and me. We'll help all we can. And you know the way it is with me, although I'd give anything for this not to have happened. You know that, don't you?'

'I know, Jonty. But let's not just stand here. Why don't I get on with the milk on my own? Nobody's going to complain if it's half an hour early, are they? On my way back I'll call in and tell Polly and maybe Grace can do the dairy work – just for this morning.'

'Okay. Harness Daisy up and give me a shout when you're ready; I'll heave the crates for you. As soon as I've told Dad I'll get down to the village and help you out. And let's not forget Marco. He'll be here at eight.'

Marco? She hadn't forgotten Marco. All through the night he'd been in and out of her thoughts. Since Monday she had hardly seen him yet there was so much to tell him. About Barney, and now about Paul. He would listen and he would understand. Once she had told Marco she might not feel so alone, so afraid.

'Yes,' she said, out loud. 'We mustn't forget Marco.' Nor how good it felt with his arms around her, how safe. She longed to be with him, loved him so much and knew, now, that she always would. 'I'll make a start. I'm sorry

430

about all this and I'm sorry I panicked, but I didn't know how I'd cope on my own.'

'Well, you don't have to, now. We'll all pitch in. Don't worry, Kath.'

'I'll try not to. Jonty, remember that I once asked you to be there if ever Roz should need you? Well, she needs you now. She won't know it, but she'll need you as she's never needed anyone in her life before.'

'I remember. Kath – if you were thinking about going back to the hostel, can you ask Flora for a little more time? Roz can't be left alone. Do you think they'll let you?'

'I don't see why not. I'll ring Peacock. Afterwards . . .'

It was a little before eight o'clock when Kath and Jonty crossed the yard at Ridings.

'Look!' Kath pointed. 'She's up. The back door's open, and I left it shut.'

The sound of early morning music could be clearly heard. Roz had switched on for the breakfast-time news. Everything appeared normal, which meant that Roz didn't know; that no one had telephoned.

'Hi!' Roz's smile was bright. 'You said you'd give me a call, and you didn't. But the bombers woke me up. Why are you back so soon, and Jonty –' She saw their faces clearly for the first time; saw the set of their mouths, the apprehension in their eyes, and the smile left her lips.

'Jonty – what is it? Why are you here?'

'Sit down, Roz?' He took her arm, guiding her to a chair, easing her into it as if she were not capable of doing so simple a thing unaided. 'The padre rang . . .'

'Last night, Roz.' Kath ran her tongue round lips gone dry. 'Only I didn't – couldn't – tell you . . .'

'Tell me? Tell me what?' She was on her feet again. 'Not Paul? Oh, God, not Paul . . .' Her lips formed the words, but no sound came.

'The padre told Kath that the pilot's name was John Wright. Roz, I'm sorry . . .'

'No. Not Sugar. I won't listen. I won't!' Her face was drained of colour, her eyes wide and wild with fear. She clasped her arms tightly around herself but it did nothing to stop the jerking of her limbs.

'A glass of water, Kath.' Jonty took a step nearer, wanting to gather Roz to him yet fearing to touch her.

In a daze, Kath filled a glass, carrying it clumsily, splashing water on the floor.

She offered it to Roz, but she turned away, putting out her hands, reaching for the fireguard but not quite making it because the floor was tilting beneath her.

'No!' Her cry was harsh. 'Paul! Help me!'

Jonty caught her as she fell then scooped her into his arms, lifting her as if she were no weight at all.

'Open the door.'

Kath ran ahead of him, up the stairs and into the bedroom, smoothing the rumpled bed sheets with agitated hands, shaking the pillow.

'There, now.' Gently he laid her down. 'Stay with her, Kath. She needs help. I'll get the doctor . . .'

'The number's on the pad, beside the phone . . .'

'Right, then. Cover her up. Hold her hands, talk to her. I won't be a minute.'

'Roz?' Furiously Kath rubbed the limp, cold hands. 'Roz, love – please? Roz, say something?' She gathered her into her arms, holding her tightly, rocking her. 'Don't look at me like that? I'm sorry. I'm sorry.'

'All right, Kath. Go downstairs now, put the kettle on. Tea, she needs, with plenty of sugar. And fill a hot-water bottle.' Jonty's voice was low and firm. 'The doctor's coming. I'll stay with her.'

She could not strike the match. She broke three in her shaking, useless fingers before she heard the plop of igniting gas.

Tea with sugar, and a hot-water bottle. Shock, that's what. Sugar for shock.

She closed her eyes, and began to pray.

The doctor was tall, his face thin but his eyes kind. Kath was glad his eyes were kind. 'Can I come in?'

He walked into the kitchen with a swinging limp. Kath had heard about that limp. He'd been wounded in Norway. He'd lain for two days and nights in the cold, his leg shattered. They'd invalided him out . . .

'She's upstairs,' Kath whispered. 'She just keeled over. Shock, I think. She's shaking dreadfully. First her gran, and then Paul, last night.'

'Her boyfriend? On the bomber that crashed?'

'We only just told her. Up here, doctor . . .'

'And you are?'

'Kath. Kath Allen.' She pushed open the bedroom door.

'Hullo, Rosalind.' The doctor knew her name and his smile was gentle. 'Well, now, let me have a look at you.'

Jonty nodded briefly, then walked to the door, closing it behind him.

'He'll see to her, now. They say he's a decent sort. Let's make that tea, shall we? I think the hot-water bottles are in the big cupboard in the back lobby. And get yourself a cup, Kath. You look as if you need one.'

'Yes, Jonty. Thanks.' He was so good, so kind, and kindness always made her want to weep. 'What a mess. What a terrible, terrible mess it all is.' She covered her face with her hands. 'She'll never get over this. *Never.*'

Roz lay still in the half-dark room. She wanted to move her head, look at the bedside clock, but if she opened her eyes Polly would notice and she didn't want to talk. Not to anyone. She just wanted to lie here, cocooned against the world and never have to speak nor eat nor laugh again. She wanted to drift up and away; wallow in time forgotten.

She ached all over. Every part of her hurt. There was a pain in her chest and a cold, gnawing ache at the place where her heart should be. Could you die of a broken heart? People did. They just faded into small, sad wraiths and people said, 'Nothing wrong, really. Only heartbreak. A terrible thing, heartbreak . . .'

Paul, my darling, *why*? Why did it happen to us? I thought my love could keep you safe. I thought you would make it, make your thirtieth. But you didn't, Paul. You were too young and good, we loved too well . . .

They had loved too well and now it was over. No more lying close, lips to lips, heart upon heart; no more taking and giving, loving and needing. No more small, sweet thrills as he touched her; never again the joy of seeing him walk toward her. Only Paul broken and burned, his beauty defiled.

She clenched her teeth until her jaws hurt. She wished Polly would go. Why did she sit there? Were they afraid she would do something if they left her alone?

Where are you now, Paul? Can you hear what I'm saying to you – what my heart is saying, or have you gone from me? Is death the end of everything or will I see you again? Will you be waiting there like always? Will you smile and kiss me, say you've missed me? Or is there nothing for us, Paul?

The door opened quietly. 'Still asleep, is she?' Footsteps across the room.

'Aye. It's that stuff the doctor gave her.'

'Poor lass. Poor little lass . . .'

Grace and Polly, whispering. Only she wasn't asleep. Whatever he'd given her only made her feel numb inside, and floaty. She would never sleep again.

'I'll come downstairs, Grace. She's hard on.'

Polly and Grace leaving her; one of them propping open the door; the fifth stair down creaking.

She stretched her cold, aching limbs, opened her eyes, looked at the clock. Ten minutes past noon yet it seemed she had lain here for a lifetime. But what was a lifetime? For Paul it had been not quite twenty-three years.

I'm glad we were lovers, my darling; I'm glad about – everything. I don't know how I'll face it, but still I'm glad . . .

Strange that there were no tears inside her, no anger. But perhaps that was because of the tablet the doctor had made her swallow.

'I'll leave two more downstairs, Rosalind. One for tonight – another for the morning . . .'

And what else had he said – that she must call him at once if she felt ill? Stomach cramps or abdominal pain or vomiting. Day or night she must call him. He'd been kind to her, yet she couldn't remember his name.

Paul, sweetheart – why . . .

'I think,' Polly said, 'that if I let myself I could scream and scream till I'm blue in the face. It's frightening, Kath. This family, I mean. Nothing but bad luck all down the years. Dogged with it, the Fairchilds – every generation beset by tragedy.'

'She was so happy about them getting married – well, not happy exactly, Polly. More like she'd believe it when it happened. But it was Paul's flying. It hung over her all the time. And he'd so nearly made it.'

'Aye. That's the way it is, when there's a war on. But hadn't you better be getting over to the hostel? Didn't you say the Warden wanted to see you? If you go now you'll be well back before I leave. Because I'll have to go, Kath. There's Arnie to see to, but him and me will move in here for a while, if they say you must go back. Somebody's got to be with her, though. She can't be left on her own.'

435

'I think it'll be all right – for a time, at least. I don't think it matters where I sleep, so long as the work gets done. Trouble is I'm not working all that much these days, am I?'

'Happen not, but Roz comes first – Mat would be the first to say it. Haytime's over, now – they'll manage, until harvest. And they've got the prisoner. He's a decent young chap . . .'

All at once, Polly had taken to Marco, Italian and enemy though he was, for hadn't he been there, with the Mistress? Hadn't he held her and comforted her last moments? She'd have been alone, if the prisoner hadn't been there. Alone and afraid, but for him. There was good and bad in all things and all men, and Poll Appleby was the first to admit it.

'Decent? Yes, he is.' Better than decent. A man she could love for all time. 'Well, if you're sure, I'll get over to Peacock Hey and have a word with the Warden. I won't be long. I'll be back as soon as I can to let you know what she said.'

It would be strange, going back to Peacock; back to the noise and chatter; to where everything was as near to normal as you could hope to find it. There might be another letter waiting for her; a pale blue lettercard with Passed by Censor stamped on it in red and Barney's name, rank and number printed across the back. If there was, would Barney have written it, or a nurse? She didn't know. All she could be sure about was that she was very tired and very unhappy; in desperate need of arms to hold her, someone to whisper that one day it would all come right.

But it wouldn't come right. It couldn't. Not for her and not now for Roz. Not ever.

She called, 'Bye, Polly. Won't be long,' and her words were harsh with tears.

The RAF truck approached her travelling too quickly

for the winding, narrow lane and Kath pulled her bicycle on to the grass verge, giving it room to pass.

With a squeal of brakes it came to a stop, then backed down the lane, weaving erratically from side to side. It came level with her and Juney jumped out.

'Kath! Gawd, girl, how's Roz?'

Her face was pale and her cap, perched on the back of her head, gave her a curiously vulnerable look. Only a kid, Juney was. She'd thought the world of Sugar's crew.

'Roz? I – I don't know. It's as if she hasn't taken it in yet.'

'It's a bugger of a war, innit? I'm going to the Black Horse tonight. I'm going to get as tight as a tick, Kath. They were a smashin' bunch. And they nearly made it. Just three more ops and they'd have been laughing. And what about Julia? What about Skip's wife, then? Did you know?'

Kath shook her head.

'There was this telegram, see. For Skip, it was, only it arrived just before they – before they took off. Afterwards – when they cleared their things out, they found it. On his bed. Someone had left it there.'

'Cleared their things out, Juney? That was a bit quick, wasn't it?'

'Nah. They always do it quick. Strip their beds, empty their lockers, pack everything up and send it to the next of kin. It's got to be like that. There'll be a new crew in them beds tomorrow, like as not. But the bod from the Adjutant's office found the telegram. He had a Waaf sergeant with him, packing their things up and he told her to open it. A little girl, Kath. Both well, it said. Skip had a daughter, only he never knew. Tell Roz, won't you – when you think she's up to it.'

'I'll tell her.'

'I'd like to see her. Paul and Roz – they were great

437

together, weren't they? Don't suppose we'll be seeing you at the Friday-night dances, now?'

'I doubt it.' Not for a long, long time. She hadn't even thought about the Friday dances. Come to think of it, she'd hardly had one coherent thought in her head since Sugar crashed. 'Do you know what went wrong, Juney?'

'Not really. There's been talk, mind, but they'll never know; not for sure. Nothing left of that Lancaster, see? But a bloke was there, right at the end of the runway and he said the plane just suddenly slewed; went out of control. A burst tyre, they're saying it was. Makes you think, dunnit? Had luck written all over them, that crew did.' Her lower lip had begun to tremble; tears shone brightly in her eyes. 'Tell Roz I was asking, will you? Tell her I'll call and see her one day.'

'She'd like that. When things get a – a bit better.'

'Not on her own, is she?'

'No. Polly's with her. I've just been to the hostel. The Warden says I can stay with her – probably I'll move into Ridings permanently.'

'Well, I'm glad she'll have someone with her. Poor kid. Talk about getting kicked when you're down. But keep in touch, Kath. Let me know how she's getting on? You can ring me on 217. Ask for the MT Pool – motor transport.'

'I'll do that. I'll give Roz your message.'

'Yes.' She climbed back into the cab, swallowing noisily, sniffing loudly. 'See you, mate. Take care.'

'So long, Juney. Be lucky.'

Marco was waiting by the yard gate at Ridings, hands in the pockets of his jacket.

'Hey, Kat! *Ciao*.' He looked up, and smiled. 'I ate my rations quickly and I come to see you, but there is no one.'

'No. Roz is upstairs and Polly will be with her. It's good to see you, Marco.'

'It's a long time since we talk. Hardly at all since the *signora* died. And now there is Paul.'

'Now there is Paul. I can't believe it, Marco. Roz is devastated. I don't think she'll ever get over it.' She slid her hand into her pocket and brought out cigarettes, offering him one. 'I can't stay to talk; not this morning. But I'll be here at Ridings for a time. Come and see me tomorrow, if you can?'

'I'll come, Kat. And Mrs Ramsden says to tell you she'll be over, soon, with soup and milk.'

'That's kind of her. Tell her Roz is sleeping, will you?'

She held out her hand and he took it in his own, touching it gently with his lips. She wished with all her heart he could have taken her in his arms and whispered that it would be all right; just as it had been on threshing day. But he didn't; it wouldn't have been right. Soon she must tell him that Barney had been wounded and maybe was even now on his way back to England.

'I'll come tomorrow – if I can,' he said softly. 'Tell Roz I will pray for her, and for Paul. Take care, Katarina.'

'And you, Marco.'

Roz heard the closing of the back door and footsteps crossing the yard and she looked again at the bedside clock. Polly, going home, that had been.

The bed was cold and clammy. Her feet were cold, too, and she wondered how long she could endure this limbo. She felt light-headed. Was it the tablet or was it because she couldn't eat? She really should try, but food tasted like cottonwool in her mouth and the feeling of nausea was never far away.

Stewart. She remembered the doctor's name. He'd been in the Medical Corps. He would always walk with a limp, but he considered himself one of the lucky ones.

She pushed herself upright and the bedroom tilted, then righted itself. It wasn't true, about Sugar. She'd been lying here all morning and she hadn't heard the phone. Best she should get up; best be there, when it rang. But Paul wouldn't ring. Never again. She had almost accepted it. When the sentries left the field in Peddlesbury Lane – when she could go there and see it for herself; when something happened, something final and indisputable to prove it was true, then she would accept it and weep for Paul, try to get on with the business of living again. Yet until it happened, there *was* hope; there must be, or how was she to bear this terrible ache inside her? How was she to endure the sight of lovers together, walking close, and acknowledge that only her own little world had ceased its spinning? How soon before the longing for him, the need of his body against hers, became bearable? How long could she suffer a life alone? Fifty years from now she would still want him. When she was old and lonely, she would still remember every word, every whispered caress.

Paul. Paul Rennie. Precious, precious love. Gran had endured this agony, and Polly, too. For all those years, those empty, unloved years they had existed.

Did you know, Paul? When death was only seconds away, did you know?

She had given him a kiss; had placed it in his hand for luck when next he took off. She hadn't known, then, it was a kiss of goodbye.

She was sick and tired of this bed and the curtained window. She wanted to be outdoors; to run across the grass shouting rage to a world that dared to go on turning and a sun that had no right to shine.

She flung back the curtains and blinked in the sudden glare of light, then walked unsteadily to the door. She was still wearing her dressing gown and she wrapped it around her, tying the cord tightly. She hoped Kath was downstairs.

Kath was sitting at the kitchen table, pen in hand. She

pushed back her chair as the door opened and stood up, not knowing what to do or say.

'Kath . . .'

'Hullo, love. Had a good sleep?'

'No. The tablet only made me feel floaty. I was pretending.'

'How about a cup of tea?'

'No, thanks. A drink of water, perhaps . . .'

'Grace came.' Kath hurried to the tap, filling a glass, offering it. 'She left soup and milk. Couldn't you try just a little soup, Roz?'

'Maybe I will. And, Kath – it wasn't your fault.'

'I know, but I didn't want to be the one to tell you.' She glanced down at the writing pad. 'I – I was writing to Barney, and Aunt Min.'

'Good old Aunty Minnie.' Roz pulled out a chair then leaned her elbows on the table. 'Any phone-calls?'

'Just one, from Flora. The Warden's going to give me a temporary ration card. She says I can stay here – maybe permanently. Since the York raid, the ARP people reckon it's not on, people sleeping in attics. Too much risk from fire-bombs. Is it all right if I stay for good?'

'Of course it is. You know that. When will you bring your things over?'

'Later.' She wished she knew what to say; wished she knew how to help make it easier. The silences were awful, the tension in the kitchen so thick and heavy it seemed as if she could reach out to touch it. 'Roz. I'm sorry. You know I'm sorry, don't you? I was talking to Juney,' she rushed on. 'She sent her love. Did you know that Julia has had a little girl?'

'Good. I hope she'll be all right. Did Skip know?'

Kath shook her head, her eyes on her fingertips. 'Juney said it was a blow-out; a tyre. It wasn't Skip's fault.'

'No, Kath. He was the best. Nobody's fault. Their luck

ran out, that was all.' She walked to the sink, her bare feet padding on the stone floor.

'Roz! Where are your slippers? I'll get them . . .'

She almost ran in her eagerness, was at the top of the stairs when the phone began ringing. She hesitated, then ran on into the bedroom, picking up the faded pink slippers, running downstairs again.

The phone was still ringing; Roz sat unmoving, staring at it.

'Helpsley 181 . . .'

'Hullo? Roz?'

'No. But she's here.' A woman's voice. Clear, but a long way off. 'I'll get her.' She held out the receiver. 'For you. Long distance, I think.'

Eyes wide with apprehension, Roz took it, murmuring her name.

'Roz, it's Pippa. Pippa Rennie.'

'Pippa.' She let go a little keening cry.

'I'm sorry, Roz. The telegram came this morning. I've just got home – compassionate leave. But you'd know, Roz. You'd know before we did?'

'Yes. It was last night. About eight o'clock. They were taking off . . .'

Her cheeks blazed red, now. Too red. Bright, unnatural spots of colour.

'I had to talk to you, Roz. I loved him, too. And I promised I would – if anything ever happened . . .'

'Paul asked you?' She closed her eyes tightly. She felt sick, again. 'It's good to talk to you, Pippa. Sad it had to be like this.' Her mouth had gone dry again and it was hard to speak. She turned, looked at the glass on the table and Kath understood, picked it up and held it out for her.

'This hurts me, too, so I'll say it quickly. Paul told me – on his last leave – that if anything ever happened I was to ring you. "Tell her," he said, "that I love her. Tell her thank you from me, and say goodbye to her."' Her voice

442

was little more than a whisper. Pippa. Paul's twin. They had shared a birth, and all their youth. It had taken a war to part them. 'And he did love you, Roz. There was only ever you. We told each other everything, and I was glad for you both. Thank you for loving him.'

'Thank you for ringing, Pippa. It was kind of you, and brave. I don't know what to say.' The room was tilting again as it had done that morning. She grasped the dresser tightly.

'Say you won't forget him. And, Roz – it's tomorrow, at three – the funeral. Think of me.'

'I'll think of you. I'll think of your parents too. Goodbye, Pippa. And bless you.'

She made a moue with her lips, a silent kiss for Paul's twin, then placed the receiver gently on its rest, making a little shrugging movement with her shoulders, letting go a small sigh.

'You heard?'

'Yes,' Kath choked. 'What did she say?'

'Not a lot. Just goodbye, from Paul. Do you know, I tried to pretend there was still hope. Some small part of me could hope, I told myself, until something happened – something like now; like Paul's sister, telling me goodbye. So that's it, Kath. I've got to believe it, accept it, now. I've got to get on with it, Kath; do what Gran would have done. She got on with it. She lost her baby, her husband and her home – or most of it. And then she lost her daughter, my mother. But she kept on. She brought me up and she kept Ridings going – well, just about. And that's what I must do. I'll keep Ridings going. I'll have to.'

'No, Roz! You can't make a religion of it.' There were tears in Kath's eyes; tears Roz should be shedding. 'Your gran thought a lot about the old house because that was where she'd been happy. It was all that was left of her Martin – of course she clung to it.'

'Yes, and she left it to me. I'll work the land and I'll

make it pay its way; I have no choice.' She lifted her head defiantly, her eyes shining unnaturally. 'It isn't a case of the Ridings past, the big house it once was, the way of life Polly remembers . . .' The bright spots of colour were back in her cheeks. 'You see, Kath, it all came clear when Pippa phoned, because really that call was from Paul. And it wasn't a goodbye, either. A goodbye between us could never have been possible, *will* never be possible. Not now. I've got no time for tears, Kath. I've got to get on with life. It isn't any use fooling myself. I won't ever see Paul again.' She smiled, briefly, sadly, then placed her hands gently on her abdomen. 'But he hasn't gone – not entirely, you see, because I'm pregnant.'

22

There was a silence, startled and stunned; no sound save the sharp inpulling of Kath's breath. Then she let it go with a gasp of disbelief.

'You – are – *what*?'

'I'm going to have Paul's baby.'

'I know. I heard what you said. God, Roz, *why*? You said you'd talk to Paul about it.' She jumped to her feet and began an agitated pacing of the floor. 'But are you sure? Have you counted properly? It's the shock of your gran. A day or two late – it's neither here nor there. You'll be all right. Shock does funny things . . .' She was shaking. All over. Roz pregnant? Oh, please *no*.

'Stop prowling, Kath. And I'm not a day or two late. I'm over a *month* late.'

'*Hell!*' Kath threw up her hands then sat down heavily. 'Oh – I'm sorry. I don't know what I'm saying, but what was Paul thinking about?'

'Paul? Listen – it takes two people to make a baby and this baby is all I've got now. Be glad for me.'

'Glad? Have you thought about the talk there'll be in the village – yes, and Helpsley, too? What is Polly going to think, and Grace? And what about Jonty? Sooner or later they'll all have to be told – and then what?'

'Jonty? Y'know, I used to tell him everything once. He was my big brother . . .'

'Well, he isn't your big brother now. The man's in love with you. It'll be like a slap in the face when he finds out.'

'Then he needn't find out – not yet; no one need. I know there'll be talk, sly digs and nods, there always is. They like their little bit of scandal in the village. It'll set the tongues wagging, all right. Roz Fairchild getting herself into trouble – now fancy that! But at least Gran never knew, and while they're gossiping about Tom they're leaving Dick and Harry alone, I suppose.'

'So you'll brazen it out down in Alderby? Don't you care at all, Roz?' The pacing began again.

'Of course I care. I've been worried sick, if you must know.'

'Then why didn't you bring Paul home sooner, like I said? You could have been married by now if you had. Paul should have insisted, once he knew.'

'I see. Marriage would have made it all right, would it?'

'The baby would've been all right. At least marriage would have made it legitimate.'

'Yes – well, I'm going to have to learn to live with an illegitimate child, aren't I? And shall I tell you something, Kath? That's the first and last time it's going to be called that. If there's any fault it's mine, not the baby's. And Paul couldn't insist, because he didn't know. I didn't tell him because I didn't want him worrying about it when he was flying. Skip worried about Julia, so I made up my mind not to say anything till the tour was finished or maybe, if – if there'd been a wedding, I'd have told Paul then. He'd have been glad about it, though. He wanted us to have children. We talked about it the other night and I almost told him. I wish, now, that I had.'

'Oh, Roz – let's have a cup of tea, dammit.'

'You have one. Water for me. Tea makes me sick.'

Sick, Kath thought dully. Why hadn't she realized? Roz, not wanting to eat; throwing down her cigarette, saying it tasted awful, looking pinched and pale with black smudges under her eyes. Like an idiot she'd thought she was worrying only about Paul.

'Roz love – why didn't you tell me sooner – share the worry?'

'Before I'd told Paul?'

'Okay. Point taken. But you'd better be seeing a doctor. You should be thinking about getting your green ration book.'

'A green ration book! Once you've got one of those you might as well tell it to the town crier.'

'But you need the extra food.' The special green ration book, giveaway though it might be, provided extra milk and the vitamin pills and orange juice an expectant mother needed. 'And if you're pregnant you don't have to queue.' A pregnant woman need only show her green book, then walk to the head of any food queue without protest.

'Kath, love, don't go on about it.' She felt sick and floaty again as though making her brave, defiant statement had exhausted her. 'I feel lost and alone and I'm trying to keep myself in check. I've lost Paul; I don't want to lose the baby, too. I've *got* to keep calm.'

'I know. But it was such a shock.'

'It was a shock to me, too, but I've had time to get used to it. I just wish I'd told Paul.'

'Perhaps he does know.'

'Perhaps.'

'So what's to be done about work, Roz? You shouldn't do anything heavy, you know. No more lifting sacks or heaving milk crates; you realize that, don't you?'

'Yes – but how will I manage without them knowing at Home Farm, then?'

'I don't know, but you will – *we* will. I'll be there to see you don't do anything stupid and we'll have to take things as they come. But right now the Warden's expecting me at Peacock for my ration book. You'll be all right for a couple of hours, won't you?'

'I'll be fine.'

'And you won't go breaking down or doing anything stupid? Promise?'

'Promise. I might even heat up some of Grace's soup and see if it stays down. Off you go.'

'Oh, lovey . . .' Suddenly it was all too much and gathering Roz to her Kath held her tightly. 'Try not to worry too much? We'll manage, between us.' She dashed away her tears with the back of her hand, sniffing inelegantly. 'And we'll love that little baby a million, won't we?'

She ran from the house, slamming the door, choking back sobs. Only a week ago they'd all been so happy. A week ago they had laughed and danced at Peddlesbury as though their luck would never run out. Yet now it was a part of another world, another life. And they had brought it upon themselves. They'd been too happy, and it didn't do. Not when there was a war on.

She pedalled furiously down the lane, past the Black Horse, wondering if there would be another letter waiting and how long it would be before Barney came home. A hospital ship from Egypt had to sail home by way of South Africa, now; the long way round, it had come to be called. The Mediterranean was almost barred to Allied ships, German and Italian dive-bombers and warships had seen to that.

Italian bombers; enemy ships. Oh, Marco, what fools we are, you and I . . .

Kath wobbled past the Black Horse then took the back lane that led to the apple orchard and Ridings. She had tied a brown paper parcel to the back of her bicycle and in one hand she carried a carrier bag stuffed with clothes. It would need another trip to retrieve her suitcase and the remainder of her belongings, but at least they had sorted out her ration book. Tomorrow she could ride over to Helpsley and register her coupons with the grocer and butcher there. Better that way, the Warden had said;

better, too, that she sleep at Ridings. Since the raid on York and the terrible damage caused by fire-bombs crashing through roofs, people had become anxious about attics. The Air Raid Precautions people had even gone so far as to insist they be emptied of everything. You couldn't deal with an incendiary bomb in an attic full of junk, they reasoned, and soon it would be against the law even to sleep in one.

Strange, Kath pondered, how sometimes things turned out for the best. Roz needed her at Ridings and the Warden needed empty attics at Peacock Hey. Pity the rest of life couldn't be that simple.

Then she stopped, smiling and suddenly happy, for there was Marco, herding pigs into the orchard. Mat had said they'd be turned out soon, to forage for themselves and eat the windfall apples. And to save precious pig-feed, too.

'Hey, Marco!' Kath felt a warmth inside her and a flaming in her cheeks, for every time she saw him the feeling of attraction was there. Marco Roselli was good to look at; lean to the point of thinness, yet his arms and shoulders were muscled, and brown from the sun. She knew how it was to feel those arms around her; how broad were his shoulders to lean on. She had never felt like this about any man and only now could she begin to understand the way it had been for Roz and Paul, the urgency of the need that throbbed between them. For that was the way she felt about Marco and no longer could the ring she wore make any difference.

'Kat.' He turned, then smiled – the smile she had come to love. 'I am thinking about you and then you are there.'

'I'll be back at the farm tomorrow and maybe Roz, too. Best she doesn't stay at home alone. We'll see how she feels in the morning.'

'How is she?'

'Trying to be brave, poor love, but I'm worried about

her. She ought to cry, but she won't. It isn't any use bottling it up.'

'*Si*. But we accept our sorrows in different ways. For me, being a prisoner is to work, not to give in; for others it is acceptance and day after day living caged, like animals. Only Roz knows how to live out her sorrow. She will know when the time to accept it has come and then will be the time for tears. But I talk too much. I will help you home.'

His hands closed over hers on the handlebars and briefly she let them rest there. Then smiling she fell into step beside him.

'So how will Roz manage? Two terrible shocks in one week. You must be kind to her – we must all be kind to her and not leave her too much alone. One day, she will accept it.'

'Yes – but when, Marco? She loved Paul deeply; she's too young to have to cope with all this. Not so long ago, when the war started, she was little more than a child – now she's – she's . . .' She stopped, remembering. 'Now she's had to grow up in the space of a week.'

And accept the responsibility of Ridings, learn to live without Paul and see her baby safely born without him. Poor Roz. Poor lonely, frightened Roz.

'But we will help her, Kat. One day she will be happy again.'

They had reached Ridings now, and he leaned the bicycle against the wall and set the carrier on the ground. Then taking her hands in his he kissed each fingertip slowly, sensuously. His lips sent need tearing through her and she closed her eyes, tilting her chin, wanting to be kissed.

His kiss was gentle, without passion, and his smile, when she blinked open her eyes, was soft as his lips.

'And you, my Kat – how is your world?'

'Fine,' she whispered, her eyes on his. 'Just fine.'

'Then that is good. Off you go and look after Roz. I see you soon, hey?'

'Soon . . .'

Kath dumped her parcels on the kitchen table. 'Marco sends his love. I told him you might be back at work tomorrow. Did I do right?'

'Yes. It's got to be faced, I suppose.'

'And you'll be careful? A farm's no place for a pregnant woman. But won't you tell Jonty? It might be better if you did, especially if you want to keep working on the farm.'

'I know. Lord, what a mess.'

Why wasn't Paul here to make it come right; to hold her close and rest his cheek on her hair, tell her that nothing in the world mattered as much as Sprog.

Sprog. That was what Paul had called Skip's baby; Skip's little girl, born yesterday.

A wave of pain sliced through her, blocking her throat in a hard, tight ball. She wasn't going to be able to cope. If it hadn't been for the baby, she'd have –

'What was that?' Kath was speaking; cutting into her thoughts.

'I said it was a mess, but we'll manage. We'll have to. There's Sprog, now.'

And Kath was right. They would muddle through. No more morbid thoughts. The baby had a name, now. Sprog was her reason for living and holding her head high. 'But I won't tell Jonty. Not yet. I've hurt him enough lately.'

'Nor Polly? She's your guardian, now. Don't you think you ought to?'

'Maybe I should, but she'll take it badly. She's like Gran – straitlaced. But I'll tell her, just as soon as the time is right.'

'Good girl. I'll just nip upstairs and put these things away. Guess what? They're having apple pie at Peacock

451

tonight and cook gave me some for our supper. She said it was for you, with her love. You'll try to eat some, won't you – for Sprog?'

'For Sprog.' Roz smiled.

It was a small, fleeting smile, but Kath saw it and was glad.

Roz sat on the staircase seat, her coat hugged to her. The sky was clear, but touched with the metallic brightness that told of rain to come.

Rain. It would do no harm, she supposed. The hay was safely in, now. Haytime. Now she would remember, every year, that at haytime Paul had died, and Gran. Hear of one death, hear of three, Polly always said. Gran, Peggy and Paul.

She shivered. She should, she supposed, walk down to the churchyard to see if Gran's flowers were all right, but she was too tired, too drained; drained of all feeling and she couldn't cope with a grave tonight.

She felt cold. She didn't know why she was sitting out here. Maybe because Kath had switched on the wireless for the news bulletin and she didn't want to listen any longer. There was heavy fighting in North Africa, the announcer had said. The British were in retreat and Barney was in a hospital bed near Cairo.

But she didn't want to hear, nor hear about last night's raids over Germany, nor about civilians at home who had died in air-raids during June. Three hundred of them. It was then she had come outside, because Gran had been one of that three hundred, and it hurt.

She hoped the bombers wouldn't be operational, tonight. Tonight she didn't want to see one nor hear one. But they'd been flying last night. Raids on Bremen and the Ruhr and on Emden. Which of those places had Paul been going to? And was it only last night it had happened?

But Peddlesbury's aircrews would be stood down tonight

452

and away already to York or Helpsley or even deciding to give the Friday-night dance a whirl.

She looked down at her watch. Was it really only a day ago? Could twenty-four hours seem this long and would every day to come be the same? Yet it was good to sit here in the ruins; to accept that these walls had stood for more than four hundred years. It made her wonder what they had been witness to, who had lived and died within them.

Her child would be born here; her child and Paul's. A January babe, born to snow and ice in the drear of winter and Paul would never see it nor hold it nor love it.

She drew her coat more closely around her and looked up again at the rooks that flew cawing homeward. They nested in the tall trees behind the kitchen garden and if they should leave, if ever they forsook their rookery, it would foretell the loss of Ridings, Polly always said. And Polly said you must always tell things to the rooks. You should stand beneath their trees, she said, and tell them of a death in the family, or a birth.

'Never mind about telling it to the bees,' she insisted. ''Tis better far to tell it to the rooks . . .'

Roz wondered if Polly had told them that Gran had died, and knew instinctively that she had. Polly believed in such things; believed in the graveyard watch, too, and would expect her to see that the gates of St Mary's were chained and locked on St Mark's Eve, just as they had been when Gran was alive. Things must go on, she would say.

And they will go on, because Paul and I have a child . . .

'Roz?'

She turned sharply, fretful at the intrusion into her dreaming.

'Jonty. Sit down.' She patted the seat beside her.

'Kath said you were here. Are you all right? Shouldn't you be in bed?'

453

'Yes, I'm fine and no, I shouldn't be in bed. You're a worse fusspot than Kath.'

'She said you aren't eating enough; said I was to talk to you about it.'

'But I had some of the soup your mother sent, and it was good. Will you tell her so and thank her for it? And, Jonty, I'll be back at Home Farm tomorrow. Mat has been good but I've felt guilty about having time off when you were so busy with the hay. Kath and I will be back to normal in the morning.'

'Sure you're up to it? You look shattered. Sure you're all right?'

'I'm fine. And did you know that Kath is living out, now? Or is it living in? Anyway, she's at Ridings, for good.'

'She told me. There's a suitcase to be collected from Peacock. Next time I'm passing with the trailer I'll pick it up for her. And I'm glad you won't be on your own, Roz. Mum worries about you.'

'So she sent you over to check up on me?'

'I came because I wanted to. I'm worried about you, too. The Roz I thought I knew wouldn't have taken things this calmly. It's wrong to bottle things up.' He made to reach out for her. He wanted to hold her close; tell her that one day the pain would ease. But he knew he mustn't touch her and he pulled back his arm, laid it instead on the back of the seat. She was still Paul's. And there was a brittleness about her that he recognized. It had always been there, even when she was very young; a clipped calm that one wrong word, one false move, could ignite into a blaze of outrage and tears. 'But if you're quite sure you don't want anything . . .' He rose to his feet.

'No, Jonty. Don't go.' She shivered again. 'Think I'll go in, now. Walk back with me?'

She felt strange, walking beside him, her back so straight, arms stiffly at her sides. Once, she would have linked her arm in his and walked intimately close because he hadn't been in love with her, then. Not since Peg's funeral, brought together by a shared grief, had they touched. But Paul stood between them now, and a grief too enormous to be shared.

At the yard gate she paused, then turned and offered him her hand. It felt childlike in his own and he held it tightly for a moment. Then he said, 'Goodnight, Roz. Try to get some sleep.'

She whispered that she would and that she'd see him tomorrow then stood unmoving as he walked away.

Tomorrow, and all the tomorrows. A lifetime of lonely, near-unbearable tomorrows.

'Goodnight, Paul,' she whispered. 'I'm glad about our child.'

Sprog. Her reason for living.

23

Wednesday. The first day of July, a day for saying 'white rabbits' and making a wish; the day, twenty-four years ago, on which she had been born. And married, Kath thought with a lifting of her shoulders. Three years since she stood with Barney before the Registrar promising love and devotion for the rest of her life.

But her marriage was cold and only half alive. The birthday she had looked forward to would pass unnoticed because there had been two terrible tragedies and no one, yet, could think about anything else. Even trying to forget was hard, because always there was Roz who seemed to have grown paler and smaller, to remind them. Roz, with her grief locked inside her with her secret. So lonely and afraid of what was to come; of the scandalized sideways glances and sly innuendoes, for not even a Fairchild could conceive a child out of wedlock and escape the rough justice of a small village like Alderby.

'At least,' some would say, 'her grandmother was spared the shame, poor lady,' whilst others – those with daughters of their own, perhaps – would shake their heads and say nothing, because if it could happen to a Fairchild it could happen to anyone. With a war on, with men and women torn apart and no one knowing what the next day would bring, folk could understand a lass getting herself into trouble, even if they couldn't condone it.

Kath pushed open the schoolyard gate and set down the crate of small bottles. Twenty-five of them. A lot of children for so small a village, but most of them evacuees, like Arnie.

She glanced back to make sure that Roz carried no

more than a milk bottle in each hand. Nothing heavy, now; no lifting crates or churns – it said so in the book she had bought in Helpsley without so much as a blush because it was all right for a woman who wore a wedding ring to buy a book about pregnancy. Only the unmarried ones – the careless ones, the wantons – were expected to hide their shame. If they were lucky, they married hastily and discreetly, but never in white. White was for purity – pregnant brides knew it and kept to the unwritten rules. Those who were not so lucky might go away to some other place; to relations who would grudgingly take them in, hide them until it was over and their baby sent away for adoption. Only then could they come home, heads defiantly high, and everyone knowing about it yet saying nothing, except with their eyes.

And there were some – the desperate ones – who safety-pinned a note to a shawl. *Kathleen. Born 1st July*. Born just before the end of the war – the *last* war – the one they called the Great War.

She pushed the crate of empty bottles to the back of the trap then clicked her tongue to Daisy who knew exactly where to go and where to stop. Just the school house, now, and the Black Horse, then back by way of the gate lodges. Daisy knew.

Kath bent to pick up an apple, hard and green, with the marks of small teeth in it; stolen from an orchard, thrown away after one bitter bite. She held it on the flat of her hand and the pony took it gently.

She wondered if Aunt Min would remember her birthday, or Barney. But Barney didn't go in for sentimentality; there would be no greeting from North Africa. Today would pass without notice and that, she supposed, was how it should be, because three weeks ago Paul had died on the day they buried Mrs Fairchild. Set beside that, a forgotten birthday was nothing at all.

'I'm going to wash my hair tonight, Roz. Be a love, and pincurl it for me?'

'Sure.' Roz flinched as a bomber flew low overhead. Circuits and bumps, this morning. Test flights, which meant that tonight the squadron would be operational. Tonight could have been Sugar's thirtieth operation. Could have been; should have been. 'I'll probably wash my own, too. And I'll have to go through Gran's desk soon. Will you be there, Kath, when I do?'

She would need help. Mr Dunston had taken the legal papers, but the little things left there were the ones which would matter. Gran's diaries, ages-old letters and photographs; precious, sentimental things a woman keeps and hopes someone will deal with gently when she is gone.

'You know I will, but there's no hurry, is there?'

'None at all. Just thought I'd mention it.' She waved to Polly hanging sheets on the clothes line and pulled her mouth into the shape of a smile. She was getting good at it. Soon, she might even find a way of laughing without laughter because she was beginning to learn she could do anything she wanted if she tried hard enough. She could even go on living.

At midday, Kath saw Marco at the gate of Two-acre field. He smiled and waved, calling, 'Hey, Kat! Happy birthday!'

'Oh, thank you! I thought everyone had forgotten.' She laughed, and all at once the sun came out from behind a cloud and every bird for miles around began to sing.

'How could I forget? Ah, Kat, if we were free – if we lived in my country, we would have such a day. I would take you to a *ristorante* and we would drink wine and kiss and be happy.'

'But this is England, Marco,' she said gravely, 'and my country is at war with your country.'

'*Si*. That is the small problem. And I cannot give you a

present – only these.' He brought his hand from behind his back with a flourish offering the flowers he had gathered; white, wild daisies, honeysuckle and foxgloves, all from the lane-side. 'They are all I can give you, but one day, Kat, you shall have roses.'

'These are beautiful – better than roses.' She laid them to her cheek and silly, happy little tears misted her eyes. 'Oh, Marco, I do so –' She stopped, biting off her words. She had no right to say it, to say 'I love you, Marco'; she was a married woman and Barney lay wounded in some faraway hospital – she had no right to happiness such as this.

'*Si*, Kat?' he whispered.

'I – I – Oh, just that you are a very dear person and I'm very fond of you . . .'

'Fond? What is fond? I would like it if you say you love me. But that is too much to ask?'

'It is, Marco. It is.' Gently she touched his cheek with her fingertips and it was the kiss she wanted to give him, the declaration of love she could not make. She wondered, for one frightened moment, if Grace was standing at the kitchen window, then all at once she didn't care.

'What do we do, you and I?'

'I don't know. I don't think we have much of a choice – not now.'

'*Now*, Kat? What is *now* for?'

'I'm sorry. I should have told you. I've been trying to, wanting to.' They were walking towards the barn, away from the window. 'I've known for a while. Barney has been wounded and I think the Army will send him home. He could soon be in hospital, in England.'

'And you will go to him?'

'I'll go. He's my husband . . .'

'Even though you love me?'

'Don't say that, Marco. Please don't. You see, I've known for a long time that I don't love him – that I never really loved him. I'd made up my mind to ask him to let me

459

go, and I shall still ask him, when he gets well. I've been trying to pluck up the courage to tell you. Don't think too badly of me?'

'How could I think badly of you, Kat?'

'Very easily, I should think. I'm a married woman standing here telling you my marriage is over and all the time my husband is lying wounded in hospital.'

'Ah, *si*.' He raised his eyes, his face perplexed. Then he threw back his head in a shout of laughter. 'It is said that a man will never understand women, Kat, but that does not stop him from loving them.'

'Perhaps so. But I must go. Thank you for my flowers, Marco.'

'I'm glad they make you happy. Kat – I'm sorry that Barney has been wounded. Like my cousin Toni, I hope that soon he is well. We'll talk again?'

'We'll talk again.'

Roz asked her, when she walked into the kitchen, where she had picked the flowers.

'Oh, here and there.' Kath smiled. 'I shall put them in my bedroom. They're lovely, aren't they?'

'But they're only wild things. If you'd wanted flowers there are loads outside. The ruins are smothered in roses. Pick them any time you want.'

'I will – and thanks.' And forgive me, Roz, for not telling you who gave them to me, but I can't – not when Paul will never bring you flowers again. 'Next time, I'll remember.'

But for all that, wild flowers were the most beautiful, and given in love they were better than roses or the rarest of orchids. She had wanted to tell Marco of her love and how she needed him, but it might be years and years before the war was over. People talked about the duration – but how many years made up a duration? And who had the right to ask?

* * *

460

It was as well, Roz said, that she had opened her diary and seen Polly's name written there.

'Lordy! It's the sixth on Monday – and I almost forgot! And Wednesday was *your* birthday, Kath. I'm so sorry . . .'

'Think nothing of it. A girl doesn't care to be reminded overmuch that her youth is slipping past.'

'Kath – you're not old!'

'I know, but sometimes it feels – oh, forget it. And we'd better see if the shop has any birthday cards in. We can pop them through her letterbox on Monday morning.'

'I'll get them. I – I'm going to see Dr Stewart tomorrow. I've missed two periods. It's pretty certain, now.'

'You've accepted it, Roz?'

'Yes, and oh, sometimes I'm so glad about it yet other times I'm afraid – not of having the baby, but of having it without Paul. And sometimes I'm angry because he'll never see it – like Skip. I often think about Julia, you know, and wonder how she's coping.'

'Don't, love. Don't think about anything. Just take the days one at a time and see how you go. Don't worry about people; not about the old biddies in the village nor anyone. You want that baby and Paul would have wanted it, too. And you won't be entirely alone. There'll be me and there could be Jonty, if only you'd tell him. And if Polly hears about it from anyone else she's going to be very hurt. Tell her, Roz – soon?'

'Okay. But when I've seen the doctor – and when the time is right. One day at a time, you said.'

'All right. By the way – I told Marco about Barney being wounded. And I told him I don't want to live with him when the war's over.'

'And what did he say?'

'Not an awful lot. We were in the middle of the yard – Grace might have seen us. We'll talk about it when we get the chance, though things seem pretty hopeless. There isn't a lot going for us, Marco and me.'

'I know. It's the war, I suppose. But if there hadn't been a war you'd never have known Marco and I'd never have known Paul. But wars are so uncertain – no one can make plans. Oh, we'll win it – nothing's so sure – but *when*? How many of our young years are we going to lose before it's over? And when it is, when they get round to releasing Marco and sending him back to Italy, how soon before the two of you can get together?'

'And will he want me, Roz – even supposing Barney lets me go? I'm a fool for loving him, aren't I?'

'Like I was a fool for loving Paul? But you don't choose who you love – it just happens and I'm glad it did. I wouldn't have had it any other way. And we did try to be careful, but Sprog still happened, so it must have been meant.

'Yet if I let myself think about what's ahead for me, I'm so afraid. Afraid of the loneliness, I mean. Like Gran and Polly. All my life alone . . .'

'Hey! C'mon, now! You're *not* alone. There's me, and the baby. Be glad about Sprog, Roz. Because some of us will never be so lucky. Not ever.'

'Good! I caught you!' Roz opened the kitchen door as Polly drew on her coat. 'I popped back early to say happy birthday before you left.' She wrapped her arms around the small woman, kissing her cheek, smiling fondly. 'Did you find the cards? We left them with the milk.'

'I found them, and I thank you both. Where's Kath?'

'Kath won't be here, just yet. Like I said, I came home a little early –'

'Then you and me have time for a talk, Roz.'

'*Polly?*' Her head tilted, her eyes took on the old, guarded look.

'A talk. It's about time, wouldn't you say? I've been

waiting for you to tell me since – since your gran was taken. Up until then it was none of my business. But it is, now. Your gran made it my business and I want you to tell me.'

'Tell you – *what*?' Her mouth had gone suddenly dry and her tongue made little papery noises as she spoke.

'About the bairn you're carrying – because you *are*. Nothing's so certain. And I'd have taken it more kindly, Roz, if you'd given me your confidence and not made me have to ask.'

'Oh – *God*! I'm sorry, Poll.'

'Sorry I've found out – or sorry you've fallen for a bairn?'

'Not sorry about the baby; not about that. But I'm sorry I didn't tell you. Kath said I should.'

'So you told Kath before you told me?' There was hurt in her voice, and sadness.

'Yes. But I didn't mean it to be that way. I just blurted it out, the morning I knew about Paul. And I was going to tell you, when I'd seen Dr Stewart.'

'But you saw him on Saturday. I was in Helpsley – saw you go into the surgery. That's when I knew for sure.'

'But how did you know? I'm not showing, yet, and you didn't know I'd been sick. So tell me how?'

'I can't. Not rightly. It's just something that's there, in a pregnant woman's face; round the eyes, it is. Just a certain sort of look. My mother could always tell. She'd know, sometimes, before the woman knew herself. And I'm not often wrong, either.'

'Did Gran know?'

'No, lass. Unworldly, your gran was. She only believed what she wanted to. When is it due, then?'

'The end of January – maybe a little later. You don't know with first babies, the doctor said; not to a day or two. But he was very good, Polly. He didn't look at me – well, *that* way, nor say anything.'

'And I should think not! Doctoring's his business, not morals. All he'll be concerned about is a healthy baby and a safe delivery. You'll be having it at home?'

'I – I'd like to, Polly.' Her heart was thudding less loudly, now.

'Then home it had better be. You'll have Kath with you if you start in the night and a phone downstairs. Mind, January isn't the time I'd have chosen, but we'll make do.' Then she smiled, conspiratorially. 'Are you wanting a little lad or a little lass?'

'Polly – you're not angry? You're not disappointed in me – not shocked? There'll be talk in the village. There always is . . .'

'Aye. There always was and there always will be. And while they're talking about you they're leaving some other poor body alone. You aren't the first, Roz Fairchild, and you won't be the last. It's how you conduct yourself betweentimes that's important, and don't you forget it. A girl, will it be? I've a fancy for a girl, though a boy would be better for Ridings. Ah, well – it's out of our hands, Roz. We'll take what comes, I reckon, and be thankful.'

'Poll Appleby – you're an old darling. I was dreading telling you. I thought you'd be ashamed of me, and angry. I thought –'

'Then you thought wrong, because there's nothing so grand as a new little bairn –' she fastened the buttons of her coat, carefully, precisely '– especially to a spinster like me that's never had one of her own. And I'll thank you,' she snapped, jamming on her hat, 'not to be so free with the *old*. A darling I may be; old I am *not*, so I'll bid you good-day. And lass?' She turned in the doorway and Roz saw that her eyes were wet with tears. 'I think your gran would have been as glad about it as I am – I really do.'

'Polly!' Roz cried, taking her arm. 'Don't go. Not just yet. There's something, you see –'

'Aye?'

'Something I want to know that I think you can tell me. The pain? When does it go? You've been through this when you lost Tom. When did you start living again? How long before I can forget?'

'Forget? Forget your Paul, you mean, or forget the pain and the hurt of losing him?'

'The pain and the hurt. And the anger, too.'

'Ah, well – I don't rightly know. The anger – now that's easy. I cried the bitterness and the anger out of me as soon as I knew. I walked, Roz, along the riverbank at Helpsley; walked and wept till I was too tired to move another step and all the tears were gone. The anger is easy got rid of; it's the pain that takes time.'

'Tell me. I've got to know. I want to cry; I ought to cry, but there are no tears there. I tell myself it's because I don't want to get myself in a state and harm the baby, but it isn't true. There just aren't any tears.'

'Then I grieve for you, lass, because tears can be a great comforter. But happen you're not ready for them, yet. Happen the shock's gone too deep. Don't upset yourself, though. Give it time.'

'But when will I be able to think about him and not hurt inside me? When can I bear to say his name? There's no comfort for me, Polly; no peace.'

'I know the feeling, and your gran knew it, too. Only your gran could never put the bitterness of it behind her. She lived with it all her life. But you, Roz – if you're lucky like I was – you'll find the day comes when you know peace. Then you'll be able to call him back whenever you want to, remember the good times and the laughter.'

'But how, Polly? And *when*?' She couldn't go on like this; couldn't live with the hopelessness of it.

'How, I can't tell you, but you'll know when, same as I did. There'll come a day when you call out to him; some day, like as not, when you want him beside you so much that you think you'll never be able to bear it. And when that day comes, you'll hear him, because that's when he'll talk to you . . .'

'*Talk?*' Oh no, she couldn't believe that. Not voices. She didn't believe in voices.

'Aye. One day you'll call out to him – not really call, but cry from inside you. And he'll answer you; all gentle and loving his voice will come to you. Like a whispering on a warm, soft wind it'll be; nothing more than that. But you'll hear him with your heart, and you'll know the worst is over.

'I never told anyone, till now – not even your gran. She didn't want to be comforted. But the day you give in – the day you stop fighting the pain and go along with it – that's when you'll hear him. He'll come to you like a whisper on the wind . . .'

'Oh, Polly, hold me. I hurt so much – so very much . . .'

'Hold you, lass? Nay! That would never do! You can't use folk as props. You've got to pull your shoulders back and stick your chin out, aye, and soon you'll have to learn to hold your head high, an' all. So shape yourself, now. There's Kath coming across the orchard and you with not so much as the gas lit under the kettle! And I'll be away. There's shirts to be washed and ironed today, and standing about isn't going to get this old war won, is it? See you tomorrow, same time. I've got my own key . . .'

'Poll Appleby – you're a terrible bossy-boots and I love you very much. But you know that, don't you?'

The woman who had come to Ridings as a fourteen-year-old servant, and stayed there through good times and bad, snorted and pretended not to hear, nearly colliding with Kath as she came in through the door.

'What's the matter with Polly? She was crying, Roz – oh, *no*! You've told her?'

'She knows,' Roz said softly, fondly. 'And Kath – she's glad about it. She's *glad*.'

'Then there's only Jonty to tell, and the worst'll be over.'

'Jonty. Yes – well – look, Kath; that's something altogether different. Men don't understand these things the way women do, you see. Leave it? I'll know when the time is right. Believe me, I know Jonty better than you do.'

'All right. But don't leave it too long.'

'Well, now, there you are.' Grace looked up, smiling, as Kath pushed open the kitchen door. 'It seems an age since I've seen you. I've missed you calling in for a drink, Kath, since you went to live at Ridings.'

'I know. Not a month ago, yet it seems like a lifetime.' She took a mug from the mantel and picked up the teapot. 'So much has happened since I came here, Grace.'

'Aye. Mrs Fairchild and Roz's young man – both gone. How that poor lass is managing, I don't know. Twice, in the space of a week. I used to think that this little corner of ours was cut off from the war, but it isn't. Nowhere is safe from it. It makes me shudder to think what more could happen. They say everything comes in threes. Good luck, bad luck; births and deaths. Hear of one, you'll hear of three. So what more is to happen, will you tell me?'

'I'll tell you, Grace, though I've tried not to. I even got around to thinking there'd been enough bad luck around here to last us all a lifetime without me adding mine to it. But Barney's been wounded. He's in a military hospital, near Cairo.'

'Kath! And you never said! You kept it all to yourself. You must have been worried out of your mind.'

'Worried?' Yes, she had been. She still was, but worried for Barney, not for herself. And sick with fear about what was to come. 'I suppose I am, though I've had a letter from him, since it happened; a nurse at the hospital wrote it and he seems just fine.'

'Then let's hope it stays that way and they send him

home. North Africa's no place to be when you're wounded – not with the Germans having it all their own way out there. Best they send him home, Kath, where he'll be safe.'

'I suppose he'll have to wait for a hospital ship.'

'Well, don't worry yourself any on *that* score. Even the Germans respect the Red Cross. They give hospital ships a safe passage. He'll be all right.'

'Yes. I know.' Shrugging, she stirred her tea.

'Then what's bothering you? Because something *is* . . .'

'Yes, it is. I'm worried about us – about me and Barney. I don't know how things will be between us. We were only a few months married when he was sent overseas. It'll be a stranger, coming home. We've grown apart, Grace. I haven't seen him for more than two years and he's still annoyed with me for joining the Land Army. He's always been against women in uniform.'

'Then he ought to be proud of you! I know Mat and I are glad you're here. But there's more to it than you're telling me, isn't there? Or am I to mind my own business?'

'No, Grace – I mean yes, there *is* more to it. And I want to tell you because I know you won't sit in judgement on me. I want Barney to come home – but not to me. I don't love him, you see. I don't think I ever did.'

'And what's brought all this on, will you tell me? Barney's your husband, Kath, and he's been wounded; the last thing he wants to hear is that you don't love him any more. But you're upset. We all are. These last few days have been a nightmare and we'd be less than human if we weren't upset. So don't do anything hasty, lass? Wait till he comes home and maybe you'll feel differently, when you see him. There's nothing wrong with your marriage that a week or two together won't put right. It's a terrible thing, being young in wartime, but give it time? Be patient?'

'Yes.' And why I'm not telling you the whole truth, Grace, I don't know. Because I *won't* feel differently when

I see him; I know I won't. And as for going back to that house with Aunt Min sleeping on the other side of the wall and listening, as his mother did; listening to every creak of that bed, every movement. Aunt Min, taking over where Barney's mother left off. 'Yes. We're all upset; of course we are.'

'So get yourself a piece of toast and dripping, lass. When our Jonty was a little boy it was always toast and dripping that made things come right. Cut yourself a slice and toast it at the fire. I'll bet you aren't feeding yourselves properly up there; bet you anything you like you're not . . .'

Toast and dripping? Oh Grace, you dear, kind unworldly woman – it'll take more than that to make it come right for me.

Problems, Kath was to think afterwards, sometimes had a strange way of solving themselves.

Tell Jonty, she had urged. Once Jonty knew, the worst would be over. And Roz had agreed, but later she would tell him, she said. When the time was right.

The time had not been right this morning, yet still it had happened. In the dairy, it had been, when Roz had taken a milk churn, tilting it toward her, rolling it to the door where the tractor and trailer stood.

Milk churns were heavy; even empty ones were far too heavy for a girl two months gone to be manhandling, and Kath had said so, angrily and loudly.

'Roz! Will you stop that! How many more times must I tell you? Nothing heavy. No lifting, no heaving! You've *got* to remember. If you don't you'll harm that baby!'

'Sorry, Kath. It's just that I don't think. I haven't got used to it, yet. When I'm not being sick or feeling sick I sometimes forget. But I *will* be more careful, I promise, and –'

She stopped, gazing wide-eyed at the door. Kath turned

and saw him standing there, and knew from his face that he'd heard. Every word.

'Jonty.' She was the first to find her voice. 'How long –'

'How long have I been here, Kath? Long enough! I heard, all right! How *could* you, Roz? How could you be so – so *selfish*! Don't you ever think of anyone but yourself? Didn't you think of your gran and the hurt you'd be causing her? Didn't you know that what you were doing was –'

'Stop it, Jonty! Stop it!' Roz's voice was tight with fury, her eyes sparked anger.

'– was – was dangerous and bloody stupid? Or was it a case of what Roz Fairchild wants Roz Fairchild takes – regardless?'

'I told you to shut up! You've no right to go snooping and listening! This baby is none of your business – none at all, thank God! So go away and leave me alone. And if you dare say one word –'

She pushed past him angrily, running across the yard to the orchard gate, fumbling with the latch, flinging it open in a fury.

He caught up with her at the ruins as she ran panting across the grass and he pulled her roughly around, holding her wrists in a grip of steel.

'Calm down, you silly little fool! Pull yourself together! I shouldn't have said what I did and I'm sorry. None of my business – you're right, but, Roz – why didn't you tell me?' His anger and shock were gone; now there was only sadness in his voice, and pain, plain to see, in his eyes.

'Will you please let me go?' she said softly, icily.

He relaxed his grip though not his hold. There were things to be said and he wasn't giving her the chance to run. 'Then don't struggle. We're going to talk, Roz, whether you like it or not. Okay – so you're going to have a baby and as you said, it's nothing to do with me. But let me help you. All right – so you want to keep it quiet and I can understand that – but have you thought what it's *really* about?'

'I don't know what you mean, Jonty, and will you let me *go*.'

'Not unless you'll tell me about it and let me help you; not unless you'll talk about it calmly and sensibly and –'

'Calmly? I *am* calm. It's you who's going on about it! And there's nothing to say. Don't you think I haven't gone over it again and again these last two months? There's nothing to talk about; nothing at all to be done. I'm pregnant with Paul's baby and that's all there is to it. And – and don't bring Paul into it, because he never knew.'

'You never told him? In heaven's name why not? He could have married you . . .'

'Oh, you're just like Kath!' She snatched her hands away then began to walk toward the house. 'Don't *you* go on about it, too. Kath said just the same. But I didn't tell him, panic him into marrying me, so there's nothing that you nor Kath nor I can do about it!'

'All right. All right.' He fell into step beside her. 'But you don't have to see this through alone.'

'I'm not alone. Kath knows, and Polly.' She lifted the loose cobblestone beside the door, taking the key from beneath it. 'Do you want to come in?'

'Yes, please. And I'm sorry if I was out of turn but it was a shock having it hurled at me. I couldn't – didn't want to – believe it.'

'Not believe that Roz Fairchild had feet of clay, Jonty?'

'Something like that. And I was jealous, I suppose.'

'Of Paul? Still?'

'Yes.' He pulled out a chair for her then sat opposite at the table. 'And I was angry, Roz. Not *with* you, but for you; angry that there'll be gossip and sneers, that the baby will be –'

'Illegitimate? A hedge child, as they call them around

here? All right – so there'll be talk – and sneers, too, I shouldn't wonder, but at me, Jonty; not at the baby.'

'So why don't you marry me?' He got to his feet abruptly, filling the kettle, setting it to boil. 'Tea?'

'No thanks. It makes me sick. And I can't marry you. It wouldn't be fair to you.'

'I wasn't thinking about me – nor you, either. I was thinking about the baby. Better if people point the finger at you and me, Roz; say we've jumped the gun. We can take it, but it wouldn't be so easy for a child. If the baby were born in wedlock it wouldn't be illegitimate, and when people had had their sniggers and gloats about you and me, that would be the end of it – a nine-day wonder, it'd be.'

'But it's Paul's child. Why should you take a load of flack for something that's nothing to do with you? This child belongs to Paul and me, Jonty – it's how I want it . . .'

She stared fixedly down at her hands, knowing that he was right. But nothing would ever change the fact that Sprog was hers and Paul's. Besides, it wasn't right to marry without love.

'I mean what I said.'

'I know. But marriage is for life, Jonty – not just to see me over a pregnancy. I'd be cheating on you if I said yes. You were always my dearest friend, until – until Paul. But marriage is for lovers, not for friends. I couldn't love you – not *that* way. It just wouldn't work.'

'Then couldn't we try to go back to the way things were? Before I fell in love with you and you fell in love with Paul – take it from there?'

'We could try, but it still wouldn't work. There would always be Paul between us, and Paul's child. 'But it's good of you to want to marry me – so good that it makes me wish I loved you enough to say yes. And I *do* love you, Jonty, but I'm not *in* love with you. You see that, don't you?'

'Yes. I see it, but if you ever change your mind or if things get too much, well –'

'I know, and I'm grateful. But be my friend?' She held out her hand across the table and he took it in his own. It felt small and fragile and defenceless and he wanted to hold her to him so that no one should ever hurt her again.

'Friends.' He smiled, walking over to the cooker, turning off the gas tap. 'And I won't bother with tea. Best be pushing off. Am I to take it that no one else knows?'

'Only Polly and Kath – and the doctor. It's best, that way, for a little while longer.'

'Okay. But I'll be keeping an eye on you. No more heavy lifting. Are you coming back?'

'I'm coming.' She followed him to the door. 'And Jonty – thanks.'

She wished she could love him as he deserved to be loved, but there could only be Paul. Fifty years from now she would still remember him and love him.

It was the way it must be.

24

It had been bad enough missing the grand opening day of the War Weapons Week, but Arnie had understood that Aunty Poll was sad about Mrs Fairchild and hadn't felt like enjoying herself. But there were things a boy could not forgive; things that made him almost change his mind about being a pilot. Dropping bombs on Hitler might not be such a bad thing after all, he thought malevolently. Because it was his fault; all because of Hitler that many a small boy's world had been ruined for ever.

Sweets, that's what. *Sweets rationed*. Terrible, wash-your-mouth-out words. Rationed to two ounces a week and two ounces wasn't worth walking to the shop for! Eight caramels, or two gob-stoppers or two ounces of dolly mixtures or two ounces of jelly babies. Whichever way you said it, it was still only two ounces.

'Not such a bad thing, really,' Aunty Poll had said. 'Sweets take sugar and we're desperate short of sugar. And sweets give you bad teeth, and toothache.'

Toothache. The Drill. Arnie considered it was a risk small boys must take. The decision should be theirs alone.

'And fair shares for all,' she'd added, well satisfied that fair shares would stop milady from Hull bringing any more bags of black market humbugs – if ever they were to set eyes on her again, that was.

'I suppose you wouldn't do a deal, Aunty Poll? If I was to swop my soap coupons for your sweetie coupons . . .'

But she had turned his proposition down flat, remarking that all he'd be getting was a clip around the ear for his cheek!

Then she had smiled and said that maybe, just maybe,

mind, if he were prepared to black his boots every night, fill the log basket without being asked and clean his teeth regular, twice a day, she just *might* let him have her own ration, as well.

Arnie had brightened considerably. *Four* gob-stoppers made more sense; sixteen caramels sounded a whole lot better than eight. Good old Aunty Poll. There were days when she was really very nice.

The breeding sow had done well, Kath considered, counting the pink and pretty piglets that squealed and nudged at the full, fat teats. Newly born pigs were engaging little creatures. Pity they would grow up fat and ugly like their mother – given the chance, of course. 'Sad that they'll end up as bacon,' she sighed, emptying swill into the trough.

'Mm. But please don't say that word – not for a while?' Even to think of bacon sizzling and snapping in a pan did things to Roz's inside.

'The swallows are low.' Kath regarded the swooping, screeching birds with a countrywoman's eye. 'Rain, would you think?'

Without knowing why, she thought back to April and her swallow-wish and the first cuckoo-call: the lucky one. 'I haven't heard any cuckoos, these last few days, Roz. Don't they call when it's going to rain?'

'You won't hear them a lot, now. They're getting ready to leave. They'll all be gone by the end of the month. Polly says they bring summer and they take it away . . .'

'They'll be taking my wish with them, then. But it could never have come true.'

'Never is a long time, Kath, and wishes can come true.'

Sometimes. But not for Roz Fairchild. No Paul. No happy ever after. Just a dull pain inside her that sharpened to a stab whenever she thought of him. She had wanted to weep at Jonty's goodness; she would have, had there been any tears inside her. But she was right not to say yes. To marry him would have been wrong, however easy a solution. It was as Polly said, 'When in doubt, do nowt,' and doubts she'd had in plenty.

She hadn't told Kath about it – not all of it; just that everything was all right again between them, and that they'd agreed to be friends.

And think of angels, for there was Jonty, now; coming into the yard with the tractor and taking Kath's suitcase from the trailer, waving.

'Looks as if the rest of your belongings have arrived from Peacock. Do you mind, Kath, leaving the hostel and the girls?'

'No. I like it here, too.' Jonty was holding something up. 'I think there must have been a letter for me, as well.'

She picked up the empty buckets and hurried to where he waited, wondering about the buff-coloured envelope and why, all at once, there should be this feeling of apprehension.

'For you, Kath. One from His Majesty.' Jonty smiled.

She took it, frowning. On His Majesty's Service, the postmark pale and indecipherable. 'Now what on earth . . .'

The address at the top of the letter was Shilton House Hospital, Shilton, Yorkshire. It was signed by the Sister-in-Charge, Ward 3A and it told her that her husband had been admitted to the above military hospital and that telephone enquiries could be made at any time between the hours of 0800 and 2000 hours.

Barney was home. He was here, Somewhere in England. And far sooner than she had ever thought.

'Read this.' She pushed the letter at Roz. 'Barney's in England, but I don't know where. Somewhere not too far away, though.'

'Shilton House. It rings a bell.'

'I'll phone. They'll tell me where, exactly.' Her heart thudded dully. She should have been glad and was ashamed

476

that she wasn't. 'I mean – Yorkshire is nearer than Scotland . . .'

'Or somewhere in deepest Devon. Y'know, I'm sure there's a Shilton about three miles the other side of York. How much nearer could you get?'

'I'll have to tell Mat. I'll have to go there . . .' Oh, dear sweet heaven, why did she feel like this?

'Ring them first. I might be wrong, Kath.'

'Wrong. Yes . . .'

'What is it? You've gone as white as a sheet.'

'I don't know. Didn't expect it, I suppose; not just yet.'

Shock, was it? Apprehension? She began to shake. God – what was she to do?

'Well, don't look so miserable. We'll ring at dinner-break. There mightn't be any delay on a call to Shilton – if it's where I think it is. And Kath – pull yourself together. It's Barney you'll be going to see – your husband, not the Gestapo.'

It proved surprisingly easy to make the call. Sooner than she had expected – had wanted – Kath was speaking to the Sister in charge of Ward 3A.

'Shilton? Yes – a few miles east of York. There's a bus will get you here. On the hour every hour from outside York station. And you are . . .?'

'Allen. Mrs Allen.' She ran her tongue round her lips. 'I'm Barney –'

'Mrs Kathleen Allen? Driver Allen's next of kin, of course.' Her voice was bright and no-nonsense and Kath tried to make a mental picture of her, but couldn't. 'Will you be able to visit him, Mrs Allen? A visit helps such a lot.'

'Yes. I'm quite near. I'll come. Maybe tomorrow. It's almost certain I can get time off. Is it – can I – I don't suppose I could speak to my husband?'

'Well – we don't normally encourage it. And they're all

out in the garden at the moment, getting some sunshine. I'm afraid it would take quite a time to get him here . . . But I'll tell him you phoned, of course, and that you'll be coming.'

'Sister? How is he? How badly is –'

'Perhaps tomorrow? And when you do come, Mrs Allen, can you first speak to me, or to the duty nurse? Perhaps then we could have a little chat. Do you have a telephone number I can reach you on? Just in case of emergencies – which hardly ever happen, of course.'

'Yes. I'm at Helpsley 181 – but I go out to work, so you'd have to keep trying,' Kath volunteered, realizing she was to be told nothing on the phone. 'I suppose my husband couldn't ring me?'

'Now that, I'm afraid, wouldn't be possible. We're a house, you see, not really a hospital, and there are only two lines. I'm sorry, but rules, you know. I *will* tell your husband you phoned, though, and that you'll be visiting.'

'Those nurses,' Kath said, putting down the phone. 'They just won't tell you anything. All I know is that I can get to Shilton on the bus; every hour, on the hour. I asked her how he was and all I could get out of her was that he was out in the garden getting some sunshine and that she'll tell him I rang.'

'Bossy, was she?'

'N-no. She sounded very cheerful.' Though she'd told her nothing she had really wanted to hear. But nurses were taught to be like that, weren't they – dead-pan and non-committal?

'I'm going to tell Mat,' she said. '*Now.*'

Shilton House stood at the far end of a pretty village not very much bigger than Alderby St Mary. The on-the-hour bus stopped outside the post office and the postmistress told Kath cheerily that if she turned to her left outside and walked down the little path between the churchyard and the vicarage, she would come out at the back gates of Shilton House and save herself a long, winding walk down the drive. She had smiled at the pretty landgirl and felt pleased that some poor wounded soldier would feel all the better for having his hand held by so bonny a lass.

Kath pulled in her breath then let it go with a whoosh. She did it three times, but it didn't do anything to calm the turmoil inside her. She wished now that she hadn't worn her uniform, but Roz had said she ought to; that Barney had to see her in it one day so why not now? And anyway, she had said, it would be easier to thumb a lift in her uniform. Drivers always stopped for a uniform – had she considered that?

So she had worn her walking-out clothes, set her hat at a too-jaunty angle and borrowed Roz's bicycle for the three-mile ride to Helpsley Halt. And please God let everything be all right; all right about her uniform and about the way she felt and oh, about *everything*. And please don't let Barney read anything in her eyes because she didn't want to hurt him; she really didn't.

There was bright purple clematis and sweet-scented honeysuckle hanging over the wall of the vicarage and normally they would have pleased her. After her brick-walls and chimney-stacks life, just to see any flower growing in sweet-smelling profusion made Kath happy. But today was different. Soon she would meet Barney; after more than two years of growing apart they would suddenly be face to face and she didn't know what she should say or do. Her cheeks burned, her heart thumped uncomfortably and she wondered if it was the same for him, too.

But Barney wouldn't know she was coming. He'd have got her message, but he wouldn't know about today – not for certain.

She looked up from her brooding and saw the big house ahead of her; saw the outbuildings and stables through two large wooden gates, standing wide open, and on them a neatly-painted notice: *Hospital. No parking outside these gates*. She walked through without thought. Somewhere to her right, around the side of the house, would be the front entrance. There, she could ask for the Sister from Barney's ward and then they would have their little talk. Why was she still shaking and why had her mouth gone so dry?

''Allo there, sweetheart! Got lost, have you?'

A soldier on crutches, wearing the uniform of the wounded, smiling cheerfully and doubtless glad to be out of the war for a little while. 'Come visiting, have you?' He swung along beside her.

'Yes. Driver Allen, though I'm looking for the front entrance, really.'

'Barney, is he called? Came a couple of days ago, didn't he? Last time I saw him he was sitting outside. Come on, then – I'll show you. His girlfriend, are you?'

'His wife. But shouldn't I let them know I'm here?'

''S all right. I'll tell Sister you've come. Over there, see? Under that big tree.' He leaned on one crutch and pointed with the other. 'Go on, girl. Be a devil, surprise him!'

'Yes – I *will*.' She smiled her thanks. 'If you'd tell Sister, I'd be grateful.'

'I'm on my way. All the best . . .'

She stood quite still, breathing deeply. Just a few steps more across the grass, though which one of the talking, laughing group was Barney she couldn't be sure, for they were all dressed alike; all wearing trousers and jackets in the colour that had come to be known as hospital blue. And soft-collared white shirts and bright red ties.

He's your husband. As Roz said, he wasn't the Gestapo

480

and he wouldn't, couldn't, make a fuss about her uniform in front of all the other soldiers.

She looked about her. The house – she could see the front of it now – was very beautiful. Exactly the place a battle-scarred soldier could get well. Old, tall trees and sweeps of lawn; flowers in surprisingly well-kept beds. Peaceful and green, away from war and wounding.

Go on, then. Go to him. Nothing to be afraid of. You can milk a cow, and drive a tractor. You're not the wife he left behind him.

Straightening her shoulders, tilting her chin, she began to walk slowly to the big tree under which he sat.

'Barney?' Still a way off, she called his name. The talking and laughing stopped, heads turned. There came a long-drawn-out wolf whistle and then more good-natured laughter.

She stopped walking, because there was Barney, looking at her; a thinner-faced, sun-browned Barney and not looking *at* her, but through her. She shouldn't have worn her uniform because he was frowning and turning his head away.

'Mrs Allen!' She spun round to answer to her name and saw a nurse, skirts flying, running across the grass. 'Mrs Allen – a minute?' A hand gripped her arm and she knew she was looking at the Sister in charge of Ward 3A. 'I asked you to call and see me first. I wanted to tell you . . .'

Barney was standing up. Blue didn't suit him, Kath thought wildly, and he'd shaved off his Clark Gable moustache. She took a step nearer and all the time the sister's hand gripped her arm tightly. Barney turned, then bent to pick up the stick at the side of his chair. It was then that she wanted to cry out, but her reaction was anticipated and the hand on her arm tightened like a warning.

'Kath?' He was pointing with his stick; his white stick. 'Is it Kath?'

Oh, God, God, *God*. Not blind? Oh, please not blind?

'Speak to him,' Sister said softly.

'It's Kath . . .'

'We're here. Over here.' Sister's voice was a brisk command and Barney walked slowly toward them, his stick moving from side to side. 'That's right . . .' Her voice guided him, her hand left Kath's arm.

Like a woman sleep-walking Kath moved to meet him, stepping to his side to avoid the probing stick. He was staring ahead, eyes unblinking and she took his left arm.

'Barney – it's all right.' She wanted to be sick.

'There now,' Sister said comfortably. 'You'll both have a lot to talk about.' She nodded toward a wooden bench on the wide, paved path in front of the house. 'Take it easy. Off you go.'

Eyes that met Kath's asked if she were all right and Kath nodded, pulling her husband's arm into the crook of her own.

'I've got you. You're all right.' Out of compassion she touched his cheek gently with her lips and she felt the stiffening of his body.

Pity. That had been wrong. He didn't want pity. It was the last thing the Barney she once knew would have wanted.

'My, but it's a fine mess you've got yourself into.' She said it lightly, testing his mood, but teasing was not what he wanted, either, though not two minutes ago she had heard his laughter.

'Yes. A bloody fine mess. Have you got that uniform on?'

'No, Barney.' She closed her eyes as the lie slipped from her lips. 'And here's the seat.' She put her hands on his shoulders, easing him nearer the bench. He reached out with his stick, tapped it, then sat down carefully.

'Imagine – you coming to a hospital so near?'

'Imagine.' His voice was dry with sarcasm. 'That's all I

can do. You tell me what it's like. Beautiful, didn't you say it was, in these parts?'

'I'm sorry. I didn't mean it like that. I meant it was a – a coincidence. Barney, please, *please* forgive me? I didn't know, you see. It was a shock – you didn't tell me. In your letter from Hafiif the nurse didn't say . . .'

'She wrote what I told her to.'

'I know. I know! Don't let's quarrel. We haven't seen each other for ages and –'

'Two years, Kath. We're strangers, aren't we?'

'And so might a lot of other couples be. Just give me time, Barney. Can you bear to talk about it? Tell me what happened. Were you on a long convoy?'

'No.' He dipped into his pocket for cigarettes.

'Shall I light it for you?' She said it too eagerly and again she felt his withdrawal.

'I can manage. They show you how and anyway, you only burn yourself once.' He lit the cigarette slowly, carefully, then took a small, round box from his other pocket and slipping open the lid, placed the spent match inside it. 'And they teach you how to smoke without setting the place on fire. I don't shave, yet . . .'

He'd said *don't* shave, Kath noticed at once, not *can't*.

'I think I like you better without your 'tache,' she offered.

'Well I don't. Some damned stupid orderly took half of it off; an accident, he said . . .'

There was a long, awkward silence. From beneath the big tree came the sound of laughter again, and beside them on the path a small brown bird searched, chirping, for crumbs.

'A sparrow,' Kath said.

Barney tapped his stick sharply against the seat and the bird flew away.

'I'm having another operation,' he offered, eventually. 'I don't know a lot about it. Sister'll tell you.'

'Good.' She was afraid, almost, to speak.

'That's why I came back to Blighty. No one out there could do it.'

'You've already had one operation? At Hafiif, was it? Barney – please tell me what happened?'

'We were on convoy duty – carrying supplies. Going from Port Said to somewhere out Tobruk way. We'd made a stop – a bivouac, sort of – and the bloke walking in front of me stepped on a land-mine. Blew him to pieces, poor sod. I just got the blast from it. Not a mark on me. Might have been better, if there had been. My eyes copped the lot.'

'And then?' She reached for his hand and held it tightly, defying him to pull it away.

'Oh, they stuck me in the back of one of the lorries and dropped me off at the nearest hospital – at Hafiif – and the rest you know.'

'I thought they would send you back, Barney, but not quite yet. I thought it would have taken longer to get here.'

'It would have, by sea. But there were five of us in that hospital, all in need of urgent surgery so they flew us home, with a nursing sister to look after us. The Air Force transport planes often go back empty, so they put us on one of those . . .'

'Are you in pain?' She was still holding his hand.

'No. Just bloody blind.'

'Don't? Please don't? There's the operation – they wouldn't operate if there wasn't a chance.'

Her heart had started thudding again and she clung more tightly to his hand to stop the trembling of her own. This was a nightmare. Not just seeing him so helpless though that was awful enough. The terrible thing had been to come upon it with such suddenness, so unprepared for the enormity of it.

She still felt sick; still felt as if some great fist had

crashed into her abdomen and left her retching with pain and shock. She wondered how it had been for him; how they had told him; how he'd taken it. Had Barney wanted to be sick, too?

A young, pretty woman walked along the path toward them. She wore the uniform of a Red Cross nurse and she smiled gently.

'Sister says if you'd like to stay for lunch, Mrs Allen, you're very welcome. Nothing posh; just pot-luck and army rations. But if you can't, will you call in and see her before you leave?'

'Thank you. I'd like to stay. Just as long as I can catch the half-past two bus back from the village. I'll miss my connection at York if I don't and there are only three trains a day to where I live.'

'And you mustn't miss your train, Kath. Whatever would the cows and sheep and pigs do without you, if you did?'

'Barney – don't!' Her cheeks flushed red and she closed her eyes, shaking her head despairingly.

'Now that wasn't very nice, was it, soldier?' the nurse admonished.

'It's all right,' Kath whispered. 'He didn't mean to hurt – I know he didn't.'

But her defence of him was futile, because he had meant to hurt her, she knew it; knew, too, that he would never accept the loss of his sight – of his manhood, it would seem to him. Until he learned to live with so enormous a tragedy, he would be dependent on those around him, especially on the wife whose responsibility he would become.

She smiled at the nurse and thanked her again, then watched as she walked away.

'Barney?' She must break through his anger; through the barrier of resentment he'd built around himself. They would both have to learn to accept this; find some way of

485

carrying on. 'I'll be writing to Aunt Min when I get home tonight. What do you want me to tell her?'

But he merely answered her with a shrugging of his shoulders as he stared fixedly ahead. She knew she had made another mistake. *When I get home*, she had said.

Oh, God, help me to be more careful? she prayed silently.

'Gave you a bad time, did he?' Sister Ward 3A demanded, handing the teacup to Kath.

'Awful. If only I'd seen you first. But someone told me about the short cut. My own fault . . .'

'He's very bitter, you know.'

'Yes, but he was big and strong and afraid of nothing once. I don't think he'll ever accept it. But he's to have an operation – another one, he said.'

'Very soon. They did emergency surgery in the Cairo hospital, but he'll be going to Edinburgh tomorrow – with two more men. There's a very fine surgeon there and a first-class unit – very well equipped.'

'Edinburgh? It's a long way away.'

'I know. And it's sad that you probably won't be able to visit. But it's his only chance. The army nurse who flew over with him will be going up there with them. She's having a few days' leave, at the moment, but she'll be back tonight. When you say goodbye to your husband, try to cheer him up a bit? Reassure him, Mrs Allen. Let him know that whatever happens, you'll always be there? So much is going to depend upon you, if – if –'

She left her words hanging on the air. She didn't have to say it; say 'If the operation isn't a success. If he's blind for the rest of his life . . .'

'I'll try. I know how awful it must be for him. When will they know, Sister – if – '

'If it's been successful? Not for several days. Perhaps, when the dressings are removed, if he can distinguish between light and dark they'll begin to hope. But either way, good or bad, he'll be coming back here to convalesce and you'll be able to visit again.

'You must never give up hope. Just tell yourself that your husband will be getting one of the finest surgeons in the country. He'll be in good hands.' She opened her drawer and took out a small cigarette box. 'I don't use these – they make me cough – but I think you could do with one,' she smiled. 'And maybe another cup of tea? Don't give up hope, my dear. Never stop hoping.'

'It was awful.' Kath sat at the kitchen table, hands clenched into tight fists, glad to be home, to be away from the nightmare. 'He was bitter – so very bitter. It wasn't the Barney I knew. He was so helpless. He's leaving Shilton tomorrow; going to Edinburgh for an operation. The Sister said there's hope, but they always say that. Barney just sat there, staring. He asked me if I had my uniform on and I said I hadn't. Just think – lying to a blind man. We didn't talk, not really. Oh, I'm just going on and on. I don't know what I'm saying, I'm sorry . . .'

'Marco knows, Kath. He asked where you were, and Mat told him. Are you sure you don't want something to eat? There are some eggs in the pantry – I could boil one.'

'No, thanks. Just another cup of tea and a cigarette. Oh, God, Roz – what am I to do? All this is my fault. I wanted to leave him and that lot up there thought, "Oh, yes? We'll see about that!" How do you leave a blind man, will you tell me? How *can* you? And had you thought? If he doesn't get his sight back he'll be invalided out of the army and back to Birmingham . . .'

'And you'll have to ask for your release from the Land Army, on compassionate grounds,' Roz finished dully, her voice a whisper.

'Yes. It's my own fault and I deserve it, but I'm so miserable I don't know what to do.'

'Then join the club, old love.' Roz reached out for her friend's hands and held them tightly. 'Misery Farm we'll have to call this place. Do you believe in God, Kath?'

'Yes – oh, I don't know. Why?'

'Well, I think all we can do now is pray. For you and for Barney, for me and Sprog. And for Marco, too, I suppose. Do you know what Polly once said? She said that when you reach rock bottom there's only one place left to go – and that's upwards.'

'I don't want to go back to Aunt Min,' Kath whispered, closing her eyes tightly against the tears.

'I don't want you to. What say we go out and get raging drunk?'

'Good idea. Wouldn't do Sprog a lot of good, though. And I suppose that since we've both of us hit rock bottom –'

'You're right. We'll both have to stick together – well, for as long as we can. But oh, Kath, I wish I could weep. I'd give anything to be able to weep. But I can't . . .'

25

The rain the swallows foretold began to fall from low, grey clouds.

'Looks as if it's set for the day,' Grace remarked, filling Kath's mug with tea. 'Can't say we don't need it, though, for the potatoes and sugar-beet. Why don't you bring Roz in of a morning, now? That lass is as thin as a rake. What she needs is some toast and dripping inside her. You should bring her with you mornings, before you start the milk-round.'

'I'll tell her, though she isn't one for breakfast.' And tea and toast thick with beef dripping were the last things Roz would want, though if the baby-book was to be believed her sickness should soon be at an end.

'Tell me about your Barney? Such a terrible thing to have happened.'

'Yes. I worried about it all night. He's leaving early this morning for Edinburgh. It all depends on the operation, Grace. I can't – I *won't* – think beyond that.' Not about Barney, raging against his blindness; not anything. 'I rang Shilton as soon as I got up. The night-sister said he was still sleeping and that he was fine. She promised to tell him I'd phoned, to wish him luck.'

'And to give him your love, Kath?' They'd be all right, now, Grace was sure of it. They'd be drawn together again. Maybe closer than ever.

'Love. Yes.' Pity, more like. Because that was what she felt. Deep, deep pity and anger that it should have happened to him. 'But I'll have to go and give Roz a hand.'

From across the yard came the sounds of the pony being

489

harnessed. If someone wasn't there to watch her, Roz could forget, and start loading milk crates on to the cart.

'Mind you put your gum-boots on,' Grace called, 'and your raincoats or you'll catch your deaths, the pair of you. Don't forget, now.'

'We won't.' *Oh, Grace – if only a soaking was all we had to worry about . . .*

'I do not,' said Marco as he helped Kath unload the milk-cart, 'like your English rain. It is very cold.'

'And wet,' Roz offered. 'In winter it freezes, if you remember, and turns into snow. I'll see to Daisy if you like, Kath – dry her down.'

'Thanks.' She needed to talk to Marco; needed his nearness, his understanding. 'You know about Barney?' she asked when they were alone.

'I know. It is bad. It is the worst thing that could happen to any man. And I know how things will be. Since I heard, I think about it a lot, Kat, and I don't like what I think.'

'That I might have to leave the Land Army – leave Home Farm; go back to Birmingham? I've thought about it too, Marco, and I won't have any choice. I couldn't turn my back on a blind man.'

'You could, but you won't. Not you, Kat. I think I am going to lose you because you won't leave him; won't ask him to let you go free – not now.'

'No.' She looked down at her boots, her voice a whisper. 'No one could do a thing like that, no matter what.'

'Jonty said he's to have an operation.'

'Yes. That's all I'm thinking about. In a couple of days, perhaps, he'll have had it and that soon he'll be able to see again. I want it for Barney – not just for me.'

'And is there a chance for him, Kat?'

'I don't know. The nurses didn't tell me anything. They can't, I suppose. But by now he'll be on his way to

Edinburgh with two other soldiers and I hope it'll go well for them all.'

'*Si*. Sometimes hope is all we have left. My mamma say that hope can be stronger than prayer. And oh, Kat, I want so much to hold you and comfort you . . .'

'Like on threshing day?' Such a fuss, over one frightened rat; a fuss over next to nothing, had she but known it, then.

'Like that day, Kat. Did you know then that I loved you?'

'No. But I was angry with myself that I'd liked it when you held me. Things are in a mess, aren't they? What's going to happen to us?'

'I don't know.' He touched her cheek with his fingertips. 'I think we must – how you say it – bear it and grin?'

'Something like that.' And take what life hurled at them, because the Fates got jealous. It didn't do to love too well – already Roz knew it. 'You'll have to go, or someone's going to catch us here together.'

'Would you care, Katarina-mia, if they did?'

'No.' Not now when all she wanted – needed – was to feel his arms around her. But later she would care, because she was married to Barney and Barney needed her. In sickness and in health, she had promised. 'Right now I need you so much, but it isn't what I need, any longer. There's Barney to think of, now.' Barney, who would never see again.

'I am *sick* of this rain,' Roz grumbled. 'It's gone on all day and the sky is still full of it. And this kitchen smells *awful*.'

Of wet raincoats on the rack above the fireplace, dungarees and socks draped along the fireguard to dry, shoes stuffed with newspaper in the hearth.

'Does it bother you, Roz?'

'Not really.' Some smells had made her want to retch,

but not so much, now. And this last week she hadn't felt quite so sick, either. In a couple of weeks, when she was three months gone, the doctor had said, it should be almost over.

Three months pregnant and a tiny, almost perfect child inside her. Hers, and Paul's. By the time harvest was over, she would be half-way there and she would feel the baby moving. Just gentle little stirrings, at first; but when it happened, her baby would be really alive.

'What are you thinking about?'

'The baby. And about lighting a fire in the little sitting-room.'

'*Another* fire? In July? We're supposed to save fuel.'

'But why not? It's been really cold today, and we've got any amount of logs. Why don't we sit in there, for a change? I could make a start on Gran's desk, then. I shall have to go through it some time. Why don't I bring some logs in?'

'I'll get the logs. You find paper and kindling. And what do you think has happened to that call? I booked it ages ago.' Kath frowned. 'Why should there be these delays over trunk calls? It never used to be like that.'

'No, but the armed forces are ringing up all the time. It's they who have put the phone lines on war work, and civilians have to wait their turn. There *is* a war on.'

'I know, but I'm going to ring the girl on the exchange again. She might have forgotten.'

'And *you* might have given her the wrong number.'

'I didn't. All I want to know is that Barney has got there and for them to tell him I phoned.'

'But of course he'll get there all right. They all will. There'll be an army nurse with them, didn't you say? But let's get that fire lit. I'm cold.'

'That's because you're not eating. There's nothing inside you to burn up into heat. All you want is drinks of water, and things to crunch. A baby can't exist on *crunch*, Roz.'

'It can, you know. I asked Doctor Stewart about it. I was worried, you see, about two terrible shocks, coming one on top of the other, and about my not wanting to eat. But he said that embryo babies are tougher than we think and I wasn't to worry, too much. He said that once I stopped being sick and began eating again, I'd probably feel really well.

'And he said that pregnant women often want to eat peculiar things in the first few weeks, and provided they aren't *too* peculiar, it's all right. I'd told him, you see, that I was desperate to crunch on a big, juicy apple. But there aren't any apples in the shops, now. There won't be any until the English apples are ripe, in the autumn. So then I hit on something else. Carrots. Well, at least they aren't in short supply and just now they're small and sweet and –'

'And crunchy?'

'Mm. Sprog is going to have a marvellous complexion.'

'And he'll be able to see in the dark, too.' Weren't carrots supposed to help people see in the blackout and fighter pilots to see at night?

They began to laugh, and it was the strangest sound. Roz, laughing. Only briefly, because laughter, now, wasn't on. But she had laughed.

'You want this baby, don't you, Roz?'

'Oh, yes,' she said softly, gently. 'More than you know . . .'

Later, Kath sat on the floor, in the fireglow. Outside, all was grey and rain-soaked, but in this little room the weather and the war, too, seemed to be happening in some other place. She recalled the first time she had sat here; that Sunday afternoon visit when Roz had shown her Ridings and the ruins, and Mrs Fairchild had said, 'Come and see us again – soon.' And had meant it.

Was it only half a year ago that Roz had reminded her not to speak of Paul. And shown her the portraits – her peculiar forebears, she'd called them.

'Remember when –' Kath sighed, then stopped abruptly,

493

said instead, 'Remember when we could have bought seven pounds of apples, if we'd wanted them? And oranges, all the year round – not just one, at the end of a half-hour queue?'

'Yes, and cream cakes for Sunday tea.'

'And now it's illegal to make cream, let alone sell it.'

'Everything nice is illegal or rationed or under the counter these days. Here – want to see one of me, when I was two-and-a-half?'

She handed over a snapshot of a small girl, unmistakably Roz, standing with toes turned inward and mischief in her eyes.

'*Rosalind Fairchild-Jarvis. Age 2yrs. 6mths*. My mother must have written that – or my father. They always called me Rosalind, I believe. It was Jonty who first called me Roz, and it stuck. Even Gran only called me Rosalind when she was cross with me.'

'Where was this taken? London?'

'I should think so. That was where we lived. That snap must have been taken only a few weeks before they died.'

It was strange, Kath thought, that Roz could speak of her parents without pain – probably because she had never really known them.

'Do you remember anything about living in London?'

'Not a thing. My life began here, seventeen years ago in December, it'll be. And Gran never spoke about the way things were – only if I asked, and then not much. Here's one of me and Jonty! Just look at those awful round glasses.' A snapshot of Jonty, holding Roz's hand tightly – loving her, even then.

'Glasses suit Jonty, now,' Kath defended. 'They make him look intellectual – donnish, sort of.'

'Well, they didn't when he was eight. They made him look like a surprised little owl. And I'm not being catty. *I'm* allowed to say things like that.'

'Because he's your brother?'

'Yes. It's nice in this little room, isn't it, Kath?'

'Yes. And cosy.' No bad memories in here.

'When winter comes, we'll sit here more often, won't we – now that we've got logs to burn?'

'Good idea.' They would use it all the time, if it meant that sometimes Roz would laugh. 'Ssh! The phone!' She was quickly on her feet to answer it; to break the spell and let in the outside world again. 'That's my call to Edinburgh . . .'

Kath placed a cup of hot cocoa on a tray, and a glass of milk for Roz. Boiling the kettle and setting the tray gave her time alone to think, to compose herself.

A nurse with a soft Welsh accent had answered her call and told her that yes, Driver Allen's party had arrived and all three were safely installed in the surgical ward.

'Your husband is second on the list tomorrow – can you try to get through in the evening? He should be over it by then and a message from you will cheer him up.'

'I won't be able to speak to him – later?'

'I'm afraid we can't allow that. But try not to worry, my dear. We'll take good care of them all.'

And that, Kath shrugged, had been that. They had told her nothing, really, except the number of his ward.

She was glad Barney was still with his friends; glad the army nurse who had looked after him on the flight home was with them. Before she went to sleep she would write to him and post it in the morning when they did the milk-round. Letters were important to a soldier – even if he had to ask someone else to read them to him.

'Sorry there's nothing crunchy.' Kath set down the tray. 'Barney's fine – settled in his ward and his operation is tomorrow. The nurse said I wasn't to ring before evening – even supposing I'll be able to get through.'

'Good.' Roz took the milk and drank it without thinking.

'And I've got everything sorted – letters and photographs and Gran's diaries. Y'know, Kath, I'd never opened Gran's desk; it was a sort of understanding between us that I didn't – just as she'd never have dreamed of opening any of my letters. The first time I did it was when I gave everything that was in the bottom drawer to Mr Dunston, as she'd said I should if – if anything ever happened to her. It felt strange, at first, but I think I've got it organized, now. It was very tidy – but Gran was like that. I think she could have opened this desk in the dark and put her hands on anything she wanted. The photographs and letters are in the bottom drawer, now, and I'll go through them all, bit by bit, when I'm in the mood for it; her diaries are all in proper order, too. I shall like reading them. Well – now that she's not here I suppose it's all right?'

'I suppose so, Roz. But I've always thought that diaries are very private. Maybe, if we knew exactly which day is to be our last one, we'd destroy things like that. I know I would.'

'You mean I shouldn't read them? That Gran might not have wanted me to know what she'd written?'

'I don't honestly know. Really, it's up to you, Roz. The only thing we can be sure about is that she didn't know the day she would die –'

'So I'd better take it that she might not have wanted me to open them?'

'No! I don't mean that at all. They might give you an insight into a lot of things, in fact. Are your grandfather's letters there?'

'Yes. Bundles of them – written from the trenches. And letters from other people, too; some with Victorian and Edwardian stamps on them. Those letters and diaries are Fairchild history, Kath. I'd like to read them through one day. With respect, I mean, and love. I'd really like to have known how Gran felt about Grandpa's death. I did look at the last of the diaries – she didn't keep one, it seems, after

Grandpa was killed, so I'm a bit disappointed about that, and that there isn't anything there about my mother and father – and me, being born. But the last one was dated 1916 and on the very last page she'd written, *Today, they killed my darling Martin.* That's all, Kath. Sort of final. Then no more entries; no more diaries. Just as if her life had ended. Just the way I felt when –' She stopped, eyes closed, face twisted with pain.

'Sssh, now,' Kath whispered. 'Lock it up, Roz? No more for tonight?'

'Okay. But I shall read them – even if only because I'm certain she knew exactly how I'm feeling, now. It might even help.'

'Yes. But another night?'

Carefully Roz locked each drawer, then closed the desk-top flap, and locked that, too. 'I wasn't going to tell you, Kath, but you know when Jonty found out about the baby and we had that terrible row? Well, he asked me to marry him – for the baby's sake, he said; so it needn't be illegitimate. He didn't expect – well – anything else, he said . . .'

'But you said no?' Kath demanded, startled.

'I told him no. It wouldn't have been right.'

'No. It wouldn't have. For one thing, you couldn't love him, Roz; not the way you're feeling now, anyway. And Jonty's too good to be used. He deserves to be properly loved.'

'I know – but I do care for him, Kath. I care enough *not* to marry him.'

'Then there's hope for you yet.' She was growing up. In so short a space of time, Roz had left her youth behind her; had accepted the responsibility for another life.

'Hope. Yes.' She placed the key in the little china dish on the desk top. 'I think I'll go to bed, now. What about you, Kath?'

'Me too. I'll just lock the doors and check that the

clothes are all right round the fire, then I'll follow you up. Off you go. Goodnight, love, and try not to worry too much. From now, things can only get better. Upwards, remember?'

She had been wrong; so very wrong, though it was to take a little time to register in her numbed brain. But she should have known, she told herself afterwards, when the warrant-officer had come to the farm that next morning. He'd walked carefully across the yard, picking his way between the pools and puddles – well he would, she considered, watching him – wearing such brilliantly polished boots.

'Will you take the milk over, or shall I?' Roz had asked.

'Best leave it. The sergeant-major from the camp has just gone into the kitchen.'

'Oh? And what does he want?'

'Dunno – you'd better ask Mat.'

'I will.' She had a right to know. It was obviously about Marco and Marco worked for Ridings, too. 'Do you suppose Mat has asked the War Ag. for another prisoner?'

'Haven't a clue, though sometimes we could do with one. But when he leaves you can nip over with the milk and ask what it's all about.'

They had left it at that, because it hadn't seemed all that important. Not then.

'It's a bit of a licker, having it hurled at you out of the blue, like that,' Mat brooded. 'And with the harvest on top of us, too. What do they want to do a damn-fool thing like that for? I said as much to the sergeant-major and he said that the camp at Helpsley was the most secure there was around these parts, and that's why they were moving the Italians out and moving Germans in. The Germans take

498

a lot of looking after; not like the Italians, he said. Seems that a lot of Italian people don't like Mussolini overmuch and didn't want to come into the war on Hitler's side. Those prisoners are easy-going; glad to be out of it, he said, but the Germans are another thing altogether.'

'So where will Marco be going?' Roz asked. 'Did you find out?'

'Not in so many words – well, he couldn't tell me, could he? But it's too far away for us to keep Marco; that he did say.'

'So will they give us a German prisoner if we ask for one, Mat?' And thank God Gran wasn't here to hear her say that – nor Kath, either.

'Lord bless you, no. Far too sure of themselves those Nazis are. They aren't going to be allowed to work out, like the Italians – left me in no doubt on that score. Couldn't trust them not to try to escape.'

'I'll be sad to see him go,' Grace said softly. 'Marco's a grand lad – always cheerful, and a good worker.'

'Aye. He'll be missed – that he will.'

Missed, Roz thought, splashing through the puddles to the dairy. And by Kath most of all. But nothing went right around Ridings and Home Farm – Ridings, especially. Ever since Gran had miscarried her son all those years ago, worse luck had followed bad. The ill-luck of the Fairchilds people called it; one generation after another, and anyone close to them, too.

She stood in the doorway of the dairy, hands spread on her abdomen as if to protect her child from it.

'There's a curse on this place, Kath. A *curse*.'

'Tell me,' Kath whispered. 'It's to do with Marco, isn't it?'

'They're moving the Italian prisoners out – moving Germans in. They don't know when, but it could be as – as soon as the end of the week. That was what he came to tell Mat.'

'End of the week?' Two, maybe three more days. 'I don't know about a curse, Roz, but Somebody up there doesn't think very highly of us.' All at once she felt very afraid. 'There's no hope, I suppose, that –'

'That they've made a mistake? No. And Mat couldn't find where they'll be going – only that it's too far away for us to keep Marco. I'm so sorry, Kath. I know how you care for him.'

'I care too much. But maybe it's as well he's going – and maybe I'll be the next to go. If Barney isn't lucky, I'll have to get my release to look after him.'

Once she had been so happy that it had been a joy to get up each morning. She should have known it couldn't last.

'Don't say that, Kath? If you were to go I don't know what I'd do. Sprog and I need you. And Barney might get well . . .'

'Yes, but he mightn't . . . Oh, Roz – I know this sounds mad, but isn't there somewhere – anywhere – we could live around here? Being in the country would be far better for Barney than streets and streets of houses. There'd be birdsong for him to listen to, and all sorts of sounds and smells. I could plant a scented garden for him – honeysuckle and roses and pinks. And even if I did have to leave the Land Army, I'd still be near to you all. Isn't there *anywhere*?'

'No. Not just now, though I know the Manchester lady won't want to stay here once the war is over. But it's *now* we want somewhere, not two or three years on. I'll try to think of something Kath – I *will*.'

'I know you will.' Her face was racked with pain and she closed her eyes tightly against the tears. 'And oh, Roz, I don't want to leave you nor Home Farm and I *don't* want Marco to go.' Never to see him again nor talk to him; not even to be allowed to write to him. And so little time left. 'Where is he working this morning?'

'On Ridings' land – up near Polly's. Are you going to him?'

'No. Later, I'll see him.' When she'd had time to pull herself together, to think it all out in her mind; convince herself that what they had had, little though it was, was no more than a bonus – something to think back on, to recall on the sad days; on days when the unfriendly streets she would be going back to were grey and cold. 'I'll see him at dinner-break, in the barn . . .'

He was sitting there when she went to the barn at noon; sitting on the floor, his hands relaxed on his knees.

'You know, Kat?'

'I know. Roz told me.' She sat down beside him.

'And what are we to do, you and I?'

'What can we do, but – well – bear it and grin? But you knew, Marco, didn't you?'

'Not for certain. But I heard things. The guards talk and they forget, sometimes, that some of us speak English good.'

'Just a few more days, that's all.' The panic that had slashed through her when first she heard was gone, now, and in its place was despair and acceptance.

'Perhaps not a few days, Kat. Some, I think, will go tomorrow.'

'And you'll be with them.' The tears were back in her throat, hurting her, but tears she would not cry, because she was married to Barney; to a soldier who was waiting to be taken to an operating theatre and praying as he'd never prayed before that when it was all over there'd be hope.

'I might be – or I might be lucky.' He reached for her hand and held it tightly.

'And after today – or tomorrow –' she whispered, 'it'll be the end, won't it? I won't see you again or speak to you. They won't let me write to you – it would be no use trying. And you can't write to me.'

'No. But there might be a way. If I could post a letter – one the Censor hadn't seen.'

'But how? How could you buy stamps? Just walk into a post office, would you – or even into a phone-box, to ring me?'

'No. I don't have any of your money. But you could give me envelopes, Kat, with stamps on them.'

'Yes, but how –'

'How do I post them? If they let me go out to work again, there might be a letterbox, nearby – though to telephone would not be easy. But I shall find a way to write to you – just as I found a way to get out of the camp. You'll give me envelopes and stamps? Today, Kat, before I leave?'

Today. Now. So he *was* going tomorrow? Once, she had brought soup here. This barn was where they had met and where, perhaps tonight, they would part.

'Tonight – before the truck comes for you – meet me here and I'll give them to you. But don't get into trouble, just to post a letter? I won't forget you, Marco; not ever.'

No one could stop her remembering; not Barney nor Aunt Min nor anyone.

'And I shall remember my Kat. Always. And be glad that a war gave you to me and sad that it took you away.'

'Yes.' She knew, now, how Roz felt, only for Roz there was no hope. She, at least, could think of Marco and know that somewhere he was alive. She could still hope in her wildest, craziest moments that one day they would meet again; meet, and say *Ciao*! and smile. That would be all, but she'd be grateful, even for that.

And yes, she would take care of Barney; she would even go back to the little house in the Birmingham street, but nothing would ever stop her wishing that she and Marco could have once – just once – been lovers.

'Have you booked the call?' Roz asked later that evening. 'To Edinburgh?'

'I did. And you're going to have to let me pay for them. Your phone bill will be awful.'

'Oh, for heaven's sake – phone bills are the least of my worries. And did you –' She stopped, letting her eyes finish the asking.

'Did I say goodbye to Marco? Yes. He said that some of them will be moving out tomorrow and I know he'll be amongst them.'

'I'm sorry, Kath. This is a bloody awful war, isn't it? Did he give you any hope – about your meeting again, I mean?'

'No. I gave him envelopes; he just might be able to get to a letterbox. I hope he doesn't get searched – that they won't find them on him. But I'm not fooling myself. We said goodbye, though we didn't have a lot of time.'

He had been there, waiting, when she got to the barn a little before six. She had gone straight into his arms, saying nothing for a little while; just grateful to be near him.

'Kat. There is something –' He'd dipped into his pocket, then, giving her a piece of paper. 'I want you to have this; it is where I live – my address, in Italy. Perhaps, one day when the war is over – well, that's where I'll be.'

'And Ridings' telephone – you know the number?'

'181. It's easy. And Mrs Ramsden and Roz – they'll always know where you are?'

'They'll know.' She closed her eyes, searching with her mouth for his. Their kiss was long and tender, touched with sadness. A kiss of goodbye. 'Don't forget me, Marco?'

They heard the truck, then, and the driver sounding the horn impatiently. He had kissed her again then pushed her a little way from him, looking into her eyes.

'*Arrivederci*, Katarina. *Ti amo . . .*'

'And I love you, my darling,' she had whispered. 'I always will. Take care of yourself.'

'I won't see him again. I know I won't, but I'll never

503

be sorry I met him. And loved him. When the going gets rough, I shall remember that there's a little place called Alderby St Mary and once, a long time ago, I had a very sweet love. And that I was happy there.'

'You're determined, aren't you,' Roz demanded softly, 'that you're going back to Aunt Min and that Barney's operation wasn't a success? But what if it has been? What if – even at this very minute – that surgeon in Edinburgh *knows* it's all right?'

'But he can't know. They won't be able to hope, even, till the dressings come off.'

'And when will that be?'

'Lord – how do I know? The only thing I'm fairly certain about is that he'll be coming back to the hospital at Shilton. I tell you, Roz, I don't know why I'm bothering to ring them. All they'll say is that he's comfortable and as well as can be expected.'

'But you *will* ring, Kath, and you'll keep hoping.'

'Yes. Hope can be as strong as prayer – at least that's what Marco said.'

Marco. Whom she must forget, because it was Barney who needed her prayers, now.

Please God – *please* – let it come all right, for Barney.

26

'He'll be back at Shilton, soon.' Kath checked her watch with the kitchen clock. 'He might even be there already.'

Saturday, the first day of August. Seven weeks since Paul's death, more than seven weeks since a German fighter snarled out of the sun and a lonely woman died in the arms of a prisoner of war. And ten days, Kath brooded, since Barney's operation and every phone call to the Edinburgh hospital the same.

'Your husband is comfortable.' Or improving or even, these last few days, making good progress. But always the half answers, the guarded statements. So why didn't they say it? Why didn't they tell her there had been nothing they could do – that they were sorry, but –

And more than a week since Marco left; a going so sudden that even now she could hardly believe it; still expected to look up and see him there, smiling, or waving, calling '*Ciao*, Kat!' But she mustn't think of Marco. It had been meant that he should go because Barney needed her, now. He had left that next day and two days later they had all been gone and more prisoners arriving by train to take their place.

Those Germans marched from Helpsley Halt under armed guard, yet they marched with heads high, arms swinging. Helpsley people stopped and stared as they stamped past, wondering if they'd been wrong to dislike the Italians so. Indeed, the Helpsley constable had had it on good authority that the new prisoners were making it quite plain that it was only a matter of time before their Führer put paid to the Russians and could fling the whole of his fury against the stubborn British. Arrogant to a

505

man, they were. It was like having a time-bomb ticking away on the edge of the village, some went so far as to mutter, because no one could say that the war was going our way; not with food getting scarce and good news from the war front even scarcer.

It stood to reason, said the man in the street. The Germans were getting it all their own way in North Africa, with only a handful of our soldiers between them and the taking of El Alamein. And in Russia the Germans had taken Sevastopol and –

'Are you going to ring Shilton, yet?' Roz broke into Kath's brooding.

Last night they had learned that Barney was leaving Edinburgh; coming back to Shilton in an army ambulance and Kath still none the wiser about anything.

'I shall give it till eight – surely he'll be there by then. And I won't be fobbed off any longer. I shall ask to speak to the Sister and *make* her tell me how he is. I can't understand it. It's as if they're going out of their way to hide something. Eight o'clock,' she said again, tapping her wrist-watch with an agitated forefinger, 'and then –'

And then *what*?

At exactly eight o'clock, Kath asked the operator at Helpsley exchange for trunks, and trunks, amazingly, connected her to Shilton House Hospital with no delay at all. And yes, the Sister said, Driver Allen had arrived and appeared to be none the worse for the long journey.

'He seems in the best of spirits . . .'

'But his eyes, Sister – the operation? I want you to tell me if it's been –'

'Ah – now there I'm afraid I can't help you. I've only just come on duty and your husband's records are with the Medical Officer-in-charge, at the moment. I haven't even done rounds, yet, nor has the MO. I'm sorry, but I can't –'

Prevarications! Side-stepping and evasions! Why couldn't

they say it? Why didn't they say 'We're sorry. We tried, but –' It was all they had to say.

'Tomorrow, perhaps? Come tomorrow, Mrs Allen. He'll be good and rested by then and the MO will have done his rounds . . .'

'When is visiting-time? How early can I get there?' And the sooner the better, she thought angrily, because tomorrow she would have an answer!

'Come whenever you like, after ten. I don't suppose Driver Allen will be going to church parade.'

Church parade? But the remark served at least to remind her that tomorrow was Sunday and her rest-day; remind her, too, that there would be no trains into Helpsley Halt and the only way to get to York, and beyond it, would be to hitch a lift.

'I'll be there as early as I can, will you tell him and – and thank you, Sister.'

Thank you for *what* – because whose husband were they talking about, anyway, and whose future?

'Tomorrow I shall *demand* to be told how he is, Roz!' Tight-lipped Kath put down the receiver. 'I shall stay there till they tell me. Why are they always like that – cautious to the point of stupidity? Do they think I'm an idiot, or something?'

'Forget it, Kath; they're always the same. When they aren't blinding you with medical mumbo-jumbo they're being evasive. It's the way they are; almost as if they're afraid to commit themselves.'

'Well, this time they've had their lot! If the ward-sister won't tell me I shall ask to see the medical officer, or whoever's in charge.'

'Why not ask Barney?' Roz suggested. 'Well, he should have a good idea, shouldn't he?'

Barney? She hadn't thought of Barney – but there had been no news from him, either. Not even the briefest of letters.

'I wonder why he didn't get one of the nurses to write, Roz? You'd have thought someone could have found a minute to dash off a couple of lines . . .'

'Mm. Something like "Your husband asks me to send you his undying love and to tell you he can't wait to see you?" Oh – I'm sorry. I shouldn't have said that – but you know what I mean, Kath? And I suppose you don't know when you'll be back?'

'Not to an hour or two – well, there won't be a train to Helpsley. But you'll be all right?'

'I'll be fine. I shall wash my hair and have a lovely long bath.' At least she would do her best. You couldn't do a great deal in five inches of bathwater. Once, the permitted water level had been six inches. Roz wondered just who had made such an earth-shattering decision; who had decreed that fuel was now a munition of war, and water, too, and if anyone *dared* to take even an extra half-inch of bathwater, they would be guilty of an offence against the war effort! Before so very much longer, she supposed, one of the faceless ones at Whitehall would be insisting that civilians shouldn't bath at all! 'Then I think I might have another look at what's in Gran's desk.'

'You won't get yourself upset, Roz? Can't you leave it until I'm there?' Roz was beginning to look a little better, Kath was sure of it; maybe because she hadn't been sick, this morning – nor yesterday morning, either. 'Why don't you have a really lazy day, tomorrow? Why not slop around in your dressing gown or put your feet up for an hour or two?'

'I probably will. I'll see how the mood takes me. But I won't do anything to get myself upset; there's Sprog to think of, now. And, Kath – I do wish you and Barney all the luck in the world. But you know that, don't you?'

Kath knew it. And if she could hold back tomorrow; if she could stop the sand in the time-glass from running out, then she would do it. Wasn't it strange that people said tomorrow never came? Because it did and it would; tomorrow she was going to Shilton. Tomorrow, she would know.

Try though she might, Roz could not call Paul back to her. Once it had been easy, yet now, since that night, she could neither see his face nor hear his voice, his laugh. It was as if he had never been, and the pain of it could only be eased when she opened the drawer in which she had placed his photograph and, sighing, recall him.

The house was full of echoes today, but it always was when she was in it alone. Carefully she unlocked her grandmother's desk. There, she was sure, would be the answer she sought and some small solace for her grief. Gran knew. Gran had lost her love and though she had never accepted it, she had learned at least to live with it. It would be there, perhaps, like a magic recipe, showing her, pointing her along the path that led to acceptance. Gran had come to terms with loneliness, and Polly too, and she, Roz, would do the same. She had Sprog. Her little unborn child was all that stood between her and despair.

She took the last of the diaries, its gold-leaf numerals still bright. *Today, they killed my darling Martin*.

She should have remembered she would get no comfort from the diaries, for after that heart-tearing sentence there had been no more words. The diary for the year to follow – for 1917 – was there, poignantly unused.

Letters, then? People wrote letters all the time in Gran's early days; so few had telephones, then. At times of bereavement, special notepaper was bought; black-edged, to be used for the first six months of the year of mourning, black-edged envelopes, too. They would be easy to recognize, those sad notes of condolence. She hoped they would still be there, and picking a bundle at random, searching through it quickly for the tell-tale black, she found one almost at once.

It was postmarked Honiton, though the date had faded beyond reading. Once, though she was too young to remember her, she'd had a great-aunt in Devon. Mary, Gran's sister.

A flush pinked her cheeks, because reading someone else's letters, even though they belonged to Gran, wasn't the thing to do. But Gran would understand, now more than ever, her need to do it.

The writing on the Honiton letter was flowing and feminine; the name of the writer was indeed Mary – a *loving sister* Mary. The words were beautiful, sad and heartfelt – this was a letter to Gran in her heartbreak.

. . . and I am sad to my soul that you lost your child – the son you both so very much wanted. To say that we must accept such a sorrow as God's will is hard to bear, but I am arranging to come and visit you and bringing with me some small comfort – if comfort you can call it.

I shall travel on Tuesday by train, staying overnight in London and arriving at York station at three in the afternoon of Wednesday next. Perhaps Martin will arrange for me to be met there?

A letter from great-aunt Mary, who would have had a carriage awaiting her at the station – or had Grandpa owned a motor car, then? Eagerly Roz opened the diary for 1903, flicking the pages impatiently.

. . . a letter from Mary, dear soul. I am pleased she will soon be here. Mary will make me smile again.

More pages, then Mary had arrived.

And such a run north. Locomotives travel faster and faster. Such speed. Mary looked tired but our northern air will be a tonic for her . . .

And then blank pages. Seven of them. A whole week of chattering and gossiping, no time for diaries. What had it been like for them, sisters together? Afternoon tea beside a roaring fire in a room that no longer existed; a dinner-party given in Mary's honour – or would Gran have been receiving, so soon after her miscarriage? Had they, at the turn of the century, gone into mourning even for a stillborn child?

The pages snapped over between her thumb and forefinger. The day was Monday.

My sister returned to Honiton this morning, leaving sadness and bewilderment behind her. I cannot believe what she has told me, though Martin has been goodness itself and we are to make all haste to set things to rights. I do not accept that such a thing can happen to us. I pray with all my heart that Mary will be proved wrong.

Wrong? What had happened during that visit, Roz frowned; what terrible thing to be faced and set to rights? Was this, then, her secret sorrow?

But surely not then? Not when she was newly-married? She must have been deeply in love, then – starry-eyed, still. As she remained until war came and a telegram bearing a date in December, 1916 . . .

January 3rd, 1904. So sad a new year. Nothing, now, is left to doubt. Mary and I should never have married, for our children will be tainted.

The London doctors told Martin that I am a carrier of haemophilia as my sister, to her sorrow, has discovered. It is no comfort to know that such a monstrosity can strike both high and low at will; that the Tsarina of Russia, even, must bear a like grief. I only know I can never give Martin the heir he so longs for. Why are we so cursed?

'Gran!' So that was why there had only been one child and no son for Ridings. 'Oh, poor, darling Gran,' Roz whispered. But wasn't it better that the little boy had not been born alive? So awful a thing, although today such a disease could be held in check – even lived with. Neither Gran nor Aunt Mary knowing about it when they married and Gran having her first baby with no trouble at all. Her first baby?

Only then did the enormity of it hit her. It slammed into

her like a great tidal wave, knocking the feet from under her and the breath from her body. Gran's *first* baby?

'Janet – my mother,' Roz whispered.

And *that thing* was passed down, wasn't it, through the female line? Haemophilia didn't affect women; they just carried it in their blood then passed it to their sons. Daughters were all right; injured, they would not bleed without stopping. Daughters could ride it out; only their sons bore the brunt of it.

'Mother!' Roz whispered. 'You must have known! Why did you have a child? Why did you have *me*?'

Her heart pounded and a dizziness washed her so that she clung tightly to the arms of the chair.

She had wanted her child to be a son; a living image of Paul. Oh, God, God, God! They had made a child as her own mother and father had done, for surely they, too, had made their child carelessly? Surely, knowing what she did, Janet Fairchild could not have deliberately conceived.

'Paul – what did we do?'

The room tipped and tilted around her. Kath! Where was Kath? Oh, please, let this not be happening!

But Jonty would know what to do! Stumbling and dazed, she flung open the door to the kitchen. Picking up the telephone she tapped the receiver-rest impatiently to demand the attention of the operator.

'Get me Home Farm,' she gasped. '223, *quickly*, please . . .'

In only a minute Jonty was with her, gathering her to him, hushing her, calming her.

'Now tell me,' he said softly. 'Take a deep breath and tell me again. You've got to be wrong, sweetheart. Your gran couldn't have had –'

'She *did*! Read that page! That was why she only had my mother, why they didn't try again for a boy because women pass it on – mother to son. Why did my mother have me? She must have known about it. And why didn't Gran tell me? It isn't something you can keep quiet; sweep under the hearth-rug. She knew I wanted to get married. She talked about it to Polly and told her she was going to let me. So why didn't she tell me then – warn me?'

'Roz, love – by that time it wouldn't have made any difference, would it?'

'All right. So we'd already jumped the gun – is that what you mean? But why didn't she warn me sooner? She *should* have told me. And, Jonty – don't tell Grace and Mat, just yet? When they ask why I wanted you to come over, can you tell them it was – was –'

'No need to tell them anything. They're both at church. They don't know I'm here. Look, Roz – come back to Home Farm – have Sunday dinner with us? You mustn't be alone.'

'Thanks, but no. They'd soon realize something was wrong. They'd be bound to ask me. Just give me time to get used to it?'

'If that's what you want – but you're shaking and cold. Sit down and I'll make you something hot to drink, then we can talk about what's to be done. It's what's best for the baby that matters; not what's best for you or what might have been or what should have been. And the first thing you must do is talk to Dr Stewart.'

'What can he do? Tell me not to worry – that what's done is done?'

'No. He's a decent sort and he wouldn't tell you that. But he *will* know what to do. It can't be all that long since he qualified; he'll know all about the best treatment – all the latest research.'

'But I don't think there *is* any treatment for it. You just learn to live with it if you're a man, and not get yourself hurt, or anything. And if you're a woman, you don't have children – or at least I *think* that's what happens.'

'But you *are* having a child, and you need help. You

can't face it alone. Won't you think again about us getting married?'

'No, Jonty. Now more than ever I can't marry you. Just think of it – a child like that – like *mine* – being brought up on a farm? How often were we told – right from being young – what a dangerous place a farm can be? But you're good and kind and thank you for coming when I needed you. Now that I've said it out loud it doesn't seem quite so bad. Just promise not to tell anyone? Not your mother or father, nor Polly? Wait till I've told Kath and had a think about it? And I *will* talk to Dr Stewart – I'll have to tell him – but not just yet.'

'All right, then. But first we'll have that drink, then this afternoon I'll come over again and keep you company. How does that suit you?'

'It suits me very nicely. And, Jonty?' She held her forefinger to her lips, kissing it, placing it to his cheek. 'Don't fall in love with anyone else? Not just yet?'

'Okay. Not just yet.' He smiled. *Not ever, Roz. There's only been you; there only ever will be.* 'If that's what you want.'

'Right now,' she whispered, 'it's what I want.'

Kath walked slowly, carefully counting the doors as she went, wishing her best shoes didn't make such a noise on the bareness of the floor; asking herself why her mouth was dry and her breathing uneven. Turn left at the top of the staircase, said the nurse she had met in the hall downstairs, then fourth door on the right, at the end of the corridor.

Now she stood, gazing at that door, wondering if she ought first to have spoken to Sister. But she wanted to get it over with and nothing anyone could have told her would make one iota of difference, now would it? Taking a deep breath she knocked on the door, hesitated, then pushed it open.

The room was very small, not a ward at all; furnished only with an iron bed, a locker and chair – a chair Barney was sitting in. Drawn across the window was a filmy curtain that shaded the room into half light which meant she couldn't see his face properly – only the dark glasses he wore and the hospital-blue uniform that still didn't suit him.

'Barney? It's Kath.'

'Yes. I thought you'd be here today.' He nodded toward the bed. 'Sit down.'

'I – I'm sorry.' She eased herself on to the high bed. 'I haven't brought anything for you, I'm afraid, but there's nothing in the shops, and –'

Her voice trailed away. She wanted to say something – anything – but her words sounded trembly and strange. 'No cigarettes at all, only under the counter. It isn't so easy to get them, now that I'm not living in the hostel . . .'

She ought to touch him, kiss him, but he'd told her to sit on the bed – *ordered* her to. There had been no mistaking the tone of his voice.

'How are you, Barney? Were they good to you at Edinburgh?'

Say it! Ask it! Say, 'Barney – is it all right, or haven't they told you, either?' But she didn't ask because the man who sat opposite was still the stranger who'd come home to her and she didn't know what to do.

'I'm very well, Kath, and Edinburgh was fine. Wish I were still there. Nothing to do, here. Bloody boring . . .'

'But you'll feel better before so very much longer. And you'll learn to do things again.'

'Like driving a lorry and reading a book, things like that?'

His voice hurt her. If he hadn't been blind she'd have told him not to be sarcastic – well, maybe she would have. But she must learn to make allowances for his swings of

515

mood; try very hard to understand how it was for him in that strange, dark world of his.

'Barney – please? Is there anything you want – anything I can do?'

'Yes – there *is* something. Next time you come, don't wear that uniform.'

'Uniform? But how did you know? All right – so I didn't tell you last time, but I didn't want to upset you. But *how*?'

'How did I know, you mean?' She was adjusting to the dimness of the room, now, and she could see his face and the set of it. 'Is it because it stinks of cows or do I know because I can *see* it?'

'See? Oh, God, you can see! Why didn't you tell me?' She didn't know if she were laughing or crying. A mixing of both, was it? 'Barney! Tell me you can see!'

She dipped into her pocket for a handkerchief but her hands were shaking so much that she gave up and pulled her hand across her eyes instead. 'Barney?'

She was on her knees beside his chair, touching his face, taking his hands in hers, but he pulled them away and the shock of his withdrawal hit her like a slap.

'Barney, you *can* see. Say it! Say, *I can see!*'

'I can see, Kath. Not properly, yet, but I *will* see. All the time, it's getting better. By Christmas I should be due a spot of leave before I'm posted back to a regiment.'

'I'm glad; so very glad!' She covered her face with her hands and wept; on her knees she wept and silently thanked God. 'Barney, it's wonderful . . .'

She found her handkerchief and mopped her eyes then got slowly to her feet, taking a backward step to the bed again, because he hadn't tried to touch her, nor hold her.

'Wonderful, is it? That you won't have the bother of a blind man? So you can go on doing what *you* want to do and to hell with what I want? Is that why you're glad?'

'No, Barney, no! I'm glad because it's all over and you

are going to see again. I'm sorry if I hurt you when I joined up without telling you – without *asking* you – but it isn't really a uniform I'm wearing and I want to carry on being a landgirl, till the war is over.'

'Then you can do what you damn-well like. It means nothing at all to me any more. You can carry on being the selfish, cold, uppity bitch I married. I'm sick of you. I want a divorce, and I want it not when you think it's convenient and not when the war is over, either. I want it *now*!'

'Barney?' A *divorce*? But he *couldn't* know! No one knew about Marco – certainly not Aunt Min! 'Barney – look at me.' He had turned in his chair so that his back was to her and he gazed steadily at the oblong of brighter light that was the window. 'Say it again. I don't understand.'

'It's simple enough. I told you I want a divorce,' he said slowly, carefully.

'But *how*?' All right – so she'd heard him the first time – but who had told him? And what was there to tell – *really* to tell? Was merely wanting a man a sin? Did loving someone else make her a guilty woman? She eased herself off the bed and walked unsteadily to where he sat. 'Tell me what I've done?' she whispered. 'I want to know.'

'Done? You've done nothing and – oh – it just hasn't worked out, Kath.' His voice was gentler and for the first time he lifted his head and looked into her eyes. 'We should never have got married, you and me.'

'But we did marry, and now you want out of it. Why?'

'Because – hell, Kath, it's a mess, and if we try for a month of Sundays it'll get no better. You were always so – so *distant*, yes, and stuck-up. Like those posh people you skivvied for. And cold, Kath. You were bloody awful to sleep with . . .'

'And that's grounds for divorce? Barney – you can't get a divorce for that! There's got to be something really serious, surely? Like cruelty or desertion or – or adultery and I haven't done any of those things. All right – so I joined up without asking you – maybe what I did was selfish. Once, just once, I did what *I* wanted to do – I admit it. But you can't divorce me for selfishness. A woman doing her bit for the war effort? You'd be laughed out of court!'

She took another long, shuddering breath, amazed at her eloquence, silently acknowledging that yes, she *had* wanted to be free – get a legal separation, even. But divorce her? Oh, no, he wasn't going to make her admit to anything she hadn't done; wasn't going to have her branded a guilty woman, just because she'd been stuck-up and – and bloody awful in bed!

So she didn't love him – she never truly had – but she wouldn't give him grounds. Closing her eyes she leaned against the wall; her legs had gone peculiar all at once, and she didn't believe any of it – she didn't!

'Kath – listen. Just *listen*. And for God's sake sit down.'

He got to his feet and placed his hands on her shoulders, guided her to his chair. His touch made her instantly wary and her eyes flew wide open.

'Sit down, will you, and stop flying off the handle. Nobody's accusing you of anything.' His voice was soft, now; coaxing, almost. 'I don't want to divorce you, girl. I want you to divorce *me*.'

'For *what*?' She didn't believe any of this; not any of it.

'I'll give you grounds. I'll give you it in writing so it'll all be plain sailing for you. Adultery is grounds, isn't it – so can we start again and talk this over like reasonable human beings?'

'*Adultery*? Look – can we go outside, or something?' She wanted to be out of this room, this half-dark, bare, awful little room. 'Will they let you go out?'

'Of course they will. As long as I tell the nurse at the door where I go, and don't leave the grounds. And keep my eyes shaded.'

'Can you see all right?'

'Well enough. Just give me your arm down the stairs.'
He picked up his white stick. 'And it won't be long before
I don't need this thing. God, Kath – it was awful . . .'

'Yes. Don't think I didn't care, because I did. It's
something that shouldn't happen to any man.' Why was
she repeating words Marco had said? And where was
Marco? Oh, dear, sweet heaven, where was he?

They walked along the path and across the lawn. She
had set her mind on the seat farthest away – to walk there
would give her time to pull herself together, tell herself that
she wasn't losing her reason. If she kept her head and got
everything straight in her mind, then maybe – just maybe
– they could work something out.

'Adultery? Who with?' she demanded the moment they
reached the seat. 'And when?'

'Now hold your horses!' He took out cigarettes and
offered her one but she shook her head. 'I've had advice.
There was a bloke – in the Medical Corps – who told
me all about it. I met him when I had that spell driving
ambulances.'

'So you discuss your private life – and mine, too – with
a barrack room lawyer you hardly know?' She'd got her
second wind now, and dammit, she wasn't going to let him
walk all over her! 'Well, thanks a lot, Barney!'

'Now steady on. I got to know him very well. And he
wasn't a barrack room lawyer. He knew what he was on
about. A proper solicitor's clerk, in civvy street, and he
told me how it's done.

'Some men only pretend at adultery, he said, to give
their wives grounds; the man usually gives the woman
grounds to divorce him – it's the gentlemanly thing to
do . . .'

'I see. And how do people *pretend* at adultery?'

'Dead easy. All they need, it seems, is some woman
who's willing to stay the night with the bloke in a hotel bedroom. Just be there, Kath – not do – well, you know . . .'

She knew. 'And?'

'And for a chambermaid to swear in court that she saw them together . . .'

'All nice and civilized but totally false, then? So where will *your* adultery take place, Barney? Where are my grounds coming from?'

'From Cairo.' He flicked away his cigarette end, watching its flight intently. 'And not *will*, Kath; *did*. I stayed the night – quite a few nights – in a Cairo hotel with her. Like I said, I'll admit it. I'll send you a letter all about it that you can use in court and I won't defend it. An undefended petition goes through quickly, he said. It's when people start making a fuss and arguing about money, that it takes time. And I want it done quickly, Kath. I want it over and done with as soon as you can. I'm asking you – *please*?'

'Why? Is *she* pregnant?'

'No.'

'And does she know all about this? I mean, I take it that the Cairo lady is the one this divorce is all about? Doesn't she mind being cited? Will she like it when she's called the – the *co-respondent*, I believe it is?'

'There are ways of keeping her out of it.'

'Well, now. You and your lawyer friend have got it all sewn up, haven't you? But there's just one thing you haven't thought about. Divorces – and divorce lawyers – cost money. Where is the money coming from?'

She was angry, and hurting inside. Not because of the divorce; that was what she wanted. But it was Barney's assumption that she would do exactly as he – and the Cairo woman – wanted, that was so high-handed and unfair. And having it thrown at her.

'Money? You've got some, haven't you? That money you've saved out of the Army allowance. You were going to buy me a car with that, Kath, so why not use it to pay the solicitor? There must be quite a bit there, now?'

'Yes.' She was so taken aback by his arrogance, by

his – yes *cheek* – that she said, 'A hundred and eighty pounds.'

'There you are, then! That'll more than cover it. We're home and dry!'

'Yes.' There wasn't anything else to say but yes and if there had, she wouldn't have been capable of saying it. 'Home and dry,' she gasped, then threw back her head and laughed. Really laughed. It was all there was to do, come to think of it.

'Oh, Barney,' she whispered when she had finished. 'You beat cockfighting, you truly do . . .'

And he stared at her, not understanding, demanded to know what was so bloody funny, but she didn't tell him. She couldn't, so she said instead, 'Tell me about it, Barney – and about her, too. I think you owe me that. And don't worry; you can have your divorce. Perhaps we both made a mistake . . .'

So he told her. About being sent temporarily to a Medical Corps unit – there had been heavy fighting and a lot of casualties, not enough ambulances or drivers to get them all to hospitals – and about arriving at a place called Hafiif and *her* being there.

'There she was, Kath – an army nursing sister with rank up – and there I was, helping carry in a stretcher case. I didn't recognize her at first and I said, "Where to, Sister?" and she said, "Straight ahead. The ward on your left, Barnaby." I tell you, I nearly dropped the poor sod. Ellie, it was. After more than three years – looking bloody marvellous.'

'You knew her before – before –'

'Before you, Kath? Yes. Going steady, we'd been, for more than a year. Then I met you and I had to have you and – well, the rest you know.'

'You jilted Ellie, for me?'

'Yes.' He lit another cigarette and drew on it deeply, blowing the smoke out through his nostrils. 'That's just about it. A dirty trick, Kath, because I loved her, you see, only she was more available than you were. You – well – *wouldn't*.'

'And she would – and did? And being you, you were determined to have the one you couldn't bed – *me*?'

'Kath!' His dismay was genuine, his embarrassment real. He had never heard her talk like that before – but it was all the fault of the Land Army. Gave women ideas when they got themselves a uniform.

'So, Barney – you and Ellie got together again?'

'Yes. Helen Bates her name is, only I called her Ellie. She always called me Barnaby – the only one who ever did. After I married you she went nursing – got qualified then joined the Army. Done well, Ellie has . . .'

'And she'll get marriage leave, will she? They'll let her come home?'

'She *is* home.' He shifted uncomfortably, looking down. 'She was the nursing sister who flew back with us on the RAF transport. It was Ellie who nursed me when they took me to Hafiif, after the land mine, would you believe?'

'And Ellie who went with the three of you to Edinburgh?'

'That's it, Kath. She's still there. And she's told them she's getting married, so they won't post her back to Hafiif.'

'Well, I wish you both luck – I really do – and Barney . . .' Now she must tell him and because it wasn't in her nature to be anything but honest and open, she must meet him half way. '. . . I want us to part friends because I know how it was for you, meeting Ellie again. I met someone, you see, only he's gone away and I won't ever see him again. We weren't lovers, but I wanted us to be.'

'Why are you telling me that, Kath?' He looked up, startled. 'You don't have to.'

'No, but I want to. As I said – good luck to you both. Does Ellie come from Birmingham, too?'

'Yes. No more than three streets away. Why?'

'Nothing, really –' Only that it might be fun to be a fly on Aunt Min's immaculate wallpaper when the two of them met. 'Well – that's it, then?' She gave a surprised and slightly disbelieving laugh. 'I – I'll get on with it, I suppose – see a solicitor.'

'Yes. Is there anything –'

'No, Barney. There's nothing I want. Just my clothes. And I suppose, now, that in the future it'll be my solicitor talking to your solicitor?'

'Reckon it will, Kath.'

'Then you'd better have my new address – I'm living in at Ridings, now. And since you'll probably be moving on from here before so very much longer, I think you should have letters sent to Birmingham.'

'Good idea . . .'

'Aunt Min can forward them on – well, she'll always know where you are, won't she? And Barney, ask her – *tell* her – not to open them first. All right?' It was her parting shot, her exit line; catty, but Barney owed her that. Rising to her feet she held out her hand and red-cheeked, he took it.

'So long, Barney. All the best.'

'So long, Kath. Be lucky.'

She walked away in a daze; across the lawn, around the side of Shilton House and through the tall gates. Then down the narrow lane between the churchyard and the vicarage, to the bus stop – and freedom.

And Marco would never know.

27

This morning she had stood at these very crossroads, thumb jabbing, wondering what would await her when she got to Shilton. A blind soldier, perhaps, raging bitterly against a mean-minded Fate that had placed him one step behind the man who had stepped on a land mine?

And by whose capricious whim had there been a nurse called Ellie at a hospital at Hafiif and why, Kath demanded, hadn't her instincts warned her? The facts had all been there, yet she'd been too stupid even to suspect. How was she to go about getting a divorce? Was it to be a sordid affair with herself the injured, complaining party, or would Barney's eagerness to be free of her make it easier? And had it *really* happened? Did she, even now, believe that suddenly there was another woman in Barney's life; that now there was Ellie, from no more than three streets away . . .

'I'd sell my soul for a mug of tea,' she said soberly, hanging up her hat, peeling off her bright green pullover. 'Just *wait* till I tell you!' Water rattled into the kettle, the gas plopped alight. 'It isn't possible! I get there, and he's fine. His eyes are going to be all right and for that, thank God. But guess who wants a divorce, Roz! Just *guess*!'

She hadn't intended telling it like that; she'd planned to relate it as it really happened, and calmly, too. But her mind was still in a turmoil of disbelief because now it was Barney asking for his freedom.

'Barney? You're telling me Barney wants out? I don't believe it!'

'Then you'd better, because it's true. He's giving me grounds and he won't defend it, either, he says. Well, I *think* that's what he said, and oh, I want to tell Marco, and I can't . . .'

All at once it was too much. She covered her face with her hands, fighting back tears.

'Please don't cry, Kath. It'll be all right.' Roz, arms close around her, leading her to a chair, offering a handkerchief, making little hushing sounds. 'I'll make the tea.' She offered her cigarettes. 'Go on – have one. I can't find a lot of use for these things, now.'

'I'm sorry.' Kath's agitated hand set the match flame shaking. 'It's a terrible thing to be divorced, Roz, but I'm glad. I *am*. In fact all I'm worried about is that I'll wake up in the morning and find it was only a dream; that I'll have to go back to Birmingham and Aunt Min – and that bed.'

'So tell me?' Roz said gently, and when she had, when Kath told how it had been at Shilton – every word they had said, and more besides, she took a shuddering breath of disbelief and whispered, 'So there you are . . .'

'So there we are, and Kath – isn't it all so clear, now? Those shirty letters – they weren't really because you'd joined the Land Army, were they? By that time he'd met Ellie, hadn't he? The long convoys we didn't understand, him actually sending you a postcard from Cairo, and all the time he was – well, you know. And now, if you please, he's graciously allowing you to use your savings to pay for the divorce!'

'I know. I'm a fool, but I want it too, don't forget. But how do I go about it, and what will it cost? Are people going to point at me and say, "Look at that one – *divorced* . . ."'

'Does it matter? Do you care what they say? So they'll be talking about your divorce? At least they'll be giving my unmarried pregnancy a rest, won't they? And as for *how* – well, I think you should ring Mr Dunston in the morning and tell him all about it. If he can't help you, he'll know who can. Then you show them Barney's confession and tell them to get on with it – pretty damn quick. And if you're short of cash, I've some I can lend you – okay?'

'Put like that it seems fairly straightforward.'

'*Fairly* straightforward. Divorces are always – well – messy. But it'll be a nine-day wonder and after all, you *are* the innocent party.'

'Innocent? But am I? All right – so Barney went the whole way with Ellie in Cairo, but I wanted to, as well. I wanted Marco like there was no tomorrow and I wish, now, that we *had*!'

'Then just be glad you didn't, because if you're blameless – technically blameless, that is – getting a divorce is going to be a whole lot easier. I wonder if Ellie is having a baby?'

'He said not. He probably wants to marry her quickly in case either of them get sent overseas again. They might have to wait years, if that happened. After all, what Barney wants, Barney must have. *Now*. It was always the same.'

'A spoiled child growing up into a selfish man?'

'Something like that. But I wish Marco could know. I wish there was some way of telling him. There'd be something for us to hang on to, then – even though the war won't be over for years.'

'Me, too. I wish Paul could have known about the baby. Once, I almost told him, but I didn't, and now it's too late. But you, Kath, are going to find Marco and you're going to tell him. Somewhere there's got to be someone who knows where they all went.

'So he's a prisoner of war and it'll be difficult, but I don't think he's all that far away, and if you love him like I think you do, then it'll be up to you. Everything is coming right for you, so go out and grab it. Because I'd do anything – *anything* – to be able to see Paul. Just once more. I'd tear down York city walls, stone by stone with my bare hands if I could see him for just a minute;

just long enough to say, "We have a child, Paul," and to kiss him goodbye.'

'Oh, Roz – *don't*!'

'No. I mustn't, and I'm sorry. But *think on* as we say in these parts. And Kath – can *I* tell *you* something, now? Will you come into the sitting-room so I can tell you and show you? And when I have, will you hold my hand tightly and tell me I'm going to be able to cope and that you'll stay at Ridings with me as long as you can? Will you?'

'What is it?' Suddenly Kath wasn't hungry and the thick slice of bread and jam she'd been longing for since she had walked, thumb jabbing, along the road that led from Shilton, was forgotten. 'What's happened? Are you all right? Is it the baby?'

'Sprog is fine – well, I hope he is, but this morning, after you'd gone, I thought I'd have another look in Gran's desk.'

The desk. 'Oh, yes?' Dammit, why was she so obsessed with raking up the past?

'I started reading letters and I found out that – well, you'd better read this.' The diary lay open on the desk. 'Look – January 3rd, 1904 – it's all there . . .'

'*So sad a new year?*' Kath frowned. 'Look – are you sure –'

'Go on. Read it all – and the letter.'

'All right, then.' Kath read the flowing words, then read them again, just to be sure. Then she lifted her eyes to those of her friend and whispered, 'Poor, poor lady. Loving Martin, loving Ridings the way she did – and no son. Ever. Cursed? You might almost believe it is, Roz.'

'You might, because we are. But think, Kath. Just *think* . . .'

'Yes, but what about? She was a lovely person. She didn't deserve that.'

'No, she didn't, Kath. And nor did my mother, nor *me*!'

527

'Oh, *no*!' She was on her feet in an instant, hugging herself, walking up and down as she always did when upset. 'Haemophilia? Isn't that the one – that – that's –'

'Handed down? That's the one. From Gran to my mother and from my mother, to me. Oh! I don't blame Gran entirely. Neither she nor her sister knew about it when they married – a just cause or impediment *that* would have been, and no mistake. But my mother had me, Kath, and she shouldn't have. Gran should have told her.'

'Maybe she did tell her? Maybe your mother and father were so much in love that –' She ran her tongue round her lips, then whispered, 'Well, you above all should understand, Roz. You know what it's like to love a man without rhyme or reason.'

'Yes, I do. But Gran should have warned me.'

'And if she had, would it have made any difference?'

'No. But I could have told Paul – given him the chance to back away, to finish it between us.'

'And would he have?' Kath demanded, crossly. 'Would either of you have accepted that? You know you wouldn't. All you could have done was to have been a bit more careful. When you love someone like that – well, I do understand, Roz.'

'I know you do. But what's to become of this poor little baby? I want it so much – I still want it to be a son. It's wicked of me, but I do.'

'A part of Paul? Don't you think I wouldn't have loved Marco's son the same way? A little living image of his father? But a son very often looks like his mother. You might have a little boy just like you; stubborn and quick-tempered and red-headed into the bargain.' Why she was saying something so facetious she didn't honestly know, because it was awful – really awful – if what Roz had stumbled on was true. 'But are you sure there isn't a mistake, love? I know it was a shock to you – but mightn't you, if you'd read on a bit more, have found somewhere that they'd got it all wrong? Haemophilia must have got into your Gran's family somehow, somewhere, so couldn't there be a time it could have left it? Maybe you are all right, Roz – tell Dr Stewart about it? He might even tell you that it burns itself out, or something, after two generations. It just *mightn't* be as bad as you think. You ought to see him. Worrying yourself to death is the last thing Sprog needs. That little baby has had all the shocks he can take, if you ask me.'

'Yes. Tell the doctor. That's exactly what Jonty said.'

'Jonty knows?'

'He came over. I was in such a panic that I rang him and he came straight away. Then this afternoon he came again, but he couldn't stay long – it was his turn for Sunday milking. But he came . . .'

He came. He always would. Jonty would never be far away when Roz needed him, Kath acknowledged silently, sadly. He'd said he would be, the afternoon they had heard about Peg Bailey. They'd leaned on the gate and talked about – oh, all sorts of things. But especially about Roz being in love with Paul.

'Be there, if she needs you,' she asked of him though there had been no need to say it.

'I still think you should do what he says – tell the doctor, Roz.'

'I will. I shall have to. But the last time I went to the surgery he said I was fine and there was no need for me to go back for a while; not unless the sickness got worse, that was. And it hasn't. It's a whole lot better, in fact.

'"Call in some time in September," he said. "By then you'll be about half way and you'll have felt the baby moving. We'll have a good look at you, then." That's what he said, Kath, so why don't I leave it at that? Can't I pretend – for just a little bit longer – that everything is all right?'

'Okay – but just as long as you tell him. And as long as

you don't worry too much. Sprog can do without worry, don't forget.'

'Yes.' She let go a sigh of relief. 'And nobody knows but you and Jonty. I haven't told Polly, nor Grace and Mat. Let's leave it as it is, shall we, because I couldn't bear to see the pity in their eyes. Not a word, Kath?'

'Not a whisper and – oh, come here, will you?' She held wide her arms and Roz went into them gladly. Kath held her tightly and whispered, 'I said we'd love this little baby a million, no matter what. We might even love him a bit more, now.'

'We will. Oh dear, he's going to grow up to be as spoiled as Barney, isn't he?'

Kath said perish the thought, but he probably would. Spoiled something awful.

But neither of them laughed.

Last year at this time, Roz considered, she hadn't even known Paul existed yet now, on this eighth day of August – the day on which clocks were put back and one of the hours stolen from night-time to help the war effort given back – she had met and loved and lost him. Soon the days would be shortening and by the end of the month, blackout curtains would be drawn by nine o'clock, though the day would be bright again, long before six in the morning.

Long before six, Roz brooded, leaning on the gate-top, chin on hand, Grace would be up, making morning drinkings for Mat and Jonty, coaxing a reluctant herd to the milking shed.

The far cornfield looked ready for harvesting, her countrywoman's eye told her; the ears of wheat golden brown, now, and if she were nearer, she would hear it swish and sigh as the breeze gentled through it to bend the poppies and daisies growing around the headlands of the field. Last year had been her first harvest; she was still a child, then, with not a worry in the world, save that somewhere beyond the bounds of Alderby St Mary a war raged – and that the faceless ones in London had announced the rationing of clothing and shoes.

Then suddenly Peddlesbury Manor, empty and decaying for almost a decade, came alive, the trees in its parkland torn out by the roots, and a squadron of Lancasters roared in. And Paul came.

But she didn't want her innocence back. She wanted Paul with every breath she took; with every beat of her cold, aching heart. Please don't let the bombers be operational, tonight, she silently begged; bombers that would heave themselves into the sky like over-full birds, fighting gravity until they became airborne and graceful once more, high in the evening sky. Please not tonight again the thrash and roar of take-off, because she still counted, still sent them on their way with fear and love, and still awoke to the first faint throb of homecoming engines.

To her left, to the east over Peddlesbury Wood, the moon was rising, big and round and gold. Soon it would be high in a darkening sky, silver-blue. No more August moons, Paul; no more bombers' moons, my love.

'Roz!' Kath was calling her, walking through the ruins carrying a bright red cardigan. 'There you are! Here, now, put this on or you'll catch a chill. What are you doing out here?' Kath, mothering and fussing; always caring for her.

'I was watching the moon rise. Look at it, Kath. Huge, isn't it?'

'And beautiful,' Kath breathed. But everything was beautiful and now she need never leave it. 'Supper's ready – only vegetable pie, but –'

Vegetable pie. An assortment of unrationed vegetables mixed with yesterday's left-over gravy and topped with a suet crust.

'I think Mat will be starting to cut the wheat any day now,' Roz remarked, shrugging into the cardigan. 'And next year, there'll be wheat and barley on Ridings land,

Kath. Next year –' She stopped, eyes sad. 'By next year, I wonder what will have happened?'

'I don't know. One day at a time, didn't we say?' She didn't want to think about seeing the solicitor at York, or that soon she must tell Grace and Mat about the divorce. Mat had agreed at once when she had asked to change her rest-day from Sunday to Wednesday – without even asking her why, he'd said it was all right. 'I shall tell Grace about me and Barney,' she murmured as they walked across the grass to the yard gates. 'It's only fair.'

'And about Marco, too?'

'No. Not just yet. Not unless he manages to get a letter to me. I'll tell her, if he does. But one day at a time is best. I'm only glad the solicitor Mr Dunston is sending me to is a woman. I won't feel so bad, talking about things to a woman.'

'Yes – and then it'll really get moving.'

But as Kath said, one day at a time, because she was beginning to learn that it didn't do to make plans or to look forward with hope. Not if you were a Fairchild.

'By the way, I told Grace about Barney and me this morning.' Kath picked up a sheaf of wheat.

'Was she shocked? Bet she was. Grace thinks all marriages are made in heaven, like her own.'

'Not shocked,' Kath frowned. 'More disappointed, and hurt for me when I told her about it – well, about *some* of it. She was more worried, I think, about what will happen to me now – a poor, discarded woman.'

'Then I hope you told her you'll be staying on at Ridings and that one day you'll be living in the gate lodge?'

'I did, and it seemed to satisfy her. But Grace judges all men by Mat's standards, and I suppose you can't blame her for not understanding. Well – just try to imagine Mat going off the rails? Or Jonty, either. I said she could tell them about it but not to let it go any farther – well, you know what they're like in Alderby.'

'I know.' Roz counted the sheaves. Ten to each stook. Stooking was considered a woman's job at harvest time and to make a stook, Kath had quickly learned, was to lay the sheaves together to form an ark; a tentlike shape with five sheaves on one side leaning against five on the other and a gap at the bottom for the breeze to blow through.

'How soon will the wheat be dry?' Kath asked of Grace who had come into the field carrying drinkings; a jug of tea, and water in screw-topped bottles to be laid in the shade of the hedge, for coolness.

'Mat always gives it three clear Sundays after cutting. Always three Sundays, he reckons it takes.'

'That's a long time . . .'

'Happen. But it took a long time to plough the fields and sow the seed, didn't it; and time for it to grow and to ripen. So you don't spoil it, lass, for the sake of the odd Sunday. Farming takes time. And patience.'

'And a great deal of fortitude,' Roz smiled, 'when the barley is harvested. No bare arms, then. Barley horns are like little sharp needles, Kath, and it's arms covered and shirts buttoned to the neck, isn't it, Grace?'

'It is, my word. But I'll have to be getting back; dinner doesn't cook itself. You'll both be eating at Home Farm, today?'

'Please. What is it?' Roz was suddenly, amazingly hungry.

'Rabbit pie, wouldn't you know, and gooseberry tart to follow. And custard. The Lord bless rabbits,' Grace murmured, though after this war was over she had taken a solemn vow never to cook another rabbit again. 'Marco liked rabbit pie, didn't he? Poor lad. I wonder where he is. We shall miss him, you know, before this harvest is over.'

'Miss him,' Kath whispered as Grace walked through the

wide-open field gate. Oh, Grace – if only you knew. 'Why is there such a stigma attached to divorce?' she demanded, for no reason at all that she could think of.

'*And* unmarried mothers . . .'

'Because I'm the innocent party, Roz. Why *should* people point a finger at me?'

'And Sprog is a love child, and wanted . . .'

'Do you suppose it's because we're young? Do you suppose Those Up There are old and grizzled and jealous of us? Is it wrong, to be young?'

'And foolish, sometimes?'

'Oh, Roz, how long is this war going to last?' All their precious years, was it to take? Would they, too, be old and grizzled and jealous before it was over?

'Don't know, old love. I'd make a fortune, if I did.' Roz waved to Jonty who had seen the arrival of drinkings and was walking toward them, rubbing the small of his back. 'Come on – let's take a break for five minutes. I could do with a drink of water. I don't suppose Grace has told Jonty, yet, about you and Barney. Why don't you tell him, now? He'll understand, Kath.'

'Yes. I think he will.' Of course he would understand. Jonty Ramsden was like that. Just about the nicest man she knew, in fact. Pity that Roz couldn't think the same.

'We'll be done by St Matthew's day,' Mat said, relieved that the corn harvest was well-dried, stored in stacks and barns. 'And the stacks thatched and netted, long before Michaelmas.'

But he had known this would be a good harvest, for hadn't the first day of September dawned gently and lengthened into a glorious day, with the air clear and bright – golden, almost. And those who worked the land knew that a fine first day of September promised good weather for the remainder of the month. Mat had had his three clear Sundays and now the wheat and barley were almost in, the harvest finished, save for this one last load to be pulled by Duke to the stack. All that was left, now, were fields of bristly yellow stubble. Even the small creatures who had lived in the shelter of the cornfields all summer – fieldmice, voles and shrews, white-tailed baby rabbits – had fled the flailing blades of the reaper and found shelter in woods and hedgerows nearby, leaving the fields to starlings and sparrows to scavenge for fallen grain.

'It's a fine, thankful sight, that final load,' Mat smiled. 'Come on, everybody. Throw up your last sheaf!'

And everyone, even Grace who had come to see the end of the harvest, just as she had been there to watch the first cut, took a pitchfork and, laughing, threw her sheaf high to Jonty, standing precariously on top of the load.

'And there goes mine!' Roz sent her sheaf upwards. She knew how to handle a weighty sheaf on the end of a long fork; unlike Kath whose arms had ached something awful until she'd got the hang of it. 'And another, for good luck!'

The pain hit her low in her back without warning, and she winced, silently. Stupid of her, really, to have thrown the sheaf with such panache. She had been careful all through the harvest, wearing loose-fitting dungarees to hide her swelling stomach and breasts. Soon, when the weather grew colder, a thick, too-large sweater and jacket would take her, disguised, into the seventh month of her pregnancy – by which time the whole village would know. But this far she had been lucky. The heavy work of the harvest had not been the problem she had feared, for Jonty and Kath had watched her like hawks for any signs of stress, and contrived to be there when there was lifting to do. She felt so well, now, with the early nausea long forgotten, and her appetite back.

'Lost your appetite and found a donkey's,' Kath had taken to complaining. 'The baby book says you aren't supposed to eat for two!'

Roz rubbed away the pain in her back and laid aside her fork. She would enjoy the celebration supper at Home Farm, tonight. Not one of Grace's grander feasts – the rationing of food had seen to that – but a young cock had already disappeared from the farmyard and there would be a piece of cold, boiled bacon, Grace said, and clove-scented apple pie. Afterwards, they would toast the harvest with a glass of carefully-hoarded parsnip wine. Made at the start of the war, it had been, just before sugar was rationed, and no more home-made wine till sugar was free for all to buy, more was the pity.

There would be seven of them around Grace's table, counting Polly and Arnie, Roz considered as she stood beside the gate for Duke's triumphant passing. No Gran, though, she yearned, and no Paul. Paul, my love . . .

'I'm absolutely shattered!' Kath sank into the kitchen rocking chair. 'Who's first for the bathroom?'

She looked at her hands, calloused and scratched, with dispassion. Every bone in her body ached; every muscle felt as if it had been pulled torturously on the rack. The thin red weals left by the barley horns on her arms would take ages to heal and, what was more, they hurt. It would all have been so much easier had Marco been there; but Marco would be working on some other farmer's corn harvest, in some other place. Scotland, even, or Devon.

'You go first, Kath. I think Grace would like it if we smartened ourselves up – just this once. I'll have a look through my dresses – see if there's one that doesn't fit too tightly.'

'You're all right, Roz? Sure you're not too tired to go?'

'Sure. And Sprog is ravenous. I'm all right, Kath. Only a bit of backache and the baby book said I might have that.'

'Mm.' Kath had great faith in the baby book. 'Why

don't you put your feet up till I'm finished – have a rest?'

Roz smiled. Fuss, fuss, fuss. But Sprog was important to Kath, too. And Kath would always be around, now. That divorce was just about the best thing that could happen, she thought, with never a scrap of remorse.

The pain came again, stabbing, as she began to undress and she cried out in surprise. A vicious pain, starting in the small of her back, grinding through to her abdomen.

'Kath?' she called over the noise of the running taps. 'I – I think something's the matter. When I threw up that second sheaf, I felt one then.'

'Felt what? Where?' Kath came at once, a strange crawling under her skin. 'And what's *this*?' She picked up a piece of discarded underwear from the floor. 'Roz – didn't you know? When did *this* start? Didn't you feel it?' There was no mistaking it. Roz had started to bleed.

'Oh, *no*! I didn't realize, Kath – I *didn't*!'

'That pain – what was it like?'

'It came suddenly. I thought – in the field – that it was because I'd overreached myself, sort of. But it happened again, just now; ended with a sort of grind.'

'What do you mean – *grind*?' Fear sharpened Kath's voice.

'Achy. Like just before the curse starts.'

'Like a period pain?'

'Yes, it was. But don't fuss, Kath?' She was afraid, now. 'Maybe I did it when I threw the sheaf up.'

'And maybe you didn't! Look – get into bed, and stay there. Don't get up. Just try to be calm. It's maybe nothing at all, but I'm going to ring the doctor. Won't be a minute,' she called as she clattered down the stairs.

'Please, *please*,' she pleaded silently as she stood, fingers drumming on the dresser top. 'I'll never, ever, ask you for anything again if you let it be all right, God. Don't let anything be happening to the baby? And God – why doesn't he answer the phone?'

The doctor inclined his head in the direction of the bedroom door and Kath followed him out, and downstairs.

'Do you have a car, here?'

'Afraid we don't. Nor at Home Farm – only tractors.'

'Pity. I want her admitted right away, and I've just sent the Helpsley ambulance to York with an accident case.'

'She isn't going to lose the baby?' Sudden fear slapped hard at the pit of Kath's stomach.

'Not if I can help it, but I want her in hospital – *now*. Pack her a few things, will you? I'll take her in myself.'

'Yes. Of course.' Why was she shaking so? And why, when she had had just about as much as she could take, was this happening to Roz? 'Shall I come with you?'

'No, thanks. There'd be no point. Just get her things into a case, will you, then ring the surgery if you don't mind; tell them where I am.'

He carried Roz carefully down the stairs. Her eyes were wide with fear; her face paper white.

Kath held open the car door. 'Don't worry. You're going to be fine.' She smiled, tucking a blanket around her knees.

'What about Grace?' Roz whispered. 'What will you tell her tonight?' Her eyes met those of the young doctor. 'No one knows, you see, about the baby . . .'

'Stop your worrying. I'll think of something – your appendix –' Kath looked at the doctor, her eyes asking help. He gave a small smile and nodded and she knew that Roz's secret was safe – for a little while longer.

Briefly she kissed her cheek then watched the small black car as it bumped across the cobbles and out through the yard gates, then burying her face in her hands she let go a long, shuddering sigh. The ill-luck of the Fairchilds, again. Not even a tiny unborn baby was safe from it.

She walked slowly upstairs. She didn't want a bath, now, but she had run it and it was unpatriotic to waste water – especially hot water. And, she thought, as she eased herself into the comforting warmth of it, she was only doing this to kill time. The truth of it was that she didn't want to go to Home Farm and lie to Mat and Grace. They were good, dear people and they didn't deserve untruths.

But Jonty would understand. When she was able to tell Jonty the truth of it, she would feel a lot better. That was something to be thankful for at least, because right now, speeding to hospital, Roz would be feeling anything but that.

She made a lather of soap and rubbed it on her arms, wincing as the hot water set the pricks and scratches tingling.

Oh, damn the barley horns and damn the war and damn *everything*!

'Ward four,' Kath murmured. 'That's what they told me when I rang.'

'And nothing else?' Jonty frowned.

'Do they ever? Not even that she'd had a good night.'

The rosebuds she carried were still moist with dew. She had picked them early, before she did the milk-round, so that Roz could be reminded of Ridings – and perhaps cheered up a little.

'When do you think she'll be out?' Their footsteps echoed loudly in the long, bare corridor, their eyes searching doors for the ward number.

'Haven't a clue, Jonty. They'll keep her here till they're sure the baby is safe. I miss her. I think even the house misses her.' It was a relief to be able to talk openly to Jonty; not to have to watch every word she said. 'I feel bad about not telling Grace – well, telling her a lie,' she murmured, 'but I suppose it can't be helped. Polly looked at me a bit old-fashioned last night, and she was at the house early

539

this morning, wanting to know what had really happened. She knows about the baby, you see. She guessed . . .'

'And Mother will know, soon enough.' Jonty knew how she worried and what she didn't know, he considered, she couldn't fret over. 'Maybe, whilst Roz is here, they'll give her those blood tests she ought to have. Will you talk to her about it, Kath? She'll listen to you . . .'

'About the haemophilia, you mean?'

'It's best she should face up to it. Poor little Roz. There are times, Kath, when you could almost believe it – the bad luck of the Fairchilds, I mean.' He stopped, pointing to an arrow, painted on the wall. 'That's it. Ward four. Fingers crossed, Kath?'

Fingers crossed, she echoed silently, that Roz was all right and the baby, too. Her pulse quickened as she pushed open the wide, double doors.

'It's Rosalind Fairchild you've come to see?' asked the nurse they met as they walked hesitantly inside. 'I wonder if you'd mind seeing Sister, first?'

Kath knew, then, without being told; knew before the Sister rose to her feet, hand extended in greeting, that something was very wrong.

'Are you family?' The Sister was pretty and dark and looked too young for such responsibility. 'By rights, Rosalind shouldn't be here at all. We are right next to the maternity ward and she can hear babies crying, you see. But I've put her in the little room at the top of the ward where I can keep an eye on her, though it isn't always possible – well, we're so short-staffed, with half the nurses away to the war. She would do better at home if there was someone to look after her.'

'We'll take care of her,' Kath said quickly. 'She hasn't any family of her own, but we're both very near to her. She and I live together – more like sisters, really. She'll be all right with me.'

'And there's my mother, and Miss Appleby, her guardian,' Jonty urged. 'But how is Roz?'

'You don't know, then? I'm so sorry. She went into premature labour in the night. She lost the baby . . .'

'*No!*' Tears rose to Kath's eyes. 'She wanted that baby!'

'I know she did. But for all that, she seemed to take it calmly. Dr Stewart came, not long after. He sat with her – told her about it, but it was as if she didn't want to know. He was most concerned.'

'*He's* concerned,' Kath breathed. 'Then just how's this for bad luck, Sister? Roz lost her grandmother not long ago – the gran who brought her up. Remember the lady who was killed in June by a fighter? Then that same week her boyfriend was killed, just a few days before they were going to be married and she's seemed to have been in a kind of limbo ever since. It went deep – you've only got to look at her eyes to know that. And now she's lost the baby, too, and he's concerned. Well, so am I, Sister. It terrifies me, just to think of it.'

'It isn't like her.' Jonty frowned. 'She's usually so – so volatile – such a fire-cracker. I don't understand it.'

'Well I do,' Kath whispered, though for the life of her she couldn't put it into words. For weeks now, Roz had been on the outside, looking in. She had forsaken Roz Fairchild; stepped out of her body to stand there, watching the grief of some other young girl.

'You'd better go in, I think. One at a time,' the Sister said.

'You first, Jonty?' Kath choked. 'Give me time to pull myself together.'

'All right.' Jonty rose to his feet. 'Best it should be me, I suppose.'

'Fine, then. I'll take you to her. And ask about the baby, will you? Try to get her to talk about it.'

Dabbing her eyes, Kath watched them go. Jonty was taking the rough of it again; but hadn't he promised always to be there when Roz needed him? And didn't she need him, now?

Jonty took a deep breath as the Sister opened the door of the little side ward. *Oh, my poor little love, I'd do anything to make things come right for you, but all I can do is offer a shoulder to cry on.*

The room was very small and bare, with cream-painted walls and blackout curtains hanging at the high, narrow window.

Roz lay there, against a pile of pillows, her hands unmoving at either side of her. She looked small and afraid and alone.

'Roz? How are you, love?'

'Fine. Just fine.'

He was standing at the foot of the bed, his eyes dark with pain. He ran his fingers through his hair and said, 'Good. Kath's come, too. And Mum sent her love, and Polly –'

'Polly? She knows about the baby.'

'Yes. Kath told her – later – how it *really* was.'

'Mm. I'm sorry about your mother, Jonty.'

'Don't be. She need never know now.'

'Oh, Jonty. All that fuss; all the lies we told and it doesn't matter, now. Because there isn't a baby – not any more.'

Paul's child, gone. Paul's precious son had slipped away from her in a haze of pain and protest.

'Ssssh, Roz. You don't have to talk about it; not if you don't want to.'

'No. I *don't* want to. But he was such a little thing. It *was* a boy; Dr Stewart told me.'

Her face was a mask of grief and she turned her head from side to side on the pillow, her hair bright against the whiteness. 'What did I do that was so wicked?'

He was at her side in an instant, gathering her to him, holding her, rocking her. He felt her body begin to tremble, then the cry came: a harsh, animal cry of pain and anguish. It echoed round the bare little room, the most heart-tearing sound he had ever heard.

'Ssssh, now. It'll be all right; it will. Just cry, sweetheart. Cry for Paul and for the baby. Don't hold back.'

The tears came in deep, jerking sobs as she cried out for her dead lover and her stillborn child. In Jonty's arms she wept away the bitterness of pain and grief while he hushed her and stroked her hair, holding her tightly, until it was over.

'I haven't got a handkerchief.' She looked up at him through swollen eyelids.

'Here.' He gave her his own and she dried her eyes then blew her nose noisily.

'Can I have a drink, please?'

'Sure, love.' He poured water from the jug at her bedside, holding the glass to her lips. 'That better?'

'Yes, thanks. Sorry about all the noise . . .' She closed her eyes and lay back against the pillows, exhausted. 'And thanks for being there. I wanted to cry. I waited till you came . . .'

'Any time at all.' Why did he love her so? And why would he love her, God help him, to the end of his days? 'Want to talk to Kath, now?'

She nodded, and taking his hand in hers, she laid it to her cheek.

'You're an old love, Jonty Ramsden. Come again to see me, if you aren't too busy?'

'I'll come.' He smoothed back the hair that lay across her face with gentle fingers. 'Soon as I can.'

'They've gone,' Roz whispered as Kath bent to kiss her cheek. 'Paul and the baby – I've lost them both. And he was such a little scrap. I asked Dr Stewart about it and he told me. A boy, he said. So tiny he could have lain on the palm of my hand. But perfect. Nobody's fault, he said. Just bad luck. Oh, Kath, that poor little thing . . .'

'Hush, love. The baby's all right. He'll be with Paul, now. Paul will take care of him.'

'Yes.' She smiled fleetingly. 'Of course he will. And d'you know what else the doctor said? I'd be all right, next time. Next time – imagine? He doesn't know there can't be a next time.'

'Sister said you can maybe come home in a couple of days – if you behave yourself and do as you're told.' Kath reached for her hand and held it tightly, tears trembling on her voice. 'I told them I was like your sister, you see, that we live together and there'd be plenty of people to look after you.'

'Well, you *are* my sister, Kath. And I do so want to come home. I – I finally had a good weep. All over Jonty's clean shirt . . .'

'I can tell. Your eyes are all puffy and your nose is red. Weep some more, if you want to. It's what you've been needing.' Kath sniffed inelegantly. 'I've brought you some roses – the pink ones you like, from the ruins. Sister's having them put in water for you. And Roz – I miss you something awful.'

'I miss you, too. And Ridings and, oh, everybody.'

'That's my girl.' Kath smiled weepily. 'Polly's coming to see you tonight – early, so she can get the last train back. Is there anything she can bring for you; anything you want?'

'Nothing, thanks.' Only Paul, and Paul's child and to be able to turn back time to a June evening. Paul kissing her goodnight; Paul saying *Fifty years from now, I'll still love you.* 'Nothing at all, Kath. I'm fine. Just fine.'

28

'That's *awful*!' Red-faced, Grace Ramsden laid aside the letter.

'From the Ministry?' Kath asked.

'It is. And the milk ration to be cut again! How, will you tell me, is a body to make out on half a pint of milk a day?'

'Do they have a choice? Grin and bear it, I suppose.' People usually did. They had to. To grumble would be considered unpatriotic, so they made do with what they could get.

'Well, I don't see the need for cutting down on milk. We're producing enough for the whole of Alderby and plenty left over for the dairy at Helpsley, so just you see to it that folk in the village don't go without.' Grace stuck out her chin defiantly. 'There's some of the old ones have seen two wars and now they're being told to make do on half a pint of milk, and rations cut to the bone!'

'Don't worry,' Kath soothed. 'They won't go short. There won't be a Ministry of Food snooper checking every bottle we sell, so think about something nice, instead – like Roz coming home tomorrow. I've missed her, you know.'

'We've all missed her, but it's because of her not chewing her food properly. There was a body in Helpsley had trouble with his appendix, and all because he didn't chew his food enough. You tell her, Kath.'

'I'll tell her. And you tell *me* how we're to make her put her feet up?' Kath hurriedly changed tack. 'No work for another week the doctor said.'

'Shouldn't be a problem. We'll manage all right. There's a week or two, yet, before we start lifting the potatoes and the beet. It's sad that Mrs Fairchild isn't here to see her first crops gathered. And Marco that helped plough all those acres of hers – sad about him, too. I miss him, Kath. I suppose he'll be working for some other farmer now – more's the pity. I wonder where they all went?'

'I wonder,' Kath echoed, turning her face to hide the sudden flush on her cheeks. 'I've finished in the dairy – shall I see to the eggs?'

'If you would, lass. If there are any cracked ones bring them in, will you, and I'll make Roz a baked custard tomorrow.'

'She'll like that. She's coming in the ambulance, but Polly will be there, so she'll be all right.'

'Aye. Polly'll see to it that she does as she's told. And let's hope the dratted thing doesn't flare up again. What with losing her gran and her young man, then getting rushed into hospital – let's hope that's the last of her troubles behind her. Unlucky, she's been – but running true to form, I suppose, for a Fairchild.'

Unlucky. Kath was still thinking about it that evening after work was over; thinking, too, that Grace didn't know the half of it. Not about the baby nor about Mrs Fairchild's diaries. Everything Roz had, now, was gone, and it was useless to reason that what had happened was for the best; that Roz need never look at her child and regret what she had passed on. Roz had wanted that baby and she, Kath, had wanted it too. Life could be so uncaring and unfair that she wanted to beat the wall with her fists, to weep as Roz had wept, for a little dead child.

The knocking, the hard, urgent knocking on the back door drove all thoughts from her mind and her eyes slid to the window.

On the doorstep was a black-haired, brown-skinned gypsy woman and a small, thin child.

'Damn!' This she did not want. A begging gypsy she could do without!

546

The knocking came again; harder, more insistent. There was nothing for it but to tell them to go.

'Yes?' Kath didn't like the gypsies. Mrs Fairchild hadn't liked them either; had never allowed them on Ridings land, Roz once told her. 'No thank you,' she said, looking at the pegs in the woman's hand.

'It's lucky to buy from a gypsy, lady.' The woman stopped, dramatically sweeping the back of the house with her eyes. 'And this house needs luck.'

'Please go. I haven't any money to give you.' Kath gazed into the blazing black eyes. 'This isn't my house. I know nothing about luck.'

'Then I'll read your palm.'

'No! No, thank you.' Defensively she stuck her hands in the pockets of her breeches. 'And I haven't any money. I really haven't.'

'I believe you, lady. You have a truthful face, and a sad one.' The child at her side began to cry, but she ignored it. 'I can tell you good things. There are children for this house; a lot of children.'

'You don't know what you're talking about!' A lot of children? How could she say such a cruel thing? There would be no children at Ridings. Roz would never marry; not now. 'Just go away, will you? And why is the little one crying? Is she hungry?'

'Show me the young thing that isn't, lady?'

'Just a minute. Stay there.' The child *was* hungry. And it wasn't the old woman's child, either. A granddaughter, probably, dragged along for a day's begging.

Quickly Kath cut a thick slice of bread, spreading it with margarine and jam.

'Here you are.' She smiled as the child bit into it, eating hungrily, noisily, mouth open.

'You like children, lady? It's a crying shame you'll have none of your own.'

'But you said – this house – a lot of children . . .'

'None of them for you.' She shook her head. 'But you'll know great love and much happiness, though none of it brought about by children.'

The woman looked down, then looked up at the sky, clucking. It had begun to rain, drops falling on the doorstep big as halfpennies. Sighing she took off her shawl and draped it around the shoulders of the child.

'You'll get wet,' Kath scolded. 'Haven't you a coat with you?'

'No, lady. Never did have one.'

'Here, then – take this.' Hanging on the peg beside the door was Hester Fairchild's gardening coat. 'Put it on. It'll keep you dry.' She dipped into her pocket, taking out all the money she had. 'This is all I've got – buy something for the little girl, but go, will you?'

The gypsy took the money, arranging it on her left hand with a dirty forefinger.

'There's luck between us, mistress. In threes. That's good.'

'Luck?' Three shillings, three pennies, three half-pennies. Three and fourpence-ha'penny was lucky?

'Three threes. Luck comes in threes. For three-times lucky I'll help take the curse from off this house. Shall I do that, lady? Shall a gypsy take away the bad luck?'

'Curse? What nonsense! Why do you say that?' And why was she saying it was nonsense? The house *was* cursed. Hester had known it, all along.

'Why? Because a gypsy can tell. I can smell luck; I can smell ill-luck. Good luck is sweet. Bad luck turns your stomach like a rotten stink. There's been ill-luck over this house for as long as I can remember.'

'And you can take it away?' Kath gasped. 'How much money do you want?'

'I've money enough. You gave me all you had and that is riches. And you gave food to the bairn and a coat for my back. I want nothing more.'

'But how? Can you do it now?'

'Nay, not I. Not alone. But we come to these parts on Luke's day and stay until Jude's day. Jude can do all things. Some pray to him for miracles, but gypsies make their own miracles, their own luck. Will we be welcome when we come, to camp here and graze our horses at the sides of your lane?'

'You'll be welcome,' Kath whispered.

'Then there'll be one of us – the old one – who can do what you ask. She'll take your curse and leave this house blessed.'

The rain stopped as suddenly as it started and the gypsy took the coat from her shoulders and offered it back.

'Keep it.' Kath shook her head. 'She would want you to have it.'

'Aye.' The woman nodded gravely. 'We'll be back on Luke's day. I'll leave a sign that will keep you all safe, till then.'

Kath stood unmoving and watched her go. She walked with her head high, her back straight. And for three shillings and fourpence-ha'penny she would lift the curse from Ridings?

Would that she could.

Polly nodded her thanks to the ambulance driver, picked up Roz's small suitcase, then shepherded her charge inside.

'Come on, now. To bed with you like the doctor said.'

'*Polly*! I've been in bed for the best part of a week and I feel fine. Let me stay downstairs for a while? I've missed this kitchen so, and this rocking chair.'

'All right, then. Just as long as you don't go dashing about undoing all the good that's been done. I'll make us a cup of tea, will I? Can you drink tea, now?'

'I can drink tea.' Her sickness was all gone, and her likes and dislikes. Her baby, too.

'Sorry, lass. Didn't mean anything by what I said. I'm

sorry about the bairn. It would have been grand – a lad for Ridings, just like your gran always wanted.'

'I know. But Gran never gave a son to Ridings, did she Polly, and neither will I, now.'

'Oh? And why not, will you tell me?'

'Because – well, I just won't, that's all.'

'You will, Roz. One day you'll be over the hurt of all this and one day, please God, you'll conceive again.'

'No, Polly! No! You don't understand. I won't. I *can't*!'

'Can't?' She poured boiling water into the teapot, her back turned away. 'There's no such word as can't. I thought your gran always made that plain to you?'

'Well, she didn't. There were other things she should have made plain to me, but she didn't. And I'm sorry, Poll, but I don't want to talk about it – just leave it, won't you?'

'No I will *not* leave it! What nonsense have you got into your head, now?'

'You don't know, Polly? Gran never told you? Then come with me to her desk and I'll show you. All written down, in letters and diaries . . .'

'Oh, I know about the desk, and the diaries.' Not so long ago she had found the desk unlocked, and letters that had plainly been read. And one of the diaries open, still, at the third day of January, 1904. 'You left that desk open. I locked it, and put the key back in the dish.'

'So do you know anything about what was in those letters?' Roz whispered. 'Did you never suspect that –'

'That there was a reason that Ridings never had a son? I didn't suspect, lass – I *knew*!'

'You knew? All along, you knew about the – the –'

'About your gran and her sister Mary? Aye. Your gran told me.'

She walked over to the dresser, opening the drawer, taking out a freshly-laundered tray cloth, setting out china cups and saucers the way she had done in Hester Fairchild's time; the way it would be done as long as Polly Appleby served tea in this house.

'When did she tell you? Were you always close?'

'No. I was but a housemaid here, and young, like your gran. She was the Mistress, remember. Servants spoke when spoken to. But that morning she was in the library – she always opened her letters in there – and I'd gone in to put more coal on the fire.'

'I didn't know there had been a library . . .'

'Oh, goodness me, yes. A grand room, it was. The door was to the right of the main stairs – about six feet away from where the staircase seat is now, in the ruins.

'Full of books, and portraits hanging on the wall. The desk stood between two tall windows that looked out on to the parkland and there were big leather armchairs . . .'

'And you were putting coal on the fire?' Roz prompted, calling her back from her dreaming.

'Aye.' A morning's work it had been, lugging buckets of coal and baskets of logs around all the rooms, seeing to it that none of the fires went out. Fires in the sitting-room, in the front hall and the morning-room and the library. And at four in the afternoon, a fire lit in the dining-room and in the bedrooms, too. Pathetic, now, the weekly hundredweight of rationed coal. 'And your gran said, "Good morning, Appleby," and I curtsied, and nodded. I was just carrying out the bucket when she cried out, so I ran to her.

'Well, we knew she'd lost her bairn – servants knew everything that went on, though they'd never have dreamed of repeating one word of it down in the village – so I thought it was something to do with that, you see, and her not being over it properly, like.

'But when I asked her if she was all right, she looked at me and began to sob; terrible tears they were, so I comforted her and then, drawing herself up all dignified and drying her eyes she said, "Appleby, you must never tell anyone that I wept. *Never*, you understand?" I think that was the beginning of our closeness – and we were pulled closer by the war, of course. The last war, I'm talking about, when we both lost our men . . .'

She lifted the teapot, making a great to-do of filling the cups, taking calming breaths, as if she were upset by it, still.

'Go on, Polly?'

'She told me, years later – it was just about the time the Master and Tom got taken – that there could never, even if he'd lived, have been another son. Her sister Mary had found out, you see. Your gran told me all about it.'

'About the haemophilia?'

'About that. And as time went by, she told me more. Ridings had been burned, by then, and your gran left with hardly enough to live on, but I still came to do. I was the only servant she had left by that time.'

'And her only true friend, apart from my mother. Did you know my mother well?'

'That I did. I carried the meals up to the nursery many a time in the good days. A pretty child; dark-haired with big brown eyes. There was a nanny, then, and a nursery maid. Aye, and a day nursery and a night nursery. Everyone waiting for a little lad to be born, no one knowing why there never was one. Not even me, then.'

'And Toby, my father?' Roz prompted. 'Tell me about him, because I've only ever seen photographs. How did they meet?' Ships and shoes and sealing-wax. Talk about other things; about anything rather than what she didn't want to know. 'Was it a love affair, him and my mother, or was their marriage arranged?'

'Arranged? Nay, not *that* marriage!'

'They had to get married, Poll?'

'*Had* to? Indeed they did not, Miss! It was a love match, right from the moment they met. There was no arranging about the way those two felt about each other.'

'Yes, I think I understand.' Like Paul and herself. Right from the very moment they'd met. Loving, wanting – crackling between them like electricity in the air. 'I know.'

'Your mother – Janet – was in London for the Season. Young lasses getting presented at Court, though in truth I often thought it was mothers trying to find husbands for them all. It was an expensive carry-on and one your gran could ill afford. But an elderly friend – a highly-titled lady – presented your mother to the King and Queen and chaperoned her at balls and parties.'

'And at one of those grand balls my mother and father met?'

'Nay. Your mother wasn't in the market for a husband – not the way things were. They met in Regent Street, in London. Your mother dropped her handbag and everything spilled out and this young man stopped to help her pick everything up. Just qualified as an architect, he had, and with hardly a penny to his name. And it happened,' Polly clicked her fingers dramatically, 'just like that. She would have no other. And he loved her so much that he accepted the way things were.'

'That any sons they had could be in danger of having haemophilia?'

'Yes. He thought nothing of it and they were wed in St Mary's. So lovely Janet looked; so very happy. And none save me and your gran knowing they'd never have bairns.'

'But they *did*, Polly. And because of that *I* can never marry. It wouldn't be fair to any child to wish a thing like that on it. I wasn't meant to marry Paul and our little boy wasn't meant to be born. Yet I wanted that baby, Polly. It was all I had left. Even when I found out about the haemophilia, I still was glad we'd made him.'

Her eyes filled with tears. Polly gathered her to her, whispering to her to let it all come out.

And when Roz had said she was sorry and dried her tears, they sat drinking their tea from the blue-rimmed china cups.

'Now then,' Polly said, 'shall I tell you something? Your gran left it to me to tell you. And only, she said, if you needed to know. It was up to me, really.'

'Yes, but I found out, Polly; doing something I shouldn't have done – reading other people's letters.'

'No, Roz, you *didn't* find out. We'd decided, you see, never to tell you. There was no need for you to know – that's why she never said a word. You see, that thing ended with your mother. Miss Janet passed nothing on. She knew she mustn't. You've talked a lot about your red hair, lass. All the Fairchilds dark, you said, and us telling you you were a throwback from a long-ago Fairchild. And your gran and me wishing you'd shut up about it . . .'

'Polly.' Roz took in a deep, disbelieving breath, then whispered, 'You're trying to say I'm not a Fairchild?'

'I'm saying it. You're *not*, thanks be. You were adopted when you were three days old.'

'Oh, God!' Not a Fairchild? Not a part of all this and no ancestors going back to long before the Tudors? 'I'm – I'm an unwanted child!'

'No! And never let me hear you say that again, do you hear me? You were wanted; more wanted than any born rightly a Fairchild and don't you forget it! And your gran loved you because you were all she had left to love and depend on to give Ridings a son. Yes, she worried about Ridings even when it was nothing but a glorified ruin! This place was important to her and it's got to be important to you because you *are* a Fairchild! You're the only one that can carry it on.'

Carry it on? Have children for Ridings, with Paul dead?

'Then who really am I, Polly – or don't you know?'

'Not rightly. And you can poke and pry till you're blue in the face, you'll find nothing that can say you're not a

Fairchild born. There was no legal adoption; no going to court, no special birth certificate. Folks – kindly folks – helped your mother and father, even though they might have broken the law doing it. They knew their desperate longing for children – and Lord only knows there were enough unwanted bairns in those days. But your birth certificate would stand up in any court of law, so you'll tell nobody about this – *nobody at all*, do you hear?'

'Nobody.' She was still reeling from the shock of it. Thrown at her, out of nowhere; right between the eyes and her head still spinning from it. She was like Kath; unwanted – well, by her real mother. She and Kath *were* sisters! Foundlings, the pair of them. Small wonder they'd grown so close.

'Another cup?' Polly demanded. 'And don't be getting yourself all upset over it. You had to be told. You'd got it into your head you could never marry – there was nothing for it but to tell you the truth. And if you've got the sense you were born with, you'll take those letters and diaries and you'll burn the dratted lot, because that's what she'd have done if she'd known her time had come. She'd have done it for sure!'

Burn them? Yes. Then no one would ever know. Because Gran had intended that no one ever should. Only Polly, her friend.

'Maybe you're right, Polly. You knew Gran better than I ever did and loved her every bit as much. She was determined I was a Fairchild – okay – so that's what I am.'

'Good. A bit of sense, at last. And I think we'll see if that teapot'll take a drop more water. Talking sense into you is a thirsty job. Want another cup?'

'Please. But, Polly – can't you even guess who I really am?'

'No. Your mother found this lass one night, wandering the streets of London and sobbing fit to break her heart. She was pregnant, that lass, and her folks had thrown her

out. Daren't go back home, she said, until she'd got rid
of the bairn. Got rid of it, Roz, and Janet breaking her
heart for a child in her arms. So she took the poor soul in
– gave her work as a servant and cared for her until her
time came.'

'It's my mother you're talking about, isn't it?'

'No, Roz. I'm talking about the lass who had you. Janet
was your mother, and never forget it. When you were born,
you were given up to be a Fairchild. And wanted by them,
and loved – *always*.'

'And that's all you know?'

'It's all Janet told your gran; that, and that the lass who
had you had bright red hair, and green eyes. And that her
name was Megan. Where she came from, where she went,
no one ever knew but Janet and Toby and it died with them
that December day, in a car crash.'

'In Scotland,' Roz whispered.

'Yes. Killed instantly. Together, as they'd have wanted
to be.'

'But in the wilds of Scotland, Polly – and in December?
No wonder the car skidded out of control. What on earth
made them go up there at that time of the year?' She had
never understood it – them leaving her at Ridings with
Gran, though afterwards she was grateful that they had.

'What on earth but a child, Roz. A baby boy they were
going for, to be adopted all legal through an adoption
society. Janet and Toby and you were going to have
Christmas with your gran, and they'd have brought a son
back with them – a boy for Ridings.'

'Oh, Polly – can't life be cruel?'

'It can and it is; the more so if you're a Fairchild, it
seems.'

'Maybe it's as well that little boy didn't come here. Just
think; somewhere there's a young man who might have
been my brother.'

'There is. A lad about seventeen, he'll be now. I've often

thought about him – hoped some other couple took him. Your gran once mentioned that she'd thought of trying to get him herself, but they'd have had no truck with her. Too old, they'd have said she was, to be adopting.'

'Poor Gran. And I blamed her for not telling me about the haemophilia . . .' She covered her face with her hands and began to cry quietly.

'Now then, lass. That's quite enough or you'll be making a mess of your face. You could never weep prettily, so off you go upstairs and wash your face. Never let me see you getting upset again about what I've just told you. And that's an order, Miss!'

'Oh, Polly – my dear, lovely Appleby – what you told me didn't make me cry. It was being wanted so much; being so very loved. That's why I was crying; for those two people who made me theirs, and for Gran, who loved me so much. And tomorrow I'll do as you say. You and I will burn those letters and diaries.'

'That we will. It don't do to hold on to the past. And if it's all right with you, I told Arnie to come straight here after school, so upstairs with you. It won't do to let him see you've been crying.'

Oh, my word no. The mistresses of Ridings didn't weep in public. They never had, and they never would!

Arnie waved to Kath who was driving the tractor into the stackyard at Home Farm, then headed for the orchard. He was glad it was too cold for the pigs to be out, now; relieved they'd been put back in their sties. A terrible waste of good windfall apples it had been, letting pigs gobble them up.

He walked to the end of the orchard, to the pippin tree. The best and sweetest in the whole orchard, that tree was, and a fair assortment of windfalls lying beneath it, an' all.

He filled his pockets, then taking the biggest and the best of them crunched his teeth into it ecstatically, wondering if he should take one for Roz.

He was glad she'd be home from hospital when he got to Ridings. He had never heard of a grumbling appendix before. It sounded very interesting, and he hoped she would tell him all about it. It even made him wonder if he should think again about working in a bank and be a doctor instead – if he got a scholarship to the grammar school.

He would have to think about it very seriously. Tomorrow, of course, because right now there was nothing more interesting than a pocketful of apples.

He smiled, broadly. Good old Roz. He'd missed her . . .

'Kath! I'm home!' Roz, in slippers and dressing gown went straight into Kath's open arms.

'I'm glad, love. I missed you. And what smells so good?'

'Meat and potato pie – mostly potato, she said. Polly left it in the oven. She's just gone; Arnie was ravenous for his supper. And Grace brought a baked custard and stewed apples and oh, it's so good to be back.'

'Roz – listen. I've got something to tell you and I don't know if you'll approve.' Kath hung up her jacket, then unlaced her boots.

'And I've got news for you, too. But yours first,' Roz demanded as Kath took the pie from the oven.

'We-e-ll – Grace brought our rations back from Helpsley with her.'

'Hm. They're in the pantry.'

'And the War Ag. told Mat they can't find a farm man for him, nor the Ministry of Labour. Goodness knows how we'll get the potato crop lifted.'

'Come on, Kath – the *real* news?'

'Oh, dear. You mightn't like it – what I did, I mean. A gypsy came yesterday. I tried to get her to go – well, I know your gran didn't allow them on Ridings land.'

'I think it was more my grandfather who didn't, and

Gran just kept it up. They did something they shouldn't have, I believe, and Grandpa had them moved on – told them never to come back to camp here.'

'Oh, my goodness. And I've just told them they *can* come back, and graze their ponies, too. Sorry, Roz. Looks as if there'll be more trouble.'

'No. Leave it. They usually arrive in these parts in October, and stay for about a week. I won't turn them away.'

'The gypsy said on Luke's Day, when ever that is.'

'St Luke's Day – about the middle of October, I think, and they move on after St Jude's Day. They've always been around Alderby at that time. They're no trouble, really.'

'Don't they steal things?'

'Sometimes – but only food. I'll tell them to keep off Mat's land, but anything they can scrounge off ours they can have. The potatoes will have been harvested, by then – they're welcome to a few turnips and any rabbits they can catch. But what led up to all this?'

And so Kath told her; every word of it.

'She says that when they come,' Kath finished, 'the old one will take away the bad luck and bless the house. She said that until they arrive on Luke's Day, she'd leave a sign to keep us safe. It was worth a try, Roz. There *is* ill-luck on this house. You've said so yourself, and your gran even wrote it in her diary. You're not angry?'

'No. And maybe they *can* lift the curse. There's supposed to be one, though nobody knows quite what, and no one talks about it openly – just veiled mutterings about the ill-luck of the Fairchilds. She left a sign, you said? Then maybe it's started already; keeping us safe, I mean, because I've had some news today. A bit of a shock too, mind, but I think our luck just might be changing.'

'Already?' Kath spooned apples and custard into dishes. 'You believe it, then?'

'I don't know – but I'd sure as heck like to. This house has had more than its fair share of trouble; you've got to admit it.' Then, because there was no way to say it gently, she murmured, 'I'm adopted.'

The clock ticked loudly in the silence. Kath regarded the custard that trembled on her poised spoon, then whispered, 'Say that again?'

'I said I'm adopted. When I was three days old, it seems. Polly has just told me. I'm not a Fairchild, except by name, and all I know about my real mother is that she was very young, unmarried, and turned out into the street by her parents. My mother – Janet – took her in and looked after her until I was born. Janet knew about the haemophilia, you see, and that she ought never to conceive. They were on their way to Scotland to adopt a baby boy when they were killed, and that's just about it . . .'

'Just about it? Are you *sure*?' Kath was still breathless. It didn't seem possible. Roz *was* a Fairchild; she just had to be.

'I'm sure, lovey. At least I think I am. It's going to take a bit of getting used to, but what Polly told me makes sense.'

'Polly knew? Did anyone else?'

'No. Not even Mr Dunston, and no one must ever know – not even Jonty. There's no way I can prove I'm *not* a Fairchild, they sewed it all up so well. But I believe Polly. Sprog,' she whispered, 'would have been all right.'

'Y'know, Roz, the gypsy said there were children for this house – a lot of them. None for me, she said, but children for Ridings.'

'And you think they'll be mine, Kath?' She shook her head, her eyes sad. 'Oh, no.'

'Sorry, love. Shouldn't have told you that, should I? But tell me about it – all of it. And Roz – get rid of those diaries.'

'I will. Polly said the same and I'll burn them. You once said Gran would probably have done it herself, if she could have known about that fighter. It's nearly half-past seven. Time for the blackout. Let's close all the curtains, then make up the fire and talk. Oh, and there's something else. My natural mother was called Megan. She had red hair, would you believe, and green eyes. It all adds up. But imagine it – adopted?'

'Ha! That's posh, isn't it?' Kath grinned, pulling down the window blind, swishing the curtains across. 'Lucky old you, being adopted. *I* was *dumped*!'

'Kath, love,' Roz whispered, when they had finished their laugh, 'you and I won't ever lose touch, will we?'

'We won't,' Kath smiled gently. 'Not ever, and that's a promise.'

September coming to its close, with bright orange suns rising over Peddlesbury Wood, and sharp, misty mornings.

'Noticed anything, Kath – the swallows, I mean? They've all gone. When I went into hospital they were gathering on the telephone lines, making such a noise, getting ready to leave. And now they're all away.'

With them had gone summer – the high summer of her love, Roz thought. Now autumn had come, cobwebs sparkling with dewdrops, brambles purple in the hedges, and elderberries hanging in shining black clusters.

'Yes. About a week ago. I noticed, one morning, that they weren't there any more.'

She had wished on her first swallow, Kath remembered; a wish that was sweet and impossible. Now the swallows had gone, the cuckoos, too, taking her wish with them. She would never have Marco; wishes were made of daydreams, without substance. What was real and dark with foreboding was a war which only a few weeks ago had entered its fourth year. And the Allies no nearer the victory – the total victory – Winston Churchill swore we would have.

In North Africa, fighting still raged, and in Russia Stalingrad had surrendered bitterly and bloodily, though some still fought on, street by street, house by house, in the outskirts of the city. But the battle was almost over and the Nazi invaders preparing to dig in for another brutal Russian winter.

'We'll be starting to lift the potatoes next week,' Roz said. This was her first milk-round since that last day of the corn harvest and it seemed, now, that the golden summer had never been, nor Paul, for it was difficult to call back their loving; call back, even, the sound of his voice or see his face in the quiet of her mind. The swallows were gone, and Paul, too.

Last year, when they met, when they had come together like two halves of a perfect, shining whole, she had not thought that one year on she would be alone, lonely and bewildered.

'Potato harvest? They call it *tattie scrattin*' round these parts, don't they?'

'They do. And it's the worst job of all,' Roz said soberly. 'Your back will never straighten up again, that I guarantee.'

'Then when your hands are cold and caked with mud and your back is about to break, you'll just have to think about all that lovely money you'll get from your acres, Roz.' And remember Marco Roselli, perhaps, who helped plough them – so long ago, it seemed.

'Wish Gran were here, to see the first sack filled.'

'And Marco.'

'Oh, heck! It's going to be a long, dark winter, Kath. What say we try to get to York on Saturday and do a flick; spoil ourselves a bit, before potato lifting starts?'

'Mm. Wouldn't mind seeing *In Which We Serve*. Or had you thought we might go with the Peacock Hey crowd to the big dance in York? There'd be room on the transport for both of us, if you'd like to?'

'Thanks, Kath, but not just yet.' Not dancing to sweet, soft music in any other arms but his; not remembering that every sentimental word of every love song were words they had once sung softly as they danced. It was so awful to have loved as she and Paul had loved, only to be torn apart. They had belonged so completely that it was inconceivable they would never again be lovers.

'Okay – it's *In Which We Serve* then, and a quick look at the shops.'

'Fine. And if we can get there before closing time, we might even come across a cosmetic queue. My lipstick is down to next to nothing and I've used up all my cold cream.'

Cosmetics had almost ceased to exist, now, and anyone lucky enough to come upon a queue when the chemist had received his quota would wait patiently for an hour if her reward at the end of it could be a lipstick, or a tub of rouge.

'Could do with a tablet of decent soap, myself. Let's see what we can find. We might be lucky.'

They might indeed, for hadn't the gypsy left them a sign and wouldn't the old one be coming soon to take their ill-luck away? If it could only be lifted, she would never ask God for anything again, Kath promised silently.

'There's a bottle of milk left over,' Roz called from the back of the milk-cart. 'Shall we let Polly have it?'

An extra pint of milk, Kath thought soberly; now *that* was what life was about these days. And staying alive, if you were young, until tomorrow . . .

Kath could never have thought – not in the wildest of her dreams, even – that this would be so wonderful a day.

Grace had been the start of it, beckoning from the kitchen window as they returned from the milk-round, and Roz had run to the house, leaving Kath to take the little pony from the shafts and lead it to the trough to drink.

'Letter for you, Kath. Postmarked Malton. And who is Jean Butterworth?' Roz demanded.

'Never heard of her.' She didn't recognize the hand-writing on the envelope, either, Kath realized, turning it over. 'But whoever she is, she's a landgirl.' Which didn't take a lot of working out, considering her address was the Women's Land Army Hostel at Kirk Sutton, near Malton.

'Kath – had you thought? It could be news of Marco!'

'*Marco?*'

She tore at the envelope with shaking fingers, then her face crumpled, tears all at once filling her eyes, making it impossible, almost, to read the words.

Katarina. I find a friend who will post my letters . . .

'Roz! It *is* from Marco!' He had written. As he said he would, he had found a way to get a letter to her. 'Where's Malton,' she demanded, thrusting the letter at Roz.

'About thirty miles away – and am I to read it? You're sure?'

'Of course I'm sure. It's a very ordinary letter – just telling me where he's working, and that he's well . . .'

Working at Glebelands Farm, in a village called Kirk Sutton. He'd signed it 'M' – hadn't even used his name.

'But it would have to be – well, ordinary, wouldn't it? When last you saw him, Barney had just come home, blinded, and for all Marco knows nothing has changed. You might even be back in Birmingham. If that letter hadn't found you, there's no knowing who might have opened it. A passionate letter from an Italian prisoner of war could have landed the pair of you in big trouble.'

'If I'd been gone, Grace wouldn't have opened it. She'd have sent it on, thinking it was from some landgirl I'd known.'

'Maybe so. But I think Marco was playing safe, for all that. He wanted you to know he was all right – and thinking about you. And hoping to hear from you, I shouldn't wonder.'

'But *how*? Do I write back to him care of this Jean Butterworth at the hostel? A bit risky . . .'

'Could be. But Malton's not all that far away. Why don't you go there – try to find him, Kath. We'll get the map out at dinnertime and find exactly where that village is. It's worth a try, isn't it – especially now you've got so much to tell him.'

'It is, Roz, and I'm going!' Her chin tilted defiantly, though what she would do when she got to Kirk Sutton and how she would find him, was something best worried about later.

She cupped her blazing cheeks with trembling hands. Marco was only thirty miles away. He hadn't been sent to Scotland or deepest Devon. He was nearer than she had ever dared hope.

She let go a deep, shuddering sigh. What a wonderful day this had turned out to be.

'Kirk Sutton,' Roz said from the kitchen floor on which she had spread the road-map, 'seems to be at the end of a one-track lane somewhere off the Malton to Scarborough road. There.' She pointed with her pencil. 'You'll be all right, I think, as far as Malton – you can get that far on the train. But after that, you'll have to hitch a lift, or walk. Seems it's right out in the wilds.'

'I'll make it,' Kath muttered. If she had to walk every step of the way, she would get there.

'Once you've found the village, you'll have to ask where the farm is, though that shouldn't attract much attention – a landgirl, I mean, looking for a farm.'

'Yes, but had you thought, Roz, that my rest-day is Sunday, just as Marco's will be. Even if I find the farm, he won't be there. I'm going to have to do a swop again, if ever I'm to see him. Mat's going to get fed up with all the chopping and changing – especially when we'll soon be busy with the potato lifting.'

'All right – so he might. But had *you* thought that you've already changed your day off to Wednesday next week. Forgotten your appointment at the solicitor's, had you – oh, surely not?'

'I had, Roz. And isn't it great that it's at ten – I can be on the train to Malton by midday, if I'm lucky.'

'What do you mean, *if* you're lucky? That gypsy must have taken a real shine to you, Kath Allen. Aren't you thrilled, and excited?'

'I – I suppose I am. I haven't taken it in properly. But yes, I *am* happy and excited. In fact I'm so darn happy that I feel guilty. Well, I should, you know, when you've had such terrible things happen to you.'

'Look, Kath – what Paul and I had was wonderful and I shall never forget him as long as I draw breath. But this world isn't going to stop turning just because – because we aren't together any more. I told you to go out and grab life by the throat, didn't I? Don't wait for tomorrow, because there are no tomorrows for people like us; not when there's a war on. If it's offered, you take it! Thank God *I* did!'

'Bless you, love. I'm glad I came to Alderby. Just imagine – you and I might never have met,' Kath whispered, tearfully.

'And you'd never have met Marco, either. Life's funny at times, isn't it? Funny-peculiar, I mean . . .'

Life could indeed be peculiar, Kath thought, staring wide-eyed into the darkness, tossing and turning, wishing she could get down from the lovely pink cloud she was floating on, close her eyes, and sleep.

On Wednesday, in just four days' time, she would see Marco – if her luck held, that was. They might even be able to talk – to touch, even, and kiss. Perhaps even say *Ti amo*.

And I do love you, Marco Roselli. I can't wait to tell you – oh, *everything* . . .

But if she couldn't tell him her wonderful, *wonderful* news, then just to see him, and for him to see her, to know she had found him, would be all she would ask – well, for just a little while.

'Right, lass, this is as far as I can take you.' The milk-lorry pulled up with a rattle of churns. 'Over there.' He pointed. 'Make for yon' church spire and you'll be at Kirk Sutton. Someone'll tell you, then, where Glebelands Farm is.'

Kath jumped down, thanking the driver, waving as he pulled away. Just across the fields was the village she was looking for and perhaps Marco, too. Or she might find Jean Butterworth, who could tell her where he was, though probably she would run into the farmer himself who might just tell her to keep her socializing with his landgirl until after working hours!

But somewhere, soon, she would meet someone who would help her, she knew it; knew it from the dryness of her mouth, the giddy beating of every pulse in her body.

She climbed the fence and began to walk across a cow pasture where a herd of shorthorns grazed, tails flicking. Today was warm for early October and she loosened her tie and unfastened the top two buttons of her shirt. Smart this walking-out uniform might be; cool, it was not.

'Hey, there! Looking for someone?' Standing by the fence at the far end of the field was a tall, slim landgirl. 'And I'd get a move on, if I were you. The bull's in with the herd today.'

'Oops!' Kath quickened her step. Shorthorn bulls were known for their aggressiveness, but they rarely gave trouble when surrounded by a herd of cows – that, at least, being a landgirl had taught her.

'Hullo.' She smiled, holding out her hand. 'I'm looking for Jean Butterworth. Do you know if she works around here?'

'She does, and she's me. And you are Kat – Kath Allen?'

'It was *you* –' Kath stopped, taking in the silver-blonde hair tucked up in a bright green snood; the smile, showing white, even teeth and eyes so blue you couldn't help but notice them. Just for a moment she knew panic. Or was she plain, old-fashioned jealous that Marco knew so beautiful a woman? '– you who posted that letter for – for . . .'

'For Marco Roselli? Yes, I did.'

'Then thanks. Thanks a lot. But will you tell me why you did it? Oh, heaven only knows I'm grateful – but *why*?'

'Why risk getting myself into trouble over a prisoner of war?' She shrugged, then smiled. 'It's because somewhere there are Italians who took a risk for my boyfriend. I owe them one, I suppose. My John is in the Navy, you see. His ship was torpedoed on the Malta convoys and he was taken to a prisoner of war camp near Naples. It wasn't a lot of laughs, he said – that's why I can sympathize with Marco, though I know I shouldn't.'

'So what happened?'

'Well, John isn't the sort to take it lying down. He got fed up with the whole set-up, so he escaped. And to cut a long story short, the Italian escape network helped him. They hid him until they could get him on a neutral ship bound for Gibraltar. Seems not all Italians like Mussolini. I think those Partisans who helped John were Communists, though he never quite found out. But I'm not complaining. He's back home and we're getting married on his next leave, so I don't mind doing Marco the odd favour.'

Relief washed over Kath. The beautiful Jean was engaged to a sailor, thanks be!

'Then I hope it won't be too long before you're applying for your marriage leave. Do you know where Marco is working today? Is there any way I can talk to him, without being seen? All right – so I shouldn't be here –' She stopped, lifting her shoulders, all at once embarrassed.

'Shouldn't be fratting with the enemy, you mean? Listen, Kathleen, what you and Marco do is your own business. And I don't mind posting letters for him – or having you send his to me. I'll see he gets them. As I said – those Partisans were good to John. And you needn't worry about being seen. In fact, you couldn't have picked a better day. There's a big farm sale on this afternoon and just about everybody around is there – except Marco and me. You'll be all right for an hour. I don't expect them back until afternoon milking.' She pointed to the corner of the adjoining field. 'See him? He's clearing the ditches. Can't miss that yellow patch, eh?'

'No.' Kath turned, smiling, and held out her hand. 'Just in case I don't get a chance later – thanks a lot, Jean. And good luck.'

'You're welcome, pal.'

Kath walked slowly, her heartbeats thudding delightfully in her ears. Then she began to run, calling his name, waving to him. He looked up and cried, 'Kat! Katarina!' and ran to meet her, scooped her up in his arms, lifting her high so she lost her balance and clung to him, laughing as he swung her round in a giddy whirl.

Then he lowered her gently to the ground, his eyes on hers, touching her face with gentle fingertips as if he couldn't believe she were real.

'Kat – it *is* you?'

'It's Kath,' she whispered tremulously, closing her eyes and lifting her face for his kiss. 'And oh, I've missed you so. Tell me you've missed me?'

'I have missed you, Kat.' They began to walk to the shelter of the hedge, arms linked, fingers entwined. 'I think I shall never see you again, and then I am lucky and sent to work on this farm where there is Jean, who helps me. But how is everyone at Home Farm? And Roz – does she still grieve for Paul?'

'Yes. She's been through a terrible time, poor love, but

she asked me to say "All the best," to you. Only Roz knows I'm here, but everyone misses you.'

He smiled, and she wondered how ever she had existed so long without that smile; wondered how she would bring herself to leave him, when their hour had run.

'And you, Kat? How is it for you?'

'For me? We-e-ll –' She sat down beside him on the sun-warmed grass, taking out her cigarettes, lighting two, passing one to him, and all the time the joy of what she was about to tell him – what she had so longed to tell him – surging through her in bubbles of excitement. Then moving closer so their shoulders touched she whispered, 'Barney wants a divorce.'

'He – *what* did you say?'

'He wants me to divorce him.' Laughter trembled on her words. 'He wants to marry someone else; a nurse called Ellie he knew long before he met me. They met up again in Cairo, and – well – he's giving me grounds for divorce. I saw my solicitor this morning and she's pretty sure we'll soon get a hearing – because Barney isn't defending it, you see. She says that with luck I could be free by next summer.' She stopped, breathless, then whispered, 'Barney's eyes are going to be all right. He had another operation in Edinburgh and already he can see. Soon he'll be back with his regiment and oh, Marco, I can't believe it; I just can't. Even when the solicitor tells me it should be all plain sailing, I still can't.'

'I am glad that Barney sees again – more glad than you know, because if he hadn't been so lucky you'd have stayed with him, I know it.'

'Yes. I would. But it turned out all right, and I could have my decree nisi in the new year.'

'Then you wait, Kat?'

'Yes. For six months. And for that six months I mustn't do anything – well – *wrong*. That's what the law says, anyway.'

'For six months,' he frowned, 'we can't meet?'

'I think not – I'll ask my solicitor. But we'll write, won't we?'

'*Si*. All the time we will write. And when I am wanting you I will tell myself that when next we shall meet – in the summer, perhaps – you will be a free lady, and I can ask you to marry me.'

'And when you do,' she whispered, holding his hand to her cheek, 'this free lady will say yes, my love. Gratefully and gladly, she will say yes.'

Tears filled her eyes, spilled on to her cheeks and he gathered her close, kissed them tenderly away.

'Katarina-mia, it is sad you must be so good, because I want so much to love you. And I want for you to stay with me; always to stay . . .'

'Me, too. But it *will* come right for us, I know it. A gypsy came to Ridings, you see – you know what a gypsy is, Marco?'

'Yes. I know.'

'Well, she said I would know great love and much happiness.'

'*Si*. I shall love you and make you happy always, Kat.'

'And you won't mind that perhaps we'll have to wait a long time before we can be together?'

'I *will* mind, but I shall, how you say, put up with it.' He jumped to his feet, pulling her up beside him. 'And let us walk or I shall kiss you and kiss you and we shall forget you must be good.'

She laughed, loving him and the nearness of him; glad it was the same for him, too.

'I've brought you some cigarettes, Marco. Flora got me some when the WVS ladies came to the hostel. And I've brought you some of my chocolate ration; and some envelopes, with stamps on them. You'll hide them, won't you? Hide them some place the guards can't find them if they search your hut?'

'I'll hide them good. No one finds Marco's envelopes and no one will find the letters you send to me.'

'But you *can't* keep my letters. It's too risky,' she wailed. 'You must tear them up – get rid of them.'

'No, Kat. I shall keep them, but no one will ever find them. They will be all I have. Soon, it will be winter and dark and cold. I shall read your letters many times, so that summer comes more quickly.'

'If I can't come to see you until the divorce is absolute, you won't forget me? You won't let it make any difference that I'll be a divorcee?'

'No, Kat – and no. I love you. Tell me you will always love me?'

'*Ti amo*, Marco. I shall always love you.'

'Don't go, Kat,' he whispered, his lips against hers.

'I must. They'll be back before long. But I'll see you again, if there's a way. I promise I'll try. Now that I've found you, I'll find a way, somehow.'

'Do you really know,' he cupped her face in his hands, his eyes dark with longing, 'how much I love you, and want you?'

'Yes, I do,' she murmured, straining closer, 'but don't ever stop telling me?'

And please, God, forgive me this shining happiness in a world so full of heartache. And let me keep it.

She looked at her watch. Their time was nearly gone.

'I don't want to leave you. Hold me, my darling. Just hold me . . .'

And he held her tightly, and whispered, '*Ti amo*, my Katarina. *Ti amo*, my love.'

Roz walked, hands in pockets, moodily kicking at piles of fallen leaves, thinking there could be no more miserable a time than this, when summer had gone and trees began to shed their leaves; when the days grew shorter and nights longer and lonelier.

She had awakened early, out of habit, listening as Kath crept downstairs and out of the house to help Mat with Sunday morning milking. She had stood at the window, watching her walk across the orchard over the wet, once-green grass.

In the east, the sky had begun to lighten, yet high in the sky to the west the half-moon still shone brightly and, with it, the morning star.

Roz envied Kath the warmth of the milking shed and the noise of the beasts, the chuck-chuck of the milking machine and oh, anything and everything that was people to talk to and laugh with.

This morning, Ridings was empty and cold, and unless she lit the kitchen fire there would be no hot water. Polly didn't come on Sundays, either. This would be an awful day, and if the Lancasters at Peddlesbury started their circuits and bumps, she would scream.

On the other hand she could, of course, stop acting like a spoiled brat. She could dress quickly, go downstairs and rake out the remains of yesterday's fire. Then she could light it, chop logs and fill the baskets and oh, there were so many things she could do. Indeed, she must learn to fill her days – if each day of the rest of her life were to be as long and lonely as this, then what would be the point of going on living?

She blushed furiously with shame. Paul would be glad to be this miserable; and Skip and Flight and the rest of Sugar's crew. And Peg Bailey, too.

'What is the matter with you?' she demanded angrily of the malcontent who gazed at her from the dressing-table mirror.

The matter, whispered the voice in her head, *is Paul. You can't accept that you won't ever see him again. You fret and fume that you lost the child you were carrying, and wonder that life dares to do such things to you, Roz Fairchild.*

'And who, really, are you?' she asked out loud of the face in front of her. 'Just who are you – and what does life owe *you*?'

Life owed her nothing, and she could either sit here, wallowing in her loneliness until Kath came back, or go out and walk until she couldn't go another step. She could walk down Peddlesbury Lane and cross the field to the wood behind which Sugar had crashed; she could go to where it happened and call for Paul with her heart, tell him how wretched she was, how lonely. Maybe he would call to her, softly tell her it was all right; that she had only to cry out to him from her heart and he would hear. If she stood calm and still, would she hear his voice, quiet as a whisper, and see his face in her mind's eye – the face that had eluded her since he'd died? Why, when she loved him to the point of madness, was he such a stranger to her, now?

We made a child together, Paul. You were real and warm, full of laughter and love of life. So why now have you left me? Why can't I call you back, remember the sound of your voice. Is death so final, so unkind?

She turned quickly, impatiently, reaching for her clothes, pulling them on, and ran downstairs to the kitchen, filling the kettle, placing it to boil. She *would* make herself busy, then this afternoon she would walk and walk as Polly once did, though she would not weep. Her tears were spent, though she wished they were not, because even tears were better than the black nothing that wrapped her round whenever she was alone and prey to her thoughts.

And so she walked, now, kicking the fallen leaves, knowing she was going in search of Paul, of his voice, his face and the sweet relief of discovering he had not entirely left her.

She hated this part of the year, when autumn's richness gave way to near-winter and everything was dying without protest. She preferred the starkness of mid-winter: leafless trees, twigged branches like black lace against a sky of grey velvet. She liked the glare of winter sun on an untrodden field of snow, pheasants kark-karking as they fluttered up to roost and a setting sun so red it made your heart glad just to see it. And cold ears and fingertips, frost patterns on the windows and tall, dead grasses dusted with silver.

Winter she could take, but the half-dead months at the end of autumn she could not, she thought, as she leaned on the field gate at the end of Peddlesbury Lane, remembering the last time she had stood here, Kath's restraining hand on her arm and the RAF sentry warning her to go no farther, ordering her away as if she had no right to be near Paul. Well, the sentry wasn't here, now. There was no-one to stop her opening that gate and walking to where it happened.

She looked ahead to the edge of the wood, where branches grew stark and jagged; Sugar, falling like a great wounded bird, had done that, two seconds before –

Before you died, Paul. Before you died on a soft June evening, filled with beauty.

She walked to the edge of the field. They said there had been a huge crater, but it wasn't there, now. Someone had levelled it, then ploughed over the field. There wouldn't be anything left of Sugar. Paul wasn't at this place. If she waited for ever, she wouldn't find him here.

She turned and walked back to where the sentry had stood, then crossed the lane, making for the riverbank and the copper-beech trees, their dying leaves waiting to fall. Once, she and Paul walked here, talked about soon being married. It was useless to wait, they'd decided, for the war to be over. All they had known was *now*, and their need for each other. But Paul had gone, and their child, and all around her was aloneness and despair.

'Where are you, my darling,' she yearned. 'How could you leave me so completely when I need you so, love you so?'

And I love you, Roz. I always will. I promised, didn't I?

'Paul?' His voice – she had heard it! After trying and trying, she'd heard him!

She closed her eyes, and his face was back in her mind's eye. He was smiling, loving her, looking just as he'd looked that night in the ruins when he'd said their last goodbye.

She waited, listening. The wind sighed gently through the copper-beech leaves and she heard his voice again, soft and tender.

I love you, Roz. Fifty years from now, I'll still be loving you . . .

Paul had come back to her! She could recall his face, hear his voice. He'd come, out of her remembering, like a whisper on the wind; a soft, warm wind from the summer of their loving. When she had stopped fighting the pain and accepted, Polly had said, then she would hear him.

Paul, I love you so. Don't go away again. Don't leave me.

Because she needed always to remember how it had been, to hear their laughter and their whispered words; needed to recall their closeness as they danced, thrill again to the love in his eyes each time they had met. And she could see him now; had called him back to her, at last.

She began to cry softly; tears of relief and love and acceptance. There was no anger in them; no bitterness. She wept for a love that would never be lost. Fifty years from now, she would still remember; see his smile, hear his voice. When she was old, he would still be young, straight-backed and handsome. And remembering, she too would be young. She smiled, not able to imagine it, not caring, knowing only that she could keep him in a small, secret corner of her heart for all time.

'And I'll love you, Paul Rennie,' she whispered as the wind took her words and carried them to him. 'Fifty years from now, I'll still be loving you.'

Her love for him would make her nineteen again, wild with youth. Even fifty years from now, when she was old, he would make her young again.

The fire glowed warmly, lighting the shadowed corners of the little sitting-room.

'The eighteenth of December, Roz – imagine, a whole year since I first came to Peacock Hey.'

'And worried sick because you couldn't milk a cow – and that Barney was going to hit the roof when he found you'd joined up.'

'And now I've got my decree nisi; I'm half way divorced.'

'And you'll be free, *absolutely* free, at the end of June. Just in time for your birthday, Kath. Then Marco will ask you to marry him –'

'Ask me *again*, Roz. Oh, I miss not being able to go near him, but until June I've got to accept that I can't.'

'Stupid divorce laws.'

'Never mind. At least we can write, thanks to Jean, and oh, it doesn't seem possible – such luck, I mean.' She stopped, red-cheeked. 'Sorry, Roz. I shouldn't flaunt my happiness so, should I; not when –'

'When I've lost Gran and Paul and the baby? Look, Kath, I've accepted it, now. I'm learning to live with it. I – I've grown up, I suppose.'

'My word, yes. You're a real farmer – you've harvested your very first crops, don't forget. Ridings is a farm now.'

'And paying its way again, thank heaven.'

They sat for a moment, gazing into the fireglow, strangely at peace.

'Kath?' Roz murmured, her eyes not leaving the flickering flames. 'Do you ever wonder about your father?'

'No. Now that you mention it, I don't. Only about my mother and why she had to leave me. Do you?'

'Funnily enough, I don't, either. I did, once, and then

I realized he mightn't even have known – or cared – that he'd got my mother pregnant. Megan, I mean, not Janet. But I do sometimes think about Megan, and hope she found happiness, somewhere along the way. I won't look at every red-haired, green-eyed woman I see, though, and wonder if she's the one. And I won't ever try to find her, Kath. It wouldn't be fair, either to her or to Janet.'

'It wouldn't. You're a Fairchild, and you must look after Ridings, for your gran.'

'Mm. Dratted old ruin.'

'No it isn't! You know you love it. And you will get used to – well – being like me. You'll accept it, Roz, as I did, and not feel too sad about it. You learned about it suddenly, you see; it came as a shock. But me – well, I always sort of knew it; always knew I was different from most other kids – an orphan . . .'

'But we *aren't* orphans. We do have mothers – somewhere. And we've got each other, Kath. Sisters, remember?'

'Sisters. But no more talking about the past, uh?' Because Roz was doing well, now; starting to live again. The sadness had gone from her eyes and she laughed more often. But she would never forget Paul. Kath knew he would always be with her, and thoughts of what might have been never far away.

'Mm. And I suppose I *am* a farmer – or I will be, when the place is really mine. I want to farm properly, Kath, just as Jonty does. Ridings can't ever be just a house again. Do you suppose, when the gypsies came on Luke's Day, that they blessed the land, as well – when they lifted the curse, I mean?'

'How do you know they lifted it? I didn't see anything happening, come to think of it.'

'No chanting, you mean; no creeping widdershins around the place? Neither did I, but I know the bad luck has gone, Kath. I can feel it has.'

'They'll come every year, now – you realize that, don't you? You're stuck with them every October,' Kath, still the practical one, reminded her.

'I know. But they didn't do any damage – only left a lot of horse muck in the lane . . .'

'And horse muck is good for mushrooms, I suppose.'

'And rhubarb.'

'*Rhubarb*? Now what good is rhubarb without sugar, Roz? Didn't you hear it on the wireless yesterday? That lot in London are cutting the sugar ration in the new year. Wouldn't it make you sick?'

'Yes, but we have had a victory.'

The winning of a battle, a *big* battle. Rommel's Panzers routed and prisoners taken, *by us*; thousands of prisoners! The light at the end of the tunnel. Not the beginning of the end, Mr Churchill said, but the end of the beginning. We *were* going to win!

'A victory – wasn't it just! And wasn't it great to hear the church bells again?'

Once, the ringing of church bells would have sent fear into every man, woman and child; would have warned them that Britain was being invaded. On that wonderful November Sunday every bell in the land had rung out joyously for the winning of a battle and the scenting, at last, of victory to come.

'By the way,' Kath murmured, placing a log on the fire, 'what were you and Jonty talking about so earnestly this afternoon?' Leaning on the stackyard gate they'd been; talking, heads close. 'You were nattering as if you were putting the world to rights.'

'Were we? I could have sworn we were talking about pigs.'

'*Pigs?*' Kath wailed. 'We're not back to pigs again? I thought you once said you didn't want them so near to the house?'

'No, I didn't. Gran said it. Ridings is a farm, remember,

and those doghouses would make good sties. Wouldn't it be marvellous to have our own bacon?'

'Well, I must say you've got a point there.'

Home-reared, home-cured bacon. Lots of it, in sizzling, spitting bacon-fat, and fried bread . . .

'Jonty said I was to think about it, and if I want to I can have two or three from Home Farm's next litter – for a Christmas present, sort of. But d'you know what I'd really like? I've got a fancy for a good breeding sow.'

'*Breeding?* Good grief, Roz – think of the trouble there'd be when farrowing time came. You know sows can be one heck of a nuisance.' She'd been a landgirl for a year; Kath Allen knew about such things. 'A breeding sow needs a lot of attention. How could you manage on your own?'

'Manage?' Roz frowned. 'I'd be all right. Jonty would help me. Jonty would be there.'

Jonty would be there. Jonty would always be there, Kath brooded, staring into the fire. He'd be there when she needed him just as he'd always been from the time she was a little thing, not three years old. Still loving her and waiting for the time she would want him . . .

'Sorry,' Kath murmured. 'What was that you said?'

'I said you were miles away. And before that I was trying to tell you there are six bottles of champagne in the cellar – didn't I show you them – all dusty and cobwebby?'

'You did not. What about them?'

'Gran put them there for my twenty-first birthday – or my wedding, whichever was first. But what say we open one for New Year's Eve? Let's have *two*? And let's ask Mat and Grace and Polly and Arnie and Jonty over. We'll blow a couple of corks for 1943! Shall we, Kath? Shall we be devils?'

'Why not!' Why not drink to a new year and a new beginning? All right – so the war could go on and on and on – who knew when it would end? But we'd turned the corner, hadn't we? We were going to win! 'And we'll drink to absent ones, won't we?'

'We will,' Roz said softly. To Marco, whom Kath would marry one day. And to Gran, who'd have been pleased about Ridings doing so well and glad about the curse being lifted. And silently, with love, to Paul. 'And Kath – I wonder where we'll all be – all of us, I mean, fifty years from now?'

'Good gracious – whatever put that idea into your head?'

'Oh – Paul, I suppose. But it's a thought, isn't it?'

Fifty years from now – a *thought*? Yes, Kath was forced to admit, she reckoned it was. Quite a thought.

'Fifty years from now . . .'

1992

Roz laid down her pen, pushed aside the list she was making and gazed at the desk-top photographs. She would rather look at her children than make lists. Come to think of it, she would rather look at her children, think about her children and talk about her children than almost anything else.

She settled her chin comfortably on her hand, smiling up at four of them. Four in six years there had been, and goodness, what an upset! Six years of morning sickness, nappy washing, floor walking and potty training; no sooner one lot of front teeth through than another baby on the way. Young Jon, Martin, Kate, then Lizzie. Grace and Polly in a tizzy of delight over each pregnancy, willing always to pram-push or babysit. Her children were all long-married, now; all but Meggy.

She turned to the little sofa-table and Meggy, who smiled back at her from a silver frame. Red-haired, green-eyed Meggy who came as an afterthought in their middle age. Such a shock – or had it been? Everyone saying how risky it could be at her age; and all the tests and scans and goodness only knew what else; things they'd never even heard about all those years ago when she was pregnant with Young Jon. That child of their middle years had been born perfect and utterly beautiful. She had cradled that soft, sweet creature to her and smiled as the midwife said, 'Well, now. A little redhead this one's going to be. Just like her mother!'

Meggy hadn't had any hair; just a haze of red-gold down where her hair should have been, and she'd stared at her mother with eyes so fiercely blue that Roz knew before so very much longer they would turn to green.

'And what are we to call her?' asked the midwife.

'Megan,' Roz had whispered. There had been no hesitation, though people in Alderby St Mary had wondered a bit about the Welsh name and remarked that they'd thought it might have been Grace or Hester, or even Janet, God rest them all.

It was Meggy who was causing all the upset now, as Meggy always had. Roz just didn't know where everyone was going to sleep, and Meggy wasn't helping in any way at all. She hadn't realized, Roz supposed, that there were so many of them. Five children, four spouses and eleven grandchildren. Jonty's grandchildren. Jonty who had aged so incredibly well; still slim-hipped and broad-shouldered, with a shock of steel-grey hair he even yet ran his fingers through when he was troubled. His eyes had changed with the passing of the years so that now he didn't need glasses – except for reading – which made him handsomer than ever.

Smiling, she gave her full attention again to the desk top; to Jonathan – Young Jon – her firstborn, farming Home Farm as his father and grandfather had done; to Martin, London gynaecologist, with a brood of his own; to dear, gentle Kate, wife of an inner-city parson; and to Lizzie, who painted portraits quite famously.

And then, when they'd thought they could sit back smugly and look forward to four weddings, there had been the joy of another Roz – or so a bemused Jonty had declared. Quick-tempered, easily upset, painfully direct Megan.

'I just don't know,' Roz said, peering over the tops of her reading-glasses to address her husband's newspaper, 'where everyone is going to sleep. There are so many of us.'

'I know,' said her husband affably. 'You shouldn't have had so many children.'

'Then you shouldn't have given me so many!'

'Now don't get upset, love. We'll manage.' He set aside his paper and gave her his full attention. And it was very easy to give her his full attention. To him she was still the beautiful, volatile girl he had married. Even five pregnancies had hardly thickened her waist. 'After all, they won't all be sleeping here. Young Jon can take five of them over at Home Farm, and surely we can squeeze the rest into three spare rooms and the big attic? It's only for a couple of nights, and Lizzie's two could sleep out, in the ruins. Next time you ring her, ask her to bring a couple of sleeping-bags and that small tent of theirs when they come.'

'You don't think it'll be too cold for camping out in April?'

'Roz! Lizzie's lads have camped out in the Lake District in February before now!'

'Mm.' She picked up her pen again. 'It's Meggy, you know, who's really putting everything out of gear.'

'Megan,' he smiled fondly, 'always did. Right from the moment we realized it was another pregnancy and not the menopause. What on earth were we about?'

'Being careless, darling, as usual. But Meggy was really *your* fault. It was your forty-ninth birthday. In your fiftieth year now, you said, and you looked so very sad about it that I wanted so much to love you. I think it was that night we got Meggy.'

'And did you mind?'

'Now you ask! But actually, I didn't; not once I was over the sickness, though she did cause a bit of an upset at the time.'

'And still does.' He smiled. 'Sweetheart – does it *really* matter that she and Richard aren't married? I thought you'd got used to the idea of them living together.'

'Living together in London is one thing; sharing a double bed in *my* house is altogether another.'

'I see. It's all right for other people's children, but not yours?'

'As I said, not under *my* roof; not at Ridings. Gran would turn in her grave.'

'Yes, and talking about – well – *that*. You're not going to have the churchyard gates padlocked again, are you? Don't you think it's time to put an end to it?'

'The gates were locked in Gran's time on Mark's Eve, and even though it's fifty years since she died they'll go on being locked. When you and I are dead and gone, I hope Young Jon will make sure they still are. It's up to us to keep the old customs going and to see that things don't change too much here at Ridings.'

'So now we're back to Megan again, and her – her –'

'Her lover,' Roz supplied matter-of-factly. 'I do try to be broad-minded about it and I know they're all doing it these days, but I simply can't – well, not here . . .'

'All right, love.' He walked to the desk beside the window and laid his hands on her shoulders. 'How about if we put Richard upstairs in the dressing-room on a single, and Meggy down here on the sofa-bed, and –'

'*And?*'

'And remind the pair of them that the fifth stair from the top creaks.'

'But of course! Why didn't I think of that!'

'Fine. Then the sleeping arrangements are settled, can we take it?'

'All settled.' She lifted her face for his kiss. 'I can manage now, thanks, though who thought up this stupid shindig I'd dearly like to know.'

'If I remember rightly,' Jonty settled himself in his chair again, 'it was your idea entirely. "Into my seventieth year," you said. "No age at all! Let's push the boat out! Let's have all the family!"'

'Then I must have been quite mad. Such a houseful, *and* Kath and Marco. Hasn't it gone quickly? Forty-five years married, I mean, and me getting on for seventy and you –'

'Seventy-four,' he supplied, comfortably.

Seventy-four. And Kath and Marco around the same age. Pity those two never had a family. They'd have made such beautiful children together, Roz sighed. But they'd been godparents to Young Jon and had claimed a share in all the others. Anyway, Kath always said they'd been so incredibly happy she couldn't expect to have it all ways.

'We'll be inviting Arnie, of course.' She added Mr and Mrs A. W. Bagley to the list. 'To the dinner, I mean.'

'Darling.' Jonty lowered his paper. 'Don't you think you should try to call him by his proper name? After all, the manager of one of the biggest banks in North Yorkshire isn't an *Arnie*. By the way, he'll be retiring next year, he told me.'

Arnie retiring? Oh my goodness, Roz fretted silently. And Mat and Grace and Polly all with Gran, and the Fairchilds gone for all time. They were the Ramsdens of Ridings now. Roz had not kept up the Fairchild name; had not wanted it to be added to Jonty's, when they married. She hadn't even added it as an extra Christian name for either of the boys. The Fairchilds had left Ridings and the curse with them, if curse there'd been. Home Farm and Ridings made up one big estate now, the farm men and their families living in the gate lodges and Ridings a happy old ruin, so very much blessed.

Jonty raised his paper again, thinking about that long-ago evacuee and how quickly forty-five years of being with Roz had passed. He thought about all the lonely years of loving her and wanting her; five years of watching every word he said; every glance. Being careful not to touch her or love her with his eyes, even. Five years of waiting until the day the tension inside him snapped and he'd taken her into his arms and kissed her; kissed her very thoroughly. She had stiffened, briefly, then relaxed against him and the explosion of anger he expected hadn't come.

'Sorry,' he'd said, tight-lipped, but she'd smiled very gently and said, 'Don't be.' Said it softly as if she were as bemused as he was at the start of their loving. Five years after Paul, that had been.

He folded the paper with a crackle and laid it aside, ran his fingers through his hair before he said, 'Do you still remember him – Paul, I mean? Do you ever think about him, Roz?'

Paul. Her first love. She took off her glasses and laid them on the desk, and her pen beside them. She did it slowly, to give herself time to think, very carefully, about what her answer would be. Then, because she was Roz who was still frank and told the truth without fear or favour, she said, 'Yes. I still think about him.' She pushed back her chair and walked to where he sat. Then, dropping to her knees in front of him, taking his hands in hers, she whispered, 'And I care for him, still. When something from the past jogs my memory; when someone talks about the old days and the way it used to be, I remember him, and I'm nineteen again.'

Times when I wander through the watermeadows or walk beneath Micklegate Bar and see the bed-and-breakfast house, I hear his voice. It comes to me still, a whisper on the wind. And it's a gentle wind, like a summer breeze. It touches my face briefly, then it's gone . . .

'And you wouldn't have it any other way, Jonty, because if I had loved you wildly and without reason and for a little time I'd carried your child, would you have wanted me to forget *you*?'

'So a woman can love twice, Roz?' There was pain in his eyes as he asked it. 'Are you saying you loved me wildly and without reason when we made our children?'

'No, love, I'm not.' She thought a while, then murmured, 'Do you know that when I was expecting Martin I used to wonder if I could ever love him as much as I loved Young Jon. It worried me, till he was born, and then I found I loved him every bit as much, but differently. All five of them were the same. And none of them planned.' She lifted his hand and placed a kiss in its upturned palm. 'They all just came – two sons and three daughters, all made with *our* love. And remember that you and I have always had a tomorrow. Paul and I didn't.'

'Tomorrow . . .' Cupping her face in his hands, he smiled into her eyes. And many a one, he supposed, would have answered his probings with *Paul? Paul Rennie, wasn't he called?* and shrugged it off. But not Roz, who had never lied to him.

'Well then, you soft old thing,' she whispered. 'Does that make you happy?'

'It does, sweetheart. And never change. Always be you. Don't ever have secrets.'

'I'm too old for things like that.'

Once, there had been secrets. She hadn't told him about being adopted until he'd asked her to marry him and she'd said, 'But had you forgotten? What about our children, Jonty?' And he'd said it didn't matter; that they'd adopt half a dozen, if that was what she wanted.

So she told him, then, about herself being adopted and about a pregnant young servant girl called Megan who'd had red hair and green eyes. She'd asked him if he still wanted her, now he knew she wasn't a real Fairchild. And he'd said more than ever, because having children together, their *own* children, would be just about the best thing that could happen to him.

Yet there was still one secret left. Only Meggy knew about the little carved wooden box with her precious things in it. Roz had locked that box a long time ago then walked through the watermeadows and thrown the tiny key into the river. Afterwards she had said, 'When I'm gone, Meggy, take that box, and burn it. Don't try to open it – just do as I ask?'

Meggy knew where the box was kept; hidden behind one of the cruck beams in the little gable-end attic, so high up she would have to stand on a chair to take it down. Only her green-eyed Megan knew about her box of secrets, her long-ago things. A brittle brown carnation, once pink; a picture postcard of Micklegate Bar; a brass button from the tunic of a wartime navigator; a leaf from a copper-beech tree; a photograph.

'Well, just one,' she smiled. 'Only a little secret, between me and Meggy. You'd let me have one, wouldn't you?'

'One. But only because I'm rather fond of you.'

'Right, then.' She rose to her feet, a little slowly, a little stiffly. 'You can get on with your paper, now. I think I've got things sorted. Only Kath and Marco to see to. Do you suppose they'll be all right at Gatwick or should I give Martin a ring and ask him to have them met?'

'*Met?* Good grief, Roz, they can get themselves across London all right. Lord knows they've done it often enough.'

Marco and Kath. They'd had to wait, too, but they'd made it in the end. And Kath and Roz close as ever. Like sisters, still.

'Mm. Think I'll give her a ring, all the same – just to be sure. It won't take a minute.'

'Want to bet?' he murmured, folding his arms comfortably, abandoning his reading.

So much change, he pondered. Once, in the old days, Roz couldn't have dialled Italy. Fifty years ago, making a long-distance call even at home had been a hit-and-miss business. There'd been a waiting-list for trunk calls because there was a war on but now you pressed buttons

589

on a bright red telephone and you were through to Italy in seconds and Kath on the other end as clear as if she were in Helpsley.

But everything had changed. The old machines were long gone and only to be seen in farm museums these days. Now great harvesters made short shrift of a field of corn, throwing it out ready threshed at one end and straw at the other. And another machine waiting to gobble up that straw and thump it into bales, all neat and tidy and easy to stack. Changes for the better, mind. Jonty Ramsden had always been a machine man. But *ready threshed*, mind you, and gone for ever the noise and dirt of winter threshing days.

He smiled, remembering Kath, fresh from the city and wide-eyed with delight. No landgirls now, bless 'em, and Peacock Hey bought by a southerner who was something in stocks and shares and travelled to London by Inter-City every day from York because it was less of a bother, he insisted, than travelling from Epsom to his offices in the West End.

The Air Force had quickly left Peddlesbury once the war was over, he seemed to remember, the aerodrome – didn't they call them *airfields*, now – ploughed up and all the ugly makeshift buildings gone. Only Peddlesbury Manor left there, just as it was before it all started, only now it was converted into four desirable residences for people with more money than sense who fancied living in a quarter of a Victorian mansion.

Fifty years gone and Young Jon farming the land, now, and Roz coming up to her sixty-ninth birthday. Forty-five good years together that had slipped past so quickly. Frightening, almost, if you were daft enough to let yourself think about it. He smiled across at her, then closed his eyes.

'Going to have forty winks, darling?' She returned the smile.

'Not if you want to talk.'

'I don't, thanks.'

No use talking about her age and feeling incredibly sad if she let herself think about it overmuch. Selfish, really, because she'd had so many happy years with Jonty and it was awful it wasn't possible to live them all over again and do exactly the same.

She flinched as a sudden clap of noise hit the room and she turned to the window automatically, but it was gone. One of the planes that sometimes flew over, now, booming and crashing, missing the treetops by inches, it seemed. No use looking. These modern bombers were gone before you knew it; only the sound of their angry passing left miles behind them. Angular, ugly, wedge-shaped contraptions; not like the graceful old Lancasters. You could see a Lancaster long before you could hear it; when it was just a speck in the sky you knew it was coming and you stood there, listening, watching it grow bigger, counting and worrying and –

'Jonty?' She pushed back her chair and walked over to where he sat. 'Why did you ask about Paul? After all this time, I mean – out of the blue?'

'Don't know, really. Just thinking back, I suppose.'

'You know I love you?' She leaned over the back of his chair and laid her cheek on his head.

'Mm.' He reached to cover the hands that lay on his shoulders with his own.

'And I always have, Jonty. I've loved you *differently*, but equally well.'

'I know, sweetheart. I know.' *And I have loved you my darling woman, as long as I can remember, and I'm too old to change now.*

'Well then. No more talk about –'

'No more talk, Roz. Away with you, and phone Kath. And by the way, I –'

But already she was gone. Quicksilver Roz. Probably

half way to Italy, he shouldn't wonder. Smiling, he closed his eyes again.

'I love you, too,' he'd been going to say, but it would keep because she knew it, and anyway there was always tomorrow.

He would tell her tomorrow.